The ANiMals of Farthing Wood

*'We must face facts!' Toad cried. 'Farthing Wood is finished.
We must find a new home. Now – before it's too late.'*

Other Classic Mammoth titles

Little House in the Big Woods	Laura Ingalls Wilder
Little House on the Prairie	Laura Ingalls Wilder
On the Banks of Plum Creek	Laura Ingalls Wilder
The Wind in the Willows	Kenneth Grahame
The Midnight Folk	John Masefield
The Box of Delights	John Masefield
The Hundred and One Dalmatians	Dodie Smith
National Velvet	Enid Bagnold
The Yearling	Marjorie Kinnan Rawlings

The ANiMals of Farthing Wood

Illustrated by Jacqueline Tettmar
Colin Dann

mammoth

First published in Great Britain 1979
by William Heinemann Ltd
Published 1989 by Mammoth
Reprinted 2000 by Mammoth
an imprint of Egmont Children's Books Limited,
a division of Egmont Holding Limited,
239 Kensington High Street, London, W8 6SA

ISBN 0 7497 1066 7

10 9 8 7 6 5 4 3 2

A CIP catalogue record for this title is available from the British Library

Printed and bound in Great Britain
by Cox & Wyman Ltd, Reading, Berkshire

For Janet

Contents

PART ONE

Escape from Danger

PART TWO

Journey to White Deer Park

PART ONE

Escape from Danger

1

Drought

For most of the animals of Farthing Wood a new day was beginning. The sun had set, and the hot, moistureless air was at last cooling a little. It was dusk, and for Badger, time for activity.

Leaving his comfortable underground sleeping chamber, lined with dry leaves and grass, he ambled along the connecting tunnel to the exit and paused, snuffling the air warily. Moving his head in all directions, his powerful sense of smell soon told him no danger was present, and he emerged from the hole. Badger's set was on a sloping piece of ground in a clearing of the wood, and the earth here was now as hard as biscuit. No rain had fallen on Farthing Wood for nearly four weeks.

Badger noticed Tawny Owl perched on a low branch of a beech tree a few yards away, so he trotted over for a few words while he sharpened his claws on the trunk. 'Still no rain,' he remarked unnecessarily, as he stretched upward and raked the bark. 'I think it's been hotter than ever today.'

Tawny Owl opened one eye and ruffled his feathers a little. 'They've filled in the pond,' he said bluntly.

Badger stopped scratching and dropped to all fours. His striped face took on a look of alarm. 'I could hear the bulldozer moving around in the distance, all day long,' he said 'But this is serious. Very serious.' He shook his head. 'I really don't know where we'll go to drink now.'

Tawny Owl did not reply. His head had swivelled, and he was looking intently under the trees behind him. Presently Badger's snout began snuffling again as he caught the scent of Fox, who was approaching them.

Fox's brush started to wag in greeting as he spotted his friends. He could guess from Badger's worried expression that he had heard the news.

'I've just been over there to look,' he called as he ran up. 'Not a drop of water left. You wouldn't know there had ever been a pond.'

'What can they be doing?' asked Badger.

'Levelling the earth, I suppose,' said Fox. 'They've cut some more of the trees down as well.'

Badger shook his head again. 'How long before . . .?' he began.

'Before they reach us?' interrupted Tawny Owl. 'Could be this summer. Human destruction moves swiftly.'

'What do you think, Fox?'

'Tawny Owl's right. In another year all of this could be concrete and brick. In five years they've dug up all the grassland, and cut down three-quarters of the wood. There are human dwellings on either side of us. We've been driven back and driven back, so that we're like a bunch of rabbits cowering in the last stalks of corn in the middle of a corn-field, listening to the approach of the harvester, and knowing we've very soon got to run.'

'And now they've taken our last proper water-hole,' groaned Badger. 'What can we do?'

'We still have the stream at the foot of the hill,' said Fox.

'It must be just a muddy trickle by now,' retorted Badger. 'With all the animals in the wood using it, it'll be dry in a few days.'

2

Tawny Owl rustled his wings impatiently. 'Why don't you go and look?' he suggested. 'There are sure to be others there. Perhaps someone will have an idea.'

Without another word he jumped off the branch, flapped into flight and disappeared.

The last faint rays of daylight were gone as Badger and Fox descended the slope into the depths of the wood. Everywhere the ground was baked hard, and even the quivering leaves on the trees sounded brittle and dusty. Only the darkness around them was any comfort: that familiar, noiseless darkness that enfolded the timid animals of Farthing Wood in a cloak of security.

Badger and Fox trotted along, shoulder to shoulder, each wondering what they would find at the stream. Neither animal spoke. Eventually they could see some movement ahead. A number of creatures were jostling together on the banks of the stream, milling about in a rather purposeless, disconcerted manner. There was a family of fieldmice, and about half a dozen rabbits, all of whom scuttled away when they saw Fox approaching.

A number of hedgehogs remained. Some of them stood their ground, but the majority quickly rolled themselves up, projecting their spines in a precautionary way against the two most powerful inhabitants of the wood.

'Tut, tut. Don't be alarmed,' Badger reassured them. 'Fox and I have merely come to examine the stream. It's the only piece of water left to us now, you know.' He smiled kindly. 'We're all in this together – big and small alike. There must be no . . . er . . . er . . .' He broke off, unable to find the right words.

'Differences of opinion?' suggested Fox, with just the beginnings of a grin.

'Er . . . quite,' replied Badger. 'How diplomatic.' He peered forward over the bank, his weak eyes straining in the darkness. 'Oh dear!' he exclaimed. 'Oh dear, oh dear!'

At this point the rolled-up hedgehogs unrolled them-selves, and the young ones began to squeak excitedly: 'It's dried up! All dried up!'

From under the trees, and from the entrance to their burrows, the rabbits edged forward again, wondering what the clever Fox and experienced Badger would decide to do. One by one they seated themselves, still a little nervously, on the bank, keeping in a group as they watched Fox and Badger discussing the situation.

The fieldmice returned too, and pretty soon their noses, like the rabbits', were all twitching expectantly.

'There will have to be an Assembly,' Fox was saying.

'Everyone must attend. We ought to discuss this problem together, so that everyone will be able to put forward their ideas.'

Badger nodded. 'Yes. It must be held without delay,' he said. 'The situation is critical. Our lives are in danger.' He looked earnestly at Fox. 'I suggest no later than tomorrow night – at twelve,' he said.

Fox was agreeable. 'Will you chair the meeting?' he asked.

'Certainly. Unless Tawny Owl . . .'

'Oh, Owl! He probably won't even come. You know what he's like. Can't bear anyone else to arrange anything,' grumbled Fox.

'He *must* come,' insisted Badger. 'I'll tell him so myself. When an Assembly is called, the whole of Farthing Wood has to attend. Five years ago, my father chaired the Assembly that was called when the humans first started to build here. There were more of us then, of course. Farthing Wood was almost a forest in those days, with a large stretch of grassland all round it, and also . . .'

'Yes, yes,' Fox cut in, a little impatiently. He knew Badger loved to talk about 'The Old Days', but once he started it was sometimes very difficult to divert him. 'We know what it used to be like,' he said. 'But *we're* concerned about what it's like at present. *My* father,' he added, in case Badger was offended, 'was at that Assembly. But no good came of it. What could mere animals do?'

'So true,' mumbled Badger sadly. 'But this time, unless we're all to die of thirst, something has *got* to be done.'

He turned towards the group of onlookers. 'Fox and I are agreed that an Assembly of the animals of Farthing Wood must be called,' he announced. 'You should all arrive at my set by twelve o'clock tomorrow night.' He began to digress again. 'There's plenty of room for everyone. Once upon a time many families of badgers lived there, but now I'm the sole survivor . . .' He sighed reminiscently: 'The last of a long line of Farthing Wood badgers, going back for centuries.'

'We must spread the word to the others,' Fox cut in quickly. 'You rabbits must find Hare and his family, and, fieldmice, you can pass the word to the voles. Badger knows where to find Weasel, and I myself will look out for Adder and the lizards. Any of you who are about during the daytime can tell the squirrels about it.'

'What about the birds?' asked one of the hedgehogs.

'We'll leave them to Tawny Owl,' replied Fox.

'Badger was right – he must play his part.'

'I'll tell him when I get back home,' said Badger. 'Now don't forget, all of you. Twelve o'clock tomorrow night.'

The smaller animals scurried away, the younger ones chattering excitedly and feeling important because of the duties entrusted to them.

Badger turned to Fox. 'You'd better impress on Adder,' he warned, 'that we haven't arranged this meeting to provide him with a wonderful opportunity to gorge himself. Remind him that every creature attending an Assembly is strictly bound by the Oath of Common Safety.'

'Your father introduced that, I believe?' Fox queried.

'He did,' replied Badger seriously. 'It was very necessary, to prevent the possibility of bullying or fighting. Do you think Adder will listen to you?'

'As much as he ever does,' Fox replied evasively. He shrugged. 'But I think even Adder respects the rules of the Assembly.'

They stood a little longer; then Badger turned to go. Fox called him back. 'What about Mole?' he asked.

'Oh, don't worry about him,' Badger managed to laugh. 'Once he hears all the feet running overhead, he'll soon surface to discover what all the commotion is about.'

Fox grinned. 'Till tomorrow then,' he said.

'Till tomorrow,' said Badger.

2

The assembly

By eleven o'clock Badger felt that everything was ready. Since he had risen, he had been busy enlarging one of the unoccupied chambers of his set to a size which would accommodate everyone who was likely to attend the Assembly. Even with his powerful digging claws, it had been exceptionally hard work. The soil was dry and hard, and he had to remove all the loose earth into one of the unused corridors. Then, outside, he had gathered together several mounds of dry leaves, and dragged them down, backwards, into the chamber, spreading them evenly over the floor.

When he had finished, he had sallied out again, this time to the borders of the wood. Underneath the hedgerows he gathered together a number of glow-worms, which he tucked into the thickest parts of his fur, in order to transport them back in bulk. Back at the set, he stowed the little insects at intervals along the entrance corridor, and with those he had left over he illuminated the Assembly Chamber, placing them in tiny clusters, just as he had watched his father do before him.

At length, satisfied with his evening's work, he left his set again to dig up a few roots and bulbs for his supper, which, garnished with a number of beetles, made a welcome meal.

It was now eleven-thirty, and Badger decided to take a short nap before the other animals started to arrive.

He did not seem to have been dozing in his sleeping-chamber for more than a few minutes when he heard the old church clock strike twelve in the distance, and simultaneously he heard voices outside. He jumped up and wriggled his way quickly to the exit. It was Weasel, who had arrived with Fox.

'Go straight down the corridor on your left, Weasel,' said Badger. 'After a little way it turns to the right. Take the first turning left after that bend into the Assembly Chamber, and make yourself comfortable. I'll join you in a moment.'

Weasel followed his directions and the glow-worm lights, and had only just disappeared from view when more voices could be heard approaching. They belonged to the rabbits and Hare and his family. Just behind them came the fieldmice.

'Fox, will you go down and keep Weasel company?' Badger asked. 'I'd better stay here to direct the others.'

'Of·course,' said Fox and, bowing his head, he eased himself into the tunnel.

'This way, everyone!' called Badger. 'Straight in there.' He used his snout to indicate the entrance. 'Just follow the little lights.'

The rabbits, in their particularly timid manner, were unable to decide on who should be the first one down the hole, and they began quarrelling until Hare, with some impatience, said, 'I'll lead.' He nudged his mate encouragingly. 'Come on dear. And you, children! Our cousins and the fieldmice will be right behind us.'

The lizards were next on the scene, though Badger did not notice them until they were darting around him like individual threads of quick-silver. After the squirrels, hedgehogs and voles had arrived, only Adder and the birds were missing.

The latter arrived together, led by Tawny Owl. He had

rounded up Pheasant and his mate, and even Kestrel, who spent most of his time hovering high in the air above Farthing Wood, had agreed to attend.

'I didn't deign to invite the other birds,' explained Tawny Owl. 'Blackbirds, starlings, pigeons, thrushes – they're all half-domesticated. They thrive when humans are around. The more humans there are, the better they like it. No purpose in them coming. They don't really represent Farthing Wood at all.'

'Do we have to go in there?' Pheasant asked Badger in some alarm. 'Soiling our feathers with all that dirt?'

'My set is quite spotless!' Badger retorted. 'I've spent all evening getting it ready.'

'We haven't come here to admire each other's plumage,' Tawny Owl said shortly. 'If you haven't anything more to offer the Assembly than that, you might as well not have come.'

'I didn't say anything about not attending the Assembly,' said Pheasant in a small voice, and without further ado he walked into the hole with his mate, followed by Kestrel.

'Vain as a peacock,' muttered Tawny Owl, and Badger shook his head.

'You go in, Owl,' he said presently. 'I'm only waiting for Adder, and then we're complete.'

Just then Fox's head reappeared at the opening. 'Mole's just dropped in,' he announced with a grin. 'He came direct. Dug a long passage from his tunnel straight into the Assembly Chamber.'

Badger laughed. 'I'd forgotten Mole,' he admitted. 'Hallo, here's Adder.'

'Good evening, gentlemen,' Adder whispered, as he slid to a halt. His forked tongue flickered all around. 'I trust I'm not late?'

'I suppose someone had to be last,' remarked Fox pointedly. 'Well, after you, Badger.'

Inside the Assembly Chamber, the expectant faces of the

young animals contrasted strangely with the solemnity of their seniors in the faint greenish glow. Badger took his place in the centre of the room, flanked by Fox and Tawny Owl as his self-appointed committee. The other animals spread themselves evenly round the Chamber against the hard earth walls. Most of the fieldmice and voles and rabbits took care not to sit anywhere near Adder or Weasel.

Without ceremony, Badger opened the meeting. 'This is only the second Assembly called in my lifetime,' he began, 'and for most of you it will be the first you've attended. My father called the last Assembly five years ago, when the humans first moved in to lay waste our homes. In those days there was a Farthing Heath, as well as Farthing Wood. I don't have to tell anybody what happened to the heath that once surrounded the whole of our wood.'

'Gone. All gone,' hissed Adder from the corner where he had carefully coiled himself up, and was resting his head on the topmost coil.

'All gone!' echoed the voles.

'But the humans weren't content with that,' Badger went on bitterly. 'They began to fell our trees. They continued to do so, at regular destructive intervals, until what was once a large wood had been cut back to the present sad remnant, not much larger than a copse.'

'What do you think will happen, Badger?' asked one of the rabbits timidly.

'Happen?' Badger echoed. 'Why, the same thing that has *been* happening. They will cut down *more* trees, and build *more* houses, and *shops*, probably a school, and offices and roads, and ghastly concrete posts and signs everywhere, faster and faster and faster still, until eventually . . .' He broke off with a despairing shake of his head.

'Until eventually we are destroyed with the wood.' Tawny Owl finished the sentence with determined pessimism.

'And all this – how long will it take?' asked Hare.

'The very question I myself asked yesterday,' nodded

Badger. 'Though all the time I suppose I knew the answer. We animals can never accurately forecast what the humans will do; we only know what they are capable of doing. And they're capable of cutting down the remainder of Farthing Wood in twelve months, perhaps less.'

There was a stunned silence for a moment, then one or two animals coughed nervously. Kestrel began to preen his wings. His livelihood was not as completely threatened as the others' by the advancing destruction.

'And on top of all this,' Badger said in pained tones, 'comes a drought.'

'The very last straw,' said Mole.

'Merely accelerating the end,' Tawny Owl muttered, more to himself than to anyone else.

'Friends, we are up against a brick wall,' Badger intoned with deadly seriousness. 'Leaving aside the threat of our extermination, if we don't, in the next couple of days, find a safe, secluded place where we can all go to drink, we're going to find ourselves in the worst kind of distress.' He coughed huskily, already feeling his throat to be unusually dry. 'This is why I've asked all of you to join me tonight. The greater the gathering, the better the chance we have of finding a solution to end our immediate danger. So I entreat you all: don't be afraid to speak up. Size and strength have no bearing on anyone's importance at an Assembly. The only important fact is that all of us live in Farthing Wood, and so we all need each other's help.'

The smaller animals seemed to receive some encouragement from Badger's remarks, and began to murmur to each other and shake their heads in bewilderment. But none of them seemed to have any definite ideas.

Badger looked at Tawny Owl, and then at Fox, but they were both scanning the circle of faces to see who was going to be the first to make a suggestion.

'Surely you birds can help us?' prompted Weasel. 'You cover a wider stretch of country than we ground dwellers.

Can any of you say where the nearest water is to be found outside our boundaries?'

Pheasant's dowdy mate shifted uncomfortably, as she felt many pairs of eyes turning towards her. 'Say something, Pheasant,' she whispered to him.

'My mate and I don't really venture outside the wood,' he said hurriedly. 'Being game birds, there is always the danger of being shot at.' He thrust out his gaudy breast. 'I'm told we're considered to be a great culinary delicacy by all well-bred humans,' he added, almost smugly.

'Kestrel, can you offer a more worthwhile piece of information?' Badger enquired, directing a withering glance at Pheasant. 'Of all the birds present, you spend more time than any outside the wood.'

Kestrel stopped preening and looked up with his habitual piercing glare. 'Yes, I can,' he said evenly. 'But I doubt if it will be of any real use. There's a sort of marshy pond on the enclosed army land on the other side of the trunk road. I haven't hunted over there for some weeks – it's never very rewarding at the best of times – and for all I know that, too, could have dried up. Apart from that, the most secluded expanse of water is a goldfish pond in a garden near the old church.'

'But that's in the old village, well over a mile away!' exclaimed Badger. 'Is there *nowhere* else?'

'Oh yes,' Kestrel replied without concern. 'There's a swimming-pool in one of the gardens on the new estate.'

'How close?'

'I suppose, for you, about fifteen minutes' travelling.'

'There'd be no cover: no cover at all,' Fox warned.

'I know,' Badger answered worriedly. 'But it's nearer. The smaller animals could never walk as far as the church and then back again, all in one night.'

'We could try!' piped up one of the fieldmice.

'Of course you could, and you would be very brave to do so,' said Badger kindly. 'But that would only be one journey.

If this drought continues we'll all have to make several journeys to drink what we need.'

'The only suggestion I can make,' said Hare, 'is for the larger animals to carry the smaller – as many as we can manage.'

'Yesss,' drawled Adder. 'I could carry several little mice and voles in my jaws, and I should be so gentle, they wouldn't feel a thing.' His tongue flickered excitedly. 'I should so enjoy carrying the plump ones,' he went on dreamily. 'And Owl could manage a young rabbit or two in his talons, couldn't you, Owl?'

'You're not looking at the situation in at all the right frame of mind, Adder,' admonished Badger, looking with some sympathy at the smaller animals, who were huddling together as far away from Adder as they could manage without actually bolting into the tunnel. 'You're merely thinking, as usual,' he went on, 'of a way in which you can benefit personally from it. I know what you're thinking, and it won't do. It won't do at all. We're a community, facing a dangerous crisis. You know the Oath.'

'Just a suggestion,' hissed Adder, with a scarcely disguised leer. He was quite undismayed by the effect his words had had on the fieldmice and voles.

'Now calm down, mice,' soothed Badger. 'Calm down, rabbits. You'll come to no harm in my set.'

When the Assembly appeared to be more relaxed again, one of the squirrels said, 'Couldn't we dig for water?'

Badger looked towards Mole. The latter shook his black velvet head. 'No, I don't think it's really possible,' he said. 'We'd only be wasting our energy, I'm afraid.'

There was silence then, while every animal cudgelled his brains for a way out of the difficulty. The seconds ticked past.

Suddenly, a voice was heard calling from the passage outside. 'Hallo! Who's there? Who's there?'

Weasel ran to the tunnel. 'I can see something moving,'

13

he said. Then he called out, 'This is Weasel! The other animals are here, too . . . Good Heavens, it's Toad!' he exclaimed.

'I've been looking all over the place for everyone,' said the newcomer, as he stumbled into the Chamber. 'I've been so worried: I thought you'd all deserted the wood. Then I heard voices.' He sat down to regain his breath. 'And I noticed the lights.'

'Toad, whatever happened to you?' Badger cried, as all the animals gathered round him. 'We'd given you up for lost. Wherever have you been? We haven't seen you since last spring. And you're so thin! My dear chap, tell us what has happened.'

'I . . . I've been on a long journey,' Toad said. 'I'll tell you all about it when I've got my breath back.'

'Have you had anything to eat recently?' Badger asked with concern.

'Oh yes – I'm not hungry,' he replied. 'Just tired.'

The heaving of his speckled chest gradually quietened as he recovered from his exertions. The other animals waited patiently for him to begin. He looked wearily round his audience.

'I was captured, you know,' he explained. 'It happened last spring, at the pond. They . . . they took me a long way away – oh! miles away! I thought I would never see any of you again.'

He paused, and some of the animals made soothing, sympathetic noises.

'Eventually, though, I managed to escape,' Toad went on. 'I was lucky. Of course, I knew I had to make my way back here – to the pond where I was born. So I started out that very day. And ever since, except during the winter months, I've managed to get a little nearer: little by little, mile by mile, covering as much ground as I was able to each day.'

Fox looked at Badger, and Badger nodded sadly.

'Toad, old fellow, I . . . I'm afraid there's bad news for you,' Fox said with difficulty. 'Very bad news.'

Toad looked up quickly. 'What . . . what is it?' he faltered.

'Your pond has gone. They've filled it in!'

3

Toad's story

Toad looked at Fox with an expression of disbelieving horror. 'But . . . but . . . they couldn't!' he whispered. 'I was born there. My parents were born there . . . and all my relatives, and acquaintances. And every spring we have a reunion. Toads all around leave their land homes and make for their birthplace. They couldn't take that away from us!' He looked pathetically from one sad face to another, almost compelling someone to deny this awful piece of information; but he received no answer.

'Filled *all* of it in? Is it . . . quite gone?' Toad's voice shook.

'I'm afraid so,' Badger mumbled. 'But, you know, there was very little left of it really. With this drought the water had nearly all dried up anyway.' He knew his words were of no comfort.

'What about the other toads?' Toad asked hoarsely.

'I think they had probably left the pond before this happened,' Fox said encouragingly. 'After all, it is May now . . .'

'Yes, yes,' Toad agreed morosely. 'I'm late. It's not spring any more, really. Not what we toads call spring.'

'This drought,' Badger rejoined, 'is a danger for all of us.

That's why I called this Assembly. There's *no* water left, Toad. None anywhere in Farthing Wood. We just don't know what to do.'

Toad did not reply. His downcast face took on a new expression. He looked considerably more hopeful. 'I've got it!' he exclaimed excitedly. 'We'll leave! All of us! If I could do it, so can all of you!'

'Leave Farthing Wood?' Badger queried with some alarm. 'How could we? What do you mean?'

'Yes, yes! Let me explain.' Toad stood up in his excitement. 'I know the very place to go to. Oh, it's miles away, of course. But I'm sure we could manage it, together!'

The other animals began to chatter all at once, and Badger completely failed to quieten them.

'We must face the facts!' Toad cried. 'What you've just told me about the pond has brought our danger home to me with a jolt. Farthing Wood is finished; in another couple of years it won't even exist. We must all find a *new* home. Now – before it's too late!'

The other voices broke off. Toad's voice dropped to a whisper. 'The Nature Reserve,' he announced dramatically. 'We shall all go to the Nature Reserve, where we can live in peace again. And *I* shall be your guide.' He looked round triumphantly.

'Dear, dear! I don't know.' Badger shook his striped head. 'You'd better tell us all about it, Toad. I don't know if it's a good idea. If it's so far . . .'

'Go on, Toad,' Fox broke in. 'Tell us about your adventure, right from the beginning.'

Toad sank back into his accustomed comfortable squat, and cleared his throat.

'You'll recall how last spring was very warm – in March particularly,' he began. 'Well, one weekend there were a tremendous number of humans at the pond; young ones with their horrible nets and glass jars – and a lot of them had brought their parents along. Everything in the pond was in a panic; there seemed to be no escape anywhere. The young humans were even wading out nearly to the middle of the pond in their eagerness to capture us. I remember I dived underwater and tried to hide in the mud on the bottom. So did a lot of others. But it was no use. They found me; and I was prodded into a jam-jar and carried away.'

'How awful for you,' one of the lizards commiserated. 'They come after us, too, with those stifling glass jars that are made specially slippery, so that you can hardly grip the bottom.'

'Ghastly things,' muttered Toad. 'I must have been kept in it for three or four hours, I should think. I was submitted to the indignity of watching my captors eat their food by the side of *my* pond, while I was left out in the sun, trying frustratedly to scale the sides of the jar, without so much as a leaf to protect me. If the weather had been any hotter, I'm sure I would have dried up.'

'I *like* to sunbathe, myself,' said Adder. 'But, of course, you amphibians have never really learnt to live comfortably on dry land.'

'Just the same as you reptiles can't adapt to swimming and diving!' retorted Toad.

'I can swim when I have to,' Adder returned.

'Well, well,' nodded Badger. 'What happened next, Toad?'

'They took me away,' he said. 'I don't know for sure how far, because I took the opportunity of having a nap during the journey. They put me in the back of their car, and the next thing I knew I was being tipped into a glass box in their garden.'

'How long did they keep you in this glass box?' asked Fox.

'I suppose about four weeks,' replied Toad. 'They put some netting on the top as a lid, and one day their wretched cat, who was always prowling around trying to get at me, knocked it off. So I leapt as high as I could, and I managed to jump out of the box and hide behind a shed. That very night I started my journey home.

'I hadn't got very far before I decided I ought to strengthen myself with a good meal. All the humans had ever given me was mealworms; tasty enough, but so boring without some change to relieve the diet. I still think you can't beat a juicy earthworm, fresh and moist from its burrow.'

'Hear, hear!' cried Mole feelingly. 'Nothing like them! I could eat them till I burst. Never tire of 'em.'

'It's a wonder there are any left at all, with your appetite,' remarked Tawny Owl.

'Oh, nonsense, there are plenty for everyone,' Mole justified himself a little shamefacedly. 'Though during this dry weather I have my work cut out finding them. They do go down so deep, you know.'

'Yes, of course,' said Toad. 'Anyway, when I had eaten my fill, my first problem was to get out of that garden. The great difficulty lay in getting round the wall. There was no wooden fence with convenient gaps in it – just a stone wall all round the garden. However, I was determined not to be disheartened, and there was one thing in my favour. The wall had bits of pebble and flint stuck into it – for decoration perhaps, I don't know – and I knew I could use these projecting pieces to climb up.

'It took so long, however, that I was sure daylight would break before I had reached the top, particularly as I fell off about four times, and had to start again. But I knew I had to get up that wall, even to have a chance of setting out for Farthing Wood.

'Well, I got to the top eventually, and walked along to the end of the wall. By that time it was just starting to get light, and I knew I would have to jump for it. I looked all round for a plant or something to break my fall, but there was nothing; only concrete all around. Of course, I couldn't possibly risk jumping on to that, so I had to lower my legs over the edge, and climb down the pebbles again. Fortunately, it didn't take as long as going up, and I was just thinking I could probably jump the last few inches when that horrible cat came out of the house. I pressed myself close to the wall and froze.'

Toad broke off, and contemplated his enthralled audience. The room was completely, utterly silent, so that you could have heard a pine needle drop. The young squirrels had wrapped themselves cosily in their mothers' thick tails, and the fieldmice and voles were now all bunched together in a large, furry mass, which was animated only by a score or so of quivering pink noses. Every animal gave Toad his rapt attention. Only Adder appeared to be taking no further interest in the proceedings. He had allowed his head to drop forward, but whether he was asleep or not would have been difficult to say.

'Would you believe me,' Toad went on quietly, 'if I told you I stayed in that spot all day, trying to look like another pebble? I couldn't risk climbing down any further because there was nowhere to hide, and if the cat had seen me it would have been the end of me.

'Fortunately, the day was reasonably cool, and as soon as it was safely dark, I let myself drop the rest of the way to the ground, and then crawled and hopped as far as I could away from the house. There were only one or two other houses nearby, and once I'd got past them I began to feel much freer. My sense of direction told me what course to take, and I kept on down to the end of the road. This was sealed off by a sort of ditch, and behind that a fence. I knew I was on the right route, and those two things didn't present much of a barrier to me. I hadn't gone far on the other side when I realized I must be in some sort of private park, because the fence stretched as far as I could see in both directions.

'Now I don't know exactly why it was, but the more I

looked at that fence, the safer I felt. I suppose it was because I knew I was on the right side of it.

'It was very quiet and peaceful in there, and a lovely bright moon was shining as I made my way along, flicking up a few insects on the way. I decided to make my bed under some trees, so I scooped out a little hole in the earth, and pulled some dry leaves round me. I slept quite well during the day because, apart from the birds, no one seemed to be about.

'When it was dusk I emerged again, and continued forward. After a while, the trees gave way to some open land, and ahead of me I could sense water. You can't imagine how excited I became at that, after all those weeks without a dip. It was another bright, moonlit night, and eventually I could see a pool ahead, where the moon was reflected perfectly. As I approached I thought I could hear one or two croaks coming from the water. I realized I had not been mistaken, when the whole party of the pool's inhabitants started croaking in unison, making a tremendous racket. It was a call I couldn't place, unlike any I had heard before. They were obviously frogs – but what sort of frogs?

'As I didn't know if they were likely to be friendly, I approached the water's edge cautiously, and just watched them for a while. There seemed to be quite a number of them splashing about in the centre of the pool, and some were just floating, with their heads out of the water. These were the ones making the noise. They were blowing out their cheeks like two bubbles in their efforts to croak the loudest.

'After I had been there for a little while, they stopped croaking, and seemed to decide amongst themselves that it was time to leave the water. They began to make for the shore, some swimming in my direction. I stood my ground. As they clambered out, one of them called, "We've got a visitor. A toad."

'They all came up to have a look, remarking that they hadn't seen me before, and that the toads who shared their pond in the spring had all been gone a week or more to make their homes on land. They made quite a fuss of me when I told them my story. They explained to me that they had just left the pond to feed, and invited me to join them.

'There was no shortage of food, and we were all able to eat our fill. Although it was night-time, I was able to discover that these unusual frogs were a definite shade of green, with darker spots, and a stripe of a paler colour down the centre of the back. When we had finished eating, they asked me to join them in a swim, and I was glad to accept.

'We swam out to the centre, and rested amongst the water-weed, and I took the opportunity of asking them about the park. Their spokesman was an old, fat male who seemed to be a sort of patriarch of their society. He told me the park was called White Deer Park, and it was a Nature Reserve.'

Toad paused for effect, and there were obliging murmurs of, 'Ah' and 'Of course – the Nature Reserve.'

'We have heard of these Nature Reserves,' said Badger. 'Do they, in fact, reserve nature?'

'Exactly as the name implies,' Toad answered emphatically. 'My friends the frogs told me all about it. A Nature Reserve is a piece of land – or water – of exceptional value and interest because of the rare animals or plants – or both – in it. There is a certain breed of human called a Naturalist, who, unlike most ordinary humans, spends his time learning about, and caring for, animals and plants. Their prime consideration is our well-being and safety. The frogs told me these Naturalists usually work in groups, and it was one of these groups that decided that *their* homeland, White Deer Park, was too valuable to be left unprotected. So, about three years ago, it was sealed off, designated a Reserve, and now no humans are permitted entry to it without a special pass. Even then, they may not remove any animal or plant from the Reserve whatsoever.'

'It sounds wonderful,' said Hare's mate. 'Peace and security all the time. No hiding. No running away. No guns!'

'And that's not all,' Toad went on. 'The Reserve is under the permanent care of one of the Naturalists, who is called a Warden. The animals' health and safety is in his keeping, and he patrols the Reserve to ensure their protection.

'Apparently, in the frogs' park there is a herd of albino deer which is unique. They themselves are a colony of rare frogs, called Edible Frogs by the humans, although luckily nobody is allowed to eat them. There is also an unusual type of water-plant in their pond, and they believe one or two rare butterflies feed in the Park. But they assured me that there is also a good representation of the commoner animals, like ourselves, who live there and benefit from the protection.'

'Why, it sounds like Paradise,' breathed Badger. 'I can't think why you wanted to leave it.' Fox looked at him meaningfully, and Badger went on quickly, 'That is, of course, I understand why you did. But . . . but . . . tell me, Toad, how far is it? It's taken you months to get here.'

'It's certainly a long way,' agreed Toad. 'I wouldn't deny it. I spent a week with the frogs, and then explained to them that I had to go on. Of course, they understood perfectly.'

'Is it a large park?' asked Fox.

'One of the frogs told me that he'd heard it was about five hundred acres, which, as you can imagine, would more than hold all of Farthing Wood! And I mean the old wood – as it used to be.

'Anyway, it took about another week to cross the park completely. Then, every day after that, I pressed on, never staying in one place more than a day. I travelled mostly in the dark hours, finding a convenient hiding-place during the day-time. I ate what I could on the move . . . and so the weeks went on. I must tell you that I was constantly buoyed up by the thought that every day, every step or hop, brought me nearer to my friends.'

'Good old Toad,' said Badger under his breath.

'When I noticed the weather was beginning to get colder I tried to hurry. I could sense there wasn't a tremendous distance left, and I wanted to get home before the winter really arrived. But I knew if I didn't eat properly, and the winter overtook me, I would die. So I compromised, I kept on going, but at a more leisurely pace, eating as much as I could find every night. Finally, I knew it was time to hibernate. The other frogs and toads, and lizards too, that I had encountered during the previous week or so, had been looking for a comfortable roost, and I found one on some farm land.

'I chose a grassy bank, by a ditch where there was plenty of cover. Food was becoming scarce by now, and I spent all day picking up what I could. Then, as night was approaching, I dug myself a nice hole under a large stone, and settled into that. It was really quite cold by then, and I felt so sleepy that I went out like a light as soon as I closed my eyes.

'Well, there I stayed until the warm spell at the beginning of March woke me up, and then I had a good meal at an ants' nest, and set off again. And . . . the rest you know, really.'

'A brave fellow indeed,' remarked Badger warmly.

'Very courageous,' agreed Weasel.

'What tremendous perseverance!' commented Fox. 'I've always admired you toads for that. Once started on something, you just won't be diverted!'

'I'd do it again, gladly, if you'd all come with me,' said Toad stoutly.

'That's fighting talk!' cried Badger. 'How about it, everyone? Shall Toad be our guide to a new home?'

'And a fresh start for everybody,' Toad added, 'away from the threat we've been living under here for so long?'

There was a deafening chorus of agreement.

'Then it's farewell to Farthing Wood?'

There were more shouts of approval. The animals were excited now.

'Better to say, "Welcome to White Deer Park",' said Mole.

'Now Mole, don't get carried away,' said Badger kindly. 'We haven't even taken our first step yet, you know.'

Mole grinned contritely. Badger looked around the chamber.

'Are there any dissenters?' he asked formally, and studied every individual face. There was no reply.

'Then I take it as unanimous. We go to White Deer Park!'

4

Preparations

There was a tremendous hubbub as all the animals started chattering at once, and the young animals ran around chanting: 'White Deer Park! White Deer Park!' in their shrill voices, as if they had already forgotten the existence of Farthing Wood. Even Adder evinced enough interest to uncoil himself and slither towards Toad to ask him for more details about the colony of frogs. He had decided these must be particularly succulent if even the humans considered them edible.

'Really, Adder, can't you forget your stomach for one minute?' asked Toad testily. 'Besides, you must promise not to hunt the frogs. They're very rare and important. We don't want to be accused of harbouring a viper in our midst, you know.'

Adder scowled, his red eyes turned to a deeper hue by the pale, greenish light in the Chamber. The pun did not amuse him.

'Quite right, Toad. We must have no ideas of that sort in our minds as we set out,' Badger agreed. 'As their prospective guests, we should be determined to be on our best behaviour. But enough of this! We have a very dangerous, harrowing journey ahead of us. We must plan! Quiet, everyone! Quiet PLEASE!

'Now, er . . . Fox, how shall we begin? I'm rather a sedentary animal. I'm afraid I haven't any real experience of this sort of thing. But you go further afield.'

'I suggest we begin by asking Toad what sort of terrain we shall have to cover on the journey,' said Tawny Owl drily.

'H'm!' Badger cleared his throat. 'Yes, of course . . . I was just coming to that. Toad?'

'To be absolutely truthful,' said Toad, 'because I don't want you to have any illusions, I can't offer you much comfort. The country we have to cross is almost all hostile. We begin by going through the housing estate, thus skirting the army land . . .'

'Hold on,' interrupted Badger. 'That's a bit risky, isn't it?'

'Well, of course we should travel at night,' said Toad.

'But supposing there were cats about? Or dogs? There might be dogs loose.'

'*I* came that way,' said Toad, a little offended. 'The army land is more dangerous. They have shooting practice – and bombs.'

'I think I must appeal to you birds,' Badger said. 'None of you, I know, is obliged to join us land animals. But we shall need you for reconnaissance. You can fly on ahead – spy out the land, as it were – and tell us if it's safe to proceed. What do you say?'

'I can't see in the dark!' retorted Pheasant.

'I'll scout for you during the day,' said Kestrel, 'but only Tawny Owl can help you at night.'

'Will you help, Owl?' asked Badger.

'Of course I will,' said Tawny Owl, very much on his dignity. 'How could you think otherwise? I brought the birds to the Assembly, didn't I?'

'Thank you, my feathered friends,' said Badger, looking so pointedly at Pheasant that he turned away and pretended to be passing a remark to his mate.

'If we're all to travel together,' said Fox, 'we shall have to do so at a speed that *everyone* will be able to maintain comfortably, from the largest to the smallest.'

'From the swiftest to the slowest,' corrected Badger. 'Who is the slowest of us?'

'Mole!' a dozen voices shouted accusingly.

'I can walk as fast as Toad,' Mole said, a little hurt.

'Not overland,' said Toad. 'We shan't be digging tunnels, you know.'

'Never mind, Mole,' said Badger sympathetically. 'We're all made in different ways. It's not your fault. None of us can dig as fast as you can.'

'We don't seem to be getting very far,' Tawny Owl broke in impatiently. 'We haven't got beyond Farthing Wood yet.'

'I think we should go through the estate, as Toad says,' remarked Fox. 'We shall all need to drink our fill where we can. Kestrel will have to direct us to the swimming-pool he mentioned.'

'Very well,' Badger conceded. 'Then that is our first objective. But we must aim to be well clear of the estate by daylight.'

'How are *we* to manage?' asked Pheasant. 'We're not nocturnal like Owl and most of you animals. We can't fly at night.'

'You'll have to follow me,' said Tawny Owl. 'You'll be able to see *me*, I suppose?'

'But how will Kestrel find his way to the swimming-pool?'

'I shall manage,' said Kestrel. 'Don't forget the estate is well lit. I shall fly slowly, ahead of the main party, and stop at the pool, where I shall hover as a signal, until the rest arrive.'

'Excellent,' said Badger. 'Now, Toad, would you care to continue?'

'Well, once we've left the estate behind,' Toad went on, 'and, remember, we have to cross the trunk road on the way – we have a long stretch of farmland to pass through; lots of fields and orchards. That shouldn't be too difficult at night. After that we come to the river. If the drought holds, that won't be much of an obstacle. Then it gets more difficult. But I can tell you more about what's ahead as we go on.'

'Yes, that's the best plan,' agreed Badger. 'We'll cross our bridges as we come to them.'

'Well, let's hope we come to one when we reach the river,' Hare said jocularly. 'I'm no water lover.'

Everyone laughed at this, and when the laughter had died down, one of the voles piped up: 'When do we start?'

'At once,' replied Badger. 'That is, tomorrow night. We all need a good rest first, so that we can start refreshed.'

Some of the animals started to edge towards the door, feeling that the meeting was over. 'We haven't quite finished yet,' Badger called to them. 'There are various officers to appoint. We've decided Toad is to be our guide. Kestrel and Owl will go ahead as scouts. But we need a leader; someone who is courageous, and able to make quick decisions. I can't think of anyone better than you, Fox.'

Fox showed his appreciation by wagging his tail. 'I, in turn,' he replied, 'should like to nominate you as quartermaster, Badger. With your good sense applied to food, I'm sure we shall all have enough to eat every day.'

'I'm most obliged to you, Fox,' he said. 'But I beseech all of you to fill your stomachs well tomorrow, before we meet. We can't know for sure when we shall eat next. Now are there any other points we haven't discussed, anyone?'

'Yes,' squeaked one of the fieldmice. 'For the benefit of the smaller animals, I'd like to ask that we all renew the

Oath tonight, in full company. I'm sure we'd feel more comfortable with the knowledge that everyone is bound by solemn oath to help all the others.'

'A worthy thought,' agreed Badger. 'We shall call this new oath, the Oath of Mutual Protection. We must all swear that, for the duration of our journey, our first consideration is for the safety of the party; in other words, the safety of each individual. Adder, I think it might be appropriate if you were the first to swear.'

'I swear,' said Adder with resignation, while actually still thinking about the Edible Frogs.

One by one the animals and birds of Farthing Wood adopted the Oath, and even the young repeated the words as their parents had done, feeling proud of the fact that they were not excluded from the solemn procedure.

'I think it would be as well,' said Badger afterwards, 'if each *group* of animals chooses a leader, who will be able to represent them at any discussions we need to have for planning our journey. They can report to Fox tomorrow, when we meet for a last talk before we leave.'

'When the village clock strikes twelve tomorrow night,' said Fox, 'I shall be under the Great Beech by the hedgerow. Meet me there.'

Badger looked all round again. No one had anything further to say. 'I now close the second Assembly of Farthing Wood,' he intoned.

The animals filed slowly out along the tunnel to the open air. Adder brought up the rear and, feeling hungry, doused the insect lights as he went.

5

Farewell to Farthing Wood

All day the bulldozers crashed forward on their path of destruction. Shrubs, young trees and undergrowth fell before the cruel onslaught of the monsters' greedy steel jaws. Old trees, stately and dignified with age, were mercilessly machined down by vicious saws. Yard by yard the forest fell back before the human despoilers; and, crouching in their burrows and tunnels, or huddled in the remaining tree-tops, or cowering under the bracken, the animals of Farthing Wood listened, shuddering, and longed for darkness.

Badger, in his cool set, heard the roaring and crashing grow nearer and nearer, but dared not stir. Fox, in his earth at the foot of the slope, panted in the heat, and waited for the chime of five from the village clock which, he had learnt, signalled the end of the noise, and the departure of the men.

The squirrels leapt from tree to tree, watching old homes uprooted in their wake, and Mole dug deeper and deeper down into the earth, trying to reach a point where he could no longer feel the terrible vibrations.

Under the hedgerows the hedgehogs lay among the leaves like a set of pin-cushions, while Toad and the lizards kept out of sight in the undergrowth.

Tawny Owl, in the highest branch of his favourite elm, ruffled his feathers and closed his large round eyes to the sunlight, while Pheasant and his mate squatted in the thick ground-ivy in the densest part of the wood, and kept as quiet as the fieldmice.

Adder had draped himself over a birch-stump to enjoy the sun, but when the machines had approached he had vanished in a flash into the thick bracken.

Only Kestrel, soaring high above the wood, was free to watch the advance of the humans and their machines. As he watched, he knew he had been right to join the animals' party, for pretty soon everything below would be desolation; and after that followed the brick and concrete.

So the dreadful hours passed, and only when evening came, bringing silence, was it possible for Farthing Wood, in the last few snatched hours, to sleep.

Shortly before midnight, Badger awoke and looked sorrowfully around. Never again would he sleep in his own chamber in this beloved set, where he had fond memories of his young days in the care of his parents, and which had been used by his ancestors for centuries.

For the last time, he shuffled along the corridors and paused at the exit, sniffing all round warily. He wondered if there were badgers in White Deer Park, and, if he should ever reach it, where he would construct his new set. It was hard that, at his age, he should be driven out from his birthplace and ancestral home by callous humans, who seemed to ignore the very existence of their weaker brother creatures.

He trotted out into the open and down the slope, glancing back every so often, and telling himself each time he was a sentimental fool, and that he must forget all about the old life now. He had new responsibilities, and these were more important. After all, the journey ahead was an exciting challenge; a chance for animals to match their wits against the clever and cunning humans. But it was difficult not to feel sad about leaving his old home.

A grey shape fluttered down from a tree in front of him. 'Oh, there you are, Owl!' he exclaimed with a slight jump. 'I'm just taking a last look round.'

'Doesn't do to be too sentimental, Badger,' commented Tawny Owl. 'Yet I must admit I'm glad I shall never witness the final end of the old place. At least we shall be spared that.'

At that moment the clock chimed twelve. 'There it goes!' cried Badger. 'Come on!' He set off briskly, half trotting, half ambling, through the trees. Tawny Owl flapped along almost at his side, sensing his need for company.

At the Great Beech they found Fox and Weasel, Toad and the lizards, and the rabbits. Kestrel was perched on the lowest bough, staring piercingly ahead like a sentinel. Pheasant and his mate had arrived at the meeting-place at dusk, and were dozing at the foot of the tree.

The elected leaders of the lizards and rabbits, in both

cases the oldest and most experienced members of their communities, took up their positions alongside Fox and Weasel as Badger and Tawny Owl arrived.

'It's a fine night,' Fox remarked. 'But the moonlight is a little too bright for my liking.'

'Should we postpone it?' asked Badger.

'No. I don't think that would be a good idea. The humans are too close now for safety.'

Badger nodded. 'It was a frightening day, today,' he agreed.

'I had to run for it,' squeaked Weasel. 'They came right on top of my burrow.'

The other animals were not long in arriving, but when Fox took the count he found Mole was missing.

'Confound it! Where is he?' demanded Fox with annoyance. 'We've no time to lose.'

'It's just as well, really,' remarked Adder spitefully. 'He was going to slow us all up as it was.'

Badger rounded on him angrily. 'He'd be better company than you, at any rate,' he snapped. 'We're not leaving without Mole. How could we leave him alone?'

Harsh words never bothered Adder. 'There's no need to get your fur in a bristle,' he said quietly. 'I was merely thinking of the safety of the others.'

'We'll give him until the next stroke of the clock,' Fox said. 'After that . . . well, we can't wait for ever, Badger, old fellow.'

'Give me a little time,' said Badger. 'I think I know where to find him.'

'All right. But do be quick!' warned Fox.

Badger trotted quickly off in the direction of his set, looking all round as he went for any sign of his friend.

He reached his old home again, and entered it, taking the passage leading to the Assembly Chamber. Once in there he went up to the hole through which Mole had emerged on the previous day, when he had tunnelled his way to the meeting.

'Mole!' called Badger loudly down the tunnel. 'Are you there?'

No answer.

'Mole, wake up and come out quickly! It's Badger! We're all waiting for you!'

Still no sound.

'Oh dear,' said Badger. 'Where *can* he be?' He decided to make one final attempt. Pushing his striped head right inside the tunnel, he took a deep breath and yelled, 'M-O-O-O-L-E' as loudly as he could manage. It made him cough a bit, and he realized again how thirsty he was. Then he thought he heard a faint scuffling noise.

'H-A-L-L-O-O-O!' he called again.

'Is . . . is that you, Badger?' came a timid voice.

'Yes,' said Badger. 'For goodness sake come out, Mole. What are you doing in there?'

'I'm . . . I'm not coming,' said Mole faintly.

'Not coming? Whatever do you mean? Of course you're coming. Now, hurry up! The others are all waiting.'

'No,' said Mole. 'It's no good, Badger. It's kind of you to come and look for me . . .' His voice broke off in a sob. 'But . . . but . . . I'd be no good to you. I'm . . . too . . . slow.'

'Oh, Mole! What nonsense,' said Badger. 'We can't bear to leave you here. How could we? Please come out.'

'They . . . said . . . I was . . . too slow,' Mole said jerkily, in between his sobs.

'Never mind what anybody said,' Badger replied consolingly. 'We're all going together. *Nobody* is to be left behind. Think how sad the others would be if you didn't come. They'd never forgive themselves.'

There were more scuffling noises.

'I'll tell you what,' Badger went on, convinced Mole was

now making his way down the passage. 'You can climb up
on to my back, and I'll carry you. I won't notice a thing.'

'Will you, Badger? Will you really?' Mole's voice
sounded closer now; and presently Badger could see him,
moving along the passage using a rowing motion of his
front paws to pull himself through the dry soil.

Badger withdrew his head, and presented his back to the
hole. 'Jump on!' he said kindly. Once he felt Mole's claws
holding firmly on to his fur, he quickly made for the exit.

'I'm sorry to be so silly,' said Mole. 'You are . . . so kind
to me, Badger.'

'Say no more about it,' answered Badger, as they left
the set. He trotted hurriedly back towards the Great Beech.
'We'll just be in time,' he muttered to himself.

The village clock chimed the half-hour as they joined
the waiting animals. Fox wagged his tail as he saw Mole on
Badger's back, but kindly passed no remark.

'Right, Kestrel, when you're ready,' he called. 'The
party's complete.'

Without answering, the small hawk leapt from his perch,
and swooped gracefully over the hedgerow. Tawny Owl
flew at his side in case of any difficulty in the dark, and the
pheasants behind them. The land animals set off in a bunch,
Fox leading with Weasel, and Toad hopping alongside.

Behind them were the rabbits, hares and hedgehogs; and the smaller creatures – voles, fieldmice, lizards and squirrels, followed close behind them. Badger and Mole brought up the rear, with Adder slithering as swiftly as he was able next to them.

Through gaps in the hedgerow the column of animals passed, all moving as quickly as they could. They stepped on to the vast expanse of dry, hard, pitted earth that had once been woodland, and where now the silent bulldozers stood like monsters regathering their strength for the next day's plunder.

Fox kept his eyes on Tawny Owl, who was flapping and gliding slowly along, about twelve feet above the ground. Ahead of them, all the animals could see scattered lights from houses on the fringe of the estate, where the occupants were still wakeful.

Fox saw Tawny Owl suddenly wheel and come flapping towards him. 'Kestrel says the street lights are out,' he called softly. 'We're in luck!' He flew off again, without waiting for an answer.

The animals watched the remaining house lights go out, one by one, as they drew nearer. Occasionally they turned their heads towards their old home, but Farthing Wood had become just a dark mass, which grew smaller and smaller against the starlit sky.

6

The long drink

At Number 25, Magnolia Avenue, the owner of the swimming-pool, Mr Burton, was standing by his bedroom window. Although he had felt very tired and had gone to bed at his usual hour of eleven o'clock, the bright moonlight shining into the room had prevented him from sleeping. So he had wearily slipped out of bed, taking care not to disturb his wife, and had gone downstairs to pour himself a consoling drink. He was gratefully sipping this now, as he stood looking out at his garden.

Mr Burton was proud of his garden. He had nurtured it carefully over four years from a patch of bare earth and weeds to something of colour and beauty. He looked down at his green, sloping lawn and his well-tended flower beds, and at his hedge of mixed shrubs. At the end of the garden, reached by a few steps, lay his new swimming-pool. Blue-painted, with imitation marble surrounds, it had been filled for only a couple of weeks, and although nobody had swum in it yet, Mr Burton felt sure it was the envy of his neighbours. Now he looked down with considerable satisfaction at the gleaming water which reflected the moonlight.

Mr Burton's eyes started to grow heavy, with tiredness.

Suddenly he saw a variety of shapes moving round the sides of the pool; and ripples appeared on the previously un-ruffled surface of the water. He wondered if he had perhaps been a little too generous when pouring out his nightcap, and he rubbed his eyes. Sure enough, there *was* some move-ment down there. Could it be cats?

He was just considering whether to go and investigate when his wife called impatiently to him to stop sleep-walking. Feeling a little guilty at being discovered with a glass in his hand, Mr Burton contritely returned to bed. So the animals, quite unaware that their presence had been detected, remained undisturbed.

Following Fox silently through a gap in the hedge, the little band of animals had arrived at the pool's edge only to dis-cover that the water was too far down for the smaller of them to reach. No matter how far over the sides they leant, it was impossible.

'Dear, dear,' said Badger. 'Now what are we to do?'

'Leave it to me,' said Fox, quite unruffled. 'Let the larger animals drink first, and then they can help the smaller.'

It turned out that only Fox and Badger were able to drink from the pool unassisted, and even they found it an awk-ward task. All the other animals watched them with concern, except Adder who persuaded Weasel to hold his tail in his teeth, while he slithered the front half of his body directly into the water.

The marble surrounds were shiny, and Fox's and Badger's claws slipped on the surface, putting them in grave danger of tumbling in as they leant over the edge thirstily lapping their first water for three days. However, no such accident occurred, and it was some time before their tremendous thirst was quenched. Finally, they raised themselves and sat back on their heels, licking their chops.

'I never knew water could taste so fine,' said Fox.

'I feel fit for anything now,' remarked Badger.

'Don't forget us,' said Mole, who had dismounted from Badger's back on their arrival.

'Of course we won't,' answered Fox. 'Now, over there are some steps leading down into the pool. The water just covers the top of the second one, so if I lie down on that, you smaller animals can climb on to my back and drink from there.' Without more ado, he jumped down and lay flat on the second step, with his head on his paws. The distance down to the first step was still too great for the short legs of the voles, the fieldmice and the lizards, and so Badger got on to that and lay down too. The smallest animals were then able to jump on to Badger's back, and from there on to Fox.

'Cling on tight,' Fox called. 'We don't want any accidents.'

The voles were the first to drink, and three or four of them were able to jump down at a time. They were followed by the lizards and fieldmice, who all drank their fill without any mishap.

Indeed, Hare's youngsters, the hedgehogs, squirrels and Mole, had all satisfied their thirst, when Toad, who had been casting longing glances at the water all through the proceedings, could withstand the temptation no longer. He took a flying leap and landed with a resounding plop about a yard out. This action, on its own, would have been no disaster, for after all, Toad was more at home in the water than on land, and he began to swim delightedly up and down. But the young rabbits, who had been getting more and more excited as the time approached for their turn to drink, took Toad's leap as a signal to themselves, and all together, in a bunch, they jumped over the edge, landing on top of Fox and knocking him into the water.

The mother rabbits, seeing their babies in the pool, followed them without a thought, and Weasel, who all this time had been on the other side holding Adder's tail in his teeth, opened his mouth to cry out a warning; whereupon Adder shot like a dropped anchor straight down to the bottom.

In a trice the swimming-pool was a mêlée of bobbing heads and thrashing feet, while the animals remaining on the edge ran hither and thither in anguish.

At this moment Kestrel, who had remained patiently hovering over the pool since his arrival, spotted the figure at the bedroom window of the house. 'We're being watched!' he called down. This increased the pandemonium in the water, as each animal struggled to reach the steps out of the pool. None of them was in any danger of drowning, as, in common with almost every land creature, they were all able to swim in their own particular way. The problem was, how to get out of the water?

Adder had swiftly surfaced after his surprise dip, but was only able to undulate up and down the pool quite helplessly. Fox managed to clamber up on to his step, where he vigorously shook his coat all over Badger.

Kestrel swooped down and perched on the hand-rail by the steps. 'All clear again now,' he said reassuringly.

Badger and Fox took up their old positions again, and one by one the rabbits were able to scramble out on to Fox's back.

It only remained now for the father rabbits, Hare and his mate, and Weasel to drink, and then their journey could continue. While this was accomplished, Adder continued to swim up and down in a tremendous bad humour, vilifying Weasel with the most insulting names he could remember.

'Don't worry, Adder,' said Fox. 'We'll get you out, once the water's had a cooling effect on your temper!'

The birds, who did not drink much anyway, were able to wet their throats with the water that had been splashed up on to the marble when the rabbits had dived in together.

'Anyone else?' asked Badger. There was no reply. He

and Fox then climbed back up, leaving only Toad and Adder in the pool.

Fox began to run up and down the garden, examining the flower-beds. Finally, he seemed to find what he wanted. After tugging vigorously at a clump of delphiniums, he ran back to his friends carrying a long, thin cane in his teeth.

'What's that for, Fox?' asked Mole.

'It's for Adder, of course,' Fox answered, dropping the cane at the side of the pool. 'Now then, Adder!' he called. 'I'm going to hold this stick by one end in my teeth. When I lower it over the side, you grip the other end in your jaws, and I'll pull you out.'

Adder agreed to this proposal, rather sullenly, and the cane was pushed into the water. 'Come on, Adder!' called all the other animals, and the snake turned in the water and swam towards the stick with his jaws open so wide that they all thought he intended to swallow it. His razor-sharp fangs sank into the end of the stick with a violence that nearly pulled it into the pool, with Fox clinging to the end.

'I think he was imagining the stick to be my tail,' Weasel whispered to Badger.

Fox slowly backed away from the pool, drawing Adder out of the water. Once on dry land again, Adder relaxed his grip on the stick, and slithered irritably up to the apprehensive Weasel.

Fox turned his attention to the pool again. 'Toad, old chap, I think you've had long enough in there now,' he remonstrated. (Toad was still splashing around merrily.) 'We've got to get on, and we need you,' Fox reminded him.

'I'm coming,' cried Toad, cheerfully blowing bubbles in the water. 'Just drop the stick over again, and I'll hang on.'

Fox lowered the cane into the water again, and Toad, clinging tightly to the end with his special grasping pads, was hauled clear.

'No time to lose,' said Fox. 'Is everyone ready?'

'We make for the trunk road now,' said Toad. 'At this hour it should be almost deserted. But we must hurry.'

'We'll meet you there,' said Tawny Owl, as he and Kestrel led the other birds away.

'Lead on, Toad,' said Fox. 'On to White Deer Park!'

The next morning Mr Burton looked with dismay at the grimy water in his previously gleaming pool. There were grubby footprints all over the imitation marble, and his clump of delphiniums was sagging. He knew that his beloved garden had indeed received visitors the previous night. Looking at the assorted footprints, he realized they had been left by a number of wild creatures, but whence they had come, or whither they were heading, he, like all the other human inhabitants of the estate, never knew.

7

Two narrow escapes

Swiftly out of the garden and into the unlit road went the group of animals, Badger once more carrying Mole. Toad led the way, hopping more than crawling, and leaving Fox and the larger animals to adjust themselves to a slow pace so that they would all keep together.

The animals chose the parts of the roads where it seemed to be darkest, and their luck held as Toad proudly led them through the maze of turnings towards the trunk road. They heard nothing and saw nothing to alarm them. There were no late cars driving home, and no dogs or cats in evidence.

As time wore on, the danger of discovery gradually lessened. The animals, all of whom had maintained complete silence since they left the garden, felt themselves to be safer and began to whisper to each other.

'Tawny Owl will be getting impatient,' Badger remarked. 'He must have been waiting a good hour and more. I've just heard the church clock chime three.'

'It's . . . not . . . much further,' panted Toad, who was beginning to tire. 'Once we get round the next corner . . .'

'Please, Badger, shall I walk for a bit?' asked Mole. 'I'm sure I'm too heavy for you.'

'Nonsense. Can't feel a thing,' Badger reassured him. 'Once we've got the trunk road behind us, we'll be able to rest.'

The animals' pace had slackened, owing to Toad's increasing tiredness. He was no longer able to hop, but could only manage a weary crawl. 'Can't you hurry up a bit at the front?' Adder hissed from his position as rearguard. 'At this rate, dawn will break and we'll still be on the estate.'

'Toad's doing his best,' said Hare. 'We've come a long way. The small animals are all very tired.'

'I'm not exactly feeling as fresh as a daisy myself,' replied Adder, 'but we've slowed almost to a halt.'

Fox, at the front with Toad, turned his head. 'Do stop complaining, Adder,' he said. 'Remember the rule we made about our travelling pace.'

'I'm sorry,' Toad said wearily. 'Of course . . . I didn't . . . do such long stages as . . . this when I . . . was alone.'

'I do feel guilty, riding like this,' wailed Mole. 'Everybody else is tired out, and I'm not helping at all. Oh dear!'

'You're helping more by staying up there than you would by trying to keep up with us walking,' Badger informed him.

'But I could keep up, Badger, you know, now you've slowed down.'

'If Mole wants to walk so much, I'll change places with him any time,' Adder murmured to Weasel. 'I'm sure I shall

rub all my scales off, if there's much more of this hard road.'

'Don't be ridiculous, Adder. How could you hold on?' said Weasel.

'I could coil myself round his neck,' Adder replied with a hint of malice.

'Don't be so unpleasant,' retorted Hare, who had overheard. 'I really can't see what benefit to our party you are at all.'

Adder merely bared his fangs at this rejoinder, and Hare accelerated his family a little further up the column.

At length the animals turned the last corner. Ahead of them, about a hundred yards distant, lay the trunk road, and beyond that the last few yards of the fenced-off army land which they had to skirt before they reached the first open fields.

Very slowly now, they advanced along the last road on the estate. Houses still posed a threat on either side, but now it was only a matter of minutes rather than hours duration. As they proceeded, four o'clock struck.

Halfway down the road they could hear Tawny Owl hooting to them; soon they could see him flying towards them.

'Thank goodness,' he said, landing beside Fox. 'I thought you'd got lost.'

'Oh no. Nothing like that,' Fox answered. 'Toad knew all the right turnings. He's been marvellous. But this walking on hard roads is terribly tiring.'

'The other birds have all found roosts and gone to sleep,' Tawny Owl told him. 'You'd better find somewhere quickly, where you can hide up during the day. It'll be light in a couple of hours.'

'Any ideas?' asked Fox. 'You've had a chance to look round.'

'There's a big gorse thicket just inside the railings of the army land,' Tawny Owl answered. 'I'd recommend that.

There's plenty of room for everyone. And no humans ever come down to that far corner. I'll go ahead now and keep an eye open for traffic. See you in a minute.'

He launched himself into flight and disappeared swiftly into the blackness ahead.

The last few yards of the road took the longest of any to cover, but the animals finally arrived together at the trunk road, where they rested on the pavement. Tawny Owl was perched on the railings on the other side of the road.

'There's no traffic,' he called across.

'Right-o, Owl,' Fox answered him. 'We'll get the youngsters across first. Hare, you can manage your family, and the hedgehogs and rabbits too. Owl will show you where to go.'

Hare put himself in charge of the first party, and under his direction they scuttled quickly across the wide road, and then followed Tawny Owl through the railings to the haven of the gorse patch.

Fox stood on the edge of the pavement, scanning the road in both directions for headlights. It was still clear.

'Come along, voles and fieldmice,' he called. 'Weasel, will you take them across? Quickly as you can.'

The second party took a little longer to cross, but reached the other side without mishap. Tawny Owl, who had returned to his perch on the topmost bar of the railings, repeated his task of guiding the animals to the gorse. They found that many of the young rabbits and hedgehogs had already dropped asleep.

'Good. Not many of us left now. Adder, you'll take the lizards across, please,' Fox ordered. Adder leered his consent. He was too tired to answer.

Everybody in this third party travelled so close to the ground that, in the darkness, the anxious Fox lost them from sight when they had covered only half the distance. He continued to scan the road in both directions. To his horror, in the far distance to his left, he saw a gleam of light. This rapidly increased in size.

'Adder, are you over yet?' he called urgently. 'There's a car approaching.'

'Nearly there,' Adder rasped. 'Come on, come on, quickly.' Fox could hear him hurrying the lizards.

Tawny Owl flew to the roadside to see if he could be of assistance. Adder and the lizards still had a couple of yards to cross, and the lights were very close now. The lizards put on a final spurt, and darted towards Tawny Owl. But Adder, with no projections on the flat surface to ease his passage, could only continue to wriggle across the road in an ungainly fashion. In the next second the lizards, who were just mounting the pavement, Tawny Owl and Adder were all caught in the beam of the car's headlamps.

'He'll never do it,' Fox whispered in horror to Badger. 'He's going to be hit!'

Then, miraculously, the beam of light swung slightly to the right, towards the animals still waiting to cross. The car was manoeuvring to turn into the estate road, and actually passed right by the struggling snake. Adder was safe.

The lizards had turned on the pavement to watch the fate of their large reptile cousin. As his head, with its sinister red eyes, appeared over the kerb, they cheered in excitement.

'A trifle close for comfort,' drawled Adder, as he slithered towards Tawny Owl.

'You're very lucky,' Tawny Owl said unfeelingly. 'Now quickly, this way. We're being investigated.' They disappeared through the railings.

The driver had stopped his car just inside the estate road down which the animals had travelled. He had first seen, in his headlights, Adder and Tawny Owl; the lizards were too small to distinguish. Then, as he turned the car, the lights had swept the opposite pavement, taking in Fox,

Badger and Mole, Toad and the squirrels. In amazement, he hurriedly stopped and got out to look.

'Quick, make a dash for it!' Fox urged them, and with the squirrels and Badger right behind him, he raced across the road just as the car driver arrived on the scene.

Safely on the other side, Fox looked round in dismay. 'Where's Toad?' the animals all cried together. 'We've forgotten Toad!'

Sure enough, at that very moment as they looked back, they saw the man bend down to examine something on the pavement. Then he looked all around for some moments. They held their breath. The man bent down again, and prodded the pavement with his shoe.

Toad, who at the best of times would not have been fast enough to escape pursuit, was so tired he could hardly move at all. As he felt the toe of the man's shoe touch him, he shuffled a mere couple of inches towards the road. His friends were all on the safe side of the road and he felt completely abandoned. The man's shoe started to move towards him again. The next thing he knew, there was a flurry of wings above him, followed by a sharp cry of pain.

Then Fox was by his side. 'Fast as you can, up my tail,' he whispered. Toad grasped Fox's thick brush, and clutching tightly with his front feet, pulled himself slowly up. Fox did not stop more than a moment. Once he was sure Toad was off the ground, he raced back across the road again, with Toad hanging grimly on behind.

Tawny Owl had stretched out his talons and skimmed the man's head, raking through his hair. The man's arms flailed wildly upwards and caught the bird a glancing blow on the back, but Tawny Owl, seeing that Fox and Toad were out of danger, flew steadily upwards in a wide arc until the man could no longer see him. Then he flew back over the road, and over the railings, landing by the gorse patch. The moment of danger had passed.

49

Tawny Owl looked through the thick, interlocking strands of gorse. Most of the animals seemed to be silent, and in the dimness he could make out various shapes huddled together.

'Thanks, Owl,' he heard Fox whisper. 'All safe now. Everyone's exhausted – no wish to talk at the moment . . .' he broke off to yawn. 'We're well hidden here . . . oh, I'm so tired . . . I think I'm the only one still awake. Toad's asleep already.'

'Goodnight, Fox,' whispered Tawny Owl.

'Goodnight, Owl,' he whispered back. 'See you in the evening.'

Tawny Owl flew slowly away to join the other birds before it grew light. The first stage of the journey was completed.

8

First camp

Mole, who had obviously been the least tired at the end of the journey through the estate, was the first to wake the next evening. It was still daylight. He looked all round at his companions, to see if there was anyone awake that he could talk to. But they all continued to sleep, their bodies rising and falling rhythmically; a gentle rhythm that had been undisturbed by the daytime traffic noise, or by passing pedestrians.

Again there had been no rain, and the air Mole sniffed inquisitively was moistureless and still. He was acutely hungry, and wondered if he should begin to dig for worms. Perhaps Badger had other ideas. When they woke, everyone would want to eat.

They had all been too exhausted even to consider food the previous night, but it had been many hours since any of them had eaten, and their stomachs would all feel uncomfortably empty. Mole looked at each of his companions again, but there were still no signs of life. He thought to himself that, after all, there would not be any harm in digging up just one or two worms – even three – to help pass the time until his friends woke.

He pulled himself out of the gorse thicket. 'Well, goodness gracious me!' he exclaimed. 'Wherever did they come from?'

A few inches away a large shallow hole had been scooped out of the ground. Inside it was a squirming mass of insects, worms and fat, juicy grubs. The temptation was too much for the famished Mole. He made a rush towards the feast.

'Oh, there you are!' he heard a voice above him. He looked up, and saw Kestrel and Tawny Owl perched side by side on a holly branch.

'I . . . I was just going to sample the dish,' Mole explained a little guiltily.

'Of course. Tuck in!' said Tawny Owl. 'We've collected it together while you were sleeping. Even Pheasant helped.'

'Of course I did,' said Pheasant from underneath the tree, where he and his mate were preening themselves. 'I unearthed most of those grubs, you know, Mole.'

'Oh. Thank you, Pheasant,' said Mole politely. 'Can I start then?'

'Go ahead,' Tawny Owl said. 'But where are the others?'

'Still sleeping,' answered Mole, as he selected an earthworm.

However, their voices seemed to have roused some of the sleepers. There were rustling noises in the gorse thicket and, after a moment or two, Badger's snout appeared through the prickles. According to his usual careful habit, he sniffed all round warily for any strange scents. Then he ventured into the open.

'Hallo, Badger!' Mole cried. 'Come and try these earthworms – they're magnificent! I can't remember ever eating such succulent ones before . . .'

'Hold on, hold on,' Badger scolded good-humouredly. 'Don't eat them all, Mole. I know your taste for worms!'

'I said to start on the food,' remarked Tawny Owl. 'Mole looked ravenous.'

'I was,' agreed Mole with his mouth full.

'Very kind of you, Owl, to get this together for us,' Badger remarked. 'I think perhaps I ought to wake the others, though, so that we can divide the food fairly.'

Mole stopped chewing, and looked guilty again. 'I say, Badger,' he said with embarrassment, 'I hope I haven't taken too much.'

Badger looked down at the pile of worms that Mole had scraped from the hollow into a heap in front of him. 'No, no,' he said kindly. 'There's plenty for all.' He lumbered off back into the gorse thicket, and presently there was a chorus of voices.

The other animals began to spill out through gaps in the bushes, uttering glad cries at the sight of food. Toad was last out, crawling rather stiffly. 'I'm still tired, but hunger comes first,' he remarked. 'Owl, I don't know how to thank you for saving me last night! I didn't get a chance to say so before – we were all so exhausted – but I'm very grateful. If it hadn't been for you and Fox . . .'

'Oh, nonsense,' Tawny Owl said, shuffling his feet on the branch uncomfortably. 'That is what our Oath is all about.'

'Nevertheless, I thought I was lost!' Toad said. 'When I felt that boot touch me, and I knew I couldn't run, I at once thought: if I'm done for, *they're* done for. It was an awful moment.'

'Well, well,' Tawny Owl nodded. 'I'm glad I could help. Now come on, Toad, eat your fill!'

Under Badger's direction, most of the animals were able to satisfy their appetites, with food to spare. But Hare and his family, the rabbits and the squirrels, and the little field-mice were unable to join in, as their diet did not include insects or worms. Since they were equally as hungry as the other animals, they had to set off at once in search of their own food.

Before they left, however, Badger consulted Fox, and it was decided that, on their return, there should be a council of the leading animals. This would be for the purpose of deciding what they should do in future about food, as, to a certain extent, they all had differing tastes.

Eventually, only Mole was left eating, while the rest of the animals lay down, replete, to await the return of the plant-eating group. The little creature was in raptures. With a blissful expression on his pointed face, he munched his way through his stock of worms, and then looked round to see what the others had left.

Finally he looked up. 'Owl, wherever did you manage to dig up such worms?' he asked. 'I pride myself on being a connoisseur, you know, and I've never tasted their equal.'

'Oh, Pheasant and Kestrel found a lot of them, I think,' Tawny Owl replied, without much interest.

'They weren't difficult to find,' said Kestrel. 'We went to the marshy ground – plenty of 'em there. Though, if there isn't some rain pretty soon, all that marsh will just dry up. A lot of it is dry already.'

A greedy expression came over Mole's face, which he quickly hid. 'Is . . . er . . . is it far to the marshy place?' he asked softly, trying very hard to appear nonchalant.

'Not for us,' replied Kestrel. 'But I couldn't say how long you'd take to get there.'

Mole's face dropped; then he looked quickly at Badger. Badger caught his eye. 'We shan't have time for that sort of thing,' he said. 'We've got to keep on the move.'

'Couldn't we . . . just have a quick look?' the disappointed Mole said beseechingly.

'We'll see,' Badger said. 'I don't think Fox will agree.'

Fox was drowsing in the last of the sun's rays, oblivious to all around him. He remained so, until the missing party returned.

On their arrival back at the camp, as dusk was falling, Fox hastily organized a meeting inside the gorse thicket.

'Well, everyone,' Badger began, 'it certainly seems that our original idea of my acting as quartermaster, and directing the collection of food for the whole party, will have to be abandoned.'

'I'm afraid it will, Badger,' said the elected leader of the rabbits, whose new position of importance had rather gone to his head. 'It's all right for you meat and insect-eaters, you know. But we vegetarians find worms and other creepy-crawlies most unpalatable.'

'We squirrels prefer nuts and things,' said their spokes-man. 'In any case, we're not used to eating – or sleeping – on the ground. We really only feel at home when we're up a tree, out of harm's way.'

'Your own individual habits may often have to be sacrificed for the benefit, even the survival, of the party,' Badger warned him. 'We decided all this before we left Farthing Wood. We shall not succeed in reaching our destination in one piece unless we conform.'

'Perhaps then, Badger, we could all eat grass for the duration of the journey?' suggested Rabbit. 'There's always plenty available. We never have to search far. It seems to me the simplest answer.'

'No, no,' Badger shook his striped head with some annoyance. 'It would play havoc with my digestion, and that of the other meat-eaters. Anyway, I wasn't referring to food just now. I was really thinking of how we travel, and where we rest. We must stick together. Safety in numbers, you see.'

'I'm afraid there seems to be only one solution to the food problem,' said Fox. 'For reasons of health and comfort we must all ensure that we eat the food we're used to – the food we like. Otherwise there's no knowing how many will fall by the wayside.'

'What do you suggest, Fox?' asked Badger.

'I suggest this. When we stop at the end of each day's journey, we go out in parties to obtain what food we need. The plant-eating animals would form one party, for instance; the squirrels another. We meat-eaters could hunt together, or individually. The birds can please themselves. But there is one point it will be necessary to agree upon: that is, the length of time allowed for searching for food. It should be the same for all, and we can decide on the amount of time we can spare at the end of each day. That way everyone will arrive back at the chosen resting-place at approximately the same time.'

The animals all agreed that that was the best plan.

'There's a second very important point to discuss,' said Toad. 'That is, the rate and distance we travel each day.'

'Surely we can't really forecast that?' Badger asked with a puzzled look.

'No, of course not. I've raised the point because our resolution to travel at a pace that would be comfortable even for the slowest of us doesn't really work in practice.'

At this remark, Mole looked most uncomfortable, as if he were quite sure Toad was alluding to his privileged position as a passenger. But he was relieved to discover that this was not so.

'The reason that we were all so tired after crossing through the housing estate last night,' Toad went on, 'was because for the slower animals, like myself and the lizards, the journey was too much for one day. Also, for the larger, quicker ones among us – like Fox, and Hare, and Weasel – the dreadfully slow pace at which they had to travel so that we all kept together, was fatiguing in the extreme. We'll have to remedy this.'

'I can give some help in that way,' said the leader of the lizards. 'We lizards have decided that it would be best, for ourselves, and for all of you, if we stay here on the army land.'

Toad nodded his agreement. But the other animals showed their amazement. 'This is silly,' said Badger quietly. 'We'll find a way round the problem. We can't just go off and leave you here. After all, you're really no slower than Adder. *He's* going on, aren't you, Adder?'

'Oh yes,' lisped Adder, who was still thinking very much about the Edible Frogs, but had no intention of mentioning it. 'In for a penny, in for a pound, I suppose,' he said.

'The truth is,' Lizard went on, 'the distance might well prove too great for us. After last night, we don't look forward to many weeks – or even months – of such hard going. And we know we'd be a burden to the rest of you.'

'I think you're very wise, Lizard,' said Toad. 'There's really nothing at White Deer Park you wouldn't be able to find here. Kestrel will be able to tell you that no humans use this corner of the army land. You're as safe here as in a Nature Reserve. They can't build here.'

'Exactly,' said Lizard. He turned to Badger, who looked as if he were about to try to persuade him to change his mind. 'You're very kind, Badger,' Lizard said. 'But I know, in your heart of hearts, you can see the sense in our decision.'

Badger dropped his head and nodded weakly. 'Well, I

suppose you're right,' he conceded. 'But I hope no one else is going to stay behind?'

None of the other animals appeared in the least disposed to call a halt to their journey.

'That's good,' said Fox. 'Now, I suggest that to recover fully from the first stage of our journey, we remain here for another day. Then, when we're completely rested, we can decide, with Toad's advice, where to make for on our next stage. Any disagreement?'

No voices were raised on this point, and the meeting ended. Lizard's intervention had prevented any definite plan on the animals' future travelling pace from being formulated.

The animals stayed in the gorse thicket until it was completely dark. Then some of them began to ask Kestrel and Tawny Owl about the water-hole in the marshy ground, and it was eventually decided that, after they had all taken another nap, Tawny Owl would show them the way.

Pheasant and his mate and Kestrel returned to their roosts, while the animals found comfortable sleeping-places. Mole decided to dig himself a short way into the earth, where he said he would sleep better, while the squirrels climbed up into a small oak tree.

Tawny Owl, who really came to life at night, and who was completely relaxed in the darkness, went and perched on a railing. Fox and Badger, who also spent most of their waking hours in the dark, elected to join him for a time, as they had too much on their minds to be able to sleep.

They sat down at the foot of one of the metal posts. Fully occupied with their thoughts, none of the three spoke for some time. Finally, Fox broke the silence. He seemed to air the thoughts of all of them when he said, 'I wonder just what chance we've got of going through with this thing?'

'Well,' said Badger, 'if we're careful, you know ...'

'I'm worried about Toad, you see,' Fox went on, as a light breeze began to blow soothingly through his fur.

'Everything depends on him really, and he's completely exhausted himself on the very first stage.'

'He made the journey before,' Badger pointed out.

'That's the whole point.' Fox gave his head a shake. 'Perhaps two journeys of such length will be too much for him. I was really thinking of *him* when I suggested staying on here another day.'

'He mustn't walk any more,' said Badger.' He'll just have to ride, like Mole.'

'I've had the same thought,' said Fox. 'I'd carry him willingly. But, apart from that, when he made the journey before, he only had himself to think about. He travelled at his own pace, within his own limits. *We've* got far greater responsibilities.'

'Oh come, Fox, it's early days yet,' put in Tawny Owl. 'It's not like you to be pessimistic.'

'I'm trying to be *realistic*,' returned Fox, a little brusquely. 'But you're right, Owl,' he added, 'we must look on the bright side and . . . well, go carefully.'

For some minutes longer, they sat there, eagerly breathing in the coolness of the breeze. Then Fox and Badger rejoined the other animals.

Tawny Owl spent a considerable time skimming noiselessly from tree to tree, enjoying the freedom of solitude and darkness. Occasionally, he hooted with all his old confidence, as he had done in the times when Farthing Wood had been intact. Eventually, deciding that the animals had napped long enough, he swooped swiftly in a graceful curve from a lofty elm branch and landed by the gorse thicket. Here he hooted again. 'If anyone wants a drink, now is the time,' he announced.

Almost at once he felt that he was standing on a small earthquake. The ground underneath him began to shake, and the earth definitely began to give way. Tawny Owl flapped upwards in alarm, and then noticed Mole's snout appearing through a hole in the ground, near where he had been standing.

'Good evening, Tawny Owl,' said Mole. 'I've had a wonderful sleep. I've quite slept off all those worms I ate.'

'You must have a *wonderful* stomach,' Tawny Owl remarked a little coldly. He was feeling peeved about showing alarm in front of Mole, an animal he felt to be distinctly inferior to himself.

'Oh yes,' said Mole cheerfully. 'I could quite easily start all over again now, and eat twice as many. Oh, I can't wait to get to that marsh. Where's Badger?'

'Behind you,' Tawny Owl said drily.

Mole gave a little jump. 'H . . . hallo . . . Badger,' he said.

'Now, Mole, Tawny Owl's taking us to the water. We're not searching for any more worms,' said Badger.

Mole looked very crestfallen. 'I didn't know you'd been listening,' he said in a small voice.

The kindly Badger relented a little. 'Well, perhaps there will be time for one or two,' he said. Then, turning, he called out, 'Come on, everyone! Tawny Owl's waiting.'

The animals began to assemble, talking amongst themselves about the drought, and the problem of finding water during their journey. Toad was still too tired to join them, and Adder's experience with water the previous day rendered him quite unwilling to make one of the party.

So this time the animals were able to set a smarter pace, and with Tawny Owl at their head, flapping like a grey ghost through the air, they moved off through the dry bracken and grass.

Every blade of grass, every fern-frond, seemed to be drooping for want of moisture. The grass stalks were dry and brittle, looking like so much straw, and everything, including the lower leaves on the scattered trees, was grimed with dust, and panting for air.

Mole, grimly clutching the brindled hairs on Badger's

back, thought only of the second feast he intended to have when they reached the marsh.

Under the animals' feet the ground felt bone hard, and it seemed to have retained a lot of the heat from the daytime sun, despite the slight breeze that blew. But after they had walked in silence for some time, the ground grew softer. It had a spongy feel to it; and from the clumps of dry reeds that abounded, the animals knew that they had reached the outskirts of the marsh, a part that had dried up. They began to tread carefully.

Fox, who was leading, saw Tawny Owl fly further ahead and then perch awkwardly on a reed tussock, there being no trees within easy distance. When the animals came up to him, he said, 'I can't go any further now. The water's just ahead. Watch how you go. The ground's very damp here.'

Fox nodded and went forward slowly, picking up his paws carefully, and gingerly testing the ground in front of him at each step. At this pace, the party went forward another twenty yards. Then Fox called back, 'I can see the water now. Everyone stay here, and I'll go forward and find a safe path.'

The animals held their breath as the chestnut body of their leader went further on, one slow pace at a time. After about thirty paces, they saw him stop and bend his head. Then he turned round. 'It's all right,' he called back. 'Just come straight forward, in single file, and don't run. You'll be quite safe. The water's cold, but very bitter,' he added.

One by one the animals went forward, treading carefully along the path Fox had taken. Mole slipped from Badger's back, and sportingly volunteered to be last in the queue.

Once behind the other animals, without Fox's or Badger's eye on him, Mole felt free to follow his own pursuits. His own short-sighted eyes could just make out Fox at the waterside, supervising the drinking. Badger was queuing along with the rest. Mole retreated a few paces and felt the ground under his feet to be promisingly spongy. Swiftly he began to dig, his voracious appetite demanding satisfaction.

Worms! Plump, juicy worms were in Mole's mind as he dug, and nothing else. He paid no attention to the muddy water that was seeping into the hole in little trickles as he dug deeper. In his excitement he forgot he was on dangerous ground.

The other animals eventually finished drinking, and collected on drier ground. All of them felt much refreshed. Fox looked all round to see if everyone was present.

'Are we all here?' Badger asked him.

'No,' replied Fox with a serious expression. 'Mole isn't. I bet he's gone off after those worms.'

'He has. I saw him tunnelling.' Tawny Owl swooped in.

'You might have told us,' Fox said shortly. 'We shall have an awful job getting him up now.'

'Since Badger gave him permission, I saw no reason to tell anyone,' Tawny Owl replied in his most dignified manner.

Fox looked at Badger in surprise.

'Well, before we set out I did just say to Mole there might be time for him to catch a couple of worms,' Badger explained. 'But, of course, he should have waited for the appropriate time. I didn't know this would happen.'

Fox shook his head. 'You're too kind-hearted by half, Badger,' he said. 'He'd eaten more than enough already.'

'I'm sorry,' said Badger, 'But, Fox, you know how Mole can sound so plaintive.'

'Yes, yes,' Fox nodded wearily. 'I'm as fond of him as you. But this is plain greediness on his part. However, don't let's waste any more time talking. Where was he tunnelling, Tawny Owl?'

Tawny Owl flew to the spot and pointed to it by extending his legs downwards over the hole, while he flapped his large wings furiously to maintain his position.

'Weasel, will you take the others back?' Fox asked. 'Badger and I will follow behind with Mole as soon as he appears again. It would teach him a lesson if we all went off and left him to get back to camp on his own, but then we'd probably never see him again.'

Weasel obliged by leading the party off in the direction of the animals' first camp.

'There doesn't appear to be anything in this hole except water,' said Fox, looking closely at the ground. 'Are you sure this is the right place, Owl?'

'Positive. Distinctly saw him go down there.'

'Well, good heavens, he'll drown!' Fox said with alarm. 'Quick, Badger, we'd better dig another hole next to this and see if we can reach him.'

The two animals furiously raked back the spongy soil, but as soon as they got about six inches down more water quickly filled up the hole. They tried three more holes, each time with the same result.

'It's no good,' Fox said, not daring to look at Badger's face. 'He must be drowned already.'

'Oh no! Surely not!' Tawny Owl exclaimed, feeling very guilty. 'He's probably branched off through a tunnel somewhere. I'm sure he'll surface again in a moment.'

At that moment their attention was taken up by what appeared to be a red glow through the trees. 'Whatever's that?' Badger muttered, and looking down, began digging again.

'Should we call him, do you think?' asked Tawny Owl, who had perched on a reed tussock.

'No point,' said Fox. 'He's more likely to feel our vibrations on the ground than to hear our voices. I'm afraid I'm not very hopeful. I'm sure that if he could, he would have surfaced by now.'

'Perhaps he's still eating?' Badger said hopelessly. 'His appetite, you know ...'

'SSSh,' hissed Fox. 'Listen!'

63

In the distance they could hear voices, a lot of voices, beginning as a whisper and rapidly becoming louder. They exchanged glances of alarm, their bodies frozen into stillness. The red glow they had noticed seemed to waver, then glow all anew.

Suddenly they saw Weasel rushing towards them, and close behind him were the hares and rabbits.

'Fire!' he yelled. 'Run for your lives! FIRE! FIRE!'

9

Fire!

Fox's first instinct was to turn and run, for, like all animals, he was terrified of fire. He knew with what swiftness it could engulf the homes of defenceless wild creatures like himself, burning everything in its path. He also knew that where there was fire there would soon be large numbers of humans, trampling everywhere with strange, frightening machines and awful noise. But Fox did not run. His sense of responsibility returned to him, and he courageously resisted this first impulse.

As Weasel dashed past him in panic, he called out, in a voice ringing with authority, 'Stop! You're running straight into the marsh!'

Weasel's headlong flight was checked, and he dutifully turned back towards his leader. The rabbits and Hare and his family followed.

'I'm sorry, Fox,' said the sobered Weasel. 'We just panicked.'

'Where are the others?' snapped Fox, one eye on the flickering glow in the distance. 'We've no time to lose!'

'They're following,' said Weasel. 'We were nearly back at the camp when we saw the flames. Adder and Toad were coming towards us, moving as fast they could, and they called out to us to go back the way we'd come.'

'Toad!' Fox exclaimed. 'He'll never be fast enough to get away. The grass is so dry the flames will just roar along. Trees, shrubs, everything will go up. He'll be overtaken in no time. I must go back – before it's too late.'

At that moment Kestrel and the pheasants alighted on the ground by Tawny Owl. 'The other animals are nearly here,' said Kestrel. 'The squirrels and hedgehogs are well ahead of the flames, and the mice are not far behind.'

'What about Toad?' Fox barked.

'He's doing his best. Adder tried to help him, but he told him to go on and save himself. I'm afraid without help . . .'

'I'm going back for him,' Fox said grimly. 'Badger, I'm leaving you in charge. You're to take the party right round the edge of the marsh. If we can get to the other side we might be safe. The damp ground here may check the flames. Anyway, it's our only chance. Wait for the other animals to reach you here; then all go together. Toad and I will join you as soon as we can. Owl, I'm relying on you to guide them clear of the water. Badger, you lead the way, and tread carefully – the ground's dangerous here. But go as fast as you can. Ah! The squirrels and hedgehogs are coming now. Good luck!'

Fox raced off in the direction of the flames. The other animals bunched nervously round Badger and Tawny Owl. The hedgehogs and squirrels joined them.

'How far behind are the fieldmice and voles?' asked Badger.

'They'll be here any minute,' panted the senior hedge-hog.

'Have you seen Adder or Toad?'

'No.'

'We must wait for Adder,' Badger said. 'Fox has gone for Toad.'

'I don't think we should wait,' said Tawny Owl. 'We

can't jeopardize all the animals' safety for one member of the party. We don't know how far away he is.'

'We'll ask the mice when they get here,' Badger insisted.

The glow through the trees was brighter now, and the animals could hear the noise of the flames. Against the black sky, the trees in the distance flickered redly.

A moment later, the furry mass of mice and voles spilled into the foreground, squeaking in alarm. They reported no sign of Adder.

'We can't wait,' Tawny Owl said again.

'We'll give him as long as it takes for two hundred beats of the heart,' said Badger.

Two hundred heartbeats, while under threat of being overtaken by fire, were obviously several times as fast as usual. Badger listened to his pounding heart and realized the impossibility of counting. But he forced himself to stay still just a little longer, in the midst of all the restless, milling animals. None of them dared to bolt, for the dangers of the marsh were directly ahead, and they felt themselves trapped between that existing danger and the approaching one.

The few agonizing moments paid off. Adder's red eyes, baleful in the darkness, were spotted by Kestrel. In a trice he had joined the ranks.

'At once now, Tawny Owl,' Badger commanded, and

Tawny Owl led the birds into the air, while the animals set off at top speed behind Badger.

'Round the marsh,' he called to the birds. 'Kestrel knows the way.'

As the animals raced on, Tawny Owl called down directions to them from his position twelve feet above the ground. Without answering, Badger religiously obeyed them, leading his party in diversions around marshy ground, avoiding holes and bunches of reeds that screened treacherous mud. With every step and every gasping breath, the animals knew they were putting the flames further behind them. Every so often Badger and the larger animals stopped to allow Adder and the voles and fieldmice to catch up; then they raced on. Weasel dropped back to take up position as rearguard, encouraging the slow ones, and keeping an eye open for Fox.

After half an hour they reached the end of one side of the marsh, and began to turn the long corner to reach the other side – what Fox had hoped would be the safe side. The younger animals were exhausted, and all of them, adults and young alike, ached in every limb.

'Owl!' Badger called up. 'We'll stop for just a very short rest. The youngsters are gasping.'

The birds landed, and the animals sank to the ground, bodies heaving violently, their throats parched and their eyes streaming. They gulped in the air with hoarse, shuddering breaths.

In the far distance they could still see the fire. They were now on slightly higher ground, and they could see the movement of the flames. Even as they watched the fire seemed to come nearer.

'Father, will we ever see Fox again?' asked one of the leverets.

Hare smiled down at him. 'Of course we will, my dear,' he said gently. 'He'll soon be back. You'll see.'

*

As he sped back towards the camp in the gorse thicket, and in the direction of the flames, Fox resolutely put every fearsome thought from his mind. He told himself to think only of Toad, and how he must save him to save the others. Without Toad they were indeed lost.

The fire grew brighter and noisier ahead of him, and soon the air smelt, and felt, hot and scorched. The heat increased continually. There was no sign of Toad.

Fox began to call him. 'Toad! Toad! Where are you?' Then, raising his voice above the noise of the burning, he shouted as loudly as he could: 'TOAD!'

Fox dared not look directly at the terrifying sight that he was swiftly approaching. He knew that to do so would mean an instantaneous loss of nerve. But he could hear the crashing of blazing boughs – sometimes whole saplings. The roar of the greedy flames was hideous, and at last he could go no further. His courage failed him, and he felt all he could do was turn and run back to safety and companionship.

Then he heard a desperate croak. 'Fox! Have you come back? Here I am!'

Toad was sitting under a gorse bush, making no attempt to move.

'What are you doing there?' Fox whispered through his parched lips. 'Come quickly. The flames are almost on us.'

'I thought I was lost,' Toad answered. 'I knew my poor speed could never get me to safety, so I resigned myself to wait here for my . . . end.'

Even as he spoke, the first flames burst upon them with a tremendous roar. Fanned by a slight breeze, the fire had accelerated, and was sweeping its greedy fingers through the undergrowth. Toad made a mighty leap as the gorse bush went up like a bonfire. The night was lit up around them, as bright as daylight, but more fitful, by the flames.

Now they heard sirens in the distance, traffic, and human

voices. Fox bent his head and gently took Toad in his jaws. Then, turning, he galloped away, back through the dry undergrowth towards his friends.

He paused only once, to release Toad and allow him to climb on to his back. Then, with the hateful roar still dinning in their ears, they raced for the marsh.

While his friends had fled for their lives, the unfortunate Mole remained completely oblivious of the existence of the oncoming fire. His insatiable appetite drew him down, deeper and deeper into the earth. Worms were plentiful in that marshy soil, and Mole ate as he delved. He only became aware of the presence of water when his feet began to get wet, and eventually he felt his fur to be wet too. Mole realized the hole he had dug was filling up, and he knew that to turn back would be to drown. So he went no further down, but continued to dig a path in a straight line, and after about another twelve inches, he clawed his way upwards.

The surface seemed to be a long, long way away. Mole had no idea that, in his hunger, he had tunnelled so far downward. As he climbed upwards he felt warmer and warmer, and he decided this must be due to his exertions in reaching for the surface. But he grew hotter and hotter, and hotter, and even the soil began to feel hot. Soon it was too hot for him to bear: his paws could no longer touch the earth without being burnt. Mole recoiled, and slipped back a few inches. He was trapped between the heat above him and the water below.

When Badger's party had rested for some minutes, and all had got their breath back, Badger and Tawny Owl led them on again at a steady pace. The distance was shorter this time, and they were not long in finally reaching the other side of the marsh.

They looked across the marsh at the fire. They seemed to

be far enough away from it now to be safe. The muddy water reflected the flames and seemed to flicker.

'Look, look, the water's on fire!' squeaked one of the young fieldmice.

'It's just the reflection,' his mother answered him, soothingly.

'Water fights fire,' Badger pointed out kindly. 'It's an enemy to fire. Humans use it, you know, to kill flames. We're quite safe. Fox was wise.'

'What will happen then, Badger, when the fire reaches the water?' asked a young squirrel.

'It will burn itself out,' Badger answered. 'It will be quenched by the water, just like you quench a thirst.'

The animals relaxed. Badger, whom they held in almost as high esteem as Fox, was confident that they were safe. They lay down, the young ones snuggling up to their mothers.

Badger called to Tawny Owl, who had perched on a low branch. 'Why don't you fly across the marsh and see if you can spot Fox and Toad?' he asked. 'I can't rest till I know they're all right.' There was some nervousness in his voice.

'I shouldn't worry, Badger,' Tawny Owl reassured him. 'Fox can look after himself.'

'Yes, but what if he couldn't get to Toad in time?'

'Very well, if it will put your mind at rest . . .' Tawny Owl flapped off the branch and flew away over the water. Badger watched him until he was too small to distinguish against the darkness.

He felt someone brush against his fur. It was Hare.

'If he *was* too late to save Toad . . . what then?' he asked.

'I don't know,' said Badger. 'We can't go back. No doubt Fox would think of something.'

Tawny Owl was not long gone. They were still gazing across the marsh when they noticed his grey shape returning.

'They're all right!' Tawny Owl called, and hooted in his pleasure. 'They're both all right!'

Badger heaved a sigh of relief. 'Thanks, Owl, for going,' he said.

'Believe me, I'm as relieved as you are,' said Tawny Owl. 'Fox is terribly tired, but he's coming as fast as he can. He's just started turning the corner towards this side. He was too tired to talk, but Toad called out to warn everyone to look out for the humans. There are lots of them coming.'

'Toad was on Fox's back?' Badger assumed.

Tawny Owl nodded, and Hare was struck by a thought. 'I wonder what happened to poor old Mole?' he said.

While his friends were wondering about him, Mole, of course, was thinking of them, and bitterly regretting the greediness which had brought him to his present danger.

'Why didn't I answer when I heard them calling?' he wailed to himself in his uncomfortable tunnel. 'Oh, Badger, if I ever get out of here, I'll never again run away because of my awful appetite! I promise. Oh dear, will I ever see him again? And Fox?' The more he thought about his friends, the more miserable and helpless Mole felt himself to be.

He knew there must be some danger on the surface, although he had no idea what it could be. He wondered if Fox and Badger, and all the others, had escaped it, and, as he wondered, the thought came to him that they might now be miles away, having given him up for lost. He was all on his own, deserted! Whatever would become of him? He began to sob violently. He was very frightened. Finally, in his misery, Mole cried himself to sleep.

He had no idea how long he slept, but he was woken by the vibration of heavy footsteps overhead. There were many of them, and they were not animal footsteps. He shuddered afresh at this new danger, for the crashing above told him humans were about.

Eventually the din passed over and the vibrations became fainter. Mole decided it was high time to move if he were ever again to rejoin his friends. He inched timidly upwards. The soil still felt warm to his paws, but he continued. He soon felt sure he had passed the spot where he had previously had to retreat. After a few more moments the soil began to feel damp, and cooler. He pulled himself upwards more quickly, and experienced a new sensation. His snout detected a smell of burning, an acrid, charred smell. Then his claws pierced the surface and he wriggled up to peer out. He could scarcely believe his eyes.

Dawn had broken. Mole found a scene of desolation around him. Everything was a uniform, hideous black. Earth, grass, rushes and shrubs had been burnt to cinders. Stunted saplings with charcoal for trunks, bald of leaves and shoots, stood like skeletons. Some of the larger trees had escaped with a severe scorching, losing only the branches and leaves close to the ground. Even those looked as if they had been severely wounded and would bear the scars for ever. The black ground was thoroughly wet, and was still smoking in places.

Mole knew that there had been a terrible fire, and that the humans had come with water to quench it. He felt certain that all his friends must have been killed, as they could not possibly have survived such a disaster.

'Oh, I wish I were dead, too!' he howled. 'I'm no good on my own. Where can I go? Oh, poor Badger!' And he laid himself down on the ashes, with his head on his paws, and wept bitterly.

Mole's poor eyesight had been too weak to notice that in

the distance, along the sides of the marsh, the fire was still burning, despite the efforts of the humans with their water and their beaters. At that moment the other animals, now rejoined by Fox and Toad, were, while far from dead, in even graver danger than before.

10

Confrontation

As Mole lay in despair, his little velvet-covered body shaken by sobs, he was unaware that he was being watched. One of the beaters had remained behind to ensure that no further fires would break out from the glowing embers. Now he had reached the spot where Mole had earlier gone hunting, and was amazed to find any wildlife remaining in the wake of the flames. He bent over the little creature to see if he was still alive, and could see evidence of Mole's breathing. When he saw the hole from which the animal had recently emerged, the beater understood how he had managed to escape being burnt to death. Cautiously he lowered a hand, and found that the animal had no wish to run away. He lifted him up and looked at him more closely. Mole did not even wriggle.

The beater was in a quandary, for he had nowhere to put the creature. At the same time he was unwilling to abandon something he was pleased to think he might have just saved, for he felt sure Mole's docility resulted from the fact that he had been injured. In the end he deposited him in one of the large side pockets of his firefighter's jacket, mopped his forehead, and went slowly on in the direction of the marsh.

*

After the initial excitement at the reappearance of Fox and Toad had somewhat abated, Toad was able to tell his friends just how the fire had started.

'I had finished with sleeping,' he began, 'and I was simply squatting restfully in the comfortable little hollow in the ground that I'd made for myself. I was alone, because Adder had slid off somewhere.'

'Just went to have a hunt round,' Adder told them with a glint in his red eyes. 'Never know what you might find . . .'

'Anyway, I remember hearing a sizzling noise,' Toad went on, 'and it seemed to get louder.' He paused for effect, looking round at the other animals, who were clustering in small groups among the grass tussocks and reeds. 'I went to have a look. The grass beyond the railings was burning. It must have been a cigarette that started it, thrown out of a passing car. The flames were advancing rapidly, and I could see that in a very short time they would reach inside the army land. I hastened off to tell Adder.

'As the flames got nearer, and I watched the gorse thicket swallowed up, I knew I could never escape the fire, being so slow. I told Adder not to wait for me – to get away, if he could. But, thanks to our brave leader, I'm still here with you.'

'If it weren't for Mole,' said the exhausted Fox, who was lying full length on the ground, 'the party would be complete.' He told Toad about the disappearance of Mole, and all the animals fell silent, thinking about their lost companion whom they presumed drowned, or burnt by the fire.

Dawn approached, and across the marsh the flames seemed to pale as the sky became lighter. But the fire did not stop.

Rabbit expressed the concern of the smaller, more timid animals. 'It's coming on! It's still coming!' he cried to Fox, as if blaming him for its continuance.

'Yes, I see that it is,' Fox replied wearily.

'But didn't you say it would stop at the marshy ground?' Rabbit persisted.

'I said that I *hoped* it would,' answered Fox.

'What if the marsh doesn't stop it?' asked Vole, and his question was repeated in alarm by his brethren.

'Fox will think of something, don't worry,' Weasel said confidently.

'At any rate,' Toad put in, 'the humans have arrived with their machines and ideas. *They'll* soon stop it. Fire is just as much their enemy as ours, you see.'

Fox drifted off into an uneasy sleep, while Badger tried to calm the growing fears of more and more animals in the party. When it was broad daylight Kestrel flew off to see what was happening.

The fire continued to roar on, and began to spread round the sides of the marsh. 'Surely we shouldn't stay here?' Pheasant protested.

'Where do you suggest, then?' Tawny Owl asked sharply.

'Well, er . . . I . . . *we* don't have to stay. We birds aren't in danger.'

'You're free to leave at any time you want,' Tawny Owl said meaningfully.

Pheasant's mate gave him a nudge with her wing, and he looked a little embarrassed.

Kestrel returned at that moment, and attention was diverted from the discomfited Pheasant. 'They're making progress,' the hawk announced. 'But I think the fire won't be mastered for a while yet. We'd better decide what to do. The flames are creeping round both sides of the water, so that there are now in effect, two fires, and, at the moment, we're between them.'

All the animals looked towards Fox, who was still sleeping.

'We'll have to wake him,' Badger decided. He went up close to his friend and gave him a shake with one paw.

Fox looked up at once. 'I was only dozing,' he said.

Badger told him of the advance of the fire.

'Then it looks as if our lives are once again at the mercy of humans,' he said with resignation. 'Only they can save us now.'

The animals looked very alarmed at these words from their leader.

'Are we helpless?' asked Hare.

'Not quite,' said Kestrel. 'From the air I could detect a sort of causeway of land, just a narrow strip, running under the surface of the water, but connected to the ground we're on now. It leads to a small island some way out in the marsh. I think you could all walk on it. Once on the island, there's no question of the flames reaching you.'

Fox was immediately alert again. 'Where is the causeway, Kestrel?' he asked. 'Let me have a look at it.'

He left Badger in charge of the party, and followed Kestrel's flight for a short distance.

'Can you see it?' Kestrel called down.

'I think so,' Fox answered, peering out over the water's edge. 'Yes! Yes, I can.'

Kestrel, hovering expertly above, watched Fox put one foot gingerly into the water, and test the firmness of the sunken ground. He seemed satisfied, and walked a little further in until his whole weight was pressing on it.

'It seems strong enough,' he called. 'Better go and round up the others.'

When the rest of the party arrived, they saw Fox standing in the water. It reached up to just below his knees.

'I'm going to walk out to the island,' Fox told them. 'Badger, will you follow behind me? We need to know how much weight it will bear.'

Slowly, with about a yard between them, the two animals moved forward along the causeway. The water reached to the top of Badger's legs.

'We can't go across there!' squealed Vole as he watched.

'We voles and fieldmice, and the squirrels and hedgehogs too, would be under the water.'

'I'm sure that won't have escaped Fox's notice,' remarked Tawny Owl.

Fox and Badger reached the island without mishap, and remained there a little while in discussion, looking out towards where the flames were now noticeably beginning to encircle the marsh. Then they ran quickly back across the causeway, with the dark water splashing up against their sides.

'We haven't got long,' Fox told them. 'We could see the humans at work on the flames, but I don't think they can stop it in time for our safety. Badger and I will have to carry the smaller of you across in shifts. The larger animals, like Hare, the rabbits and Weasel should be able to keep their heads above water. Kestrel, will you get airborne and keep Badger and myself informed as to the progress of the fire? Now then, Fieldmice, up on my back.'

In the urgency of the moment, the excitable little mice, always rather highly strung, all made for Fox's bushy tail, expecting to climb up. But there were too many of them. They got in each other's way, bumping and pushing in their scramble to be the first up.

'Ow! Stop this!' yelled Fox, who felt as if his brush would soon be pulled off. 'Calm down, and climb up one at a time.' He looked across at Badger, who had lain himself down, the better to enable the voles to climb up his sides.

'Now, wait, all of you,' said Fox, and followed Badger's example. The fieldmice scurried up on to his back, and, with Badger ahead of him, Fox stepped down again on to the causeway.

Having deposited the tiny creatures safely on the island, Fox and Badger ran quickly back for the second load. Already the awful roar and crackle of the fire could be heard again, and the animals were able to smell the scorched, ashy air wafting towards them.

'Now, squirrels!' cried Fox. 'Badger and I can manage you all between us. Rabbits, Weasel, follow us. Hare, you must bring your family. Quickly!'

The animals leapt on to the spit of land, Fox and Badger carrying their furry burdens like two grey cloaks that had suddenly been invested with life. Hare followed, with his mate behind him, each carrying one of their babies. The water completely covered their bodies, leaving only their heads ar.d necks above the surface, and the leverets, hanging on to their parents' neck fur by their teeth, were all but submerged.

The rabbits, with their shorter legs, sank even further down in the water, and while the adults were just able to keep their noses, eyes and ears in the dry, Rabbit had to tell the youngsters to stay behind for Fox and Badger to collect them, leaving them in the care of Hedgehog.

'Hurry up, Fox!' Kestrel called, as he hovered above them, his eyes turned towards the fire. 'The flames are racing this way! Quickly, quickly!'

Weasel, having watched the plight of the rabbits, knew that the water would completely cover his low-slung body if he endeavoured to walk across. So, with grim determination, he entered the dark water and began to swim towards the island.

Toad and Adder were quick to join him, and, keeping their various pairs of eyes fixed firmly on the little island where their friends were cheering them on, they struck out bravely.

Adder undulated swiftly through the water, only his small head above the surface, and as he neared land, Fox and Badger were running back across the causeway for their third load.

While Badger carried the young rabbits, Fox managed the small hedgehogs. As they stepped towards the brink again, the fire was roaring at them from both directions.

'You'll have to swim for it too!' Fox panted to Hedgehog

and the other adults. 'No time to come back again.' As he and Badger raced for safety, the flames burst upon the hedgehogs, who leapt in one bunch for the water.

Kestrel dropped from the sky like a bullet, while Tawny Owl and the pheasants had long ago flown to join their companions.

Adder and Toad, both of whom were excellent swimmers, had soon reached dry land again. All of the animals were now safe from the fire, although some were still struggling in the water.

The hedgehogs, and Weasel too, were good swimmers, but their feet were continually becoming entangled in the weeds and reedy water-plants. This made the crossing doubly tiring, but they helped each other and shouted encouragement, as did all the animals already on the island, until finally, the last dripping body emerged from the water on to dry land.

With a quite unconscious movement, all the animals clustered closely together as they watched the dancing flames across the water. Standing in a tightly-knit group, each individual experienced a comforting feeling of security and mutual affection.

Fox voiced their common feelings. 'In the face of danger,' he said, 'we have managed to forge a community. We are all members of one unit and we can never be divided.'

Although he spoke the words quietly, there was some emotion evident in his voice which communicated itself to all of them. Every animal and bird felt that, whatever else might happen to them on their journey, this particular moment would always retain a vivid significance.

Then they heard the voices. They were human voices, calling directions and advice to each other as they fought the fire. They saw tall dark shapes, in helmets and thick coats, wielding huge pipes, which gushed water at the flames. Other men were beating the ground with stout staves to which were fixed heavy fireproof cloths.

'The humans will soon win this battle,' Tawny Owl declared knowingly. 'You can already see the flames receding.'

'All this damage and horror was caused by one foolish human,' said Toad. 'And all of it has to be put right by these others of his kind who had no hand in it.'

'They're certainly a strange species,' agreed Badger. 'I never pretended to understand them.'

As the animals watched the flames gradually diminishing under the efforts of the firefighters, many of them felt, for perhaps the first time, an unusual kinship with the humans who shared their desire to see the fire, their mutual enemy, quenched. Yet this kinship, they each understood, was to be short-lived. For as soon as the fire was finally overcome, the very presence of the humans at such close quarters posed a new problem for their freedom. As long as the men remained on the other side of the causeway, the animals' safest escape route was blocked.

Fox turned towards Badger, and found his eyes on him. He saw they reflected his own thoughts. Fox beckoned his friend aside, and motioned to Tawny Owl and Kestrel to join them.

'I think we shall all have to swim for it,' Fox said.

'Not quite all of us, of course,' Tawny Owl needlessly corrected him. 'But I see your point. The humans are far too close for comfort.'

'We still have one advantage,' Badger pointed out. 'They haven't spotted us yet.'

'Don't rely on that,' the pessimistic Owl warned him. 'At the moment they're too intent on their work to look about them. I don't think we should fool ourselves. There's virtually no cover of any value on the island. As soon as they've mastered that fire, we shall be noticed.'

'Tawny Owl's right,' Fox agreed, grimly nodding his chestnut head. 'As I see it, we've two alternatives. We can swim across to another side of the marsh, or we can wait until the fire is put out, and then make a dash for it back across the causeway.'

'Right under their noses?' Kestrel asked in amazement.

'The element of surprise could give us just the few minutes we need to get clear,' Fox answered.

'Better still,' suggested Badger, 'the birds could create some diversion – I don't exactly know how – that might enable us to slip past without even being spotted.'

'I'm afraid you're forgetting two very important points,' Tawny Owl said somewhat pompously. 'First of all, it will take several trips across that causeway before you're all back on the mainland again; just as when you were coming on to the island. Secondly, even when the fire is out, the ground will remain red-hot for some time. None of you animals could possibly set foot on it, and as for Adder – why, he'd be roasted alive.'

'Of course,' muttered Fox. 'I must say, Owl,' he added after a moment, 'your judgement is of the greatest value.'

Tawny Owl passed off the compliment with the words, 'I merely wish to help,' but he was not entirely successful in disguising an expression that was a little smug.

'What do *you* advise?' Fox asked him.

'If all of you were powerful swimmers, and if there were no juveniles, I shouldn't hesitate to advise you to swim for it straight away,' Tawny Owl replied. 'But even the fully grown hedgehogs, and Weasel, had the utmost difficulty in swimming to the island. So I think there's only one course open to you. You will simply have to stay put, and trust in the good nature of the humans, or in the likelihood of their being too exhausted, after their efforts, to bother about a handful of wildlife.'

Badger and Fox knew there was nothing they could say to refute Tawny Owl's statement.

'However,' Kestrel added, 'although I'm sure you've correctly summed up the situation, Owl, there's still a possibility of we birds diverting the humans' attention, as Badger suggested.'

'Only for a few minutes, surely,' argued Tawny Owl.

'Unless we can attract their attention, and make them follow us far enough, and for long enough, to leave the coast clear for the animals to get away.'

'Sounds like a very long shot to me.' Tawny Owl shrugged his wings.

'It's worth a try,' Kestrel said pointedly, and with some irritation.

While the four of them were debating the point, a gleeful shout, repeated by all the other animals, reached their ears. 'There's Mole! There's Mole!'

They broke off their conversation, and Fox and Badger looked at each other in astonishment. They hastily rejoined the others, who were all craning their necks over the water, and standing on the very edge of the island, completely disregarding the danger of their toppling in.

On the edge of the marsh there were now only one or two isolated pockets of flames. One of the firefighters, who appeared to have only recently come on to the scene, had removed his jacket and was mopping his brow. He had quite carelessly dropped the coat in a bundle on to the ashy ground, and from one of the deep pockets Mole had half emerged, and was peering short-sightedly all around.

The man had fortunately not heard the animals' cries of excitement, which to him would merely have sounded like a chorus of yelps and squeaks, but Fox at once told everyone to remain silent.

The animals suffered unbearable tension as Mole, not seeming to be in too much of a hurry, pulled himself right out of the pocket, and stepped off the jacket.

'He'll burn himself!' said Tawny Owl.

But Mole seemed to feel no ill effects, and began to wander aimlessly around over the ashy ground.

'Quick, Kestrel, and Owl, I beg you, go up in the air and catch that man's eye,' said Fox urgently. 'I'll try to reach Mole myself.'

The birds glanced at one another for an instant, and then together swooped into the air, uttering their loudest cries.

'Hoo-hoo-hooooo,' called Tawny Owl.

'Kew-kew-kee-kee-kee,' screeched Kestrel, soaring like an arrow way up into the sky, and then diving downwards again, as straight as a javelin.

The man, still holding his handkerchief in one hand, looked up at the cloudless sky. Kestrel and Tawny Owl began to loop round and round each other like two giant gnats, still hooting and screeching as loud as they could.

With one eye on the man, Fox stepped down on to the causeway and streaked towards the shore. The two birds continued to make such a racket that the noise of Fox's splashing was quite unnoticeable.

He reached the other side safely, and realized at once why Mole had appeared to walk quite comfortably over the burnt ground. The gallons of water squirted from the pumps had cooled the surface tremendously, and though it still felt warm, the soft ashy deposit was extremely comfortable to the feet. This encouraged Fox a great deal, and in a few bounds he had reached Mole.

At the suddenness of Fox's approach Mole began to make little twittering noises of alarm. The two animals exchanged not a word as Mole quickly climbed on to Fox's back, and Fox at once turned back for the causeway.

At this moment the man, who had been staring up at the two birds, found his eyes beginning to water, and was obliged to look down again. Out of the corner of one eye he saw a blurred shape dash past, and turning round, saw Fox, with his passenger, jump into the water and run back towards the island.

'Well, I'll be . . .!' he muttered, walking quickly to the water's edge to look more closely. He saw at once the promontory of land running underneath the water, and, looking along its length, soon spotted the little collection of creatures on the island.

'Good – ness gra – cious!' he exclaimed loudly, and began to call his colleagues. 'Quick, lads, come and look at this! There's a regular zoo over there! Just look at them!'

Most of the other men joined him at once, leaving only two beaters at work on the remnants of the flames. Standing in a line by the waterside, they stared pop-eyed at the animals gathered on the island. Even as they stood, unable to speak, Tawny Owl and Kestrel dropped from the blue and landed amongst their friends.

'It's . . . it's uncanny,' one of the men whispered. 'Where have they come from?'

The animals, with their party once again complete, faced the humans with a feeling of solidarity. Behind the men, now joined by the last two beaters, stood the huge scarlet engine, like a dormant monster, in an expanse of black and ash-grey. The fire was out.

And so the two groups confronted each other: human faces staring at animal faces, and animal faces staring back, both wondering who would move first.

11

The storm

While the animals and the men had all been absorbed in watching or fighting the progress of the fire, they had not noticed a dark formation of cloud moving slowly towards them. Only Kestrel, sporting with Tawny Owl in the sky, had seen this bank of cloud, but the significance of its approach had not really impressed itself upon him. Now, as the party of animals on their little island stood wondering if they were once again in danger, the first rumblings of thunder could be heard.

The men looked at each other questioningly, and then upwards, noting for the first time the gathering clouds. The slight breeze that had prevailed had blown up into a strong wind, and so the clouds came on apace. The end of the long drought was at hand.

It was only a matter of minutes, while the two groups still stood somewhat uncertainly facing each other, before the first heavy spots of rain fell on the scorched ground. The reverberations of thunder became louder and louder, and it grew steadily darker. The sun was blotted out. Finally lightning began to flicker across the dark sky, and the rain started to fall in real earnest.

The animals felt the welcome wetness on their bodies,

and Toad, who always enjoyed really wet weather, leapt joyfully off the bank into the water, and paddled up and down croaking happily.

The men, who only minutes earlier would have rejoiced at the rain, now instinctively behaved as all members of the human race do in such a situation. They dispersed to find shelter from the downpour.

This was the very chance Fox had been hoping for. He hastily called Toad out of the water and on to his back, while he bid Mole take up his usual position on the back of Badger.

'Now, follow me!' said Fox in urgent tones, 'as swiftly as you can!'

On to the causeway he jumped, with the larger animals following close behind.

Three trips Fox and Badger made through the heavy rain before all of the animals were safely on land again.

'Which way do we take?' Fox asked the passenger Toad.

'Straight ahead,' he replied. 'That will bring us to the fence on the other side of the army land. Then we're into the farmland. We'll have to go carefully, but there will be plenty of shelter.'

Water pouring from their drenched fur, and their heads bent beneath its fury, the animals slunk through the downpour. Only Toad and Adder, who had no fur to worry about, seemed to enjoy the feel of the rain. Toad tried to croak a little tune to cheer up the others, but the deafening noise of the peals of thunder unfortunately smothered his good intentions.

Tawny Owl and the other birds had been flying on ahead for short distances, and then waiting for the rest of the party to catch them up.

'This is most unfortunate,' the soaked Badger remarked to Tawny Owl as he passed him again. 'First the fire, now a torrent of water. We really couldn't have been more unlucky.'

'You should remember, Badger, that it afforded us just

the diversion we needed,' Tawny Owl pointed out.

'Yes, I suppose we should be grateful that we've come this far and are still all together.'

'I'm the luckiest of all,' said Mole. 'I was given up for dead.'

'You would have had only your own greed to thank for that,' Tawny Owl said sternly.

'Oh well now, Owl,' Badger said, 'I'm sure he's learnt his lesson.'

'Thank you, Badger,' Mole said timidly.

Tawny Owl flew on ahead again, and the animals remained silent for some time.

Suddenly, Mole said, 'But we're *not* all still together.'

'The lizards?' asked Fox quietly.

'Yes.'

'I was rather hoping no one would mention them,' Fox said.

'If only I could have persuaded them to have stayed on the journey,' Badger said miserably. 'I knew they were taking the wrong decision. And now . . .' he broke off, unable to finish the sentence.

'They *may* have escaped,' Fox said with false heartiness, but he knew it was no comfort to Badger, who refused to be consoled.

Presently they crossed beyond the limit of the burnt ground which marked the extent of the fire in this direction, and after that the soil became increasingly spongy and soggy. The small animals, with their lighter weight, were able to run over the surface fairly easily, but the heavier animals began to slow down considerably.

The rain continued to pour down, and soon Fox, Badger, and the hares and rabbits, found that their paws were sinking into the softening ground. As they trudged on, the situation worsened. They sank up to their ankles in mud.

'We'll have to keep on.' Fox barely turned his head to call behind him. 'There's no shelter here, and this mud will only get worse.'

Toad had long since ceased his singing, and was peering ahead through the rain. 'Yes, there it is!' he suddenly cried. 'I can see it! I can see the railings! Not much further!'

Heartened by the news, the line of animals put on a little spurt. Soon they could all see the line of metal posts and rails which was the boundary of the army land.

Beyond the fence was a thick hedgerow of shrubbery and thorn trees, where Kestrel, Tawny Owl and the pheasants were already sheltering, while they preened their drenched feathers. They watched the animals threading their way underneath the rails. They looked a sorry sight, with their fur plastered down, and streams of water dripping from their sides.

Fox led them into a thick mass of holly shrubbery, where the closely packed leaves had kept the ground underneath comparatively dry. They sank down with dejected faces and empty stomachs.

The mother rabbits and mice had to quieten their hungry children. There was no possibility of looking for food until the storm abated.

Their shelter was periodically lit by a dazzling brightness as the lightning flashed directly overhead. Some of the animals endeavoured to sleep.

Toad wanted Adder to join him in a foraging expedition, but the snake declined. 'I'm too tired,' he drawled. 'I haven't been riding all the way like you.'

'Please yourself.' Toad shrugged, and wandered off into the teeming rain to look for slugs and worms.

The other animals looked at each other miserably. They felt very wet and very uncomfortable.

Badger thought of his old, dry, comfortable set and wondered what had become of it. 'It'll be many long weeks before I can build another one,' he thought to himself.

Weasel and the voles, and Fox and the rabbits, also wished they were in their snug underground homes. Mole wondered if he dare dig a tunnel for comfort, but feared Badger's disapproval.

So the merciless rain lashed down. Toad, returning from his hunting foray, found the animals' makeshift shelter was getting damper and damper. Eventually they were as wet as if they had remained in the open.

'It's no use,' said Fox wearily. 'We'll have to move and look for a drier spot.'

'If I remember correctly,' said Toad, 'there's a barn not far away.'

Fox wanted to know how far.

'I can't be exactly sure,' replied Toad. 'It's so difficult to see anything at the moment, except the rain.'

'But do you know in what direction it is?' asked Fox.

Toad pondered for a minute. 'I'm sure I could find it,' he said at length.

'Then we put ourselves in your hands,' said Fox. He shrugged his shoulders. 'In any case, we can't stay here.'

So the animals wearily formed another line in the rain, their still wet bodies taking a second soaking, and Fox led them off, at Toad's instigation, across the field that lay before them.

In one corner of this field they encountered a stile, which they were all easily able to circumvent, and it gave on to a narrow path which ran between the fields beyond. In one of these a herd of black and white Friesian cows, with a number of calves, were doing their best to shelter under a large oak tree.

Toad advised Fox to continue along the path, so, after satisfying himself that no humans were near, he led the animals slowly down it, keeping well in to the side by the hedgerow border.

They found that the path led into an orchard, where pear and plum trees had recently finished blossoming. At the far end was a long, low wooden building with small windows.

'Is that the barn?' whispered Fox.

'It's not the one I saw before, but it looks as if it will suit our needs,' Toad answered.

The animals lost no time in running over to it, and for once they were lucky. It was open.

'It's a storehouse,' remarked Fox. But at that time of year there was no fruit to store. There were a few empty boxes lying around on the floor, and a few odds and ends on a shelf that ran the length of one side. At one end there were the remains of a bale of straw that must have been used for packing. Apart from this the storehouse was quite empty.

The straw and the floor were dry. 'This is marvellous,' said Hedgehog. 'We'll be snug and dry in no time.'

The rodents had already begun to pull lumps of straw from the bale. Fox stood irresolute, his head down. His fur dripped continuously, and a little puddle of water had

formed at his feet.

'What's troubling you, Fox?' asked Badger, who was fashioning himself a comfortable nest of straw in one corner.

'I don't like the idea of that open door,' Fox said. 'Why should it be open if the storehouse is not in use?'

'I can't say,' said Badger. 'But if it had been closed it would have been no use to us!'

'You're right, of course,' said Fox, still not moving.

'We can stay here until this storm is over, at any rate,' Badger reassured him. 'Nobody will be about in this rain – not even farm workers.'

'When it stops we shall have to look for food,' Fox said. 'However . . . yes, we'll stay here for the present, and rest.'

Tawny Owl alighted in the doorway. 'Kestrel's in one of the plum trees, keeping a lookout,' he announced. 'Pheasant's agreed to relieve him in a while. I'm joining you until dark.'

The owl fluttered up to a vacant piece of shelf and there

he perched. For a time he watched the animals preparing their nests from the straw; then he closed his eyes.

Badger, having finished his own arrangements, directed the voles and fieldmice in forming their own little ball of straw.

The larger animals laid out a generous, thick expanse all over the floor, and lay down side by side. Even Adder was content to entwine himself round some of the strands.

The squirrels, however, objected to sleeping on the floor. 'It's just for now – just this time,' Badger told them. 'There's not time enough to build a proper nest on the shelf.'

So Weasel and Mole joined Badger in the corner, Fox lay down with the rabbits and hedgehogs, Hare and his family joined the squirrels, and Toad snuggled up with the mice. Only Adder found that no one wished to sleep near him.

As they listened to the rain lashing down outside, the animals from Farthing Wood were all the more grateful for the snug dryness of the storehouse. One by one they dropped into sleep, forgetful of their empty stomachs.

There was not one of the party left awake when Kestrel arrived on the threshold having completed his watch, his dry feathers showing that the furious storm had at last abated.

As Kestrel joined his sleeping friends, the safety of the party was now entrusted to Pheasant.

12

Trapped!

Tom Griggs had been in a black humour all that morning. He had lost another chicken the previous night, from right under the nose of his guard dog, a big bull-mastiff. The animal was worse than useless; it always seemed to fall fast asleep just when it was needed most. This latest theft had brought the total of stolen chickens to four. And now the hens were in such a frightened state that they would not lay. Oh, if he could just get his hands on the guilty fox!

To cap it all came the storm. After weeks of drought which had dried up his crops, those that had survived were now being beaten flat by this merciless rain. 'I shall be ruined, Betsy, I'm sure of it,' he muttered angrily to his wife, as he stood watching the storm dash itself against his windows.

Mrs Griggs could offer him no comfort. Weather was its own master; mere humans had no control over it. She went on preparing the midday meal, keeping silent except for an occasional word to the farm cat, which sat shivering in the kitchen, soaked to the skin.

The rain finally stopped as Griggs was moodily munching the meat pie his wife had made. He pushed his plate away.

'No more for me, my dear,' he said. 'I must go out and have a look round.'

He got up, ignoring the protestations of his wife concerning the unfinished meal, put on his gum-boots and mackintosh, and, taking up his ancient shotgun from the corner, went outside.

The sky had lightened considerably, but the ground was awash with puddles.

The bull-mastiff strained at its leash as it saw its master. 'Down, Jack!' called the farmer. 'You're no use to me!'

It lay down again, sadly, and watched him out of sight.

It took Griggs about an hour to examine his fields for damage, and he found what he had expected to find. This put him into an even blacker humour.

As he trudged unhappily back through his small orchard, a gaudy cock pheasant rose up from the long grass, and, putting his gun to his shoulder, he shot clean through it. The glossy, multi-coloured bird crumpled, and plummeted to the earth.

At the sound of the shot, the pheasant's dull-marked mate also took to the air, uttering a loud, startled clatter. Griggs promptly fired his other barrel at the hen pheasant, and she, too, dropped to the ground.

He collected the two limp bodies and then, noticing his wife standing by the storehouse, with the now unleashed Jack by her side, he called out, 'We're in luck, Betsy! A brace of pheasant!'

'You come and see what I've found!' she called back.

Griggs was somewhat struck by the way in which his dog remained by the shed, bolt upright, and did not bound towards him at his approach.

'Look through the window if you want a surprise,' said Mrs Griggs, indicating the storehouse.

Her husband put his face to the glass, and a gasp escaped him. For a moment he remained immobile, then he moved away and looked at his wife, round-eyed.

96

'It's . . . it's full of animals!' he said in a tone of disbelief, handing the pheasants to her absent-mindedly.

'Including your fox,' she added meaningfully.

Griggs looked at his gun. 'Caught him red-handed,' he whispered.

'I came out to give Jack his dinner,' his wife informed him. 'I just chanced to wander round here, and there was our store-shed full of animals – and birds – all fast asleep. When I saw the fox, I quickly shut the door on 'em all.' She paused to examine the two unfortunate members of Fox's party who were not inside, and which her husband had just killed in the orchard. Then she motioned to the shed. 'There's an owl on the shelf, and a sort of hawk thing,' she reported. 'I reckon they must have all run in there out of the storm. Did you ever see such a thing?'

'No, I *never* saw such a thing,' said Griggs emphatically. 'And I won't ever again. The culprits won't get away from me this time.' He seemed to think the other animals had also played a part in the theft of his chickens.

'Now, Jack,' he admonished his dog, 'you sit there, and don't stir till I say so. We've got work to do.'

The bull-mastiff did not show the slightest inclination to do anything but sit exactly where it was, its teeth partially bared in anticipation of its forthcoming moment of success.

'What are you going to do, Tom?' asked Mrs Griggs, following her husband indoors.

Griggs brandished his shotgun at her. 'I'm going to clean and oil this,' he said. 'Then I'm going to re-load her, and *then* I'm going to settle a little score with our friend the fox.'

'What about the other animals though?' asked his wife.

'Those we'll see about later,' he replied. 'There's plenty of time.'

Fox had woken with a start as he heard the door close on them. It was not a loud noise, and most of his companions continued to sleep unawares.

'Are you awake, Kestrel?' Fox whispered, as he saw the bird stir.

'Yes,' Kestrel whispered back. 'Was that the wind?'

'No, I can hear someone outside,' Fox replied. He walked to the door and tried to peer through the crack underneath. At once there was a loud growling noise. Fox quickly retreated.

'There's a human and what sounds like a very large dog,' he informed Kestrel.

'We'd better wake the others,' suggested Kestrel.

'No,' Fox said sharply. 'Not yet. We don't want any panic.' He sniffed all round the sides of the shed, pushing at various boards with his paw.

'Have a look at the windows,' he said finally.

'No latches,' Kestrel reported. 'In any case, none of you animals could climb up here.'

Fox nodded and went over to Badger's corner. A gentle prod roused him.

Badger noticed at once the door was shut. 'Oh dear,' he said. 'Now we're in a mess.'

'I'm afraid we are,' Fox said. 'But there *must* be a way out.'

Badger stood up, unintentionally disturbing Mole. 'What is it, Badger?' asked the sleepy animal, with a yawn. 'Are we going?'

'Sssh!' Badger cautioned. 'We're thinking. Go back to sleep, Mole, there's a good fellow.'

But Mole sensed there was something wrong. 'Oh! We're shut in!' he shrieked. 'We're caught!'

'Be quiet!' snapped Fox fiercely. 'Do you want everyone to wake up?'

There were sounds of stirring amongst the straw. They heard the lazy hiss of Adder's voice. 'Mmm. It seems our exit is sealed,' he drawled. 'I knew it was a mistake to put that stupid, vain bird on guard. Pheasants are only good for eating.'

'No use saying that now,' remarked Badger. 'What's done is done. What we've got to do now . . .' he broke off as they heard the unmistakable report of a gun.

The animals looked fearfully at each other. There was a brief silence; then they detected the alarm call of a pheasant followed immediately by a second gunshot.

'Sounds as if Pheasant's done for,' Fox muttered.

All the animals were awake now, milling about in the centre of the floor, and bombarding Fox and Badger with frightened questions.

Finally Fox shouted for silence. 'Please! Everyone, quiet!'

He began pacing up and down the shed, a few feet one way, then a few feet back. 'Now, I admit we're in danger,' he said in a low voice. 'There's no point in denying it.' His head was down, and he seemed to be merely thinking aloud, not addressing the others. 'But if you all keep calm,' he murmured, 'we'll think of a way out.' He continued to pace.

'There's only one way out, of course,' Tawny Owl observed.

All faces turned to him.

'Dig,' he said.

'Dig?' asked the squirrels.

'Dig?' asked the fieldmice.

'Of course!' exclaimed Fox. 'Dig! We'll dig our way out.'

At that moment they heard human voices calling to each other outside. It was Tom Griggs telling his wife about the pheasants, and she replying to him about her find in the store-shed.

The animals fell silent again. The next minute they saw the farmer's face pressed to the window. In his eyes they read amazement, then anger, and finally resolution. They saw him turn away, and heard his and Mrs Griggs's footsteps receding towards the farmhouse.

'Right,' said Fox. 'No time to lose. Who's our best tunneller?'

'Mole,' replied Badger.

The little creature visibly swelled with pride. At last he was to be of some use to the party. It was all he could have wished for.

'Come on then, Mole,' said Fox. 'Show us what you can do.'

'Just watch me,' said Mole ecstatically. Then he looked up at Fox in consternation. 'But where do I begin?' he asked miserably. 'I can't dig through that.' He pointed with his snout at the wooden floor. He was so disappointed that he could feel the tears beginning to collect.

'Leave that to us,' said Squirrel, and gathered the gnawing power of his party together.

'We can gnaw too,' said the hedgehogs.

They were joined by the rabbits and the voles and mice. Opening their mouths, they presented over a score of sets of powerful teeth to the floor and began to gnaw.

The din was terrific as they set to work. The bull-mastiff heard the rasping and scraping of their teeth and began to growl again.

'They've left the dog behind,' Kestrel said to Fox. 'How are we to avoid him?'

'I think that's where I come in,' hissed Adder, and slithered towards the crack underneath the door. Here he stationed himself, keeping the farmer's dog at bay by alternately hissing and lunging at its inquisitive muzzle.

The thin planks of wood that formed the floor of the shed soon succumbed to the concerted efforts of the rodents. When the hole was big enough, Mole squeezed through, and began to dig vertically downwards through the soil underneath as fast as his expert claws could manage.

As the hole in the floorboards was enlarged, Badger was able to climb into Mole's pit, and, following in the tracks of his friend, he widened the tunnel as he descended. Presently he reached a junction in the tunnel where the industrious Mole had turned off horizontally, carving out a straight path that would eventually take him right underneath the shed, to emerge again in the orchard.

'Where are you, Mole?' Badger called softly as he stopped. 'Are you outside yet?'

'Not yet, Badger,' he heard a muffled voice reply from the darkness ahead of him.

'How do you know?' Badger asked. 'You'd better dig up to the surface to see.' He was afraid that Mole, in his enthusiasm for being useful, might get carried away and dig too far.

'All right,' he heard Mole answer him.

Badger waited patiently. A little later he heard Mole's excited squeak. 'Yes! I'm out! Badger, I've done it!'

'Good fellow,' said Badger warmly. 'Now, come back to me. If we work quickly, we'll all be safe in a few minutes.'

Mole, an elated expression on his face, returned along the tunnel to Badger.

'Now, I want you to go back to Fox,' Badger told him. 'Tell him to organize a chain of animals to pass the earth along that I'm going to dig out. He'd better stay at the

entrance of the tunnel to pile the earth in the shed. Off you go!'

A moment later Weasel appeared. 'Fox said to go ahead,' he informed Badger. 'You push the soil back to me, and I'll pass it on to Hare. Behind him is Rabbit, then Mole, and finally Fox at the top.'

'Good.' Badger nodded. 'I'm going to dig fast, so be careful you don't get buried.'

Without another word he began to move forward along the tunnel, kicking large sprays of earth behind him with his powerful back feet. Weasel worked overtime to keep his part of the passage clear, furiously pushing the earth behind him to Hare.

As they progressed down Mole's tunnel, more animals were needed in the line to keep the soil moving all the way back to the entrance, where Fox was busily spreading it over the floor of the shed. By the time Badger reached the point where Mole had started to dig towards the surface, nearly the whole of the party was helping with the work. Only the tiny animals, the voles and fieldmice, the very young, and Toad and the birds remained in the store-shed, assisting Fox where they could.

Adder had remained at his post all the while, and had succeeded in holding the attention of the bull-mastiff so well that the dog remained completely unaware that the animals had almost tunnelled their way to safety.

Badger soon saw daylight ahead and cautiously inched his way to the surface. Pushing out only his head, he saw that he was back in the orchard, about six feet from the shed. Only a matter of inches round the corner sat the bull-mastiff. Badger sniffed elaborately in every direction, and then stepped out of the hole.

Looking down into the tunnel, he could see Weasel, his fur and face covered in lumps of earth, climbing up towards him.

'Pass the word back to Fox that we've finished,' Badger

whispered, 'and that he must get everybody through the tunnel as quickly as he possibly can. I'll stay here at the exit to help everyone out.'

Weasel turned to whisper the message to Hare, then joined Badger on the surface. The procedure was repeated by all of the animals in the tunnel, so that when Hedgehog, who was the last in the line, finally repeated Badger's words to Fox, most of the party was already hiding in the long grass of the orchard, ready to race for safety.

Fox had just finished distributing the last quantity of earth over the floor. 'Down you go, my little friends!' he called to the youngsters, who descended into the tunnel under the care of the voles and fieldmice.

Toad, Tawny Owl and Kestrel went close on their heels, the birds half fluttering and half walking along the tunnel.

Fox glanced towards Adder. 'Can you hold on just long enough for us to get clear?' he asked.

'Of course,' replied Adder. 'We must all play our part.'

'We won't forget this,' Fox assured him. 'We'll wait for you as soon as we reach a safe spot. I'll send Kestrel back to show you the way.'

'You'd better get going,' Adder hissed. 'I can see the farmer on his way back.'

Fox called a final farewell and leapt into the tunnel.

13

Pursued

Now left entirely alone, Adder prepared himself for escape. He stretched his full length tight against the wall, so as to be as inconspicuous as possible. As soon as the farmer and his dog entered the building, he would slip through the crack while their backs were turned.

He could still watch the approach of the farmer towards the shed, but now all he could see were his boots trudging ominously forward. He heard Griggs call to the bull-mastiff; then the footsteps stopped, and the door was swung back.

The dog bounded inside, barking furiously. Then, seeing that the shed was empty, it began to run round, nose to the floor, whining in frustration.

'What the devil . . .!' was the unfinished exclamation from the farmer as he stepped into the shed, his gun half raised to his shoulder. He stood staring in disbelief at the earth spread evenly over the floor, and the neat hole in the floorboards.

Behind him, Adder slithered under the open door and out on to the path, making as fast a pace as he could manage towards the nearest long grass. He could hear the commotion in the store-shed, as the cheated farmer cursed and shouted angrily at his dog. The shouting was followed by a loud yelp, which, Adder decided, was the result of a well-aimed kick from the farmer.

He reached a patch of cover adjacent to the orchard, and hid himself in some wet twigs and leaves amongst a clump of couch-grass. Here he intended to stay until he judged it was safe to proceed further.

The farmer came out of the shed like a bolt from a gun, his miserable dog slinking at his heels, its tail held low. He went straight to the orchard, where he fell to scanning the grassy ground. His eyes soon picked out what he was searching for – the exit hole of the animals' tunnel. With an angry snarl, the farmer directed the muzzle of his shotgun down into the hole, and fired both barrels. Some clods of earth flew upwards, followed by a thin wisp of smoke.

'That'll teach 'em!' growled Tom Griggs, and he stumped off, frowning hideously, back to the cottage where his wife was waiting at the door.

The bull-mastiff continued to skulk around the hole as if it did not intend to be fooled twice.

Adder, in his temporary hideout, wondered how far away his friends were. He knew that they would have put as much distance behind them as they were able, before they rested.

Through the network of twigs and grass-stems in front of his red eyes, Adder saw the bull-mastiff suddenly turn its head from the tunnel and put its muzzle to the ground. It sniffed vigorously over the grass, and having picked up a scent, followed it closely under the trees of the orchard. Adder was sure the dog was now on the trail of Fox and his party.

The bull-mastiff increased its pace, and barked excitedly. It was a deep, throaty bark; a fearsome noise.

Adder decided the coast was clear, and slithered into the open. He wound his way to the next piece of cover, an isolated patch of stinging-nettles, where he paused to consider what he should do next.

106

After some serious contemplation he decided there was really very little he could do, except wait for Kestrel. He had no idea in which direction his companions had gone, and there was no way in which he could warn them that they were being pursued. In any case, the dog was making enough noise to wake the dead. They would have plenty of time to get out of its way. Having reassured himself on that point, Adder settled down patiently for a long wait.

It had taken a matter of only a couple of minutes for Fox to race through the tunnel, clamber up the exit shaft, and prepare the waiting animals for immediate flight. It needed only a short consultation with Toad before they decided on their direction.

On Toad's advice Fox led them out of the bounds of the farmer's land, on to a footpath that wound its way past several neighbouring farmsteads and orchards, on to a stretch of open common land, where it then led sharply uphill.

'Are you quite sure this is the right way?' Fox asked, as they rested for a minute amongst some shrubbery at the foot of the rise.

'Oh yes,' declared Toad. 'I recognize all this. Of course, it took me an age on my own to cover the same ground.'

'I don't much like the look of what's ahead,' Fox admitted. 'We can be seen far too clearly, for my liking, as we climb that hill.'

'Don't worry about that,' Toad answered. 'It's a very stony, uneven path. Humans don't use it much. I would guess. In any case, the sensible ones are still indoors after that storm.'

'I hope you're right,' said Fox. 'What's on the other side of the hill?'

'The path drops steeply down to a sort of copse. Beyond that there are more farm dwellings and fields. When we've got those behind us, there are green meadows ahead, as thick and lush as you've ever seen. They will lead us to the river.'

'Can we reach the copse today?' Fox asked briskly.

'Oh, it's not too far,' Toad assured him. 'We'll be quite safe in there. Nothing but a few rooks to bother about.'

Fox looked round at his friends, most of whom were too tired and hungry to talk. 'One last effort now and we'll soon be able to rest and eat at our leisure,' Fox promised them. 'Can you do it?'

All the animals nodded, some more wearily than others.

Fox took the lead as they moved up the hill at walking pace. As they climbed, rain began to fall again. But this time it was gentler; there was no fury in it, and it refreshed them.

Wearily they plodded on. Tawny Owl and Kestrel flew to the brow of the hill and called back encouragement to their struggling companions.

'You can see the river from up here,' Tawny Owl cried. 'It looks just like a tiny stream in the distance.'

'You're nearly up,' Kestrel called. 'Keep going.'

When they were about halfway up, Fox suddenly stopped. 'Did you hear anything?' he asked Badger, who was behind him.

'No,' said Badger.

'Keep going! Keep going!' Kestrel shrieked. His hawk's eyes had picked out an ominous shape way back on the footpath. 'Don't stop now!' he cried. 'Make haste!'

Fox knew now that he had not been mistaken. A faint bark came to him from the distance. 'It's the farmer's dog,' he said to Badger. 'We must hurry.'

Standing to one side Fox egged on the other animals to fresh exertions. Eventually they all passed him, and he was left watching their ascent anxiously.

'Badger, I must entrust you with the party again,' he called after him. 'You get them to the copse. I'll try and delay this customer.'

He added in a lower voice, 'Well, Toad, I'm afraid you'll have to make your own way for a bit. I'll join you as soon as I can.'

'Of course, I understand,' Toad replied, and instantly leapt to the ground from Fox's back, and hopped after the main party as quickly as he could. 'Look out for yourself!' he called back over his shoulder.

The bull-mastiff was just beginning to climb the slope, so Fox descended part of the way to meet it. Needing all its breath for running uphill, the dog had at last ceased to bark.

'Here I am!' Fox shouted down, standing his ground. 'I'm the character you're after! You can ignore the others!' He glanced quickly behind him to see how his friends were progressing. They were about three-quarters of the distance up the rise.

'Yes, it *is* you,' gasped the dog, looking up towards the small chestnut figure. 'You're . . . the . . . culprit. My master . . . wants you . . . dead.'

'Your master wants every fox dead,' came the reply. 'I could see the hatred in his eyes when he saw me in the shed.'

The bull-mastiff paused, a few yards from Fox. 'He wants *you*,' the dog replied. 'You killed his chickens. He wants his revenge.'

'He's got the wrong animal,' Fox said calmly. 'I never killed a chicken in my life. They don't suit my tastes at all – too many feathers.'

'A likely story,' growled the guard dog. 'Strange isn't it, that you should be found lurking just round the corner from the chicken-coop?'

'You may call it strange,' said Fox. 'I was not lurking, as you suggested. I and my friends merely entered the shed to shelter from the storm – and were shut in.'

'I don't believe a word of it,' the bull-mastiff said savagely. 'Oh, I know you foxes are all supposed to be very cunning and clever. But you don't fool me. I'm taking you back.

Then perhaps I'll get some thanks, for once, from my master.'

It advanced a step towards Fox, warily.

'I'm afraid you'll find you're mistaken, if that's what you're expecting,' Fox said evenly.

'What do you mean?' growled the dog, hesitating a fraction.

'Your master doesn't want *you* to obtain his revenge for him. He, and only he, wants that satisfaction. Nothing else will do. Believe me, I know all about human feelings.' Fox shrugged. 'You domesticated creatures are blinded by humans' generosity. They feed you, groom you, give you a home. You don't notice their faults. Now we wild animals are different. We observe human ways from a distance, and we understand them better. Animals, and their needs, are of little consideration when they conflict with their own. That's always been the way of it, and it won't alter. So I say again, you'll get no thanks from your master for killing me.'

The bull-mastiff seemed to waver. With less confidence in its gruff voice it said, 'Then I'll take you back alive.'

'That's quite impossible,' Fox replied at once. 'I'm no match for your size and strength, but if you want to take me back, you'll have to kill me first.'

'Confound your clever talk!' the bull-mastiff swore. 'My master blamed me for not catching the fox that killed his chickens. Now I *have* caught a fox, it seems he won't want it.'

'You should have caught the right fox,' said Fox smoothly. 'I've got nothing against you,' he went on. 'Every creature to its training. But whatever killed those chickens was clever enough to elude you. It won't help you now to kill the wrong animal.'

With wonderfully contrived coolness, Fox turned on his heel and walked off up the slope after his friends, who had now disappeared over the brow of the hill.

110

He steeled himself to continue at a sauntering pace, knowing full well that this show of confidence would convince the bull-mastiff once and for all that it had made an error.

At the top, Fox found Toad waiting for him. Only then did he permit himself to look back. The bull-mastiff was standing, with a baffled expression on its once fierce face, looking up the slope towards Fox. It had not moved one inch forward. As it saw Fox turn, it slunk away, back the way it had come.

Toad was unable to contain his excitement. 'Fox, you were superb!' he exclaimed. 'I heard everything. It was magnificent. Wait till I tell the others about it. Such coolness and poise. Well, you certainly browbeat him!'

'When you live by your wits and senses, as we wild creatures do,' said Fox, 'it's not so difficult to win an argument with one of his sort.' He smiled. 'Now, come on. Up you get, my friend. We must catch the others up. It's a long time since we ate, and I bet there are all sorts of good things to be found in that copse.'

14

The copse

Badger and the rest of the party made much of Fox when he and Toad caught them up. The respect and admiration which they already felt for their leader was now heightened by his latest success.

Dusk was falling as they entered the copse. Rooks were circling the tree-tops, cawing noisily in their evening ritual, before settling one by one, on their nests for the night.

The immediate objective of the animals was to satisfy their gnawing hunger, and, after establishing their camp amongst some elm shrubbery, they set off on their separate forays.

The squirrels were so overjoyed to find tall trees which they could run up and down, that their quest for food was temporarily suspended as they chased one another up the trunks and along the branches. The sleepy rooks cackled irritably.

When the animals had all found and eaten as much as they needed, they made their way directly back to the camp. Fox called a council of the leaders of each group, and they decided unanimously to remain in the copse for some days, to rest and build up their strength. After the danger and hardship which they had encountered in the last few days, when they had run from one crisis to the next, all the animals agreed that they had found the ideal haven of safety for the time being. Here they could comfortably prepare themselves for the many hazards that lay in their oncoming travels.

'What are you going to do about Adder?' asked Weasel.

'Adder!' Fox exclaimed. 'Good heavens, we've forgotten him! Whatever will he be thinking of us!'

'Leave it to me,' volunteered Tawny Owl. 'It's pitch black now. I'll fly back to the farm and find him. Don't worry.'

He flew off through the trees and into the open country.

'You mustn't blame yourself,' Badger said to the downcast Fox. 'You've had a lot on your mind.'

'But I promised him,' Fox said miserably. 'He depended on me.'

'It's much safer for Adder to travel at night. The two of

them will be far less noticeable,' Weasel said comfortingly. 'Tawny Owl will get him here by the morning. You'll see.'

All afternoon Adder lay hidden amongst the thick stinging-nettles, wondering, while he felt comparatively safe himself, about the safety of his friends.

He watched the farmer's bull-mastiff race away on their trail, bellowing horribly. The dog's barks had gradually dwindled into the distance, and Adder was left wondering what the fate of Fox, Badger and the others would be.

He would not admit to himself that he was worried, but he found it difficult to maintain his chosen character of an uncommitted, unfeeling individual. He felt decidedly uneasy. This feeling grew as the time wore on; in fact until the time he saw the bull-mastiff return.

There was something so altered in the manner of the dog, as it slunk through the long grass of the orchard on its way to its kennel, that Adder guessed at once that it had been bested in some way by his friends.

His feeling changed to one of mild excitement, and he felt sure he could soon expect the arrival of Kestrel.

The rain stopped again, but the sky remained cloudy, and soon it was dusk. Adder began to hope Kestrel would not be long in arriving; otherwise, if it grew too dark, they would certainly miss one another.

But Adder was still alone when night fell. He decided it was pointless to remain any longer under cover in the darkness, and he sallied forth to search for food.

He kept well away from the bull-mastiff's kennel, and slithered round the other side of Farmer Griggs's cottage, keeping close to the wall. There was an old water-butt at one corner, and next to that an ancient vegetable box, full of potato peelings and other scraps. Here Adder was fortunate enough to catch himself some supper in the shape of a rat, which had been looking for its own supper amongst the kitchen leavings.

He decided to eat his meal in comfort, away from the human dwelling where there would be no fear of being disturbed. So, with the rat clutched firmly between his jaws, Adder made his way back to the patch of stinging-nettles.

In the middle of his meal, he was interrupted by a familiar hooting sound. So Tawny Owl had come for him! He made haste to reach the orchard where Tawny Owl was flitting to and fro like a huge bat, calling him softly in his flute-toned voice.

The bird's powerful eyes soon discovered Adder signalling him from the grass.

'Glad to see you, Adder,' said Tawny Owl.

'Likewise,' drawled Adder. 'What kept you?'

Tawny Owl related all that had happened.

'I'm just finishing my supper,' said Adder afterwards. 'Have you eaten yet?'

'Only lightly,' Tawny Owl replied.

'Will you join me?'

'With great pleasure.'

They both repaired eagerly to the stinging-nettles, and made short work of what was left of Adder's meal.

'I'll catch you another,' said Tawny Owl, 'and we'll share it out. One good turn, you know . . .'

Adder described where he had made his catch, and Tawny Owl flew away.

He was not long in returning with a second rat, and Adder complimented him on his prowess as a night hunter. They set to together, and devoured their additional snack in companionable silence.

'Now I think we should get under way,' said Tawny Owl. 'It's going to be a fairly long haul for you, Adder. I'll swap some hunting yarns with you as we go.'

In the early hours of the following morning, just before daybreak, Adder and Tawny Owl paused on the crest of the hill, before their descent towards the copse. Tawny Owl took the opportunity of relating to Adder how Fox had triumphed, by persuasion, over the fierce farm dog.

Adder enjoyed the tale. 'Yes,' he said afterwards, 'he's a clever chap, that Fox. I shouldn't be at all surprised if he sees us safely through after all.'

Tawny Owl, whose wisdom even Fox admired, was a little envious of the praises heaped on his friend, considering that he himself had played a leading part in the animals' escape from the farm by his suggestion of digging.

'He *is* clever,' admitted Owl, 'but I'm sure we've all been of some assistance, at one stage or another, on the journey.'

Adder saw where Tawny Owl's thoughts lay, but, a trifle spitefully, pretended ignorance to afford himself some amusement.

'Of course,' he hissed, 'there's no question of anyone else assuming the leadership of the party.'

'Er . . . no, of course not,' said Tawny Owl.

'And yet, if Fox should fall sick or something . . . there would have to be some changes,' Adder went on. 'I suppose Badger would step into his tracks in that case.'

'I really couldn't say,' Tawny Owl said shortly. 'Badger has a good heart, and he's kind. But I don't know if he's got *all* the necessary qualities . . .'

Adder could not resist replying: 'But then who else is there?'

'Well,' Tawny Owl said, ruffling his feathers importantly, 'I . . . um . . . would always . . .'

'You were perhaps thinking of yourself?' Adder suggested.

'Well, Adder, you know I myself would never have mentioned it,' said Tawny Owl, 'but as you began on the subject . . .'

'Did I?' said the teasing snake. 'Yes. I must have done. Ah well, I suppose we all have our aspirations, but whether we ever succeed in them is another matter.'

Tawny Owl felt that Adder was making him look foolish. He tried to retrieve some dignity. 'For my part,' he said, 'I shall be content to act as counsellor when called upon to do so. Fox, I know, relies on me in that respect.'

'Oh, quite,' returned Adder. 'Er . . . shall we move on?'

As they continued towards the copse, Tawny Owl was uncomfortably aware that, without any distinct confession on his part, Adder had exposed a very private feeling of his, the existence of which he had scarcely acknowledged to himself.

It was dawn as they entered the copse. They found their friends astir, their slumbers having been interrupted by the first noises from the rookery. They were greeted with enthusiasm by the whole party, but as soon as possible they pleaded tiredness and went away to find resting-places. For Tawny Owl, in any case, it was customary to sleep during the daylight hours, so this arrangement suited him admirably. The other animals busied themselves exploring the copse.

Thus the best part of the day was spent, and when most of them, apart from the squirrels, had returned to the elm

scrub after their wanderings, they were joined by several visitors.

These were a number of the male rooks who, flying down from the elm-tops, came waddling towards the animals, their iridescent purplish plumage reflecting the shafts of late sunlight that broke through the thick greenery. Naturally they were curious to know what had brought such a miscellaneous group of animals to their particular copse, but there was no trace of resentment in their tone.

Fox explained why they were there, describing their travels as he did so.

'I must tell you,' said one of the rooks, interrupting him after a while, 'that we did wonder if you could be that party of animals we had heard about.'

The animals exchanged surprised glances.

'Word spreads quickly in the bird world,' said the rook, 'and, of course, such an event as a fire is soon common knowledge in the neighbourhood. We've all heard of your escape from that, and how you ran through the storm. But I've never heard tell of a White Deer Park, so there must be a good long way ahead of you yet.'

This observation brought Toad into the conversation, explaining that he was acting as guide because he had already travelled the distance once on his own.

The rook shook his head in admiration. 'I wish I had your pioneer spirit,' he said. 'But I'm too old for that sort of thing now. This rookery's been my home all my life, and I expect to end my days here.'

'Oh! we're not all youngsters in this party,' chuckled Toad. 'Badger and I have both reached double figures, you know.'

'Then I admire you all the more,' said the rook, who seemed to be the patriarch of the copse rookery. 'But now that you're here,' he added, 'I hope you won't leave us too soon, despite your long journey. We don't see many ground folk here, and we rooks always enjoy a good chat.'

'We've already decided to spend a few days here,' Fox told him. 'We need some uninterrupted rest before we move on.'

'You've made a wise decision,' replied the rook, who failed to recognize the veiled hint in Fox's remark. 'It's secluded and peaceful here,' he went on. 'Nobody ever comes near the place. We're really delighted to have your company.'

He looked round at his companions. 'Are we singing tonight?' he asked.

'It was fixed for tomorrow,' replied one of the younger rooks.

'We fellows have a bit of a sing-song some evenings,' the old rook explained to the animals, 'when the ladies are in the nest with the young ones. We gather under the trees. If you'd care to join us tomorrow evening under the tall elms, we could have a longer chat too.'

'I'm sure we'd all like to come,' said Fox. 'How kind of you.'

'Till tomorrow then,' said the old rook, opening his wings for flight.

'Till tomorrow,' said Fox.

15

The river

The animals were made so welcome by their new friends the rooks, that they were all very reluctant to leave the copse. The days drifted by, free of any danger, and all the members of the party were able to enjoy their first freedom from intrusion since before they had left Farthing Wood.

Badger found an old disused set, part of which he soon cleaned and lined for his own quarters, while the rabbits occupied some of the other chambers.

Mole, Weasel, and Fox, too, slept in the old tunnels leading to this group of chambers. The voles and fieldmice made their home under the exposed roots of an ancient sycamore, and Toad contented himself with retiring into a discarded jam-jar that he had found amongst some ground-ivy.

The squirrels, of course, built makeshift dreys of old leaves and twigs in the tree-tops, but far enough from the rookery for them to enjoy some privacy.

Only the hedgehogs and hares remained on ground level, and Hare found it necessary to accommodate his family on some dry grass well away from where the hedgehogs collected to sleep, owing to the fact that they *would* snore so.

Nobody knew where Adder hid himself: one or other of the animals would sometimes stumble across him sunbathing in a warm spot in a glade, but he seemed never deliberately to seek anyone's company.

Kestrel hunted by day, in the open country and farmland that surrounded the copse, and in the evening he returned. When it grew quite dark, Tawny Owl flew away on his nocturnal wanderings, and between them the two birds kept the party informed of anything outside the copse that could pose a threat to the continuance of their journey.

It was so easy for them all, now they had the opportunity, to slip back into their usual habits of foraging, eating and sleeping, and with the occasional diversion of a party and a conversation with the rooks, many of the animals began to wonder why they had to move on at all.

Fox, however, saw the danger of their being lulled into a false sense of security, for he felt quite sure there was something significant about the absence of any resident animals in the copse. So, one morning about ten days after they had first arrived, he made a tour of the copse and rounded everyone up, including Adder, telling them to be ready to leave at dusk on the following day.

That night they had their last sing-song with the rooks, and, despite their friends' efforts to persuade them to stay a little longer, they made their farewells.

At the appointed time, the animals gathered in the elm-scrub, and when they were all present, Fox led them out of the copse, to a chorus of good-luck caws from the rooks, who had stayed up late to see them off.

Their way took them first through a wide area of farmland. After their recent experience with the bull-mastiff, the animals were far more cautious of straying too near human dwellings or livestock enclosures, where other fierce dogs might be on guard.

Following Toad's directions Fox led them on a route that skirted most of the farm buildings, and which always had sufficient cover for them to lie up in during the day.

Emerging from their communal hiding-place at dusk each day the animals would spend some time searching for food. They would eat together, as far as this was possible, and then set off for their night's travel, stopping to drink on the way as soon as they found the opportunity. Water was no longer a problem as, ever since the May drought had ended, showers of rain had fallen regularly.

For as long as Toad informed them that they were still in the vicinity of human habitations, their pattern of movement and rest never changed, and as the days wore on they drew close to the river.

Finally, one night, they passed the last farm on their side of the river, and when they rested at daybreak the animals could see the green meadows, many dotted with vivid yellow buttercups, sloping gently away from them down to the water's edge.

They looked their fill at the peaceful scene, before finding a corner in one meadow, overgrown with thick shrubs, nettles and dock, where they could sleep during the day.

As they settled down to rest, Hare asked Toad what they would find on the other side of the river.

'More meadows,' replied Toad. 'When we've passed those, as far as I can remember there's a long stretch of common land. Don't worry, it'll all come back to me when I see it again.'

'Is the river very wide?' asked Vole.

'Not very,' said Toad. 'None of us will have any trouble crossing it. There's a stretch of water, just a few yards along the bank from where we will arrive, which is almost still, the current there is so slow. Leave it to me, I'll see we all get across at the right point.'

This assurance satisfied all the immediate queries regarding what lay ahead of them, and, without further ado, the animals prepared for sleep.

Kestrel declared he was tired of hunting at dusk, when

his piercing eyesight was of little use, and that now the sun was coming up, he was going to make the most of it.

'Poor old Kestrel,' Tawny Owl sympathized. 'I'm getting the best of the arrangement at the moment, travelling at night, sleeping by day. It doesn't suit him at all, of course. It's a complete reversal of his usual habits.'

'We have to plan every move with an eye on safety,' said Fox. 'I myself am not averse to a spot of daytime hunting for a change; but for a party, it's far safer to go off foraging when it's dark, and, of course, to journey by night.'

'Dusk,' hissed Adder, 'is the best time for hunting activities. I've found that it's then that all the tastiest little creatures are stirring.' Here he was unable to avoid casting a meaningful glance at the fieldmice, making them quail. 'And it suits me . . . er . . . right down to the ground, as you might say.'

The larger animals and Tawny Owl chuckled at this quip, but the fieldmice and the voles shifted uneasily. They were still unsure of the snake's intentions towards them, even as travelling companions, and were more than glad of the reassuring presence of Badger and Fox.

As the sun rose higher, bees and butterflies began to appear, skipping from one buttercup to another, or settling on the white clover flowers. Weevils and beetles, grasshoppers, ants and earwigs were all busy amongst the grass stalks, and the morning was filled with their rustlings and murmurings.

Drowsiness soon fell on all the animal band, and they gratefully shut their eyes.

Another day passed, and Fox led them through the cool meadows to the bank of the river. They paused, looking down into the clear water that reflected the starry night sky in its blackness. Then they drank greedily before they undertook the important crossing.

Toad led them upstream a short way, looking carefully for the spot where he himself had crossed before. Eventually he came to a halt.

'I'm sure this is it,' he told them confidently. 'There's a hole in the bank here just like the one I hid in last time. It must be the same one.'

The animals drew themselves up into a bunch, and all of them started to jostle at the water's edge in their efforts to examine the state of the river.

'You're right, Toad,' Fox declared. 'The water here seems scarcely to be moving.'

'It looks a long way to the other bank,' squeaked Fieldmouse.

'Don't worry,' said Toad kindly. 'I'll go across first. You can watch me. I'm about your size, and if I can do it . . .'

'You go ahead,' Fox told him. 'The rest of us will take to the water together, and help each other. Good luck!'

Toad gave them a smile and sprang from the bank, landing in the water with a modest little plop. The animals watched as the regular backward-kicking of his strong hind legs propelled his small body across the river in a series of jerks.

As he reached the middle, he was lost to their view, but a few minutes later they heard his croaks of triumph from the opposite bank.

'I've done it! I've done it!' he called. 'Come and join me! The water's lovely.'

Fox sent Kestrel and Tawny Owl across to join him. The animals paused on the brink, waiting for directions.

'We'll all go together,' Fox repeated. 'Line up along the bank, everyone.'

The voles and fieldmice took the middle position, flanked by the squirrels and hedgehogs. The rabbits, Hare and his family, and Badger took up their positions on the far right. Weasel, Fox, Mole and Adder were on the far left.

To Toad's encouraging cries, the long line of assorted animals entered the inky water together.

Mole and Badger were soon ahead of the rest, both being excellent swimmers, and the hares and hedgehogs found no difficulty in paddling their way across. Fox and Weasel swam well within their capabilities in order to keep an eye on the rest, who were not faring so well.

Strangely enough, of the slower swimmers the voles and fieldmice were the most adept. It was merely their size and comparative weakness that made the crossing of the river a daunting task. Yet they kept bravely on, their tiny heads poking above the surface, and their even tinier pink feet paddling furiously.

Adder, who was not really a keen swimmer, seemed to be making reasonable progress. The rabbits and squirrels were the slowest.

These animals were the jumpiest and the most nervous of the party. Although they all possessed the ability to swim, once they were in the water they seemed to lose their heads. Instead of striking out for the opposite bank, they went round and round in circles, thrashing the water in a kind of panic, and paying no heed to Fox and Weasel who attempted to calm them.

Toad watched the proceedings with considerable anxiety. Although he had been able to see all of his companions when they lined up on the bank in the moonlight, once they had entered the blackness of the water he could see only the reflected stars and the heads of the largest animals, Badger and Fox. The only evidence of the presence of any other animals in the river was the noise of their splashing, and the widening rings on the surface of the water that had been caused by their entrance. It was only when some of them reached what was about the halfway point, that Toad, peering over the water, could distinguish their features.

He spotted Mole, swimming dexterously, alongside his

friend Badger. 'I can see you, Badger! I can see you too, Mole!' Toad shouted excitedly, and in another minute he was welcoming their dripping bodies as they pulled themselves on to the bank.

Badger shook himself like a dog, and sent a shower of water over Tawny Owl. Ignoring the bird's protests, he turned back to see how his companions were managing.

The hedgehogs, who actually seemed to be enjoying the swim, had almost reached the shore. Behind them, in the gloom, Badger noticed Hare's mate, swimming comfortably, while Hare himself was paddling between his two young ones, holding them on course.

Soon the members of the party safely on the bank numbered nineteen, including the two birds, and with the arrival of the undulating Adder, the number became a round twenty.

Next into sight were the voles and fieldmice, who had formed one closely-packed mass, so that they appeared to Badger like one creature, with an infinite number of heads.

These brave little animals could hardly find the strength to climb out of the water after their exhausting efforts but, needless to say, their friends on the bank all rallied round to help them up to safety.

'I knew you could do it,' said Toad, 'if courage played any part in the matter. You'll be surprised to see that a lot of the larger animals are still in the river; so you've really set them an example.'

'Wherever can Fox be?' asked Badger, with a note of concern in his voice. 'I can't see him at all.'

Straining his weak eyes for a glimpse of his friend, he walked along the bank a few steps, and then returned to go in the other direction, a puzzled expression on his face.

'Fox!' he called. 'Are you all right? We can't see you.'

The only sounds that reached his ears were the continuing splashes that had been audible ever since they had all first entered the river.

'Fox!' he called again, more loudly. 'Are you there? Rabbit! Weasel! Can you hear me?'

A muffled reply from he knew not whom followed his cries. He could not distinguish a single word.

'What was that?' he shouted. 'I can't hear you.'

Just then Weasel's head appeared out of the darkness, and the squirrels were with him.

'Bit ... of ... difficulty,' he panted, as he paddled nearer. 'The rabbits . . . took fright. Swam in . . . all directions, except . . . the right one. Fox is . . . trying to calm . . . them down. Squirrels . . . all right now.'

Badger called the rabbits all sorts of names under his breath.

'Can he manage?' he asked, as the squirrels, somewhat shamefaced, and Weasel joined the throng.

'I don't know for sure,' replied Weasel. 'He's tiring. I told him to leave them, but he wouldn't.'

'Just like Fox,' said Badger. 'Perhaps I should go and help him,' he added. He scrambled down to the water's edge.

'Let me come too! I'm a good swimmer!' cried Mole.

Then, suddenly, Hare shouted: 'There they are!'

The heads of the rabbits and of Fox were at last visible. Fox was swimming behind them, trying his best to keep them on course; for even at this stage the rabbits were still in a state of alarm at finding themselves in deep water, and none of them was swimming in a straight line.

The weary Fox was paddling furiously to one rabbit, who was threatening to swim away from the group, only to see that, having put *this* animal straight, another, at the other end of the line, had started to swim back to the far bank.

Badger and the rest of the party who had successfully made the crossing, were absolutely amazed at the rabbits' stupidity, and in their sympathy for the gallant Fox, began to shout angrily at them.

'Where are you going? This is the way!' shouted Weasel.

'What are you turning round for?' Vole called in his shrill voice.

A chorus of protests were directed at the jittery rabbits. Fox looked pleadingly at the animals on the bank, but the damage was done. At the sound of the shouting voices, the already nervous rabbits really panicked. Pandemonium broke loose as they all set off in different directions, colliding with each other, and pushing the young ones under the surface with their struggling bodies.

The despairing Fox swam into the midst of the mêlée, and tried to shepherd the frightened animals towards the bank.

Badger was still poised on the edge, in two minds whether to enter the water to assist Fox, wondering if one more animal in the river would only add to the rabbits' confusion. He happened to look upstream, and what he saw made him shudder.

A huge mass of debris, containing twigs, leaves, grass and even whole branches, was drifting in the middle of the river, and bearing down directly on Fox and the rabbits. It was so large that Badger saw it when it was more than thirty yards off.

If Fox had been alone in the water he would have been in no danger, for the debris would be slowed down considerably by the slack water of the crossing-place, and he would have had ample time to reach safety. But Badger knew that Fox would never abandon the rabbits, and so, unless he acted quickly to save his friend, all the animals in the water would be carried away downstream, and perhaps drowned in the swifter currents.

'Quick, friends! They're in danger!' he cried. 'Every able body into the water. Each one of you must rescue one rabbit; I don't care how. I'll look after Fox. Be quick, lives are at stake!'

Badger dived into the river, just ahead of Weasel, Hare, Mole and the hedgehogs. Even Toad followed, determined to help if he could.

Each of them singled out one rabbit, and, with one eye on the approaching debris, either coaxed or forced the animal to the bank. Toad took one of the youngsters in charge, and eventually, by some means or another, all the animals were within striking distance of the river bank.

Only Fox and Badger were now left in danger. Fox had used all his strength and stamina in his heroic efforts to save the rabbits, and when Badger reached him in midstream, he was on the point of sinking with exhaustion. With Badger's assistance, he was able to manage a painfully slow paddle.

The debris was about ten yards away. Badger noticed with relief that all the other animals were now safe on dry land. They seemed a long way away. He looked again at the approaching mass. With a feeling of horror he realized he and Fox could never reach the bank in time. Fox knew this too.

'Badger, please,' he begged, 'leave me. You've still got

time to save yourself. Go back to the others. They'll need you . . .' He could not manage any more words.

Badger did not reply, but steeled himself for the coming impact. He heard the alarmed voices of Tawny Owl and Weasel, and the various squeaks of the mice and voles, and of Mole. Then a cold, sodden mass struck him on his left side, and enveloped him completely.

He was pulled underwater, his legs and head entangled in the choking mass. He fought to free himself, but was dragged further and further down into the dark depths of the river.

16

A new leader

The animals on the bank watched with horror the drama taking place in the river. The sight of Fox, the leader of their expedition, and Badger, whom all, except perhaps Tawny Owl, acknowledged to be his deputy, in such grave danger of drowning, sent a shudder through every one. They could all see that the mound of floating debris was about to engulf both the swimmers; and there was nothing they could do about it.

They saw Badger's head disappear under the surface, while Fox caught a blow from one of the floating branches, and was carried away downstream, his feeble struggles being powerless to prevent it.

In one mass movement the animals raced along the bank to keep Fox in sight, while Tawny Owl and Kestrel flew directly over the river, following its course.

After some twenty yards or so the debris reached the swift-flowing water, and in no time Fox was hurled away out of sight of the animals, though the birds continued to follow overhead.

There was a large rock in the river at this point, and the debris broke into two pieces, half of it rushing past one side, and the other piece on the opposite side. A lot of the grass and leaves caught against the rock, and were trapped there.

The animals were about to retrace their steps along the bank, all of them in the depths of despair at the tragedy.

'Stop!' cried Toad. 'There's something amongst that mass of vegetation out there.' His voice rose in a feverish excitement. 'It . . . I think it's . . . Badger! Yes, I can see him! Badger's there!'

The animals held their breath. Sure enough, there in the thick of the swirling grass and weed, was the unmistakable striped head of Badger – motionless.

'Is he . . . is he . . . ?' faltered Mole, in a shaking voice.

'I'm afraid there's little hope of his still being alive,' said Weasel, and did his best to comfort Mole, who began to sob inconsolably.

'Look! Look!' shrieked one of the young rabbits. 'He's moving!'

'Come on, Hare,' said Hedgehog. 'We must get him out.'

Without hesitation he jumped into the water and, using all his strength to combat the faster current, struck out for the rock. Hare and Weasel were not slow to follow his action.

To the smaller and weaker animals on the bank it seemed an age before Badger's rescuers managed finally to reach the dead water behind the rock. Weasel tore savagely at the vegetation round Badger's body to free him, and when he had cleared a space, he and Hedgehog got on either side of Badger's head, and using their small bodies as props, kept it just clear of the water. Hare, the strongest of them, took up his position directly behind Badger, and as they began to swim for the shore, he pushed the helpless body along with a series of nudges from his shoulders.

At last, to the intense relief of Mole, all four reached the bank again. They had to push Badger to safety, as he was unable to stand.

He was a pitiful sight. His eyes were barely open, his coat matted with mud and rotting grass, while his sides heaved violently as his lungs gulped in air. Presently he coughed up about a pint of water.

The animals surrounded him, touching his aching body affectionately, while Mole leant his little black velvet head against one of Badger's legs, and wept as though his heart would break.

'Now, Mole,' Adder reprimanded him. 'Badger's safe now. That's enough of that.'

'It won't help him, you know,' said Rabbit.

Weasel turned on him fiercely. 'How dare you utter a word,' he snarled. 'You, and your cowardly kind, are to blame for this.'

Rabbit quailed before Weasel's furious glare, and coughed uneasily.

'Well, we all panic at times,' he muttered uncomfortably, looking away. 'We rabbits don't like flowing water – we're not good swimmers, you know. You're more fortunate . . . Ahem! I'm sure we're all very sorry for the . . . um . . .'

'Please,' Badger managed to gasp. 'Don't let's quarrel. We're all . . . all safe now.'

Weasel looked at Hare, and Hedgehog exchanged glances with Toad. Badger was obviously unaware of the fate of Fox. Weasel made a little sign to them all that they should keep quiet about it for the present.

'What you need more than anything is a good rest,' he said to Badger kindly. 'You'll feel better after some sleep, and we'll have something ready to eat when you wake up. Do you think you can manage a few steps to the clump of undergrowth just over there?'

With help from all his friends, Badger reached the shelter and fell into a deep sleep as soon as his head touched the ground.

The animals went off to look for food, and when they returned they found Tawny Owl waiting for them.

'We lost him,' he told them. 'Kestrel's snatching some sleep . . . I left him back there. He's going to continue to search when it's light . . . far better eyesight than mine.'

'Surely Fox will be far away by then?' said Hare.

'Kestrel flies like a bullet,' said Tawny Owl. 'It's not long to daylight; he'll soon make up lost ground. I suppose . . . no news of Badger?'

The animals had forgotten that Tawny Owl was still ignorant of Badger's rescue. They all started talking at once.

Tawny Owl was both pleased and relieved to hear that Badger was restored to them, but there was, nevertheless, a certain reserve in his reply that was probably only recognized by Adder.

'When Badger wakes,' said Weasel gloomily, 'someone will have to tell him about Fox.'

The animals looked at each other. There were no volunteers for the task.

'Don't despair,' said Tawny Owl. 'Let's keep our spirits up, at least until Kestrel returns. He may have some good news for us.'

'What will we do if it's bad news?' asked Mole.

'Carry on,' said Toad. 'We must.'

'Without Fox?'

'If we have to – and we ought to face the possibility of it.'

'Of course. What else can we do?' said Tawny Owl. 'We'll manage – Badger and I – somehow.'

A crafty grin spread over Adder's face. Without intention, Tawny Owl found his eyes turning towards the snake's, and when their glances met he turned away again uncomfortably.

'I'm sure we'll *all* play our part,' Weasel remarked, a little huffily. 'I don't believe Fox ever named a deputy.'

Adder's grin became wider. 'It seems,' he drawled, 'that we have several pretenders to the throne.'

'Badger will lead us,' declared the loyal Mole stoutly. 'Fox has already relied on him once or twice to lead us in his absence.'

'Well,' said Tawny Owl, looking at his feet, 'I really don't know if Badger will be quite fit enough. Not at once, I mean,' he added hastily.

'How can you all stand there arguing about who is to be the new leader?' demanded Toad. 'Surely you're forgetting something? Our first concern is for news of Fox. He may even now be on his way back to us.'

'Well said, Toad.' Hare remarked. 'He's only been out of our sight a matter of hours. What *would* he think if he could hear us?'

'I suggest we all retire straight away,' said Hedgehog, to change the subject. 'Kestrel will soon wake us on his return.'

'How will he know where we are?' asked the short-sighted Mole.

'You obviously don't know the expression "eyes like a hawk",' said Tawny Owl. 'He'll spot us a mile off.'

The animals began to make a move to join Badger.

'Aren't you sleepy?' they asked Owl.

'I'll join you later,' he replied. 'I've a spot of hunting to do.'

*

The animals woke of their own accord during the following day. From the position of the sun, Adder, an expert in such matters, judged it to be about noon. Only Badger remained sleeping, and as Tawny Owl was nowhere in evidence, they decided he, too, must still be dozing in one of the nearby willow trees.

They immediately began to discuss the plight of Fox but none of them could feel very hopeful about his return.

Toad decided to go for a swim while they were waiting for Kestrel. Out of bravado, Mole said he would accompany him.

'You'd better come with me to the slacker water,' said Toad, and they set off along the bank.

When they reached the spot where they had made the crossing, Mole asked, 'Will it be safe here in the daylight?'

'Yes, if we stay near the bank,' answered Toad, 'We're both small enough not to be noticed.'

They went in together, and splashed around happily. Toad began to enjoy himself, frequently diving out of sight, and then surprising Mole by surfacing right in front of him.

'I wish I could do that,' said Mole enviously.

'I'll show you if you like,' said Toad. 'Now, watch me.'

He performed two small dives, and Mole tried to copy him but without success.

Toad dived again, and was gone for some minutes. Mole was just beginning to feel worried, when Toad reappeared with an alarmed look on his face.

'Quick, get to the bank,' he said urgently, and Mole obeyed without hesitation.

When they had pulled themselves clear, Toad blew out a long breath. 'Phew! That was close,' he said. 'Look!'

Mole peered into the clear water, and saw a huge pike, about three feet long, skimming about with its cruel mouth jutting forward as it sought for food.

'It didn't see me; I hid behind some weed,' explained Toad. 'Thank goodness it was not around last night.'

Mole shuddered. 'Perhaps we'd better get back?' he said. 'This very minute,' agreed Toad.

When they arrived back at the camp, the two animals found Badger awake, and surrounded by his friends. They were told that he had woken refreshed, and had made a reasonable meal of roots and grubs. He had told everyone that he felt a great deal better, and of course had enquired about Fox. Tawny Owl had volunteered the information of Fox's disappearance, trying to sound as hopeful about his return as he was able to.

Badger was now describing his own experience in the river. 'As I was drawn under the water, deeper and deeper,' he said, 'all I could think of was that if I drowned Mole would have to find someone else to carry him.'

'How kind you are,' said Mole, nestling close to the fatherly Badger, 'to think of others when you yourself were in such danger.'

'Well, you know,' Badger went on, 'I really thought I *was* going to drown. I was literally bowled along by the pace of the water, and my limbs were fettered by that ghastly mass of vegetation. My lungs were bursting. Then there was a sort of jolt, and everything became still. The hateful weed seemed to be pulled away from me, and I felt myself floating upwards. The next instant my head broke the surface, and I was gulping in air as fast as I could.'

'That was when we saw you,' said Hedgehog.

'Not quite then,' replied Badger. 'I remember striking the surface, but nothing after that. I must have passed out. I do recall feeling rather light-headed. Then . . . nothing.'

'We found you by that large rock,' Weasel pointed out.

'Exactly,' said Badger, with some excitement. 'That rock was my saviour. The weed caught against it, thus freeing me. I don't mind telling you, it was a near thing.'

While Badger had been talking, Rabbit had been shifting his gaze from the face of one animal to another, and then back again. Never once did he look at Badger. Finally, when Badger stopped speaking, he shuffled forward sheepishly.

'I . . . er . . . that is, on behalf of all,' he began, 'that is, all the rabbits. I mean . . .' He stopped, looking very confused. Nobody spoke. He struggled on. 'What I was trying to say,' he mumbled, 'was . . . um . . . we all hope you'll forgive us, Badger, for being such nuisances yesterday. We . . . er . . .'

Badger relieved him. 'It's all forgotten,' he promised graciously. 'We all have our weaknesses. We'll say no more about it.'

Rabbit's expression changed to one of gratitude. He smiled at Badger, and Badger smiled back.

'I wonder how long Kestrel will be,' said Mole.

'Patience,' admonished Tawny Owl. 'He won't come before he has something to tell us.'

As the minutes passed, and then the hours, all the animals stopped talking. Instead they sat together, scanning the sky. Some of them fell asleep as they waited.

At long last their patience was rewarded. Hare spotted Kestrel, just a speck in the blue, speeding towards them.

'It *must* be Kestrel,' he declared. 'Only he flies so fast.'

They craned their necks. Kestrel hovered and, as swift as an arrow, swooped in to land. When he saw their expectant faces turned eagerly towards him, his heart sank.

'It's bad news,' he forced himself to say.

'I managed to find him,' he told them, 'soon after dawn. I kept him in sight for a long way. He was still floating on the surface, half clinging to the driftwood. There was a weir. But Fox came through it, still on top of his wood, although the debris had broken up. After that the river broadened. There were boats – small ones and pleasure steamers. Somehow Fox's little pile avoided them all. Then it floated under a bridge. I waited on the other side, but he never came out. All I saw was a small boat, a motor one, but no pieces of driftwood, and no Fox. I waited and waited, but he didn't reappear.'

'Lost!' whispered the animals in horror.

'I even flew under the bridge, and I looked everywhere,' said Kestrel. 'He was not there.'

There was an awful hush. None of the animals dared speak. Mole wept silently against Badger's side. Rabbit looked ghastly. He stumbled away, with his relatives following, and sank to the ground in misery.

'I can't believe he's gone,' Badger whispered. 'Surely, Kestrel, you're mistaken? He couldn't just have disappeared?'

Kestrel was unable to speak.

After some minutes, Badger shook himself.

'We'll move on tonight,' he said. 'There's no point in staying here. Do you hear me, everyone? The journey continues. Be ready to leave tonight.'

There was a new authority in his voice which was unmistakable. Tawny Owl said nothing. There *was* nothing to say. Badger had recovered, and he was the new leader of the party. It was as simple as that. No one wanted to dispute the fact, and, strangely enough, Tawny Owl felt himself quite content with the situation.

17

Which way?

As dusk fell, the animals set out on the next stage of their journey.

Badger informed everyone that he was fully rested, and assured Mole he would not feel his weight on his back. Toad climbed up on Hare, and the party moved off silently, all of them with their minds full of thoughts of their missing leader.

It was a cool, breezy night with clouds chasing overhead, behind which the moon struggled to shed some light.

The rabbits looked a particularly forlorn bunch, for, despite Badger's forgiveness, they still felt the rest of the animals held them to blame for the loss of the courageous Fox. They shuffled along in the rear of the party, faces down, not caring to meet the eyes of their companions.

The grassy meadows they were passing through smelt sweet and lush, and some of the rabbits, mostly the younger ones, paused to nibble at the scented stalks.

'Come along! Come along, you youngsters!' called Rabbit harshly. 'No dawdling! We don't want any more trouble.'

After some time had elapsed the animals began to feel the need to talk. It was Weasel who broke the silence.

'Somehow,' he said, 'I still have the feeling that Fox is

not lost. Perhaps even now he's making his way back to us.'

'Swimming *up* river?' suggested Adder sarcastically. He had no time for those who would not accept facts.

'No, no, of course not,' said Weasel. 'It's just that . . . well, nobody knows for *sure* what happened to him.'

'But we *are* sure he's no longer with us,' Adder persisted, 'and we should therefore get used to the idea that we have to reach our destination without him.'

'Now, Adder,' Badger felt obliged to cut in, 'there's no harm in hoping, you know.'

'Oh, as to that,' the snake replied in a whisper, 'I hope for a lot of things.'

After this exchange silence prevailed again for a spell. The animals entered the last meadow.

'What do you see ahead, Owl?' Toad called to the bird, who was fluttering a little in advance of the band.

'Looks like open country,' Tawny Owl called behind him after a moment.

'Good,' said Toad. 'It's as I expected.' He raised his voice so that all could hear. 'A stretch of easy going now,' he announced. 'Cheer up, everyone. Things aren't so bad. We've come a long way.'

'Yes. *We* have,' Mole said pointedly, in a small voice.

'Try not to distress yourself too much,' said Badger to him. 'Fox wouldn't want that, you can be sure.'

'I'm sorry, Badger,' said Mole. 'I know he would wish us to go on. But . . . Oh dear!' he sighed miserably, and stayed silent.

'I'll get you there,' said Badger encouragingly. 'You'll see.'

The animals left the meadow and found themselves on wide, open downland. Underfoot the rich grass rippled beneath the breeze with a gentle waving motion. The air was bracing, the grass springy and soft to walk on. The little party found their spirits lifting despite themselves.

Toad and Mole were determined to share the exhilaration

of their friends, and took to their feet, walking side by side.

Hare, freed for a while of responsibility, could not resist the urge to run and jump about, and he called to his mate to join him. Together they gambolled about, chasing each other and racing away at breakneck speed, their long hind legs and lean bodies as supple and elastic as if they were on springs.

All the animals relaxed and travelled at an easy pace. They forgot the anxious moments of the past, and, confident that for the present no danger or hardship was at hand, were determined to enjoy their new sense of freedom.

Badger looked up at Tawny Owl. 'Won't you join me for a moment, Owl?' he asked. 'Come and have a natter.'

Tawny Owl obliged willingly, and fluttered to the ground by Badger's side. 'I'll walk a few steps with you,' he said.

'You know,' said Badger, 'this is the first time since we left Farthing Wood that I haven't wished I was back in my old set. I really feel a sense of adventure at last.'

'I know what you mean,' agreed Tawny Owl as he strutted along, his wings folded comfortably on his back. 'I think we've really put our old life behind us now, haven't we?'

'Yes,' said Badger. 'And I'm glad we weren't there to witness the wood's final destruction. At least we have our memories untainted.'

They strolled on, talking of the old days. The party had scattered and spread out into little groups of two or three, but a few walked alone like Adder and Weasel. For once the animals did not feel confined; they were enjoying the extra space.

Suddenly Toad halted, and looked all about him. He looked puzzled. The others stopped too. Some yards away Hare and his mate sat down and looked back.

'Anything wrong?' asked Weasel.

'It's strange,' Toad muttered. 'I'm sure we go straight ahead here, and yet something is nagging at me, drawing me away to the left.' He shrugged and hopped on in the same direction. His companions continued slowly, keeping their eyes on him.

He halted again after a few more yards. 'It's no good,' he said. 'This feels wrong to me. I'm not comfortable. My legs want to turn left. And yet . . .' He looked all round again. 'Can't understand it,' he murmured.

'Perhaps we've taken a wrong turn somewhere?' suggested Squirrel.

'No. No, that's just it. I remembered everything quite clearly as we came along.' Toad was emphatic.

'Shall we try the other direction,' Badger asked, 'if it seems right to you?'

'All right,' said Toad, and swung left. The animals reformed into a bunch and followed him.

But Toad did not look happy. He shook his head in a puzzled way, although he did not stop.

'This should prove interesting,' Adder drawled. 'Looks as if our guide has lost himself.'

'Good gracious!' exclaimed Badger. 'I hope not.'

Toad ignored this remark, but continued on with a somewhat grim expression, continually turning his head in all directions, as if searching for a clue.

In the face of Toad's doubt the travelling began to lose its enjoyment.

Tawny Owl rejoined Kestrel in the air. Kestrel honoured his return with an aerial loop. Tawny Owl was unimpressed. The hawk's dexterity in the air was a simple matter of fact to him. Now it was night, he, Owl, held sway in his natural element.

The next moment Kestrel's words seemed, unbidden, to acknowledge the situation. 'I'm afraid I can't be of any use in the dark,' he began, 'but you can see. Why not fly on ahead and spy out the land? Then Toad will know if we're on the right track.'

'Surely you don't imagine I hadn't already decided that

for myself,' the owl replied haughtily.

'You said nothing,' retorted Kestrel. 'I'm merely trying to help.'

He watched in annoyance as Tawny Owl flapped his powerful wings harder, and flew away without a word. 'Can't bear to be told anything,' Kestrel muttered in disgust.

'Where's Owl off to?' Mole inquired of Badger.

'We shall soon see,' replied Badger. 'Tawny Owl never does anything without a reason.'

Toad had no need to ponder over the owl's action. He realized at once what the bird was doing. He felt relief, and at the same time alarm. If it should prove he was leading the party in the wrong direction, he knew they would all feel he had let them down. Would they not then lose faith in their guide? Toad shuddered. Every one of them depended on him so much – on his memory. They had trusted him completely so far, and he had not made one error. And now? He longed for, yet dreaded, Tawny Owl's return. Nevertheless, the strange unseen influence that had made him turn left still beckoned. He plodded on.

Badger could sense Toad's anxiety; he could feel a definite tenseness in the air.

'Don't worry,' he said kindly, and so quietly that only Toad could hear. 'If you've made a mistake, no one is going to blame you.'

Toad looked up at the familiar striped head and smiled as their eyes met. He could not bring himself to say anything.

'I suggest we stop for a bit,' Badger said more loudly. 'We'll wait for Tawny Owl.'

Toad nodded unhappily and the animals came to a halt behind him. Most of them stretched out at their ease on the soft grass. Kestrel joined them.

They did not have long to wait. Tawny Owl's grey shape appeared in the gloom. Every eye was turned on him as he came to rest amongst them. Only Toad failed to look up. His flat, broad head was bowed, as he waited with bated breath.

'It's the wrong way,' Tawny Owl announced with an air of finality. A medley of gasps and sighs followed his words. 'We're almost back at the river. We've travelled a complete circle.'

Toad felt all eyes were on him, accusing him. His error had cost the animals precious time and effort. Time and effort that was completely wasted.

'I . . . I'm sorry,' he sobbed.

Badger was about to speak, while Mole nuzzled their miserable guide, but Tawny Owl had not finished.

'No need to be sorry,' he said. 'It's quite obvious what's happened. Your homing instinct has begun to work, just as it did when you were captured before and then escaped on your own. It's leading you back to your pond at Farthing Wood – your birthplace.'

Toad looked up. 'Of course,' he murmured. 'The irresistible urge – pulling me the wrong way.'

The other animals felt they had become victims of a mystery; an age-old mystery over which they had no control.

'What . . . what do we do now?' asked Fieldmouse.

'Simple,' said Tawny Owl. 'Turn round and retrace your steps.'

'But what about Toad?' said Vole. 'How can he guide us now?'

'Fortunately, Toad still has his memory,' replied Tawny Owl. 'He can no doubt remember what lies ahead of us on our route.'

Toad nodded.

'But,' said Tawny Owl, 'in future you will have to rely on my guidance by night . . .'

'And mine by day,' said Kestrel.

'Will it work?' asked Squirrel.

Tawny Owl drew himself up. 'Of *course* it will work,' he said pompously.

18

The butcher bird

The travellers, in fact, made little progress under the guidance of Kestrel and Tawny Owl, but through no fault of theirs. Several of the mother voles and fieldmice presented the party with additions to its number during the next rest period, and these events proved to be a turning point in the journey.

It was obvious to all, particularly to the despairing Badger, that the vole and fieldmouse parents concerned in these births would no longer be able to travel, and a conference of the group leaders was arranged in the resting-place they had chosen in some heath scrub.

'It looks as if our ranks are to be depleted further, then?' said Weasel.

'There's no other solution,' Badger said miserably. 'We can't put a halt to our journey until these young ones grow up.'

'It was bound to happen,' remarked Fieldmouse, 'but nobody ever mentioned the subject.'

'If we had reached White Deer Park I would have been delighted with the whole thing,' said Badger.

'But we haven't,' said Tawny Owl.

'Oh dear,' sighed Badger. 'I wonder what Fox would have done.'

'That question shouldn't arise,' said Tawny Owl impatiently. '*We* have to decide.'

'There's really no decision to make,' Adder chipped in. 'If we're to continue on our way these new broods of our friends the mice must be left behind. If we can't bring ourselves to do this, then we must all stay here and sing silly songs while they grow big enough to walk. Believe me, there's no doubt in *my* mind what we should do.'

'If it had been left to you, none of *us* would have been here in the first place,' said Vole angrily, steeling himself to ignore the horrific leer which served as Adder's reply.

'Please, please,' Badger interrupted hastily, 'this isn't getting us anywhere.'

'Adder's right, of course,' said Tawny Owl emphatically. 'The parent mice concerned will have to do the best they can for their babies, and that is to stay behind. We can help them to look for a home in the area. Then we *must* go on. All of us are committed to it.'

'Well, Owl, you know,' Badger nodded his head as he spoke, 'I must admit I'm in agreement with you.'

'Well, I am *not*!' retorted Vole. 'The issue is not so cut and dried as far as we voles and mice are concerned. These creatures are our kith and kin, and we can't just abandon them here.' He looked at Fieldmouse for support. 'I say, if some of the mice stay, we *all* stay.'

Badger looked distinctly alarmed. 'Please don't take that view, Vole,' he begged.

'Well, you *must* realize, Badger,' said Fieldmouse, 'there will be no second opportunity for these animals to press on to White Deer Park – even when their babies have grown. I can see Vole's point of view. How *can* we take the responsibility of leaving our relatives behind to await – who knows what fate?'

'*I* will take the responsibility,' said Badger stoutly. '*I* am your leader now.'

'But you're not a vole or a fieldmouse!' snapped Vole. '*You* don't see the situation in the same light.'

'I really don't see,' drawled Adder, 'why everyone is getting so concerned about something they had no part in.'

Vole and Fieldmouse glared at him.

'I think you're forgetting something, Adder,' said Badger. 'Before we began our journey we all swore an Oath, including *you*. That Oath meant that the safety and well-being of any member of the party was the concern of all the others. You should reflect on that,' he finished in a schoolmasterly tone.

It was not in Adder's nature to apologize. He merely grinned disarmingly.

Vole and Fieldmouse turned to Badger again.

'Then *surely*, Badger,' Vole said, 'if that Oath meant anything at all, how can you talk about leaving even one of us behind?'

'Because, Vole, you know as well as I do that the parents with their babies can't attempt to travel. But, for the safety of the *whole* party, we must complete our journey as quickly as possible; and, having come this great way, the rest of you mice should be moving on with us. We'll do everything possible to find them a safe home here,' he added. 'I'm sure they'll be quite comfortable, you know. It's a secluded spot.'

'Thank you, Badger,' said Fieldmouse, who was inclined to be more reasonable than his cousin. In a persuasive tone he said to Vole, 'Badger's in a difficult position, don't you see? He didn't ask for this to happen, and he has to think of everyone.'

'At this moment, *I* am thinking primarily of my own kind,' said Vole. 'You should be, too, Fieldmouse. We have to stand by them. I can't go on if any of them stay behind.'

'I'm sorry, Badger,' Fieldmouse muttered. 'I'm afraid Vole is right.'

'If that is your decision I shall have to accept it,' said Badger sadly. 'But our priority is to reach our destination. In Fox's absence, I have to see that the rest of us succeed. I'm sorry.'

Vole shrugged and left the meeting without another word. Fieldmouse lingered, as if in two minds, but finally followed his cousin.

'It's natural they feel so concerned,' said Weasel.

The conference broke up with the intention of searching for the best settling-place for the voles and fieldmice as soon as it was daylight.

Badger wandered off alone to think. The break-up of the party that had already travelled so far preyed on his mind, and he found himself thinking how happy he would have been if he had had Fox to consult. But the animals depended on *him* now, and he must see them through.

As soon as it was light, a number of the animals, led by Badger, set off to look for a new home for the mouse contingent. It was not a difficult task, as these small creatures' requirements were modest.

On the advice of Fieldmouse they chose a spot in a thicket of birch scrub, where the leaf litter was thick and soft, and there was plenty of cover in the way of twigs and bracken. Vole agreed that the sunny hillside nearby would make the area ideal for his group, and the animals hastened back with the news.

The mice and voles were soon comfortably installed in their new home and, after all the farewells had been made, the main party continued on its way with Kestrel as guide.

As the sun rose higher, the day grew hotter and hotter, and the animals' pace became correspondingly slower. They were relieved to find a little stream at which to quench their thirst, and the shallow gurgling water was so inviting that several of the animals followed Toad's example and stepped into it to cool themselves.

The countryside seemed so empty and peaceful that Badger decided to pause awhile, until they were all completely refreshed.

Kestrel and Tawny Owl flew on ahead to spy out the land, and the sunny, quiet day lulled the animals into a state of drowsiness. Toad was floating blissfully on the stream's surface, buffeted gently by the ripples, his limbs spread out, and his beautiful jewelled eyes glinting as they reflected the sun. He was half asleep.

Suddenly he returned to full consciousness with a jolt. He heard a violent squeaking noise and saw a small, fierce bird flying overhead with a tiny, wriggling fieldmouse clamped firmly in its beak.

Toad paddled briskly to the bank, and watched the grey-headed bird making off with its prize. Badger, Weasel, Hedgehog and Hare came running.

'It might be one of our mice!' cried Toad.

'Quickly!' said Badger. 'Hare, Weasel, come with me. Hedgehog, will you stay here, and get everyone under cover? Oh, *where* are Kestrel and Owl?'

The three animals raced off in the wake of the robber, Hare at once taking the lead.

Burdened by its victim, the bird fluttered along slowly,

and the fleet-footed Hare was soon directly beneath it. He slackened his pace, and was about to cry out. But, as he looked up, he saw that the poor mouse was dangling limply from the bird's cruel hooked beak. It was quite clearly dead.

Hare knew it was useless to follow further. The bird looked down with an air of invincibility, and uttered a muffled 'chack'. Then, turning its handsome chestnut back on the powerless Hare, it flew triumphantly away, disappearing into the very birch scrub where Hare knew the voles and fieldmice to be.

He looked round. Badger and Weasel were still a long way off. He followed the bird into the scrub. An excited 'shrike, shrike' betrayed the creature's whereabouts, as it was greeted by its mate from a prominent perch on a birch sapling. What followed made Hare's blood run cold.

The chestnut-backed bird made for a neighbouring blackthorn bush, and, with a vigorous stab of its beak, skewered the tiny mouse on one of the projecting thorns. It then promptly rejoined its mate on the branch where they clacked excitedly, wagging their long tails from side to side.

Hare found himself drawn towards the thorn-bush, almost against his will. A few feet away he stopped, scarcely able to credit the horror of what he saw. The bush was covered in bodies: bumble-bees, large beetles and grasshoppers, and tiny, almost furless mice, all neatly impaled on the sharp thorns.

Hare whispered to himself: 'The butcher bird!' All wild creatures had heard tales of the horrible 'larder' of mutilated victims which was kept by the red-backed shrike, the 'butcher bird'.

Hare shivered. He was struck by a thought he hardly dared acknowledge. Where *were* the voles and fieldmice? He began to search amongst the leaves and twigs underfoot, more and more desperately. He looked everywhere. None of the mice was to be found.

He heard Badger calling. 'Hare! Where are you?'

He quickly left the scrub. The shrikes were both sitting bolt upright on their perch, turning their heads jerkily in every direction, searching for fresh morsels to catch.

Hare was determined that Badger should not see what he had just seen. It would be in that kindly animal's nature to blame himself for what had occurred, and if he saw that awful larder he would feel he had sent the voles and field-mice, or at least their helpless babies, to their death.

'There you are!' cried Badger, as Hare emerged into the open. 'Where did the bird go? Did you see?'

Hare sadly shook his head. 'The little mouse –whoever he was – was dead,' he said. 'I saw *that*.'

'What kind of bird was it?' demanded Badger.

Hare had to think quickly. 'Well, I'm not sure,' he said evasively. 'It had a red back, grey head, and a hook-tipped beak.'

'The butcher bird,' said Weasel immediately.

Badger looked at him in horror. 'Ghastly creatures,' he said. 'There used to be a pair on the borders of Farthing Wood . . . more dangerous than Adder when it came to hunting small creatures.' He stopped talking and looked round.

'But the mice . . . the voles . . . where are they?' he muttered, moving towards the scrub.

Hare held his tongue, but lamely followed him. Inside, Badger looked around again.

Suddenly they heard the rustling of leaves underfoot, and, from beneath a pile of leaf litter, one by one, came the voles and fieldmice.

'Is it safe?' whispered Vole.

'Yes, come quickly,' said Hare; and he, Badger and Weasel, shepherding the mice between them, ran from the birch scrub towards a hollow tree. Once inside, they rested, panting heavily. No one spoke for a while.

Then Badger said, 'You see, Vole, what happens when you leave the safety of the party? You small creatures are too vulnerable to be left on your own. How many have died?'

'All the babies,' Vole said brokenly. 'I'm sorry, Badger. I should have known you were really thinking of our good.'

'We'll stay with you now,' said Fieldmouse. 'The poor parents are agreed – otherwise there'll *be* no voles and fieldmice.'

'Come on,' said Badger resolutely. 'We can't leave Hedgehog any longer. Who knows what other dangers threaten us?'

The animals made their way back to the stream, where Hedgehog trotted out to meet them, 'All safe here,' he announced.

Badger explained what had happened. 'It's been a tragedy,' he admitted. 'But this won't happen again. You have my word on it. From now on we shall travel in close formation – and we shall stop only to drink and eat and sleep. One of the birds will always be on guard in the air, where they will be able to detect the approach of any foreign creature.'

He looked all round. His voice took on a warm, benign tone. 'There will be no more lives lost while I'm in charge; I promise it. I hope now you will all trust in me?'

The animals responded unanimously to his plea.

'I thank you all,' said Badger. 'Adder, you look as if you want to say something?'

Adder's face took on a sardonic grin. 'A very moving vote of confidence,' he drawled. 'I'm sure if it were possible for me to applaud, I should do so now.' He chuckled noiselessly.

But nobody took any notice of him. For there *was* a new confidence in the party, despite the recent setback. They had survived the catastrophe of the river crossing and the loss of Fox who, a natural leader, had seemed irreplaceable.

They felt that Badger had now stamped his authority on the leadership and would rise to the occasion. Whatever hardships were still in store for the animals, they sensed that, having come so far, it was unlikely they could now be diverted from their joint purpose.

Ignorant of the fate of Fox as they were, most of them could not believe him dead, and still felt in their bones that, eventually, he would rejoin them. Yet, with or without Fox, however long it might take, the determination of each creature was now reinforced. Their journey could end in only one place – within the boundaries of White Deer Park.

PART TWO

Journey to White Deer Park

19

Fox alone

From the middle of the river Fox watched a huge mass of driftwood and debris floating downstream towards him. He was tired – terribly tired – and he knew he was too far from the shore to avoid the impact. In a few seconds the mass was upon him, engulfing him. One of the larger pieces of wood dealt him a sharp rap on the head, and he was carried away on the current.

Despite his struggles, he was unable to resist the pressure exerted by the heavy brushwood, and he was carried helplessly along. In a last, frantic, backward glance, he saw his friends on the bank running, trying to keep pace with him, but he knew it was impossible for them.

In a few minutes, Fox was entirely alone. All his effort was concentrated on keeping his head above water.

Eventually he was carried into a stretch of calm water, and here he managed to ease himself a little. He was able to pull himself far enough out of the river to rest his front legs on the collection of large sticks and branches surrounding him. In this position he travelled a considerable distance, while day gradually dawned.

The water was cool and refreshing, and as he was not able to swim – enmeshed as he was in the driftwood – he had very soon recovered a good deal from his previous exhaustion. But as he floated downstream on his tiny island, farther and farther away from his friends, Fox wondered if he would ever feel solid ground underfoot again.

The wood-pile carried him over a weir, from which he emerged none the worse except for a fright and a good ducking. He floated into less peaceful water, becoming more and more of a speck in the broadening river. He drifted past anglers and picnickers, past houseboats and rowing-boats; he drifted underneath overhanging willows and alongside big pleasure-steamers thronged with passengers in thin summer clothes. But nobody saw him. Nobody remarked on the waterborne fox.

He had begun to feel quite convinced that before long he would be washed out to sea – that vast, terrible expanse of water he had heard tales about – when his situation suddenly changed.

As he floated under a bridge, there, directly in his path, was a small motor-boat. The man inside had obviously been fishing, for he was getting the last of his tackle aboard. The wood surrounding Fox caught against the outboard motor, and finally came to rest.

Fox did not dare to attempt to climb into the boat, although it was low in the water, but he thought there might be a chance for him to reach the bank at last, if the angler was going to moor his boat.

When he was quite ready, the man began to paddle his boat in a leisurely fashion out from the bridge without once looking behind.

A little further on the river split, flowing either side of a large island. The man paddled into the left-hand channel, and Fox saw ahead two large wooden gates, right across the water. As they approached these gradually swung open, and the man continued to paddle right inside.

Suddenly the boat was motionless. Fox found he was in a narrow channel of water, locked in by two tremendously high, slime-covered walls on either side, and two sets of great double doors, before and behind. Looking directly upwards he could see human faces peering over the tops of the walls.

He heard a gushing sound, and the next thing he knew, he was slowly being raised upwards on the water. The green slippery walls slid past on either side of him, and the faces above came nearer and nearer. Surely they would notice him!

All at once he heard a child's excited cry. The faces peered further over the walls. Fox began to feel nervous and vulnerable. He heard the sound of human voices growing louder, and he saw the man stand up in the boat, and look towards him.

Fox tried to shrink back against the branches and sticks, hoping to camouflage himself. But he was too late. More and more faces were staring down at him. Hands and fingers pointed excitedly. The chattering voices increased in number. Fox was almost on their level.

The water was rising more slowly now. The man in the boat had been obliged to sit down again, and prepare to move his craft. The lock gates in front of him were swinging open, and he was taking hold of his paddle.

Fox saw that unless he did something quickly, he would be towed on down the river. His head was now level with the top of the wall. Arms reached out to him, but he did not wait to see if they might be helping arms. He snapped his jaws twice, viciously, and the arms were withdrawn. With a half-leap he scrambled clear of the brushwood and, for a fleeting moment, balanced himself before jumping on to the pathway.

Legs, human legs, everywhere. Straight through them he dashed, before anyone could prevent it. He saw the river bank and raced for it. Then he ran as he had never run before in all his life, away from the humans and their noise, and straight for the first cover he could find.

But humans seemed to be everywhere. Shouts followed him. Humans were in front of him as well as behind him. They were strolling, sitting or lying on the grassy bank. Some did not even notice Fox dash past. Others stepped back in amazement, uttering little shrieks.

Fox sped along the tow-path, with the river on his left and fences, hedges, walls, houses on his right. He was hemmed in, but still he kept running.

Soon, looming in front, was the bridge he had floated under only a short time ago. The path ran directly underneath. Fox did not stop.

The sun and the air were drying his fur, wet for so long. He felt strong and refreshed and courageous, and was spurred on by the thought of the friends he was running back to join. Suddenly the fences ended, and there on his right were trees and wide fields with cows or horses in them.

He turned into the first field. The grass felt cool and supremely soft under Fox's feet, and as he put the human path further behind him, he felt secure. A little, winding stream ran through the field, and he drank from it in great gulps.

A Friesian cow that was drinking a little further upstream, raised her head and looked docilely towards him. 'You're a bold one,' she said. 'Farmer's in the next field.'

'I . . . I was lost,' Fox replied. 'I'm trying to find my way back.'

'Are you far from home?' the cow asked.

'I'm a long way from what I used to call home,' answered Fox. 'I have no home now. I'm on my way to a new one, only I've been separated from my friends.'

The cow wanted to know if she or her companions could be of any assistance.

'You have been already,' said Fox gratefully. 'I shall avoid the next field. I must get on – I've a long way to go.' He thanked the cow, and ran off, skirting the neighbouring field, and entering the adjacent one, keeping the river in sight in the distance on his left.

There was a solitary black horse in this field, and from its grizzled haunches and neck, Fox could tell he was old. He was leaning peacefully against a chestnut tree, blinking his eyes and lazily swishing his threadbare tail against the flies.

'Good day!' Fox called pleasantly, as he trotted past.

The old horse started and looked down. 'Oh, hullo!' he wheezed. 'Must've been dozing again. Very warm today.'

'Isn't it?' said Fox, stopping for a moment to snap up a stag-beetle that was lying on its back, all six legs waving feebly.

The horse turned his head away in disgust. 'Ugh! Don't know how you can,' he protested.

'That's the first morsel I've had for a good many hours,' Fox replied.

'If you're hungry, my manger's half-full over there,' the horse said hospitably. 'My teeth are going – I can't crop grass so well now. And my appetite's not what it was.'

'Very kind of you,' said Fox, 'but I don't really go in for that sort of food.'

'Oh well, come and have a chat anyway,' wheedled the

161

ancient horse. 'I get so bored here by myself all the time.'

Despite his haste to rejoin his friends, Fox felt it would be impolite to refuse the invitation, especially as the horse was behaving very civilly towards him.

He wandered over to the chestnut tree and lay down, panting, in its shade. The sun was very hot.

'That's right,' nodded the horse. 'Make yourself at home. It's cooler under here.' He continued to lean against the trunk of the tree. 'I don't get much company these days,' he went on, turning his rheumy eyes on Fox. 'Not since my old pal, the bay, died last summer. After the wife went, we became very close, although, of course, he was only working class.'

'The bay?' asked Fox.

'Yes. A draught horse, you see.'

'And you are . . . ?'

'I *was* a hunter,' replied the black horse. 'Best in the stable, with a long pedigree. Seems funny, my talking to you like this, after a long career chasing foxes.'

Fox started and pricked up his ears. 'Fox hunting?' he whispered.

'That's right. Oh, I don't uphold it. It's a wicked sport really. But the racing, the leaping, the scarlet coats – that part of it's grand.'

Fox shuddered. The old horse's words took him back to his childhood, and the terrifying tales he had heard from his father of the mad, baying hounds, the thundering hooves, and the torment of the exhausted, solitary fox forced to run to its death.

The old horse noticed Fox's discomfort. 'You must excuse me,' he said humbly. 'Just an old creature's thoughtless reminiscences. Believe me, I used to be as relieved as you would be, when the animals I chased got away.'

'That's good of you,' said Fox. 'I never suspected anything else. Only humans could practise such cruelty as exists in hunting any smaller or weaker animal to its death.'

162

'I agree with you,' the old horse nodded. 'And yet, those same humans have always treated me well – like a life-long friend.'

'Well,' Fox shook his head. 'A different relationship, I suppose.'

'Of course.'

'Thank heaven, I've never been involved in a hunt,' said Fox. 'But my father told me of his experiences. He was lucky, but *his* father and mother were both caught. The hounds tore them to shreds.'

The black horse nodded his grizzled head. 'I can give you a word of advice,' he said seriously. 'I shouldn't stay in this part of the country any longer than you can help. It's all hunting country for some miles round here. I wouldn't want anything to happen to you.'

'Thank you, but don't worry,' said Fox. 'I'm just passing through. I'm on my way back to rejoin my friends up river. I was separated from them last night.'

'Really? What happened?' the old horse wanted to know.

So Fox explained that he had been swept away while try-

ing to help some frightened rabbits to cross the river. Then, seeing the look of disbelief on the horse's face, and feeling that it would do him good to rest for a little while longer, Fox settled down to tell the whole story.

He explained how all the animals of Farthing Wood had been driven from their homes by the humans, and how, having heard from Toad of a wonderful place, White Deer Park, a Nature Reserve where they could live in peace again, they had banded together to make the long and difficult journey. Fox trembled as he recounted the various dangers they had met on the way, remembering particularly the terrible fire they had survived, and the storm, and the angry farmer with his gun – and, finally, the horror of the river crossing. Stirred by renewed anxiety for his friends, Fox brought his story to an end as quickly as he politely could, impatient to be on his way again.

The horse had listened in silence, except for the occasional snort of disgust. When Fox stopped talking, he commented sadly, 'It's happening all over the country. You wild creatures are being driven back on all sides. Humans have always been greedy, particularly where land is concerned. But it's to the credit of those among them who appreciate your existence that they're setting aside at least a few chunks of land where you can live in peace. I've heard about this White Deer Park you mentioned. For a horse it wouldn't be a long journey from here. But if it's necessary for you to travel at the pace of mice, then obviously it's another matter.'

'I sometimes wonder if any of them will reach our destination,' admitted Fox. 'The journey is really too harrowing for such small animals.'

'I wish you luck,' said the horse feelingly. 'I mustn't detain you. Your friends will be worried.'

'You've been good company,' said Fox politely. 'Perhaps one day you'll hear news of our success.' He got up and shook his coat.

'I hope so,' said the horse. 'I'll be thinking of you every day.'

Fox opened his lips in a smile. 'Goodbye,' he said.

'Goodbye, my friend,' said the horse. '*Bon voyage*!'

Fox left the field without a backward glance. He had a long run ahead of him still.

As he trotted along, keeping as much as he could behind a screen of undergrowth or shrubs, he recognized various landmarks he had passed as he floated down the river. Some of the boats were certainly familiar, and, looking across the broad stretch of water to the other side, occasional aspects of the landscape brought again to his mind the thoughts that had occupied him as he passed the spot earlier.

Most of the time he had been endeavouring to think up some means by which he could get out of his predicament, but the plight of his friends, without their leader, had also been uppermost in his mind. He had constantly hoped, too, that Badger would send Kestrel to search for him, and as he retraced his journey, he kept scanning the sky for a sight of the bird. His friends seemed so far away.

After some hours, Fox knew he would have to stop for a rest. Although he could not really afford time to sleep, he realized that it was essential to refresh himself with a nap, in order to have any chance of rejoining Badger and the others. Apart from a few minutes when he had fallen into an uneasy doze as he drifted helplessly along, trapped amongst the brushwood, Fox had been far too alarmed to sleep properly. He started to look round for a likely spot of cover.

There were still many anglers and picnickers too close for comfort, so he kept going at a slackened pace. Traffic on the river was confined at this point to one or two small motor or rowing-boats, and Fox thought he could see that the opposite bank had drawn just a fraction closer. Presently he came to a spot where a thick grove of willow trees grew right down by the water's edge. Here it was impossible for any human to approach the river from the bank, and so Fox decided it was an excellent place to hide himself.

He crept under the trees and laid himself down under the thick leaves of a tree whose boughs bent so low that some of them brushed the ground. Here Fox was sure he was invisible from the river too, and he gratefully laid his head on his paws and let out a long sigh. A few hours' rest and he would be fresh on the trail again. He was so sleepy that he was able to ignore the pangs of hunger that had begun to make themselves felt in the pit of his stomach. A gentle breeze rustled the willow leaves, causing them to stroke his fur. In another moment Fox had fallen into a deep sleep.

20

The vixen

It was completely dark when Fox was woken by a strong breeze blowing through the sheltering willow trees. He got up, feeling refreshed but appallingly hungry. After stretching all his limbs in turn, he emerged from his bower and set about finding something to eat.

In his ravenous state, Fox had no scruples about snapping up any small creatures that happened to be abroad. Beetles, slugs, worms, snails were all tasty titbits to his keen appetite. When he had taken the edge off his hunger, Fox continued on his way at a smart trot, remembering the warning of the old horse.

At night the river was quiet; there were no longer any noisy motor-boats about, and no humans sitting or strolling on the river's banks.

A complete day and night had now passed since he had been swept away by the river debris, and he had seen no sign of any of his companions coming to look for him. He realized that the distance he had been carried in the water was far too great to allow anyone but one of the birds to set out in search. He wondered if he might have missed Kestrel while he had been sleeping, but as many hours of daylight had passed without any sign of the bird before he had stopped to rest, Fox gradually became certain that his friends had given him up for lost. He felt terribly alone.

As he went on, he reflected that the sort of community life he had been living during the last month or so on the journey had changed him. He had lived in a rather solitary style in Farthing Wood – a typical fox's life, sleeping during the day for the most part, roaming and hunting alone at night. Of course, Badger had always been his friend, and there had been other acquaintances, notably Tawny Owl. But, in those days, he had not been in the habit of inviting the company of others. Now Fox found himself so in need of companionship that he could feel a definite physical ache inside. What worried him most at that moment was that, if the other animals had indeed decided he was lost to them, they would move on, continue their journey, leaving him further behind. The one consolation was that, alone, he could travel a great deal faster than the party, obliged to travel at the pace of the slowest. He increased his pace to a canter, which he knew he could maintain quite easily.

He still cherished a faint hope that, now it was night, Tawny Owl might be on his way to him. But as time wore on, this hope waned.

Constantly wondering about the fate of Badger and the rabbits, who had still been struggling in the river when he was swept away, Fox suffered real anguish in his ignorance. There was very little to take his mind off these thoughts as he travelled through the cloud covered, breezy night.

He felt he was making some recognizable progress when he spotted the weir a little way ahead of him. The sound of the furious, swirling water made him shiver again, and he forced his tiring legs to a still faster pace.

Soon pale streaks of grey appeared in the sky, the clouds seemed to lighten in hue and with the approach of dawn, the breeze dropped.

As the light gathered, Fox's weariness became more acute. These two things progressed together, so that the thought came to Fox's mind that as soon as it was broad day, he would drop from exhaustion.

At length he stopped running, and, his head hanging between his legs, his breath came in long panting gasps. He descended the river bank, and lapped up the cool, treacherous water, while his weakened legs quivered like a hovering kestrel's wing-beats.

When his great thirst had been slaked Fox knew he could go no further. If he was ever to catch up with the friends who needed him, he must keep his strength up by eating and sleeping sufficiently. He felt satisfied with the progress he had made during the night, and started to look round for a resting-place.

There was nowhere with sufficient cover by the riverside, so Fox moved further away from the water, towards the fields and meadows where there were thick, concealing hedges. In a corner of one field, under the hedgerow, he found a large burrow. He first sniffed very carefully all round the hole, and then put his head inside and sniffed again.

He thought he could smell fox, but as there was no sound, he very cautiously ventured inside. The hole was dark, warm and empty. It could indeed have been a fox's earth, he decided, but how recently it had been occupied he could not tell. He went back to the entrance once more and looked out. There was no sign of any animal nearby. Fox turned his back on the daylight and made himself comfortable on the bare earth floor. It was quite soft enough to send him off to sleep almost at once.

He awoke with a jump as he felt something touch his body. In the darkness it was some time before he could see what it was, but his strong sense of smell conveyed to him at once the unmistakable scent of a female fox. He scrambled to his feet.

'Don't be alarmed,' said the vixen soothingly. 'Stay and rest as long as you like. It's dusk, and I must go in search of food.'

'I . . . I didn't know the place was occupied, you see,' Fox stammered, 'It was empty, and I . . .'

'It's only one of my retreats,' explained the vixen.

Fox looked puzzled.

'I haven't been in this area for some time,' she explained. 'I was passing, and I could hear your breathing.'

'I was very tired,' Fox explained.

'Have you been travelling? I don't think I've ever seen you before.'

'Travelling?' Fox smiled. 'Yes, I have. It's a long story.'

'I'd be interested to hear it – if you feel like telling me.'

'I should enjoy it,' said Fox. 'But you said you were about to go hunting. I haven't eaten either – and . . . well, perhaps we could hunt together and bring our food back here. Then, after we've finished, I'll tell you how I came here.'

'That's a marvellous idea,' said Vixen. 'Shall we go straight away?'

'Rather,' replied Fox emphatically. 'I'm ravenous.'

Vixen led the way from the earth, and Fox trotted beside her, experiencing a new feeling of companionship, quite different from anything he had felt before.

As they crossed the darkening fields, Fox now and again glanced at his new acquaintance. He thought Vixen was the most wonderful creature he had ever seen, and he intended to make her aware of it when the time was right.

Together they hunted, and together, through the moonlight, they slipped back to the earth with their catch. All this time neither of them uttered a word.

Safe underground again, they devoured their supper and Vixen invited Fox to tell his story. So he told her of Farthing Wood and his friends, of their journey to White Deer Park, of the calamity in the river, and how he was on his way to rejoin the band as their leader.

Vixen listened with the greatest interest and admiration for their exploits. 'How brave you all are,' she murmured when Fox had finished.

'And you?' asked Fox. 'Tell me your story.'

'Oh no!' Vixen laughed, and shook her head. 'There isn't any story really. I've always lived in this part of the country. Fortunately *my* home has not been taken from me by the humans, although I've had my brushes with them.'

'The Hunt?' Fox asked in a low voice.

'Yes, but I've been lucky. I've heard it in full cry more than once, but always in pursuit of another animal.'

'Poor creatures.' Fox shuddered.

'It's part of our existence.' Vixen smiled. 'We learn to live with it. One day it might be my turn, but until then . . . I'm free.'

'I can't bear to think that you . . .' Fox began – but broke off.

'What were you going to say?' Vixen asked gently.

Fox did not reply at once. Then he said, 'I couldn't help but look at you while we were hunting. You're the most marvellous creature I've ever seen – so swift and lithe. How your eyes shone! And your coat is beautiful – glossy and soft.'

Vixen was silent. She looked away shyly . . .

'I wish you were my mate,' said Fox. 'Then you'd have nothing to fear. I would protect you – from everything.'

Vixen looked up and smiled. 'I believe you would,' she said softly. 'Gallant Fox.'

'Then will you come with me as my mate, and help me to find my friends?'

Vixen fell silent again, and stared down at the earthen floor as if thinking. Fox held his breath. Eventually she looked up and met his eyes in the darkness.

'I will travel with you until you find your friends,' she said finally.

Fox's spirits sank. Her reply was less than he had hoped for.

Vixen sensed his disappointment. 'I cannot promise more at present,' she said. 'But as we travel, by and by I shall make up my mind.'

Fox understood her at once. He had to prove himself to her. For her caution he admired her even more.

He made a resolve. 'I shall be worthy of you,' he said solemnly under his breath. Aloud he said, 'Then I can hope?'

Vixen laughed. 'Of course,' she said. 'I shouldn't want it otherwise.' She lay down on the floor.

'You must be tired,' said Fox. 'I've rested, and I'm ready to start. But you must have your rest, too. While you sleep, I'll speak to the night creatures. Perhaps they will have news of Badger and the others. I'll return before dawn. Sleep well.'

'I shall,' said Vixen, resting her head on her paws.

Fox left the earth and made for the nearest wood. If the local owls were about they would be sure to have some knowledge of the Farthing Wood party. He *must* find out which way his friends were heading.

The wood was quiet and very dark, save for silvery patches of moonlight filtering through the gaps in the trees.

The mellow, liquid notes of a nightingale assailed his ears, and he quickly followed its direction. He found the songster perched on a hawthorn branch.

'I compliment you on your voice,' said Fox diplomatically, 'and I wonder if you could help me?'

'Thank you,' replied the nightingale, 'I *am* reckoned to be the finest ballad singer in these parts. I certainly haven't heard a finer.'

Fox, who did not have a lot of faith in the good sense of songbirds, was not particularly surprised at the empty answer he had received. He decided to have another try.

'I can well believe it,' he continued. 'I think some friends of mine might have passed this way recently, and they would certainly have appreciated such music. I wondered if you might have seen them?'

'What do they look like?' inquired the bird without much interest.

Fox described the leading members of the party.

'Humph!' returned the nightingale indignantly. 'Snakes and toads and such-like have no ear for music. Only birds such as myself can be relied on to judge such things. No, I haven't seen your reptilian friends.'

The absurdity of the bird irritated Fox, but he wasted no more time on him, for he had espied the ghostly form of a barn owl flitting from tree to tree. He hurried over as it alighted in the fork of an old ash.

The owl looked down at him with its huge eyes.

'I'd like a word with you, if you've the time,' Fox called up.

'Certainly,' came the prompt reply. 'On what subject?'

'I'm trying to trace my friends,' said Fox. 'Have you seen anything of a group of animals travelling through these parts?'

'I'm afraid I haven't,' said the owl. 'I don't seem to see many foxes in the wood these days.'

'Not foxes,' Fox corrected him. 'A mixed party of

animals – a badger, a mole, a weasel, rabbits, hares, squirrels and so on, all travelling together and accompanied by a tawny owl and a kestrel.'

'Ah! Now I'm with you. No, I haven't actually seen all of them. But your friend the tawny owl was around . . . oh, a couple of nights ago. I had a conversation with him.'

'Are they all safe?' Fox asked quickly, suddenly recalling with a jolt that he had no idea what had happened to Badger. 'Was there a badger with them?'

'Oh yes. Your friend the badger is their leader, is he not?' replied the owl, who had no reason to assume he was only a deputy. 'The tawny owl mentioned some mishap, but I think they're all safe now.'

'That's good news,' said Fox. 'So I am on the right track.' 'You've all come a long way,' the owl commented 'according to your friend. But how did you come to be separated from them?'

Fox explained.

'I understand.' The owl nodded, blinking his great eyes. 'Well, I hope you find each other again. It would be a shame if your adventure failed to end happily.'

Fox asked the owl if he could give him any idea of the direction the party had taken. The bird shook his head. 'On that point *your* owl was not forthcoming,' he replied, 'and I imagine that his hesitancy was deliberate. After all, the less their plans are known the safer will be their journey.'

'It's true our route was known only to one member of the group all along,' Fox admitted. 'And, of course, it is better kept that way. But at least I know I'm in their vicinity.'

'I'm sure your sensitive nose will prove more than equal to the task of discovering them,' said the owl. 'Good luck to you.'

Fox thanked him and, without pausing for words with any of the other denizens of the wood, returned to the earth. Vixen was peacefully asleep.

21

Vixen decides

The morning was warm and sunny when Fox and his new companion left the earth and set off towards the river.

Their swift pace and alertness helped them to avoid the few humans dotting the riverside that day. In a few hours they had reached the piece of slack water where the Farthing Wood party had swum the river, and where Fox's troubles had begun.

Fox, however, now had reason to think differently about his misfortune in the water. Although it had separated him from his old friends, he had found a new one, and he felt grateful to the river for enabling him to meet Vixen.

His loneliness had disappeared, but he was more anxious than ever to catch up with the other animals. He felt so proud of his beautiful new companion that, for a reason he would not have been able to name, he wanted his friends to meet her and like her.

As they trotted, nose to tail, along the river bank, Fox felt he wanted only one thing more to make his happiness complete – for Vixen to see him leading the animals into White Deer Park.

Every now and then he would steal a glance at her, or turn quickly to meet her eye. In the bright sunlight he

175

thought she looked even more beautiful. Her silky fur seemed to glow, and her eyes sparkled with liveliness and intelligence.

When they reached the crossing-place, Fox bade Vixen keep out of sight while he searched for some clue as to the direction his friends had taken.

The first thing he found was the animals' sleeping-quarters, where the long grass had been flattened by their bodies. Shortly afterwards, he detected a narrow track through the first meadow, beaten down by many assorted pairs of feet. He barked a signal to Vixen, and they continued on their way.

Using his sharp eyes and sense of scent, Fox was able to keep on his friends' track. During the afternoon the two foxes left the last meadow behind them and found themselves on the open downland.

Rather than press on until they caught sight of the other animals, Fox decided it would be better to look at once for a resting-place, and to make an early start again the next morning. Had he been able to foresee the consequences of this decision, he would have continued his journey that day, and all the following night too, even to the point of exhaustion.

However, in the late afternoon, Fox and Vixen hid themselves in a thick growth of bracken, and dozed during the remaining hours to dusk.

When at last it was dark, Fox was on his feet first. He stretched – first his front legs, and then his hind legs. He looked down at Vixen who was still napping. When he shyly nuzzled her, she awoke.

'Are you hungry?' Fox asked.

'Very.'

'I'll see what I can rustle up for you,' said Fox. 'You stay here; I won't be long.'

'You're very kind,' said Vixen, and smiled at him.

Fox felt a warm glow spread under his skin, and he smiled

176

back. Jumping over the fern-fronds, he ran off into the darkness.

While Vixen awaited his return, a gentle shower of rain fell, sharpening the rich smell of bracken and the scent of grass, and producing an intoxicating fragrance of damp leaves and soil.

Fox returned, carrying a generous supper in his jaws, and his fur sprinkled with glistening raindrops.

'I'm sure we shall catch up with them tomorrow,' he said as they ate. 'I can sense we're close.'

'What a surprise they will have,' said Vixen, 'if they think that you were . . .'

'. . . lost,' finished Fox. 'Oh, it'll be so good to see them all again! Dear old Badger, and Owl, Kestrel, Toad – even Adder! They're *all* my friends.'

'You're lucky to have so many,' remarked Vixen. '*I* never did . . . not many . . . well, until you . . . turned up.'

'And now you'll have a lot more,' promised the beaming Fox. His voice dropped. 'That is, if you agree to come with me, as my mate.'

'I'll give you your answer tomorrow,' said Vixen.

The two foxes rose with the dawn and slaked their thirst at a cool puddle in a hollow of the ground. They were soon on the animals' trail again. They had not been travelling for long when Fox suddenly stopped and looked all round with a puzzled expression. Then he sniffed the ground closely, to the left and right of him, for some distance.

'That's very odd,' he remarked. 'The trail seems to divide here. They can't have split up!' He sniffed more closely. Then he shook his head. 'No, the same scents run in each direction. For some reason they must have made a turn, and then doubled back. Perhaps something was after them . . .'

'Could it have been a wrong turn?' suggested Vixen.

Fox looked up. 'Yes, you're probably right,' he agreed.

'The question is, which is the right way? If we take the wrong direction we're going to waste a lot of time.'

'There's only one thing to be done then,' said Vixen. 'We must separate; I'll go left, you go right. If you are on the wrong track, turn back as soon as you realize it, and catch me up. If I go wrong, I'll do the same.'

'Vixen, you're wonderful,' said Fox with admiration. 'What an asset you could be to our party. Oh, if you would only join me!'

'We'll see about that,' said Vixen mischievously. 'But I must wish you farewell for now.'

'But not for long?' begged Fox. 'Now that I know you, I couldn't bear to lose you.'

'You may not have to,' said Vixen with an impish grin as she turned away.

Her reply put new heart into Fox, and he took his direction in a joyful mood.

As he paced over the downland, following the familiar scent of his friends' trail, he occasionally stopped and turned, expecting to see Vixen in the distance, running towards him. Then, as the gap widened and he still did not see her, he began to expect to find very soon that it was he who was on the wrong track.

Nevertheless, he plodded on faithfully, and eventually came across a sign that pointed without any doubt to the fact that his friends had indeed travelled *his* route. On reaching a patch of birch scrub he found that the scent he had been following all along continued past it. But a second scent, which smelt to him fresher than the other, led right into the scrub itself. It was not long before the smell of carrion made him stop and look around in alarm. A few yards away he saw a thorn-bush littered with bodies, amongst them tiny, new-born voles and fieldmice.

As Fox moved nearer he noticed, to his horror, that two of the baby voles bore a striking resemblance to those with whom he had been travelling only a few days ago. Shocked, he noticed two adult voles, who a few days ago had actually been travelling with him, impaled on the cruel thorns. There was no doubt in his mind now – his friends had suffered some misfortune. Perhaps they *had* lost their way, or been split up?

Fox felt he could not rest until he knew what had happened. He was convinced that at least *some* of his friends were very close, and he had to find them.

He thought of Vixen. *Surely* she must have discovered by now that she was on the wrong track. He dashed out of the scrub, confident he would see her running towards him, but she was still not in sight.

He was torn between retracing his steps to collect her, and leaving her to make her own way back to him while he pressed on in pursuit of the other animals.

With each passing minute he was becoming more worried about the fate of his friends, and he felt that to double-back now would be to waste vital time.

With a heavy heart, Fox decided in favour of his old friends from Farthing Wood. He picked up the trail again and followed it as swiftly as he could.

When the scent Vixen had been following ended abruptly, she realized Fox had taken the correct trail, and that she must rejoin him as they had agreed.

She sat down and pondered. Now was the time to make her decision. Did she wish to rejoin Fox or not? If she did, there was no time to lose. If she did not, then here was her chance to leave him without causing him the pain of rejection.

It took Vixen but a few seconds to read her own heart. Of course she wished to rejoin him! He was kind, handsome and courageous. She wanted to go wherever he led. Yet still she did not move.

While every muscle in her body prepared to spring her forward in the direction Fox had taken, her mind would not give the command. Something at the back of it told her she was losing her freedom. She had always been completely free. She had lived the life of the wild with only herself to consider, only her needs to satisfy. If she followed Fox now, that freedom – to go where *she* chose to go – would be lost.

But in the end, Vixen's heart decided the matter. At the moment that Fox, with anguish, decided not to go back for her, Vixen was already running after him.

Sadly, her moment of hesitancy was to put her life, and that of Fox, in the gravest danger.

22

The hunt

Fox had been quite correct in assuming that his friends from Farthing Wood were not far ahead of him.

On that very morning Badger had led his somewhat dejected party out of their night shelter in a nearby ditch, on to the downland again.

Their journey now took them up a rising piece of ground, the slope of which was very steep, and because of the voles and mice progress proved quite slow.

Rabbit had begun to mingle with the other leading animals again, as the recent distressing event convinced him that his and the other rabbits' part in the loss of Fox, was now forgotten.

'You might be interested to know,' he remarked to Hedgehog, 'that if it weren't for us rabbits, this grassland would all grow out of control. No sheep round here, you notice. What do you think keeps the grass nice and short like this?'

'Cattle?' suggested Hedgehog.

'Nonsense! No cattle about. It's rabbits!'

'I always felt sure you creatures must have some usefulness,' replied Hedgehog, 'though I could never think what it might be.'

'Hmph!' snorted Rabbit. 'More use than any hedgehog,' he said witheringly.

'On the contrary. The place would be overrun with insects and slugs if we didn't find them so tasty,' said Hedgehog.

Rabbit's argumentative nature was not equal to finding another retort, and he contented himself with muttering peevishly beneath his breath. Hedgehog left him and joined Weasel.

Badger and Mole were in conversation. Mole had been dismayed to hear Badger's gasping and panting as he plodded up the steep slope.

'Oh dear,' he thought to himself. 'Here I am, on Badger's back, and he's finding it such an effort.'

Then, aloud, he said, 'If you stop for a moment, Badger, I'll get off.'

'Don't be silly . . . not much . . . further,' panted Badger.

'Please, I'd like to walk for a change,' said Mole.

'Not worth stopping now,' replied Badger. 'Wait till we get to the top.'

This was just what Mole was trying to avoid, so without speaking further he leant to one side, and slid down Badger's coat, finally dropping the last few inches to the ground.

'Ow! Don't tug so, Mole!' complained Badger. 'You just stay put.'

'Oh dear, he thinks I'm still on his back,' Mole said to himself, and hurried in his attempt to keep up with the larger animal's strides.

He heard Badger continuing to talk, but he had already dropped behind so much he could not hear what his friend was talking about. He dared not make it obvious that he had played a trick on him, for it would only make Badger look foolish. So Mole, as he struggled upwards, bellowed, 'Yes, Badger,' and 'No, Badger,' or 'Just as you say, Badger,' at intervals, hoping Badger would not discover him.

Mole's pace was so slow that gradually all the other animals, including the mice and voles, passed him. In the end he was left cursing his own misplaced good intention of lightening Badger's load, while he watched the rest of the party leaving him further and further behind as they mounted the steep slope.

He knew that Badger would be very cross indeed when he reached the top and found he had been talking to himself for most of the way. As Mole's eyesight was so very poor he eventually lost sight of the other animals altogether, and this made him feel as if he were climbing the hill completely alone.

Supposing they left him behind? He reassured himself quickly. That could not happen. Badger, or somebody, would notice he was not with them. Badger would come back for him. But by the time he was missed, they might be miles ahead! No, no, surely they would pause for a rest at the crest of the rise?

'Oh dear, oh dear,' Mole wailed, as he inched his way

upwards. 'I'm always causing trouble! If I had only done as Badger said, this wouldn't have happened.'

Suddenly his small velvet-clad body froze to the ground. His sensitive feet and acute hearing had caught a series of vibrations. The vibrations strengthened. Mole knew it was not the light tread of his friends that he could sense. The vibrations were too many, and too loud. They increased at a tremendous rate.

Then Mole heard voices – human voices – and the excited bark of dogs. At the moment they were still distant, but with every second the noise, and the thudding of the ground, increased.

Mole looked round in horror. Of course he could see nothing. But that tremendous din, that thud! thud! thud! approaching so swiftly, the scattered barks and human cries, could mean only one thing. The sound that every creature of the wild, however great or small, dreaded beyond all else. The sound of the Hunt!

For a moment Mole's senses reeled in panic. He was terrified, not for himself, but for his friends – particularly Badger and the hares. He knew he could dig himself to safety in a matter of seconds, and in any case the Hunt was not interested in such small quarry as he represented. But what about the others?

With all his strength, and the added speed of fear, Mole hauled himself up the hill after his friends.

He was almost at the top when the first of the dogs appeared, cutting across the side of the hill. Others followed, tongues lolling. Mole sighed thankfully as he watched them make their way down the slope. His friends on the summit were safe.

The scarlet coats of the huntsmen, and the black coats of the women riders came into view on bay, black and grey horses. But the animals were at a mild canter, and Mole realized that the hounds had not yet found a scent; their pace was far too leisurely, and their cries, though excited, were without any trace of that awful frenzy that typified, more than anything, the terror of the Hunt for wild creatures.

At the top of the hill Mole found a small spinney, and from the confines of the trees in hesitant pairs, or singly, appeared the forms of his friends.

'Oh, Mole! You're safe!' cried Badger. 'Whatever made you do it? We all thought you were lost again.'

'I'm sorry, Badger,' Mole said contritely, 'but I did it for a very good reason. Please believe me. It was for your sake.'

Badger could say nothing more. He merely gave Mole an affectionate, understanding nuzzle.

'Did you see . . . the . . . Hunt?' Mole faltered.

'We heard rather than saw,' said Weasel. 'We buried ourselves among the trees.'

'I fervently hope no foxes are abroad today,' said Toad.

The other animals all turned to him, the eyes of every one of them showing that they were occupied with the same thought.

Suddenly a startling new cry was borne to them on the breeze. The hounds were giving tongue in a wild, unearthly baying. The animals rushed in a body to the edge of the slope and peered down.

They saw the hounds now racing over the downland, the riders galloping after them with coat-tails flying, in the direction of a small wood.

'They've picked up a scent,' said Tawny Owl grimly. 'Some poor creature's got the race of his life ahead of him.'

It was in fact the unfortunate Vixen, on her way back to join Fox, who had attracted the interest of the pack. In an attempt to make up for lost time, she had taken a short cut through a wood, expecting to be ahead of Fox when she emerged on the other side of the trees.

Halfway through the wood, she heard the hounds. Her

first thought was that they were on the track of Fox, and she was engulfed by a feeling of mingled horror and helplessness, so much so that she stopped stock still.

Then, in mounting waves of terror, she heard the baying and the galloping coming nearer, and she knew that it was she they were after!

Her first reaction was to turn about and run back the way she had come. Then, in a moment of startling clarity, she realized that, once in the open again, she would have little chance. By far her best manoeuvre would be to remain in the wood and, amongst the close-knit trees and saplings and shrubs, to zig-zag, feint and double-back, in and out and around the undergrowth and groups of trees, so that she would tie the hounds up in knots and break up the pack, while the horsemen would be constantly impeded by the low branches. Then, when she had got them into such a state of confusion that they would waste many priceless minutes extricating themselves, she would streak for the nearest edge of the wood, and with the lead she would have earned, race so fast across country that she stood a fair chance of losing them for good.

With wildly beating heart, Vixen forced herself to stay still until the first hounds should reach the wood and locate her. While all her senses and every nerve screamed at her to run, to fly, she retained an outward composure.

The horrible, deafening baying grew nearer . . . nearer . . . nearer . . . Soon she could even hear the jingling of the harness of the first horses. Then, with a crash, a shock, the hounds were into the wood, sending clouds of leaves, twigs and mould into the air, and trampling down undergrowth and seedlings beneath their furious feet.

Away spurted Vixen, away from their baying and their gaping mouths, away from their gleaming fangs. She ran under the taller trees of beech and oak, and dived into a thick shrubbery of elm and holly bushes. The hounds followed her.

186

Emerging swiftly from this, Vixen made a complete circuit of the shrubs, so that she was in effect then behind the leading hounds. With a swift glance she saw the main body of the pack threading its way through the trees on her right. She rushed off towards a thick stand of birch saplings, slowed enough as she entered them to make sure the hounds followed her direction, and then looped her slim body first round one trunk, then another, in and out, with the suppleness of a snake.

She heard the hounds yelping frustratedly as they attempted to push their bigger, stouter bodies between the close-packed saplings, and she heard the curses of the riders who had ventured into the wood as shoulders were buffeted, or heads assailed by the protruding branches of large trees.

She broke from the group of saplings, and ran exultantly into the more open part of the wood. Her plan was proving successful. Now she saw ahead a thick screen of brambles and ferns. If she could once enmesh the maddened hounds in its clinging prickles and stems, she would still have breath

and strength enough to run out of the wood and race far and fast across the open downland.

She had achieved her main object of separating the hounds. They were coming after her singly now, or in pairs, with long gaps between them. Others were barking in bewilderment, trapped amongst the saplings; some that had broken free had lost considerable energy in doing so, and their continued baying was at half-strength. Some again had lost all sense of direction and were sniffing the air, or unthinkingly following the lead of other hounds and becoming in turn entangled in the shrubbery.

But now the greatest test of courage faced Vixen. For to ensure that a good number of the hounds followed her into the undergrowth, she herself would have to delay entering it until they were but a few feet from her. Otherwise their training would tell them merely to bypass this obstacle, surround it on the outside, and wait for their quarry to be forced into the open by their master.

Her heart thudding madly, Vixen allowed her pace to slacken, gradually, until, as she neared the undergrowth, she had almost stopped moving. Now the hounds gave tongue to a new note, as if they sensed their triumph. Their baying became shriller in its excitement, and they increased their pace. Some of the bewildered hounds began to make straight for this corner of the wood as they saw and interpreted the leaders' commotion.

Vixen glanced behind and, despite herself, felt fresh waves of fear explode through her body. The hounds were almost on her! With a tremendous bound she leapt forward, and landed in the midst of a thick mass of fern. At once she began to inch and crawl her way through the intricate mass of stems.

She heard the hounds scrambling after her, and knew that if she could just manage to pull her body through the tugging heap of undergrowth without trapping herself, she could almost certainly escape.

As the minutes passed the confused and furious noise behind her told her that more and more of the foxhounds had penetrated the brambles and bracken. Angry human voices – calling voices – ordered the remainder of the pack away. Vixen continued to edge forward, at times with her stomach almost flat to the ground.

A little more, a little further, and she would be free. She saw, through the tunnel of undergrowth, bright sunlight ahead, and an absence of trees. She was about to emerge on the other side of the wood! There were only a few feet of undergrowth remaining for her to pull her body through! Brambles had torn at her fur and skin, springy ferns had struck her face again and again, making her eyes stream water, but ahead was clear, open space. She struggled on.

The next time Vixen looked up, her heart almost stopped. In that wide empty space of downland she had almost reached, she now saw a forest of horses' legs, stamping the ground impatiently as their riders waited for her inevitable appearance. Between those legs were blazing eyes and open mouths – cruel, red tongues and bared, snapping teeth. Foxhounds!

Despite her superb cunning, the humans had bested her. Realizing the futility of remaining in the confining wood, they had ridden back into the open, and moved round the outside of the trees to the very spot she had been working towards, unaware. They had taken with them those slower hounds which had been prevented from entering the undergrowth.

Now Vixen saw her stupidity in underestimating the skill and experience of the huntsmen. Behind her the hounds who were struggling in fury through the brambles and ferns were inching closer. The game was up.

23

Fox to the rescue

The noise of the Hunt had, of course, soon been picked up by Fox as he ran across the downland, hoping every minute to see some sign of his old friends.

When the first yelps of the pack reached him he stopped dead, just as Vixen had done. His ears pricked up, and he sniffed the air cautiously. He judged the Hunt to be some distance away, but directly in the line of his present path.

Like Vixen, Fox wanted to run as far as he could in the opposite direction – to keep running until those ghastly sounds became memories only. But he had already decided once that day, that to be reunited with his friends was his most important objective. Those friends, who needed him, were somewhere ahead, and not far from him.

Now Fox realized that to reach them, he would have to run the risk of encountering the Hunt. He had one advantage. He was upwind from the pack, and if he made a wide skirting movement from his present course, he might well avoid detection.

He looked behind him again, and stood for some moments, motionless, but there was still no sign of Vixen. Fox suddenly experienced a feeling that he might never see her again, but he immediately cast it from his mind, and set off on his decided route.

As he ran on, the noise of the dogs and the hoofbeats of the horses became louder. Soon he heard the frenzied baying of hounds following a scent. For a moment Fox felt that selfish feeling of relief produced by the knowledge that it is another, and not oneself, in danger. Then he wondered whose scent they might be following.

Fox had no doubt that there were a good number of foxes in the vicinity, any one of which might be the unfortunate animal now being pursued. He was thankful that Vixen was behind him, out of danger's reach. But suddenly his protective instinct told him he ought to find her and make quite sure she was safe. After all, he did not know for sure where she was at that instant.

The realization of this struck Fox with the impact of a heavy blow. He felt dreadfully afraid, not for himself, but for his lovely companion who, it now appeared, he might

have abandoned at the very time she needed his presence and protection the most.

He wanted to run back then and find her at all costs. But what if she were not behind him? If she had been, surely she would have caught him up sufficiently to be visible in the distance at least? The awful thought that his beloved Vixen might at that very moment be the quarry of the hounds made Fox shudder with horror. The more he tried to shut the thought out, the more he became convinced that that was the dreadful truth.

He raced back on to his old path, and made a bee-line for the direction of the Hunt. Fear lent wings to his feet. 'I'm coming!' he called, while knowing full well nobody could hear him. Then to Vixen he vowed in a low voice, 'They won't catch you while I'm still alive!'

Soon he could see the wood, and the dogs plunging into it, the riders following more cautiously. For a few minutes they were out of sight, under the thick screen of the trees. Bound by bound Fox lessened the distance between them.

When he had only a few hundred yards to run, he saw the scarlet coats emerging again from the darkness, and spurring on their horses as they raced round the side of the wood, taking with them a bunch of eager, dancing hounds.

Fox saw them pause at a point on the east side of the wood, all of them looking down expectantly, and he set himself to run right into the teeth of danger.

He seemed to feel no fear at all as he spurted across the springing turf towards them. His mind, his whole existence, was occupied with one idea – to save Vixen, whose scent at that moment he himself detected for the first time.

They saw his coming with surprise, pointing and shouting their astonishment to each other. They had not expected a fox to appear from that quarter; and so headlong and fierce was his rush that the hounds themselves were taken aback, and gave way.

Fox dashed straight between the impatient legs and hooves of the horses. The amazing sight of a wild animal actually running to meet them had quite thrown the hounds off balance. But with Fox's russet back now turned to them, the hounds regained their composure.

The horn blew, the dogs howled, and the horsemen prepared once more to give chase. None stayed to await the emergence of Vixen from the undergrowth. They were no longer interested in ambush, but only in the glory of speed, in skilful horsemanship, the feel of the wind dashing against their faces, the vibrations of thundering hooves: all the excitement and exhilaration of pursuit.

Fox kept close to the trees, and continued to run round the perimeter of the wood. He felt strong, fresh and keen.

He felt confident no hound could ever catch him. He would show them what *real* running was!

Nevertheless, he was not going to make it easy for them by staying in open country. Like Vixen, he realized the value of trees in impeding the progress of the hounds and, particularly, the horses and their riders. He entered the wood through a wide gap between the trees.

Of course, the Master called off the dogs from following into the wood a second time. He was not going to have this tactic repeated, with its accompanying frustrations to pack and riders. However, by electing to stay on the outside of the wood, he was at a loss as to which direction to take, as there was absolutely no knowing from which side the fox would appear again, and there was no way of surrounding the whole wood.

In the end, he realized he was temporarily beaten. He would have to allow the hounds into the wood again; otherwise, what possible chance was there of getting his quarry to leave it?

So under the trees they went again, baying continually. But the Master had lost this round of the battle. His indecision had given Fox a valuable lead, and he had already run through the length of the wood, and was now in the open again on the other side, going full-tilt across the grass towards a steep rise he saw ahead of him.

In the meantime Vixen, who had of course been a witness to Fox's heroic action of leading off her ambushers, found the coast clear again. Scrambling free of the thick under-growth, she burst into the open only seconds before the hounds who had followed her into the brambles also broke free.

And so the pack was now neatly divided into two sections, each giving chase to different foxes and each group unaware of the existence of the other. Here was a problem for any Master of Foxhounds, and the one concerned was at that moment following the hounds in the wood, ducking gingerly to avoid low branches and beginning, like the rest of the riders, to think it a very bad day's hunting.

However, Fox was not to have it all his own way. Strong as he was, he had made a grave mistake in heading for the grassy slope he saw ahead. For it was steeper than he had imagined, and a short way up he began to tire. His heart pounded horribly, his legs quivered, and his breath became more and more laboured.

And now the hounds began to gain on him. They were out of the wood and, after their brief rest, they were running better. Had it not been for the start Fox had on them he would have been in a hopeless situation, for the hounds' greater stamina made light of climbing the slope.

For the first time Fox began to feel the likelihood of being caught, and at the thought of what that meant his blood turned to ice. He was only a little more than half-way up the slope, and now he could hear the hounds' harsh breathing as well as their usual din.

Then, as if in a dream, he heard well-loved, almost forgotten voices shouting to him in familiar tones from the top of the slope. Badger, Mole, Weasel, Hare, Tawny Owl, Kestrel, Adder, Toad, and all his other friends had been watching from the very beginning the fluctuations of the Hunt in unbearable excitement, little realizing until now that the poor pursued animal was their own beloved Fox. They had believed him dead, and now, when he was on the point of being restored to them, he was in greater danger of losing his life than ever before.

It took the dazed Fox a little time before he could accept that what his senses were telling him was in fact real. He had found his friends again. Now everything would be all right.

With renewed effort, he managed a final spurt and reached the top of the slope, staggering into the protective circle of his old friends. At once they led him into the copse where earlier they had themselves hidden from the Hunt.

This time, however, the hounds were not passing by. The animals looked from Fox to the approaching yelling pack, and then back again. They saw Fox's exhausted form sink to the ground. How were they to save him?

'It's . . . no good,' the brave animal gasped. 'I'm done for. I . . . can't run . . . any more. Don't . . . stay with me. Hide yourselves. It's . . . me they want. Leave me!' He rose on to his tottering legs and took a few steps away from them.

They would not leave him.

'We haven't just found you to lose you again at once,' said Badger. 'Don't worry, Fox! We shall win yet!'

'They're coming! They're coming!' shrieked the squirrels who had, of course, taken to the trees.

Badger and the other animals, realizing their only chance was to fight to the death, instinctively surrounded Fox, and awaited the onslaught.

In agonized silence, their mostly defenceless little bodies frozen in fear, they waited. The painful throbbing of their hearts seemed to each animal like a continual thunder-clap. They continued to wait; every second that passed seeming as if it would be their last.

Human shouts and galloping horses told them the riders had reached the top of the hill. Then the horn sounded, horribly close. Yet still no hounds appeared through the trees. They had even stopped barking.

The animals could not understand what was happening. They could not move. There was nowhere safer to go. The unbearable tension began to feel worse than the fate they had all expected.

'For goodness' sake, Kestrel,' Badger whispered hoarsely, 'put us out of this misery. Go and see what's happening.'

Even as Kestrel flew out of the copse, the animals heard more human cries, the hounds gave tongue again and, miraculously, these sounds and the horses' hoofbeats became fainter.

'They . . . they've gone,' whispered Mole in amazement.

'Yes.' Fox's weary voice came from the midst of them. He alone of all the Farthing Wood animals could guess the reason for the Hunt's change of course. 'It's Vixen,' he said.

The animals looked at him for an explanation. Weary as he was, Fox was obliged to tell them of his meeting with Vixen, and how they had travelled together.

'I thought I had saved her,' he muttered, in a tone of utter despair.

He had no time to say more. Kestrel was flying towards them in great excitement.

'There's another fox,' he said quickly. 'Some of the hounds were already following it. They must have broken off from the main pack that came up here. Now the Master has set all of them after it, and the horses are right behind. He stopped the hounds from coming in here – I don't know why. I suppose the Hunt can't chase two animals at once. Anyway, it's our lucky day. We must get out of here at once,

while there's time. The other fox is making straight for this slope.'

'Where else is there for us to go? We can't possibly escape,' said Badger. 'How can our party outrun those dreadful hounds? They would tear us to bits.'

'Listen, Badger, listen,' said Kestrel impatiently. 'Don't you see? They're chasing the other fox, not us. As long as we get away from this copse, out of the path of the huntsmen, we're safe. They're bound to catch the other fox – it looks all in, though I've never seen such a fast runner before. Once it's caught, their sport's over for today.'

'How can you be so callous?' snapped Mole, who could see the groaning Fox, his head on his paws, weeping in the most pitiful way.

'You wrong me,' said Kestrel. 'You wrong me, Mole. I loathe and despise this human trait of hounding smaller creatures to death, with large numbers opposed against one solitary animal. But, don't you see, it's the law of the wild. This poor fox is sacrificed today to the humans' cruelty. But we can't stop it. I wish we could. Surely you believe that? I'm thinking now of our own party's safety. You can't blame me for that!'

'You want us to profit by another creature's misfortune?' said Mole.

'No. I merely want us all to escape,' said Kestrel, with a puzzled look. 'Is that wrong?'

'You mustn't blame Kestrel,' said Badger. 'He's thinking of us, and rightly so. He doesn't understand the situation.'

'What situation?' Kestrel asked.

'The other fox is . . . a female,' explained Badger with some awkwardness. 'She's our Fox's friend.'

'Oh no! How awful!' Kestrel exclaimed. 'Fox, do forgive me. I didn't know.'

Fox was not able to reply.

'It's all right,' Badger smiled kindly on his behalf. 'You

weren't to know. I know Fox won't hold it against you. But I'm afraid he's quite overwrought.'

'Look, Badger,' Kestrel whispered, beckoning him aside. 'Friend or no friend,' he went on, when they were out of earshot, 'I must say again, she will be caught. She'll never keep ahead up this hill, not after all the running she's already done. You *must* go now. Don't you see? Time's running out.'

'I do see,' Badger said gravely. 'But we can't leave without Fox. And he would never come with us, and desert her. He's obviously lost his heart to this vixen, poor fellow. Just look at him now!'

'Then it was a sorry day for our party when he did so,' Kestrel remarked, as he looked at Fox's pathetic form. 'For it means we shall probably all suffer her fate.'

'You are absolutely right in everything you've said,' Badger agreed. 'But we must stand by Fox now, come what may.'

They returned to the other animals, and as they heard the noise of the Hunt approaching yet again, led on by Vixen, Fox, despite himself, could not remain hidden. He felt bound to share her fate. He got up, and moved to the edge of the copse to watch her last gallant efforts. Behind him were the rest of the party.

She was nearer than he had expected her to be. Her head was drooping in the extremities of exhaustion, and her tongue lolled lifelessly from her open jaws. From where he stood Fox could hear her hoarse, racking gasps for breath. He shuddered to hear it. Somehow her legs kept moving. It was a mechanical action, with no conscious effort behind it. The leading hounds were only feet away, their blazing eyes already anticipating the kill.

Amazingly, Vixen kept running. Inch by inch the hounds gained. She looked up, and Fox saw her glazed expression. Yet he knew she had seen him.

For a few seconds, her pace quickened perceptibly. The

hounds, snarling in anger, lost a little ground, but by now the first riders were level with them, led by the Master, who urged them on.

Nevertheless, with each stride Vixen was drawing further away. The hounds, tiring rapidly, seemed to acknowledge that they were beaten. Their efforts were unavailing. Vixen was approaching closer and closer to Fox. Soon she was a matter of yards away.

And then, in horror, the watching Fox saw the treachery of human nature laid bare. By any natural laws, Vixen had won this race. If there was any fairness to be had in the dealings of humans, who regarded the drawing of innocent blood as sport, then she deserved to go free. But the Master thought otherwise.

Seeing that his hounds were beaten, he took the matter into his own hands, and spurred on his horse. Mercy was not to be shown by any rule in his book. He came up behind Vixen and raised his whip-handle, his arm poised for one heavy blow that would knock her gallant little body back into the hungry jaws of his hounds. He leant over the side of his horse, at the same time reining it fiercely back, to make sure of his aim.

Suddenly, in the grass under his mount's front feet, a glistening, mosaicked head reared up. It was Adder. With red eyes glinting, he lunged forward with the force of an uncoiled spring, and buried his fangs deep in the horse's left fetlock.

The horse let out a scream of pain, and reared on to its hind legs, its front ones pounding the empty air, and threw the unbalanced Master to earth with a sickening thud. He lay unmoving.

In the next second Vixen reached Fox, and all of the animals retreated once more into the copse. The hounds were halted by the band of huntsmen arriving on the scene. These looked down with concern at their companion, a vivid splash of scarlet sprawled on the green turf.

'My leg,' he gasped, his features white and drawn. 'I can't move it!'

His horse, with a frightened look, was limping about by his side.

'Perhaps an act of Providence?' one of the other riders was heard to whisper.

The day's hunting was finished.

24

Reunited

Behind the screen of trees, the animals watched the scene with bated breath. The huntsmen had called forward one of their number who was obviously a doctor, and this man was kneeling, grave-faced, by the injured Master. It was now the turn of the humans to be in difficulties. But the animals' only concern was to be quite sure that the Hunt was leaving.

They watched its slow retreat down the slope with its casualty supported as comfortably as possible, a limping horse in need of attention, and a pack of subdued hounds. Only when the last sounds of the assemblage had died away did the animals feel safe.

Adder came slithering nonchalantly towards them over the leafy soil. The whole party greeted him like a hero.

'You can save your breath,' Adder said sourly. 'What else could I do, when that monster was just about to tread on me?'

The animals ceased their praises at once, but Adder's excuse had not fooled any of them. They realized he must have deliberately positioned himself on the slope in the chance of being some help to the exhausted Vixen.

'This is indeed a happy day,' said Badger joyfully. 'Our

dear friend, whom we thought to be lost, is restored to us. And now, it seems, we have a new member of the party to welcome too.'

He looked across to where Fox and Vixen, the latter still panting heavily, were sitting side by side, each content to feel the other's nearness without the need for speech.

Fox knew he would never have to ask Vixen that important question again. The adoring look her eyes gave him told him all he wanted to know.

Presently Fox looked up and smiled at all his friends. 'We've all got an awful lot to tell each other,' he said, 'but now isn't the time. I suggest we have a brief rest here. Then we should move to a safer spot. In addition, Vixen and I are consumed with thirst. I wonder if someone . . .'

'Leave it to me, my dear Fox,' Kestrel interrupted. 'I'll scout round for the nearest stream; it won't take me more than a few minutes.' He flew up towards the tree-tops and vanished into the steely blue sky.

The other animals found themselves automatically looking to Fox again for directions. The usual pattern had soon been re-established.

Kestrel returned with good news. 'We're in luck,' he said brightly. 'There's a disused quarry about a quarter of a mile away, completely fenced off from the outside, and there's a great pond inside it with ducks and water birds and I don't know what else. We'll be quite safe there.'

And so, eventually, at a leisurely pace, the reunited party of animals, with Badger walking proudly by the side of Fox and Vixen at its head, made its way down the south side of the slope, with Kestrel hovering a few feet in advance.

When they had almost reached the quarry, Toad let out a cry. 'I feel right again!' he shouted. 'This is marvellous! I feel I'm going the right way at last.'

The animals looked at him curiously.

'Don't you see?' he croaked happily. 'My homing instinct is working again, only in the opposite way. Farthing Pond has no influence any more. I'm too far away. Now I can feel a pull to the other direction – the direction of White Deer Park!'

'Hooray!' cried Mole. 'Good old Toad! Now he can really guide us straight to our new home.'

'Hare, will you stop please?' said Toad gaily. 'I feel as if I can leap all the way myself.'

With a grin, Hare complied, and Toad sprang forward energetically in front of Fox and Vixen, determined to lead the column into the quarry.

The animals soon arrived at their temporary destination, but found the fencing to be of the net type, so that only Toad, the voles and the fieldmice could climb through. Adder was able comfortably to slide underneath.

'Leave this to me,' offered Mole proudly, and he began to dig a broad furrow underneath the fence. So quickly did he work that the leading animals found themselves unprepared, and were liberally sprayed with earth from top to bottom, as Mole kicked it back vigorously.

'Steady on, Mole,' protested Badger, giving vent to a sneeze, and hastily moving back a few steps.

The channel was soon deep enough to allow the hedgehogs and squirrels to pass underneath the fence and Mole,

having deepened it considerably on the outside, went under himself to perfect the other end.

'That's it. It's done!' he squeaked excitedly, and the rest of the animals entered the quarry.

They saw before them a huge, deep pit of bare chalk with a wide, man-made pathway, now encrusted with weeds and bushes of gorse and broom, leading steeply down one side. In the centre of this crater was a large pool, dotted with islands of vegetation, where several varieties of water-bird seemed to have made their homes.

Fox and Vixen hastened towards the water, leaving the rest of the party to follow as they wished. Side by side the two foxes drank their fill, and in the clear water they had time to admire each other's reflections.

'Oh, it's so peaceful here,' said Vixen afterwards. 'I can hardly believe it's the same world.'

'All this countryside could be peaceful if only the humans allowed it to be so,' remarked Fox grimly.

'Yes, but let's be quite fair,' returned Vixen. 'There are many humans who detest the idea of hunting as much as we do.'

'The ones they call Naturalists?' asked Fox.

'Those, certainly. But there are others,' said Vixen. 'Otherwise why do they keep what they call pets?'

'I must confess I shall never understand humans,' Fox said, shaking his head. 'In the wild, certain animals prey on others who, in turn, prey on smaller ones. Every creature knows what is his enemy, and also what he has no reason to fear. But those humans, who a short while ago were clamouring for our deaths, will probably go home and play with their dogs and talk to their horses with real affection.'

'Well, at any rate, let's forget the Hunt now and everything connected with it,' said Vixen. 'We're lucky to be here, safe with your friends. Let's enjoy ourselves.'

'By all means, my sweet,' said Fox warmly. 'And don't forget – they're *your* friends, too.'

205

Vixen pointed, with a chuckle, to where, on the edge of the pond, Kestrel and Tawny Owl were busily ruffling up their feathers, preparatory to enjoying a bathe. The two birds squatted down in the shallowest part, and scooped the water over themselves using their wings. They made little flurried movements, sending a procession of ducklings out to a quieter spot in the middle.

Soon all the other animals were in a line by the pond edge, lapping and sucking water greedily. Toad found a quiet place where he indulged in his favourite pastime of bathing.

As the sun began to sink, the pond took on a wonderful reddish glow, like a huge molten ruby. The animals had remained in its vicinity, and they stood transfixed by its beauty.

'How quiet and still everything is,' Hare's mate remarked. 'This place is a sanctuary. Why is there any need for us to go further? We could live here quite happily.'

'Impossible, I'm afraid,' said Squirrel. 'No trees.'

'Hares don't need trees,' she pointed out. 'Neither do most of the other animals.'

'Well, we've come this far. Seems a bit faint-hearted to stop now,' Squirrel persisted.

'He's right, my dear,' Hare said. 'Of course, I see your point. But Toad was saying earlier there isn't much further to go. I think we should carry on.'

The discussion was interrupted by the approach of a heron, a very tall fellow who had been standing motionless in one corner of the pond almost all day.

'I bid you good evening,' he said in a lugubrious voice to the animals, stepping jerkily forward on his stilt-like legs. 'Your friend the owl has been telling me of your exploits. I heard all about the Hunt.'

'We were very fortunate,' said Fox, not wishing to have the subject brought up again.

'You were indeed,' replied the heron. 'A lot of foxes have

been killed round here recently. I heard the racket going on earlier.'

'Actually, we're trying to forget the whole incident,' said Badger diplomatically. 'It was a frightening experience for all of us.'

'Oh yes,' said the heron, 'I can imagine. I was shot by those humans once, you know. Look.' He opened out one vast wing which had a neat hole through the middle.

'Gracious! Can you fly?' Kestrel asked.

'In a rather wonky fashion, yes,' the heron chuckled. 'The wind makes a lovely whistling noise through that hole when I flap my wing.' He beat it up and down a few times to demonstrate.

The animals let out little cries of surprise.

'My friends all call me the Whistler,' the tall bird went on. 'They always know when I'm coming.'

'It's a good thing you don't hunt in the way I do, then,' remarked Tawny Owl. 'I'm quite noiseless, of course – have to be.'

'Everyone to his own trade,' said the heron. 'I'm a great fish-eater myself. There are plenty in this pond: carp, tench and perch. I've always preferred carp.'

'Fish would certainly be a welcome change to *our* diet,' said Fox.

'Really?' exclaimed the heron. 'Tell you what, I'll catch you a few tomorrow, if you like.'

'Would you? How very kind,' said Vixen.

'Oh, no trouble, I assure you,' said the heron. 'I enjoy the sport. Perhaps we can take breakfast together?'

'Do please join us,' said Fox. 'But don't wake us too early,' he laughed, 'it's been a very tiring day.'

'You can rely on me,' said the heron. 'I'll say goodnight, then.'

'Goodnight,' said the animals in chorus.

They watched the blue-grey back of the lofty bird as he

stepped away towards his own resting-place. Then, as if by common consent, the whole party of Farthing Wood animals, with Vixen, huddled together into an intimate circle and listened as Badger and Fox exchanged stories of their adventures while they had been separated.

Some of the drowsy youngsters amongst the squirrels and mice fell asleep against their parents' sides. One of them forgetfully leant against a hedgehog and was given a rude awakening.

But the adult animals and birds, despite their tiredness, talked far into the night about the hardships they had survived, and of what might lie ahead. Exhausted as Fox and Vixen had been earlier, the talk and good company revived them, and nobody retired until Tawny Owl broke up the party by saying he wanted to stretch his wings, and glided off into the night.

The following morning the animals were awakened by a persistent whistling sound. They had slept in the open, without any need for cover, so far from danger did they feel now. They all stumbled to their feet to find their new friend the heron waving his damaged wing vigorously, and pointing his beak towards a glistening pile of freshly-caught fish.

There were many cries of enthusiasm at this sight, but the vegetarian animals, after greeting the heron, went their own way to find some breakfast.

'As I caught them I brought each one up here,' Whistler explained. 'Early morning's the best time for fish, I find. I could see dozens of 'em dashing about. Anyway, there's plenty for everyone, I think. I don't know about you, but I'm starving.'

'You *have* done well,' Fox congratulated him.

'Well, have a look and take what you fancy,' said the heron generously.

Fox chose some plump carp for Vixen and himself, and Whistler, with his long beak open in a grin, his rigid stance making him look as if he were standing to attention, watched as Badger, Weasel and the hedgehogs took their share. Kestrel and Tawny Owl followed, and even Adder ventured to swallow whole some of the very small fish. Mole said politely that he thought such rich fare might upset him, and went to dig for worms with Toad at the pond side.

The heron began hungrily to stab his beak into the pile that remained, and the animals were intrigued to see the way he tilted his head right back and gulped the fish down his capacious throat.

When all the animals had satisfied themselves, they lay back on the ground to allow their digestions to operate comfortably, and congratulated themselves that there was no need to be moving on that day.

'Mole and Toad must be hungry,' Badger remarked with a chuckle. 'They're still eating.'

Mole, who was not far away, heard him. 'I didn't know Toad had such an appetite,' he squeaked in amazement. 'As soon as I dig the worms up, he pounces on them. I've hardly had a look in.'

At that very moment Toad snapped out his long tongue and dexterously flicked up another worm, then used both his front feet to cram the protruding ends into his mouth. He gulped it down, inch by inch, in a series of huge swallows that shook his whole body, and at each swallow both his eyes closed in ecstasy.

'You'd better catch *yourself* some,' laughed Weasel, 'otherwise old Toad will burst himself in a minute.'

Mole's breakfast was eventually assured by a fall of rain. The raindrops caused a change to come over Toad. He abandoned the worms, and took on a distinctly lively air as he felt the moisture on his skin.

'I always feel like singing when it rains,' he declared, and began to jump about every time he felt a fresh raindrop. He broke into song with a rather high-pitched series of croaks, which resembled the cries of the ducks on the pond.

209

Mole paid him no heed, but ate all the worms he could dig up. For some ridiculous reason, he had felt a little stab of jealousy when the other animals had laughed at Toad's good appetite. He felt that his own reputation for voracity was being obscured and, perhaps because this was his only noteworthy feature, he started at once to reinstate himself as the greatest worm-eater.

It was a vain move because, as the rain grew heavier, most of the animals looked for shelter, and his greediness was unobserved.

Toad's antics, meanwhile, had carried him into the water. As he paddled about, he did not notice the dark shape beneath him, but suddenly he was seized by a fish, whose great size betrayed its age.

This old denizen of the pond, unable to get a good grip on Toad's slippery body, tried to gulp him down its throat as quickly as possible. This proved difficult, since the huge quantity of worms that Toad had put away had considerably distended his stomach, and he was too plump a morsel to swallow whole.

So Toad, half in and half out of the old fish's jaws, croaked loudly for help. He was not able to call out for long as his captor's next move was to dive promptly for the depths of the pond. As Toad felt the water close over his head, he decided his time was up unless he quickly wriggled free, and he kicked manfully. Not an inch did he gain. He was held fast. Although he could last without air for a few minutes, he knew the old fish would remain on the mud bottom now until he was drowned.

Luckily, though most of Toad's friends had not noticed his disappearance, one creature had seen everything, and this was Whistler. He quickly alerted Fox and Badger and then waded into the pond, peering down into the water, his view partially obscured by the raindrops.

'Can you see anything?' Fox asked anxiously.

The heron did not reply, but Badger gave Fox a meaningful nudge. He knew silence and stillness were of paramount importance now.

After what seemed an age, Whistler suddenly lunged downward with his long beak, and when he drew it up again, there was the old fish, a great carp, threshing in its grip, with Toad (a very limp Toad) still held fast in its jaws.

'Bravo, Whistler!' cried Badger, as the heron deposited the fish far up on the bank, where it squirmed and wriggled like an eel. It was not long before it was obliged to open its mouth, and Whistler immediately snatched up Toad and laid him gently at the feet of Fox and Badger.

Eventually Toad recovered his breath and got unsteadily to his feet. 'My dear Whistler,' he panted, 'I . . . I'm indebted to you.'

'Entirely *my* pleasure,' replied the heron.

Toad looked at the dying fish, gasping out its life on the bank. 'I wonder,' he said, 'if you could perhaps do me another favour?'

'You only have to ask,' murmured Whistler.

'Then will you return that poor creature to the pond?' requested Toad. 'He is old, and I should like him to die peacefully when the time comes. For the old, a violent death is all the more terrible.'

'Do you mean it?' asked the heron in amazement.

Toad signified that he did, and without further ado the tall bird gently raised the fish in his beak, and stepped solemnly back into the water to release it.

'You're getting too soft, Toad,' said Adder, who had hitherto been a silent witness of the events. 'That creature would have been your death if it had had its way. To spare such a life is senseless. It merely gives the fish a second chance to try the same thing.'

'I know there's no streak of mercy running through your twists and coils,' said Toad coldly, 'but fortunately some of us have a gentler nature. Having just stared Death in the face myself, and been rescued, how could I ignore the plight of another creature in the same straits?'

'Even when it tried to kill you? Oh, that's *very* sensible,' Adder commented sarcastically.

'Now, Adder!' Badger remonstrated. 'An act of compassion is dictated by the heart, not the head.'

'Pooh!' said Adder. 'Don't talk such airy-fairy nonsense, Badger. When it's a question of survival you, like me, take the only course open to you. If another's death means my life continues, then so be it.'

'The difference being,' Toad remarked, 'that my life was already safe.'

'Don't be too hard on him, Toad,' Badger whispered. 'Remember the Hunt. He saved us all you know.'

'*I* haven't forgotten, believe me,' said Toad quickly. 'Only I think old Adder is trying to. There's nothing he likes less than being regarded as a hero, and he's doing his best to change our minds. His action was a blow struck for all of us, not just himself as he would have us think. It revealed a layer of sympathy in him, and he's trying hard to cover it up again.'

'I'm sure you're right,' acknowledged Badger. 'But at least we know now we can depend on him in a tight corner. I always wondered about it before.'

Adder slithered away in a huff, as Whistler rejoined the animals.

'To be fair to your friend Adder,' he said, 'I must say I agree with his view. Although I admire your request, Toad, it seemed an unusual one to me. In addition, that fat old fish looked a tasty morsel. I've been trying for years to catch him, the wily creature. Now I don't suppose I ever shall again.'

'For that I'm sorry,' said Toad contritely. 'It wasn't the right way to reward you for rescuing me.'

'You know,' said Fox, 'I think the dangers and hardships we've suffered on our journey have changed us. Back home in Farthing Wood, none of us, including Toad, would have allowed that fish to escape. But I suppose fighting for our continued safety every day was bound to bring about a change in our behaviour.'

'Live and let live?' suggested Whistler.

'Exactly.'

'I must say,' said the heron thoughtfully, 'the more I talk to you fellows, the more I begin to wish I were travelling with you. You've got a purpose in life. You struggle on, but there's a reward at the end of it. Of course, I'm quite safe here. But nothing ever happens. I'm inclined to wonder if there mightn't be a charming young female heron living in White Deer Park who would love to meet me.'

The animals laughed.

'You're perfectly welcome to join us,' said Fox. 'We've already acquired one new member of the party' – he looked tenderly towards Vixen – 'and one more would be no strain on our resources.'

'I could be of some use to you, perhaps, too,' Whistler said excitedly. 'Oh, I should love to come.'

'Then it's settled,' said Fox. 'Tonight we'll have a celebration and you can meet everyone personally.'

'What a wonderful idea,' said Whistler. 'By the way . . . um . . . will you be needing any fish ?'

25

The celebration

As dusk fell that day the animals began to gather. Close to the pond Fox found a comfortable area of soft grass, screened by reed tussocks. There the animals lay down where they wished and Badger, who was to be Master of Ceremonies, counted his friends as they took their places.

Whistler had been looking forward to the event all day, and had been striding up and down the pond side in an effort to disguise his impatience for things to begin.

Mole, whose unnoticed attempt to eat a record number of worms had caused him to feel quite sick, had found it necessary to drink vast quantities of water during the day, and he now felt as bloated as a balloon. With every hesitant step he could hear the pond-water slurping inside his stomach, and he decided to fast rigidly for the next twenty-four hours.

As for Toad, after his fright in the early morning he had not ventured to swim again, but had contented himself with sitting in the mud in a cool spot, enjoying the rain, and lazily flicking up mayflies and gnats that strayed too close to him.

But the rain had stopped in time for the celebration, and it was now a warm, still evening with a sky whose stars were obscured by scudding clouds.

'Has anybody seen Tawny Owl?' asked Badger. 'And where's Adder? I hope he's not going to be silly and stay away.'

'Tawny Owl's flying over the pond,' piped up one of the little hedgehogs. 'He looks like a great big bat.'

There was a chorus of giggles from the other youngsters, which was checked instantly by Owl's arrival, and a stern look from Badger.

'I would never have believed it!' Tawny Owl exclaimed, with an almost indignant look. 'It's just too ridiculous for words!'

'What is it, Owl?' asked Badger. 'Do find a perch, old fellow, and settle down.' The latter remark was addressed to Whistler, who had hurried up to hear the news.

'I don't perch very much,' he replied. 'I'm more a statuesque sort of bird. I like my feet on terra firma.'

'Just as you like, of course,' Badger said politely, 'but don't walk off again, will you? Now then, Owl . . .?'

'It's Adder,' Tawny Owl explained irritably. 'He's in the pond, swimming up and down and causing as much commotion as a miniature Loch Ness monster.'

'Whatever for?' demanded Badger.

'You may well ask. Adder doesn't take to water too readily. It's my guess he's after that fish.'

'Oh, surely not!' cried Fox. 'Adder's got more sense. He can't *see* anything.'

'But this is serious,' Whistler said slowly. 'If Tawny Owl's right, he's more likely to end up the hunted than the hunter. That old carp could soon bolt down a long, thin morsel like Adder.'

Badger and Fox glanced at each other.

'How can we get him out?' Fox wanted to know.

'Nothing could get him out while he's in that sort of mood,' said Tawny Owl.

'Yes, yes, there *is* a way,' Mole squeaked excitedly. 'Listen, please listen, everybody. I know, I know!'

Fox smiled at him in a patronizing way, and Tawny Owl did not look pleased with Mole's dissenting opinion.

'All right, Mole,' said the kindly Badger, 'let's hear you.'

'All the mice and all the voles must sing – as loud as they can,' Mole announced, 'and I . . . I'll join them, and perhaps Toad could join in, if he feels able.'

'And will that fetch him out?' Badger asked gently.

'Of course not!' Tawny Owl interrupted contemptuously. 'I know what idea Mole's got in his head, but it won't work. Adder wouldn't be able to hear.'

'Well, what *is* the idea?' enquired Fox.

Mole looked round at the mice and voles shyly, and then at Fox. 'It's a little difficult to say now, Fox,' he said awkwardly.

Tawny Owl was not so shy. 'No good beating around the bush,' he said. 'We all know Adder's very fond of mice in his diet. Can't resist them. Their squeaky little noises in the dark act like a magnet to him.'

The voles and mice in one mass began to jump around in alarm, making nervous twittering noises.

'No, no!' they cried. 'We won't! We won't sing!'

Mole looked at Tawny Owl with an expression that plainly said: 'Now look what you've done!'

'It's all right, calm down,' said the owl. 'You don't have to worry. If we all sang at the tops of our voices he wouldn't hear.'

'Then we have to leave him?' asked Fox.

Whistler began to flutter his damaged wing a little, producing a very slight whistle. 'Of course, there is one answer to it,' he said meditatively. 'I could always do a spot of fishing.'

Fox looked for a moment as if he might agree to the suggestion. Then his eyes looked away. 'No, I couldn't allow it,' he said. 'Adder would never forgive us for humiliating him – and in front of everyone, too.' He looked at the heron again. 'But it was a good idea,' he admitted.

'We shall just have to do without him,' said Badger resignedly. 'Will everyone take their places again, please?' He waited patiently while his friends, including the placated members of the mouse family, rearranged themselves comfortably.

'This is a double celebration tonight,' Badger began. 'We're celebrating the safe return of our dear friend here – Fox; and we're also celebrating the fact that we have made two new friends – our very charming Vixen and, more recently, the amusing Whistler.'

Here the droll heron bowed with a flourish, causing his damaged wing to make a long, solemn note, at which the small animals giggled loudly.

Badger went on: 'This will probably be our last opportunity for a proper break before we reach White Deer Park, so we must make sure we all enjoy ourselves tonight.'

He looked at Fox, who appeared eager to say something, and nodded.

'Thank you, Badger,' said his friend. 'I just wanted to say, everyone, before we show our neighbours the fish and the ducks how to sing, how lucky I consider myself to have such good friends. After wondering for quite a time if I should ever see you all again, now that we're so happily reunited, I value your company more than ever.'

There were cheers at this juncture, and many of the animals called, 'Good old Fox!'

Fox continued, 'We've been through such a lot together already that there's no doubt in my mind we shall eventually win through. After all, if we can survive the Hunt, I am sure we shall prove the match of whatever dangers lie in our path ahead.'

The animals shouted excitedly at Fox's fighting talk. Some of them felt they were as good as in White Deer Park already.

'Just one last thing,' said Fox, 'and then, I promise you, we'll sing all night if you want to. When I was on my own, I met an old horse, an ex-hunter, and he gave me some good advice. He told me that this open country hereabouts, and the neighbouring enclosed fields, is all part of a hunting area, and that I should get out of it as soon as I could.

'And so, my friends, that is what we shall do. Now we're all together again, and thoroughly rested, we should be ready to push on tomorrow night, at our swiftest pace, and to stop only when it's vital. We shall continue in this way every night, sheltering by day, until we've put this danger- ous stretch of country behind us for good. It'll be hard going – there's no point in denying it – but I promise you this: if we all make the utmost effort, and help each other, we'll see it through, I'm sure of it. And then what stories we'll have to tell the creatures of White Deer Park!'

Fox smiled as he saw the resolute expressions on the faces of his friends. From the smallest to the largest, they all looked as if they had decided that, having come so far, noth- ing could stop them now.

'Well, Badger,' he finished, 'I'll leave it to you now to put us in a more light-hearted frame of mind.'

'Thank you, my dear friend,' Badger returned. 'Well now, who's going to start the singing?'

'I am,' said a low, drawling voice from behind. And there was Adder, his tongue flickering busily as he slid through the grass, his scales gleaming with wetness. 'I feel in a musical sort of mood,' he hissed, making no mention of his recent aquatic activities. 'Tiddle-tum, tiddle-tum, let me see, how does the tune go? Ah yes . . .' And in a rather monotonous, unmelodic lisp he sang a song about the first snake who had ever lived in the world, and who had had six legs, each one of which had broken off when it had told a lie, until in the end it had been obliged to slither around on its stomach.

The animals all applauded politely, but Adder was no singer, and Tawny Owl was heard to remark, 'Same old thing; he doesn't know any others.'

'Well, I'm sure we all enjoyed that,' said Badger. 'Who would like to follow?'

'I'll sing you one,' said Kestrel, flying up to a prominent branch, where everyone could see him. 'This, of course, is a song about birds,' he announced, 'and in it I shall imitate a lot of birds' cries, so I want you all to listen very carefully and see how many you can recognize.'

He began to sing, but there were so many different bird calls in the song that there seemed to be more of those than the words, and they all came so quickly one after another that the animals found it confusing and forgot half of the ones they had already identified. However, they all laughed very much when Kestrel gave a beautiful impression of Tawny Owl's flute-like hoots, so that the rather pompous Owl thought they were laughing at him, and looked offended.

But he soon cheered up when Kestrel finished his recitation with a few whistles that sounded exactly like their new friend the heron.

'How many did you know?' Kestrel asked afterwards, and it was discovered that Vixen had the best ear for bird calls. She had remembered nearly all of them, and Fox was proud of her.

'That was marvellous, Kestrel,' Badger complimented the hawk. 'But now, let's have one with a chorus where we can all join in. Anyone got any suggestions?'

'I know one,' said Toad. 'It's the one we toads sing every spring when we gather in the ponds. The frogs have a slightly different version. It's called "The Song of the Tadpole".'

However, nobody seemed to be acquainted with the words apart from Toad, although Fox said he had heard the toads and frogs croaking away at it in Farthing Pond many times.

'There must be something we all know,' said Badger.

'What about that song the rooks taught us?' Mole suggested timidly. 'You know, the "Freedom Song".'

'Of course!' cried Badger. 'The very thing. Well done, Mole, old chap!' He beamed at the delighted Mole, and asked everyone to sing up.

'We all know this one,' he said. 'Ready! One . . . two . . . three . . .' And in a dozen different pitches that nevertheless blended beautifully, from the squeaks of the mice to Fox's bark and Tawny Owl's hoot, the animals happily chanted the verses the rooks had taught them underneath the elms of the copse.

From then onwards the feeling of comradeship glowed in every member of the party. Animal after animal volunteered to give a song. Some were solo songs, some had choruses, and the night air vibrated with their lively voices.

Even Whistler, who confessed he did not know any songs, agreed to give a recitation, which he accompanied with many varied musical sounds from his famous wing.

At length the water-fowl, unable to sleep, gathered from their damp nests and resting-places and swelled the number at the celebration, quacking or chirping good-humouredly with the others.

It was left to Badger to give the final performance of the evening. Before announcing his choice of song, he smiled in a paternal way at the company of happy birds and beasts before him, the younger ones amongst them already lulled to sleep; and the companionship and mutual trust that was visible on the faces of the motley collection of creatures moved him so much that he had to blink hard several times before he spoke.

'Well, friends,' he said finally, 'we've had a wonderful time, and now at last it's my turn to entertain you. I knocked a little song together this morning, while we were eating, and now is the moment to give it an airing.'

He cleared his throat very deliberately, and in a voice that was rather gruff and off-key, sang to them a song which was about their own travels. Not one incident was left out: the fire, the storm, the farmer's dog, the river, the chase – everything was included. And, very cleverly, Badger managed to give at least a couple of lines to everyone in the party, bringing in Vixen and Whistler at the end.

The song proved to be so popular that everyone wanted Badger to sing it all over again. But he declined, saying it was getting late.

'I'll tell you what, though,' he promised, 'as we continue our travels, I'll add a few more verses as we go along, and when we finally reach our destination I'll sing the whole thing to you.'

The other animals all declared that it was a bargain, and Mole remarked that it made him all the more eager to get to White Deer Park. So, in the best of spirits, the celebration broke up, and everyone retired, full of confidence for the next stage of their journey.

26

The motorway

The animals left the security of the quarry late the following evening. Fox once again took his place in the van of their formation, carrying Toad. On one side of him he had Vixen, and on the other Hare with his mate and offspring.

Badger, carrying Mole, and Weasel guarded the rear, and Adder slithered along with them.

In the middle mass the rabbits and hedgehogs were at the front, voles, fieldmice and squirrels behind.

In the air there were now three members of the party, Tawny Owl, flying in advance of the day-birds, Kestrel and Whistler. The animals found that the regular, musical wing-beat of the heron above them was a reassuring sound of the party's compactness. But Tawny Owl secretly disliked this noise, past master as he was himself of stealth and silence.

When dawn first suggested itself it was the animals' task to find a safe resting-place as soon as they were able. Here they hid up and slept during the day. At dusk they would forage and drink, then, when it was quite dark, continue their journey.

They proceeded in this fashion throughout the month of June, and the beginning of July found them only one day's

travelling short of the end of the downland where, Toad
told them, they would have to cross a very wide, new road
that was still under construction. Once across this obstacle,
their troubles would be very nearly over, for the only remaining hazard they would have to encounter was a town,
and this they must pass through in order to reach the Park.

During these weeks they had not seen or heard any further
evidence of the fact that they were in hunting country.
Their narrow escape from the Hunt, and the terror they
had all experienced had, with time, become little more than
a bad dream.

However, while in the resting-place Fox had chosen for
their last daylight hours on the downland, the animals'
memories were very suddenly and unpleasantly jolted.

It occurred during the afternoon while they were sleeping. Only Kestrel was awake. He never seemed to find it
necessary to take more than a few hours' rest. He had left
his friends snoozing peacefully in the midst of a thick stand
of thorn bushes, and was enjoying his solitude, alternately
soaring and floating in the cloudless July sky.

His superb eyesight picked out various objects moving
across the green expanse far below him. There were little
groups of people picnicking, couples strolling with dogs,
other birds forever flying from tree to tree and point to
point, and motor traffic, in a moving rainbow of colours,
flashing like beacons as the glass and chrome reflected the
sun.

Kestrel looked out for the new road that Toad had
mentioned. He knew in what direction it lay, but it was
screened from his view by a high bank and a long, straight
swathe of trees. Had he seen it, he would have been obliged
to report that it was not at all the sort of thing they were
expecting. As it was, a blur of scarlet in the far distance in
another direction was an abrupt reminder of a danger they
had almost forgotten.

Kestrel hovered, trying to assess the distance of the threat.

There was no doubt that it was moving slowly towards him; he could see the ripple of movement running through the tightly-packed mass of hounds, and the pattern was repeated by the horses carrying their scarlet-coated burdens. He decided they were at present far enough off for him to remain calm, but not far enough away to be ignored altogether. He flew back to the camp to wake Fox and put the matter to him.

Fox thought they should move at once to be sure they kept ahead of the hunters, but he woke Vixen for her advice.

'Yes, we *should* leave here at once,' she said emphatically. 'We can't afford to wait and hope they won't come this way. If we did, we might find we'd left it too late to get away.'

Fox nodded. 'My thoughts exactly,' he said. 'But there's no cause to alarm the others, is there?'

'I think they'd be less likely to worry if you tell them *why* we're moving on,' Vixen said.

'I expect you're right,' admitted Fox. 'You always are,' he added admiringly.

Vixen smiled and helped Fox and Kestrel to rouse the sleepers.

Some of the animals grumbled at first at their slumbers being interrupted, but Fox soon acquainted them with the seriousness of the situation.

'Now there's no need for any panic or alarm,' he pointed out coolly. 'As long as we keep to a good steady pace, there will be no danger. And when we've got safely across the new

road, we'll have put the Hunt, and everything connected with it, behind us for good.'

'How long till we reach the road?' asked Hedgehog.

'I couldn't say exactly,' Fox answered, 'but it's just beyond that line of trees. Now, are we all ready? Come on, Toad, up you get.'

He looked all round to make sure everyone was with him. 'Mole, are you all set? Good, I think that's it, then. I can't see Adder. I suppose he's here?'

'I'm right behind you,' said the snake. 'If you remember, you woke me before anyone else, and I've been waiting ever since.'

'Yes, I'm sorry,' said Fox good-naturedly. 'All together then?'

With a tuneful whistle, Kestrel was accompanied into the air by Whistler, but Tawny Owl continued to hold himself aloof, keeping a few feet behind them now that it was daylight.

Keeping their target of the line of trees constantly in sight, the animals made good progress across the last stretch of downland. No sound of hounds or horns reached their ears, and, apart from a few cautious pauses and detours to avoid other humans who were out enjoying themselves, they had little to worry about.

However, as the outline of trees gradually assumed a more definite shape while they approached, another kind of sound became increasingly noticeable. It was the sound of motor traffic.

As the nearest road in that vicinity was the one Toad had seen being built, Fox became more and more apprehensive. Eventually he called Kestrel down, and asked him to go on ahead and investigate.

The animals watched the hawk diminish into a black speck in the sky, and finally disappear beyond the trees. In a few minutes he was back.

Whistler and Tawny Owl escorted him to the ground, and the animals stopped for his report.

'We might have guessed it,' was Kestrel's preliminary remark. 'Toad's new road has been finished, and it looks as if it's been so for some time. There are six lanes of traffic on it, with an island in the middle, and high banks on either side.'

Some of the animals looked accusingly at the dismayed Toad, as if he were responsible.

'Oh, heavens!' he croaked. 'I . . . I'm sorry, everyone.'

'Nothing to apologize for,' said Fox. 'It's a good while since you passed this way. Humans build quickly, as we all know to our cost.'

'What's to be done?' asked Squirrel nervously.

Adder chuckled without humour. 'We shall have to cross it, of course,' he drawled.

'But it's impossible! We'll all be killed!' wailed Rabbit.

'We wouldn't have much trouble getting across one half,' Kestrel told them. 'There's a big traffic jam on the side nearest us: a mass of cars and huge lorries stuck fast, nose to tail.'

Fox looked at him quickly. 'And they are not moving at all?' he asked sharply.

'Only at long intervals, it seemed,' answered Kestrel.

'But by the time we get there, who knows?'

'Surely it's safer to wait until night-time to cross?' suggested Weasel. 'The road might be almost clear by then.'

'There wouldn't be so *much* traffic,' Fox agreed. 'But this is obviously a motorway, and motorways are never entirely clear.'

'Even so, we'd have more chance then,' Weasel insisted.

'I'm not so sure about that,' Fox returned. 'If we reach the road while this hold-up continues, we have a very good chance of at least reaching the centre island safely.'

'Yes, and there we'd stay,' Weasel said a little irritably, 'while hundreds of human eyes looked on. No, I don't like that idea at all.'

Fox lifted up a back leg and scratched himself thoughtfully. 'We're in danger of forgetting one thing,' he said evenly, 'the thing that decided us in the first place to travel at this time of day instead of during the dark hours.'

'Well, we've heard nothing so far,' Weasel pointed out.

'Quite right,' agreed Fox. 'However, we must ascertain our position.'

Kestrel needed no bidding. 'If you'll just be patient for a minute . . .' he said, and flew upward again to discover the whereabouts of the hunters.

What he saw was disconcerting. 'They're much closer,' he told Fox. 'I think the hounds might be on your trail again.'

'Right. That answers your question, Weasel,' said Fox decisively. 'Press on, everyone. There's no time to lose now. There's not much further to go, and they can't follow us beyond those trees. I think you'll agree a lot of stationary cars is rather less dangerous than a maddened pack of hounds?'

'Caught between two fires,' muttered Adder.

The animals kept moving as quickly as they could, and the traffic noise was soon really loud and very frightening to them. Fox tried to keep everyone calm, but the fact was that none of them was at all used to being so close to heavy traffic, and the nearer they approached to the line of trees, the more nervous they all became.

'This is ghastly,' said Rabbit. 'I don't see why we can't wait for the road to clear. Even if the Hunt should come this way, they're not likely to be concerned about us small fry. Fox and Vixen can go now if they want to.'

This last remark he made in a much lower voice, which showed that he did not have the courage of his convictions, and that it was intended to be unheard. But Hare swung round on him. 'You're an utter disgrace,' he said witheringly. 'Surely by now even your small mind has grasped the fact that Fox decides on the best course for all of us. There's to be no splitting up. And I might add that *you* wouldn't get far on your own without others to think for you.'

As usual Badger was the peacemaker. 'Please, please, Hare, you know quarrelling is never any help,' he said beseechingly. 'And, Rabbit, you should try to be more unselfish. Fox is in a very difficult position.'

'I know,' admitted Rabbit. 'I'm sorry, Badger. I'm just feeling scared, I suppose.' Only to Badger would the animals admit their faults.

His old striped face lit up with a smile and he said, 'Of course you are, Rabbit. Nothing to be ashamed of. But we've been scared before, haven't we? Nothing new to us, h'm?' And he gave him a reassuring poke with his muzzle.

It was not long after this conversation ended that the animals heard for the first time proof that the Hunt was again on their tail, and closing the gap. The fear they had experienced on their previous encounter with the furious dogs and riders, when they had so narrowly escaped, returned to them in a moment, and Fox and Vixen unconsciously began to run faster.

Although the sounds of the baying and the shrill blasts of the horn were faint in the distance, all the animals knew only too well how swiftly this faintness became louder, and, taking no risks, every one of them began to streak across the remaining few hundred yards towards the trees.

Fox, Vixen and the hares were first to arrive, and they waited in the shade, in trepidation, as they watched their friends drawing nearer.

One by one they came up breathless, and Fox counted them all in. With all the little mice and voles safely arrived, only Adder was to come.

The animals strained their eyes to see him slithering through the grass, but no one could spot him.

Kestrel went off to discover his progress, and the rest of the party momentarily turned their attention to what lay before them. As they stood together under the shade of the trees they could see just a few yards more of grass in front of them, running up into a high bank that obscured the motorway at that point. Whistler volunteered to fly over the bank to report on the latest state of the traffic.

As he left, the animals looked back towards the downland they had just travelled through. There was no sign of Adder, but they could now see the first hounds breasting a slight rise, not half a mile away. They exchanged glances of alarm, but none of them spoke.

Mole broke the silence. 'Do you think they're coming for Adder?' he asked timidly. 'You know – in revenge?'

'Oh no, not at all,' said Fox. 'But we can't wait for him. He'll have to manage by himself,' and he involuntarily shivered as he continued to watch the hounds' approach. With a visible shake of his head, he tried to pull himself together.

'Come on, everyone!' he said peremptorily. 'Up to the top of the bank.' And he nudged Vixen forward.

Together, the animals ran across the last open space and

up the grassy bank overlooking the motorway. The bank was topped by an open wooden fence, which was no obstacle to them. They merely passed underneath the lower rail, and once on the other side they felt considerably safer from the sound of the Hunt.

However, there were now no more barriers between them and the motorway itself, and the crossing had to be faced.

The bank sloped straight down in front of them to the margin of the road, and a few feet beyond that was the nearest lane of traffic: cars and lorries of all shapes and sizes stretching as far as the eye could see in either direction, and all unmoving. Two similar rows of such seemingly peaceful monsters were lined up parallel to this, their gleaming metalwork baking in the heat, and from the end of each monster there issued a constant feathery column of smoke, that hovered for a little in the air and then seemed to vanish.

Separating these ranks of motionless vehicles from those that were roaring by in the opposite direction, was a thin strip of paper-strewn grass and weeds bounded on both sides by low crash barriers.

In one spot of this narrowest of islands, comfortably standing between the crash barriers, was the imperturbable Whistler. His back was turned to his friends on the bank, and he appeared to be completely engrossed in watching the fast traffic on the far side, for his head was turning rapidly from left to right as each vehicle flashed past.

'He looks as if he's been mesmerized,' whispered Weasel.

The animals had taken in the scene before them at a glance, and at the sight of all the humans ranged in lines in their stationary cars so close to them, they instinctively dropped to their bellies, while the nose of every creature, big or small, wrinkled in disgust at the tainted air.

Fox knew they would have to make a move very soon. Save for Vixen, he more than anyone felt they could not risk remaining still, with the threat approaching them from

231

the rear. Although he believed that the possibility of the hounds being allowed to go further than the line of trees was remote, that was enough for him.

Kestrel found them on the top of the bank, watching Whistler.

'I couldn't see him,' he said, referring to the missing Adder. 'I think he's done this deliberately, in case he might be needed again to halt the advance of the Hunt.'

'Hmph!' Tawny Owl grunted. 'That last exploit must have gone to his head then.'

'I don't think so,' Fox said soberly. 'Adder's not like *that*, whatever else you might say about him.'

Above the roar and whine of speeding cars and lorries, and the low hum of idling engines, the animals caught again the hubbub of barking on the air.

Fox got up and looked behind him, then quickly dived down again.

'We'll have to move,' he said bluntly. 'It shouldn't be difficult. There's plenty of space under the backs of the cars. We can run in and out of those lines of cars and join Whistler before we've even been spotted.'

'But, Fox, supposing they start moving when we're half-way across?' demanded Fieldmouse. 'Even just a few inches' movement could squash most of us, particularly the tiny ones.'

Fox looked again along the lines of traffic in both directions before he answered.

'There doesn't seem to be any likelihood of that,' he said, 'but the sooner we go the better.'

'Perhaps there's a footbridge over the road somewhere?' suggested Rabbit.

'Yes, and perhaps it will have tiny little steps up to it made especially for the convenience of mice,' said Fieldmouse sarcastically.

'I hadn't thought about that,' said Rabbit with embarrassment.

Fox turned to Kestrel, who had perched on top of the fence running along the ridge of the bank.

'Kestrel, will you stay and keep an eye open for Adder?' he asked.

'Of course I will. Both eyes,' he said merrily. The present difficulty facing the animals, as indeed with most of those they had already surmounted, did not affect him or Tawny Owl in the least.

'Well, my friends,' Fox said, turning to the rest, 'will you come with me, then?'

He looked round with just a trace of shyness on his face. He knew that most of the animals felt they were safe where they were for the time being, but the thought of the Hunt was, naturally, never out of his own mind.

Without a word Badger got to his feet and, with a look, bade Mole take his place on his back. Hare rose too, and hustled his family together.

Vixen, who had caught the almost pleading expression on her hero's face, nuzzled his side sympathetically and lovingly licked his fur.

One by one the other animals stood up. The rabbits were the last to do so. Tawny Owl flew off first to tell Whistler the heron to stay put.

Then Vixen ran quickly down the slope, shepherding the mice and voles in front of her, and in a trice they were lost to sight as they threaded their way through the traffic, under bumpers and between wheels, until they emerged on the island.

Fox let out his breath in a sigh of relief. Gathering the squirrels together, he made haste to follow in the steps of Vixen. Hare and his family went close behind him.

Weasel joined the hedgehogs, and eventually the rabbits, who were at last persuaded that the crossing was not as hazardous as they had believed, condescended to move.

Badger and Mole brought up the rear, so that in the space of a few minutes the whole party had safely crossed half the motorway, and was gathered in the precarious haven of the island between the two crash barriers.

Only Kestrel remained on his look-out post on the fence, searching in vain for a sign of the missing Adder.

As Fox and the rest of the party sat amongst the litter and weeds pondering their next move, they could see human faces looking at them in astonishment from the imprisoning cars and the cabs of lorries. Excited children gesticulated to their parents, their mouths *oohing* and *aahing* in silence behind the glass. The line of traffic nearest to the island held humans who were a matter of inches only from the animals, and before long tentative arms groped towards them from open windows. Fortunately for the animals they remained just out of reach, and as the vehicle occupants were all aware of the law prohibiting walking on the motorway, they were safe from any interference.

However, they did not greatly enjoy the closeness of the humans, and they all looked despondently from the roaring traffic on the other side of the road to their audience in the stationary rows, feeling very exposed.

But unknown to the animals, a mile away, where the jam started, traffic was starting to move forward at last. Like an imperceptible wave rippling to the shore, the movement was passed back down the long queue until finally it reached the spot where the animals had crossed. So the vehicles inched forward, taking away the amazed passengers. The animals were soon forgotten as their various journeys and errands reassumed their prime importance in the humans' minds.

'They're going! They're going!' cried Mole.

'How right you were, Fox, to cross at once,' commented Weasel.

'I'm very thankful it has proved so,' Fox acknowledged.

'Not such good news for Adder, though,' remarked Toad seriously. 'He's more or less stranded now.'

'Hallo! Here comes Kestrel,' announced Badger. 'I wonder if he's seen him.'

Kestrel alighted suddenly on one of the crash barriers. 'The Hunt has turned back,' he said with an air of drama. 'The hounds were called off when they reached the line of trees. Now they're all going back the way they came.'

'Thank heavens that's the last we shall ever see of *them*,' said Hare grimly.

'I'm afraid Adder hasn't shown up,' said Kestrel, 'though once the Hunt has disappeared there's nothing to keep him in hiding.'

'Will you continue to watch for him?' asked Fox. 'Otherwise, if he can't see any of us, he won't know which way to come.'

'I'll go and have another search for him,' Kestrel replied promptly, 'but what about you? You can't get across there.' He motioned with his head to the speeding traffic that had not diminished in volume one jot.

'Not at the moment, no,' admitted Fox. 'But surely it can't go on like this indefinitely. There must come a lull sooner or later.'

'And then you'll risk crossing?' Kestrel asked in surprise.

'What else can we do?' demanded Fox. 'This strip of debris isn't exactly my idea of a sanctuary. We'll have to do it in bursts, when there's a long enough gap between bunches of traffic.'

Kestrel shook his head. 'I honestly wonder if any of you except Hare are fast enough runners. Don't forget you've got three times the width of a normal road to cross, and vehicles that initially appear far distant come up in a matter of seconds. Their speed is unimaginable to us wild creatures.'

Fox's brow creased with concern. 'We have no option,' he said gravely.

'I think I may be of some use here,' Whistler said. 'Should it prove necessary, I could do a sort of portering job with the smaller animals – you know, ferry them across in my long beak.'

'What a wonderful idea!' Fox exclaimed. 'But we can't start until this dreadful traffic clears a bit. There don't seem to be any gaps at all.'

The animals sat and watched in dismay the unceasing stream of fast traffic. Where they sat, the stuffy air was thick and heavy with petrol fumes. Some of the young rabbits and Hare's leverets began to feel sick.

Kestrel flew away to take up his perch on the top of the bank.

'Why is there any need for *me* to wait?' queried Whistler, beginning to flap his damaged wing slightly, as if in preparation for flight. 'I can relieve these youngsters' discomfort straight away.'

'Where will you take them?' Fox asked.

'I'll unload them on the top of the opposite bank,' replied the heron. 'They'll be quite safe there, and the air will be a little fresher.'

'All right,' said Fox. 'Rabbit, Hare, get the little ones ready.'

'It'll have to be one at a time,' Whistler explained, and he advanced upon the first rabbit, beak at the ready. Then,

236

with extreme gentleness, he picked up the furry little body, using the blunt middle part of his beak and, holding it with just sufficient firmness, flew off to the safety of the far bank.

One by one, in trip after trip, he carried the young animals to safety. Tawny Owl stood guard on the other side.

'I might as well do the job properly,' the heron observed to Fox, and began to ferry the voles and fieldmice across. Gradually the number of animals on the island dwindled in the face of Whistler's continuing return trips, until finally Fox and Vixen, Badger, Mole, Toad, Weasel, Hare and his mate, and the adult rabbits, squirrels and hedgehogs remained – about half the party in numbers.

Fox looked round approvingly. 'We're progressing,' he said.

'I haven't finished yet,' said Whistler. 'Come on, Toad – you're next.'

Mole followed Toad, and the slender, light Weasel followed Mole. The squirrels, Whistler declared, were just about manageable, but once he had transferred all of *them*, he confessed himself beaten.

The party was now split into three groups across the breadth of the motorway. On the downland side were Kestrel and, somewhere, Adder; halfway across, the hedgehogs, adult rabbits and hares, and Fox, Vixen and

Badger were waiting; and in complete safety on the far side all the youngest, smallest and lightest animals were gathered under the joint guardianship of Tawny Owl and Whistler.

This situation continued for a little longer, without any chance of alteration. Then, as was inevitable, the fast traffic began to thin out, and small gaps began to appear.

'Hare, you'd better be ready,' Fox warned him. 'There's a longish gap approaching.'

Hare and his mate accordingly slipped underneath the outer crash barrier, and prepared for a lightning dash. As soon as the last car was level with them they hurled themselves across the three lanes of road and, without slowing down at all, raced up the bankside to join the others. They reached the top of the bank before the next cluster of traffic went past.

'Fox, you and Vixen must be next,' said Badger. 'You're faster than me. I may have to wait a little while yet.'

Fox did not dispute this. He felt he should remain behind until he had seen all the party get safely across, but he was also concerned about Vixen's safety, and so held his tongue.

The two foxes positioned themselves on the outer edge of the island and, at the next gap in the traffic, streaked across. They were not as swift as the hares, and they had barely reached the other side before the next traffic came up.

'I don't think we've got much chance,' Hedgehog said gloomily to Badger.

These two, the other hedgehogs and the rabbits were now the only occupants of the island.

'We'll certainly have to be a little less adventurous than those four,' Badger said.

Another quarter of an hour went past. It seemed as if they might be stranded.

Whistler flew over with a message from Fox. 'He says, even if we all have to wait for the rest of the day, you're not to budge until you're sure you can risk it.'

238

'Thank him,' said Badger. 'You can put his mind at rest on that point.'

Eventually Badger saw a really promising space open up behind a group of cars that were fast approaching, and he got all the hedgehogs and rabbits lined up outside the barrier, alongside himself.

'Go!' he shouted gruffly as the last car flashed past, and all of them began to run desperately for the bank, himself included.

Two of the older hedgehogs fell behind as the main bunch began to cross the second lane, and seeing the other animals increasing their lead, they began to lose heart. With such a small margin between danger and safety, a second's hesitation was fatal. Badger and the rabbits and the faster hedgehogs reached the bank and turned round to see if they were all across. The two slower animals were just crossing the third lane, but the whole party could see they were not going to make it.

As the first cars roared up, the two hedgehogs instinctively adopted their habitual posture of defence, and rolled themselves into balls; the very worst thing they could have done. It was all over in a trice. The rest of the party gasped in horror, and amongst them a deadly silence fell.

Another dangerous obstacle had been passed. The animals were one step nearer White Deer Park, but two more lives had been lost.

27

Some comforting words

Sadly, silently, Fox led the party down the other side of the bank and into the first field, a cornfield, that lay before them. Here the motorway was not only out of sight, but its awful roar and din had become just a murmur in their ears. Whistler alone remained on the bank top to watch out for the return of Kestrel.

The animals lay down together in the midst of the tall green corn, listlessly watching a group of tiny harvest mice climbing from stalk to stalk, using their little feet to balance on the stems as they ate. The thought of death lingered in their minds, and the hedgehogs were all wearing solemn, even severe, expressions. Only Toad, of all the animals, was feeling in good spirits, though he tried not to show it because of the others' demeanour. He was feeling excited because, now they had crossed the motorway, he knew they were really not far from their destination.

Whistler, standing like a sentinel on the ridge, kept his eyes fixed on the bank opposite, ignoring the traffic still streaming below. Kestrel suddenly swooped up from the direction of the downland and alighted on his piece of fence as before. He looked across the road and, seeing only Whistler, flew over to him.

'Yes, they're all over there in the cornfield,' Whistler replied to the hawk's first enquiry.

'No mishaps?' Kestrel asked.

Whistler told him of the hedgehogs.

'I suppose we should count ourselves lucky to have lost so few,' Kestrel said philosophically.

'And Adder?' prompted the heron.

'Oh yes. *He's* all right,' replied Kestrel. 'He should reach the top of the bank over there any minute. You might just manage to catch sight of him from here. He'd been hiding in a ditch – said he didn't want to be trampled. Of course he emerged once the Hunt had gone back.'

'Well, let's fly over and meet him,' said Whistler.

The two birds took to the air. When they reached the opposite bank, they could see Adder's sinewy body winding itself through the grass of the slope.

'I trust I shall not be expected to apologize for lateness,' he remarked drily as he arrived on the ridge. 'Four legs are faster than none.'

'Fox is waiting for us with the others in a cornfield on the other side of the road,' said Kestrel. 'If you're ready, we ought to join him at once.'

'My readiness doesn't have much bearing on the situation, I'm afraid,' Adder drawled. 'I fail to see how I am to venture on to a road such as that without immediately becoming transformed into an integral part of the tarmac.'

Whistler winked at Kestrel. 'You lead off,' he said. 'They're in the first field. You'll soon spot them from the air.'

Kestrel at once flew up high, the better to pick out his friends from the green mass of the corn, and Whistler, before Adder had comprehended what was to happen, opened his long beak and snatched up the startled snake from the bank.

The animals in the field had the double surprise of seeing Kestrel suddenly plummeting towards them from the empty sky, followed shortly afterwards by a whistling sound which announced the arrival of the heron, carrying an indignant Adder dangling from his beak like an enormous earthworm.

The amusement they derived from the scene served to divert their minds, at least temporarily, from the recent tragedy. They began to chatter again, while Toad chuckled in his croaky way quite openly.

With the return of Adder, the threat posed by the Hunt was at last over – for good.

The cornfield became the animals' resting-place for the following night.

The foxes were the last to settle down. Although Vixen was quite ready to fall asleep, Fox was very restless and seemed unable to get comfortable. Vixen watched his vain attempts, and knew there was something bothering him.

She moved closer. 'What's on your mind?' she asked quietly.

Fox turned his head to look at her as she lay down among the stalks of corn. 'Oh,' he said. 'I can't seem to relax. My head's going round and round, and I can't clear my mind of things.'

'You're worried about something, I can see,' said Vixen in a sympathetic tone. 'Can I help?'

Fox smiled. 'I don't want you worried as well,' he said.

'If I am to be your mate,' said Vixen with a touch of shyness, 'I must share everything with you.'

'That's very comforting to me,' Fox said. 'You are the dearest creature.' He licked her face affectionately.

'I can't stop thinking about those hedgehogs,' he explained. 'Oh, I suppose it was no one's fault. If anything, their age was to blame, poor animals. But whenever there's a mishap, you see, I feel responsible.'

'I know you do,' said Vixen, 'and it's understandable. But you can't control everything that happens. It's not in your power to prevent such occurrences. Fox, you must put all this out of your mind. Nobody is blaming *you*.'

'Of course, I realize that,' Fox conceded. 'They're all such good-natured beasts. Even Hedgehog himself has avoided the subject ever since . . . but . . . but well, it's just that I can't stop wondering now if it *would* have been safer if we had waited until dark to cross.'

'So that's it!' said Vixen. 'I thought as much. You're feeling guilty because your decision to cross was influenced by the Hunt.'

'Yes,' said Fox. 'You already know me pretty well, Vixen.'

'Oh, how can I convince you that you did the right thing?' Vixen cried. 'You think that the Hunt was only interested in you . . . and me?'

'They were,' said Fox in a low voice. 'The others might have been safer staying on the bank until dark. I can't rid myself of the nagging doubt that two lives might have been sacrificed . . . to me,' he finished in a barely audible voice.

'What nonsense!' Vixen exclaimed. 'Don't humans hunt hares . . . and badgers? And do you think those hounds, if they had caught us up, as they would have done on the bank, would have singled *us* out and spared all the others? The whole party was in danger, and you did the only possible thing. You removed the danger from all of us.'

Fox was silent for a long time. Finally he said, almost timidly, 'Do you really think so, *dear* Vixen?'

'I've never been more sure of anything,' she answered confidently. 'And the others would agree with me.'

'I'm so glad you feel like that,' Fox said. 'Perhaps I was right after all.'

'Dear old Fox,' said Vixen, nestling up very close, 'don't you know you're already a hero to most of the animals? Just remember what you've led them through. You could never lose their respect now. And in only a short while, all this heartache will be over.'

'Yes,' said Fox. 'I really do believe we're going to get there. How I long for that day!'

'So do I,' murmured Vixen. 'I long for the peace and rest it will bring us all, and the feeling of uninterrupted safety.' Her voice became a whisper. 'But most of all I long for the day when I can have you all to myself, to be just *my* hero, instead of everyone else's.'

'Am I not your hero already then?' asked Fox playfully.

'Why else do I follow you everywhere?' Vixen smiled and, laying her head against his, closed her eyes with a blissful sigh.

28

The deathly hush

The sound of humans close by woke the animals early the following morning, and they at once prepared to move on. Once again they found themselves surrounded by farmland – only this farmland was different from any they had seen before. There were no hedgerows dividing the fields, no thatched farm cottages and no ancient lopsided barns. Everything was conducted in this area in a far more calculated, professional manner. Vast expanses of cereals and root crops grew mathematically in unbordered squares, without a wild flower or grass showing its head, even in corners. All unnecessary plants had been totally cleared away, and the fields had a cold, clinical look about them which seemed unnatural. The few trees that still existed were giants which had proved, in this cost-obsessed world, too expensive to move, and so they remained.

The farmhouses were modern, brick-built and efficient buildings without so much as a leaf of ivy growing on their walls, and the lanes and paths were cemented or gravelled.

Animals – farm animals, that is – could be heard cackling or grunting to each other, but they were never seen. It seemed they had all been shut away in the long, low concrete and steel outbuildings that were prevalent. In the overheated interiors they were probably quite unaware of the existence of lush green grass spread with buttercups, or blue sky, or the fresh feeling of a shower of rain.

Because of the lack of cover the local wild creatures appeared to have deserted the area completely, and only domesticated sparrows, blackbirds or pigeons were in evidence. The wild creatures from Farthing Wood found great difficulty in making any progress, for they felt too exposed in these wide open spaces. In addition there seemed to be an army of farm workers about, driving the very latest and biggest monsters of machinery, and manipulating the very newest gadgets and tools.

The animals all wanted to escape from this world, where they were clearly intruders, as quickly as they could. It was a manufactured world, devoted to human needs and requirements where anything animal or vegetable from the

natural world was not only unwelcome, but considered a pest or weed, and treated as such.

So the animals felt it necessary to remain hidden as much as possible during the daytime, and to continue towards their destination in the dark hours when the presence of humans was not such a risk. But, as the days passed, and nothing happened to alarm them seriously, they grew bolder.

Kestrel returned from his morning reconnaissance flight one day to where his friends were sleeping under a discarded tarpaulin. The weather was warm, dull, but very still. Not a breath of wind was blowing.

As usual Kestrel went straight to Fox and gently woke him. 'There's not a soul about,' he whispered. 'Everything's as quiet as Badger's old set out there. If we leave now, we could get away from this unpleasant area today. There are only a few fields for you to cross, and then you'll be just outside the town.'

Fox rubbed both his eyes in turn with his paw, and then scratched thoughtfully. He found Vixen's sleepy eyes watching him.

'Let's go, Fox,' she urged. 'I've hated these last few days. It's been so uncomfortable. Have you noticed how little everyone has been speaking?'

'Yes, I have,' said Fox. 'It must have been the quietest period of the whole journey.'

'It's the influence of this awful district,' Vixen said. 'I've never been anywhere like it before. It's so lifeless. And there's almost nothing to eat.'

'I'll have to wake Badger and Owl, at any rate,' said Fox. 'I won't be a minute.'

Tawny Owl, who had also of late been complaining of the shortage of food, had found himself a sleeping-place in the only tree that could be seen for a mile or more around. Badger was snoring contentedly in a fold of the tarpaulin, quite away from the others. Fox woke him first, and related to him Kestrel's information.

Badger stretched himself while he carefully sniffed the motionless air in every direction. 'Hm!' he grunted. 'It is *remarkably* silent. Can't hear a thing. No humans about. Nothing about, by the sound of it.'

'What do *you* think then?' Fox asked him.

'I think we should get out of this ghastly place at the first opportunity,' he answered. 'Which is, it seems, now.'

They trotted over to Tawny Owl's tree together, and called him. Tawny Owl did not at first reply, and they called again. A muffled sound, something like a hoot, yet more of a sigh, was heard.

'Oh, it's you, Fox,' said the sleepy owl, peering down at him. 'And Badger.'

'Will you come down, Owl?' said Fox. 'We can't see you; you're quite hidden, you know.'

'We've something important to put to you,' added Badger.

'All right,' replied Tawny Owl wearily and, with his wings fully extended, he dropped down between them.

Fox told him of Kestrel's suggestion. 'I suppose we might as well make use of the quietness,' he finished.

'Certainly,' Tawny Owl agreed immediately. 'No time like the present. And perhaps we'll be able to get a square meal tonight.'

The three of them went back to the tarpaulin, and rounded up everyone.

Adder was especially pleased with the early move. 'I can go a good time without food,' he whispered, 'but this place has really been disappointing. There's simply nothing to get one's fangs into.' With a malicious leer at the voles he added, 'I was really beginning to think I might have to look elsewhere for my sustenance.'

'Now, Adder,' Badger remonstrated, 'why will you make remarks like that? See how you've made them quiver. They look quite frightened.'

'Oh, pshaw!' Adder exclaimed contemptuously. 'They should be used to my ways by now.'

'We shall never get used to your unkindness,' said Vole in a hurt tone of voice.

'Come on, now,' Fox broke in. 'That's enough, Adder. Let's get under way. We can all have a good feed tonight. Lead on, Kestrel.'

Following Kestrel's direction, the animals entered the first field – a wide, flat expanse of potato plants. Not a sound could they hear but their own footsteps and breathing. There was no bird-song, no buzzing of insects, and no breeze.

'It's . . . uncanny,' said Mole. 'If we couldn't see the sun, it would be just like being shut in one of my tunnels. Even then I can hear things above me.' Unconsciously he found himself whispering, which increased the feeling of eeriness.

'I don't like it at all,' Fox admitted to Vixen. 'Everything's so unnatural. Look at those plants. They look almost artificial.' He pointed with his head to the potato plant leaves, which indeed had a strange, waxy look about them.

'Yes, they look sort of shiny, don't they?' said Vixen.

'Not at all appetizing in appearance,' said Hare, who was close behind them. 'I wonder what they taste like.'

'Don't do anything silly, Hare,' said his mate sharply. 'Leave them alone. They don't look right at all.'

'I was merely wondering,' said Hare. 'No need to worry.'

'Leverets,' his mate admonished her young ones, 'on no account must you eat anything in these fields. Not so much as a nibble, d'you understand?'

The leverets promised their mother obedience.

The potato field ended, and just a dry strip of dead grass separated it from the next one, which supported sugar-beet.

Keeping Kestrel in sight, they skirted this field and began to cross another, where a crop of cabbages seemed to be flourishing. The rabbits' eyes grew big at the sight of the rows and rows of juicy green vegetables, and their empty stomachs ached for them.

Rabbit called to Fox. 'Can't we stop?' he pleaded. 'We're all so hungry. A few plants wouldn't be missed, after all, and there's simply no one about.'

Fox halted, and the rabbits and young hares, despite their mother's warning, looked at him eagerly.

'It's that very thing that makes me suspicious,' Fox said. 'I don't like this quietness one bit. There's some reason for it, which we don't know. In my opinion we shouldn't risk stopping.'

'Quite right, Fox. Keep going,' said Badger, who felt his friend needed support.

'Fox, *please*,' Rabbit begged him. 'We may not get another chance like this. None of us has eaten properly for days.'

'We hares won't touch anything,' said Hare's mate categorically, and her little ones' faces dropped.

'More fool you,' said Rabbit with contempt. 'There's nothing wrong with those cabbages. They're perfect. Look how fresh they are! You can still see the raindrops on them!'

Fox walked up to a large plant and looked all over it carefully, sniffing each leaf. 'There's certainly some moisture on them,' he agreed. 'The soil underneath is damp too. But it can't be rain. It's been dry for a long time.'

'Is it dew?' Mole piped up. The damp soil made him think of worms.

'I doubt it.' Fox shook his head. 'Not at this time of day.' He sniffed the plant again, more vigorously. 'I'm not sure,' he said slowly, 'but there seems to be a strange smell about them, a sort of mineral smell. Rabbit, you'd know better. Will you have a try?'

Rabbit went to the cabbage, and his nose quivered excitedly. 'No. Nothing different,' he observed, although he *had* detected the mineral smell. He was determined to persuade Fox to give way.

'I still don't like it,' Fox said uneasily. 'I'm not convinced they're safe. And this silence is getting me down. Where are all the insects we usually hear? I'll bet you wouldn't find a single caterpillar on those plants. They look *too* perfect.'

While the animals continued to debate the matter, Mole slipped down from Badger's back. His keen appetite was beginning to master him again. He had been deprived of his usual quota of earthworms for some days, and he had never been without a gnawing feeling of emptiness. The thought that, at last, in this field, there was a good chance of finding a satisfying number of worms proved too much for him.

To his credit, he fought the temptation for at least a few seconds, but Mole, above all creatures, found it difficult to deny the promptings of his stomach. He crept stealthily away from the other animals, until they all had their backs to him. Then he scurried behind a large cabbage plant and began to dig furiously.

'I should . . . be able to . . . catch a few . . . and get back again . . . before they miss me,' he panted as he dug, his whole mind devoted to the thought of plump, pink, wriggling worms. He was soon hidden from sight.

Fox and the rest of the party had not reached a decision.

'I say don't be tempted,' Weasel was saying. 'The plants may be delicious, but surely it's better not to risk anything than to be sorry afterwards?'

'It's all right for you. You don't eat cabbages,' Rabbit said angrily, 'otherwise you wouldn't be so indifferent.'

'Well . . .' Fox began.

'No!' said Badger. 'Fox, don't waver,' he whispered to him. 'Let's get out of this place while the going's good. It's broad daylight. Humans could appear at any moment, and we'd be spotted.'

'I don't like to seem hard on them,' Fox said doubtfully.

'They'll soon forget it, and be glad we went on,' Badger urged. 'I think we . . .' He broke off, as the sound of Whistler's wing made them all look up.

The heron was racing towards them, accompanied by Kestrel and Tawny Owl.

'Come on! Keep going!' they called.

'What is it?' Fox asked, alarmed.

The birds landed together. 'This place is a graveyard,' said Kestrel, and shuddered.

'Poisoned,' said Tawny Owl. 'Nothing's safe.'

'Poisoned?' gasped Rabbit.

'The whole area,' Whistler nodded. 'There's an orchard just ahead. The ground is littered with bodies of bullfinches, chaffinches, blackbirds . . .'

'Then the moisture . . .' began Rabbit.

'POISON!' cried Fox.

'But surely no one has eaten . . .' faltered Kestrel.

'No,' said Fox. He gulped at the danger they had escaped. 'You were in the nick of time.'

'The whole farm has been sprayed with chemicals,'

Tawny Owl explained. 'All wild life has fled. Some were too late,' he added.

'For goodness' sake, everyone, let's go,' said Fox.

It was only then that Badger began to look for Mole, who was at that moment emerging from the hole he had dug behind the cabbage.

Badger saw the soil on his friend's fur and feet. 'Oh, Mole!' he wailed. 'What have you done?'

'Worms,' said Adder. 'Infected worms. Mole, you've poisoned yourself.'

Mole looked at them in consternation. 'But I haven't eaten any worms,' he said. 'They're all dead!'

29

The naturalist

Fox soon acquainted the wandering Mole with the reason for the death of all the earthworms, and the narrow margin by which Mole himself had escaped being poisoned made the little animal feel as weak as water.

'Now, Mole, let that be a lesson to you,' Badger told his erring young friend. 'No more creeping away with deceitful little plans. You're jolly lucky to be with us still.'

Badger was really as relieved as Mole at his escape, and after lecturing him, smiled with pleasure at the animal's return.

Now the animals' horror of the place lent wings to their feet, and with the ghostly feeling all around them of the silence that meant death, they hurried on.

In the orchard, the pitiful corpses of birds who had committed no greater crime than that of finding it necessary to eat, sent shudders down the spines of the animals from Farthing Wood.

In another field they saw more lifeless creatures: poisoned fieldmice and beetles, and pretty butterflies which had unavoidably been tainted with the death-dealing spray. Even bees, useful to humans, had ignorantly strayed into this area where only machines and the mathematical minds of men were permitted to hold sway. These innocent makers of honey had perished too.

'I shall feel like a good wash once we're away from here,' Vixen said to Fox.

'We all will,' he answered grimly, as he resolutely led the band onward.

At last they reached the far border of this soulless farmland – a stout hawthorn hedge which ran as straight as a Roman road along its edge.

Fox found a gap for them, and they followed Vixen through into a cool green meadow, where cows were grazing and where golden buttercups grew in such profusion it was as if the sun had settled on the grass.

It was so inviting and refreshing after their recent ordeal that they sank down together in the lush verdure, letting out sighs of contentment. Tawny Owl, Kestrel and Whistler joined in their enjoyment of rest and relief.

'Yes, it's amazing to what lengths humans will go to preserve their own species,' Tawny Owl said wisely, with a sense of importance.

'How can poisoning help them?' Toad asked.

'It helps them because it doesn't poison *them*, 'said Tawny Owl.

'But how can humans avoid coming into contact with it, when it is they who spray it around?' demanded Weasel.

'None of us could answer that,' Tawny Owl replied, 'as we have never been witnesses to the awful practice. What we all *do* know about, however, is the infinite cunning and cleverness of the human race. This alone is sufficient to tell us that the operation is probably undertaken by some of their lifelike machinery – under their control, of course.'

'But what do they do with all those poisoned cabbages and things?' Rabbit wanted to know.

Tawny Owl began to feel that, on this subject he might have bitten off more than he could chew. But, unfortunately, having once given the impression of being knowledgeable, he was obliged to continue displaying his wisdom.

'All those plants we saw,' he said, 'are eaten by humans.'

'EATEN!' shrieked all the rabbits together. 'THEY'RE POISONOUS!'

Tawny Owl racked his brains for an explanation. To his chagrin, Whistler stole his thunder by answering first.

'It seems extraordinary, doesn't it?' he intoned in his lugubrious voice, 'but it's really quite simple. Although at this moment those crops we saw have enough chemicals on them to poison many of us, there is probably not sufficient strength in the poison to kill a human, although he would certainly suffer to a degree. But, of course, the essence of the matter is that the plants are not going to be eaten *now*. We can only assume that, in their usual efficient way, the humans have rid themselves of any competitors for their food by spraying them with chemicals which will have completely disappeared by the time they are to be eaten. The chemicals are produced to *serve* humans, not the other way about. Therefore they would be quite sure of their own safety in the matter before they ventured to use them.'

'I wonder,' mused Fox. 'Can humans always be right? It must need only a small error for them to put themselves at danger, using such terrifying materials.'

'That we shall never know,' Tawny Owl declared in his wisest tone, hoping to regain his status.

But Adder, as usual, seemed to be able to analyse his motive. With a chuckle as dry as a withered leaf, he said sarcastically, 'Tawny Owl is such a *sage*.'

While they lay talking in the lush grass, a man came into the field through a gate and, avoiding the cows, walked slowly along, looking down at the ground all the time as if he had lost something.

Kestrel noticed him and drew the others' attention to his presence. Normally, they would all have run at once into hiding, but for some reason the appearance of this particular human did not seem to them to pose a threat to their safety.

He was dressed in a duffle-coat and was carrying various instruments, some slung round his neck and others hanging by straps from his shoulders. The animals saw him stop suddenly and, excitedly disencumbering himself of the objects he carried, drop to his knees and look closely at the grass.

The animals looked from one to another in astonishment.

The man, whose excitement seemed to increase, began to write feverishly in a notebook, pausing every now and then to look at the particular spot on the ground that interested him. When he had finished writing, he put all his apparatus on one side and sat down two or three feet from the spot. Then, notebook in hand again, he endeavoured to sketch what he had been so closely examining.

The animals continued to watch with more curiosity, and they were particularly struck by the care and gentleness of the man's actions as he sketched, quite unaware of his audience. He finished his sketch and put away the notebook. Then, taking one of his instruments, he cut into the turf with the utmost delicacy, and removed a small sample of some plant that had obviously been the focus of his attention, and carefully put it into one of his containers. Having written the relevant details on the label, he lifted the container up to the light and began to study his sample from every angle, with a look of profound pleasure.

A total silence had descended on the watching beasts and birds, and the sound of Toad clearing his throat seemed excessively loud.

'My friends,' he said in an awestruck tone, '*that* is a Naturalist.'

The animals' faces took on an expression of wonder, almost of reverence.

'I have seen such humans before,' Whistler admitted. 'I remember two occasions when the quarry was visited by a human, like this one carrying all sorts of boxes and equipment, who had come to look at the waterfowl.'

'Why do they do that?' asked Squirrel.

'Strange to say, there *are* some humans who are interested in the welfare of wild creatures,' the heron explained.

'It's these very people we have to thank for White Deer Park,' Toad pointed out eagerly. 'It is they who are responsible for the creation of those havens for wild life they call Nature Reserves.'

'It's only when you learn of such kindness and interest in us creatures,' said Badger, 'that you recall that the human race is, after all, a brother species.'

'I shall never consider myself even remotely related to a race who can deliberately arrange to poison every living thing in an area, for reasons that arise solely from their own arrogance and greed,' said the fatalistic Adder.

'Those are strong words, Adder,' said Fox, 'but I'm sure we all take your point. In my view, which may be a selfish one, cruelty of a sort where there is some purpose to it, is not as bad as the senseless cruelty practised by those humans who delight in hunting a wild creature to its death, simply for what they call sport.'

'And don't forget shooting!' said Hare. 'That's *sport* too!'

'But even then, you see,' said Fox, 'it has a purpose, when they afterwards eat what they shoot.'

'It really is extraordinary,' said Vixen, 'that one species can produce specimens who differ so much in their behaviour that they could themselves become enemies. I'm thinking of our Naturalist, and the huntsman. One is so friendly to us, he feels he must lend us his protection; the other sees us merely as something to torment for his own enjoyment.'

'One seeks to preserve, the other to destroy,' Whistler summed up.

'I shall never understand humans,' said Mole.

While they had been talking, the Naturalist had taken a pair of field-glasses and was scanning the sky in an idle moment for something to watch.

'Kestrel, why don't you help him out?' suggested Fox. 'There doesn't seem to be anything for him to look at.'

'Yes, don't let's disappoint the poor creature,' said Adder sarcastically, 'when he's come all the way here to look at nothing.'

Fox could not help smiling. 'Adder, really . . .!' he began. 'Don't you have any sympathies at all?'

'Not for humans,' drawled the snake.

'But surely even you recognize that the Human Race isn't all bad?' persisted Fox.

'Pooh!' said Adder. 'Humans like that one you all seem so fond of are very much in the minority. And don't think he wouldn't change towards us if *his* food supply ran out.'

'You're such a pessimist, Adder,' said Toad.

'I'm merely stating the obvious,' he said. 'Humans always have, and always will consider themselves and their needs first. Oh, there might be a few of your precious Nature Reserves around. But if land should become scarce, and humans find what they've got is not enough, they'll jolly soon forget all about their high ideals of protecting their brother species! They'll take every inch before they remember our existence.'

'There's no need to be so bitter,' said Toad indignantly, feeling in his heart of hearts that Adder was right, but not wanting to admit it.

'You all know as well as I do,' Adder insisted, 'that if it should ever come to a choice between *their* continued existence and *our* continued existence, not one human would hesitate a second before deciding.'

The animals fell silent. Adder seemed to have found an irrefutable argument that was infinitely depressing to them. He looked round at them triumphantly.

'Let us hope, then,' said Vixen, 'for their sake, as well as ours, that situation is never reached.'

'I'm sure it won't be – in our lifetime,' Badger said, in an effort to be comforting. 'Perhaps it never will be.'

For some reason Toad felt himself bound to defend the conception of Nature Reserves. 'I don't know why you bothered to join us,' he said in an aggrieved tone to Adder, 'if you have no faith in White Deer Park.'

'I didn't think my faith was in question,' the snake replied easily. 'The point I was making was what might occur if and when our human friends find they are short of land. I realize it's something that will only occur in the future. Nevertheless, you won't have to look far to find a good illustration of my point. The very reason we are here now is, in case you've forgotten, because land that was once left wild was seized, without compunction, by humans for their own purposes.'

'But Farthing Wood,' argued Toad, 'had not been set aside specifically for the use of wild creatures as a Reserve.'

'Can't we get off this dismal subject?' asked Weasel. 'We can't foretell the future, thank heavens, and I've a suspicion that neither can our clever, all-knowing humans.'

'I agree,' said Fox. 'This sort of argument doesn't help any of us. We're in danger of losing sight of our objective – our only objective – which is to reach White Deer Park.' Despite himself, he found his voice rising as he spoke and he finished up glaring at Adder.

'I'm sorry,' said Adder with a leer that belied his words, 'I meant no offence. I shan't say another word.'

'Good,' said Toad under his breath, but just loud enough to be overheard.

The innocent Naturalist who had prompted the discussion was preparing to leave the meadow, having found nothing else in which to interest himself.

'It seems such a shame when we're all here so close,' said Fox. 'Kestrel, won't you go?'

'Delighted,' said Kestrel, and uttering one of his loudest cries, launched himself upwards with the speed of a rocket.

Against the broad backcloth of sky, he began to under-take a series of acrobatics of the utmost virtuosity: hovering, diving, somersaulting with such breathtaking speed that his friends below felt like cheering.

'Kew, kew,' he called continually as the Naturalist, forgetful of his collection of instruments and paraphernalia, followed his every movement through the field-glasses in spellbound admiration.

It was not long before Whistler decided he, too, had things of interest to show this appreciative human spectator and, after executing a number of preparatory whistles as he flapped his wings, eventually joined Kestrel in the air at a considerably lower height.

There was not much he could do, apart from showing off the majestic motion of his huge wing-beats, but the animals watching the Naturalist's reaction, all felt that he now found the larger bird's appearance of more interest. Kestrel seemed to have the same feeling for, after a little longer in the sky, with a particularly spectacular dive he plummeted to the ground, and rejoined the party.

Fox next tried to persuade Tawny Owl to fly a little.

'No, I shall not make an exhibition of myself,' he answered pompously. 'Besides, I'm sure he's not only interested in bird life.'

'Would he be interested in me?' Mole squeaked excitedly. 'I could show him how quickly I can dig a tunnel!'

Fox laughed. 'Mole, really! How would he see you if you're inside a tunnel?'

'Well, yes, I forgot that,' said the subdued Mole.

'I'll tell you what we'll do,' said Badger. 'He doesn't want to see a lot of animals trying to show him how clever, or agile, or swift-running they can be. He's not at a circus. I'm sure what would interest him more than anything is to see us all simply walking in formation through the field together. I bet *that* would surprise him more than anything. After all, how many humans can have seen a motley collection of wild life such as we are, all strolling amicably in a bunch? Why, he would never forget such a sight to his last day.'

'An excellent idea, Badger,' Tawny Owl was gracious enough to admit. 'I'll join you in that with pleasure.'

The animals waited until Whistler finally returned, and then, automatically taking up their usual travelling positions, they filed slowly and deliberately through the grass, keeping about twenty yards' distance from the Naturalist. Mole and Toad insisted on walking too, and the three birds fluttered along in advance of the column.

Without saying a word, Adder had tagged along behind, and none of the others dared remark on it for fear of upsetting him.

The Naturalist spotted the movements of the birds first, and then the procession on the ground caught his eye. He pressed the field-glasses harder and harder against his face, unable to believe what he saw. But as the movement continued, he realized that what he was witnessing was, in fact, a unique wonder of nature. When the animals reached the far end of the field, he sank to the ground and began to scribble feverishly in his notebook. They watched him then for some time.

'Your idea certainly seemed to create an impression, Badger,' said Fox.

'We've made his day,' Badger chuckled gleefully. 'He'll never forget us.'

'*We* all seem to have forgotten something, though,' said Tawny Owl. 'Our empty stomachs!'

30

The church

The animals spent the remaining few hours before darkness out of sight under the thick hedge. When it was dark enough, they set off singly, or in small groups, to forage and satisfy their ravenous hunger. Fox told them they could have all the time they wanted to accomplish this very necessary and enjoyable task, as they were to have a day's complete rest before continuing their journey through the nearby town. Only Kestrel and Whistler were left in the meadow, intermittently chatting and dozing through the night. Their needs had been satisfied while the daylight held out; Kestrel had hunted from the air, while Whistler had flown a considerable distance before finding a stream where he could indulge his favourite pastime of fishing.

Mole, too, had no need to leave the meadow. He merely looked for a soft piece of ground, and with a speed greatly accelerated by his hunger, dug himself towards his dinner.

On the animals' return, they went straight to sleep in the thickest part of the hedge and slept the clock round until dusk the following day.

They woke in stages, completely refreshed, and with healthy appetites again. This time Fox told them to eat enough to last them for the next stage of the journey only, and to be as quick as they could about it, as their route now ran through the town, which they could only risk crossing at the dead of night.

When they were ready to leave, the night had become several degrees cooler, and a gusty breeze was blowing. Toad had told them that if they were careful there was not a lot to worry about, as it was quite a small town and had been very quiet when he had passed through it before during the night hours. At his direction Fox avoided the main street, but led the animals along a series of lanes and alleys, each of which was bordered by high brick walls.

The party kept close against these walls, on the darker side of the alleys, and were really quite inconspicuous as the passages were very murky and badly lit. When they came out of the last lane some spots of rain began to fall. This increased very quickly to a heavy shower, but the

animals felt it was to their advantage, as the few humans who might be abroad would be looking for shelter.

'The next bit's the worst,' said Toad. 'We have to cross the town square. But don't worry; it should be deserted at this time of night.'

They crossed the road that lay in front of them and entered the square from one corner via an empty shopping colonnade. This square contained an island of flagstones and trees, surrounded on all sides by roads, pavements and shops.

They quickly crossed to the island, and at once froze. Under a pair of lime trees, whose thick foliage afforded excellent shelter from the rain, a group of about a dozen humans, mostly courting couples, was standing.

'No use stopping, Fox,' whispered Toad. 'You must go on. They're not likely to do anything.'

Fox and Vixen broke into a trot, and the other animals followed suit as they passed the lime trees, and made their way to the far end of the island. Luckily the dim lighting in the square and the hard rain combined to screen the column of animals from detection.

They left the square and, turning a corner, found themselves in a market-place. Empty crates and boxes and small heaps of straw, paper and squashed fruit and cabbage-leaves lined the sides of this deserted spot, normally so crowded with eager, jostling shoppers.

'Ugh, what filth these humans make,' growled Adder, as he slithered across the muddy cobbles.

The rain fell harder and harder, and the wind dashed it against their faces in squalls, almost blinding them.

'We can't take much more of this, Fox,' Fieldmouse called from the midst of the soaked, struggling mass of mice.

'It's not much further now,' Toad encouraged them. 'Once we're out of the town we can stop.'

The animals made the best progress they could, and

eventually the last shop, the last pavement, the last house was passed. Now that they were able to stop for a rest, they did not at all want to do so. There was absolutely no shelter from the stinging rain. They were surrounded by open playing-fields, devoid of trees or any kind of wind-break.

'This is dreadful,' wailed Squirrel. 'Our fur is so drenched and matted together, we'll all catch our deaths.'

'We came through a storm before,' Hedgehog observed. 'I don't think any casualties were suffered.'

'Nevertheless, it's no less uncomfortable the second time,' Squirrel insisted.

'What about us?' said Vole. 'We voles, and the fieldmice, will be drowned if we stay here in the open.'

Fox looked all round, his brow furrowed as he strained to make out some object in the vicinity where they could take shelter.

'I can't see *anything*,' he said in despair to Toad.

'I can,' said Vixen. 'It looks like a church. At any rate, it's a big building – on the other side of these fields – look!'

Fox could just make out a dark mass looming in the near distance.

'Come on, my gallant little friends,' he urged. 'One last effort and we're home and dry.'

'Just to be dry would be something,' Squirrel muttered.

'Supposing it's shut?' said the pessimistic Vole.

'If it *is* a church there's sure to be a porch we can shelter under,' said Fox, trying to sound confident.

'Well, don't let's waste time,' said Squirrel, in a weary sort of whine.

Fox started off across the fields, Vixen at his side, with Badger, the hares, Weasel and the rabbits close behind. The squirrels, their usually bushy tails plastered with wet, were a sorry sight as they ran nimbly in their wake. The hedgehogs, whom rain did not bother very much, and the soaked voles and fieldmice were last, save for Adder.

266

There was a second hazard for the mice, for, because of their size, the heaviness of the drops was an additional hardship. Yet the sight of the church looming nearer and nearer drove them on, with its promise of eventual comfort and shelter.

So the animals arrived beneath the building's towering dark walls, tired, cold, soaked and shivering. The mice were the last to arrive, uttering piteous little cries of misery.

Fox looked at them with a forlorn expression. 'I . . . I'm afraid there's no porch,' he told them hesitantly.

Some of the voles and fieldmice broke down at the news. To have come through all they had, and then to find no relief, was too hard to bear. They huddled together on the muddy ground and sobbed heartbreakingly.

'But just a minute, my little friends,' said Fox, 'perhaps we can get inside. We're not beaten yet. Badger, look after them. I'll have a scout round.' After shaking his saturated coat with a single vigorous movement, Fox began inspecting the walls.

The animals watched him despairingly, while the cruel rain relentlessly lashed down as if it were trying to beat

them into the ground. Tawny Owl flew up to the steeple and took up a perch in the belfry, where it was dry. Kestrel joined him, but Whistler remained on the ground standing with his great wings extended as an umbrella over the cowering mice.

Fox disappeared round the other side of the church.

'How much longer will this rain continue?' groaned Rabbit. 'I'm sure we shall all end up being drowned.' He looked with distaste at Toad who, alone amongst the animals, was enjoying every minute of the rainfall, and was busy splashing about in a large puddle.

'Extraordinary habits he has,' Rabbit muttered to Hare.

'Yes,' Hare replied, 'water is certainly a tonic to Toad. Just look how his skin glistens – as if he had put on a new one.'

A shout from Fox made them all prick up their ears.

'Quickly! Round here!' he was calling from round the corner. 'We're in luck!'

In one mass the party of animals scurried round to the other side. Fox proudly indicated a greyish shape that was draped against the brickwork.

'Well, what is it?' Badger asked, almost irritably.

'It's a hole!' said Fox triumphantly.

'There's no hole there,' said Rabbit peevishly. 'What have you . . .?'

'Of course, you can't see the hole,' Fox interrupted him. 'They've covered it with this material' – he indicated the greyish shape which in fact was canvas – 'but we can soon get behind that!'

He at once began to paw an opening, tugging the material away from the wall.

'Ooh, there *is* a hole!' cried one of the fieldmice.

Fox climbed over the broken brickwork that framed the hole and looked back at the animals, all of whom were still watching him, except Vixen who had at once followed him inside.

'What are you waiting for?' Fox asked. 'It's dry in here. It smells strongly of humans, but it's as dark as Badger's set. There's no one about.'

The animals needed no second bidding, and they scrambled together through the hole, Whistler stepping awkwardly after them in his upright gait. Adder was the last to slither between the canvas and the bricks.

'I think Tawny Owl and Kestrel ought to be with us,' Fox said. 'Whistler, will you fetch them?'

The heron cheerfully stepped back into the rain, and soon the three birds appeared together on the threshold.

'Are we complete?' asked Fox, beginning to see through the gloom.

'No,' Adder drawled. 'It seems that Toad finds the rain preferable to our company.'

'Oh, drat the fellow!' exclaimed Fox. 'All right, I'll go this time. Vixen dear, would you help Badger look for a suitable hiding-place? We want somewhere dry and inconscpicuous, and free from draughts.'

'But I can't see anything, Fox,' she protested mildly.

'We could do with your glow-worms now, Badger,' chuckled Weasel.

'Leave it to me,' pleaded Mole. 'Darkness is nothing to me. I'm used to it. I prefer it to sunlight really, you know,' he added, trying to impress. 'Oh yes, the darker the better.'

'No wonder he's as blind as a bat,' said Adder maliciously, under his breath.

'He's just trying to be helpful,' said Badger pointedly, rounding on the snake. 'But, of course, *you* wouldn't understand that.'

Adder remained unabashed.

Mole led the party, at a necessarily slow pace, down one of the side aisles. The animals' feet produced a variety of clipping and padding noises against the worn stone floor, while Adder's scaly body made a dry, swishing rasp as he writhed along behind them. In the almost total darkness

269

the animals had no idea where they were going, and followed the confident Mole quite blindly.

The little velvet-coated animal went forward purposefully, using his instinct to find the darkest corner of a thoroughly dark building. He turned a few corners, and threaded the line of animals between pews, and eventually stopped in the narrow space behind the organ. Here it really was pitch-dark, but in its musty seclusion it was as dry as dust and completely sheltered from any unwelcome draughts.

'Where have you brought us, Mole?' asked Badger.

'I don't know,' Mole replied, 'but it . . . um . . . *seems* all right.'

Fox, in the meantime, had brought Toad into the church, and was sniffing and groping about for a sign of his friends.

'Do you see anything?' Toad asked him.

'No,' he replied, 'but I can smell their damp bodies.'

An unexpected flapping of wings above them made them both jump, but Tawny Owl had appeared to guide them to the hiding-place.

'Good old Owl,' said Fox, trying to mask his momentary fright. 'Well, we should all get a good rest tonight.'

'I'm not so sure I approve of sheltering in a place that seems to have such a magnetic influence over humans,' Tawny Owl remarked. 'But I suppose there is no choice.'

'It's certainly better than being out in the rain,' Fox laughed.

'Personally, I don't like these very dry spots,' Toad said, shaking his head. 'I always wonder if my skin might crack.'

'Nonsense,' Fox told him. 'Anyway, it's only for a day. I should have thought you were tired.'

'I am,' admitted Toad, as Tawny Owl alighted on the back of a pew and then fluttered to the ground.

When all the animals were together, they began to ask Toad in sleepy voices how far away they now were from their destination.

'About a day's travelling, I should think,' he answered. 'However,' he added, as assorted squeals of delight and excitement were heard, 'I can't be absolutely sure, because we've gone a little bit out of the way in our search for shelter. I didn't ever come past this church before, but I do know that, having come through that town, the Park is now very, very close.'

'Do you think we'll have any difficulty in getting back on the correct route?' asked Hedgehog.

'Of course not,' Toad said cheerfully. 'It only needs Kestrel to do a little flying some time tomorrow, provided this rain has stopped. Why, I'm sure he could see the Park from here.'

'As soon as it's light enough . . .' murmured Kestrel, as he tucked his head under his wing.

When he emerged from the building early the next morning, leaving his friends sleeping, Kestrel was pleased to see the countryside looking so clear and fresh. The air was cool and crisp, and the sky blue again, as if washed clean of clouds. The wet grass gleamed and sparkled in the sunlight.

Kestrel flew lazily aloft and stretched his wing muscles. After enjoying a series of swoops and dives, he began to look around him, at the landscape. Sure enough, in one direction, an area of parkland was easily discernible. Kestrel could see stretches of fencing and rolling grassy country, with dark patches that he recognized as bracken, and clusters of trees that were copses or woods. The Edible Frogs' pond was not visible from Kestrel's position, but he decided to fly and have a closer look. There was no longer any doubt as to the park's identity when, as he approached he saw several white blobs moving over the grass, which gradually took form and shape as the very white deer that gave the park its name. As he drew near this place that the party of animals and birds had been struggling to reach for so long, Kestrel felt that their arrival, which now seemed inevitable, should

271

be suitably memorable, and a plan began to form in his mind.

Back in the church, his friends were not feeling so confident of finally reaching their new home or even of getting safely away from the building, for daylight had brought workmen along to continue their repair work on the broken wall. The sound of human tools banging and chipping at the very place they had expected to use as their exit and, worse still, raucous human voices, awoke and seriously alarmed the animals. In reply to a barrage of questions all more or less

encompassing the one demand of what was to be done next, Fox replied grimly that for the present they should sit tight.

'That's all very well,' said Rabbit. 'But what if those men wall us in?'

'There are such things as doors in churches, you know,' Tawny Owl remarked testily.

Rabbit felt foolish, although he tried not to show it. In this he failed dismally. 'Anyway,' he said sullenly, 'there's no knowing when the doors will be opened.'

'Oh, it won't be long.' Fox tried to sound unconcerned. 'Somebody's bound to come sooner or later, with these workmen here.'

'Actually, Rabbit has got a point,' said Hare, surprising his distant cousin by siding with him for once. 'If a human *does* come to open one of the doors, we might well be too slow to get out before it's closed again, and in any case he's hardly likely to hold it open for us while we file through.'

Fox started to think and, as he had begun to do more and more, consulted Vixen.

'It's safer to stay here at the moment,' the animals heard her say to him in a low voice.

Fox looked round at his companions, studying every face. 'Does anyone want to make a dash for it now?' he asked.

No one replied, but there were sounds of shifting feet and one or two coughs.

'Vixen and I are quite ready to accompany any of you who wish to chance it now, rather than finding we might have left it too late,' Fox said.

'We'll probably have a better opportunity later,' said Badger in his soothing voice. 'I think an attempt to leave now might prove to be rather foolhardy.'

The concerted murmurs of the party seemed to express approval of Badger's opinion.

'Then it's decided,' said Fox. 'We wait.'

The noise of the workmen continued unabated, and the animals remained in their hiding-place, listening with sinking hearts to the ceaseless hammering and shouts, and wondering what Kestrel was doing. After some hours, during which time none of them spoke very much, the noise came to an end. Fox looked at each of his companions significantly, as if mentally warning them to be ready.

They waited for the voices of the workmen, who were obviously preparing to leave, to diminish. The light inside the church, filtering through the coloured panes, and striking straight through the clear glass, had moved gradually round the building. A shaft of sunlight, illuminating a thousand dancing motes of dust, now shone obliquely on to the organ pipes, in front of which the crouching animals were all geared for flight.

The rough voices were retreating; there seemed to be only a matter of seconds longer to wait, when a swooping form suddenly alighted in front of them. Kestrel had returned.

'It's no good,' he said immediately. 'Stay where you are. There's a throng of people on the way here, and two of them are just about to open the main door.'

Even as he finished speaking the noises of a handle being turned, followed by creaking hinges, reached their ears. Instinctively they all cowered closer to the floor. New, quieter human voices could be heard.

'What about the wall?' whispered Fox. 'Surely we could still make a dash for it before any more arrive?'

'No, it's hopeless.' Kestrel shook his head. 'They've bricked up the lower part of the hole completely. There's only a small gap left now, about four feet from the ground.'

'Oh no!' Fox groaned. 'We're stuck fast.'

'But we can't remain here,' protested Hedgehog, in an agitated voice. 'It's not dark any more. We'll be discovered in no time.'

'On the contrary,' Fox told him. 'We're as safe as we can be under the circumstances. We're screened all round pretty well, and there is no room for any humans to come close to us. And don't forget, they don't know we're here. They won't come looking for us.'

'I'm sorry I didn't leave with you now, Kestrel,' said Whistler, who always slept well and had not woken as early as the hawk.

'You needn't have come back,' Fox remarked. 'Now you're stuck with us.'

'Kestrel's a good friend,' said Mole.

'Well, I didn't want you to move from here,' the hawk said, smiling in a pleased way. 'I thought I might have been too late to stop you.'

More voices came through the open door, and more steps echoed on the stone floor. There was a scraping of chairs, and one set of footsteps came nearer and nearer to the animals and then stopped just the other side of the organ which sheltered them. A sound of rustling papers and the varied noises of someone settling himself into a seat were then audible, so that they knew one of the humans was very close.

'Just when we're so close to home,' muttered Toad.

His unconscious use of the word 'home' to describe somewhere none of his companions, except Kestrel, had ever seen, acted as a tonic on the whole party. It reminded them all with a peculiar force that not only was their long journey nearly over, but that in a matter of hours their lives would no longer be governed by the factors of how far they could walk in one day, or how to negotiate some difficult obstacle. They all realized that their escape from the church represented the very last of the obstacles which they had to surmount, before they could begin to enjoy a normal and peaceful life again – something they had almost forgotten how to do. So the thought of that home, and all it meant to each weary creature in his own particular way, produced a resolve, stronger than at any time on their journey, that they would not be stopped now from reaching it by any power, human or otherwise. Each animal sensed this fresh upsurge of moral strength in his companions, and felt his confidence rise.

'We can wait a little longer,' said Weasel philosophically.

'It's only a matter of time,' remarked Mole, who was already feeling pleased at Fox's indirect compliment on the hiding-place he had found them.

'As far as I can see it's a *waste* of time,' whispered Adder. But the party settled down silently, while the echoing footsteps and the low-pitched human voices increased in number.

Finally the shuffling of feet, and the creaking and scraping of pews and chairs, and even the whispering voices subsided, and it seemed as if the church and its people had entered a period of quiet, of expectancy.

The animals had all begun to think that their ordeal might, after all, not be so grim when, with a deafening, blaring shock, the organ pipes behind them suddenly pealed forth.

The noise was so terrifying and sudden that the whole party of animals leapt up, panic-stricken, and scattered all over the church in a sort of zoological eruption.

The birds flew up to the rafters where the terrible sounds of the organ reverberated tremendously, causing them to fly in every direction in their efforts to escape the noise.

Fox and Vixen dashed straight down the nave in blind terror, and more by luck than judgement found themselves at the open door. The voles and fieldmice, the rabbits and hares and the squirrels scurried to every corner, some of them getting under chairs, producing shrieks and screams of alarm from the female congregation. The men, no less astounded, uttered gruff shouts and exclamations, while the Vicar, who was about to perform a wedding ceremony, dropped his book as Badger lumbered against his legs. Weasel, Mole, Toad and the hedgehogs made for the opposite end of the church, each taking a different and completely motiveless route, their only thought being to get away from that horrifying machine. Only Adder, fortunately for him, was not noticed as he slid his slender body along every hidden crevice and crack he could find to reach the door.

For a few moments pandemonium held sway, but with the ceasing of the wedding music by the astonished organist, the animals' panic was calmed sufficiently, to turn their flight towards the one safe direction.

With the gradual disappearance of the swifter-running animals, the congregation's initial amazement changed to excitement, and soon a general buzz of chatter filled the church.

As Fox and Vixen hurtled forth from the doorway, the bride, with her escorting father, and bridesmaids, were just approaching it. They stopped dead, speechless, only to see, after a short interval, a badger, an assortment of rabbits, squirrels and hares and a weasel gallop out of the door and race off in the direction the two foxes had taken.

The bride looked towards her father, as if silently asking him if this were some sort of omen for her imminent marriage, but his amazement prevented him from forming any words and he merely stammered incoherently. Eventually he seemed to recall their reason for being there, and he began to lead his daughter forward again.

As they were about to enter the church, two birds shot past like bullets, and a third one, of huge proportions, flew directly at their faces, flapping its wings frantically in the confined space, and only veered upward at the last minute, making a rhythmical whistling as it soared higher and higher.

The poor bride shrieked with fright, and four sympathetic echoes came from the bridesmaids. The father's alarm now turned to anger. Telling them to wait on the threshold, he entered the church to discover who was behind the production of what he deemed a very bad effort at a wedding prank. No sooner was he inside than his legs were assailed by a group of scuttling hedgehogs who managed to scramble past him into the open. He began to call out furiously for the member of the congregation whom he thought was responsible for perpetrating such an outrage on his daughter's wedding day. Of course nobody replied, and the Vicar came forward, wringing his hands, and with a soothing voice tried to calm the irate gentleman.

After a minute or two the bride and bridesmaids could no longer bear being kept in ignorance of the matter, and they entered the church in their turn, unaccompanied by the expected strains of the organ.

While the humans stood around and debated, some heatedly and others more calmly, the cause of such an extraordinary occurrence, the smaller animals still inside the building were able, one by one, to make their escape unnoticed. Mole was the last to reach the door, but just outside he found Toad and Adder, trying to look inconspicuous by the wall.

'They went that way,' Toad said, indicating the direction the swifter animals had taken. 'They'll probably wait for us somewhere.'

'I can't see anyone,' said Mole, peering ahead.

'Of course you can't,' said Adder impatiently. 'I'm surprised you could even see your way to the door.'

'Oh, Adder, don't be unkind,' said Mole, badly hurt at the reference to his purblindness. 'Let's . . . let's go on together, shall we?'

'Not much else we can do,' muttered the snake, who felt Mole was to blame for their present position by choosing their hiding-place by the organ pipes.

'I'm sure when they've recovered themselves, Fox will send someone back to help us,' said Toad confidently. 'It'll probably be Kestrel.'

A little further on they caught up with some of the mice, who had been constantly looking back over their shoulders in dire fear of being pursued.

The humans, however, were far too busy arguing and talking inside the church for any of them to think of looking for the cause of the disturbance outside, and pretty soon all the animals had put enough distance behind them for the renewed sounds of the organ not to reach their ears.

31

The final lap

'It's not like Fox to forget about us,' remarked one of the fieldmice, after they had been walking together for some time through the soaked, glistening grass.

'Don't worry,' said Toad. 'They'll all be waiting for us in a safe spot somewhere. We'll keep going.'

'I'm almost as wet as I was in the storm,' grumbled Vole, who had been one of the last animals to get out of the church. 'This long grass is drenching me.'

'Well, our troubles will be over soon,' said Mole happily. 'I can scarcely believe it, you know,' he added to Toad.

'I shouldn't get carried away just yet,' warned Adder. 'Anything can happen.'

'Pooh, nonsense!' said Toad. 'We're as good as there. There's no doubt in my mind, at any rate.'

'Will you live in the pond with the Edible Frogs?' Mole asked him.

'Certainly not,' Toad replied. 'I shall visit the pond, of course. But, after the places I've seen, my horizons are wider than the narrow world of mud and weed they cling to.'

Adder's face took on a subtle expression. 'You must

introduce me to these friends of yours,' he lisped. 'They sound most interesting.'

Toad looked a little embarrassed, and feigned deafness. But the snake persisted. 'You will, won't you?' he urged. 'I want to meet them.'

Toad coughed awkwardly. 'H'm, well . . . er . . . the trouble is, you see, Adder, it's really a question of . . . er . . . whether they want to meet *you*.'

Adder was not offended. He chuckled drily, and leered at Mole.

Soon after this, Toad's faith in Fox was found to be justified. They heard the unmistakable sound of Whistler's wings, and they called out together to him: 'Here! Here!'

The heron landed and, having greeted them, stepped along with them on his stilt-like legs. As he made no reference to Fox, Toad was forced to prompt him.

'Is it good news or bad news?' he asked unobtrusively.

'Oh, good news,' replied Whistler brightly. 'Very good news.'

He said no more and lapsed into a pensive mood. His companions were puzzled.

'Is . . . is everyone all right?' Mole enquired.

'Yes. They're fine. I'm sorry,' said the heron, rousing himself, 'the nearer we get to our destination the more I find my thoughts turning to . . . er . . . well, to put it delicately, the chance of . . . er . . . perhaps meeting someone of interest in the Park.'

Only Adder divined the meaning behind these words, but as such matters did not interest him in the least, he remained silent. Mole and Toad were completely nonplussed.

'Well, have we *far* to go?' Vole asked the huge bird irritably.

Whistler apologized again. 'I'm so sorry,' he said, 'I've been keeping you in the dark – very wrong of me. They're all waiting for us . . . er . . . under a holly bush, actually. It's not too far now.'

281

'So the party's complete?' asked Toad.

'Yes, when *we've* arrived,' said Whistler. 'We're very lucky.'

The smaller creatures, who felt they had been quite inconspicuous before, felt considerably ill at ease while Whistler, dwarfing them all, continued to step slowly along at their side. They all felt sure he could not have directed more attention to them if he had been a notice board, but none of them, not even Adder, liked to ask him to go further off, when he had come back specially to look for them.

In fact, Whistler was so absorbed with his thoughts about 'the interesting creature in the Park' that he might meet, that he was not even aware that he was on the ground instead of in the air, and the idea that his noticeable size might attract unwanted attention to the little group completely escaped him.

However, within the half-hour they all arrived safely at the holly bush, and the whole company began to feel very merry, congratulating each other and joking, and beginning to talk about the things they were going to do when they reached the Park.

'I shall eat a huge meal, and then sleep for a week,' declared Tawny Owl, who had had more than his fair share just recently of sleeping and waking at the wrong times.

'I shall look round at once for a suitable spot to construct a new set,' said Badger. He sighed. 'How nice it will be to sleep underground again, without fear of being disturbed – all on my own again, too. How peaceful!'

'Oh, there's nothing like an underground home,' agreed Mole. 'I shall build the finest network of tunnels any mole has ever dreamed of,' he boasted.

'I'm looking forward to living a normal life up a tree,' said Squirrel. 'Ever since we left Farthing Wood, we squirrels have lived what is for us a completely unnatural existence. We've walked great distances over land, and we've slept at ground level. So just to race up and down some good solid oak trunks, and to enjoy the springy feeling of branches and twigs under our feet will be our reward for all that.'

'To be able to run free, with my family, in any direction, is my dream,' Hare told them.

'To be able to nibble at leisure,' remarked Rabbit.

'To swim when I want to!' cried Toad.

'To go foraging in the moonlight,' said Hedgehog.

'And to feel free from the constant necessity of hiding oneself,' said Weasel.

'To have the time to look for the best berries,' murmured Fieldmouse.

'And seeds,' added Vole.

'To meet someone of one's own kind again,' sighed Whistler, 'er . . . that is, of *particular* interest.'

The animals looked towards Fox. 'What about you?' they asked him.

Fox looked lovingly at Vixen. 'There's my answer,' he smiled.

Vixen smiled back.

'To be, above all,' said Kestrel, 'safe from interfering hands, and to know our home is safe from encroachment.'

'And,' drawled Adder, 'for this everlasting trek to come to an end.'

The animals laughed heartily, and as they fell silent, found themselves all beaming at one another afresh.

'Well, everyone, what do you say?' asked Fox brightly, catching the mood of the moment. 'Shall we go on now, or wait until tonight?'

'Now!' cried the majority of the animals immediately.

'Any dissenters?' asked Fox.

'I think I speak for all of the fieldmice, and us voles, when I say we would find it more comfortable to travel later,' Vole announced. But he had miscalculated. A good number of the tiny creatures contradicted him, by declaring themselves as ready as anyone to leave at once.

'Good, that's settled,' said Fox promptly. 'I'm afraid you're very much in the minority, Vole. Everyone is eager to go.'

'And why not?' Kestrel wanted to know. 'The weather is fine and clear; it's the time when most humans are indoors eating; and we can all be inside the Park in an hour or so,' he added persuasively. 'Wouldn't you say so, Fox?'

'Er . . . probably. Toad, what would you say?'

'I should say, now that Kestrel has put us back on the shortest route, two hours at the most,' Toad calculated. 'I can *feel* the nearness of the Park, but we might be just a *little* slower than usual, because . . . well, if you've no objection, I'd rather like to walk the final stretch myself.'

'Yes! Yes! And me!' cried Mole predictably.

'Very commendable of you, Mole,' remarked Badger, raising an eyebrow, 'but are you quite sure? You know . . . er . . . we don't want to be held up at the last minute?'

'I shan't hold anyone up,' Mole said hotly. 'I've just walked all the way from the church, and I'm not a bit tired.'

'Good chap, good chap,' Badger muttered consolingly. 'I'll walk with you.'

'Right.' Fox got up. 'Toad, you must head the column and lead us in.'

'Very appropriate,' Kestrel agreed. 'Just what I'd hoped for.'

This allusion to some arrangement or idea of his own carried no significance for any of the party, and Kestrel's plan retained its secrecy.

Then, with Toad proudly walking in front, his skin glistening with moisture and his beautiful eyes glowing like twin jewels in the sunlight, the animals set off across the rain-spangled ground on the very last stage of their journey.

No more than a thousand yards away, the inhabitants of White Deer Park were grouping at an agreed point a short distance from where the heroic band from Farthing Wood were expected to enter the Reserve. At the instigation of Kestrel, who had paid a visit early that morning, the assorted birds and beasts were preparing a jubilant welcome for the creatures whose exploits they were all now familiar with.

Carried for the most part by the winged population of that part of the country, word had spread of the approach of the Farthing Wood community, although precious little had actually been seen of them because of the extreme caution they had exercised all along their route; something that they had gradually developed into a fine art. But sufficient glimpses of one or more members of the party had been caught, particularly during the Hunt and at the motorway, for their expectant hosts at White Deer Park to feel impatient for their arrival as creatures from the real Wild. The fact that the travels and adventures of Fox and Badger, Mole and Toad, Kestrel and Tawny Owl and Adder, and all their other companions, were already something of a legend, served to heighten the impatience of the indigenous fauna of the Nature Reserve.

The Edible Frogs were the inhabitants most inspired by the Farthing Wood odyssey, because they recognized in the animals' guide the very Toad whose acquaintance they had made four seasons ago, and who had spoken to them of the old home to which he must return. They were additionally excited because he alone of the already famous group of animals had made the perilous journey twice, once on his own, and now, retracing his steps in triumph, as the trusted guide of a wonderful brotherhood of wildlife.

So when Kestrel had actually flown into the Park on that morning and spoken to the old White Stag, the doyen of the deer-herd and acknowledged overlord of the Park, news had spread like wildfire of the approaching event that all had been waiting for, friend and foe alike. Natural enmity and rivalry were forgotten as the entire population massed to welcome their new neighbours.

Through his various lieutenants and subjects, the old Stag arranged the various groups of creatures by an ancient oak-stump, a focal point of the Reserve that was known to everyone. There were badgers and foxes and stoats, rabbits, moles, squirrels, hedgehogs, dormice, fieldmice and voles. There were weasels and shrews, toads and frogs, lizards, slow-worms, snakes and newts. There were rooks, crows, jays and jackdaws, pheasants and owls, nuthatches, tits and warblers. There were nightingales and hawks, pigeons, finches and woodpeckers, and there was one very interesting female heron. This magnificent assemblage of Nature spread like a moving tapestry of colour over the glistening grass, and was enhanced by the superb herd of white deer, mustering two hundred head, all of whom stood behind the massive form of the great Stag.

All through the afternoon they waited, every eye turned on the broken piece of fencing where Kestrel had promised he and his friends would enter their new home. At last the moment came.

The old Stag visibly stiffened as his weaker eyesight made out what the creatures all round him were already talking about. He held himself straight and erect, looking every inch a lord of the wild, as he prepared himself for his welcoming address.

Kestrel had alighted on a fence-post, indicating that the

party of travellers was about to appear. Sure enough, a few minutes afterwards, the column of animals came into sight, led by the faithful Toad. As they reached the fence, the animals stopped, looking in bewilderment at the vast array of creatures gathered to welcome them.

'Go on, Toad,' Kestrel said affectionately. 'You ought to go first.'

Kestrel's lack of hesitancy was enough to tell his friends that the welcoming party was no surprise to him. He smiled at their quizzical expressions.

'Don't keep them waiting,' he said. 'They've been expecting you for a long time.'

Toad looked from Kestrel to the reception and back again with some nervousness, but finally, with the urging of the other animals jostling behind him, he gave himself a little shake and passed through the gap.

The old Stag watched them come. Toad, whose speckled breast began to puff with pride as he advanced, was followed by Fox and Vixen, Weasel, the hares and rabbits; then came the hedgehogs and squirrels, the fieldmice and voles, and after them Mole, Badger and Adder. Finally, in the very rear, the three birds, Tawny Owl, Kestrel and Whistler, actually walked the last few yards.

The old Stag remained motionless until it was clear that the last of the party had entered White Deer Park. Then he lowered his great antlered head, and at once a tumultuous sound of cheers broke over the newcomers. There were shrieks and cackles, roars, squeaks, barks and croaks – in fact, welcoming shouts in every conceivable register of voice.

The old Stag walked forward to meet them and, beginning with the delighted Toad, greeted everyone personally, down to the very smallest and youngest fieldmice.

After this ceremony had been performed, the mass of cheering creatures flocked forward and surrounded the weary heroes, congratulating them anew with the utmost enthusiasm. Then, as if at a signal, they fell back as they divined that the great Stag was about to speak.

'We have all looked forward to this day,' he said, speaking for all the inhabitants of the Park, 'ever since we first heard from our feathered friends of your journey. Nothing I can say can add to the tremendous greeting you have already so deservedly received, except by summarizing everyone's feelings here today. On behalf of *all* the inhabitants of White Deer Park, may I say, quite simply, welcome.'

'Thank you most sincerely,' said Fox, 'for a welcome as heart-warming as it was unexpected. We had no idea our journey was of such interest to you.'

'Oh, my friend, you're all celebrities, you know,' returned the Stag. 'We all want to hear about your adventures, and

there's no one more eager than myself. But I know you must be tired, and we've no wish to exhaust you. Fox, if you'll bring your friends this way, we've prepared a spot where you can all rest without fear of disturbance for as long as you wish.'

'What wonderful kindness,' Fox responded on behalf of all.

The animals, after again exchanging many personal greetings with their new neighbours, followed the old Stag and his escort of young hinds to a soft, ferny hollow, surrounded by whispering birch trees, and strewn with dry grass specially cropped by the finest teeth of the herd. None of them was long in availing himself of this luxury. In reply to the Stag's kind enquiry as to when he might return, Fox said that by dusk they would all be completely refreshed, and would welcome his company and that of all his friends.

'What a marvellous reception,' Mole said when they were alone.

'I think I know whom we have to thank for the arrangements,' said Tawny Owl drily. But Kestrel just winked.

When the animals awoke, the ground had dried and the moon was gleaming, pouring its silver light through the leaves of the birch trees. Beyond the trees, it shone on the white coats of the assembled deer, giving them a ghost-like appearance.

Seeing signs of life in the hollow, the deer moved forward, and behind them, around them, above them, and intermingling with them, the other creatures of White Deer Park came to hear the story of the journey from Farthing Wood.

This pleasant duty was, of course, assigned to Badger who had finished composing the song that he had sung to his friends in the quarry.

Just before he began, the old Stag signed for everyone to be silent as, along a makeshift path behind the hollow, stepped a dark human figure.

'It's the warden on his rounds,' explained the deer. 'Nothing to fear from him.'

An excited cry from Vixen arrested every creature's attention. 'It's our Naturalist!' she cried. 'Look!'

And sure enough, now divested of his various accoutrements, the long-travelled band of animals was still able to recognize their friend from the cattle pasture, who had been so enthralled by their appearance.

'A cheerful ending indeed to our journey,' Badger remarked and, smiling happily at his audience, began his song.

Epilogue:
In the park

Now that the animals had at last reached their journey's end, they all found themselves so busy for the first week or so, establishing new homes and adapting themselves to a new life, that they scarcely caught a glimpse of each other.

For all of them the wide spaces of the Reserve were theirs to explore, without fear of hindrance or any human intervention. Unaccustomed to such peace, after weeks of stealth and caution on their journey, the animals spent whole days selecting and then rejecting sites for their new abodes, determined to settle only in areas that were the perfection of their individual ideas.

But eventually each animal was content, and then the bonds of mutual sympathy and comradeship that had been forged during their travels began to tug at every one of them.

There was a day when Mole, who had constructed a network of tunnels close to Badger's new set, dug his way into one of Badger's chambers, just as he had done in Farthing Wood.

As it was only early in the evening, Badger was still dozing. He grunted, and looked up. 'Oh, hullo, Mole,' he said drowsily. 'Well, this is a surprise.'

'A pleasant one, I hope?' Mole asked, a little hesitantly.

'Of course it is,' Badger replied quickly. 'Where have you been hiding yourself?'

'Oh, I've been busy making myself comfortable,' replied the little creature, wiping some stray specks of soil off his nose. 'So have you, no doubt.'

'Yes, indeed,' Badger nodded. 'But it's all done now.' He got up and shook himself. 'I haven't seen any of the others recently, have you? At least, not to talk to.'

'No,' said Mole. 'I only saw Weasel one evening, when I had to surface for a drink. I was thinking how nice it would be to see them all again.'

'Yes,' said Badger. 'We really ought to arrange something. I know where Fox and Vixen have settled. We could go and pay them a visit later on, if you like.'

'That *would* be nice,' agreed Mole.

The two animals continued talking while the evening wore on, exchanging views about their new home and neighbours, and about how quiet everything seemed. When

they sensed that it was quite dark outside, Badger led his friend to one of the exits and, after he had thoroughly tested the air for strange scents, they emerged together.

They found Vixen at home who told them Fox was out foraging, but he presently returned, accompanied by Tawny Owl.

All the creatures expressed great delight in seeing each other again, and Fox remarked that the need for companionship seemed to be making itself felt at about the same time in many of the Farthing Wood party, for on the previous day he had encountered Toad and Hare who had both suggested that they all meet in the Hollow.

It appeared, when they began to compare notes, that all of them had seen at least one of their old friends in the last day or two. Tawny Owl had been sought out by Kestrel, and the hawk had also spotted several of the voles and rabbits while he had been flying over the Park. Eventually, it transpired that the only one nobody had seen or, at least, heard of was Adder.

'He was never the most gregarious of fellows,' remarked Tawny Owl.

'Oh, Adder's all right when you get used to his strange ways,' said Badger. 'You've got to learn to take him with a pinch of salt.'

'At any rate we couldn't agree to meet up and leave him out,' said Mole loyally.

'I think I know where I might be able to find him,' said Fox.

The others looked at him, but he would not be drawn.

'Leave Adder to me,' he said. 'I'll get Toad to help me locate him. The rest of you can round up the others tomorrow, and we'll meet in the Hollow the next night.'

His friends agreed enthusiastically with this arrangement, and they parted happily.

The next day Fox found Toad, and mentioned his idea of Adder's whereabouts to him.

'The pond?' echoed Toad. 'Oh yes, he's been there watching the frogs every evening.'

Fox nodded. 'I thought as much,' he said. 'Let's go and see him.'

So Toad and Fox made their way to the pond, and there, by the water's edge, they found Adder slyly watching the antics of the plump green frogs with a greedy eye. He evinced not the slightest embarrassment at the arrival of the two beasts. 'Good evening,' he said calmly. 'I've been trying for some time to introduce myself to our new neighbours here, the Edible Frogs.'

'I don't know if you'll ever get the chance, as I personally advised them to spend as much of their time as they could in the centre of the pond,' Toad told him with some irony.

Adder again showed no trace of his feelings. He merely slid away from the pond's edge, and asked them to what he owed this unexpected pleasure.

'The whole party is meeting again tomorrow night,' said Fox. 'Will you come?'

'Certainly I'll come,' replied Adder, 'if you're sure my presence will be desired?'

'Of course it will,' Fox assured him. 'I'm sure the animals haven't forgotten that our success in reaching the Park is owed, to a large extent, to a certain action on your part.'

Adder, typically, was not inclined to acknowledge the compliment. 'Where do we meet?' he asked.

'In the Hollow,' answered Fox.

'I shall be there,' said Adder.

Fox and Vixen were the first to enter the Hollow on the next night, and they recalled how it had been the animals' first resting-place after their arrival in White Deer Park.

Their friends arrived at intervals. Tawny Owl came first,

and very soon Badger and Mole joined them. The squirrels turned up with Kestrel, whom they had awakened from his roost. He was still yawning.

Then there was a flurry of activity, as most of the animals yet to come arrived together – the voles, the fieldmice, the hedgehogs and the rabbits. While greetings all round were still being exchanged, Weasel, accompanied by the hare family, joined the gathering.

Shortly afterwards, with a slightly bashful air, Whistler stepped carefully into the Hollow, attended by another heron who looked round shyly.

'I hope you don't mind,' Whistler said apologetically as he introduced her to everyone, 'but my young friend here and I have lately become . . . well, almost inseparable.'

'We're delighted,' said Vixen. 'And how attractive she is.'

Whistler beamed, and the female heron coyly murmured something polite.

'A very *interesting* arrangement,' Tawny Owl said sarcastically, parodying Whistler's remarks during the final stages of their journey.

'There you are, Owl. It's not too late for you to follow suit,' Vixen replied with an impish grin, turning the tables on the other bird.

'Humph!' snorted Tawny Owl, ruffling his feathers in a rather disconcerted manner, and trying very hard to appear indifferent.

Fortunately the arrival of Adder diverted the party's attention and Tawny Owl was able to regain his composure.

'You're quite a stranger these days,' Badger remarked to the snake good-humouredly when it was his turn to greet him. 'Can we blame your seclusion on the wiles of a charming young female?'

'There's no need to blame my seclusion on anything except my choice in not visiting anybody,' Adder replied. 'However, if I should happen to come across a creature of the sort you describe, I suppose I shall be seen even less.' His sharp words were belied by a very deliberate grin which caused Badger to broaden his smile.

Some moments elapsed before the animals realized that the only member of the party who had not shown up was Toad. They all went to look out for him.

'Very strange,' Fox murmured. 'He can't have forgotten?'

'I hope he's all right,' said Mole, looking concerned.

'Oh, he'll be along in a minute, I'm sure,' said Badger. 'Don't worry.'

It was Tawny Owl who spotted Toad's approach first. 'I can see him,' he announced coolly. 'He seems to be taking his time.'

Soon afterwards most of the others could see him too.

'Whatever's he doing?' asked Weasel. 'It doesn't look as if he knows the right direction.'

'He's certainly not coming by a very direct route,' remarked Squirrel. 'He's meandering all over the place.'

297

They watched the solitary Toad in fascination. He was swerving from left to right and then back again. Then for a while he came steadily on, on a straight course, only to veer away at a tangent quite abruptly, for no apparent reason.

Tawny Owl lost his patience. 'Come on, Toad!' he called irritably. 'We are all waiting for you.'

At the sound of Owl's voice, Toad stopped dead. He seemed to notice the presence of his friends for the first time.

'Hallo!' he called, and followed the salutation by a strange noise – something like a cross between a croak and a hiccup. He then began excitedly hopping towards them, his final hop sending him head-first into the Hollow.

While he righted himself, the animals exchanged puzzled glances.

'How wonderful to see everyone again,' he said in a loud voice. 'I'm sorry I'm late, but I was diverted out of my way. I fell into a puddle! Tee-hee-hee!' Toad collapsed into a fit of giggles, and then hiccupped loudly several times.

'Toad, whatever is the matter with you?' asked Fox.

'He's drunk,' drawled Adder. 'I've seen humans act the same way.'

'I *am* drunk,' Toad shouted. 'And it's marvellous!'

'Now calm down and tell us what happened,' said Fox.

'I had been down at the pond, you see,' Toad explained, 'and on my way here I came past the Warden's lodge. I suddenly became aware of a delicious smell – a strong smell: sort of tangy and sour. I was looking round to see if I could find what was making it, and I blundered into a little pool of golden-brown liquid. Immediately the wonderful aroma was all round me, and I couldn't help tasting just a little drop. It was absolutely delicious. I had another drop . . .' Toad paused and looked round with a wide smile for effect.

'The rest of the story is, I think, predictable,' Fox commented wryly.

'Well, really, I only had a mouthful . . . or two,' Toad said mischievously. 'More of the liquid was trickling down into the pool from a big wooden container that was lying on its side just inside the Warden's fence,' Toad explained. 'It must have been seeping through a crack.'

'What did it taste like?' Mole asked excitedly.

'Something like the smell. Only sweeter. And . . . well, almost a musty flavour.'

Mole looked towards Fox, but did not dare ask what was in his mind.

Fox, however, had no trouble in reading his thoughts. 'No, no, Mole, I couldn't allow it,' he said emphatically. 'It wouldn't do.'

Quite unexpectedly, however, Badger for once took an opposite view.

'Oh, I don't know, Fox, really,' he said reasonably. 'The stuff's probably harmless enough. After all, Toad seems to be quite all right.'

Fox divined there was some self-interest behind Badger's

attitude. 'Well, it's up to you, Badger.' He shrugged. 'It's your responsibility.'

Immediately all of the party, except Vixen, began to mill around Badger. Toad's face brightened even more, if that were possible.

'We'll just drink each other's health,' Badger said, trying to moderate the animals' excitement. He turned round. 'Well, Toad, will you show us the way?'

'Gladly,' cried Toad.

The little band of animals moved off full of anticipation, Fox and Vixen following in their wake reluctantly.

'Do you think it might be possible for us to move at least part of the way in a straight line?' Adder asked drily, after a while. But Toad did not hear.

Eventually they arrived at the famous puddle and, once Badger was assured that the youngsters in the group were safely under the control of their mothers, he allowed the male animals forward to sample the liquid.

One by one they lowered their muzzles, snouts and beaks to taste. Toad stood on one side, watching for their reactions with immense interest.

It had genuinely been Badger's intention to allow Mole and the other animals to satisfy their curiosity only, but he had not reckoned with the persuasive properties of the brew. He himself was the last to drink, and as he stepped back smacking his lips to get the full benefit of the flavour, he felt a warm glow begin to spread through his body.

He looked at his friends, who were all smiling at each other, and he smiled himself, knowing they were experiencing the same beneficial feeling as he.

Gradually, in ones and twos, the animals went forward for a second taste of the liquid that made them feel so good.

'Toad was right!' piped up Mole. 'It *is* delicious.'

'Fox, do try some,' said Badger.

'Yes, go on, dearest,' Vixen urged him in a low voice,

not wishing that he should be the odd one out. 'I shan't mind,' she added.

Fox walked forward with a distinct lack of enthusiasm. He lowered his head. Then he looked up again at his friends. 'I drink the health of each and every one of you,' he said warmly, and drank from the pool. He raised his head and smiled. 'It *is* very good,' he admitted.

There was now a rush as all the animals scrambled forward to drink Fox's health, and then Vixen's, and then each others'. Even Toad joined in.

'I propose a toast to all the creatures of White Deer Park,' said Toad noisily.

'Particularly one creature,' added Whistler, throwing his head back so that the liquid in his bill ran down his throat, while the young creature in question looked on smilingly.

'Let's drink to all the female animals from Farthing Wood,' said Hare gallantly, thinking affectionately of his own mate.

The animals' heads went down again.

By now the full effect of the warming properties of the liquid had made itself felt, and the animals began to laugh at each others' glowing faces and sparkling eyes. Fox sensibly rejoined Vixen.

The rabbits gambolled off in sheer high spirits, running rings round each other. This was a spur to Hare, who raced after them and, getting on his hind legs, pretended to box each one of them.

The squirrels shinned up and down the Warden's fence, flicking their tails like quicksilver, while the hedgehogs looped themselves in and out of the palings as if they were trying to knit them together with their prickles.

Tawny Owl went and hung himself upside down by one foot from a tree inside the Warden's garden. Then he swung backwards and forwards, making hooting noises.

Adder, whose capacity for strong drink seemed to exceed

everyone else's, continued to imbibe from the pool, completely heedless of the voles and fieldmice who frolicked round him in their new-found courage.

Suddenly, Badger sat down heavily and burst into song, and Mole, recognizing the refrain as the one of Badger's own composition, joined in heartily.

Weasel, who was lying comfortably on his back, took up the tune, and Kestrel, perching on top of the fence, screeched his own unmusical accompaniment. Soon all the animals who knew the words of Badger's song joined in, while those who did not hummed, and Tawny Owl continued to hoot as his contribution.

So the story of their journey from Farthing Wood was retold – not to an audience, but for their own amusement and enjoyment. And as they sang, they relived their adventures, the hazards and the excitement of that long march. Even Adder paused in his drinking and lent his lisping voice to the concert, and the animals found themselves unconsciously drawing together into one group as the priceless feelings of friendship and loyalty entered again, and for ever, into each heart.

The voices reached a crescendo as the song ended with their arrival at their new home and then Fox, without a word, led the column of animals and birds quietly back to the Hollow where they quickly fell into the most peaceful and undisturbed sleep.

So the creatures from Farthing Wood began their new life, and as the months passed their first winter in the park approached.

One day Toad met Adder near the pond. 'Well, it looks as if your waterside vigils will soon have to be curtailed,' he said to the snake. 'My friends the frogs tell me the mud is nice and thick at the bottom of the pond, and it's almost time they settled there.'

Adder's self-possession was, as usual, unaffected. 'There are a few days yet before the ice forms,' he replied enigmatically. 'Those frogs will have the pleasure of my company a little longer.'

But he never did succeed in catching any.

The Wind in the Willows
Kenneth Grahame
With original illustrations by E.H.Shepard

*The dusk advanced on him steadily,
rapidly, gathering in behind and before;
and the light seemed to be draining
away like flood-water.*

The Wild Wood seems a terrifying place to
Mole, until he finds that it's full of friends -
kind, sleepy Badger; brave and lively Ratty; and
the irresponsible Mr Toad, famous for his
wealth and his car smashes.

But there are also the sinister weasels and
stoats, and when they capture Toad Hall,
the friends know they must fight together
to save it.

The Hundred and One Dalmatians
Dodie Smith

'Goodbye, you horrid little beasts. I shall like you so much better when you're skins instead of pups.'

Cruella de Vil is delighted when Pongo and Missis become the proud parents of fifteen Dalmatian puppies. She can't take her eyes off them, or her mind off the fact that they will make a wonderful fur coat. When she steals them away to her fur factory, only Pongo and Missis can rescue them.

With the help of all the dogs in England, they set off on a thrilling quest to save their pups – and the eighty-four others soon to fall prey to Cruella's wicked plans.

The Yearling
Marjorie Kinnan Rawlings

*A spotted fawn stood peering from the edge
of the clearing, wavering on uncertain legs.
Its dark eyes were wide and wondering.*

For Jody, growing up in the backwoods of
Florida in the early 1900s, school is the forest,
land and river, and lessons are in farming,
fishing and hunting.

But Jody misses having a special companion
and when he discovers the fawn, a new world
of sharing and friendship is opened up to him.

An unforgettable story about a boy's
coming of age.

Winner of the Pulitzer Prize

National Velvet
Enid Bagnold

'Velvet'll sit on a horse like a shadow and breathe her soul into it . . . I never seen such a creature on a horse.'

When Velvet Brown wins a piebald pony in a raffle, she's the laughing stock of the village. But Velvet and her friend, Mi, know that this is a special horse.

Together they can realise a dream: Velvet and the Pie can enter the Grand National, the greatest horse race of all time.

Made into a classic film, *National Velvet* is probably the most famous and well-loved horse racing story of all time.

Little House on the Prairie
Laura Ingalls Wilder

'Here we are, Caroline!' said Pa.
'Right here we'll build our house.'

The sun-kissed prairie stretches out around the
Ingalls family, smiling its welcome after their
long, hard journey across America.

But looks can be deceiving and they soon
find they must share the land with wild bears
and Indians.

Will there be enough land for all of them?

The second of the three acclaimed
Little House stories.

The Box of Delights
John Masefield

'And now, Master Harker, now that the
Wolves are Running, perhaps you could do
something to stop their Bite?'

A magical old man has asked Kay to protect
the Box of Delights, a Box with which he can
travel through time. But Kay is in danger:
Abner Brown will stop at nothing to get
his hands on it.

The police don't believe Kay so when his family
and the Bishop are scrobbled up just before
Christmas, he knows he must act alone . . .

The Midnight Folk and this, its sequel, were
described in *The Times* as 'two of the greatest
children's books ever written.'

Contents

List of Illustrations

Foreword

On May 11th 1979 a remark was reported in the *New Statesman* that my father, Oswald Mosley, 'must be the only Englishman today who is beyond the pale'. This statement was made about a man of eighty-two who had not been active in politics for fifteen years: who when he had been active – a period of world-wide violence and crime – had been convicted of no offence (he had been acquitted of one charge of assault and one of riotous assembly) and whose policies had for the most part been ignored and had come to nothing. The remark seemed ridiculous but in one sense apt – as being representative of what undoubtedly were many people's feelings about him. The phrase 'beyond the pale' gives an impression of something taboo: of a person not just whose attitudes had once been strongly disagreed with (he had been leader of the British Union of Fascists in the 1930s) but in contact with whom even now there might be danger. The commentator in the *New Statesman* continued – 'Nobody would flinch if you'd come back from Moscow and said you'd lunched with Kim Philby'. This implied that the news that someone had lunched with Oswald Mosley, in contrast to the news that one had met a notorious traitor, might cause almost physical alarm.

My purpose in writing this book is not to provide a biography of my father nor to give a comprehensive account of his politics: these tasks have been done admirably by his biographer Robert Skidelsky. I have tried to write a personal story of him and of my efforts to understand him: his child had to make these efforts to make sense of himself. The story might be of interest to others because in so far as it is true that there was something akin to a taboo about my father, then an understanding of this might give an insight into the nature of human beings and society.

My father was adored and hated, respected and feared, pitied and reviled. But both those who abominated him from a distance and those who were charmed by his presence (most people were) had the impression of something awesome about him that could not quite be put into words. It was as if he were a Greek tragic hero to whom disaster had occurred (or which he had caused to occur) which had set him apart: the power of the taboo in this tradition resides in the paradoxical impression that the disaster both is, and is not, the person's fault. The history of the twentieth century has revolved around men who through overweening pride and force of circumstance have felt themselves set apart: who have both ridden on, and felt themselves driven by, the slavish adorations and hatreds that others have felt towards them.

It is difficult for an academic biographer or a political historian to write about such paradoxes: it is their tradition to deal with what is seen as a world of facts. It has been the job of dramatists and novelists, traditionally, to try to relate facts to what might be seen as patterns and recurring predicaments of mind: to try to write of human experience as if what human beings were was not separate from it.

I myself am by vocation a novelist. My father did not read novels: he thought it was the task of an individual to try to order reasonably the world of facts. But his relationship with me, his eldest son, was often paradoxical. From my side at least there was loyalty and some hostility, anger and bewilderment, nearly always love. Towards the end of his life he cut me out of his will on the grounds that I was 'not his sort of person': yet the very last time I saw him, ten days before his death, he announced that he wanted me to inherit all his papers. I had told him that I hoped to write this book. It was as if when death approached he did not retract anything he felt about power (money, to him, was a form of power) but he knew as part of him had always known that if anything was to survive of what he had cared about it would be to do with efforts at truth.

CHAPTER 1

Tom

My father Oswald Mosley was born on November 16th 1896; he was in line to be the heir to a Staffordshire baronetcy and estate. His mother, Maud Mosley, had three sons in quick succession and then she left her husband – on account (this was the family legend) of his insatiable and promiscuous sexual habits. Maud Mosley was a woman of piety and rectitude; she moved to Shropshire to be near her own family. There, without the sort of money she might have expected, she brought up her three sons of whom her favourite was the eldest Oswald. She called him her 'man-child': he became the man-about-the-house. He wrote years later of how he had always been 'passionately devoted' to his mother: how even as a child he had repaid her devotion to him by 'gratuitous advice and virile assertion on every subject under the sun'. Apart from members of her family there were no further male influences in her life, he said, 'other than an occasional preacher of exceptional gifts'.

The chief male influence in Oswald's early life was his paternal grandfather, also called Oswald: he too had quarrelled with his son and did not see much of him. There was thus an alliance between the grandfather and the grandson Oswald, and the latter's childhood alternated between his mother's comparatively small house in Shropshire and the stateliness of his grandfather's house Rolleston Hall in Staffordshire. Grandfather Oswald was an imposing, paternalistic figure nicknamed John Bull: he too, like his son, lived apart from his wife. Rolleston Hall was a Victorian mansion with a full complement of grooms, gardeners, coachmen, indoor servants and so on. Life in both Shropshire and Staffordshire revolved mainly around horses and dogs, as it was apt to do in upper-class county families. There was hunting, steeplechasing, shooting and fishing. It was held to be much easier in those days, my father wrote later, to show emotions towards animals than to human beings.

The exception to this in some ways seemed to be his father, the ne'er-do-well, also called Oswald. This Oswald was a rake, a gambler; one of his bets had been to do with a game of golf down Pall Mall; another with shooting out all the street lights in Piccadilly with a pistol from a hansom cab. He had for a time set himself up in an inn in a village next to Rolleston in opposition to his father: there he had entertained women: it was said he was trying to emulate one of his ancestors who had been known as The Tutbury Tup (Tutbury was the name of the village; 'tup' the local name for a ram). Another story was that the last straw that drove his wife Maud to leave him was not just the sum of his infidelities, but her finding a bundle of letters to his mistresses which showed that he was saying just the same things to them, and even giving them the same presents, as he was to her.

What grandfather Oswald objected to was not so much the fact of his son's relationships with women but that these should be flaunted publicly. Grandfather Oswald was not averse to 'recompense' (his grandson wrote) so long as it was conducted 'with the utmost discretion and dignity'. However there was a tradition amongst the three Oswalds – grandfather, father and son – that their quarrels should be aired publicly. Each father challenged his son to a boxing match in front of assembled servants: grandfather Oswald once fought his son with one of his (the grandfather's) hands tied behind his back: the son was knocked out. Years later this Oswald, the rake, challenged his son, my father, to a match: he was again apparently on the point of being knocked out when the bout ended. This Oswald (his son wrote) had on the mantelpiece of his bachelor apartment a contemporary drawing of an ample lady in a very tight skirt with a monocled dandy walking behind her: it bore the caption 'Life is just one damned thing after another'.

My father used to claim that he had made a study of psychoanalysis in later life and had decided that the violent complexities of his childhood had had no effect on him whatever. He would explain – the healthy psyche can throw off an injury which in the weak becomes a complex. But also – 'It is possible to go even further, and to say that additional strength can come from an early injury'. This assertion seems somewhat to contradict the former: also, additional strength can take the form of numbness or armour plating.

There was a story my father told in his autobiography of how his mother had been hurled out of a pony-cart which was being driven recklessly by his father just before the birth of one of his brothers: from her diaries, however, it appears that the child about to be born was himself.

His mother kept a daily diary from the time of her marriage for over fifty years. When she died she left these to her youngest son; whom my father persuaded to hand them over, and then he burned them – all except those to do with the first four years of his life, and one of a slightly later date which survived half scorched. My father also tore out, and preserved, the entry for the day of his mother's birthday (January 2nd) from each of the diaries that he burned. But what was it that he wanted to eliminate by this *auto-da-fé*?

In his autobiography my father wrote movingly of his childhood: of the orderliness, the hierarchical but somehow classless patterns of life in his mother's house and in the semi-feudal grandeur of the estate at Rolleston. His grandfather ran a champion herd of shorthorn cattle: he was a passionate advocate and producer of unadulterated wholemeal bread. In the pursuance of good stockbreeding and correct land-management everyone on the estate seemed to work willingly and to accept his allotted place: there were few incitements and few opportunities to change. All his life my father retained a love of the English countryside and of its seasonal pursuits. But there were also things in him that seemed to rage against this tradition, and to demand change.

What he did not remember perhaps or indeed tried to cauterise memories of in the burning of his mother's diaries was that running parallel to the orderliness of country life was also a tendency ferocious and dismal which haunted people with too many servants and not enough to do: there were the quarrels, the separations, the lawsuits, the punch-ups; much of the emotions seemed to be taken out on horses as things to spur on or be spurred by. But even in the pages that remain of his mother's diaries before he was four she tells of an instance of my father being bullied by his father: 'Had a miserable time W teasing Tom and I trying to defend him; and finally W caught hold of my wrist hurting it badly'. (W is for 'Waldie' – the name by which the middle Oswald was known: and Tom is the name by which my father, the youngest Oswald, was known and will be known here).

And then in the diary that survived the flames, Tom's mother wrote of a fortnight's visit that he and his younger brother Ted had to pay to their father: the year was 1909; Tom was twelve and Ted nine.

During their stay their father repeatedly urged them to kiss the Parlourmaid (before her) and the Cook. He went into the children's

bedroom with nothing on but a nightshirt and talked to the P.maid
who was there calling them. Told Tommy how he had a box at the
Gaiety each night for a month and took the actresses out to supper
and he would do the same . . . they would go to the Metropolitan and
sit in the front and yell the choruses. Had rats down from London
in a box (3 doz) and let the dogs worry them. No bath, hat on in
house, altogether low.

Compared to this, life in Tom's mother's house must indeed have
seemed lofty: nothing much seemed to happen to her other than tea-
parties, shopping, going to church, and bad weather. Tom in the
holidays hunted and went ferreting. But perhaps the very lack of
impositions of such a life – and freedom for the most part from his father
– gave him confidence. From his young boys' school in Shropshire he
wrote to his mother in the only surviving letter of his childhood – 'We
had a preliminary debate last night, and I made a speech which came
off tremendously'.
     He was sent to a preparatory boarding school at the age of nine, and
to his public school, Winchester, at the age of twelve. He hated both
schools unashamedly and with an intensity that went on into old age.
He made few friends: he wrote in his autobiography – 'the dreary waste
of public school existence was only relieved by learning and homo-
sexuality; at that time I had no capacity for the former and I never had
any taste for the latter'. His escape was into the gymnasium where he
became a boxer and a prize-winning fencer. He won the public schools
championships in both foil and sabre at the age of fifteen: both the
double victory and the early age were records. His mentors at
Winchester were his boxing and fencing instructors Sergeant Major
Adam and Sergeant Ryan: he wrote about these in later years with
something like love.
     At home he had been able to go his own way: at school, he was forced
to be a subordinate member of a group. His dislike of this situation, and
his determination to be trapped within it for as short a time as possible,
seemed to stay with him for the rest of his life. He persuaded his family
to let him leave Winchester when he was just seventeen: he went to
Sandhurst to train to be a regular soldier.
     At Sandhurst he had to submit to strict and almost brutal discipline
while on duty and on the parade ground; but there was toleration of
quite anarchic behaviour out of hours. What the cadets liked to do in
the evenings was to pile into cars (this was 1913) and go up to London
and there provoke fights with the chuckers-out at places like the Empire

Music Hall (might Tom have bumped into his father?): the point of these expeditions were the fights, more than the pursuit of women. Then when the cadets arrived back at the barracks somewhat battered and drunk they would be helped to bed as if by nannies by the same sergeants who, the next day, would revile them for any indecorum on the parade ground. My father used to call this 'the corinthian tradition': and it seemed to represent, as if in some echo from childhood, a condition by which group-life might be possible for him. He described how on his arrival at Sandhurst he had picked out to be his cronies 'some fifty to a hundred boys who seemed to me particularly objectionable'. Team spirit was made palatable so long as there was at the back of it the chance of swashbuckling, or revolt.

The gangs of toughs, however, were apt to fight amongst themselves. In one dispute about a polo pony there were insults, threats of horse-whippings, violence; and in the subsequent fracas my father, while attempting to evade pursuers, fell from the ledge of an upstairs window and injured his leg. The details of this story are confused: such goings-on were common at Sandhurst: what is indubitable is that my father accepted even if he did not originally provoke a fight, which for a time he seemed to be winning, and then he ended up a victim.

By the time the war came in August 1914 he had recovered from his injury and he was commissioned into a smart cavalry regiment, the 16th Lancers. He spent some time in Ireland and then, because there did not seem to be much chance of the cavalry being used in the war, he volunteered to join the newly formed Royal Flying Corps who were in need of observers. These did not need much training. Like many young men at the time he was afraid that the war might be over by Christmas and that he would have missed it. By Christmas he was in fact in France flying in one of the flimsy aeroplanes that were used mainly for purposes of observation. He and his pilot were shot at from the ground and they could not retaliate; though pilots and observers occasionally shot at enemy planes with rifles and pistols. There were not more than about sixty men in the RFC actually flying at the time; this was war in an élitist tradition even more than it might have been with the cavalry. In Tom's words he and his fellow airmen were 'like men having dinner together in a country-house-party knowing that some must soon leave for ever; in the end, nearly all'. They were heroes: but, suspended in the air in their flimsy machines, very much in the tradition of being in some sense sacrificial. There was a song popular among the men of the RFC at the time which was called *The Dying Aviator*, in which there was described, with the lugubrious humour that the English traditionally make use of in times of stress, how a crashed airman's mutilated body had become inextricably intermingled with parts of his machine.

One incident in the war which stayed in Tom's mind came during the second battle of Ypres in April 1915 when he had been detailed to take a message by car from the RFC to some Canadians in the front line; he had stayed drinking with the Canadians longer than had been intended; he had to make his way back on foot. Then he saw, from the vantage point of a hill, massed German infantry regiments moving with parade-ground precision to the attack – to what might be either success or annihilation by machine-gun fire. He seems to have been half enthralled, half repelled, by this spectacle. He wondered about such dedication: was it necessary for it to be involved with such prospects of death?

In the spring of 1915 he went to train for his pilot's certificate at Shoreham in Sussex. He wrote in his autobiography 'My flying was not bad though I was weak on the mechanical side ... my argument was that once in the air you could do nothing about it if anything went wrong, and on the ground the machine was looked after by our friends the mechanics and riggers'. This attitude was a forerunner of his attitudes in later life – his belief that mundane day-to-day jobs could safely be left to what he called 'professionals'.

He got his pilot's certificate. But soon after, when he was being watched from the ground by his admiring mother who had come specially to see him, he decided to show off, did not notice that the wind had changed, came in too fast to land; then – 'the machine hit the ground with a bang and was thrown high into the air'. Still flying, he realised that the plane's undercarriage was damaged: he had to circle and make a pancake landing which involved stalling just above the ground. He managed to do this, but from too great a height: the floor of the cockpit was driven up against his legs. The leg which he had injured a year ago was crushed again but this time more severely. Once more, what had begun as an act of bravado had ended with his being a victim.

His leg was patched up. Then he was called back to his cavalry regiment who were now fighting as infantry and needed their officers. During the winter of 1915–16 he was on and off in the trenches or marching to and fro; much of the time he was in deep mud and water. The bones of his leg had not properly healed: they became infected: he was sent home, and there was talk of his leg having to be amputated. He persuaded the surgeon to try to save it; and this the surgeon did, replacing the infected parts with other bits of bone from the leg. Tom finished his active service in the war with his right leg an inch and a half shorter than the other.

There is something unfulfilled about Tom in the war: this is one of the areas his mother's diaries might have shed light on. He had flown bravely in the RFC: but it is evident that when in the trenches he was involved in no attack, and it seems unlikely that he had to undergo a large-scale enemy attack or he would have mentioned this. In his autobiography he tells as one of the highlights of his time in the front line a story of how when an attack was expected his colonel came round and told the junior officers that they would be recommended for the Military Cross if they held their ground: then the attack did not materialise. The way Tom told such a story (it would seem to have been improper for a commanding officer to have held out the bait of an MC to anyone for doing something so ordinary as resisting an attack) suggests that he wanted to establish as much as possible that he had been close to direct fighting. He certainly suffered under bombardments: he endured the nerve-breaking business of tunnelling for the placing of mines. But having set out with courage to be something of a hero, he found that he was to survive the war through a series of misfortunes.

The war's last two years he spent working in London in the Ministry of Munitions and in the Foreign Office. He read a lot, and entered into what used to be called London society. This was for him a time of transformation. He himself described how before this he had been intellectually dim: he had loved boxing, fencing, and horses. He had also been much on his own and usually at odds with the people around him. Now, having done his duty, and as a wounded soldier returned from war, he made up for lost opportunities. He read 'voraciously' – about history and politics; often, the speeches of famous politicians in history. He wanted to train himself for what he wanted to become. He thought of going to a university; but it seemed to him that other requirements were more pressing.

The war had affected him deeply: he was appalled by human stupidity – by what seemed to be the wilful waste of human life and resources. He had also observed, and tried to emulate himself, a sort of dashingness which seemed to surmount the waste: which might be a way to prevent it, if only it could be harnessed to reason instead of to destruction. He determined himself to try to do this.

It was during these years at the end of the war that he first got his reputation as a seducer of women. Up till now he had wanted to be a hero among men: but in London during 1917 and 1918 it would have been difficult to avoid the challenges, and opportunities, provided by

women. Women like wounded soldiers – who can be mothered, as well
as admired. And Tom must have felt himself ready to try a new
form of conquest. He was taken up, at first, by somewhat older married
women: it was the convention of course in the society in which he
moved that young men should have affairs only with married women:
unmarried girls were to be worshipped from afar. Tom became a lover
of Margaret Montagu, who was a hostess in Leicestershire; of Catherine
D'Erlanger, of Maxine Elliott, who entertained on the outskirts
of London. Through the latter he met for the first time eminent
politicians – Lloyd George, Winston Churchill, F. E. Smith. His
successes with women gave him confidence with older men: confidence
with politicians of course added to his successes with women. It cannot
be known what sparked the whole process off: there was something
sudden about his reputation for brilliance and wit. When, years later,
people used to ask him how it was that someone like himself had
emerged from such a family background he would say – as if it were
a quotation and poking fun at himself – 'when fire meets oil, then
springs the spark divine' – fire being his father and oil his mother – and
then he would laugh; especially if this was said in the presence of his
mother.

The older men whom Tom liked at this time he admired for their
toughness, their cleverness: it is unlikely he much admired them for their
politics. They, having won the war, seemed to be not so much resting
on their laurels as selling off bits of them to bidders. There was little will
amongst older politicians to re-order the world with burning enthusiasm
and in the light of reason. The old political games went on in the old
way played by the 'hard-faced men who had done well out of the war'.
The difference between Tom and other idealists of his generation was
that he, in addition to his idealism, felt that he had the skill to take on
the older generation at their own machinations.

The reputation for brilliance he had won in social and political salons
meant that he was soon approached by Conservative and Liberal whips
to see if he would stand for Parliament: both parties wanted young
candidates who might seem some leaven to the hard-faced lump. Tom
was asked if he would stand as a Conservative for the Stone division of
Staffordshire; also for the Harrow division of Middlesex. He chose the
latter, ostensibly on the grounds that he did not want to seem to be
taking advantage of family connections, but also because thus it would
be easier to maintain his social connections in London. He made it plain
he did not care about political party labels; he was going into Parliament
to represent the war generation – or himself.

The war ended on November 11th 1918; a general election was set for December 14th. Tom's election manifesto set the tone for much of the rest of his political life. What he undertook to fight for were – high wages, nationalisation of transport and of electricity, ex-soldiers to be offered smallholdings, grants for housing and educational scholarships to be provided by the state, fiscal protection for home industries and trade with the colonies, prevention of immigration by undesirable aliens, and the promotion by all possible means of the strength and prestige of the British Empire. These were fine words: he was no different from other politicans in not elucidating how they were to be implemented.

Tom was officially the candidate of the coalition government: his opponent, Mr Chamberlayne, a sixty-five-year-old solicitor, was standing as an Independent. Tom joked – 'An Independent is someone on whom no one can depend.' Mr Chamberlayne attacked his opponent for his youth, his wealth, and what he said was his inflated war record. Tom won the argument about this (the dispute had been about the date of his commission): and retaliated by saying he would not follow 'into the political gutter' such 'aborigines of the political world'. He was not yet good at making set speeches; but he had from the beginning, a talent for fighting back; for vituperation. He was duly elected the member for Harrow with a majority of 10,000. He became the youngest MP. He was just twenty two.

His successes had been sudden and startling but his talents were still those of the individual fighter; on unaccustomed ground he could be awkward and shy: he still had little aptitude for the business of working in a group. One cause he did take up was the promotion of the embryonic League of Nations. But a contemporary remembered him in his early days in the House of Commons as being 'a lonely, detached figure wandering unhappily about the lobbies of the House, uncertain of his mind. The war, he would say, had planted the seeds of doubt; parties were changing, new political creeds running molten from the crucible of old faiths; and he did not know which way to make his own.'

He had got into Parliament by his individual skills: it perhaps seemed to him that he would not make his way far in Parliament unless he could find some sort of status, some vantage-point, which would balance his solitariness and haughtiness and enable him to work with other people or from which to impose on them his personality. He needed to turn people's view of him from that of a somewhat louring if elegant lone-wolf into someone more approachable. He needed, in fact, something personal. He was very good looking. He was practised at love.

At the end of 1919 he went down to Plymouth to help Nancy Astor in the by-election in which she was campaigning to become the first woman MP. There he met a fellow helper, a girl whom he had come across once or twice during the last year. She was Cynthia, second daughter of Earl Curzon of Kedleston, the Foreign Secretary in Lloyd George's coalition government. He fell in love with Cynthia: he had not fallen in love before. He asked her to marry him. At first she refused. She had, it seemed, heard something of his reputation. He pursued her with letters. He tried to make legible his strange, angular handwriting.

My mother Cynthia was always known as Cim or Cimmie, just as my father was known as Tom.

> Betton House
> Market Drayton
> Shropshire

Cim darling.

Do not forget dinner Tuesday 7 pm. Really that is only an excuse to write to you — and I do so hate writing letters! I could write such wonderful letters if I could only dictate them like a speech or a newspaper article; but with a hand like this how can any sentiment or expression be other than ridiculous. An authority on these matters told me once that my writing could only mean genius or lunacy: in my youthful arrogance I welcomed the former conclusion, but since the present obsession I am driven to believe that the latter alternative is true. Not very complimentary to you! but a consuming disease of this intensity can be nothing short of lunacy. I remember Disraeli said somewhere that it was better to doubt of the creed in which you have been nurtured than of the personal powers on which you have staked your life. I now so agree with him. I have always believed, and so far found it to be true, that the will of men could conquer all emotion or pain whether spiritual or physical and mould the world to be just a reflection of its own personality. And now I have discovered an emotion, or is it a disease of the mind, which is more powerful than even the human spirit. What nonsense I write!

I have come down here after a strenuous League of Nations trip; staying alone with my mother until Monday, return London *mutatis mutandis*. A good meeting on Friday at Leamington. I became embroiled with some Roman Catholic priests – Canon Barry and others – who are opposing the League. Sir Ernest Pollock's ministerial dismay at the prospects of a brawl between the clericals and myself

in his constituency was very comic! However after a slightly acri-
monious debate we got a nearly unanimous resolution in the League's
favour. They have now asked me to take over the League of Nations
campaign throughout the country as the chairman of Campaign
Committee at Headquarters. It entails several hours of work a day at
their London office in addition to everything else, but I think I must
do it as it is in the greatest of all causes, and really the more I am
smothered in work the better.

I have thought so much of things down here in the lull after the
storm. As you too have heard of these dead things from my short but
weary past – as it now appears to me – I wonder whether you set out
in some strange idea of avenging anything your sex has suffered from
me? If so I must congratulate you, for few mortals have attained so
complete a measure of success in even their most facile aspirations! I
do not believe it to be true; for – worst of all – I think you were not
even sufficiently interested for that! I would surrender the present
with the ages to come and those past, just once to make you cry as
I have made others cry; and then instead of leaving as I have always
left tears, to kiss those tears away. Whatever you feel for me whether
nothing or everything will never affect my love for you. I do want
to marry you and always shall: but until you also feel as I do, if indeed
you ever do, I am so happy just to be with you in a way I never
thought possible between men and women. I shall have been a whole
week on Tuesday without seeing you and I do want to be with you
so often and will not make love to you (yet awhile!)

Tom

CHAPTER 2

Cimmie

Cynthia or Cimmie Curzon was from a background odder than Tom's, and was thought by her friends to be herself unconventional.

Her father George Curzon was the eldest son of an aristocratic Derbyshire family, the Scarsdales, who had been from time to time on visiting terms with the Mosleys. George Curzon had emerged from an upbringing by neglectful parents and a sadistic nanny, had flourished at Eton and Balliol, had travelled across Persia on horseback, had been a founder member of the social élite called The Souls, had entered Parliament at the age of twenty seven, and had seemed set for a remarkable political career. His only hindrance was that as heir to a not very rich estate and with his father Viscount Scarsdale still alive, he did not have much money.

Cimmie's mother was Mary Leiter, the daughter of Levi Zebidee Leiter, a Chicago millionaire. It would seem from the names that the Leiters were Jewish; but apparently in origins they were Mennonites, a protestant sect originating in Holland. The Leiters had emigrated to America in the eighteenth century. Levi Leiter made his fortune in Chicago real estate in the 1860s: then, at the insistence of his wife, he moved to Washington, in order that the family might exercise its fortune at one of the centres of American social life. That the Leiters successfully managed to do this was largely due to the charms of the eldest daughter Mary. Before her eighteenth birthday she was being hailed as the belle of innumerable balls, and was on socially intimate terms with members of the political and literary intelligentsia. Having 'conquered' Washington and New York (girls in the 1880s were talked about in those terms) she moved on, with her mother, to Paris and London. There, in 1890, she met George Curzon.

George proposed marriage in 1893: Mary accepted: they professed undying love. George said he wanted to keep the engagement secret in order to consolidate his political career by travelling in India and Afghanistan: they were with each other for only two days in the next two years. When they were finally married in 1895 Levi Leiter settled £140,000 on his daughter and an additional income of £6,000 a year. George had hoped for £9,000 but had 'no doubt that we can perfectly well get on with less'. There is a legend in the Leiter family that on the eve of the wedding George asked for more money from Levi Leiter. Whatever the truth of this, there seems to have been little liking between the two families.

The couple settled in England in London and then at Reigate Priory in Surrey. George was appointed Under Secretary of State at the Foreign Office. Mary was unhappy; after the social successes of her youth she now found herself often alone. George's old friends seemed to ignore her: perhaps she did not want to play the game by which English upper-class married women made themselves sexually available. George was much of the time in London.

George's family was not much help. When visiting Kedleston, the Scarsdale home in Derbyshire, Mary noted that George's father was:

> very fond of examining his tongue in a mirror. When he sits reading or writing he makes the most fiendish grimaces. He sleeps with his feet 2ft higher than his head with no blanket over him in the midst of winter, he has 18 thermometers in his sitting room and the tables are covered with magazines and railway almanacs of 1839.

A first child, Irene, was born in 1896. By the time my mother Cimmie was born on August 23rd 1898 things were looking better. George had just been appointed Viceroy of India at the extraordinarily young age of thirty nine. Mary (she wrote to her mother) was about to fill 'the greatest place ever held by an American abroad'. There were interviews with Queen Victoria: enormous expenditures on clothes and jewels. It was accepted that Viceroys had to find huge sums out of their own fortunes. Mary asked her father for more money. But all this happened just at the time when Mary's brother Joe Leiter, in Chicago, had attempted to 'corner the wheat market', which meant borrowing huge sums of money to buy up, literally, all the wheat in America with a view to pushing the price up before selling. In the end he had been outwitted by a rival who imported wheat from Canada across the frozen Great Lakes by means of ice-breakers: so now Joe was in debt to the extent of nine million dollars. There was a conflict of interests – and indeed of styles – within the family, that came to a crisis now and lasted for generations. Joe Leiter, Levi's only son, was an outlandish character: once when there was a strike at one of his coal mines he hired an armoured train with machine guns on it to carry blackleg labour through the pickets; in the last coach there were a gang of ladies.

Levi Leiter managed to raise two million dollars for his son, and another million for his daughter. The Curzons departed in state for India.

A nanny and a wet-nurse had been engaged for the new baby Cimmie: George Curzon had insisted on interviewing the applicants himself. The wet nurse was sick most of the way across the Bay of Biscay.

Children have imprinted on them patterns they observe from their parents: George and Mary's relationship was enigmatic. They were often professing their love; yet in fact they seem to have been curiously removed from one another. The most telling description of George Curzon has been given by Elinor Glyn, who became his mistress for a number of years after Mary's death. Much of this description might also have applied to Tom at the time he met Cimmie.

He has always been loved by women, but he has never allowed any individual woman to have the slightest influence on his life ... He likes their society for entirely leisure moments ... He likes them in the spirit in which other men like fine horses or good wine ... They are on a different plane altogether.

He is the most passionate physical lover, but so fastidious that no woman of the lower classes had ever been able to attract him. Since his habit is never to study the real woman, but only to accept the superficial presentation of herself which she wishes him to receive, he is naturally attracted to Americans.

He never gives a woman a single command, and yet each one must be perfectly conscious that she must obey his slightest inclinations. He rules entirely: and when a woman belongs to him he seems to prefer to give her even the raiment which touches her skin, and in every tangible way show absolute possession, while in words avoiding all suggestion of ownership, all ties, all obligations, upon either side. It is extremely curious.

When the Curzons arrived in India they found themselves in a world in which they were almost always on show, almost always surrounded by obsequiousness, almost totally dependent on each other for companionship. They were like royalty but even more solitary, not being members of what are usually large royal families. Mary wrote to her mother that she felt as if she were on a stage; she did not seem to mind this, perhaps because in recent years she had been neglected. George, as was his custom, threw himself into work: he became obsessed with details: he did not delegate responsibility. Mary was still, except when acting like a queen, very much on her own. She and George showed their devotion to each other by writing passionate but hurried notes from opposite ends of Government House. The children were in the hands of nannies, nurserymaids, wet nurses. My aunt Irene remembered of the time when she was three or four:

> we used to drive in a landau with three nurses, two red-liveried men on the box, and two standing up behind. When we were out in the morning in our rickshaws there was an army of attendants including the Viceroy's policeman who usually carried one or two of our broken dolls ...
>
> According to my mother I was a very hard child to handle, whereas Cynthia was a saint. I was often naughty to 'saintly Cim': I kicked her savagely one day and this ended in a fight. I recall my father smacking me and locking me in the bathroom.

There is a mystery about the reign of the Curzons in India. They were in most ways immensely successful: George Curzon pushed most of his administrative reforms through: he embarked on a programme for the restoration of historical monuments which makes him still (1982) the best-loved viceroy in Indian memory. He was not always popular amongst his compatriots: when two Indian servants were murdered by some drunken 9th Lancers and the regiment found itself unable to find the culprits, he stopped the leave of the entire regiment, and for this was booed by the fashionable crowd on Calcutta racecourse. But Mary was always popular in her role of Vicereine; she backed up her husband and made people warm towards him; and his practical achievements were undeniable.

Then after seven years, half way through a second term of office which against precedent had been given to him, George Curzon began to antagonise everyone around him. He wrote letters home which infuriated even his oldest friends in government; at work, he became increasingly intransigent and appeared to be heading for some sort of breakdown. The point at issue was an important technicality of army administration – about how far the army should remain under the direct orders of the Viceroy. George Curzon was probably correct in his insistence that it should; but his methods of attacking head-on the commander-in-chief, Kitchener, resulted in his own defeat. He resigned; and came home to some sort of ostracism at the hands of his old friends.

Mary found herself in an odd position in all this: as was her custom she manoeuvred ostensibly in support of her husband; but in doing so she seems to have carried on a more or less serious social flirtation with two of his arch enemies – Balfour, the Prime Minister in 1905, and Kitchener himself. She herself became ill: she wrote 'the bell will go, and India will kill me as one of the humble inconsequent lives that go into the foundations of all great works': and it did become the legend that the Indian climate killed her. But in fact she had flourished in India; and she had been for the first time seriously ill when she was on leave in England in 1904. George had then wanted her to remain in England, but she had insisted on rejoining him in India, and there she had again flourished while he had begun to crack up. Then after he had resigned and they were back in England she took to her bed again; and while she and George were once more writing love-notes to each other from the opposite ends of a not-so-enormous house, half way through 1906 and without much explicit cause, she died. The newspapers called it a heart-attack. She was only thirty four. In her last note delivered to her husband by a footman she had apologised for her 'devilish ills' and had said that she feared she was going out of her mind: George had replied that 'nothing else matters except to make my darling well again'; but then he had gone 'crying to bed' without seeing her. As she was dying he had sat beside her and had made notes of the tragedy. Then he set about constructing an elaborate monument to her in the church at Kedleston.

Cimmie was seven when her mother died. George Curzon and his three young daughters (a third, Alexandra, had been born in 1904) settled in their large and now somewhat lifeless houses at 1 Carlton House Terrace in London, and Hackwood Park in Hampshire. These houses were paid for largely by Leiter money which was now in trust to the children – Levi Leiter had died in 1904 and this had been one of the terms of his will – but George Curzon had the use of the income.

Life for the children continued to circulate around nannies, nursery-maids, other servants, horses and dogs. They saw their father at week-ends when they would help him with the tasks that he still insisted on performing himself around the house – holding the ladder for him while he hung pictures; carrying a basket of old bread with which he rubbed out finger-marks on doors. He continued to interview the children's maids and governesses, questioning them during meals on obscure historical subjects and then appearing appalled when they did not know the answers. He would also turn this sort of teasing against himself: many of the pompous sayings for which he later became notorious ('I didn't know the lower classes had such white skins' when he saw soldiers bathing) were acted out partly as a parody of himself, by which it seems he felt he might protect himself.

As time went on his old friends returned and there were Saturday to Monday parties at Hackwood at which once again were played the games of The Souls that were erudite and childish – charades, clumps; paper-games in which it was required that one wrote verses in a certain style, or composed witty telegrams from given initial letters. The children were brought up on the edge of all this: there were the more straightforward games they themselves played with their father: he would describe a historical scene to them and they had to recognise what it was; there was one particularly lugubrious game which consisted of just writing down the names of all the famous people one could think of beginning with a certain letter.

At the outbreak of war in 1914 Cimmie was nearly sixteen. The Belgian Royal Family came to stay at Hackwood as refugees: Cimmie corresponded with the young prince Leopold in a schoolroom code fashionable at the time. She corresponded with young men at the front, and during the next four years they replied to her in hundreds of letters in the tiny, meticulously pencilled scrawls on lined or squared paper that are the memorials of men hunched up in mud or dug-outs. These letters are brave, flirtatious, cheerful, correct: they give off the smell as it were of huge and terrible events and yet say almost nothing. Cimmie had four or five correspondents who seem to have been servants at Hack-wood or Carlton House Terrace: there is some sort of straightforward-ness about their letters that is missing from the usual upper-class style: 'I think it would take all my strength to bear another winter': also – 'I have never been so happy as I have been during this war: I sometimes think it may be because I at last find that I am of some use in the world. If it were possible to make a wish and have that wish granted, I should just wish for health and strength to continue the fight and to become a billet for the last bullet fired, don't you think that would be a glorious end?'

These men sent her presents ('It is a genuine Sennussi earings and necklace presented to me by one of those ladies in return for a small kindness I was able to render') and she sent to them cigarettes, cakes, clothes, a mouth-organ. Like most young girls (and indeed almost everyone at the time) she found it difficult to get a hold in her mind of what was going on: people wrote so passively and laconically about horror: no one seemed much interested in stopping it. Cimmie kept a diary on and off during the war: much of it was concerned with the trivia of everyday life. She was still having trouble from the naggings of her sister Irene; she was ashamed of not being more 'constructive' herself. She made her good resolutions: but she felt there was little use in these unless there was:

> a Big Solemn Comprehensive idea that holds you and me and all the world together in one great grand universal scheme ... Religion is the perpetual discovery of that Great Thing Out There ... Marriage has got to be a religious marriage or else it is a splitting up of life; religion and love are most of life, and all the power there is in it; therefore they can't afford to be harnessed in different directions ... I love people loving me more than anything in the world. I am going to try to make people love me more. No one knows how it hurts when someone I adore doesn't adore me. I must say very gratefully it has never happened for long.

Cimmie went to a boarding school at Eastbourne in 1916. There she became the centre of a rather tomboyish, dashing circle of girls. In the winter of 1917–18 she worked as a clerk in the War Office: in 1918 she was on a farm as a landgirl. She liked this because it gave her freedom – far more than would have been allowed to a girl such as her before the war, or indeed after it. Then she did a short welfare course at the London School of Economics including social work in the East End. She maintained her reputation for being somewhat wild, anarchic: a rebel with a conscience.

In 1916 George Curzon had become a member of the War Cabinet: also President of the Anti-Suffrage League. In 1917 he married again, a Mrs Duggan, the widow of a South American millionaire. Cimmie's rebelliousness coincided with her father increasingly being seen as a pillar of the conservative establishment. Cimmie found her relations with him difficult; but she continued to respect much of what he stood for in the way of dedication to duty and hard work. She wrote concerning her confusions about all this to Elinor Glyn, her father's ex-mistress, who had earlier been to her some sort of mother-substitute. Elinor Glyn had had to make her own way in the world: she had been a romantic novelist, a business woman, and a courtesan. She replied:

Get to the real meaning of things and the *real values*. True socialism should be to help conditions so that every child has a chance till it comes to fifteen say, and then sift the chaff from the corn. But lawlessness can never accomplish this, only reason and self-control. Therefore when you say you have 'Bolshevick' feelings examine them. They are probably only the unrest of overstored energy and the evolution of sex, which unconsciously works in every normal and healthy human being. If I were you dear child I would pull right up and examine where I was going and what I *really* wanted to *become*. I *fully* understand that spirit you have and sympathise with it, only it must be turned to fine ends, not disastrous ones. Just think of the *wonderful* power you could have if you wanted to! No hampering poverty or small position: you could be a leader of splendid things if you liked. I would set myself a model to rise to and *nothing* of personal weakness or foolish desires should be allowed to stand in the way of it; make myself into the most beautiful and cultivated and *attractive* young woman in England, so that when the right man came along he would not have to *blink* at certain aspects of me but would worship me as a queen; not take me as a 'jolly girl' or 'good old sport' or because he could not obtain me for his mistress in any other way, as is the attitude that most modern young men approach their choices with. You should *reign* – not be commiserated with as 'Poor dear Cim, what a mess she has made of it!'

There was something in Cimmie, evidently, that might accept being taken as a 'good old sport': perhaps her tomboyishness covered a vulnerability. Many of her boyfriends from childhood and to whom she had written in the war had been killed; it was not unusual for people to protect their feelings by an armour of gaiety. This was what young men in the trenches had done. Cimmie wrote to Lady Desborough whose *Family Journal* had just been published in praise of her two sons Julian and Billy Grenfell who had been killed – 'Words cannot express how I wish I had known those boys: always I have longed to be friends with people like that: I feel I have missed something that perhaps I may never find again.'

Tom Mosley remembered that one of the first times he saw Cimmie was on armistice night when she was at the Ritz Hotel draped in a Union Jack and singing patriotic songs: later that night (in her sister Irene's description) 'she tore round Trafalgar Square with the great crowd setting light to old cars and trucks to the horror of my father'. Tom himself was filled with sadness at the memory of his dead friends. However, a year later when he met Cimmie at Plymouth what he loved about her perhaps was her exuberant energy. He asked her to marry him. But when he wrote to her of his lunacy, his sufferings, the phantasms attendant on his unrequited love, she did not see, at first, what she might love in him. Perhaps she wished for a less histrionic attack. To his letter quoted at the end of the last chapter she replied:

> Hackwood
> Basingstoke
>
> I was carried off tonight and didn't have a chance of saying good-night and thanking you for giving me dinner and wangling me such a wonderfully good seat — so this is just to thank you now very much indeed. I do think it splendid the League making you Chairman of the Campaign Committee, I am glad and shall love to be roped in if there is any mortal thing I could do. Also remember the clubs in Hanwell, and that Phyllis and I are only awaiting further instructions.
>
> And now Dear about your lunacy, don't let it be a disease, don't let it obsess you, don't *please* go on wanting to make me cry or thinking me avengeful — I am really terribly compassionate, and having to hurt you hurts me dreadfully though you mayn't think it. I am not so hard as you imagine or even I make out; I just, well, I can't love you as you love me. Don't think I am merely callous saying that, it seems to me the only thing. I love being with you, I love talking to you, I should adore to be the really glorious friends we could be: please be satisfied with that, I know it's a rotten poor return for all you meant to give me, I am so intensely aware of all you would like to give me, I know how you love me, I am wonder- even awe-struck by it: but Tom, I can't give you anything like that back. Forgive me for saying that my dear ... only I would like to be of comfort to you instead of a disease. But I send love and blessings and again if only you could be devoted to me just as I am to you and not any other way — Goodnight Tom dear. Cim (I am not a humbug and don't think I am asking the impossible).

Tom was not much abashed by this; there has to be a fight if one is to be conqueror. He pursued her by letter to Switzerland, where she had gone to ski.

Cimmie darling,

I expect by now you are with the snow and sun and all beautiful things forgetful of this land of mist and sorrows. I rather love it tho', despite its sadness, perhaps on account of it, especially down here in my beloved Leicestershire where I should always be so happy with horses and hounds if it was not for the other people! I have buried myself for the weekend in the midst of that community which poor Wilde in his arrogant days prescribed as 'the unspeakable in pursuit of the uneatable'. Middle-aged survivors of the 'unseemly brawl' [the war] which interrupted their activities still carry on melancholy intrigues with the strenuous married women of the Melton district. The famous charms and antics of the latter now appear to me in a more garish light even than of yore. I suppose everything in life is comparative! ...

No politics or clamour for a little while. In detached moments such as these the struggle seems rather distasteful, tho' we revel in it while the fight is on. The incentive of mere personal ambition, except as a means of achieving our conceptions, seems more ludicrous than usual, and the ideas behind it all stand alone as the force that drags us back and will do so until the end.

The House starts again on February 10th but I fear I shall be forced to do a weeks speaking tour in the country about January 20th. I return tomorrow to hear L.G. evade the Irish issue and to compare notes with fellow Bolsheviks. Next session promises embittered controversies as of old ...

Come back soon but not before you want to. I do hope you are very happy out there and that life is wonderful. I am sure it always will be for you because life only gives us but a reflection of ourselves. I think this is the longest letter I have ever written in my ridiculous handwriting. It may carry to you a little of the dull things and a little of the joyous things that occupy me in this interval of existence if nothing of the things to which I look beyond it.

                                                        Tom

So long as Tom talked of 'the dull things' Cimmie could reply in kind:

So dreadfully sorry not to have answered your letter before really very very apologetic as I loved getting it and have meant to write and say so for days but always there seems something to be done ...

And so on. But then, a week or so later, Tom returned to the attack.

> I do so want you to marry me you see as I tried to explain that last wonderful night at the fancy party. I am tired of next session and all its dull things and duller people and only want to love you – perhaps this bores you – I cannot tell – it is for you to settle but please do so *quickly!* My life has been such a hustle that I seem to have acquired the habit and people in a hurry are usually unpleasant to others ... Write and tell me what you feel about it all and I only pray that this and every other decision in your life will bring you happiness which is all that matters to me ...

But then, Cimmie was immediately on the defensive again.

> Darling child, don't be tired about next Session, please, and don't be unhappy, but I am very very sorry, I don't want to marry you. I hate just putting it like that, it seems so horrid, but you said you were an impatient person and I must let you know. Don't think the idea of you loving me bores me (as you say) you never would bore me and I loved getting to know you and talking to you. But I am sad that I should make you sad now whereas I only so much wanted to help and make you happy. *Please* be happy and full of interest in your job and let me know that my being unable to love you in the way you want isn't going to spoil things for you between us ...

'Being unable to love you in the way you want' probably included a reluctance on Cimmie's part to risk herself in the area in which she knew Tom was renowned. She was safe so long as she remained in Switzerland. But when she was back in England, Tom seems to have brought the style of his pursuit as it were down to earth. He arranged for Cimmie to stay in Leicestershire and go hunting with him. After this he wrote:

> Funny Baby, Please do not be cross or distressed with me for tonight's few moments or above all frightened ever of me, because I would rather anything than ever hurt you for a single instant. I fear that side of me is very vital and strong and indeed if it was not I should not be much use in this life of struggle! But I do love you with all the strength of the other side, which is the only side that matters and which I have never given to any other woman.
>
> My real love for you will always prevent the original wild animal hurting or distressing you because in me the spirit always wins when

it is interested or affected. How crudely expressed: but you will understand, and I am so anxious that you shall never be alarmed or weary with me. I adored being with you in the places that I love – and I adore you – all of me does!!

Tom

Cimmie was a practical, sensuous person and she seems to have adored Tom and never to have ceased from adoring him once her sexuality was aroused. Soon he was writing to her – from his bachelor apartment, and in a note now torn down the middle but still as it were carefully legible:

His own darling Cim ...

It occurred to me that Molyneux might possibly let me his flat for us to go there in the day time while he is away. If you know him well enough will you ask him, as this place is alright for Tom but not very congenial for his one. He feels so lonely tonight! It is all wrong!

Bless her. X.

By March 26th 1920 they were engaged.

CHAPTER 3

Marriage and Politics

Tom and Cimmie were married on May 11th 1920 in the Chapel Royal, St James's. Cimmie had wanted a quiet wedding: the Chapel Royal, in the words of a contemporary newspaper, was 'so small that the guests scarcely have room even to study one another's gowns – but the privilege of being married in this building is a highly prized favour'. King George and Queen Mary were present, as were the King and Queen of the Belgians, who had been flown across the channel in two two-seater aeroplanes specially for the occasion. Outside the Chapel there was such a crowd that it had to be held back by police. Cimmie's wedding dress had a design of green leaves in it, in defiance of a superstition that green at a wedding was unlucky: there was also a superstition that it was unlucky to be married in May. Cimmie herself chose the music: during the handing-over of the ring the *Liebestod* from Wagner's *Tristan and Isolde* was played; though the organist, a newspaper reported, did his best to make it inaudible. Another newspaper commented that 'Mr Oswald Mosley, the bridegroom, was in the happy position of arousing little attention'. Photographs of him at the wedding show him, almost without exception, like an actor acknowledging the applause of a crowd. Cimmie's younger sister wrote to her 'You must tell Tom for the sake of his political career to put on a less footling expression when photographed'.

Before the wedding there had been one or two voices advising Cimmie not to rush in too quickly. A war-time boyfriend wrote 'There is a reason for knowing your Tom very thoroughly, but this is best discussed with a married woman'. But Tom himself, it seems, had already discussed this sort of thing with Cimmie. Cimmie had wondered what her father would make of the engagement; in the event he was relieved at her choice of Tom, since he knew of what were only half jokingly called her 'bolshevick' tendencies. He wrote to his wife Grace 'It turns out he is quite independent – he has practically severed himself from his father who is a spendthrift . . . He did not even know that Cim was an heiress'. For the rest there were just hundreds of letters saying how perfect everything was. Nancy Astor wrote 'This is just a line of real love and I do love Tom too. You will be *just* the kind of wife he needs and wants. I feel he must have a great soul, or he would never have asked you to share it.' Elinor Glyn wrote to Cimmie 'One day you will rule England.'

They went for their honeymoon to Portofino, in Italy. There Cimmie taught Tom how to swim; before, he had had a terror of putting his head under water. (He wrote in his autobiography that he considered this due to his having been nearly smothered at birth, which was not in line with his view that early traumas had had no effect on him). About the house where he and Cimmie stayed he wrote – 'Both Dante and Napoleon had slept in the mediaeval fortress; across the lovely bay you could see at Spezia the tragic water wine-dark with Shelley's drowning; along the heights which linked Portofino with Rapallo strode Nietzsche in the ecstasy of writing Zarathustra; Cimmie and I followed the same route more prosaically riding donkeys'.

Cimmie's two sisters Irene (sometimes called Nina) and Alexandra (always called Baba) felt, in their different styles, an almost personal involvement in the wedding and with the honeymoon couple. Irene, aged twenty-four and unmarried, wrote immediately after Cimmie and Tom had left the reception at Carlton House Terrace:

My 2 'tweets' Tim and Tom
    This is a tiny little breath of a lonely house left behind: thinking of you so hard: my thoughts will fly to you both tonight with all the prayers and wonder and sacredness that surround that little wedding-ring – my sweet Cim. May all the stars twinkle and bless you tonight and all the divine fresh green trees and flowers whisper spring – spring – spring – with your two hearts.

Your Nina

And Baba, a schoolgirl of sixteen, wrote after she had heard from Cimmie at Portofino:

My most pessus darling Tim,
    I am *so so* happy that it has turned out so wonderful as I have thought about you such a lot and longed for it to be like a perfect dream. I am just living for the time for you to come back . . .

For Tom his honeymoon was the beginning of the twelve years of his life during which, he wrote later, 'the summits of private happiness were balanced by the heights of public acclaim'. He not only loved Cimmie: he had seen her as someone with whom in partnership he might set out to alter the world. Cimmie had felt him as her child when she had been reluctant to marry him: she now also felt him as her conqueror. And she too had been brought up to think that in such a partnership she might alter the world.

What is striking about Tom's early years in Parliament is that he was on the 'liberal' or progressive side in almost every issue of any importance. From the first he saw that the coalition government under Lloyd George which had been elected to 'make a land fit for heroes to live in' had little intention of trying to do so: elderly men who had not been in the war were making a country profitable to themselves. Tom saw himself as the champion of the young versus the old: he became President of a body called The League of Youth and Social Progress: but even this, he found, was in fact run by 'a smooth and smug little Liberal ... typical of the middle-aged politicians who in each generation exploit youth.' He could use his talent for vituperation however as a speaker on its platforms: in his inaugural address as chairman he declaimed – 'Beware lest old age steal back and rob you of the reward ... lest the old dead men with their old dead minds embalmed in the tombs of the past creep back to dominate your new age, cleansed of their mistakes in the blood of your generation.' Such violence of phraseology got him publicity: he was still not at this time an impressive speaker when controlled.

His more serious efforts were to do with his championing of the new League of Nations: he cared above all about means for preserving peace. He had already been made Chairman of the Campaign Committee in England to publicise the League: he made speeches up and down the country. His mentor in this work was Lord Robert Cecil, the British representative at the League; of whom Tom later wrote (probably his highest recorded compliment about any living politician) 'he was nearly a great man and he was certainly a good man; possibly as great a man as so good a man can be'. Together in Parliament they condemned the British annexation of a former German island in the Pacific for the sake of its phosphate deposits: Tom declared this represented 'the worst days of predatory imperialism'. He described General Dyer's slaughter of Indian civilians at Amritsar as an example of 'Prussian frightfulness inspired by racism'. When British troops were used against the Bolsheviks in Russia he protested – 'It went to my heart to think of

£100,000,000 being spent in Russia supporting a mere adventure while the unemployed are trying to keep a family on 15s a week.' Then in 1923 when Mussolini's troops occupied the Greek island of Corfu he called for the League of Nations to impose sanctions against Italy. His whole political life, he wrote later, was 'predetermined by this almost religious conviction – to prevent a recurrence of war'. He felt that this might be done by the refusal by Britain to become involved in any aggression or even adventures; and by Britain's backing all internationally controlled efforts to prevent aggression by others. About the means necessary to do this he did have a different view from Robert Cecil: the latter had an almost mystical trust in the triumph of human reason so long as conflicts of opinion could be aired. Tom at this time had no illusions that even if a majority of nations agreed on some solution to a conflict, this might not have to be imposed on a minority by at least a show of force. In later years he himself came to have an almost mystical belief in his own powers of reasoning: but by then there were fewer illusions about the efficacy of the use of force.

The issue however with which Tom became most notoriously embroiled during his early years in Parliament was that of Ireland. After the 1918 election the Irish MPs elected to Westminster had unilaterally declared Ireland to be a republic: the Irish Republican Army was formed to gain independence from Britain by force. By 1920 the IRA were in control of much of the country: Lloyd George chose not to fight back openly – this might have alarmed public opinion – but rather to organise, or allow to be organised, gangs of mercenaries who would take on the IRA in their own style. These toughs became known as the Black and Tans from the colour of their uniforms: they found themselves engaged in a prototype of modern guerrilla warfare in which there were atrocities on both sides – especially the use of torture to extract information. Tom, in Parliament, railed against the government both for its responsibility for the Black and Tans and its denial of responsibility: the government was engaged in activities like 'the pogroms of the barbarous slav': it had 'denials on its lips and blood on its hands'. He was booed and jeered by Conservative MPs: he replied that he was 'unperturbed by the monosyllabic interjections of the otherwise inarticulate'. On November 3rd 1920 he left the Conservative benches and sat with the Independents: he had lasted as even a nominal member of the Tory establishment for less than two years.

The Irish nationalist leader T. P. O'Connor wrote later to Cimmie – 'I regard him as the man who really began the break-up of the Black and Tan savagery'.

Tom had made his mark in Parliament as someone who would fight for the rights of the oppressed and underprivileged: but he was in a position of being able to object to government callousness and to government duplicity because he himself was only a critic and he was not in a position of power. He was outraged at the methods of the Black and Tans not only because they were wicked (he approved of the controlled use of force to prevent aggression elsewhere) but because they were stupid: in the event, they aroused support for the IRA. But still, what else was to be done? He suggested when not in a vituperative mood that the Government should take personal responsibility for the fight against the IRA by means of a properly organised Intelligence Service: thus it 'should' be possible to round up the 'murder gangs' without recourse to one's own terrorism. But within the word 'should' there lies all the difference between those who have power and those who do not. Tom, in later life, when faced with a form of violence against himself, felt it right to reply in some sort of kind – even to become involved in inevitable duplicity.

Tom's sitting on the opposition benches in the House of Commons meant that he fell out with most of the old men who had earlier befriended him. He seemed to relish attacking the men at the top: he accused Winston Churchill, whom he saw as being responsible for the attack on Russia, of 'borrowing his principles from Prussia . . . but my complaint is that he is an ineffectual Prussian . . . it is no good keeping a private Napoleon if he is always defeated'. He said of the editor of the *Observer*, James Garvin, that he was a 'musical doormat which plays "See The Conquering Hero Comes" whenever Mr Lloyd George wipes his boots upon it.'

He became involved in attempts to form a Centre Party which would stand against the corruption and inefficiency of Lloyd George's Coalition and might draw support from both Tory and Liberal malcontents and even Labour. He wrote to Robert Cecil in April 1921 –

A real opportunity presents itself for a confederation of reasonable men to advance with a definite proposal for the reorganisation of our industrial system upon a durable basis and a concurrent revision of the financial chaos . . . The trouble is we are so immersed in the detail of everyday existence that we lose the *a priori* mind – the only attribute in the world that matters . . . One loses entirely the vision splendid of politics within the four walls of the H of C. It was so much easier in the past with such long intervals for dreams!

Lord Cowdray, the industrialist, was approached, and gave an undertaking that in certain circumstances he would provide money for a Centre Party. Lord Grey, the Liberal Foreign Secretary at the outbreak of war, was asked if he would emerge from his retirement and be its leader. Cimmie and a dozen other wives of interested politicians wrote to him – 'We see in your return to public life the best hope of an effective rallying together ... of all the stable progressive elements in the country'. But Tom found, as he found in later life repeatedly, that however much men might like to talk about new alignments of forces in the play-grounds of the political arena, their attitudes usually changed when anything more than talk was proposed. Lord Grey replied:

> Even if I were not under the disabilities of bad sight and of being in the House of Lords I should feel that the possible results of my taking an active part in public affairs are being greatly overestimated by my friends. I do not believe that any remedy for the present discontent is to be found in politics, but I will not enter upon a discussion of that large question now ...

And then Robert Cecil himself, when Tom approached him to be leader ('I am convinced it lies within your power to change the whole course of the history of the decade') replied:

> I think we should go on as heretofore saying as little as we can about our personal position and continuing to hammer the Govt and set up our alternative policy. Believe me it is facts that count in politics and they seem more and more going against the Govt ... It is no use chopping and changing, and until I see a very clear advantage in moving again I think it would be better to stick where I am. I have practically dropped the word 'conservative' ...

Years later Tom wrote of Robert Cecil that he 'embodied the mature, experienced and traditional wisdom of statesmanship not only in mind, but in the physical presence of an age-old eagle whose hooded eyes brooded on the follies of men while they still held the light of a further and beneficent vision.' Of Lord Grey he wrote – 'I always found him a singularly tedious and ineffective figure.' He liked Robert Cecil and he did not like Lord Grey. But whatever his personal predilections, he was learning, for the first of many times, that if one wants to pursue 'the vision splendid of politics', it is likely that one finds oneself at the head of the field alone.

The fact that Tom was breaking away more and more from his conservative and establishment background meant that he and Cimmie found their relations increasingly strained with her father George Curzon. Curzon had become Foreign Secretary in 1919; but such was Lloyd George's insistence on keeping most of the strings of foreign policy in his own hands (Curzon took responsibility for Asian affairs) that on the issues about which Tom at first was outspoken he and his father-in-law seldom found it necessary to clash. However Curzon's tentative approval of Tom as a son-in-law became, over the Irish question, tinged with alarm. His wife Grace wrote to him 'What a fool Tom Mosley is making of himself! If he goes on you should talk to him.' But then when George Curzon tried to be fatherly to his daughter and his son-in-law he ran into further difficulties. To one invitation to a very grand dinner at Carlton House Terrace Tom's secretary replied – 'Dear Lord Curzon, Mr Mosley asks me to say that he and the wife will be glad to dine with you and the King and Queen on the 15th prox.' Lord Curzon replied to his daughter in his own handwriting in a letter which began 'In the first place your secretary should address me, if he must address me at all, as My Lord . . .' and continued with pages of detailed instructions about correct modes of address and the answering of invitations. Tom remarked that this information was 'most useful'.

But the chief matter of contention between father and daughter and son-in-law was about money. After Mary Curzon's death in 1906 her Leiter money was held in trust for her children. George Curzon was able to get hold of the income from this on the grounds of his providing suitable homes for the children; but then, under the terms of Levi Leiter's will, when the children came of age the income was supposed to go direct to them. Irene, at twenty one, had demanded that she should have her money: her father had protested. Cimmie, even after her marriage, had for a time left part of her income with her father because it seemed to her unfortunate that he still had comparatively little money of his own to spare (his father Lord Scarsdale had died in 1916 but most of the Scarsdale family money went into the upkeep of the estate at Kedleston). But now, in 1921, Cimmie claimed the whole of her income; probably because Tom had got into financial difficulties in Harrow. When local newspapers had given up printing his speeches about Ireland he had himself bought one of the papers in order to air his views: later the paper had failed, and there were debts. George Curzon protested about Cim's proposal to claim her money: Cimmie wrote him a letter in which (he reported to his wife) she called his attitude 'mean, petty, unwarrantable, unaccountable and incomprehensible'. George Curzon replied that he was 'unwilling to continue any controversy on the matter'. Relations remained broken off. When in 1925 George Curzon was dying, he was still not on speaking terms with his two elder daughters. Irene, when she went to make her peace with him, was turned away at the door by a footman (she would tell this story in later years with much distress: she professed an undying love and respect for her father). There is no record of Cimmie having got as far as the door.

Tom was also engaged in cutting himself off from his own past and his family. His grandfather whom he had loved had died in 1915: his father had nominally inherited the Rolleston estate, but his grandfather had arranged that much of the money bypassed his son and went straight to Tom. In 1919 Tom persuaded his father to put Rolleston up for sale 'foreseeing the ruin of agriculture which politics were bringing, and feeling that I could best serve the country in a political life at Westminster'. Tom claimed that this was 'a terrible uprooting causing me much sorrow at the time': but it was a deliberate decision to sell what had been built up by past generations and with an eye to the future, for the sake of Tom's short-term political advantage. Rolleston was bought by a developer and pulled down. By the time Tom died in 1980 there were very few family heirlooms left from what had once been the admittedly rather hollow magnificence of Rolleston.

Cimmie and Tom were acting instinctively, emotionally, in this cutting-off from their pasts. Tom even sold his hunters and his polo ponies: he wrote 'politics had become for me the overriding interest and required singlemindedness'. He wrote of Cimmie that she 'reacted strongly against the splendours of Conservatism so faithfully reflected in her early surroundings, and this led her to seek close contact with the mass of the people and to prefer simplicity in her own home'. But at no stage of their life did this claim make much sense: it was not that from now on they hob-nobbed single-mindedly with the working class, but that they substituted one smart social set that they found boring for an even smarter one that they did not. This was a time when they began to go abroad for many of their social amusements to France and to Italy.

The social life by which Tom and Cimmie were taken up at this time was what nowadays might be called international jet-set. Tom wrote in his autobiography – 'What was the purpose of it all, this going into society? Apart from fun, which is always worthwhile so long as you have the time, meeting people is clearly valuable, particularly people with influence in divers spheres ... There was too the "open sesame" into the world of culture, literature, music and art ... It was a university

of charm, where a young man could encounter a refinement of sophistication whose acquisition could be some permanent passport in a varied
and variable world.'

Tom described the style of this 'university of charm'. The hostesses
in the cities of Europe during the nineteen twenties were mostly
American: they had the money. In Paris there was Elsie de Wolfe, who
had 'made a considerable fortune in New York as an interior decorator'.
On Sundays she usually had 'twenty or thirty people of all nationalities
and professions to luncheon or dinner ... Miss de Wolfe's conversation
was distinguished by immense vivacity rather than intellectual content
... When nearly ninety she was still doing what she called her morning
exercises which consisted of being flung about by two powerful men
of ballet dancer physique. Her gentler entourage included two well-
known characters of the period called Johnny and Tony who were
always at festive board and had a more delicate appreciation of haute
couture than of high politics.' Then in Rome and Venice there was
Princess Jane di San Faustino, another American, who 'regaled the
fashion world with the extremities of scandal floodlit by her unfailing
and eccentric humour'. She would sit at the beach at Venice and
'unnerve' newcomers with some 'searing comment' or her 'basilisk
stare'. She would tell the story of her husband who, when he left her,
had 'signalled the coachman to stop, teed up on the kerbstone as if for
a golfshot, and hit her as hard as he could over the head with his
umbrella'.

Compared to these, the leading London hostesses of the time – Lady
Cunard, Lady Colefax, Mrs Ronnie Greville – might indeed have
seemed rather tame.

Tom would explain that he saw social life as some sort of antidote,
or balance, to what might have otherwise become the grim and over-
riding obsessions of politics. What was required, he used to say, was a
'Ganzheit' (wholeness) for the attainment of 'the complete man'. But
the style of people in Tom's and Cimmie's social world does not seem
to have been very different from that of politicians: there was more wit,
perhaps: but this was still the Proustian world of Paris or Venice in
which personal relationships, even love, were matters of intrigue,
conquest, possession, power; everyone was in the business of becoming
one up on everyone else. Certainly there seems to have been little in it
of music, literature, art: not much of that austere standing back by which
Proust transmuted what was tawdry into beauty.

What these *salons* were useful for, of course, was the business of men
picking up women. Tom had a phrase for this – 'flushing the covers'

– a reference to partridge or pheasant shooting, in which birds are put up by beaters. There are different opinions about how long Tom was faithful to Cimmie after their marriage: her sisters imagined possibly a few years: Tom's second wife, Diana, suggested a few months. He would not have remained faithful for long while moving in this café-society world: what would have been the point? Talk of art and literature was known as being a cover under which lurked the availability of young married women. Another form of camouflage was that provided by the life of an MP. As one of the wits in Tom's entourage put it – What other job gives one such a valid excuse to be away from home night after night till 1 am?

Tom had embarked on his social and political life as a conqueror: it seems to have been agreed by both him and Cimmie that their marriage should in some sense spur him on – she as well as he wanted him to do 'great things'. But then what is this style of 'greatness'? And what is the style of a wife who has pledged herself to support her husband thus faithfully?

CHAPTER 4

Love Letters

Cimmie's first child, a girl, was born on February 25th 1921. She was christened Vivien Elisabeth. The nanny that came to look after her had been Cimmie's nurserymaid in India. Nanny Hyslop stayed with the family in one capacity or another for over fifty years.

Cimmie and Tom had settled into a house in London – 8 Smith Square – within easy reach of the Houses of Parliament. For weekends and holidays they rented houses in the country or abroad. In the summer of 1921 Nanny and Vivien were in Devon while Tom and Cimmie were in Scotland: in 1922 they were on the Norfolk coast while Tom and Cimmie were in Venice. In the winter of 1922-23 the family were together in a house, Lou Mas, in the south of France, on Cap Ferrat near Nice. Tom had to leave early to go home to speak in Parliament about a crisis in Mesopotamia: Cimmie stayed behind with Nanny and Vivien and her sister Baba who had come to stay. Cimmie was five months pregnant again and had been told to rest. This was the first time that Tom and Cimmie had been away from each other since their marriage for more than two nights. During the ten days that they were apart they each wrote to the other almost every day: Cimmie's first letter to Tom had been written even before he had left: Tom's first letter to Cimmie was written in the train so that he could post it at his first stop at Cannes. The letters talk of their love; their dependence on each other. Tom told the story much later to his second wife Diana that during this time when Cimmie was pregnant he was having an affair with a mutual friend with whom they had been in Venice the previous summer: Cimmie had learned about this and it had caused her upset; also upset (this was Tom's theory) to the child. This might have happened after the time of the letters. The child Cimmie was pregnant with, was myself.

I have cut some of the repetitions: but these letters show, as nothing else can, the peculiarities of the relationship between Tom and Cimmie; also something of the style of social life at the time.

Monday 12 February am. Lou Mas.

My beloved precious beloved
You haven't gone yet but my heart is aching so I write now so as for you to get a lett from me soon soon after you get back.
Be happy, be happy I do love you so frightfully I want you to miss me but to be happy too. Will be back soon and till then kiss you every morning every night, think of you every moment.
Bless you my precious I do love you so.
Kisses and love and love and kisses from

Your own Tim

Monday 12th February. Cannes

My own darling
   I am so terribly unhappy at leaving you – nothing would have made me go if I had realised what it meant and nothing will again. Please, please do not be too sad and look after your wonderful darling self for your T who adores you. I never understood before I left you on the platform quite how much I loved you. You have brought all the beauty and holiness and wonder with you that my life has ever known or ever will know – something apart from – higher – and yet wonderfully interwoven with my stormy existence – all that has rendered it possible. Come back to me soon my beloved.

Tom.

Monday 12th February pm. Lou Mas.

My sweetheart, I hope I didn't make you too unhappy when you went off. It just suddenly seemed too awful and my heart nearly broke. I don't know really how I shall get through the next week. I am so utterly dependent on you, you don't know how my every thought is of you, I really have no 'me' to speak of, only *you you you*: a *you* to adore, a *you* to look after, a *you* I admire, a *you* that fills my entire horizon. You have made such a difference to my life – filling it completely – making it *so* happy, blissfully happy and content – content in having found someone really big, really worthwhile, a life and a person worthy of one's whole endeavours and furthest effort. I do hope I give you back a little of the ... [rest of the letter missing].

Tuesday February 13th Calais.

My own darling,

Afraid missed Paris letter as train did not get there until 10 and went on eleven – Tommy still in bed and by time he had dressed was going on. Now only short let as feeling very sick – train rocking terribly – if it is rough on channel disaster may ensue. Already his insistent and plaintive cries of woe have evoked the compassion of fellow voyagers. Truly so terribly wretched and depressed without my one – such lonely little meals and sad feeling bring home to me every moment how much you have become to me in all the little as well as the big things in life. I nearly jumped off the train when she milked out and would have done so if others had not been there to think was too foolish. Shall be so mis without you but terribly realise how much you mean. Please do not be too unhappy but go on loving your adoring Tom and get well and strong to have a lovely time in a few days when you get back.

Tom   X for Mum   x for baby.

Train very good for Odie [Nanny] and baby: she would be very comfortable at other end of single compartment, they are much better than double.

Tuesday February 13th Lou Mas.

Blessed heart of mine, I can't tell you what your beloved letter has just given to me such a joy, such a love and such aching tears – Oh Bill I do miss you so. Perhaps almost it's a good thing you went away tho' you must not ever ever again – coz without you here I am overwhelmed by how much you mean to me: but my sweet, I am also sadly conscious of how little I let you know how *infinitely* much you *do* mean.

Dear heart I am so sorry for the way I harry and worry you – have made too high a mountain out of the molehills of your faults and let them so much exclude the sweet shining light of your love and darlingness. No one has ever had a sweeter man an I do appreciate everything, all you give me. I have been silly and overwrought and I am sure awfully difficult – no doubt thoughtless things you never dreamt I'd notice or mind well I have minded and have been mis and hurt and hopelessly grumpy. I have let you get the capacity to hurt me more easily than the capacity to please – No – that is too far, but anyway I have been a bit upside down tho' never for one instant loving you less. All the time the only great integral vital thing in the whole world that matters to me is You, my loving You, You loving me – it's so wonderful and beautiful and from now on I am going to make so much better use of it. Help me will you my sweet. I am now feeling awfully well, awfully resolute, intensely sorry for my shortcomings and failures – aching to be back with you to do anything I can. I wish I could explain better. I feel we have a good bit been box and cox – very often when you have been sweet and charming to me, or when you have wanted gaiety from me, or when you have wanted to talk serious matters with me, I have still been grieving over some row or trouble we've had and which you have already completely forgotten. I have resented you forgetting what seemed to me so easily – not realising that maybe I oughtn't to have, as it were, wallowed in being hurt. I have been too sensitive and have lost elasticity in recovering.

I really have been abnormal about everything connected with you – too proud too intricate too naked too introspective too violent. The beauty the peace the greatness the real sympathy between us so far and away miles and miles transcends the pettifogging puerile unnecessary squabbles. Let's have no more of them. You do your part will you as sometimes my pet it is your own sweet fault. And I swear I will do mine. I look forward so much to coming back to you and the time to come, peaceful happy unclouded. I wonder however the seven days will pass that are left here.

It is too bad, weather perfection and just when you have gone. I am out of doors in the deck chair writing this on my knee – we go Nice this afternoon shopping. It's really broiling. Tomorrow we start at 10 the Colefax expedition to go to St Paul and Grasse. Thurs I take Baba to Cannes and leave her with the Coates – Lady Rock has just written to Bab asking her and us to dine one night. We are going to ring up and ask if she will give us lunch Thurs instead. Nothing more so far except going with Connie to see her house. I have got all the necessaries for our journey Tuesday.

My beloved one I think of your sweet woolly head and the corner of your eye where I love to kiss – and how sweet you look in your new smart shirts, in your chic black 'smoking'. Dicks has just been up. She had two very exciting new engagements, at least one dullish, Mary Pease to a Mr Lubbock: the other thrilling to me, I wish you were here to guess – about the only girl friend I have left – one you like very much – can you guess –

Darling I wonder whether you will ever ever wade through all this. Oh I am so lucky to be married to you my precious fellow – you are

so miles and away above and beyond all others – I am so privileged
to be sharing in that wonderful star of yours –
Never doubt yourself. Never doubt me for one second.
You will never fail you. I will never fail you.
How I long to touch you and hear your voice.
Infinite love and a kiss on your dear wicked mouth
                                                    from you own Tim

                        Tuesday night 11pm. Smithers [8 Smith Sq]
My own darling fellow,
    Back in Turtle land after many adventures – Dined at the House
with M. Wood who has been made Liberal whip under Phillipps chief
whip in place of Hogge sacked for intruging with L.G. – great
uproar in Lib circles. Oh he is so lonely in Sweet Smithers without
his one and does long for her return. I have become so accustomed
to having you with me that I am so lost and foolish without you in
addition to such ache in heart. My crossing was perfect and who
should be on the boat but old Bob [Cecil] with P. Baker [Philip Noel-
Baker] from Lausanne – great political talks – he asked me what I was
going to do and I replied with truth I did not know. Feels a lost mut
[drawing of an animal like a sheep with the tail crossed out] tail should
not be there as he left it behind at Cap Ferrat. Please soon take up her
little crook.
    I have talked to Whitly and expect to speak tomorrow or Monday
– terrible lot of requests for me to speak etc – not much for you, and
those I am refusing. Bless you my own beautiful treasure. I do so miss
my wonder one and her baby. X for Mum x for baby. So tired and
lonely in bye [another drawing of an animal] Tiny mut in big
pen all alone. Does love her.

                                        Wednesday   Lou Mas.
My darling one I am so bitterly disappointed – no lett from you
today. I so badly wanted one on my return from Cannes. I felt so
dreadfully lonely and was so sure one would be waiting on the hall
table. Naughty puss you can't have posted one in either Paris or Calais
or it surely would have been here by now. Write me all you can
belovedest – it's all I have of you to carry me on and altho' I promise
you I am feeling very well and quite serene-ish still, I am a bit desolate.
Now *all* alone. I think and think of you and us 2 and have remembered so many little funny sweet episodes in our life together that I

had quite forgotten for the while. Now I'll tell you about yesterday and today.

Well yesterday Colefax and a nice little old man (55 to 60-ish) called Johnson started off in one car Baba and I in another, and went to St Paul (right behind Cagnes) where a large grey Rolls Royce was already drawn up belonging to Kennard; he then joined on to us we saw a church and town and then went on to Grasse stopping on the road for a picnic lunch. Lovely lovely day, magnificent scenery. At Grasse we went over the scent factory – Oh, I never knew before how scent was made it's revolting and interesting. We emerged after $\frac{1}{2}$ an hour smelling like civet cats. Then we went to see the Croisset villa (daughter just married Charles de Noailles) its supposed to be wonderful. I have never contemplated any such atrocity.

We came back a splendid road through divine little old towns and gorgeous scenery. Had tea in Nice then home. Box left today for Florence.

Now I am writing in bed and wondering how ever I shall get through the days that remain. I am bored and longing to have you here oh my sweetheart if only you could just walk in now and start going to bed I could put my arms around your neck and kiss you. I want to touch you so, and have you up against me. Blessed heart I wonder if you acutely miss me as I do you, if you have an ache all the time.

8 Smith Square. S.W.1
Wednesday

My own Darling,

He has just got the sweetest letter of all his life – thank you so much – it nearly broke my heart when she milked out – do hope now a little bet – only a week more today and five days only when you get it.

Just been to the House – fine bout between Lady M.P. [Lady Astor] and J. Jones [Labour member]. Opening rounds with references to J.J.'s inveterate consumption of spirits, and counters re her making money through illicit whisky selling. N.A. finally takes the count with peach of a punch as follows – The Speaker: Millionaires are useful people – N.A.: Hear hear! – J.J.: They have been some use to you! The worst day we've had for weeks, fog and cold terrible. Tiny T very depressed and longing for the return of his precious fellow. All love in world for his beloved.

Thursday 15th February. Lou Mas.
My own sweetheart, it's already 24 hours longer than I have ever been away from you before. I do wish you hadn't had to go but I am longing to hear from you whether or not you really think you were right in leaving: are you going to speak or take any part? I hope you will be able to, but my sweet remember if you can't be good be careful: *no* nasty personal allusions to Pa.

Am dreadfully disappointed no lett *all* yesterday and none this morning's post. Now we are just off to Cannes where I leave Baba after lunching with Rocks.

Hope so much there will be one waiting when I get back.

Will tell you about yesterday and today when I write tonight. Poor Tinkie *all* alone at Lou Mas.

My belovedest I love you so.

Blessings from your own Tim

Friday 16th February. House of Commons.
My own darling,

Just got the let which she wrote prior to his departure – delayed owing inadequate stamping & 6d to pay!! Rather glad he came back – speech apparently *immense success*. Scores of fervent congratulations and cheers. R. MacDonald came up and said he so wanted to talk to me in his room. So look out for bolshie boy in red tie when you return. Just a few quips at Marquis [Curzon] which were greatly appreciated. Please not too cross – not too bad! Great hurry for post. Elsa Maxwell in London. Very bored with everything except his Tim. Only thing in world that matters to him.

My own darling. X.

Friday AM. Lou Mas.
My sweetheart pet, so happy and glad to have your lets at last. Was wanting them so badly nearly burst all Wed: all Thurs no line: then Fri morning 2 at once the Calais one and the Smithers. Precious one they have make me so happy tho' have made me ache ache ache for you. I do miss you *too* terribly and wish with all my heart you had jumped out of the train. She couldn't help her milk out.

His letts are so *sweet* she does treasure them so. She'll look after his tail so carefully and bring it home. Poor lonely fellow in the big bed. Darling one can't help saying she is glad he is missing her, is glad he finds a gap instead of her fussing around.

How nice for you meeting Bob, was he very Tory. Sidney Greville has just been up to say goodbye he leaves Maryland tomorrow for Monte and goes home Wed. I am just going to Rosemary now to see Dicks before she goes off to Genoa to join Con and to get Evelyn's address to write to her. Having lunch early going into Nice for 'grand shopping'. Joan coming to tea then lonely evening doing bills and accounts.

This is just before I go to sleep. Have just read all your letts over again my Billy boy you are too darling for words I am so lucky to have such a sweet one for a husband. So many of the little things you write, the little divine things, the drawings, every single sweet thought, every touch, is treasured so passionately – by me. The little 'you and I' touches, the 'muts', and the 'tiny fellow in the big bye': I am so glad we are like we are and not just ordinary hus and wife. I *do* appreciate you so – your tenderness and un-ordinariness about things that matter so much to me.

                                    Saturday 17th Febuary. White's.
My own darling,
I expect this will be the last let you get before you jump on to the Blue Train and are wafted away from flowers and sun to the dingy little retreat where adoring Tomby awaits his beloved fellow. Just had a lovely lunch all by himself and is settling down for a *lonely* weekend – won't see a soul until Monday – poor lamb. Last night Oggie [Olga Lynn] had a very amusing dinner party of about 20 – usual people with additions of Maxine Elliott, Gladys Cooper type, wonderful shouts: Viola Tree funnier than you would believe. A new stunt – 'learning to skate'. Napier Alington and Lois did some dances and everyone was at very zenith of form. Did so long to see his round-eyed one honking out her pleasure or looking in pawky disapproval like a shocked baby as occasion might arise. A new and enchanting lyric has taken our more esoteric circles by storm – as follows, to the tune of the Old Pink Lady Valse –

            A wonderful bird is the pell-i-can
            His beak holds as much as his belly can
            Some say that he can pass
            This beak right up his ass
            But I'm damned if I see how the hell-he-can!

The evening was appropriately concluded by Mr W Rummel rendering the 'Entry of the Gods into Valhalla' and the rest of his concert programme in Nice. Such fun; but I did so want his pretty one to enjoy it too. Oggie says we will have another when you come back *if you like*. Tomby thinks he ought to be rather political for a bit as things are developing. Has enjoyed this little bit of gaiety; as having spoken, could do no more. Lots more multi-congratulations. But *he* thought he was bad: what does *she* think?

Saturday evening. Lou Mas.

Belovedest, isn't it thrilling this will be almost the last letter I will be able to write to you. It won't go till tomorrow Sunday and you will get it the very day before I at long long last get back to you. I will write just one more Monday for you to get Wed morning as really I couldn't bear to let a day go by without writing to you. I wonder if you have been bored by my endless screeds – I have *had* to write tho' it has appeased a little my loneliness. I have loved sort of getting into contact with you as it seems. Fancy I have written practically twice a day every day since you left. I wonder if you got them all? Did you get the one I wrote even before you had left? You cannot imagine my loneliness and want of you – I literally have felt all these days that there has been 'no spirit left in me' no resilience, no capacity for enjoyment; only aching void, the French word 'lasse'. I don't mean physical health at all, as I really am feeling awfully well, awfully rested and keen to get back, I know I am quite collected and serene and more vital than I have been for months – it's just YOU YOU YOU I must have – I must have. Quite honestly if you died (as I don't contemplate anything else on heaven or earth ever ever separating us) I should never never be the same again. Something would go out of me for ever – everything mortal and immortal that one human being can give another I have given you – All the good and bad and little and big – You are everything in life to me – I really mean it. The sort of affection one gives parents children brothers sisters friends the comrade element of life you have *all* of that, I rejoice utterly in you as a perfect gay heart free companion. No Mum has ever passionately loved a baby boy or a splendid grown up son as I do you. No brother or sister have ever felt the complete accord I feel to you. No two men, no 2 women, no child ever looked up to a parent as I do to you. And then above and beyond all that I can't write at all of what I feel about you as my husband and lover. No words in the world could ever tell you that, only if you could look with my eyes and heart how would you know. Don't think me stupid but I must tell you.

I wish I knew what you were doing tonight just so as to picture and visualise you. I wonder apropos of what I said awhile back of your meaning every thing and person in the world to me whether I am too wrapped up in you (can one be) expect too much from you, ask for *nothing* from *any one else*, only *all* the time things from you. Poor you. And then when as is only human you sometimes can't give, then I think you are bored with me – I think you ought not to ask anything from anyone in the world but me – I am afraid I am narrow and stupid but the excuse is that I am dotty potty about you almost (I believe this to be very nearly true) to insanity. I must steady myself. I think this week has done a great deal towards steadying and will you help when I get back to you – help by being not too moody, not too fierce, not too getting into rages and finding fault. I really am looking forward with the utmost confidence to a time of great peace and enjoyment of each other and no worries, anyway in our real inner lives.

My heart I love you so, trust you so, respect you so, and yet again love and adore you so. Goodnight.

Saturday night. 8 Smith Square.
My own most beloved darling,
Just a very last line in hopes you may just get it before you go – I have missed you so terribly – I do adore you more every day I live and I realise so terribly through this parting how tragically dependent I am on you – My own treasure darling I long to see your wonderful face again (kisses its pic every night) Only 4 more days and I shall on Wednesday be waiting on the station for my adored wife.

X.

Sunday evening. Lou Mas.
My sweet one, I believe I have it in me to find fault with you this evening – you are a worse correspondent than ever I had anticipated or else the posts have been bad. Another 2 days without letters at all. I got one Tuesday, none on Wed, none Thurs, then 3 on Friday almost *too* good, then none Sat, none Sun – I wonder how all mine to you have arrived, have you received them every day? I hope so, you ought to have. I have had so little to do, so many long hours alone, I have had much more time at my disposal than you. I find myself awfully bad about going out without you, I really have been the week I have been alone alone here an absolute hermit, all my meals alone, I have refused practically every invitation to go out and am terrified and shy and woefully haughty and *un*selfconfident. Went to lunch at Maryland today, arrived 20 minutes late because of our damn fool clocks, found Princess Louise, Lady Londesburgh, Jack Wilson,

Muriel Ward, husband, Harry Stoner etc: got on pretty well with Muriel found her easy and charming went up with them to Rosemary this afternoon the same party as the other night with Eric Mackenzie and Lady Maidstone extra.

I am very ill at ease with those sort of people they talked of nothing but bridge and smoking how could I join in – I tried desperately hard to be friendly and gay – I think I was all right ...

I wonder what it will feel like seeing you, having you, touching you again. Your actually going away was so *far* worse than I had anticipated I hope perhaps actually meeting may be better: though it would be hard, my anticipation is *so* running riot ...

My last goodnight to you in writing, I wonder if you'll get this before me – you ought to – I put my arms around you tight tight and kiss your dear eyes and mouth I love and worship you and send everything I can across the land and water, between every line is my love for you, filling every corner of the envelope even as it fills every corner of my life – I keep back just a tiny bit extra for Wed – no – I needn't as I shall have such a lot over and to spare all Monday Tues and till Wed evening I shall be bursting.

My precious heart
Your fellow
Our baby has been so sweet and an unbelievable joy and comfort.

CHAPTER 5

Politics and Society

I was born on June 25th 1923; almost immediately I became very ill. My mother did not feed me: it was not the custom at the time for upper class mothers to feed their children: my nanny however told me later my mother wanted to, but could not. A wet-nurse was hired – a Mrs Green – and while my mother and father went off in August for their summer holiday to Venice (it was also not the custom for such wives to become socially unavailable to their husbands who it was thought needed them more than babies) myself, my sister Vivien, Nanny, Stella the nurserymaid, Mrs Green and Mrs Green's own baby, all went off to a rented house at Birchington, in Kent.

Nanny wrote every other day to my mother at the Excelsior Hotel on the Lido at Venice and at the Palazzo Priuli in the town. She reported on how I was getting on with Mrs Green. I was vomiting, I could not swallow, I cried most of the time, and my motions (as Nanny called them) had become, aptly, green. Doctors were called and recommended that I be 'put on' first bismuth, then castor-oil and barley water, then something called peptonised milk: but all this was only in preparation for being 'put back' to Mrs Green. Nanny became alarmed ('I am sure the 3 oz he lost last week was all from his face'); on her own initiative she took me up to London and got a specialist to see me in a sitting room at the Grosvenor Hotel. The specialist recommended that I should be fed with nothing but 'sherry whey'. Nanny wrote 'He has had nearly a whole bottle of sherry this week, little tippler, he loves it'. Thus, it seems, my life was saved. Later it was found that Mrs Green (this story is not in the letters to my mother: it was told to me later by Nanny) had all the time had a crate of gin bottles under the bed. Surprisingly or otherwise, I am not yet (1982) an alcoholic.

Nanny continued to rescue the lives of myself, my sister and my brother for many years. She was one of sixteen children of a working class family (her father was a gardener) who, having helped her mother to bring up her younger brothers and sisters, had gone out to work aged fifteen as a nurserymaid to America; then had joined my mother and her two sisters in India after Baba had been born. As the sisters grew up and Nanny had had to leave, she had promised Cimmie that she would come back to her when she, Cimmie, had children; she had done so when Vivien was born. Nanny Hyslop represented everything steadfast, trustworthy, down-to-earth, in our childhood. The world of our parents seemed to do with ambitions and passions like that of gods on Mount Olympus.

My mother seems to have tried, in a way beyond what was usual at the time and for her class, to be a 'good' mother: she was certainly seen as such: but it would have been almost impossible for her to take much of her allegiance away from Tom. Tom himself tried (for the sake of 'Ganzheit'?) to be a good father: but it was his theory that the upbringing of children should be left to 'professionals': this was the same sort of theory that had led him to believe that the maintenance of aeroplanes should be left to professionals when he had crashed in 1915. The conventions of the time were that upper-class children should visit their mother in her bedroom after breakfast, and that they should go down to be on show in the drawing room after tea; but for the rest of the time their place was in the nursery, which was in relation to their parents' world as real life is to a stage.

Cimmie's and Tom's political life was in transition at this time: they were moving from being members if only peripherally of the conservative establishment to something more adventurous and left-wing. This was reflected in their choice of godparents for my christening in the summer of 1923. One was Nancy Astor, the Conservative MP for whom Tom and Cimmie had campaigned in 1919; others were Violet Bonham Carter and Archibald Sinclair, both prominent Liberals. A certain mystery however seems to have hung over my other godfather, or godfathers. Prince George, the youngest son of King George and Queen Mary, had been approached and had accepted; he had become a friend of Cimmie's in the south of France earlier in the year. But now he was a friend of her younger sister Baba and there had been stories about the possibility of their marriage. Prince George wrote to Cimmie from Buckingham Palace 'I hope you don't mind my asking you not to say anything about my being Godfather but there has been such trouble already about Baba that they would be furious if there was anything else seen in the papers'. So it seems that I had an additional godfather – Mr B. A. Campbell, General Secretary of the 'Paddy's Goose Boys' Club' in Shadwell, East London. Mr Campbell wrote to Cimmie 'You know I would love to have the honour and privilege of being godfather to your boy ... there is only one difficulty ... I only have one suit – an ordinary working suit – and if I can attend in that I will'. I myself never knew that Mr Campbell was my godfather until I came across this letter in 1981.

Tom's political disillusionment with his establishment friends came to a head during the summer holiday of 1923 when he and Cimmie were in Venice, I was with Mrs Green at Birchington, and Mussolini invaded Corfu. Tom hoped that sanctions against Italy would be ordered by the League of Nations: he left Venice for Geneva, where Robert Cecil was the British representative. Robert Cecil too favoured sanctions: he went to consult Stanley Baldwin, the Prime Minister (a Conservative government had taken over from Lloyd George's coalition government in 1922): Baldwin was taking the waters at Aix-les-Bains. Baldwin told Robert Cecil that he should do whatever he thought fit: Robert Cecil had hoped for firm orders. He returned to Geneva dejected. Tom was repelled both by Baldwin's inability to give orders and by Robert Cecil's need of them. He wrote 'Will was not available, because in such men it is only aroused by intense emotion': they had remained passive when 'by an act of cold will fortified by the calm calculation they had every prospect of victory and their opponent had none'. (He later compared this attitude to the 'white-hot emotion' with which such men had started what he saw as a profoundly risky war in 1939).

Tom advocated, in theory, the use of calm calculation as a prelude to decisive action: but what he himself often used calculation for, as do nearly all politicians, was skilful prevarication. In the general election of 1922 he had stood again for Harrow, but now as an Independent. The local Conservative Association had tried to pin him down about his opinions before they decided to back him. However the President of the Association reported:

We found it extraordinarily difficult to bring Mr Mosley to the point. He could never be persuaded to give a direct answer to a direct question, and developed an unrivalled skill in qualifying any written or spoken statement he could be induced to make with some loophole by which, if convenient, he could escape from the obvious meaning of his words. This feature in his conduct became so marked both in private discussions and meetings of the Executive that we were gradually forced to the suspicion that Mr Mosley was merely temporising with us and that he intended at his own time and in his own way to throw over his Party in his constituency as he had already thrown it over in the House of Commons.

But the reason for his prevarication, Tom stated, was:

I cannot enter Parliament unless I am free to take any action of opposition or association, irrespective of labels, that is compatible with my principles and is conducive to their success. My first consideration must always be the triumph of the causes for which I stand; and in the present condition of politics, or in any situation that is likely to arise in the near future, such freedom of action is necessary to that end.

One of the charges that could be laid against Tom perhaps throughout his political career was that he claimed for himself the rights of manipulation and prevarication that were part of the normal game of politics, while he seemed genuinely outraged by the use of such methods by others. This was a self-deception that created an impression of honesty; though in the end, as with all self-deceptions, it worked to his disadvantage.

The Harrow Conservative Association decided not to back him, and to put up an official candidate against him. Tom, as an Independent, appealed to the electorate:

The war destroyed the old party issues and with them the old parties. The party system must, of course, return in the very near future, but it will be a new Party system ... My intention not to wear a label which at present, may be confused with past controversies, does not mean that I adopt the empty independence of men who can agree with no one. I am not a freelance incapable of such cooperation, and am prepared to work immediately with men who hold similar opinions in the face of the great new issues of our day.

At the election Tom had got in with a majority somewhat reduced but still over 7,000. This was a personal triumph. His oratory, his dashing style, his ability to arouse devotion irrespective of party loyalties – all this had maddened his opponent who had, as before, been driven to personal abuse; accusing Tom of treachery about Ireland and about India. Tom, it was claimed, had incited Indian students to revolt against British rule. Tom threatened a libel action; his opponent unreservedly withdrew. Tom wrote 'I had very speedily in self-defence to develop a certain ferocity in debating methods ... or I would not have survived'.

This independence meant that he was increasingly isolating himself politically: but he must have known he was unlikely to be effective in British politics if he remained without allegiance. Both the Liberal and Labour parties were in need of young and energetic men: they were out to catch him: it had been significant that neither had put up a candidate against him in 1922. It seemed natural at first that he might turn to the Liberals. As early as 1920 Margot Asquith, the wife of the Liberal ex-Prime Minister, had written to Cimmie about how highly her husband regarded Tom: now Violet Bonham Carter, Asquith's daughter, wrote:

> Father came into my bedroom last night on his return from the House to tell me that your Tom (may I call him Tom?) had made the most brilliant speech he had almost ever heard: I have never seen him more completely swept away.

Tom and Cimmie went to stay with the Asquiths at their country house The Wharf: the Liberals began to talk of them as 'one of us'. But Tom was probably doing some of the 'calm calculation' that he advocated for men of action. At the 1922 election the Labour Party had been the chief gainers with an increase in the number of MP's from 63 to 142 (the Liberals had 117). When Baldwin called another general election at the end of 1923, on the issue of protectionism versus free trade, Labour became the strongest Party in the House of Commons with 191 seats and the Liberals, although their fortunes had improved at the expense of the Conservatives, were even further behind Labour with 159. A Labour Government was formed. It seemed obvious that if Tom was going to put an end to his isolation by joining a party – and with an eye to being part of a government in the near future – it made sense if one's feelings were more for Labour than for Liberals.

Another impetus to join a party was the fact that in the 1923 election his majority at Harrow was down to 4,600: his old conservative supporters were leaving him. It had been, as, usual, a vituperative campaign. His old friend F. E. Smith, now Lord Birkenhead, had come down to speak for Tom's official conservative opponent and had referred to Tom as 'the perfumed popinjay of scented boudoirs'. Tom took umbrage. He did not mind, he said, the reference to boudoirs; but he seemed to think that 'popinjay' was a slur on his performance there.

There is little record of Cimmie in politics during Tom's years at

Harrow. At the time of her wedding she had received a letter from Tom's mother handing over to her the position of 'political leading lady': she had made a speech of thanks to the constituency for their wedding present after which a local newspaper reported that 'her victory was greater than her husband's at the polls 18 months ago': she had helped, together with his mother, in Tom's electioneering campaigns. But she never seemed to have had much time for the Harrow style of politics. Most of the first four years of her marriage was spent in settling into the house in London, giving birth to two of her children, and making the complicated arrangements for holidays, servants, dinner parties, and so on, for Tom's cosmopolitan entertainment. There is no evidence that she ever indulged in the game of upper class married women being available for love affairs: she was always available to use her social charms for the advancement of Tom. But as Tom moved closer to Labour her involvement became more political. As early as May 1923 she was entertaining the Labour leader, Ramsay MacDonald, to lunch: she struck up some sort of flirtatious relationship with him. Later that summer she invited him to join her and Tom on holiday. He replied:

> Thank you very much for your letter inviting me to stay with you in Venice when I am passing through. Sidney Arnold is with me and the two of us would I am sure be too big a handful for you. But in any event let us have a feast together.
>
> I hope the little person who I saw had come to smile on you both gives you much happiness ...

When the first Labour government was formed in January 1924 with Ramsay MacDonald as Prime Minister Tom made a strong speech in Parliament abusing the Tory record ('drift buoyed up by drivel') and wishing the Labour well ('tonight the army of progress has struck its tents and is on the move.') It now seemed only a matter of time before Tom joined the Labour Party. His Liberal friends were annoyed. On January 19th Margot Asquith wrote:

> Dear Tom, You and Cimmie are very dear to me. I am old and you are young. I have watched politics closely since I was 15, having 3 great friends – Gladstone, Morley, and A. Balfour – 3 very different men. Clear conviction and patience, courage and ambition and not too much self-love with perfect self-control go to make leaders of men. I have watched men of great ability – 1. Rosebery 2. Balfour,

Winston and Birkenhead, all ruin themselves in turn. I am not persuading you to be a Liberal and you can change from Tory to Liberal or vice versa: I am writing to warn you to take *long* views. Your future might be a great one in the Liberal Party; possibly, Cim says, in the Labour Party. But I myself see little difference between the extremes of left and right; I have never seen anything more selfish, jealous and petty – apart from gross and pathetic ignorance – than Labour; and every word you say of Tory is true. Class consciousness devours both. I have not seen you lately but before joining Thomas – a liar: Ramsay – a coward: I should think twice.

Tom made a joke about this letter saying that Margot Asquith had abused his best friends. But in fact it was his old acquaintances who were, as usual, abusing him. The main criticism of the prospect that he might join Labour was that he would be pandering cynically to a desire for power: that he saw his own future brighter in the Labour Party in that he wanted to be a 'big fish in a little pond'. But these accusations made little sense. Tom could have done as well as he wished in the Conservative Party if he had not been outraged about matters of principle; there was little enough talent among young Conservatives for him to have felt much danger of being outshone. And although there might be an initial glamour about himself as an aristocrat joining Labour he was clever enough to know that there would also be reactions and repercussions. He felt drawn to Labour because of what he felt as the sluggishness and corruption of the establishment parties: and in so far as it was true that he could do something about this only as a member of a group, then the Labour Party was the one most likely to act in the way that he desired.

There is some truth, however, in the charge that he saw politics largely in terms of what might be a platform for himself: he was always, and he thought justifiably, something of a one man party band. Even at this time (he was twenty seven) he was imagining that it was the democratic tradition of a government being harried by an opposition that prevented things being done: this was the 'drift buoyed up by drivel'. If words were to be turned into action, this would be through unencumbered power being given, albeit democratically, to a single group led by a single responsible man. He seldom prevaricated about this. In every attitude he had taken (and was to take) in politics he stood on some principle: and he said to other people in effect that they could either follow him or not as they chose. This was something unusual in

English politics – where the tradition has been to manipulate and manoeuvre possibilities. The one charge it was difficult to bring against Tom was that he manipulated what he saw as his principles for the sake of success: if he had, he might have succeeded.

At the time when he was attracted to Labour and Labour was wooing him his mother wrote to him:

> I must pen a line to try and tell you how enormously I admire your amazing courage and self-sacrifice of most things that appeal to men of your age and up-bringing; and how I pray with all my heart that your dreams for the benefit of struggling humanity may come true, and that I may live to see your present attitude justified by results and the world appreciate that far from being a pushing self-seeking politician you were in fact willing to be a martyr for your Religion – for it seems to me that is what your Politics are.
>
> And oh darling how I wish with all my heart and soul I could honourably back you up ... I do honestly believe that if the 'Labour Party' meant what you and some of those in the party are striving to make it every one of us would back you. But to my mind the tragedy of it all is that the vast mass of your often very ignorant supporters do not mean what you mean by Socialism ... It is an old story – as old as the Bible. When the Jews found following Christ meant the cross and not an earthly sovereignty and defeat of the Romans they turned on him and crucified their Lord ...

Tom's mother, a pious Christian, seems to have been the first person to see – and almost to welcome – that there might be something self-immolating in Tom's heroic stands. In the meantime there was the formal business of his application to join the Labour Party. To this, on March 27th 1924, Ramsay MacDonald replied –

> My dear Mosley,
>
> Although I have welcomed you into the Party by word of mouth, I would like to tell you in writing how pleased I am that you have seen your way to join us and to express the hope that you will find comfort in our ranks and a wide field in which you can show your usefulness.
>
> I am very sorry to observe in some newspapers that you are being subjected to the kind of personal attack with which we are all very familiar. I know it will not disturb you in the least, and I assure you

it will only make your welcome all the more hearty so far as we are concerned.

With kind regards
I am yours very sincerely,
J. Ramsay MacDonald

CHAPTER 6

Rebels

In the spring of 1924 a young German newspaperman, Egon Wertheimer, attended a meeting of the Labour Party in the Empire Hall in
south-east London. He wrote:

> Suddenly there was a movement in the crowd and a young man with
> the face of the ruling class of Great Britain but with the gait of a
> Douglas Fairbanks thrust himself forward through the throng to the
> platform followed by a lady in heavy, costly furs. There stood
> Oswald Mosley, whose later ascent was to be one of the strangest
> phenomena of the working class movement of the world ...
>
> The new man spoke ... unforgettable was the impression, the
> visual and oral impression, which the style of the speech made on me.
> It was a hymn, an emotional appeal directed not to the intellect, but
> to the Socialist idea, which obviously was still a subject of wonder to
> the orator, a youthful experience. No speaker at a working class
> meeting in Germany would have dared to have worked so un-
> restrainedly on the feelings without running the risk of losing for ever
> his standing in the party movement ...
>
> But then came something unexpected; something that, by its
> spontaneity, shook me; although it was a trifling thing and seemed
> a matter of course to all those around me. From the audience there
> came calls; they grew more urgent; and suddenly the elegant lady in
> furs got up from her seat and said a few sympathetic words ... She
> said that she had never before attended a workers' meeting, and how
> deeply the warmth of this reception touched her. She said this simply
> and almost shyly, but yet like one who is accustomed to be acclaimed
> and, without stagefright, to open a bazaar or a meeting for charitable
> purposes. 'Lady Cynthia Mosley' whispered in my ear one of the

armleted stewards who stood near me, excited; and later as though thinking he had not sufficiently impressed me, he added 'Lord Curzon's daughter'. His whole face beamed proudly. All around the audience was still in uproar; as at a boxing match, or a fair.

Another commentator, John Scanlon, viewed this sort of scene with some despair, and said that whatever Tom's entry into the Labour Party had done for him, it was a disaster for the Party.

Stories of his fabulous wealth had spread themselves all over the country, and coupled with that was the fact that his wife was the daughter of Lord Curzon. The press lost no point in this human story, and those of us who had visions of a dignified working class steadily gaining confidence in itself as the future owners of Britain had our first shock of disillusionment. No sooner had Mr Mosley come into the Party than there began the heartbreaking spectacle of Local Labour Parties stumbling over themselves to secure him as their candidate. At that time there was not a particle of evidence to show that he understood one of the problems in their lives . . . It was truly an amazing and saddening spectacle to see these working men, inheritors of a party formed by Keir Hardie in the belief that a dignified Democracy could, and should, run its own party, literally prostrate in their worship of the Golden Calf.

These two commentators were Marxists: Marxists are often amazed and disappointed at the ways of the working class. The British Labour Movement had been little influenced by international Marxism: its loyalties had been given to trade unions; or beyond them to the nation. Also in Britain, Tom used to say, there had always been an instinctive and emotional sympathy between the aristocracy and the working class who (in Lord Randolph Churchill's phrase) were 'united in the indissoluble bonds of a common immorality'. Together they showed disrespect for the puritanism both of left-wing intellectuals and of the bourgeoisie.

But then, in turn, it was natural that Labour intellectuals should distrust Tom after having been tempted to be charmed by him. Beatrice Webb wrote in her diary:

We have made the acquaintance of the most brilliant man in the House of Commons – Oswald Mosley. 'Here is the perfect politician who is also the perfect gentleman' I said to myself as he entered the room ... So much perfection argues rottenness somewhere ... Is there some weak spot which will be revealed in a time of stress — exactly at the very time when you need support — by letting you or your cause down or sweeping it out of the way?

This was the feeling also of such Labour Party stalwarts as Hugh Dalton and Herbert Morrison, who had worked their way up diligently through the ranks of the Party and resented Tom's sudden jump half way to the top. Almost immediately Tom had more than seventy invitations from constituencies to stand as their candidate for Parliament.

Tom's power was in his use of words: as a public speaker he could go over the heads of the Labour hierarchy and appeal directly to working class audiences. As soon as he had joined the party he was taken on a speaking tour of the midlands and north: the editor of a Birmingham newspaper wrote — 'His power over his audience was amazing; his eloquence made even hardened pressmen gasp'. He had learned to speak without notes (a trick he had learned, he wrote, by getting someone to read to him a leading article from *The Times* and then speaking in reply to it 'taking each point *seriatim* in the order read'). He had an amazing memory for figures. He liked to be challenged by hecklers, because he felt confident in his powers of repartee. But above all what held his audiences and almost physically lifted them were those mysterious rhythms and cadences which a mob orator uses and which, combined with primitively emotive words, play upon people's minds like music.

This power that Tom had with words did not always, in the long run, work to his advantage. There were times when his audience was being lifted but he himself was being lulled into thinking the reaction more substantial than it was. After the enthusiasm had worn off like the effects of a drug an audience was apt to find itself feeling rather empty. (In the same way Tom's girlfriends, one of them once said, would feel somewhat ashamed after having been seduced.)

Tom never understood the limitations of the power of words. He was apt to think that once a case had been reasonably and passionately stated the cause had been won: that if a difficult question had been parried or skilfully avoided, it had somehow disappeared. He did not see that it was often his very skill in the manipulation of words that made people suspect he might not be quite serious: for what is serious about a person who does such clever tricks with the difference between words and things? People reacted sometimes as the Conservative Association had reacted to him at Harrow: they admired his ability to spellbind, to bluff, to hit, to parry: but what had this got to do with what actually was required?

While he was on his speaking tour he wrote to Cimmie from the Durham and North Yorkshire Public House Trust Co:

His own darling Moo–Moo,
Does so miss her, but lucky she did not come as life is like the Great War – billets – no sheets etc – everyone very kind but a tiresome tour, lots of little 500 meetings, not my form at all, same kind friends also always accompanying, so have to improvise a different speech each time. Longing to return to wiz land and hopes to do so 10 p.m. tomorrow Monday (great excitement). All love in world from adoring
         her fellow.

Cimmie herself had joined Tom as a member of the Labour Party. The jibes which hitherto had been directed at Tom for his anti-Tory activities now also began to be directed at her. There were comments in the newspapers about her money: if she and Tom were socialists why did they not give the property away; why did they live in a house with sixteen rooms; why did Cimmie appear on Labour platforms in jewels and 'costly furs'? To this she and Tom replied that it would not help others in any serious way if they gave away their money and they could be of more use to socialism by themselves using it to finance organisation and propaganda. As for Cimmie's 'jewels' – they had been, in the instance quoted, she explained, bits of glass in a dress bought for a few shillings in India. There was then a peculiar wrangle with the Press on the subject of family titles. Tom was reported as having said he would not use the 'Sir' of his baronetcy when his father died; Cimmie as having remarked, rather irrelevantly, that she wanted to drop the 'Lady' Cynthia and be known as plain Mrs Mosley but that unfortunately there was no legal way of doing this. Tom summed up: 'In any case inside the Labour movement my wife is always known as Comrade Mosley and what she is called outside does not really matter.' But the Labour Party rank and file apparently did not want to let the matter rest: about a meeting in London the *Daily Mail* reported:

a series of quarrels were in progress among the audience about whether Mr Mosley is a duke, a knight, or a commoner. The Chairman attempted a compromise by describing him as 'Comrade Mosley' but this found disfavour with a row of very young women in front. Mr Mosley, caressing his miniature moustache with one hand and gaily slapping his razor-like trouser-leg with the other, beamed delightedly at the girls. One of them put his titular dignity beyond all doubt by exclaiming – Oh! Valentino!

Tom had gone on his tour of the midlands and north partly in order to choose a new constituency: he had decided that it would make no sense to stand for Labour at Harrow. The constituency he settled on was Ladywood, in central Birmingham: the sitting member was the conservative Neville Chamberlain. The Chamberlain family enjoyed almost feudal political power in Birmingham: it would be an extraordinary feat if Tom could even get near to dislodging him. Tom had been offered a number of relatively safe seats, but he seemed to ʹsense that the initial euphoria in the Labour Party might, if he took too easy advantage of it, turn against him; and thus it would be most sensible for him to become involved in a serious fight.

The Labour Government of 1924 lasted less than a year. During the run up to the general election in November it appeared that there was such support for Tom in Ladywood that he might even win: then there was the Zinoviev letter – a document published just before the election purporting to come from the Communist International and encouraging British Communists to infiltrate the Labour Party but in fact a Tory forgery – and this had the effect of a number of hopeful Labour candidates just losing. At Ladywood it appeared at the first count that Tom had lost by seven; at the second count he had won by two; then at the third he lost by seventy seven. It was said that a Tory official had been seen 'disappearing towards the lavatory with a pile of votes'; but Tom discounted this, knowing that such stories were apt to crop up in close-run elections.

He did not seem to mind, in fact, the prospect of being out of Paliament for a while. This would give him time, he said, to sort out and to formulate his ideas: and he could probably choose when he liked a by-election by which he might be returned to Parliament.

Tom did in fact use the next two years to take stock of his position and to prepare for the future. He was twenty eight: he had had an extraordinarily crowded and successful career: but he had become known primarily as a critic with a cutting tongue and without much steadfastness or commitment to policy. It was essential, if he was to continue to claim to act on principle rather than on expediency or conventional party loyalties, that he should have a policy which would give substance to his principles.

During 1925 he and Cimmie went on a trip to India. The long journey by boat gave Tom an opportunity to read. He took out with him versions of the Vedas and the Upanishads ('every aspect of Indian religion had to be studied'); but the book that at this time made the most profound impression on him was one he picked up by chance in a bookshop in Port Said – Shaw's *The Perfect Wagnerite*. In the book Shaw takes the story of Wagner's *Ring* and interprets it as a parable about the collapse of capitalism and the emergence of a classless type of man to lead the proletariat: but Shaw cuts his own parable off before the last act of *Siegfried* and claims that from then on Wagner loses his grip on his serious theme and resorts to the histrionics of grand opera. But the point of the final dramas of the *Ring* is to illustrate how even the highest human intentions can be wrecked by human frailty; that the hopes of the most glorious leaders fail if frailty is not recognised. Tom, at this time, seemed to accept Shaw's truncated view of the allegory: drama might properly end with the hero in control. During the second half of his life, however, Tom wrote an essay which showed that he agreed more with Wagner than with Shaw.

One of the highlights of Tom's trip to India was a meeting with Gandhi: the latter was acting as chairman of a stormy meeting between Moslems and Hindus: Tom wrote – 'Throughout the uproar Gandhi sat on his chair on a dais, dissolved in helpless laughter, overwhelmed by the comical absurdity of human nature.' Tom seems to have loved India ('land of ineffable beauty and darkest sorrow') but at the time he did not seem to feel there was much in its paradoxes to be learned by him. He saw that India was being 'lost' by the 'bad manners' of Englishmen: but he did not easily think of politics in terms of what were and what were not good manners.

Another of the books he read on the journey to and from India was Keynes's *Tract on Monetary Reform*. Before this, his interest in politics had been mainly to do with matters of foreign or Irish policy – with the business of keeping the peace. He had made one important speech in 1921 on tariff reform; but for the most part he had felt no passionate concern with economic affairs. But when he joined the Labour Party he had seen, because he had been shown the manifestations of them, the most terrible and urgent problems of post-war England – poverty and unemployment. During his tour of the midlands he had been taken round the slums of Liverpool: he had written – 'The rehousing of the working classes ought in itself to find work for the whole of the unemployed for the next ten years.' This was typical, from now on, of the style of his thinking: if there were both unemployment and poverty, then surely, logically, it was the job of the government to use the unemployed to get rid of the poverty: questions of how, and using what money, should be secondary to the decision. But perhaps he did not have the confidence to expand on such theories until he read Keynes.

Tom's understanding of Keynes happened at a time when few English politicians were paying attention to him and there had been little in Tom's background to have made it likely that he would be the one who did. There were two strands of orthodox economic thinking at the time: one was the liberal laissez-faire attitude which insisted that world trade and the functioning of markets should be left to themselves: government interference not only threatened individual liberties but actually made economic conditions worse: this was a sort of ecological argument like that about the dangers of trying to manipulate the balances of nature. This made sense when the British, as pioneers of the Industrial Revolution, had been at the centre of the manipulation of world manufacture and world trade: it made less sense now, when British exports of machinery had resulted in a situation in which other countries, with cheaper labour, were now manufacturing more cheaply goods which had previously been almost a British monopoly. The second attitude was that of protectionism, which sought to keep out of Britain the products of other countries' cheap labour by imposing tariffs on imports. The trouble with this was that it required a market which would continue to accept, without imposing retaliatory tariffs, British manufactured goods which Britain needed to sell in order to be able to buy raw materials. Such had been the imperialist policy of Joseph Chamberlain and the Conservatives. But imperialist politics presupposed that colonies should be kept as producers of raw materials and buyers rather than producers of manufactured goods, and thus in a state of subjection. This not only seemed immoral but, in the face of world opinion and the threat of war, impractical. Thus British manufacturing industries, with the lack of a clear policy, continued to lose ground. There was poverty and unemployment.

Keynes's *Tract*, published in 1923, suggested that the government, by deliberately controlling and manipulating the supply of money, might affect the economic life of the country in areas which previously had been thought to be at the mercy of almost inexorable forces of nature. Tom became interested both in this new attitude to money and in the idea of government manipulation. In India he had been struck by the self-defeating attitudes of what had been up to now a mixture of laissez-faire and imperialism: he had seen the cotton mills where Indians worked 'for five shillings a week often with modern machinery supplied by

Lancashire for its own suicide: this was no monument either to the humanity or to the intelligence of the British Raj'. By the time he came back from India he had begun to work out his own theory – stimulated by Keynes, but arising from his own powers of reasoning unconfused by the complexities of academic training; also from his faith, now, that there were few human problems that could not be solved by reasoning.

Tom's economic theories became known as the Birmingham Proposals – after his candidature at Ladywood, he had made a political base in Birmingham. The proposals were outlined in speeches that he made to the Independent Labour Party Conference and Summer School in April and August 1925: they were of such importance to Tom's thinking and indeed to his whole political career that they deserve a chapter to themselves. Tom himself used to say in old age that he would like best to be remembered for his economic thinking; and all his subsequent economic thought – with its original vision and practical weaknesses – was for the most part an elaboration and elucidation of the Birmingham Proposals of 1925. Tom presented his theory in a pamphlet called *Revolution by Reason*: and in the very title can be seen something of the optimism and idealism of Tom's ways of thinking.

In 1926 Tom and Cimmie travelled in America. They tried to keep out of conventional smart society, though they were fêted by William Randolph Hearst and had a fine time as usual in esoteric café society. There was a big lawsuit going on at the time between Cimmie's Leiter relations: an English branch of the family, the Suffolks (Mary Curzon's younger sister Daisy had married the Earl of Suffolk in 1904) were suing an American branch, headed by Joe Leiter, who had become senior trustee of the Leiter Estate and whom his sister Daisy Suffolk was accusing of misappropriating funds. The Curzon branch of the family were nominally backing the Suffolks but were trying to keep clear: in Chicago, where the capitalist lawyers were at work, Cimmie and Tom painstakingly ensured that they were entertained by the Socialist Party of America. The chairman of this however telegraphed to them in rather grandiose style: 'It is a rare privilege to join with the good Comrades in Chicago in giving a royal welcome to these notable and high-souled comrades and making them feel they are at home in the hearts of their comrades in the glorious international'.

Tom and Cimmie also went on a fishing trip with Franklin Roosevelt on his yacht: they became friends: Tom thought Roosevelt 'a compassionate man' but with 'scarcely an inkling of the turmoil of creative thinking then beginning in America'. This creative thinking seemed to Tom to give support to his proposals in *Revolution by Reason*: he noted that 'the Ford factory produced the cheapest article and paid the highest wage in the world': was not this evidence that 'mass production for a large and assured home market is the industrial key'? He did not notice, or at least did not mention, that in Chicago for instance in 1926 there was enormous corruption.

When Tom got back to England he found that there was a by-election pending in Smethwick, a neighbouring constituency to Lady-wood in Birmingham. Tom was asked almost automatically if he would stand. He agreed. All the old skeletons were dug by the Tory Press out of their class-obsessed cupboards: Tom and Cimmie were supposed to drive up to Birmingham in a Rolls Royce and change into an Austin Seven in the suburbs: Tom was accused of having bribed the previous member of Parliament to retire (he was ill and died three months later): there were cartoons of Tom as a jewish-looking money-lender bribing the poor with bags of gold. Even Tom's father, the reprobate and by now somewhat alcoholic Sir Oswald, was unearthed by the *Daily Express* and in an interview said that Tom had been 'born with a golden spoon in his mouth...lived on the fat of the land, and had never done a day's work in his life'. Tom replied that he had been 'removed from the care of my father when I was five years of age by a court of law and since that date my father knows nothing of my life'. At the election meetings there was some violence: Tom's conservative opponent was, ironically a coal miner: when he referred to Tom's aristocratic background he was shouted down by Tom's followers singing *The Red Flag*. When this was reported scathingly in the Tory press a group of 'socialist amazons' tried to manhandle reporters in a press box. One of Cimmie's old school friends wrote to her from Scarborough – 'It isn't true, is it, that *you* climbed up on a wall and helped to shout down your opponent...My dear, I simply dare not own up that I know you here!'

But an editor wrote – 'If I were an elector of Smethwick the vicious personal attacks that are being made on him [Tom]...would certainly lead me to vote socialist'. And after Tom had got in, by a largely increased Labour majority of 6,582, the *Birmingham Post*, his chief opponent among the local papers, admitted that it had been unwise with its abuse: 'left to himself he would have fouled his own nest'.

Tom announced to the crowd outside the Town Hall – 'You have met and beaten the Press of reaction...My wonderful friends of Smethwick, by your heroic battle against a whole world in arms I believe you have introduced a new era for British Democracy.'

The Smethwick Labour party asked him whether, now the election was over, he and Cimmie would at last consent to appear in their Rolls Royce for the victory parade. Tom had to explain that the car really was part of a myth.

CHAPTER 7

The Birmingham Proposals

Tom's Birmingham Proposals, which he regarded as central to his political thinking, were an attempt to move beyond both laissez-faire economics which allowed British manufacturing industries to be undermined by the produce of cheap foreign labour, and imperialist-protectionist economics which depended for success on colonial exploitation and the risk of war. Tom called his pamphlet *Revolution by Reason*. 'Revolution' was necessary because of the urgency of the problem: 'time presses in the turmoil of war's aftermath...crisis after crisis sends capitalism staggering ever nearer to abysses of inconceivable catastrophe to suffering millions'. A solution by 'reason' was possible because men had not yet taken all peaceful steps available in the matter of control.

With laissez-faire economics there was by definition little government control. With imperialist-protectionist economics there was still the threat of foreign retaliation and the country's vulnerability to it. Tom's 1925 proposals claimed that the problem could be faced in the first place exclusively in terms of the home market – over which, it might reasonably be thought, a government might have control.

The problems at home were poverty and unemployment. A cure for these was available, it was suggested, once a connection was seen between the two. The reason why there was industrial unemployment was because there was no demand for manufactured goods: the reason why there was no demand for manufactured goods was because there was so much poverty that people could not afford them; the reason why there was poverty was because there was unemployment. There was no way out of this vicious but almost ridiculously simple circle so long as laissez-faire dogma ordained that any government interference would only make things worse, and protectionism increased no one's ability to buy manufactured goods. What was required was that the government should make life-giving injections into this otherwise moribund circle – injections of money from State banks, so that the whole process should be reversed.

The injections of money were to take the form of credit being made available to the poorer sections of the community so that their new purchasing power would stimulate a demand for goods. This demand would in turn create employment in industries hitherto moribund, and this increased demand for labour would mean that in a short time the poorer sections of the community would be employed and earning their own keep. The whole scheme seemed rather magical: you just touched with a wand the viciously circular economic pumpkin as it were, and the national economy turned into a golden coach. Tom perhaps felt himself justified in having a certain contempt for people who seemed not to have thought of it before.

The reason why people had not talked much of this sort of thing before was of course a fear of inflation. If the government just pumped more money into the economy then it was likely that the effect would be simply that prices would rise and real purchasing power be lessened. To counteract this Tom proposed that the availability of credit should be commensurate with the production of goods: 'new and greater demand must of course be met by a new and greater supply of goods or all the evils of inflation and price rise will result. Here our socialist planning must enter in . . . the whole of Socialist strategy must be directed to preventing any attempt by Capitalism to avoid meeting the new demand with a greater supply of goods and to play for a rise in prices'.

To safeguard against this, it was essential in the first place that the money made available should get into the right hands: it should go, simply, to the poor and not to the rich. 'Money in the hands of the workers means demand upon the great staple industries in which men and machines are now idle'. In the hands of the rich 'it concentrates in sudden whim upon some unprepared industry or rare commodity: prices soar and an unhealthy boom begins': then the rich man's fancy changes, and there is collapse and unemployment. The traditional means of making credit more easily available was to lower the rate at which money could be borrowed from banks; but this 'encourages the least desirable kind of borrower . . . a rush of speculators follows in order to borrow cheap money from the banks to buy and hold up commodities in expectation of a rise in price . . . little of the new purchasing power percolates through to the working class'.

In order that credit should be made available to the workers, banks would have to be nationalised: also an Economic Council 'vested with statutory powers' of supervision and direction would have to be set up. This Economic Council would give directions about where credit should be made available to consumers and where it should not: moreover it would direct where and how credit should be made available to the producers, the industries. This was the second essential factor in the task of ensuring that the supply of money would not be greater than the supply of goods and cause inflation.

The business of this Council will be to estimate the difference between the actual and the potential production of the country and to plan the stages by which that potential production can be evoked through the instrument of working class demand. The constant care of the Economic Council must be to ensure that demand does not outstrip supply and thus cause a rise in price. It is evident that the new money must be issued gradually and that industry must be given time to respond to the new demand. If the whole working class were suddenly given a £1 rise in wages one Saturday night, an all-round rise in prices would be inevitable... The Council would feel their way gradually to the maximum production. Sometimes they might enforce a wage rise of 3d or 6d a week. Sometimes they might cry a halt until supply had time to catch demand.

The way in which it was suggested that credit would best be extended both to the working class and to industry would be through a method whereby credit was given to certain industries on condition that they paid higher wages: thus money would be made available for both workers and producers at the same time. 'The Economic Council would fix from time to time wages which individual firms or amalgamations were to pay. The State Banks would then grant overdrafts for the payment of these wages until the Economic Council directed that the industry could shoulder its own wage bill by reason of its increased prosperity. No additional overdraft for wage purposes would then be granted.' In this way, increased production of goods would balance an increase in money and inflation would be avoided. All this would not affect the responsibility of the State for 'the proper maintenance of human existence' at a more basic level: suitable sums would continue to be paid to the unemployed through Labour Exchanges. But by the manipulation of credit for wages and the production of goods it was expected that the unemployed would quite rapidly be absorbed.

This method of controlling credit to industries for the payment of higher wages would also ensure:

1 Luxury trades need not receive the accommodation and could be closed down as and when desired. The operatives could then be maintained on unemployment pay while they were trained for absorption in useful industry.

2 The extra profits arising from the new demand created for consumers would be automatically absorbed by wages to whatever extent was decided. The Economic Council would arrange the gradual cessation of overdraft accommodation . . . Special taxation to deal with excess profits would thus be unnecessary.

3 Wages could be forced up in the highly skilled trades as their production increased simultaneously with the rises in the less-skilled and lower-paid occupations.

4 The firm grip of the Socialist State over the whole remaining field of Capitalist activity would be finally established. All industry would owe money to the State banks. The Constitutional Government would wield the vast powers now exercised by private bankers.

One of the chief aims of the operation, in fact was to take away power, and profit, from the hands of private financiers, and to give power to government and profit to workers and producers. Even if there was a small amount of inflation this would work to the detriment of financiers who obtained their money through fixed rates of interest, and it would be to the benefit of workers whose income was flexible. The whole scheme was one of 'summary socialism': if it worked it might indeed be some 'revolution by reason'.

The area of weakness in all this and one that Tom did not explore – as he had not yet explored the weaknesses of Shaw's interpretation of Wagner's *Ring* – was the fact that the scheme depended on human beings to make it workable. The Economic Council would have almost dictatorial powers: it is the case with human beings who have great powers unrestrained by traditional safeguards that they become corrupt or at best inefficient: even more, schemes that depend for their health on the near-miracle working of human beings usually carry with them the seeds of an almost deliberate self-destruction – as if the imposition of such responsibility sends people mad. Tom's proposals for the over-riding powers of an Economic Council were forerunners of what later came to be his views about the necessity of a corporate Fascist state: it was his belief, possibly rational in theory, that only by such powers could something decisive be done about situations of crisis. Tom in fact usually exaggerated the imminence of crises: but even in so far as he did not, he mistook something about human nature: he believed that human beings, when it had been clearly explained to them what were their vital needs and necessities, would not only altruistically but selfishly become honest and reasonable: they would sacrifice what might be short term advantages for long term ends. What he never saw was that in politics as in other forms of human activity human beings are for the most part interested in some sort of struggle, in manoeuvrings for power, in risks and even unpleasantnesses; and that these are often in direct opposition to what might reasonably be seen as long-term ends. Tom always saw himself as the perfectly reasonable man at the head of something like the proposed Economic Council: about other people, he was torn between imagining they were like how he imagined himself, and being dismissive of them when he found that they were not. If he had had talent for introspection or had allowed himself much practice at it, he might have seen that within the area of his own short-term drives and obsessions there were possibly seeds of self-destruction: he had a gambler's love of challenge and risk: the way he showed his contempt for his fellow politicians, for instance, was unlikely to work for his long-term ends. But his refusal to see that a consideration of what human beings are actually like is a vital part in any scheme about what human beings can actually do, is at the heart of the failures of this story.

Perhaps what allowed him to be so impervious to rumination about human nature or himself was the tendency of his critics to be just the same. It had been the tradition of economists to assume without argument that human beings were reasonable: this was a rule of the game: how else could they carry on as though their pronouncements were scientific and not at any moment likely to become nonsensical? It had been the tradition of left-wing politicians to make out that however much capitalists and conservatives had been and always would be corrupted by power, the revolutionary working class would not be: how else could they go on playing the game of protesting that as representatives of the working class they were incorruptibly driving for power? But whereas most of these people for all their lack of facility for introspection did seem to have some unspoken instinct, in England at least, about what human beings were actually like – they usually in fact withdrew before the probable consequences of their words had had much effect – Tom, by reason perhaps of his upbringing or nature, did not: he had the aloofness and perhaps the arrogance to believe that reasonable words, at least his own, might in fact mean what they implied. This was one reason why he could so often make rings round his opponents by reasoning: he believed in it; while they, although they said they did, ultimately did not. Yet what they felt instinctively, and might have answered Tom by, was traditionally unspoken. They could not say to him in effect – Look, in your reasoning you leave out of account something about human nature: you leave out the fact that human beings with part of themselves like turmoil and something to grumble at and perhaps even failures to feel comfortable in: your economic perfect blue-print will not work simply because people will not want it to. They could not say this to him because this sort of language was not in the area prescribed for politicians. But then they could not argue with Tom because he could beat them by his un-trammelled faith in reason. As a result they had to answer him by ostracising him and hardly answering him at all. This had the effect on Tom of making him think that his arguments were unanswerable: and so a new vicious circle was set up – that of Tom having contempt for his opponents for their silence, and they, stung by this, having no reply except a hatred that might indeed sometimes seem contemptible.

Tom might have learned something of the paradoxes of human nature, it might have been thought, from his relationship with Cimmie: but the convention was overwhelming that human beings might be one sort of thing in their private lives, but were something quite different and altogether more straightforward in politics. Every now and then Tom did seem to have an inkling of where the demands he was making on people by his proposals might lead were they ever put into effect – of how there might be failure unless a demand for something more than economic rationality was met. But then – what was a proper attitude to the risk of failure? Towards the end of even such a staid document as *Revolution by Reason* Tom dropped his tone of logic and entered into the rhetoric which was his other special talent, and which he used to try to persuade people when he felt the sands of reason running out; also, perhaps, to cover doubts that he must sometimes have felt yawning beneath himself. The style of the pamphlet suddenly changes: the substance of the rhetoric – and this is characteristic of the perorations of nearly all Tom's speeches – is permeated by a concern that has nothing to do with reason. The final tone of *Revolution by Reason* is a call for sacrifice and a bid for glory:

> We have reached a supreme crisis in the history of humanity. We stand, indeed, at the cross roads of destiny. Once again in the lash of great ordeal stings an historic race to action . . .

We must recapture the spirit of rapturous sacrifice. That immortal spirit was evoked by war between men of many common interests for purposes still obscure or frustrated. Why cannot a greater spirit be summoned forth by the war of all mankind against poverty and slavery? In our hands is the awakening trumpet of reality. Labour alone holds the magic of sacrifice. Dissolved are all other creeds of baser metal beneath ordeal by fire.

CHAPTER 8

Nursery World

My own consciousness as it emerged into this setting of strangely mixed reason and rapture was such that very little remains in it of these early years: I remember nothing of the country houses in which we stayed during the summers before I was four: and of the London house in Smith Square – where we lived on and off till I was eight – I remember a few scenes but with myself as a spectator as it were looking down on myself rather than as a participant. 8 Smith Square was a Queen Anne house or more accurately two houses knocked into one: my father used to say it was too small because the family were so much on top of each other: literally on top were the day nursery and night nursery on the third floor. In the night nursery the cots of my sister Vivien and myself were side by side and at night we would tell each other fantastic stories about children who had run away from their families and who lived in jungles or on rafts. When Nanny came to bed we would try to lie awake and watch her in half dark and through half closed eyes as she performed her amazing trick of undressing and putting on her nightdress without appearing at any moment to be wearing anything less than her full complement of clothing. In the day nursery there were cupboards full of toys all along one wall and life there seemed to be mainly a matter of being ready to do battle with my sister about minuscule matters of possession or prestige: however spoilt we were in our vast quantity of toys, there was still the desire for what the other had got and the possibility of a fight almost to death against dispossession. If my father had wanted to learn about human nature, he might have come up more often to the nursery.

From the square below – we were usually in London during winter – there would come from time to time strange noises that did seem to emanate from some jungle: the sound of the muffin man with his bell, who carried his tray on his head; the cries of the any-old-iron man with his horse and cart who seemed to be calling for dead bodies. In the evenings there was the lamplighter with his long pole with a star on the end like the wand of a magician.

Each year there was a great festivity in the streets, which was boat-race day. Two men would appear very early on opposite corners of the square selling pale-blue and dark-blue rosettes. Huge crowds seemed to gather and drift past. The part of the river where the race took place was miles away, as indeed was anything to do with Oxford or Cambridge from most of the people who liked so arbitrarily and passionately to take sides. My sister and I, for no reason, were dedicated to Cambridge.

Most mornings our normal routine was for Nanny, Vivien and myself (at first in a pram) to go up Great Smith Street, past Parliament Square, across Birdcage Walk, and into St James's Park and then on to Hyde Park if Nanny felt energetic. In St James's Park we would feed the ducks or the pelicans: we were dressed very smartly for this: I remember buttons on boots and gaiters which were fastened with a sort of torture-instrument with a hook. One of the points of being immaculate in the parks was so that Nanny should not lose prestige with other nannies. Before she had come to us, Nanny had been for a time with a branch of the Rothschild family: we met, and had to keep up with, their children Rosemary and Eddie.

In the afternoons we would go down to our mother in the drawing room when she and my father were there. I remember nothing of these times. One of my sister's few memories (she was at Smith Square on and off till she was ten) is of our mother reading a story to us in the drawing room and then having to break off and rush away to vote in the House of Commons – a bell which had been installed in the house having gone off like a burglar alarm.

Sometimes my mother and father would come up to the night nursery to say goodnight before they went out to dinner. I have more memories of my father than my mother at these times, perhaps because he tried to be funny. Once he was going to dinner at Buckingham Palace and he was wearing full evening dress with medals: he showed us how he had pinned these medals on his behind. I remember thinking this enormously funny.

My sister Vivien is two and a half years older than I. When I was born, my mother reported that she was 'very gentle and attentive': Nanny reported that she exclaimed 'I'll bite him!' A year later Nanny wrote 'Vivien gets so excited when he walks and usually yells so loudly that it frightens him and down he flops'. By 1925 she was recording – 'Nicko tries so hard to turn cartwheels and somersaults like the clowns but Vivien's one ambition is to hold him high above her head with one hand.' My stepmother Diana used to say that my sister and me were like the characters in the *Peanuts* cartoon, Charlie Brown and Lucy. We were very close, and loved each other, and fought, and doubtless did much to save each other's lives.

Nanny's letters to my mother were beautifully written in a clear unadorned style. They began 'Dearest Lady Cim' and ended 'Love from Odie' – which had been Cimmie's nickname for Nanny when she herself had been a child. Nanny was a brave, strongwilled woman without a trace of subservience: she seemed to look on most of the grown-up world as children. She accepted some conventions of the time about upbringing which would now be thought idiosyncratic: she would keep my sister and me for what seemed hours (and I think sometimes was) on our pots: we became adept at moving about the room on them like hermit crabs: our word for shit became – in the light of Nanny's injunctions – 'try-hard'. I have wondered what Freudians would make of this conjunction of shit with 'try-hard'. It was also about this time that I apparently got an obsession about taking keys out of doors and putting them down lavatories.

The time when I first seemed to become a participant rather than an onlooker in my childhood scene was when my mother and father bought a house near Denham, in Buckinghamshire, at the end of 1926: this was to be our home for the next fourteen years. Denham was only twenty miles from London but in those days it was in farming country: the house when we bought it was called Savoy Farm but my mother changed the name back to its more ancient form of Savehay Farm which was more in keeping with what she liked in the way of rustic simplicity. It was an Elizabethan farmhouse with six bedrooms and four reception rooms and a huge garden surrounded by water. My mother and father added a new wing at the back which contained four more guest rooms and servants rooms and a servants' hall. We moved into Savehay Farm in the spring of 1927 and the best of my childhood seems to have been nurtured by this house: I can remember details of every room in it: I still sometimes dream that I have bought it back, and am living there. I suppose it represents some Garden of Eden.

The river that ran past the end of one of the lawns of the garden was the Colne, a tributary of the Thames. There was a punt and a large canoe on the river and these could, with difficulty, be manoeuvred by my sister and me along a sidestream that ran right round the house – over a waterfall and under bridges – a notable adventure. There were two weirs on the river, one at each end of our land (a hundred and twenty acres of farmland which went with the house): across one weir there was a bridge that led to an island thick with undergrowth like a jungle; across the other a bridge led to a thatched cottage, empty, like something in a fairy tale. During weekdays my father and mother were usually away: Nanny miraculously (or because she had been brought up in a home of sixteen children) did not take too much notice of what went on out of her sight: my sister and I were thus allowed much freedom. We would devise fantastic explorations and obstacle courses for ourselves: these were known as 'mucks': from branch to branch of trees, along the tops of walls, down over a water-wheel, up through high barn windows. (There were huge high barns unused because of the state of farming at the time in England). The bridge across the weir to the magic island jungle had partly collapsed, but it could still be crossed with legs on either side of the handrail: beyond the island there was a gigantic railway viaduct and beyond this, like an ogre, someone called Sir Robert Vansittart lived, who was an enemy of my father's being something to do with the Foreign Office. In the thatched cottage at the other end of the river my sister and I were sometimes allowed to camp; like Hansel and Gretel having been freed from their fairy tale.

What meant most to me about Savehay Farm I think was that for the first time I was able to be alone: before this, I had had to go under bedclothes and pretend to be in a one-man submarine before I felt alone. At Savehay Farm there was space – also room to hide. I remember the need for, and feeling of safety in, places to hide. There was a carved-out hollow in a thicket of bamboos: a passage through brambles and nettles: a disused tank in the rafters of a barn. In such places I could crouch, and listen, and hear the cries of huntsmen and steps of predators going past. The huntsmen and predators were only my good nanny and sister – those denizens of my unconscious. But my main memories of Savehay Farm have become to do with my own five senses: the hot buzzing of flies above nettles; the high ribs of the viaduct from which cold drips dropped down; the soddenness of weeds like bodies against the grating of a weir; the acrid smell of old plaster coming off the walls of the thatched cottage like dead skin.

Even when my parents were at Savehay Farm they often dallied in other parts of the garden. There was a rose-garden where my father sometimes walked: he would go to and fro, up and down; preparing his speeches, I suppose, by which he might order the world. In summer he would sometimes walk there naked: Nanny would warn us – Do not go near! God walked thus, I suppose, in the Garden of Eden. So by seeing my father, or God, naked, might one know the difference between good and evil? I would creep along the passage on the first floor to where there was a window that looked over the rose-garden: this was risky because the window was in my father's bedroom: but if he was in the rose-garden he could not – or could he? – be in two places at once? However then, after all – how white and gentle and vulnerable he looked! So what was all the fuss about our not being allowed to see him in the rose-garden?

My father was, it was true, sometimes frightening. He had a way of suddenly switching from being the benign joker to someone with his chin up, roaring, as if he were being strangled. He would usually roar when he was not getting what he wanted – from servants; from my mother. Once when he was trying to work in his study and a small dog that belonged to my sister and myself was outside on the lawn barking, he leaned out of his window with his shotgun and fired off both barrels in the general direction of the dog. The dog stopped barking. My sister and Nanny were somewhat outraged at this: but I remember thinking – He would not have missed, would he, if he had been aiming at the dog? And how more efficiently do you stop a dog barking?

Nanny would tell stories of my father's terrible rudeness to servants: but she would add – 'He was only once rude to me.' Then she would wait, looking stern; and we children would understand that she had perhaps just looked thus at my father. She also told a story about Mabel, the parlourmaid, an equally formidable woman who was the friend of May, the gentle housemaid. Once my father had been rude to Mabel and then to her too he had never been rude again: she had answered him back with a very rude word. We knew it was no good pressing Nanny to tell us what was this word: it was something that grown-ups could tell stories about, but not utter.

Life for the children revolved, as usual, around Nanny, Mabel and May, and Andrée, my mother's lady's maid. Andrée had been with my mother before she had married: she stayed with the family, as Nanny did, after my mother's death for more than twenty years. She was a small determined Frenchwoman; indeed it is difficult to imagine my father being rude to her. I think my father must have got his reputation for rudeness from his relationships with manservants; which is probably why they do not seem to have been permanent figures in my childhood. There was for a time a Mr Cox, the butler, who hung about in a striped apron in the pantry and was the guardian of a huge knife-sharpening machine like a butter-churn, and another machine which curiously could sharpen two pencils at once. I have no memories of any cook; they too must have come and gone: my mother had no reputation for caring about good cooking.

There were three staircases in the house – one at my father's and mother's end, one in the middle between the day and the night nursery, and one in the new wing between the guest rooms and the rooms of the servants. The only person who had a room regularly at my mother's and father's end of the house was my Aunty Baba; she was put in a rather grand room with a seventeenth century fresco on the wall of men in striped knickerbockers playing golf. Aunty Nina was always put at the other end of the house. To the children, in the middle, it often seemed as if we owned the house; it was we who remained, and the people looking after us, when everyone else had gone.

My mother's and father's end of the house was somewhat secret; taboo. You went along the passage, up three steps, were on the threshold of mysteries. My mother's bedroom was large and blue and airy and had a mass of small glass ornaments on shelves: they were of animals and birds and of a kind that would now probably be thought rather vulgar: my mother collected these when she went abroad, especially in Venice. My father's bedroom was smaller and brown and looked out on to the rose-garden: there was a scrubbed oak chest in it that was always locked. Of even deeper mystery were my mother's and father's bathrooms – there were two side by side across the passage. My mother's bathroom had the usual array of bottles and bowls and powders and creams; my father's had an enigmatic apparatus that hung on the back of the door and looked like a gutted octopus. I knew it was no use asking Nanny about this: the subject would be unmentionable like the word used by Mabel the parlourmaid. I worked out later that it was an apparatus for giving enemas.

When the children came down in the evenings at Savehay Farm we went not to the formal drawing room which was used only when guests were in the house, but to my mother's sitting room which was known as the Garden Room. This had low beams and a huge open fireplace and glass walking sticks hanging on the walls: there my mother would read to us. Once my father was persuaded to read poetry: he read Swinburne, and I fell asleep, and when I woke was covered with confusion. I wanted to ask – But might not such beautiful noises be supposed to send you to sleep?

There were certain moments of the year when it was the tradition that mothers and fathers should make special efforts with their children; the most striking of these was Christmas. After the usual opening of the stockings at Savehay Farm and the going to church with Nanny (my mother and father never went to church) and after further presents and the christmas lunch, we had our special ritual. My father would say that he had to have a short sleep; we would exhort him not to, because after lunch was the time when Father Christmas arrived and my father might miss him. My father would promise that he would only have a nap, and be there for Father Christmas. But then at about three o'clock we would hear Father Christmas's sleigh-bells outside – this was my mother and Mabel the parlourmaid tinkling away in the garden – and we wanted to wake up my father but it was held to be too late: we were rushed out of the house by Nanny: Father Christmas was said to be already arriving at the top of the chimney. Father Christmas was of course my father, who in his study having dressed up in Father Christmas clothes complete with realistic beard and mask was now climbing up the Garden Room chimney on a stepladder held by May the housemaid while we were hoping to see him coming down from the sky at the top. We were again too late! Father Christmas was already on his way down the chimney – we were rushed back into the house just in time to see him emerge into the Garden Room down the steps held by May. All this was expertly handled by my mother – or else we children were rather thick. But my father was a very good actor: he spoke in a slow exhausted voice: poor Father Christmas! with all the other children in the world to get round to! one should not ask too many questions. And of course he had to wear a mask, to protect his face from soot. Anyway there was not much time: after we had got our presents from his sack we were rushed out of the house to see if we could catch him coming out of the roof: we just missed him again! but couldn't we hear the sleigh bells? And then after a suitable time of chasing bells around the garden there was the business of running back to my father's study and accusing him of being, yet again, so greedy and lazy that he had to go to sleep after lunch and miss Father Christmas! After a time I think I came to believe that Father Christmas must come from Harrods. Neither my sister nor I saw through my father's act while he was doing it.

There was a further ritual on Christmas evening which my father once more dominated and by which he charmed his children as indeed he charmed women. Just as my mother, when he was being loving towards her, was his mutton, his moo-moo; so were his children, as his term of endearment, porkers. When we children were making too much noise in his presence he would intone, as if it were some mystic mantra – 'What is it that makes more noise than one porker stuck under a gate?' – and we would groan, because we had heard the answer so many times before: and then he would give the answer himself – 'Two porkers stuck under a gate!' – and then he would laugh, with a strange clicking sound behind his teeth. On Christmas evenings, then, we would gather round the Christmas tree and we would all hold hands and my father would begin one of his mantra chants and this would go faster and faster as we went faster and faster round the tree until we all fell down and my father's chant would be just – Porker porker porker...

All this was rather magical for children: the gods descended, and played, and put on a tremendous performance. But still, when the excitement was over, what was the world from which the gods came down? It did in fact seem that much of ordinary grown-up life consisted of things like making remarks that did not require answers with a distant look in one's eye; uttering noises which had the effect of everyone's falling about roaring with laughter. My awareness of my mother's and father's friends at Savehay Farm belongs to a slightly later time in this story: but what I remember from an early age about the grown-up world – not the world of Nanny and Mabel and May who stayed around and got things done but the world of god-like figures who came and went – was the way in which people did in fact seem to be making noises that were more like a baying, a trumpeting, than the telling of anything: noises just to let other people know that they were there, perhaps; or to give warning; or possibly to attract new friends. These noises most often came from behind closed doors: grown-ups did not seem to want to perform their most esoteric rituals in front of children. But at Savehay Farm I would creep down from time to time and would listen outside the dining room door which was just at the bottom of the nursery stairs; this was when my mother and father were having what Nanny called a dinner. The uproar seemed to be talk: but what on earth were they talking *about*; and who was listening? It was like the cries of the any-old-iron man; the bell of the man selling muffins. It was the roar of some jungle: not the nice quiet jungle across the broken bridge over the river: it was as if there were a forest fire.

CHAPTER 9

The Legend

When Cimmie arrived back from America in 1926 she gave an interview to an American newspaper in which she explained about what had been thought from her youth to have been her 'bolshevik' views, and why she had become a socialist.

> If you are to understand my position, you must take into account all the facts in my upbringing. You will understand that either I had to give in absolutely to the past – to ignore all that was happening in this country and the rest of the world – or to resist upon every issue. I suppose my father and I were two very typical figures, and that the same drama has been enacted in many homes; only I do not know another man who was so splendidly, so utterly symbolic of the old world, the pre-war world, as was my father. I should like to think that I am as typical of the new world, the post-war world.

When George Curzon was dying in March 1925 and he was already not on speaking terms with Cimmie owing to the quarrel over her money, she and Tom had just returned from their trip round India. George Curzon was told a story about how Tom, when in India, had been present at an official dinner at which the King's health had been drunk and he, Tom, had refused to raise his glass. At first Curzon had not believed this story; then, because he learned that so many other people had heard it, he believed that it 'must be true'. All this was related back to Cimmie by a Curzon aunt. A few days later her father died.

The story of the wine-glass in India is typical not only of the sort of stories that were told about Tom but of his own and other people's reactions to them. It is inconceivable that the incident in the story could have been enacted by Tom deliberately: such a gesture would have

seemed to him just silly. But there were of course people who would
want to imagine such a story; and Tom did little to persuade them it
might not be true. The Curzon aunt who related the story to Cimmie
finished her letter with – 'But why does Tom not take steps to deny
these stories?' – and her question seems relevant to something that might
be true.

Members of the aristocracy in those days had put upon them some
of the fantasies that are now put on to pop-singers and film-stars: they
were the stuff of newspaper gossip: people queued up in streets to see
them. Cimmie had become a somewhat legendary figure at the time of
her marriage: there were other upper class girls like this: but there was
no one quite like Cimmie after she had become Labour.

In the Labour Party Cimmie and Tom took upon themselves a new
form of adulation: it seemed part of the new legend perhaps that they
should also suffer calumny. Cimmie's old friends took trouble to write
to her about things they had overheard at dinner parties or on the tops
of buses – 'It's enough to make 'er father get up out of 'is grave and
smash 'er, vulgar little beast'. But if she and Tom started to worry about
replying to such remarks, they might not be able to be able to maintain
their energy and dignity as pioneers. People who become legendary
must have something in them that wants to be like this: they must be
impervious to, thrive on even, something of calumny: part of their
strength, and their magic, is that they should seem to scorn herd-
reactions. This can be a danger, as well as a strength. Tom sometimes
went to great trouble legally to take action about libels against him: he
almost never, in the light of what people said about him, showed much
personal concern or modified his behaviour.

What Tom in his possibly for the most part unconscious heart seems
to have wanted to do is to create a legend: this was more fundamental
to him than that he should acquire power. Tom's biographer, Robert
Skidelsky, has written about him that 'he was a complete professional
in everything except the winning of power'. This was not just through
mischance: it is an aristocratic attitude that says – Take me or leave me;
I am as I am; either follow me or do not. It is this sort of attitude, also,
that creates legends. And there is a way perhaps, in which the world in
the long run is more affected by legends than by the manipulation of
power: legends alter the way people think: this is on a higher level (if
they are recorded) than that of power.

This would not have been worked out by Cimmie or Tom; there was
something of it inevitably in their natures. They both came from
backgrounds in which what mattered was more what you were than

what you did: aristocrats are supposed to have star quality – they are not simply actors. Both of them moreover seemed to have had some need of the aura that surrounds legends: as if only by this could they live up to the expectations they had found themselves landed with. They had to have constant reassurance – as if to placate demons.

With Tom there was his compulsion to be so frequently running after, and conquering, women: by this he got reassurance. He also used his seductive powers politically. A Labour colleague remembers being bowled over by Tom's flattery; then seeing Tom's eyes going past him to a waiting crowd.

Tom was good at telling Cimmie how wonderful she was: his letters contain almost endless protestations of love. He and Cimmie were known to quarrel: he had a terrible temper: he sometimes abused her publicly. Yet in all his letters to her there are hardly any words of reproach. It is as if, so far as letters were concerned, what was important to him was the use of gentle and reasoned words to retain her love: this was more important to him than efforts to face facts or get at the truth. He willed that he should retain her love by telling her so often how she had his own.

> My own most precious in the world, take care of her darling self and be strong and well for his return and fun with him. My own beloved – give a kiss to herself from her adoring Tom

With Cimmie, there had always been her recognition that she needed protestations of love: she had written of this as a schoolgirl: her mother had died when she was seven: her father, whom she admired, had fought her: she had needed to put herself at the centre of a group of adored and adoring friends. She would have accepted Tom's protestations simply because she required them.

> I do think it's been a good thing to be apart just for once, it may even be a good thing some time again, but please not for a very very long time. I so adore your letters, but I do so terribly miss you.

Then by joining the Labour Party, Cimmie opened herself to a whole new form of adulation: she became like some star actress suddenly offered a stage. She and Tom became the special favourites of Independent Labour Party politicians from Glasgow – James Maxton, Pat Dollan, John Wheatley. Tom was in great demand as an orator: he was loved for his rhetoric, his style. Pat Dollan wrote to Cimmie 'He has leader qualities but he must be prepared to fight every inch. I like him when he is combatant because his combatant temper is what we need'. Glasgow politicians did not much like his pamphlet *Revolution by Reason*, because its reasonable socialist proposals would interfere with the freedom of Trade Union bargaining. But Cimmie began to be almost as much in demand as Tom: this was due not to her power with words, but simply to her ability to get herself loved. Pat Dollan wrote after an Independent Labour Party summer school – 'Yourself were one of the best of sports and everybody was pleased with you for your fun, fellowship, adventure and readiness to help. There is big work for you to do for the ILP and Socialism, and you can do it.'

The Independent Labour Party had been formed at the end of the nineteenth century to keep pure the creed of socialism at a time when many groups which called themselves Labour had not been sure about what alliances might be made. It still in the 1920's saw itself as the power-house of true socialism. It held its summer schools at Easton Lodge, a house belonging to Lady Warwick; where, in Tom's words 'very serious discussions' were rounded off in the evenings by 'charades, songs and dances'; also 'elements of the modern love-in'.

During 1925 Cimmie received many offers herself to stand for Parliament: she accepted one to become the Labour candidate for Stoke-on-Trent. This was not far, but perhaps, far enough, from Tom's constituency at Smethwick.

In London Cimmie had for some time been giving dinner-parties for Labour politicians – Ramsay MacDonald, Arthur Henderson, J. H. Thomas. James Maxton refused – 'I make a point of steering clear of all social functions.' Ramsay MacDonald continued his rather flowery flirtation with Cimmie – 'That disgruntled left-winger, Providence, has given me a nasty knock since we whispered "Easter" to each other and Tom made the scandalous proposal that I should take you to Corsica whilst he went to the ILP conference'. But then – 'I shall do what you like on Tuesday, dine in or out, go to a solemn or gay play (the latter preferred)'. Cimmie sent him a Christmas present for which he thanked her:

> One corner of my books shelves says to the other 'I was given by so-and-so' and looks most self-satisfied. Another answers 'Poof! do you know what Lady Cynthia gave *me*?' and puts its nose in the air.

Cimmie became something of a guardian angel to men who were now working with Tom and who might have been somewhat in awe of him but who found Cimmie approachable. Foremost amongst these was Allan Young, the son of a railway worker in Glasgow, who came to Birmingham as Labour agent for Tom and later became his full-time political secretary in London. He wrote to Cimmie after a weekend in the country in 1926 –

My thanks for a jolly weekend are delayed but sincere. I blush occasionally in fear that my crude behaviour may have irritated you but you will be kind and tolerant I am sure. After all I was 'born to the thong and the rod' and my body and mind are perhaps not yet attuned to sweeter things ...

Then later, when he had been with Tom and Cimmie abroad –

You gave me beauty – pictures that will live for ever: space – in the sense that I was separated from the vortex of petty problems: privacy – in the sense that your fine culture (which is feeling) enables you to refrain from interference. I shall *dream* no more of France and Italy – I shall enjoy their beauty because I have absorbed it. The sun will stay with me now, and the added width and scope of my life and imagination will enable me to appreciate to the fullest the sweetness and generosity of your friendship.

Another of Tom's Birmingham colleagues that Cimmie took under her wing was John Strachey, five years younger than Tom, son of St Loe Strachey the editor of the *Spectator* and cousin of Lytton Strachey. He had joined the Labour Party before he had met Tom; then Tom helped him to get a constituency at Aston in Birmingham. John Strachey was unlike most of the people who worked in politics with Tom and Cimmie at this time in that he was upper or upper-middle class: he had been to Eton and Oxford. He hero-worshipped Tom. He was some sort of cavalier to Cimmie.

During the summer of 1925 he had spent much time with them and he was their guest in Venice in August. He and Tom there worked together on *Revolution by Reason*; later John Strachey wrote a book with the same title as Tom's pamphlet. Bob Boothby was also a guest of Tom's and Cimmie's in Venice that summer: he wrote years later – 'Every morning Tom Mosley and John Strachey discuss *Revolution by Reason* ... This was the period when Mosley saw himself as Byron rather than Mussolini ... He was certainly a powerful swimmer and used to disappear at intervals into the lagoon to commune with himself.' When

Strachey's book was finished he dedicated it to 'O.M. who may one day
do the things of which we dream.'

John Strachey was by far the closest of Tom's Labour associates: he
was an intellectual: he was the only friend who without much difficulty
straddled, as Tom and Cimmie apparently so effortlessly did, the world
of Birmingham socialist politics and international high-life in Venice.
In 1925 he wrote a thank-you letter to Cimmie:

> Dear, dear Cim
> (I can't rise to Bob's beginning).
> When one has stayed with someone off and on for about six
> months there is something rather comically inadequate about writing
> a Collins. Still I do want, somehow or other, to thank you for Venice.
> I quite literally can't tell you how much I enjoyed it. But almost more
> than that it has somehow *meant* a most tremendous lot to me. In some
> obscure way I feel quite different to before I went – altogether more
> capable of *coping* with life. Of course it is largely that one feels so
> marvellously well – with deep reserves of sun-energy in one.
> And I do terribly want to tell you how grateful I am to you. I know
> very well my many imperfections and shortcomings as a guest, so I
> realise *how* nice of you it has been to bear with me so many months.
> But Venice was marvellous. I ran through, in that month, as many
> kinds of emotions and experiences as would last in England for a year.
> It somehow enlarged and liberated one. (Bob felt it – as he showed
> in that never sufficiently admired letter of his!) A little more and we
> shall, as he put it, strike the big notes again.
> I am talking nonsense – I only mean that when we were all together
> we sometimes seemed able to strike points, moments, sparks, of
> enjoyment, of *fun*, which set the place on fire.
> A more incoherent letter than usual. But please, please, take it as
> a symbol, a token, of something felt very deeply, even though not
> expressed at all. You were, you are, the centre round which we all
> radiated. Thank you.
>
> John

Bob Boothby was a young conservative MP. He disagreed with Tom
politically: but he believed, and continued to do so during a friendship
which lasted for the whole of Tom's life, that there were more important things in life (and indeed in politics) than political agreement. The
letter he wrote to Cimmie and which John Strachey mentions in his
letter, was:

Darling Lady Cynthia,

(I humbly apologise – all other words are hopelessly inadequate). How can I thank you as you ought to be thanked? An impossible task! I enjoyed – rapturously – every moment. No, there was one – at Faustino's entertainment – when I had drunk too little and too much – that which produces the 'grumpy' stage – and I was a credit neither to you nor to myself: but I withdrew once more to 'commune alone with the sea' ...

I can truthfully say that never in my life have I experienced such sustained enjoyment at so high a pitch. It was MARVELLOUS (one l or two? one I think). I thank you 1000 times ... If and when I do return I am going to ask you to let me spray myself with your palm oil and sit, at intervals, within hail of your 'cabano' and throw a medicine ball at you and give you dinner at the Luna – if you will. I did a crazy thing the night I left – took the fastest motor boat in Venice and flew to the Lido and looked at the moon, which was farcical, and lay on the sands and got bitten by sand-fleas, and vastly overpaid the motor-boat man, and came back god knows when in a 'vapore' and the slowest gondola in Venice. But it was exquisite and I loved it.

I think your husband (damned Socialist though he is By God) will be Prime Minister for a very very long time, because he has the Divine Spark which is almost lost nowdays, and getting less and less. They had it once – all of them. I've just been reading here a life of Chopin: a medium composer maybe, but a tremendous man. Broken by his own powers of emotional feeling – a hitch in some paltry love affair enough to send him to bed in a decline for months – what reduces us to inane guffaws reduced them to a temperature of 104, consumption, and death. The result being that they produced creative geniuses by the dozen – and what do we produce? The Lido beach. It's a little disheartening.

I'm so sorry about this outburst but I learnt with you what some have tried in vain to teach me – that the only possible thing to do is to steep oneself in the XVIIIth and early XIXth centuries and try to understand (if not try to catch a touch of) the spirit that moved them. For this – for the gondola, for the palatial drawing room, the food, the champagne, the fun both in and out of the water (bar that appalling boat that sank, and a dive I can never quite forget) the arguments (not least the one about Torcello) and the staggering hospitality in every direction – I thank you ...

Yours ever most gratefully and sincerely
Bob Boothby

> PS. I am conscious of having been, on the whole, *not* a success. But I think I have *one* conquest to my credit. Mabel (that Great Woman) said 'Goodbye Old Man' – and I *thought* her voice broke.

There were many people who at this time wrote to Cimmie similar (if not so good) letters: they tell of her gaiety; of her ability to give enjoyment; of how under her attention people seemed to expand and feel transformed. This ability to produce warmth and wit in personal life seemed as important to her as was the ability to produce enthusiasm in the world of politics: it seemed important to Tom too, who got pleasure from social life far beyond the taking up of opportunities for flirtation and conquest. Before he had met Cimmie he had of course shone in this area, but perhaps without much ease: throughout his married life Tom depended for naturalness in social relationships largely on his wives. But in 1925 it would have been the problem for both him and Cimmie to try to relate – if they wanted to – the world of Venice and the South of France to that of the Birmingham and Clydeside politicians.

Sometimes Cimmie was warned of such a difficulty by more a serious voice than those of newspapers which continued to ask simply – How could anyone be a socialist and go to Venice and have fun? Tom's and Cimmie's answer to this sort of question continued sensibly to be – their money could be put to better socialist uses by themselves than if it was given away: also class barriers are genuine, and they can better be dealt with by suitably crossing them rather than by pretending they don't exist. But the trouble with this type of answer was that it had traditionally been held by socialists that it was just the possession of unearned money that was the evil in capitalist societies and not the uses to which it was put. (Lenin had remarked that a 'good' capitalist was worse than a bad one because he delayed the revolution.) A Marxist acquaintance wrote to Cimmie to ask – had she faced the serious dangers inherent in what she was trying to do?

> You an aristocrat and I a petty bourgeois are equally unreliable in the world situation of today because however good our principles, honest our intentions, and steadfast our will, we cannot be relied on to crush in our own characters those inborn tendencies which carry us back to our own sets in any crisis – we *may* be faithful when the time comes, but we cannot be sure of it until the time. The declassed aristocrat and the declassed artist are individual tragedies which simply don't matter when civilisation is at stake. Within our private lives we may have compensations ...

Tom and Cimmie at their wedding in 1920

Nanny Hyslop, at Vivien's christening in 1921

Irene and Cimmie canvassing in Harrow

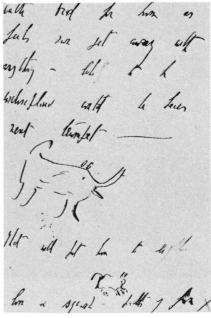

Letters from Cimmie to Tom, 1923 (left), and from Tom to Cimmie, 1925

Savehay Farm

Independent Labour Party Summer School, 1926:
Fenner Brockway (centre) with John Strachey and Tom

On the loggia at Savehay Farm, 1927: Dina Erroll, Tom, Nicholas, Cecil Beaton, Ivan Hay, Dick Wyndham, William Walton, Georgia Sitwell, Cimmie, Vivien, Sacheverell Sitwell

South of France, 1928: Tom, Bob Boothby, Mrs Shaw, John Strachey, Eileen Orde, George Bernard Shaw, Cimmie

Antibes, 1929: Paul Casa Maury, Fruity Metcalfe, Baba Metcalfe, Tom, Rudolph Messel

Cimmie was never a Marxist: nor was Tom: the difference between their sort of socialism and communism was that they believed openly (communists might put their trust secretly) in the role of heroic leaders. But then there was still the business of having to explain to people – those whom they wished to vote for them for instance – how the 'compensations' of their private lives did not interfere with their commitment to the cause of the working class. B. A. Campbell (my putative godfather) wrote to Birmingham newspapers a sort of testimonial for Tom and Cimmie, after there had been renewed attacks on their private life:

> I happen to have had the intimate friendship of Mr Mosley and Lady Cynthia for many years, the last sixteen of which have been spent living in the heart of East London engaged in all forms of social work. Amongst many who have helped me in this work, not merely by giving money but by giving service, which those of us who share the lives of the people have learned to value far more than money, have been those two friends ... I may mention that, as far as they are concerned, the accusation of 'living in large country houses with motor cars and luxurious expenditure and making no kind of personal sacrifice for the poor' is not applicable. At present their town house is a very modest sized one (and by a curious coincidence condemned by the London County Council) ...

This sort of defence made sense on the level of words: it was what Tom and Cimmie themselves were good at. But the problem remained – What is the effect of such justification on reality?

There is a letter from Nancy Astor to Cimmie of this time in which she says – 'Tell Tom not to allow on a platform what he is not willing to do himself.' There had for some time been the feeling amongst Tom's old friends that his very skill with words might result in cutting-off from reality. It seemed that some testing would occur now he was with Labour.

But if Tom and even Cimmie were allowing themselves to be set up as people slightly above the normal run of things – as legendary – then how was it that they were to be tested? Tom made no pretence about the fact that he believed that it was his right, almost duty, to ask to be judged on a rather superhuman level. And Cimmie, in her capacity of being someone who liked to be adored, sometimes found herself for good or ill, stranded on this sort of level too.

Allan Young wrote to her:

> My wish for you is that you should be surrounded by friends who do not irritate, who do not criticise, who are never exacting, but who interest you and help you to express your real self ...
>
> It is a great joy to me that in the circle in which I have met you you help me to understand the meaninglessness of material things. You make life less lonely because of your capacity to '*feel*'. Ideas and actions are the playgrounds of life – but to feel is to live greatly.

CHAPTER 10

Rules of the Game: Philandering

When Tom re-entered Parliament in January 1927 as Labour member for Smethwick he had for the first time both a policy and what must have seemed a suitable political base from which to launch it.

He was not popular in Parliament. He had first been Conservative, then an Independent, now he was Labour. He could say with justification that he had put his principles before party loyalties; that he had been right to explore different territories: but this was objectionable to those who felt strongly about party loyalties not only because they might distrust his motives but because they might feel guilty about their own – they might themselves feel more strongly about loyalties, that is, than about principles, because their livelihoods depended on their so doing while Tom's and Cimmie's did not.

There was also still Tom's arrogance, his air of disdain, his cutting tongue. Looking around in Parliament at the chosen representatives of society around him, he would remark 'A dead fish rots from the head down'. When people heckled him he referred to their 'zoological noises striving to attain the heights of human speech'. The Conservative Party was 'sublime mediocrity at the head of inveterate prejudice': Baldwin, its leader, was someone who 'may not be a good companion for a tiger hunt, even for a pig hunt; but every time he runs away he proves afresh the honesty of his convictions'. This was good stuff for the legend: it was of not much help in fostering the personal bonhomie which, apart from the battle, is necessary if there is to be any exercise of power according to the rules of a game.

To most MPs Parliament was a place where issues were raised, passions aired, votes taken: then after these activities had done their job as a safety-valve as it were, the machinery of government could be left to go on its way. Tom never saw Parliament like this: he imagined it as a sort of officers' discussion-group before orders should be given for an attack. This was due to an ingrained habit partly of seeing contemporary circumstances as always on the edge of a crisis – 'Pleasant sleepy people are all very well in pleasant sleepy times, but we live in a dynamic age of great and dangerous events' – partly of assuming that the right methods of dealing with a crisis were those of war. In 1927 there was a certain justification for this attitude. He left his audiences in no doubt about how he saw the enemies at the gates.

> Unemployment, wages, rents, suffering, squalor and starvation, the struggle for existence in our streets; the threat of world catastrophe in another war; these are the realities of our present age. These are the problems which require every exertion of the best brains of our time for a vast constructive effort. These are the problems which should unite the nation in a white heat of crusading zeal for their solution. But these are precisely the problems which send Parliament to sleep. When not realities but words are to be discussed, Parliament wakes up. Then we are back in the comfortable pre-war world of make-believe: politics are safe again; hairs are to be split, not facts to be faced. Hush! do not awaken the dreamers! Facts will waken them in time with a vengeance.

In order to find an audience that would listen to what he had to say in the style which he felt suitable to say it in he went increasingly outside Parliament; he continued to address mass meetings in the midlands and in the north. He had already made his mark as a champion of the miners at the time of the General Strike in 1926: before it, he had in theory opposed the idea of a strike – he had thought both that it would not succeed and that if it did it would have meant revolution by violence. But when the strike was on he had backed it by organising, and paying for, the publication of a strike bulletin in Birmingham, and had given a considerable donation (£500) to the miners when their own strike dragged on into the autumn. From 1927 onwards he was a regular and popular speaker at the annual Durham Miners' Gala: he became a political and personal friend of the miners' leader Arthur Cook: he learned from him some of the rhythmical, hypnotic techniques of mob oratory. Beatrice Webb described Arthur Cook as being 'a mediumistic, magnetic sort of creature ... an inspired idiot, drunk with his own words, dominated by his own slogans'. Tom said that he had 'one of the coolest and best heads among the Labour leaders'. With the help of Arthur Cook and his union Tom was elected to the National Administrative Council of the Independent Labour party; then to the National Executive Council of the Labour Party itself. In Birmingham, where he seemed personally to be winning the city from the grip of the con- servative Chamberlain family, Tom's legendary qualities were taking a bizarre hold: newspapers reported that children went through the streets singing 'Oswald is merciful! Oswald will save us!' There were cartoons of him in top hat and tails like a conjuror; then as an anarchist with a cloth cap and huge boots and a small man behind him with a bomb. Tom's characteristic reply to this sort of thing was just to complain that the cartoonist had not given him enough hair. There were also, inevitably, the cartoons about money: a money-bag labelled 'advantages of high birth and wealth' was being put away by Tom for the time being in a cloak room. But in fact of course Tom had no intention of hiding his money: he used some of it to buy an interest in one of the papers that was pursuing him – the *Birmingham Town Crier*.

In 1928 Tom's father died. He had lived apart from his wife and children for nearly thirty years. Recently there had been some rapprochement: his grandchildren (myself and Vivien, with Nanny and Granny) had been to visit him in 1924: there is a photograph of a rather young-looking middle-aged man like a professional cricketer holding me up like a trophy. Tom's mother had written to Tom – 'I'm trying hard to forget things that have made my life bitter for twenty five years.' But then there had been the Smethwick bye-election in 1926 and his father's story about Tom having been born with a golden spoon in his mouth, and Tom had again become bitter. When the news reached him that his father was dying Tom was in the South of France; he was in the middle of one of his long, hot summers; he declined to move in response to a telegram from his brother Ted. Ted, who was with their father who was himself in France, wrote 'I am disgusted to find that on the one occasion I have asked you to help me you have let me down ... I can assure you I should not have asked you to come here if I considered that your presence would disturb my father at this time.'

Tom went to the funeral: there is a photograph of him and his mother and his brothers at the graveside. In the South of France, just before he left, I remember Nanny telling Vivien and me that our grandfather had died, and so our father was now a baronet. I watched out of the window (so many childhood memories are of myself looking down at grown- ups out of windows) and saw my father on the terrace walking up and down, up and down; wondering, perhaps, about how both to be, and appear not to be, a baronet.

Tom was not mentioned in his father's will: it seemed to be becoming a habit in the Mosley family that eldest sons should not be mentioned in their fathers' wills. But much of the family money had gone anyway to Tom from his grandfather over his father's head. His father left what money he had to his 'housekeeper Mary Elisabeth Hipkiss' who had 'served me faithfully and looked after me in various illnesses for over sixteen years'.

The question of family money is of interest because there was so much about it in the papers at the time that it seemed to have gone, like so many things about Tom, into legend. The rumours were that he was a multi-millionaire. It is difficult to give exact figures when so many family assets were in settlements, trusts, and property whose capital value could not be realised: but it seems that Tom, when his father died, came into control of an estate of about £250,000: before this he had had a yearly income from trustees of £8–10,000. Much of the estate however was in the form of land in Manchester which the Mosley family had once owned but which in the last century had been made over to leaseholders on 999-year·leases – one less 9, my father used to say, and the family would indeed be multi-millionaires. But the income from this land was fixed: so that with inflation and the threat of further inflation it was difficult to find a buyer for the leases. Thus Tom was rich but not extravagantly so: and not nearly so rich as legend suggested. There was also, of course, Cimmie's income from the Leiter Trust – about £8 or 9,000 a year – but here there was no chance of the capital being touched.

Tom had found the dubieties of his financial position useful during the Smethwick by-election of 1926 when he had been able to say 'I own no lands and neither does my family: I doubt if there are half a dozen acres in the family.' This was after Rolleston had been sold, and just before Tom bought his 120 acres at Denham. But it is doubtful if the electors of Smethwick would have been put off even if Tom had not been able to play down the stories of his wealth. Such concerns were those of the newspapers: there was still little evidence of envy amongst the working class.

John Scanlon wrote in *The Decline and Fall of the Labour Party* with reference to workers' further reactions to Tom and Cimmie:

> Instead of believing that salvation for the working class would come from the working class, they still had the superstitious notion prevalent in all simple minds that salvation would come from above ... Heaven to them was a place where only rich people congregated and where was an abundance of rich food, rich drink and rich raiment.

To most of them it was quite unattainable, and therefore when anyone chose to leave this perpetual nightclub in order to mix with the workers, their love and admiration knew no bounds.

The 'perpetual night-club' world which Tom and Cimmie were supposed to frequent and occasionally come down from for the delectation of the workers – this was a fancy that had some slight relevance to facts. But Tom and Cimmie had gone to great lengths to break out of the conventional upper-class night-club world; and it was more that they themselves descended to it only from time to time for their own delight. Upper-class London 'society' at this time consisted of about six hundred people (Tom used to say) who all knew each other and knew much of what was going on between each other but who kept this secret from the outside world: the rules of the game were like those which require honour amongst gangsters, that one should not talk. A view of this world, which is indeed like that of some hellish underworld, is provided by Cimmie's older sister Irene who kept a daily diary from 1926: in this she also provides contemporary glimpses of Tom and Cimmie. Irene had inherited the same income from the Leiter Estate as Cimmie had: on the death of her father in 1925 she had become a peeress in her own right – Baroness Ravensdale. (George Curzon had managed to have this subsidiary title created for himself in 1911 when it seemed certain he would have only daughters and no son: the title could pass for one generation through the female line but then had to revert to male inheritance – to the annoyance of my sister). Irene Ravensdale never married: she was rich, titled, and unencumbered by ties: in later life she did much good work with charities and with East End clubs in London, but mostly during these early years she did what she liked. The life that she lived was the sort of life that Cimmie and Tom might have led if they had not chosen to be socialist politicians.

Each winter she would go to Melton Mowbray for the hunting; there she kept a house with four or five servants, several horses, and a groom. She would hunt four or five days a week – with the Quorn, the Cottesmore or the Belvoir. Having exhausted herself and two or three horses during the day she would spend the evenings almost invariably playing poker or bridge – at which she lost also almost invariably. (Entries in her diary end with a phrase such as 'Lost £15 as usual' with the frequency of Pepys's 'And so to bed.') Often at night there were parties at which people quarrelled, tried to swap husbands and wives, and got drunk. When there was no hunting Irene would stay in bed till lunch time: much of the time she felt ill. She had lovers; but did not find anyone for whom she would give up her freedom or who would take it on. When the hunting season was over she came with her servants to her London house for the summer season of parties and balls: there were special occasions like Derby Day, Ascot, the Eton and Harrow match; there were the Opera and gala matinees and tableaus; the night-clubs The Gargoyle and The Embassy. In the autumn she would travel, sometimes round the world – like a mythical figure in the expiation of some guilt. From time to time she drank too much, and she did a cure. She had hundreds of friends whom she loved and who said they loved her, but she was for the most part lonely. She was a good, warm hearted woman with nothing at this time to commit herself to.

Her relations with Cimmie and Tom were enigmatic. Cimmie had been her loved yet envied little sister when they were young: Cimmie had complained of her domineering ways. Then when Cimmie married and had children Irene seemed to claim a corner of these experiences. (When Vivien had been born she had written 'It is all so sacred, wonderful; it will remain in my mind as one of the great lovely mysteries'.) Tom told a story of how she had been to bed with him during some romp at Melton Mowbray; yet she was heavily censorious of Tom's extra-marital relationships and especially of causing Cimmie pain. She took no interest in Tom's and Cimmie's politics except for a week in 1929 when she went to canvass for Cimmie during her cam-paign at Stoke-on-Trent. In her diaries in their early days at least Tom appears as a rather fragile figure: Cimmie is still the envied sister. But it is likely that Irene saw and noted in her diaries mostly what she wanted to see.

Just after Tom's Labour victory in the 1926 election she was staying for Christmas with Nancy Astor at Cliveden – a powerhouse of con-servatism. Irene observed:

> Cim and Tom came down to dinner and everyone was very decent to them tho' Geoffrey Dawson and Bob Brand hate him. They were both very pathetic – Tom even looking lonely and lost for once, tho' she was utterly at her ease. After dinner we played charades. Nancy Astor was inimitable as a rich Jew and a fat girl with that bulging mask, and Bobby as a tango teacher.

Another entry in another diary of this time seems to corroborate this unexpected view of Tom and Cimmie. Zita Jungman, who later became one of Cimmie's greatest friends, first met the Mosleys in August 1927 when she was taken by Bob Boothby to a picnic on the islands off the coast of Cannes. She had not expected, from what she had heard, to like Tom; but in the event she found him gentle and attentive and it was Cimmie who was —'pretty, rather fat, strong, and ruthlessly direct'.

That Tom appeared vulnerable at this time does not in fact conflict with the other view of him as the dashing, debonair buccaneer. Newspaper reports of him talked of his 'distinguished bearing, singularly handsome face, much charm of manner'; but also that — 'shyness still hides the reckless spirit which is shown by his political career'. Part of his charm and ability to get away with things was that at this time he could appear to be both savagely dominating and yet open to being hurt: like this he had something of the attractiveness of a child. Both in politics and in private life people looked up to him and sometimes wanted to protect him: this is perhaps a characteristic of people who succeed in leadership. It was only later that Tom seemed to be the potentially all-powerful figure whom people thought might do everything himself.

Certainly in front of Cimmie there was something of the child still in him that liked to show off, to be given approbation, as well as to be looked up to. In 1927 Tom and Cimmie began to see more of her younger sister, Baba, who in 1925 had married Major Edward 'Fruity' Metcalfe — who was known as the Prince of Wales's best friend. Tom liked to tease Baba: to be boyish in front of both her and Cimmie. He wrote to Cimmie:

> Today lunched with Fruity and Baba — showed them the new Bentley. Babs very envious and says we now 'stink of money'. Bentley is marvellous, but I break into a sweat when I think of the mutton at the wheel. With this light body acceleration is terrific — much more than Merc — you are up to anything in a few yards — must be careful. Body very good but a trifle flash. Silver wheels and red seats!

He liked showing off to Cimmie too, about his harmless social conquests. Once when Cimmie was in Stoke-on-Trent and Tom was in London he was asked to dinner by Sylvia, the wife of his brother Ted. He wrote:

> Wednesday night dined with Sylvia. She elected to appear for the occasion in a bright scarlet costume — everything blazing red from her lips to the heels of her shoes. Afterwards she desired to go to the Embassy Club. I advanced rather diffidently across the floor behind this 'People's Banner' but nevertheless our entry appeared to cause a

certain sensation. Even the granite features of Lord Blandford assumed a momentary mobility.

About Tom's more serious flirtations it is difficult to tell just what, at this time, Cimmie thought. It was a convention of the world in which she moved and had been brought up that husbands were expected to take some interest in other people's wives: their own wives seemed to have evolved a state of mind by which they both did and did not notice what was going on. There were rules-of-the-game about what was acceptable; and so long as Tom kept to these – the purpose of which was to ensure that the whole business remained somewhat childlike – then Cimmie could perhaps treat him as her naughty boy. For a time Tom did seem to stick to the rules. He would go over to Paris, which was a different world; there he had a mistress called Maria. (When he came across her later in America and sent her flowers and asked when he could see her she replied 'Darling friend, I prefer not to see you at all and have very good reasons for that.') Perhaps the reason then was that Tom was by this time pursuing Blanche Barrymore, the wife of John Barrymore, the actor: she herself was an actress who used, Tom remarked in his autobiography, to act Hamlet in competition with her husband. Perhaps this pursuit was stagey enough to come within the rules of the game. Also in a manner stagey but not, one would have thought, within any recognisable rules, was his brief affair with his step-mother-in-law, Grace Curzon; with whom, at St Moritz, while Cimmie skied (Tom could not ski because of his injured leg) he would drive around in a horse-drawn sledge. Tom would usually go after the women who would be the biggest challenge to him by possessing the greatest prestige. He never, like his father-in-law George Curzon, saw the point of pursuing anyone who might not be passed off as upper-class.

Thus when he became Labour and a whole new game might have opened up because this was the time when to be left-wing and intellectual was to be an advocate of easy free love – Tom did not take very enthusiastic advantage of this situation. He had a brief walk-out with one of the wives at the ILP summer school: but soon after this he coined a witty slogan – Vote Labour: sleep Tory – and reverted to type. He became involved with the wife of a Conservative MP who managed to get hold of a photograph of Tom without any clothes on (this was Tom's own story): the photograph was passed round the Tory benches while Tom from the Labour front bench was making a speech: Tom, made aware of what was going on by the resulting laughter, considered that this was outside the rules of any game and threatened a fight.

For almost the first ten years of her marriage it does not seem from her letters that Cimmie kicked up much of a fuss about all this: she felt that, the rules being what they were, Tom would always return to her: she seemed essential to him, politically and personally. It was essential politically that there should be no public scandal: but it was personally that he still seemed dependent on her in spite of what he admitted were his 'tiresome ways'. He would assure her of this dependence in his adoring, child-like letters full of baby-talk and drawings of animals: he would call her 'My own blessed Moo Moo': 'My own darling baby bleater': 'His own darling soft-nosed wog-tail'. He would sign himself by his own baby-names – porker, mutton: he would dash off his drawings of animals in his wild primitive hand. All this –itself a game – was to show that the other game – that of affairs and flirtations – was the lesser: it could not stand up to the heartfelt, caring, genuine dependence of children-husbands on their mother-wives.

Own Beloved,
   Promise be happy. Don't work too hard. Rest and be strong for lots of fun Friday. Does love her so. If he didn't he wouldn't be tiresome. Life impossible without her.

Or:

Wishes he could make his mutt [drawing of animal] less of a goat [drawing of animal with horns] loves her so.

And Cimmie would reply:

My belovedest,
   It was so wick of me to have wasted that whole long day when I had you and now when you aren't here my heart aches for you. I will really try and be bet, not maddening or cross, but do believe nearly all my stupidity comes from excess of love which makes me often overwrought, not anything else. I so frightfully love you and do above everything in the world want to be a perfect wife to you ...
   Oh my Bill I do so adore you, my lovely one, so beautiful and so brave, such a clever one and so tender and beloved. Such a hero and yet such a baby boy. Your own Moo moo.

Cimmie and Tom were now approaching the zenith of their political and social careers. Their progress in the Labour Party was still triumphant: the Tory press campaign against them was wearing off. Tom was even being asked to write articles by Lord Beaverbrook. People were beginning to speak of him as a future Prime Minister. The house at Denham was filling at weekends with people from the more exotic and enlightened fringes of the 'perpetual night-club world': also with writers and musicians and painters and designers – Sacheverell Sitwell, William Walton, Cecil Beaton, Oliver Messel. These mixed in with the old political friends – John Strachey, Bob Boothby. All these people felt perhaps closest to Cimmie; but Tom was the attraction. However much people felt him somewhat removed, awkward, they caught the glow of his company. This sort of social life at Denham was interspersed with visits from constituency socialists or representatives from the Durham Miners Gala. Cimmie had her 'ups and downs': she wrote that her curse was to be 'either so frightfully hap or so frightfully mis'. Tom came and went like (as a French journalist put it) 'the young Alcibiades ... driving too fast in a big car, trailing after him many entangled hearts, many sarcasms, and a few confidences'. And somewhere in the middle of all this were the children telling themselves stories about how to get somewhere on a raft.

CHAPTER 11

Savehay Farm

Into the peaceful mundane world at Savehay Farm which consisted of myself and Vivien, Nanny, Mabel and May, and Mr Streeter the gardener in his cottage beyond the woodshed, there would erupt from time to time, like Vikings in their long-boats from the east, invaders, who were my mother's and father's weekend guests. Then there would be the business, for myself at least, of being always ready, like some villager, to hide. Savehay Farm was a good house within and around which to observe without being observed: there were the nooks and crannies I had discovered in my explorations with my sister Vivien: there were vantage points from which one could look down, as I liked to look down, upon the behaviour of these sophisticated hordes. There was a way out from the first floor nursery across a sort of roof-patio and then in through another door to a gallery above a loggia. Within this loggia some of the more esoteric rites of the grown-up world took place – the conversation, the badinage, the drinking, the horseplay – and even if a watcher were on the point of being caught, there was a further escape-route at the far end of the gallery which went across a cluttered loft with a ceiling too low to allow for easy pursuit and down into a mysterious area known as the End Room where were stored huge trunks containing bric-a-brac from the time when my mother had been a child in India: and this refuge was almost impregnable, because the key of the door from the outside had nearly always been lost.

Once or twice a year there were seasonal invasions of a type different from usual: enormous trestle tables would be set up on the lawn: tea-urns and trays of sandwiches would be carried from vans: then masses of people wearing thick dark suits and with hats would emerge from buses and would stand about looking cheerful like people do when they think they might be photographed. These were Labour party workers

from Smethwick or Stoke: the occasion was known as The Garden
Party. This festivity was especially terrifying for children because the
impression had been given that it was more than an arbitrary duty for
them to appear – it was a moral and political duty – something that
might be of importance in their parents'. careers. So there we were, my
sister and I, amongst the tea and buns and smiling faces like victims
being led to sacrificial altars.

At another time of year there would be tents like those of Red Indians
suddenly in the field across the river: large boys in long khaki shorts
would appear carrying pots and pans: in the evenings they would sit
round a camp fire and sing songs. These were the denizens of Mr B. A.
Campbell's Paddy's Goose Boys' Club, on their annual holiday outing.
With regard to them, too, there seemed to be some sort of moral
obligation to go and visit: grown-ups even suggested that one might
cheerfully join in their sad songs.

But for the most part the weekend invaders were as unlike constituency party workers or members of the Paddy's Goose club as could be
imagined. On Saturday mornings in the summer garden-beds of wood
and webbing would be set out in front of the loggia: mattresses and
coloured cushions would be arranged; there would be a portable
gramophone and perhaps an umbrella; it was as if a stage-set were being
prepared for some ballet. Then in twos and threes from the house where
they had arrived the night before when the children had been in bed
or from the place where cars were parked by Mr Streeter's cottage there
would emerge the people who were my mother's and father's special
friends: the men perhaps in white trousers and dark blue jackets: the
women in short skirts with waists falling down towards their knees.
They would gather round the beds in front of the loggia: they would
laugh, talk, recline; they would sway in front of each other like reeds.
But what on earth were they *doing*? And what were they *saying*? All this
was observed with eyes through some slit-hole at the bottom of a
window; on hands and knees in the gallery above the loggia. These
representatives of the grown-up world always seemed to be *acting*: they
would gesture, jerk their hands in their pockets, fiddle with pearls; but
who were they acting *to*; and what was it *for*? A man might go down
on one knee, a hand on his heart, as if making some passionate declara-
tion: a woman would lean back, kick her legs in the air; but was this
in acceptance or disdain? There would be lunges, shrieks, and cumber-
some runnings-after. Someone would be caught, and carried, and
dumped on a bed: but were all these struggles yes or no? Of course, it
was all a game. But did anyone win? And was it fun?

The portable gramophone would be wound up with a handle and play tunes like *Just A Gigolo* or *You're Driving Me Crazy*: people might dance a little in a desultory, am-I-or-am-I-not-being-watched way. They would do this as if in front of cameras: often, in fact, there was a camera – my mother had a primitive box-like cine-Kodak that you held at your waist and looked down into: she was one of the first people to make home movies fashionable. In front of the camera people of course were expected to perform: they would do the Charleston flicking their legs sideways and back; they would put their arms round each other's waists and trip to and fro like Sugar Plum Fairies. They did not seem to be involved so much in dancing as in the business of trying to find out what to do about being watched. A few games would begin: two men would get down on their backs on the lawn; they would face one another and each would put a leg up and hook it round the leg of the other; the object was to force the other person over on to the back of his head. The women would hop about like birds round carrion. Then there was a game in which two people were blindfolded and lay on the lawn and held hands and whacked at each other with rolled-up newspapers: this was called, for some reason, *Are You There Moriarty?* When all this had gone on for some time the women would drift back to the beds and perhaps file their nails and croon snatches to the gramophone.

There were more formal games. Half way down the drive there were two tennis courts side by side: I do not remember anyone playing much serious tennis. The point seemed to be the badinage, usually in mixed doubles. My aunt Irene had a very slow underarm service that her opponents could deal with as they liked, depending on what they felt about my Aunt Irene. When my father served he would flash his eyes at the same time as he flashed his racket and he seemed to be trying to hit his partner on the back of the neck.

There was even a realistic duelling game that the men played on the lawn: they would dress up in fencing jackets and masks; they would march away from each other back to back carrying pistols; then would turn and fire with bullets of uninjurious wax. The women would watch this as if rather at a loss: traditionally, had not women liked men fighting over them with some danger of death?

There was a thing called a pogo-stick with a spring on the bottom on which you jumped up and down like a kangaroo. One day Dick Wyndham slipped and broke his jaw: there was a queer funeral cortege down to the river – to throw in not Dick Wyndham, but the pogo-stick.

In the river there was swimming from a wooden landing-stage or diving-board in an area that was supposed to have been cleared of weeds by Mr Streeter in the punt. We children were allowed to bathe here as soon as we could swim. There were stories of how weeds stretched up like tentacles and dragged you down.

We would fish with nets for tiddlers in the river. Sometimes the movements of grown-ups seemed to be curiously like those of fish; they would seem all to be facing one way; then they would suddenly dash off and face in another.

One summer at Savehay Farm the play-acting did seem to have some practical or rather aesthetic point: my mother and father set out to make, with their box-like camera, a film with a story. What the story was is obscure since only one uncut reel of it survived: the rest was tidied and burned by a house-maid in the South of France who thought that the bits and pieces in the process of being cut and stuck together were rubbish. From the one reel it seems that my mother was a dairy maid who was being pursued by both John Strachey and Dick Wyndham – the former was some sort of rustic, and the latter a dashing man who turned up in the Bentley. These two had a terrible fight on the big bridge over the river: first John Strachey got hurled into the water; then he climbed out and ran back on to the bridge and hurled Dick Wyndham into the water; this scene seemed to be repeated, over and over. Then there was a brothel scene in which Cecil Beaton was the *Madame* made up to look like Margot Asquith: one of the girls in her charge was, again, my mother. Dick Wyndham returned in the Bentley and there was another struggle – with revealing close-ups of legs and thighs. Towards the end of all this Cecil Beaton went off to drown himself in the river; but it was his wig that kept on coming off and floating away like Ophelia. There was an odd blind boy, very beautiful, played by Stephen Tennant; who sat and made daisy chains by the river.

All this was scripted, directed, and filmed by my father. It was shot in a rather German-expressionist style, with reflections in water of poplar trees and clouds moving.

One of the more bizarre activities that grown-ups liked to indulge in at weekends was to play practical jokes on one another. In the downstairs lavatory there was a box which held the paper and when you pulled a snake jumped out: Olga Lynn had hysterics, and the door of the lavatory had to be broken down. Then there was a story of how my father once arranged to have soap on toast served to his dinner guests as a savoury: Oliver Messel was warned by Mabel the parlour maid, and went behind a screen with a pack of cards which he let fall to the floor thus making a sound as if he were being sick. Nanny used to recount to us these stories: it seemed to be accepted that they were about just the sort of things that grown-ups did.

Nanny, in fact, had her own fund of such stories, which we children asked her to recount to us over and over again. When she had been a nurserymaid in the employment of George Curzon she had stayed in the house of his father, Lord Scarsdale, where there was a butler who tyrannised over the other servants. One day Nanny, and her great friend Sarah the still-room maid, put some sherbet in the butler's pot, so that when he peed at night it foamed: he, too, was supposed to have had some sort of fit. Then there was Lord Scarsdale himself who was known to be mean about food: one night Nanny and her friend were having a midnight snack when they heard a scuffling outside their bedroom door and they opened it and found Lord Scarsdale on his hands and knees trying to see underneath. The impression from all these stories was that, of course, the grown-up world was mad: why else, indeed, did they have to have people like nannies to tell us stories about them?

In the evenings after guests had gone my sister and I would come down to the Garden Room where there were the glass walking sticks on the walls and we would pick up bits of family life after the invasion. My mother would read to us or at a slightly later date would play with us one of the upper-middle-brow games that she had played as a child with her father. There was the game called 'I see' in which a famous historical scene was described and the children had to guess (or rather to know) what it was – Julius Caesar on his way to the Senate: Napoleon on St Helena. Sometimes my mother would rope in my father to describe a scene; but after a time he would get bored, and begin – I see a tall dark handsome man – and we would all start groaning, because we knew he was describing himself. Similarly if my father was ever prevailed on to play the enervating game of compiling lists of famous men beginning with a certain letter he would with mysterious quickness finish his list and wait till the end of the allotted time and then when invited to read out his list would announce just – whatever the letter – Mosley! And so there would be more groans: and my father's strange clicking laugh. I continued to think this sort of thing very funny. This was the pattern of my father with his children: he would become the joker: he would be no longer distant, removed: what better could he do?

Then there were more of the strange mantras, or slogans, that he used to declaim in response to what he might feel were unnatural demands on him. On the comparatively rare occasions on which all the family were having a meal together and Vivien and I were being obstreperous and he was appealed to to keep order, he would intone, with the far-away look in his eye:

> Let us see if Nicky can
> Be a little gentleman
> Let us see if Viv is able
> To behave herself at table —

Or if there was some dispute about plans — between our two aunts, for example, who kept up a rivalry sometimes about who should do what with which of the children — he would murmur just:

> Whoever would you rather be —
> Aunty Baa or Aunty Nee —

and then would drift off, laughing again, leaving myself at least thinking that something magical had happened. I did not know why: I think it was something to do with grown-ups being able to laugh at their own pretensions.

There were the other sayings my father would use to discourage earnest personal speculation. When the question came up, as it often did, about the oddity of his emergence from his background, he would declaim, as alternatives to the 'when fire meets oil then springs the spark divine' remark quoted earlier:

> The Lily, its roots dug deep in the dung of the
> earth, yet rears its glorious head to heaven —

Or —

> Nurtured as I was in the rough usages of camp and field —

Or —

> Staffordshire born and Staffordshire bred
> Fat in the bottom and fat in the head —

all these being said as throwaway lines, real or made-up quotations, self-mockery to do away with boredom or embarrassment. Then there was a line that he would intone as he entered the sea to swim in the Mediterranean — And bluer the sea-blue stream of the bay — which meant that he was peeing.

My father was an arch-manipulator of words: it seemed that at these moments he was mocking the pretensions of words. But there were also his rages.

He never directed, any violence against us children – except perhaps once, when Vivien and I had been having a fight in the rose-garden and Vivien, accidentally, had kicked me in the balls and I had flopped about like a footballer in the penalty area. My father hauled Vivien up to his room and smacked her. He examined me solicitously. But this incident stands out for its rarity.

The scarcity of memories about my mother has resulted in those scenes that do remain being lit portentously. There was a day in London when my mother and father and Vivien and I were walking along the Mall (this is by far the clearest memory I have of my mother and father in relation to each other): we were turning up by St James's Palace and my mother was asking me why I did not like the child of one of her friends whom she had hoped I would like; I was saying I did not know why: (I cannot remember now how much in fact I did not know or how much I was declining to pass on childhood secrets). My mother was saying that of course I must know – that if one had feelings about not liking someone one must be able to describe them – and I was beginning to feel miserable: I was thinking – surely, feelings are sometimes too complicated to be put just into words? My father was walking ahead with my sister Vivien: my mother called out to him – Was it not correct, would he not say, that if one had feelings then these could be put into words? I remember my father turning, at the bottom of St James's Street, and saying no, surely, there were some feelings that could not well be put into words. I think I felt some sort of liberation.

But it was about this time, when I was about seven, that I began quite badly to stammer. My mother had recorded in notes that she made about our early childhood – 'Vivien was inclined to be a bit bossy and Nic was led a good deal of a dance always having to play second string, he was much more highly strung than her, and occasionally used to have stammering fits.' But my own consciousness that I stammered came later when both my mother and my nanny in the night nursery – this scene again is portentously etched – were standing over me and telling me earnestly that I must try to speak carefully: up to that time I had not realised that I did not. There is a lesson to be learned by parents here: if your child stammers, do not remark on this when he or she is young: the stammer may naturally go: but if you remark on it, the child has to struggle and the stammer may get dug in.

There are psychological theories about stammering that have seemed to me to make sense. One is that it is a sort of protection against the verbal aggression of others (it is difficult to be rude or sarcastic towards a stammerer): another and deeper theory is that it is a protection against the stammerer's own potential aggressiveness towards others – an aggressiveness which, without the stammer, would be alarming. But it has seemed to me also that stammering on some level is simply a protest against a too easy flow of words; against one's own and other people's terrible tendency to bury living things under a verbal lava-flow.

In the notes that my mother made in her photograph book of our childhood were sayings attributed to me at an early age: one was 'Isn't it lucky that Mummy didn't marry Mr Strachey?' Another – 'I think we are really dead, and we think all this is a dream.'

In my mother's Garden Room, when she was away, there were certain explorations to be made amongst the piles of glossy magazines that lay on a table behind the sofa. Some of these magazines had been sent from Russia; some from Paris. In the former there were pictures of enormous industrial complexes with pipes and cones and spheres: these seemed like very advanced children's toys. In the magazines from Paris there were reproductions of modern paintings and drawings which took one out of the world of toys towards some secret that might lie at the back of the grown-up world. There were women with no clothes on lying on their backs with their knees in the air – Egon Schiele perhaps. But why was this so strange? And apparently for grown-ups as well as for children?

At the not-often-used end of the house on the ground floor beneath my mother's and father's bedroom there was a panelled hall with portraits of Mosley ancestors on the walls: these were almost the only relics (apart from library books) that had been saved from my father's abandonment of Rolleston. Each year after the Christmas Tree had been cleared away (here we had circled to the incantation of porker, porker) for the rest of the winter I was allowed to make this room my own. Here I would set about building or rebuilding – the Mosley ancestors looking primly or benignly down – a whole model village, a landscape, an estate: the basis of this was a beautifully made set of toys called The Belgian Village (given to us children, I think, by my mother's childhood friend the Queen of the Belgians). This consisted of houses, gardens, churches, shops, inns; it could be set out on the floor of the empty hall and extended into parkland, farmyards, animals, railways, cars, buses – these taken from my other sets of toys. Thus a whole new world could be created; which unlike much of the real world was orderly, aesthetic and exact. I would work at this painstakingly through much of the winter holidays: the task, and the result, seemed to be of mysterious significance. I knew it would be cleared away by Nanny and May the housemaid in the spring: but it could always be taken out of its boxes again and made the same and yet slightly different: and perhaps it was this ordering of something beautiful that seemed to make life worth while.

CHAPTER 12

Labour Politics

In 1927 Cimmie, in the train to Dover wrote to Tom, who was at 8 Smith Square:

> Sweetie old boy, be a happy one and be a good one – miss his Mum a good deal but don't get plooey. Get Mabel to fix up people to come and see you. Try and make the Docs start doing something in the way of treatment. Anyway suggest a tonic to keep your strength up.
>
> Why not also have the spermy doc to see you as well, his add is on envelope on dressing table, name of Kenneth Walker. Talk to Kirkwood about the French specialist from Bagnolles and get Mabel to ring Eva up and find out when he is coming over.
>
> Darling fellow let's have loveliest happiest time yr 31st year. I will do all I can. As well as our work-y good times let's have fun-y good times. Let's really try and achieve the ideal modus vivendi! *I do so love you* and as well as that I'm frightfully fond of you for yr sake too. Feels like a Mum as well as a Mistress (can one be the Whore as well as the Bore or vice versa?)
>
> I do think we are trying to give better chances and more happiness to people in general and ought to give just our 2 selves a really good chance too – a chance to be a better happier couple than any other – it would help in the long run and I am quite sure we have a duty to ourselves as much as to everyone else. A Frenchman opp has just blown his nose and released by flourishing his hanky such an odious cloying scent I feel sick. H. G. Wells on the train, can't make up my mind whether to speak to him or not.
>
> Let's arrange a party soon after I'm back (if you're well) and go to Greta Garbo.
>
> Love and kisses my belovedest.

Don't leave this about it is stilted and restrained as it is just for that very fear.

Loves him Loves him Loves him Loves him.

Does think him a bloody marvel, really, and as the train rushes her farther and farther away is inclined to reconsider her opinion that he is evil and wick (doubtful tho') and thinks – Oh Hell, I don't know what I think.

But I do know you are often a pet and adorable and are quite without rival in public life and that all the time I love you except when I hate you so much it must come quite near to love and be mixed up with it. God bless your schemes and plans. Don't get fed up with the silly old Labs yet awhile. Give Jimmy my love and fix up some NAC fun for me. Play your new grammy and think lovingly and kindly of your Simple Sincere Suburban Sim!!

It seems that at the time Tom was quite often ill or on the edge of being ill: or he was something of a hypochondriac; he liked to put his trust in glamorous doctors whether or not there was very much for them to cure. But he had genuine recurring trouble with his injured leg. Cimmie wrote to him from Stoke-on-Trent – 'My poor sweetie old fellow I am miserable at your being phlebitic it really does seem that yr troubles are unending and cumulative (is that the right word?) always piling up – oh I am just longing for Tues when we can settle peacefully down to being normal decently idle creatures.' Ramsay MacDonald wrote to Cimmie regretting 'that Tom's illness is to drag', but making a date with her to go to the theatre.

In October 1928 Tom and Cimmie went on a motor trip with Ramsay MacDonald to Vienna, Prague and Berlin. In Berlin Mac-Donald addressed the Reichstag and made a passionate plea for dis-armament: the press seemed more interested in Cimmie's clothes. 'Lady Cynthia, the famous champion of the proletariat, was in an evening frock of grey tissue with a rich grey cloak ... slowly, and with an air which a great actress might envy, she went to the place assigned to her followed by her husband and Mr Ramsay MacDonald ... a shawl of snowy white ermine fell from her gracious shoulders.'

While in Berlin Tom and Cimmie were taken round the night clubs by Harold Nicolson who was Counsellor at the British Embassy. Tom wrote about this in his autobiography – 'Cimmie and I had never seen anything like it ... the sexes had simply changed clothes, make-up and habits of nature ... scenes of decadence and depravity suggested a nation sunk so deep that it could never rise again. Yet within two or three years men in brown shirts were goose-stepping down these same streets round the Kurfurstendamm'. Tom does not seem in this description to have been being ironic.

Ramsay MacDonald did not go with them on the tour of the night clubs: his own raffish behaviour on this trip was to do with becoming involved again with an Austrian lady who had previously been his mistress. Tom too became involved in this affair. In a passage which he dictated for his autobiography but then left out he told the story of this odd incident and its aftermath.

In Vienna we met a woman who as a type seemed to me something of an old Viennese tart: faded blonde, very sophisticated, very agreeable. And being young people, and never thinking that people much older than ourselves could have love affairs, Cimmie and I thought nothing of it. In Vienna the old pair used to go and look at museums.

A month or two later MacDonald suggested that we all go down to Fowey in Cornwall, and named the party which he wanted to take – a gay party and altogether different from MacDonald's colleagues. Just before we went he said to me 'My little Austrian friend whom we met in Vienna is in England. It would be such fun if she could come. Will you explain it to the others?' So we said all right. He used to read poetry to her, and they wandered off together making a strange couple.

Then we went into the election. We fought it and we won, and I found myself sitting in the Treasury as Chancellor of the Duchy. Then one day I was informed that a Mrs so-and-so wanted to speak to me. I said 'I'm delighted to hear you're in London but we're all very busy'. She said 'I'm living in a flat in Horseferry Road,' – at that time almost a slum area – I've got serious news for you. The Government may fall. I must tell you'.

So I went round and there was this old girl. She said 'I rang you up, you're very young, but you're the only man in this government who knows anything of the world at all. So I had better tell you'.

She went on 'I'll come straight to the point. I was once a very rich woman. The Prime Minister, when I used to meet him in Switzerland, was a very poor man and I helped him a lot in those days. Now he's got the whole Treasury of Great Britain behind him.'

So I said 'Dear Lady, you can't have the Prime Minister putting his hand in the public Treasury to support his lady friends.'

Then she got very nasty. She said 'I went to Downing Street, I was admitted, and I told him I had to get some money. He saw me in the Cabinet Room and became completely hysterical and began to bang his head against the wall. Isobel came in in the middle of this performance. Then he took me by the shoulders and pushed me out in front of all the porters in Downing Street.'

I always remember how her story ended – 'I fall down, I break my lorgnettes, my eyes they are blinded with tears. The policeman, he pick me up and put me in a taxi'.

So I told her it was terribly shocking, the Prime Minister was tired and overworked.

She replied 'I've got letters from him. You know, he's a very innocent man and he wrote to me letters which were pornographic. They were written from Lossiemouth in his own handwriting but he's cut off Lossiemouth with a pair of scissors.'

I said to her 'Now look, no newspaper will publish them here, and if you try to blackmail the Prime Minister he will be Mr X in court and you'll go down for 10 or 20 years.'

She knew a trick worth two of that. 'You may be able to stop me here, but I shall go to the Quai d'Orsay and the whole thing will blaze in the French press.'

So then I pulled a real bluff, because you can imagine in a Labour government anything of that kind would wreak havoc. But with her being a central European I thought she might fall for it. I said to her 'Do you really think a British Government is going to be brought down by one lonely woman? You have no friends, you have no helpers at all. You've got to go by train to Dover and on the channel boat to Paris. Do you think you are ever going to get to France?'

It worked. She was in floods of tears. She said 'Please, I want to leave, please don't!' I said 'Of course not, we're friends, everything will be gentle. Take the advice of a good friend, don't go near the Quai d'Orsay, very, very, dangerous. Go back to Vienna as fast as you can get.'

As Tom told the story, there were further repercussions. Years later, when he had founded the British Union of Fascists, he was approached by a man who wanted to join him who had previously been a secret service agent: this man told Tom that the flat in Horseferry Road had in fact been bugged so that the incident, and Tom's part in it, was known to the security people. And the story, the man said, had continued – the

Austrian lady had indeed returned to Vienna but then had reappeared in 1931 or 1932 and 'Jimmy Thomas was sent with £3,000 of Abe Bailey's money to buy the letters ... he went to Paris, met her there, came back without the three thousand and without the letters.'

Then many years later, Tom related, Charles Mendl, who had been at the British Embassy in Paris, told Tom that he had once seen the allegedly pornographic letters and that all he remembered of them was a poem which contained the line –

Porcupine through hairy bowers shall climb to paradise.

Back in 1928 – it seemed that Tom and Cimmie were in various ways trying to make themselves useful to Ramsay MacDonald. He came down to Savehay Farm to work: he was photographed writing a draft of his election manifesto in the loggia. There was even talk that in a future Labour government Tom might be made Foreign Secretary. But Ramsay MacDonald's way of going round with the rich and fashionable had led to hostile comment within the Labour Party: Beatrice Webb wrote sourly of MacDonald's liking for 'the Mosleys, De la Warrs, and other lithe and beauteous forms – leaders of fashion or ladies of the stage attended by 6ft tall and well groomed men'. And it might even have been true, as Harold Nicolson wrote later, that 'Cimmie Mosley's hold on Ramsay is one of the things that makes it difficult for Tom to be specially favoured.' Also Ramsay MacDonald might have sensed a growing hostility to himself in Tom at this time: it was their Berlin trip, Tom wrote later, that first opened his eyes to 'the deep element of hysteria' in Ramsay MacDonald's nature: such men might be 'figures of infinite worthiness, the models of public virtue and private decorum': but because they were 'products of the Puritan tradition' they were 'entirely different animals in all things, great and small, to the masters of action whom history has revealed to our judgement'. This feeling arose, he would explain, not of course as a result of the discovery that Ramsay MacDonald had a mistress but because of his failure to deal with the situation with dispatch. But Tom made his own odd calculations in this area: and in the coming three or four years he might at times have reflected back on himself the comment he made on Ramsay MacDonald – 'It seems to me that men in high office ought to live like athletes ... statesmen are poor fish if even for the few years at the height of their responsibilities they cannot be serious'.

There was some confusion at the heart of the Labour Party about what should be a proper attitude to puritanism. One strand of Labour thinking, represented by the ILP, was dedicated to socialism as if to some kind of puritan religion: this was in the tradition of Marx, Lenin, Trotsky: socialists had to keep clear of even social contacts with establishment ways of living for fear of almost moral contamination. But this had never been the attitude of the majority of Labour parliamentarians: for them, just as socialism would evolve out of capitalism without a revolution, so new social attitudes might be grafted without too much trouble on to the old. It was Tom, ultimately, who became distrusted by both sides in the confusion – by the puritans for being too much of a rake, and by the compromisers for being too much of a rebel.

From the evidence of Cimmie's 1927 letter there was a danger even then of Tom's becoming disillusioned with Labour: neither the puritans nor the moderates seemed to be much interested in getting things done. The former declaimed passionately about theory without much interest in what was possible: the latter, with their eye on the possible, held to no theory to spur them on. Tom did what he could from his position of not being quite in step with anyone to suggest what might be done.

In 1927 he was made a member of a sub-committee of the Labour Party National Executive to prepare a draft programme for the general election which would come at the latest in 1929. He wrote a personal letter to Ramsay MacDonald in which he expanded on the Birmingham Proposals of two years earlier; in particular he advocated the setting-up of an Economic Council with far-reaching powers to interfere in the economy. MacDonald was sympathetic to some of the ideas about ways in which credit might be provided to stimulate employment: what he objected to (and what most of Tom's critics must have objected to although for the reasons suggested it seemed they could not say this) were the methods that Tom proposed were necessary if the policy was to be put into effect. Tom claimed that there had to be dynamism with authority from the top: MacDonald wrote in his diary 'quiet cautious leadership is what I think is wanted'. But it was under just such cautious leadership that the economy had for years been failing.

The Labour Party programme that was prepared for the 1929 election under the title of *Labour and the Nation* was in fact largely written by MacDonald; it was a compendium of pious hopes that socialism would benefit all sections of the community without much mention of how this miracle might occur. But it served the Labour Party well at the time of the election.

The reason why the men whom the Labour Party and indeed the

country trusted found themselves more and more tending to ignore
Tom seems to have been not just that his proposals for political action
alarmed them, but also because there was something in his personal style
that they felt might justify this alarm. It was about this area that it was
difficult to talk – it was the political tradition that politics should be
talked about in terms of politics, and questions of what human beings
were should be kept to another context. But Tom as a person was such
an obvious oddity on the political scene that personal pronouncements
by political commentators kept on mysteriously breaking in: there had
been Beatrice Webb's view of Tom – that 'with such perfection there
must be some rottenness somewhere'. Ellen Wilkinson wrote 'The
trouble with Oswald Mosley is that he is too good looking ... he is not
that kind of nice hero who rescues the girl at the point of torture but
the one who hisses "at last we meet!" ' The suggestion seemed to be that,
with so many talents, the temptation to be out for oneself must be
overwhelming. But there were many confusions here: what might have
been a serious point about an ambivalence in Tom's moral attitudes
became lost in what seemed to be fear or envy of his energy and even
his sexual drives. There might have been serious points to be made about
these too: but not in the traditional context of judging who was to be
listened to on the National Executive.

During the summer of 1928 Tom and Cimmie were visited by her
sister Irene at Denham and in the South of France. There was an evening
at Savehay Farm in May when, having listened on the wireless to
Stravinsky's *Oedipus Rex*, Cimmie 'gave us a long socialist dissertation
and was so earnest and heart-whole one could not argue with her'. Then
a weekend or two later Cecil Beaton and Stephen Tennant came down:
they dressed up in Mary Curzon's old clothes and – 'did the most
fantastic dances as passed description for effeteness tho' brilliance was in
every line'. Tom seems to have been a bit aloof from all this. Cimmie,
Irene reported, 'seemed on the edge of a breakdown'. Then in August
at Antibes there was a hugely successful birthday party for Cimmie to
which there came 'the whole world and his wife': a few days later – 'I
talked for the first time in my life for 2 hours to Cim over the misery
of her present life and Tom's insulting behaviour to her: it killed me to
hear of her rending loyalty to him saying he had never been unfaithful
she only wished he would not make a fool of her in public.' Cimmie
herself however seems to have been a ringleader in the party-going
activity: certainly she never seems to have tried to get Tom away from
the areas in which he could so easily hurt her.

It was Cimmie's very devotion to Tom, probably, that allowed him to feel free and confident in this world: people from time to time encouraged Cimmie herself to flirt; even to take lovers: she used to say she did not want to. No one advised her to get out. On the evidence of her own letters there was something self-destructive, almost provocative, about her obsession with Tom; she would say this herself – that her possessiveness was making her nagging and sending her 'mad' without reference to whether Tom was going after anyone else or not. So, by behaving as he did, what had Tom got to lose? And by his endearments it seemed he could always mollify her. And at this time Cimmie did probably believe that Tom's flirtations could for the most part be explained in terms of the social game which was to do not with love but conquest; that apart from doing what was natural to him, what Tom was looking for was prestige. And she could try to convince herself that it was not unreasonable to want prestige.

Tom tried to justify his behaviour on the grounds that it was to do with 'wholeness', with health, with a necessary refusal to deny what was his nature: such behaviour balanced, and gave him energy for, the rigours of his life in politics. But in fact he seemed quite often to be ill. Cimmie wrote that she wished they could settle down for a time and live like ordinary people: but she did not arrange a time, even a holiday, in which this might be possible. She herself could not pretend that she flourished at the social game: but she, as much as he, seemed trapped by it.

A pattern was emerging of Tom as the swashbuckling, vituperative rebel in public life who in private life became also something of a naughty boy; who, having shown off, could return to its mother for forgiveness. (Tom's mother wrote to him at this time – 'It seems almost incredible to me to realise "The Honourable Gentleman" is my very beloved fat *obstinate* baby of so little while ago, and yet you haven't changed much.') Cimmie was now becoming seen as the angelic martyr mother: but she knew that there was something daemonic in her own attitudes to Tom: she both wanted and did not want him to be as he was: she saw him as both saint and devil. She did not, from the evidence of her letters, seem to be all that much interested now in his day-to-day politics: what he liked to do was to bring her news of them and she liked accepting this: it was as if he were saying to her – Look, what a good boy am I! People who want to be heroes perhaps also have to be somewhat like children: Freud said that anyone who has been the undisputed favourite of his mother keeps for life the feelings of a conqueror. With Tom there had been pushed out the image of the father – which inculcates the faculty for being discriminatory; self-critical.

Thus the would-be hero has no recognition of the dark side of himself:
he sees the devil only in others. In himself, he feels a power that can be
used. And so he goes out to do battle with a make-believe confidence
and with make-believe attitudes to the world: he cannot distinguish
between reality and what is imposed by childhood patterns. In this he
is cheered on by his mother – or by the mother-figure he has chosen and
who accepts him. All Tom's baby-talk with Cimmie – the porkers, the
mutts, the moo-moos – seem to have been tapping some childhood well;
he needed perhaps to draw strength from this before going out to fight
– with his words, his tongue – the terrible dragons. But heroes continue
not to see the dragons that are in themselves.

> My own beloved moonbeam one
>   Adored his weekend so with all his blessed fellows – big, tiny and
> very tiny [drawing of three trees]. Hated going back so to this
> turmoil.
> Last night a thrilling discussion, but not for paper!
> All love in world my own socialist one. Tom

Tom went on a speaking tour of the country as a run-up to the general
election: Cimmie involved herself with her constituency at Stoke. They
each wrote solicitously about their own and the other's health. Tom –
'Good meeting here but my voice going badly at the end – three
meetings and long motor drives in a night – will return I hope to find
his sweet sausage lying down.' Cimmie – 'Stayed in bed all day and only
had 4 cups of milk and a compôte of apples ... You were quite right
when you said things went wrong when I thought of myself – I will
try not to!' They were both driving themselves hard. They must have
felt this necessary, if they were to take on the world seeing themselves
and others as heroes or demons.
    At the end of 1928 – in reply to a letter from Cimmie reiterating her
sorrow at not always being able to live up to the high hopes she had
for both of them and pleading for further 'special efforts' – Tom wrote:

> My own darling Moo-moo,
>   Yes let us be happy when you come back – life and especially youth
> is so short. In our life it is so difficult to preserve the steel that
> withstands great strain with the sweet gentle things that make life
> happy – so hard to meet an age of turmoil and yet to be fit inhabitants
> of the world we wish to create. Yet to excel in the fulness of life the
> great incompatibles must be combined. Let us make together that

great attempt on which so far all have failed – the attempt to reconcile the epic life with gentle sensitive things. I would inscribe my name on the page of my epoch in letters of flame and of rose – success would be the first shadow of the superman on earth – it will probably fail, but better the empyrean flight and disaster than earthbound crawlings – let us live always with the epic sense. Tom.

But even Tom could not quite let things rest on such a note of hyperbole, and added:

This really means he thinks her the only one in the world for him – is sorry he has been a bit overwrought lately and is feeling a bit up in the air tonight – loves her so very much and does so passionately want her to be happy – sorry he is such a difficult one – she is a bit diff too sometimes but that is his fault for putting her in such a dogfight. Don't mind any *little* things my sweet one – though he will try and be better.

But it was the little things to which they were vulnerable – those dwarves that come up from the underworld and penetrate heroes' armour. In May 1929, just before the general election, Irene was at Denham with her eye again ready to perceive chinks in armour –

A most tragic and painful row took place between Cim and Tom at dinner over the cars for the election and he was vilely rude to her and I tried to argue to both long into the night but they both seem to be at deadlock. I wish at times he could disappear off the face of the earth as he only brings her endless agony. And to make it worse, she thought of all things she was in for a baby.

Cimmie was in fact pregnant. Irene went to help her in her campaign at Stoke. The election there had aroused enormous interest because Cimmie as a rich socialist had drawn on herself all the publicity and abuse that Tom usually attracted, and there was the added appeal of her being a good-looking woman. The old stories about wealth and duplicity were trotted out: Cimmie was supposed to have a penniless brother in America whom the heartless family allowed to live in a workhouse: Tom and Cimmie ran factories where they paid their workers eighteen shillings a week. Irene heard a woman telling such stories on a bus, and remonstrated: the woman called Irene 'a bit of scum'. At a meeting of Cimmie's conservative opponent, Colonel Ward, a group of Cimmie's supporters challenged him about the spreading of such stories: in the resulting confusion Irene:

> had to yell that I was her sister and knew more about the Leiter fortunes than Colonel Ward and my grandfather did not corner wheat. The chairwoman yelled for the police. Ward was white as a sheet. I left the room taking ¾ of the clapping and shrieking women with me and I was cheered all the way down the streets.

Irene and her band of maenads in fact so alarmed Colonel Ward that he announced that as a result of 'organised hooliganism' he had decided to cancel his further meetings on the grounds that 'the socialists have determined to put an end to free speech in this country'.

At her eve-of-poll meeting Cimmie herself received:

> the wildest reception ... We went on to Fenton Town Hall Square where she had another thundering welcome save for a small group of hysterical booers one of whom, a woman, tried to tear everything off Cim. To get away we had to have barriers of strong young men to prevent us from being torn to shreds by the yelling crowd.

Cimmie got a 7,850 majority over Colonel Ward – his majority at the last election had been 4,500. She doubled the Labour vote from 13,000 to 26,000: she recorded one of the biggest swings to Labour in the country. Later that day she was again 'nearly torn to ribbons' when she met Ramsay MacDonald in London: she was rescued 'shaking with emotion'. Four days later, on June 6th, she had a miscarriage.

At his own eve-of-poll meeting at Smethwick Tom had joked with his audience – 'I have got the wind up. I am afraid my wife will get a bigger majority than me.' She did. Tom's majority was 7,340.

After Cimmie had had her miscarriage Irene reported – 'Poor old Tom was pretty hard hit.' But Irene herself seems to have caught something of the fever of heroic politics. With Cimmie and Tom both now in Parliament and with Tom obviously set to enjoy his first taste of practical, ministerial power, she wrote to Cimmie:

> I don't want you to think it was all the election, because I think Bonny found your inside unsatisfactory and you might have had a real tragedy later whereas now if you rest peacefully for 10 days or more and let it get pitched right again then you stand a far better chance of having a real strong baby and being yourself strong too to carry

it. I don't want you to feel the bitterness of this too much, my very dear one. Great things have come to you and Tom in parliament things – this is indeed a heartbreak in the midst of it – but have faith it was for the best.

CHAPTER 13

Rules of the Game:
Ministerial Office

In the General Election of May 1929 Labour won 287 seats, the Conservatives 261, and the Liberals 59. Ramsay MacDonald formed a Labour Government with Liberal backing. The rumours that Tom might be made Foreign Secretary did not materialise. There were too many party stalwarts who had to be satisfied; and in any case Tom's reputation, both political and personal, was probably thought not yet to be sufficiently secure. He was made Chancellor of the Duchy of Lancaster with special responsibility for unemployment – a ministerial post outside the cabinet. His boss within the cabinet was J. H. Thomas, the Lord Privy Seal, ex-secretary of the railwaymen's union.

Tom entered his one year of ministerial power with an enormous task placed somewhat nebulously above his shoulders but with no effective administrative apparatus by which to handle it. He was given a room in the Treasury, and as his private secretary a Treasury official who had been an assistant to Keynes: he personally employed Allan Young, his agent from Birmingham, as his political secretary. But even in government he seemed fated to be very much a lone voice. Winston Churchill described him as being 'a sort of ginger assistant to the Lord Privy Seal; and more ginger than assistant I have no doubt'.

J. H. Thomas was a flamboyant character, a 'card', the inspirer of innumerable comic stories. When he arrived in his minister's office in 1929 he was said to have remarked 'What a bloody awful 'ole more privy than seal.' Lord Birkenhead found him with a hangover one morning complaining 'I've an 'ell of an 'ead': Lord Birkenhead said 'Why not take a couple of aspirates.' Once at a railwaymen's meeting a heckler called out 'Jimmy you're selling us!' and Thomas replied 'I'm trying but I can't find a buyer!' Tom remarked in his autobiography that it was difficult personally to dislike a man who could make a remark

like that. But it was also difficult to work at the huge and largely
uncharted problem of unemployment with someone whose talents,
however endearing, had been for negotiating, bargaining, disarming
people, making them laugh. He had never shown much interest in
transforming society.

The other members of the government put on to deal with unemployment were George Lansbury, First Commissioner of Works, a
70-year old party stalwart with (in Beatrice Webb's words) 'certainly
no capacity for solving intellectual problems'; and Tom Johnston,
Under Secretary of State for Scotland, a man of intelligence but carrying
little weight. These four – Thomas, Mosley, Lansbury and Johnston –
were supposed to work together; but there was no timetable nor
structure by which they regularly met, and they had no control over
machinery for implementing their decisions if they did. After some
months, Tom Johnston wrote that he was uncertain even whether or
not he was in fact on the 'Unemployment Committee'. The only
discernible difference in administrative machinery from that used by the
previous government was that whereas before responsibility for providing both work and benefits for the unemployed had resided with the
Ministry of Labour, now the responsibility for providing work had been ·
taken away and given to J. H. Thomas and his staff in the Treasury –
consisting of four civil servants seconded from the Inland Revenue, the
Board of Trade, and the War Office – and the responsibility for
implementing any recommendations remained invested with the Board
of Trade. So that what in words had seemed to be a step in the direction
of setting up an economic supreme council with executive powers such
as Tom had always advocated, in fact turned out to be a bureaucratic
proliferation of functions which made effective action more difficult
than ever.

This perhaps in some ways suited J. H. Thomas. His biographer
wrote of him that at this time 'the projects that seethed in his mind
ranged from a bridge over the Zambesi river to a traffic circus at the
Elephant and Castle: he saw civil servants, businessmen, local government authorities, trades unionists, engineers, scientists, post office
officials, railway directors'. He was the chairman of an unending succession of committees, thrashing out the feasibility of railway schemes,
harbour schemes, road schemes; for drainage, forestry, electricity and
slum-clearance. But after all the talk, nothing much happened. Nothing
much in fact could happen unless the government provided money; and
J. H. Thomas and the other members of the Cabinet knew that it was
unlikely that money would be forthcoming. Thomas agreed with

Snowden, the Chancellor of the Exchequer, that above all there should be no departure from strict free-trade principles: no subsidies to industry; no danger of inflation. But then, what on earth did a government think it could do about unemployment if it had no money with which to employ people? All the talk, all the committees, began to seem as if they were just noises to cover up the silences of nothing being done; while the government waited helplessly for world trade to pick up on its own.

Tom for a time tried to work loyally with Thomas. Just before his first speech in Parliament for the government front bench on 4th July Thomas told him to announce that between 75 and 100 million pounds would be spent on the electrification of Liverpool Street Station. Tom announced these figures: later in the debate Thomas reassured members anxious about the fact that money might at last be poured out that of course his colleague must have been referring to 'the total amount of all possible electrification schemes under consideration'. Tom wrote later – 'It was the only time in my life I ever gave to the House of Commons a fact or a figure which was not valid.' To Thomas, all this was part of the game of making noises that might reassure people in one way, knowing that noises could be taken back and used to reassure people in another.

Tom liked to tell a story of how he was going in to a committee room with Thomas one day and he noticed how Thomas was holding an object under his coat-tails. The committee was on the subject of Post Office expenditure; in particular on the cost of a new box for telephones that was to be put on the walls of houses. Thomas had been told by his civil servants that the wooden box they recommended would cost fifteen shillings: in the committee, Thomas produced from beneath his coat with a flourish a tin box and announced – 'Four bob!' The civil servants explained that the wooden box itself cost three shillings: it was what was inside it that cost the other twelve.

During July Tom did manage to pilot through the House of Commons a Colonial Development Bill which contained provisions about safeguarding native labour. A newspaper commented – 'His name will live as the minister responsible for the first Act laying down important principles to protect native labour from exploitation.'

He also – working in his 'semi-dungeon high up in the Treasury' (Lansbury's phrase) – produced his own plan for creating vacancies for young people in industry by offering those over sixty-five better pensions if they retired – increasing the payment to married couples from 10s to 30s a week. The Treasury said that the cost of this was prohibitive. Tom then suggested that pensions could be offered to those employed in certain depressed industries – coal mining, iron and steel, ship building. While the Treasury was working out ways in which to discourage this, Tom went off on his summer holidays.

Just before he left, at the Durham miner's Gala at the end of July, he declared – 'I would rather see the Labour Government go down in defeat than shrink from great issues, because from such defeats men rise again with strength redoubled.'

During August 1929 – two months after the Labour Government had taken office with their urgent and primary commitment that of dealing with unemployment – all the four responsible ministers were out of England. Thomas was in Canada, Lansbury and Johnston were on holiday in Scotland. Tom's life in the South of France will be described in the next chapter.

During the summer of 1929 the unemployment figure was just over a million: it had been much the same for six years. Unemployment was held to be a great evil both because it was not seen how the dole could reasonably be raised above a level of barest subsistence, and because wasted potential productivity seemed to be an affront to accepted ideas about progress. On his return from holiday Tom returned to the attack about pensions: 'a man of sixty who has worked all his life will not suffer much demoralisation from living in idleness but a man of 20 may suffer irreparable harm'. He worked out his scheme in even greater detail: all insured workers who reached the age of sixty by a certain date were to be offered a pension of £1 a week for a single man and 30s a week for a married man on condition that they retired from work within six months: the cost of the scheme could be spread over fifteen years. By this, Tom estimated, 'at one stroke we reduce by one third the wholly unemployed'. The scheme was put to the cabinet: the cabinet appointed a sub-committee: the Treasury told the sub-committee that the cost (£22 million) was still prohibitive because they were traditionally committed to annual budgeting and could not think in terms of fifteen years. They put up the further argument – how could it be proved, until it happened, that the young would in such a scheme be absorbed into industry? Tom replied – How could anything, in fact, be proved until it happened? The Treasury's argument was for never doing anything.

Tom started a new line of attack by proposing a national programme for building roads. At the moment there were less than 4,000 men throughout the country employed in road-building: the business was entirely in the hands of local authorities. Tom planned an additional national scheme in which high wages would be offered to those in areas of the worst unemployment to build trunk roads and motorways. This scheme was received with ridicule. Did Tom not see, his critics said, that local governments would simply shelve their own schemes in the hope that the Labour Government would take over their costs? And how would a national organisation fare any better in the lengthy business of going through the formalities of acquiring land and so on than local authorities were already faring? And in any case, how could it be proved, again, that the building of roads would be of long-term assistance to the national economy? But above all – would not providing money for roads involve withdrawing money which might have been used by industries engaged in the export trade: and the encouragement of this, in the Treasury's view, was still the only hope of the country's recovery.

To this Tom replied that it had been the blind faith in the export trade that had led the country to its present moribund predicament: with every country giving priority to exports in a free-trade world, only those would get along which produced the cheapest goods by paying the lowest wages. In fact the Treasury itself had very little to suggest as a cure for unemployment except a reduction in wages – but then other countries could reduce wages more. Tom referred back to his Birmingham proposals of 1925 in which he had advocated that a closed economic area should be created in which a strong central government should have control over investment in industry, the buying of raw materials, and the manipulation of wages and prices. In the face of questions about how a central organisation would effectively control myriad local interests and organisations Tom simply asserted that of course if it was to be effective it would have to be given powers to do just this: that if it was not, then of course this implied that effective action was not wanted. But it was in the face of this sort of argument of Tom's that people found it easiest not to answer him at all: there was no accepted political language by which it might be stated that in certain circumstances, in the face of the danger of greater evils, it might be better perhaps even in such a grave area as that of unemployment if in fact things only got talked about and not much was done.

In the middle of all this argument, or silence, there was the Wall Street crash of October 1929 when the bottom as it were, seemed to fall out of capitalists' lives in skyscrapers. Tom's prophecies seemed to be being fulfilled – there was indeed something suicidal about a world in which it was imagined that progress could be maintained by everyone competing against others to produce ever cheaper goods. J. H. Thomas had returned from Canada where ostensibly he had been to try to stimulate trade: it became evident that he had stimulated little but an anxiety about himself. By December he was reported by Beatrice Webb to be 'completely rattled and in such a state of panic that he is bordering on lunacy: Henderson reported that the PM feared suicidal mania'. Arthur Henderson suggested that Thomas 'must be sent away for a rest and Oswald Mosley installed under the Council to carry out agreed plans'. But the trouble was there were no agreed plans; and within the existing organisation there was no hope of carrying them out even if there were.

Tom had been on a speaking tour of the country trying to get support for his own plans: 'Every citizen should enrol himself in the great national army that is fighting unemployment.' But what, apart from building roads, was this army actually to do? Tom poured out schemes that were sometimes as bizarre as J. H. Thomas's: he admitted they were 'some hopeful, and some a little fantastic'. He wrote to the Air Minister suggesting – what about a roof over Victoria Station, to make a mid-city aerodrome?

MacDonald himself had for most of this time been occupied with Foreign Affairs: he had been in America successfully discussing naval disarmament. For the first six months of the Labour government he remained popular: he was the sort of Prime Minister that people liked: he was handsome, had a fine speaking voice, and he uttered noises of reassurance. In December 1929 he and Philip Snowden, the Chancellor of the Exchequer, were made freemen of the City of London: Beatrice Webb reported that during his speech to the assembled financiers at the banquet at the Mansion House 'his handsome features literally glowed ... which enhanced his beauty – just as a young girl's beauty glows under the ardent eyes of her lover'. In contrast, there sat 'Jimmy Thomas in the front row gazing at the ceremony, his ugly and rather mean face made meaner and uglier by an altogether exaggerated sense of personal failure'.

It seemed that Thomas was to be the scapegoat for the government's failure to deal with unemployment. But no government since the war had managed to deal with unemployment; and Tom, whatever he felt about Thomas, was not interested in questions of who was to be scapegoat. He went to see MacDonald in December and told him that he, Tom, was preparing a memorandum in which there would be put together all his proposals during the last six months. He would then ask MacDonald to put this before the Cabinet.

MacDonald went to his home at Lossiemouth, in Scotland, for the Christmas holidays. From there on December 30th he wrote in his own handwriting a letter to Tom.

My dear Mosley,

I had no chance of renewing our conversation about unemployment but I have thought much of what you said. Indeed for months I have been concerned with the state of things.

1   I am troubled about the lack of cooperation amongst the Junta to which the problem has been handed over. I was hoping that you would have all pulled together and hammered out from your diversity of view some agreed policy. I must admit the facts. That has not happened, and into whys and wherefores the crowded state of my own work has prevented me from going. I thought I could safely leave it to you all and took on things which I should not have done had I thought that you would not have all pulled together ...

2   The Economic Advisory Committee will be set up soon but there are various things to be provided for which at the last minute have caused delay. I am dealing with them here. That would be helpful but of course its fruits would not ripen in a month.

3   I am disturbed that the main features of our work hitherto has been to give further allowances for distress ... On outsiders it is having a depressing effect and is certainly lowering production. I have seen a good many old supporters and have had rather voluminous letters from others. The general tone is one of warning against those who are sponging and clamouring.

4   I have been looking into the pensions at 60 to relieve the labour market and I am quite certain it will not do that to any appreciable extent ... When one thinks this idea down to its essence, it is that we are overpopulated: that that old ruffian Malthus is right. The condition of the derelict areas is of the same class of problem. The whole thing must really be tackled in a way other than money aids ...

5   As I see the problem (dimly) we must hang on to what we are doing but weed out the spongers all round ... At the same time we should tackle the problem systematically. For instance the Department should present to the Treasury its views upon the financial and taxation policy – the Economic Advisory will soon do this I hope – for a situation has to be handled and not merely theories applied. We ought also to have really sound information as to expenditure upon unemployment, if for no other reason than to assure ourselves and enable us to defend ourselves against the attack which will soon be launched upon us.

But I must stop. My guardians here demand my presence for a walk. Only now am I feeling the work of past months in consequence of which I can tell C [Cimmie] a most bloodcurdling adventure in dreamland – a real good horror.

Unto you both much affection.

Yrs.   JRM

Tom was already preparing his memorandum. He worked on it through the Christmas holidays: he showed a draft to Keynes in the middle of January. Keynes remarked that it was 'a very able document and illuminating'. Tom sent a copy to MacDonald on 23rd January.

What became known as the Mosley Memorandum is a 15-page document in which Tom reiterated his proposals of the previous four years and put them into a form which, if the Cabinet still ignored them, he could use to appeal over the Cabinet's head first to the Parliamentary Labour Party and then to the country. The style of the memorandum is conciliatory and even tentative: it is emphasised that the aim is not to suggest clear-cut answers, but to set out unavoidably the serious questions which had to be discussed with a view to finding answers.

The second and third sections of the memorandum deal with long-term and short-term plans for providing work. It is pointed out that there is a certain conflict of interest here: long-term plans rely on the rationalisation of industry – on the bringing of industry up to date in both matters of technology and uses of manpower – and this may actually increase short-term unemployment. Thus it is all the more necessary that short-term employment should be treated as an urgent and separate issue.

To deal with short-term employment the memorandum concentrates on road construction. There are proposals concerning the technicalities by which movement and employment of labour should be handled sensibly by cooperation between national and local authorities. The whole short term scheme could be financed by 'a loan based upon the revenue from the Road Fund'. The cost to the taxpayer should be little more than the equivalent of 'a sixpenny tax on unearned income'. Such moderate expenditure, Tom suggested, would hardly cause such inflation as would involve a 'flight from the pound'. Then, discussion on long-term plans could begin.

But the success of the whole scheme depended on the proper working of the administrative machinery by which it would be operated: and it was just this area – that dealt with by the first and by far the most important section of the memorandum – that Tom's critics found it difficult not just not to reject, but even to talk about.

It was suggested that at the head of the Executive Committee to be

set up should be the Prime Minister himself and under him, as if in a
war-time inner Cabinet, the Chancellor of the Exchequer and five or
six other ministers of relevant departments. Under this Executive
Committee, which would meet once a week, there would be standing
committees to implement its decisions headed by the relevant ministers.
As part of a permanent executive machinery there would be a secretariat
of twelve top civil servants who would also provide the information for
the committees on which they themselves would serve. There would
also be a research committee of economists and an advisory committee
of financiers and businessmen to work with the committees of politicians. Finally, there would be attached to this apparatus an Industrial
Bank, which would provide credit for the rationalisation schemes,
higher wages and industrial development, as ordered by the Executive
Committee or the Standing Committees. The aim of the whole was,
simply, that authoritative action should be made possible. 'An attack
upon the economic problem can only be effective under the auspices of
the Prime Minister himself who should be armed with an adequate staff
for such a purpose. He alone possesses the power to secure coordination
and the authority to enforce action when decisions are taken.'

But it was just this suggestion that produced the silence·amongst
Tom's critics. Everyone in government circles knew that the organisation under J. H. Thomas was not working: Thomas himself was breaking down: his lieutenants on their own were powerless: even what
committees there were were seldom meeting. And unemployment was
growing. But it seemed to be the case that in this situation most people
in positions of authority continued to think that they should make noises
of lamentation – and do little else. Their fear, of course, was that if Tom's
proposals were put into effect, there would be danger of some sort of
dictatorship – with its attendant corruptions. But if such methods
seemed to be the only way to cure unemployment, how could they say
they were not interested? It was the tradition that politicians were
supposed to say they wanted to get things done.

Tom sent his memorandum to Ramsay MacDonald on January
23rd 1930. Shortly before this, he had mentioned to J. H. Thomas that
he was formulating some opinions about unemployment which he
would like Thomas to see in due course. Ramsay MacDonald tele-
phoned to Thomas early in February to ask if he knew of the Memorandum. Thomas said he did not. Then there ensued the sort of game
by which politicians effectively evade talking about things that matter,
by getting in a state about things that do not.

Thomas wrote to MacDonald complaining that Tom had improperly gone over his, Thomas's, head; and so he, with much regret, had no alternative but to offer MacDonald his resignation. MacDonald wrote to Thomas saying that he quite understood his, Thomas's, hurt feelings; but he had no alternative but to refuse his resignation out of considerations of national interest ('we must endure however hard the road may be'). MacDonald also wrote to Tom saying how very surprised he, MacDonald, was about Tom's behaviour which had been quite properly resented by his boss, Thomas ('I need not explain why that should be so'). But the best thing of course, all round, MacDonald suggested, would be to patch the whole matter up and say no more about it. In the middle of all this John Strachey, who was now Tom's Parliamentary Private Secretary, left a copy of the Memorandum lying around in his house when journalists were present and its contexts were 'leaked' to the press – whether by design or accident, of course, people could hint darkly. This gave Thomas further opportunities to demonstrate hurt feelings. With all this posturing going on the memorandum itself could be, and quietly was, put on the shelf – to be considered in due course by a Cabinet sub-committee consisting of Snowden, Greenwood, Margaret Bondfield, and Tom Shaw – who were all known to be hostile to Tom's ideas. This committee then could, and did, push it even further to the back of the shelf by sending it to the Treasury for a thorough examination. There it would lie, as if in some morgue.

In all the business about the Mosley memorandum – concerning both the contents and the reactions of people to it – there was a confusion, barely conscious, not just about the nature of the political game, but about the nature of language and even about human nature itself. Tom had been brought up outside a political tradition: he believed that, politically, words should mean roughly what they said. He had become a socialist because he thought it vital, amongst other things, that the unemployment problem should be solved: that the socialists, when they got power, should try to fulfil their election pledges and give priority to doing this. But then, when they achieved power largely through holding out hopes by their promises, they seemed to be doing nothing serious about the problem at all. Tom was outraged by this. He thought – If you say you want to solve the unemployment problem then you set up machinery by which the unemployment problem can be solved; if you do not, then this means that you do not want to solve the unemployment problem. You should then admit this: any other attitude is cheating.

Those who had been in the Labour Party or indeed in any political tradition for a long time knew that in some sense all this had to be a game: you had good intentions: you honestly professed them in your manifestos: you hoped by this to get power: none of this was cheating. But when you did get power of course there were often realities which were stronger than the good intentions you had had: you were forced to adapt yourself to realities not because you were betraying your good intentions, but because if you did not you might be betraying other good principles more severely. There was often a choice of evils: you had sometimes, possibly, to do almost nothing. But you could not quite say this. Political language had to be about will, and dynamism, or there would never be hope of improvement.

At the back of this there was a question of how one might see human nature. Tom thought, or believed (or wanted to believe: the words are difficult) that human beings are rational: that if human beings are rational then words should properly mean roughly what they say. There seemed to him no sense in the idea that sometimes a game with words might properly by played in which the point was that they are not quite believed: but such words are none the less valid because this non-belief is recognised by the participants from a higher point of view. In certain areas human beings play games because the demands on them are too paradoxical to make sense if they do not: in the area for instance to do with the necessary exercise of power and the salutary limitation of power it is not in the simplicities of words that there is truth; but in the recognition that there is something that can be honoured beyond words' limitations.

Tom's critics in the Party, however much they said they believed in the rational processes of socialism, yet believed in their bones, most of them (they had been brought up with less opportunities for self-deception than Tom) that human affairs were for the most part irrational and there had to be safeguards against the dangerously over-rationalising tendencies of human beings and of words. When Tom made his proposals for strong central governmental machinery they could not attack him directly because, as socialists, this is what they had always been advocating; how else could they have got as far as they had with evolutionary or revolutionary change? But it was by instinct that they feared the exaggerated implementation of government control: there is nothing more irrational, they knew, than human beings who have been given total power – even to act in such a way as they think is wholly rational. But still, they could not quite say this, or how would they ask for, or be given, any power at all? Both they, and the people who voted for them, had to pretend they could be trusted with power: and it was still in fact by dealing in limited power that people could strive and hope bit by bit for reasonable change. But all this only made sense if it was held together by rules of an instinctively accepted political game – rules that were known, but not stated, on a supra-rational level. So what did such people do when someone came along with rational arguments that did not take into account styles or levels of understanding – who did not see from some metaphysical level what had to be, and what was not, a game? It was safest, presumably, to ignore such a person, if he could not properly be spoken to. One of the rules of the game was that you could not exactly explain what was and what was not a game: if you did, then the someone who did not accept that there was a game could simply make you seem a hypocrite.

Tom might have understood some of the complexities of games-playing if he had pondered more about himself. Of course, he himself played games: his letters to Cimmie were genuine games: how better could he write to her? It was on his perceiving something like this that there might have been truth. He seemed to have to insist that other people were not playing games: it is difficult to imagine how, in his private life, he succeeded in thinking this of himself.

CHAPTER 14

Entertainment

Cimmie had her miscarriage early in June. She took her seat in the House of Commons at the end of the month. In August the family went for their usual summer holiday to Antibes.

Cimmie's sister Irene joined them there. She recorded in her cloudy, anarchic style what life in the South of France was like. Tom and Cimmie and the children were staying at the Eden Roc hotel. the other *dramatis personae* in Irene's account were in the hotel or in villas round about. The chief attraction of the long hot summer was the film star John Gilbert, who had recently been acting with Greta Garbo, and was with his wife Ina Claire. In supporting roles in Irene's story were – Baba and Fruity Metcalfe, Cimmie's younger sister and her husband; Bobby and Paula Casa Maury (the latter Tom was currently pursuing); John Strachey and his recently married wife Esther; Dick Wyndham, a painter and Cimmie's confidante; Babe Barnato, a racing motorist; Rupert Belville, a banker; and Americans Ben Finney and Dudley Malone. Irene had been enraged by overhearing Tom at a dinner party speculating in whispers to Paula Casa Maury about which of the three Curzon sisters would succeed in the contest to attract John Gilbert – 'the heavyweight, the lightweight or the middle' (Irene, Baba or Cimmie.) The evening had ended in uproar, with Tom accusing Cimmie of being drunk. The next day:

> Tom was so foul to Cim when she asked him about her birthday plans saying he did not care and was fed up with all of us I lost my temper and called him a cad. So we left him and went with the children to the beach. The weather was too vile for Ben Finney's party by boat to Monte Carlo so a lot of us joined up. Bowls and bowls of punch were made as we flopped about on mattresses in the drawing room

– Dick, Cim and I were sober adjuncts to a very stewed party. Ben suddenly brought in 'Miss America' who had won the world's beauty competition – utterly out of it and left crying in about an hour. It was discussed and discussed what we should do for hours till it resorted to more punch and sandwiches – and a marvellous dish of Ben's, chili and rice and meat. Ina was thoroughly drunk and gay and sweet Fruity was well over the odds with Baba very annoyed. He disappeared and made up like John Gilbert and came in with Gilbert and Cim and proceeded to circle all the ladies as the great lover and was very funny. The fun was entirely ruined at 10 pm by Maurice and Miss Stephenson both dead drunk being pressed together asleep and she gently fondling his hair and we all left the room in disgust and found bed the only solution. Tom emerged when we got back in haughty solitude having been away alone in a huff.

Went to the beach with the children. Cim came very late and I felt from her face and eyes Tom had been tiresome again. Poor Fruity was carried off having nearly cut his foot in 2 with glass from a bottle on the Cannes beach. Fearful arguments with Ben and everyone as to whether we should have his boat party. Ben Finney's dog did the most lovely dives for us and simply loved it.

August 23rd. Cim's birthday.
Gave Cim a black bag for the House of Commons. She got some lovely 'presies' and Tom came up to scratch with a lovely modern Metropolis Cocktail Set and Lamp. Had a family bathe with the children on the Roc, and a family lunch with the children and Baba. Joined up with Babe Barnato's big party at the next table ... tore across the ocean in Barnato's speed boat ... played vile tennis with Barnato and 2 tiresome men with 4 dirty tennis balls getting lost the whole time. Had a swim and gave Cim another bag, an exquisite one, before dinner. She gave the most perfect party down on the rocks: lovely lit tables all round, huge cinema lights making wonderful effects on everything, a marvellous band that did turns walking about and sitting out on the diving boards. Dudley Malone made a speech to Cim after a bad effort by Finney. Diving races went on with Babe Barnato, Rupert Belville and John Gilbert. I had Gilbert and Finney for dinner and had an absorbing talk with Gilbert on his view of women – *his* women – and he told me he was going off alone as things were screw-eyed with him and Ina. The whole trouble is he needs an alsatian dog like Ben's for a wife – absolute obedience. Went to the Beouf about 1.30. Tom deliberately took Ina to see Fruity and

left her there. Gilbert, losing her, went mad, tore back to the hotel
thinking she was left behind, came back to find her dancing and
savagely dragged her into the street where Cim and Dudley witnessed
a fearful scene. A bit later Bobby found him walking into the sea and
drove him round Cannes to steady him. Then he came back and Baba
and Cim had hour after hour battling and appeasing Ina and him. It
was the most fantastic evening I have ever witnessed. Dudley finally
took Ina to his villa for the night and exhausted with waiting on other
people's rows Knottman drove me home at 5 am. No one knew what
happened to Gilbert. I saw him vanish down the road with Baba
before I left. Rupert Belville had got very drunk at dinner and said
filthy things about the rich socialists – about Esther and John and Cim
and Tom – which Esther overheard, and she got up and left the table.

The next day Tom left by train for London – to get back to work on
his plans for the unemployed. John Gilbert, it was discovered, had also
left at dawn by taxi for Paris. He had told the driver – 'Don't have an
accident: my face is my fortune.' Irene stayed on for a few more days
with Cimmie and the children: she had a talk with Nanny about how
they thought Cimmie was becoming 'awfully callous'. Cimmie wrote
a letter to Tom – 'It has been incredibly quiet since you left ... John
G returned late that night after getting to Lyons in his taxi before
coming to ... Dick is getting well away with his countess, and has
already had a flog.'

Cimmie returned to London. Tom was working in his semi-dungeon
in the Treasury. They both made efforts that autumn to sort out their
own problems – or at least to view them rationally. Tom was becoming
more impatient and scathing with Cimmie publicly. Cimmie wrote for
advice to Dick Wyndham, who had stayed on in the South of France
to paint. He replied:

Darling Cimmie, Your letter did rather upset me, and I wish I could
give you some advice that would make your life happier. There seems
no solution because you have had the misfortune to have been born
a naturally happy person. This sounds like a paradox, but it isn't.
Nearly all intelligent people are born naturally miserable. I am sure
that Tom is just as unhappy and probably more so than you. And if
you take all our friends – for instance Sachie, Hutchy, William – if
you could see their real thoughts, how dismally sad you would find
them! their quite unexpected hopes, regrets, and longings. And even
I, who am supposed to lead such an ideal life with my painting,

freedom and money, live, in reality, a life of acute misery, worry and loneliness relieved occasionally by moments of great exaltation; but these happen far too seldom to make life worth while. I suppose only the human sheep are able to lead a continuously happy life; they have their 'dope' – religion, the Empire, their hire-purchase furniture; other sheep to look down upon; their aspidistra; and finally a respectable funeral and a very white marble or speckled grey granite tombstone. They have no moments of exaltation: they don't want them. But your natural happiness refuses to admit such an unpleasant state of affairs. You feel that having been born in a world filled with so many beautiful things one should be allowed to enjoy it without hindrance and help others to enjoy it. How right you are! But just because you are filled with such capabilities of enjoyment you are constantly being disillusioned and hurt. You are still like a child who sees an infinite source of fun in every object around him only to find that they are all protected by those words – 'you mustn't touch'.

On reading through this rigmarole I find it hasn't got us very far. The only logical solution seems to be that you must damp your natural happiness in order to be immune from the misery of a miserable world; and that is a remedy I would hate to advise. It comes under the heading of innoculation of which I disapprove.

The only thing I can suggest is to make a list of the things that don't matter so much – such as the mastif,* and even an occasional flit to Paris: they are annoying, but no more so than an occasional attack of flu. Then make a list of all the things you do really mind about like hell. Make up your mind never to say a word about the less important things for fear that in time you might find yourself perpetually nagging. Not only don't mention them, don't think about them, *don't mind them.* About the things that matter make a real *definite stand* – raise hell, throw things, do and say anything you like. But you must make your two lists and stick to them.

You will probably say that it is just the mounting up of the relatively small things that is so unbearable – I know – but if you start by disregarding them they won't mount up, they will never have been born.

I shall be leaving here in a few days now, all my four paintings having come to a bad end; so we soon will be able to have a 'crack'.** I shall devote some of the time to extracting the name of the 'old friend' who has fallen in love with you ...

* *Tom had recently bought a large dog.*
** *talk.*

Rules of the Game

This letter was posted on October 20th 1929. On October 21st Tom posted his own long letter to Cimmie. He had come to Denham to rest. Cimmie was in her constituency.

Savehay Farm
Denham
Bucks

Meanderings of a sick mutt.

My darling fellow,

Lying in bed with this wretched cold I have thought so much of our relationship and my mind moves to these conclusions – write and tell me if you agree.

(1)   The thing that matters most is our love and alliance in all things. That should be our absolutely fixed and unchanging relation – a basis of life in which we both have complete confidence – sure that never in any crisis or misfortune will it fail us.

(2)   The next most important thing is the individual happiness and development of each of us – without that, many of the gifts and powers we have to give to the world must be damaged and reduced: without happiness and a sense of all-pervading freedom and power we cannot be complete people. Yet none but complete people can succeed in the stupendous task that we have set ourselves

Our problem is how to reconcile and to blend into a perfect life these 2 premises of our existence: (1) our marriage and alliance in all things (2) our individual happiness and freedom which are essentials of the full personality.

To achieve this we must put away all small things. We really deny ourselves (2) because our confidence in (1) is not enough.

Each of us is afraid that the small incidents of (2) may destroy (1): each of us consequently is inclined to snatch small bits of (2) for himself or herself while striving to thwart rather than to assist the other. That situation is a commonplace in the marriage of all remarkable people – it is small, contemptible and atavistic – in our case it should be entirely lacking because (1) is so much stronger than in almost any other example of which one can think. We have not only love, a great companionship, children, home, etc – we have also a tremendous alliance in public life which has bound us together against the whole squalor of things as they are in face of a storm of hatred and mean lying abuse which no other couple has ever had to face. That is a great alliance which should be far above every factor in the sphere of (2). Yet I believe it is really our unexpressed fear that (2) will affect (1) that leads to trouble in sphere of (2). From my side such apprehension might perhaps reasonably be stronger as you are so much younger and less sophisticated in sphere (2) than me – I know I should not be affected by it – you might be – yet even here I might be more reasonable to you in sphere (2) if I did not feel that in past and even present you had there severely restricted me. Such a feeling of course must arise on both sides and has created a vicious circle.

The way out I feel is this – we should not only acquiesce in (2) for each of us – we should be as much partners there as we are in (1). We should have such confidence in the permanence and inviolability of (1) (our marriage and alliance in all great things) that we should not only be unafraid of (2) (personal freedom and happiness) affecting (1), but we should actively promote complete confidence in each of us developing in sphere (2) with the assistance of the other – we should have no feeling of fear and regret of any kind if one of us enjoyed things apart from the other – we should realise that the complete development of each individual contributed to the success and greatness of the whole alliance.

We must of course do all things in the light of our position and mission in the world – we must never disarm before the enemy – only before each other. That is what I mean by 'Tenue'.

We are in a sense conspirators together against things as they are and conspirators cannot take the enemy into their confidence. To lead what we believe to be a moral life in our immoral society some concealment and even subterfuge is necessary if we are to retain our power to change that society for the great end we seek. Together we can retain our greatest power in public life to change the miseries of present society to live a full and human life.

We already have a great comfort in (1). Let us also have a great comfort in (2).

Let us have such confidence in the permanence and the superiority of our marriage and love over everything else in life that we can be partners in promoting the freedom and happiness of each of us as well. I believe it is possible – it means an end of all small things – of all small jealousies and fears – it means the triumph of the modern mind. I believe we are capable of it. Let us try to have a great compact – a great alliance in all things. (This reads like a very muddled and badly delivered political speech but it means he loves her very much and wants both of them to be happy fellows).

It was perhaps a saving grace of Tom's that he could write a bracket such

as at the end of this letter – at moments he could laugh at himself even
when he was being carried away by one of his more extreme flights of
self-justifying rationalisation and rhetoric. But, between the rhetoric
and the laughter there was not much sign of guilt. The same evening
that he posted this letter he played one of his more extravagant practical
jokes upon his sister-in-law Irene. She was giving a large after-dinner
party in her house at which her guests included Lord Beaverbrook, Ivor
Novello, Beatrice Lillie and Arthur Rubinstein. Then (Irene recorded)
– 'Some brute (a joke we presumed) rang me up as from Scotland Yard
and tried to infer some of my party were thieves and were wanted'. The
voice instructed her to keep all her guests with their hands up facing the
wall until further notice. Irene paid no attention. When later she discovered the joker was Tom, she refused to speak to him or Cimmie for
a week.

Cimmie received Tom's long letter when she was in Stoke: she
travelled down to London and handed her reply to Tom.

Darling Darling Darling Darling. I am so glad you wrote that letter
– I agree with every word of it and *will* try – all the things you said
are true. Now taking your two premises – it always has been because
I have never been quite sure of (1) that I have been tricky about (2).
You started off with (2)s so very soon after marriage before I had
ever got confidence either in myself or you while you were my *whole*
horizon literally in every way. I have never been persuaded you really
really appreciated me, you were always finding fault, and liking
people so utterly different to me, it made me apprehensive and always
on the defensive.

I must say I do not agree that you should be more apprehensive
of me than I of you. I have only been driven to my small successes
in sheer self-defence. In fact till very recently I have had none – and
that alongside of your varied assortment has been very bad for me.
I always felt you had so much more success (not generally speaking,
I know I am all right as a general success, but I mean a 'particular'
success) and that gave me an inferiority complex. You don't know
the agonies I have gone through time after time when you have got
off with lovely ladies and I have been left; it has very often nearly
driven me dippy. I am sure you will never realise how even a success
with nonentities like Mario Pansa, Ridal or Rochefoucauld restores
my confidence, and you take it away again by sneering at the
'quality' of my fellows. You see while we are about it I had better
be quite frank: I have always felt that you won on the swings and

roundabouts; that if it came to complete freedom inside category (2) you would profit by it much more than me; you would have more successes greater fun – have your cake (i.e. Mum) and eat it!! While I, well, I would have no cake at all – no fun on swings or roundabouts. I think maybe I am wrong but you must remember nothing really matters one toss to me except you and the children. I am terribly frightened on my own, and a good deal bewildered.

My success with Gilbert and the Frenchies last week was balm and oil to my 'tortured spirit' but believe me does not go very far. I am sure my whole trouble is I am small enough to feel that under such arrangement you would get much more than me and that stops me risking it. You have it in your power to hurt me so dreadfully – you have hurt me so dreadfully –

If only my confidence in (1) could be assured but I so often feel we only stick together because of our public position and not because we really do love and value each other. Now if we could have a perfect (1) all else follows. I will try. But do you see my point: if only I had more confidence, less of an inferiority complex; and you the one person in the world who could help most always finding fault, always criticising, always belittling me, making it worse; any efforts I do make on my own mocked and derided.

I retaliate in the obvious silly way – it *is* a vicious circle as you say. How are we to get out of it: if you were kinder to me, more considerate, I know I would 'respond to treatment': but in order for me to be nicer to you you *must* be nicer to me: I am not capable of the martyr-like effort, it may be very small and petty but I am not going to make an effort alone.

Oh dear even writing those few lines I feel resentment rising in me, and that I must not allow. But I think even you will allow making a success of living with you is hellish difficult if one also strives to keep one's own individuality and end up. I do hope this won't appear as a very one-sided sort of letter as yours was *so* fair – forgive me if it is – I think this a very good moment to really have a grand try at (1) and (2) and let us become experts at avoiding all minor exasperations; they cause endless bother and with skill can be avoided.

Remember this, I do adore you, unless in a mood (generally engendered by you) when I could kill you. I would die for you. You and the children are always the only things that really matter. I am not a bad sort of person neither are you. We both want to be happy – well here's to it. And bless you my love. Be my sweet Tommy I fell in love with. Help Mum to be the grandest sort of person she can be. Kisses and devotion. Timmy

This is not nearly a nice enough letter. I did *love* yours and do thank you for it and *am* glad you wrote it and do love you.

Is your cold better?

I hope so.

In this letter Cimmie seems to have faced truly something of the predicament she was in with Tom: Tom had more energy, a more daemonic quality than she: he had the power to use words apparently rationally to justify his drives and ambitions: he could claim his own freedom and feel safe in it, because he could make impossible her own. Cimmie was a good woman; she loved Tom; she felt she could not challenge the whole process of their lives without losing him; but then, she did not seem to want to challenge this for herself. When he hurt her, she cried out; she tried to answer him back in kind; she did not turn away from him. Tom did not see that part of his energy and his success might depend on his having someone who adored him and whom he could manipulate: whom he could, when his own supremacy was threatened, mock and deride; and then win back with his endearments. Tom tried to sort out his problems with Cimmie in terms of reason: he thought – as he did about politics – that human problems could and should be solved by the presentation of a case so rational that it was unanswerable. It is not clear how often he had glimpses into his manipulations: even his laughter was something of a protection: soon with Cimmie, as in politics, the grandiose words would take over again – the 'mission to the world': the 'stupendous task'. But how did he and Cimmie imagine that with their quarrelling, their baby-talk, they were achieving 'the triumph of the modern mind'? This mind was to be controlled by will: but how was there to be any reality of will if there were no observations of the nature of the self that was wielding it?

Cimmie's innocence (as Dick Wyndham had said) was to believe not in the efficacy of manipulation, as Tom did, but just that life could be made beautiful by efforts at honesty and truth. She believed this with regard to Tom: she believed it with regard to her politics. She had almost as little sense as Tom had of the irony of the contrasts between private and public life.

Soon after she got back from the summer holiday she made her maiden speech in the House of Commons. It was on the occasion of the second reading of the Widows', Orphans', and Old Age Contributory Pensions Bill, which aimed at providing pensions for the first time for half a million widows. Cimmie said she welcomed the bill because it 'definitely takes us along the road towards the abolition of poverty and destitution': it was 'an approach towards the full acceptance of the fundamental truth that economic insecurity is socially created and should be provided for by the social services until it can be abolished by socialism'. To the opposition's suggestion that a working man or working woman might possibly be a better citizen if they were not too much looked after by the state she replied:

> I have noticed a word that has been greatly in use since this measure was brought in and that is the word 'demoralisation' – demoralisation of getting something for nothing. That is ground on which I am very much at home. All my life I have got something for nothing. Why? Have I earned it? Have I deserved it? Not a bit. I have just got it through luck. Of course some people might say I showed great intelligence in the choice of my parents, but I put it all down to luck. And not only I, but if I may be allowed to say so, a great many people on the opposite side of the House are in that same position – they also have always got something for nothing. Now the question is: are we demoralised? I could not answer that question for anyone but myself – but, looking at members opposite, may I be allowed to say they don't look too demoralised physically, though their mental and physical condition is beyond me to determine. I stoutly deny however that I am demoralised –

Cimmie got many congratulations for her speech – one from the Prime Minister ('excellent matter and excellent style'); one from Bob Boothby ('It was so good, my dear, that if I said all I want to you you wouldn't believe it'); one from an anonymous 'Mother of Ten' – 'You are splendid, you are magnificent ... those who as you say have all their lives had something for nothing cannot imagine what it is like to be all one's life giving all and getting nothing – their health and strength, their love and sacrifice, their leisure their pleasure, yes even life itself – that is the fate of the working class mother'.

Neither Cimmie nor Tom by instinct or by upbringing were equipped to do what in fact most people do whatever their idealism or protestations – which is to try their best in whatever areas are available to them, and about the rest not too much to worry. This was just what Tom and Cimmie objected to about people like J. H. Thomas and Ramsay MacDonald – who talked of stupendous tasks and then did nothing. Tom and Cimmie were too proud: they had had too many expectations pinned on to them: they could not be satisfied, as so many Labour people seemed to be satisfied, by having simply 'arrived'. They had the curse – whether of a good or a bad angel – to want to alter the world.

Humdrum politicians have almost necessarily to feel that idealism is dangerous: they feel it upsetting their day-to-day plans. Their jobs in administration, it seems, are properly to do with preventing anything disastrous being done by idealists. Tom, an idealist, was correct in thinking that such people were out to thwart him. It was perhaps their tragedy, as well as his, that at this time some idealism was probably necessary if there was not to be a drift towards chaos or war. It was the curse of the humdrum politicians that they had no use for the talents of someone like Tom: it was the curse of Tom to treat what he saw as their lethargy only with contempt. Few people at the time seemed capable of seeing a pattern into which they themselves and others of a different temperament might fit if all this was observed as it were from a higher viewpoint. Tom, certainly, did not see how his energy might be effective if he submitted it to the restraints of its being for a while thwarted. Everyone was accustomed to think in terms of antagonism – in one sort of view, or characteristic, not embracing but cancelling out another.

In war Tom had had little experience of the terrible helplessness of people even with good intentions when in authority: he for the most part had been war's victim. But it is people who have had actual experience of responsibility for life and death who have often learned that there is little good that can be done except in ways of steadfastness, and hope, and painstaking bit-by-bit efforts. And it is those who rage against the fact that there are victims, who want to alter the world; and so are apt to make victims of the people round them.

CHAPTER 15

Resignation

On May 9th 1930 the Cabinet sub-committee headed by Snowden, the Chancellor of the Exchequer, recommended that the Mosley Memorandum be rejected. Their reasons were – the Prime Minister could not take on the added burden of direct responsibility for employment; the proposed Executive Committee would undermine the tradition of the individual responsibilities of ministers; the road-building scheme ignored the rights of individuals and local authorities; the memorandum as a whole paid no attention to the one programme for recovery that in the long run would work – the encouragement of exports. Whatever might be useful in the scheme would have to be done at the expense of other things that might be useful: so it was best to play safe, and carry on just hoping that world trade would get better. What the Labour Cabinet objected to in fact was that the Memorandum was too socialistic: the arguments they put up against it were those of conservatism. But these were the arguments which, as Tom and other socialists had pointed out before the election, were resulting in society's breakdown. It seemed that socialists did not want to govern: they wanted to continue in the role to which they had become accustomed – that of being in opposition to any exercise of power.

The Cabinet set up another committee to consider the report of the Snowden committee – and to confer with Tom, Lansbury and Johnston. Discussions went on for ten days. The point at issue now was mainly about how to initiate some sort of road-building scheme: did you just raise money and get on with the job (Tom): or did you do nothing about money till you had worked out detailed plans with local authorities, (J. H. Thomas and Herbert Morrison, the Minister of Transport) – and then wait for the Treasury almost certainly to say that there was no money anyway. Tom was accused of wanting to

'Russianise' the government: Herbert Morrison said that he spoke 'like a landlord addressing his peasantry'. The issue was becoming simply between someone who wanted to give priority to getting something done over the probable cost, and the others who did not.

On May 19th Tom and Cimmie dined with Sidney and Beatrice Webb. Tom said that he intended to resign his ministerial post: what he found impossible was not so much the disagreement, but the fact that under Ramsay MacDonald there was no desire for serious practical talk at all. Meetings between ministers, he said, were more comic than anything in Bernard Shaw's *The Apple Cart*. Beatrice Webb noted that the Mosleys seemed 'sincere and assiduous in their public aims'.

Tom felt, correctly, that during the year he had been in office his energies had been used as a safety valve but there had never been a serious intention to get anything he recommended done. He had been quite cynically put in a position where his energy could be expended and his ideas ignored. He either had to resign, or to resign himself to the sort of game that during all his years in Parliament he had abominated. ·On May 18th Bob Boothby, a conservative, had written to him:

My dear Tom,
From France I have been contemplating the state of politics with a jaundiced but more or less unbiased mind: and I beg of you not to resign. I cannot see that you would achieve anything: and you might well do yourself irreparable damage. It is a God's mercy that the existence of your memorandum is known to the public.

That was essential; but for the moment it is surely enough. I care about your political future far more than about any other single factor in public affairs, because I know that you are the ONLY one of my generation – of the post-war school of thought – who is capable of translating into action any of the ideas in which I genuinely believe. Consequently I can conceive of no greater tragedy than that you should take a step which might wreck your chances, or at any rate postpone the opportunity of carrying through constructive work.

If you stay where you are that opportunity is bound to come soon. Go, and where are you?

The example of Randolph Churchill is significant and appalling. You deliver yourself into the hands of every enemy, and they are not a few. Your own front bench will heave a sigh of relief, consign you to the Mountain, and take no more risks.

They will point to their own life-long services in the Labour cause, and contrast them with yours. They will regret that they are apparently unable to proceed at a pace sufficient to satisfy the desires and ambitions of a wealthy young 'aristocrat' in a hurry.

Picture the parliamentary scene. You will make your case against the government – a formidable one – but nine-tenths of the audience will be hostile. Snowden will reply with all the venom at his command (I am sure his recent outburst against me was an oblique thrust at you.) He will quote from your speeches at Harrow ten years ago. All the pent-up fury which you have deliberately, and I think quite rightly, roused in so many breasts will simultaneously be released.

The Tories will cheer vociferously and savagely.

Your own orthodox back-benchers will be against you because they will feel that you have delivered a fierce blow at the Government which may well involve their defeat at the next election ...

The cumulative effect of so many hostile forces would overwhelm Napoleon himself.

I don't see how you could hope to stand up against them.

You can't return to us.

And however impelled you may feel to work once more with the 'gentry', you would be wretched if you did. I know to my cost the limitations of the existing young conservatives. They are charming and sympathetic and intelligent at dinner.

But there is not one of them who has either the character or the courage to do anything big ...

What is the alternative?

Surely to remain within the official fold and by making yourself increasingly oppressive and uncomfortable to what Ellen Wilkinson so aptly describes as 'The Bright Old Things' consolidate and strengthen your power. The forces economic and political now at work must assist you.

With every increase in the unemployment figures the position which *you are known* to have taken up becomes more impregnable and easier to justify ... Why should you not work with, and ultimately direct, a moderate Government of the Left?

You occupy a key position at the moment. For God's sake don't chuck it away. Incidentally, if you have a moment to spare, you might modify the divorce laws.

My own difficulties do not diminish with the passage of time and the march of events ...

Good luck to you.

Don't think of answering this.

Yrs ever
Bob

But this letter, with its admirable advice, was about how to play the political game: it was about techniques of how to win by appearing for a time to be steadfast in losing. Tom did not want this: the people with whom he had been playing the game had been making such a nonsense of it for so long that he wanted to give it up altogether. His revulsion was personal rather than political. But then, as Bob Boothby had asked, did he really think he could take on the whole accepted political machinery single-handed? If he would not play according to the rules, did he think he could alter the whole tradition of games playing?

On the afternoon of May 19th Tom had been to see Ramsay Mac-Donald and had told him he thought he should resign: MacDonald had asked him to reconsider. He found Tom (he wrote in his diary) 'on the verge of being offensively vain in himself'. Johnston pleaded with members of the Cabinet that there was still time to use Tom's talents which had been 'trampled on and ignored'. But people wanted to ignore Tom's talents.

On May 20th he handed his letter of resignation to MacDonald. In it he reiterated that his Memorandum 'was not advanced in any dogmatic spirit' but that he found it 'inconsistent with honour' to remain a member of a government that would not even seriously discuss its election pledges. The letter was written in a tone, MacDonald said, of 'graceless pompousness'. MacDonald added (these comments are in his diary) 'Test of a man's personality is his behaviour in disagreement: in every test he failed.' Most of the newspapers the next day however praised Tom for his courage. The *Daily Herald* added a warning – 'What Mosley needs is a break in his success: he has been a wonder child for too long.'

On May 22nd there was a meeting of the Parliamentary Labour Party to which Tom, now out of office, could present his proposals over the heads of the Cabinet. G. R. Strauss, a young MP personally unsympathetic to Tom, recorded that Tom's speech to the Parliamentary Party was a 'magnificent piece of rhetoric' and that most MPs were obviously of the opinion that the Memorandum 'should be carefully considered'. J. R. Thomas in a 'lachrymose and emotional vein', announced that it was 'the most humiliating day of his life': but then Arthur Henderson, an experienced tactician in the party game, played one of the traditional moves: he appealed to Tom 'in very moving language to take the noble line' of withdrawing his censure motion against the government to allow further talks to take place – for the sake of party unity. John Strachey whispered to Tom that he should refuse

– 'What people want is action'. Tom did refuse. In the words of G. R. Strauss – 'instantly all the support and sympathy he had received deserted him'. A junior minister remarked 'Pity he didn't withdraw, he would have done himself a lot of good': whereupon Cimmie, over-hearing this, said 'He didn't care for his own good, but only for his party!' Tom lost the vote by 29 to 210. His failure to withdraw was seen as a grave tactical blunder. But it made sense in the light of his deter-mination not to go on playing the parliamentary game: and it added to his already somewhat legendary reputation for courage.

And there were, in fact, outside his own party, people who saw precisely that the real battle was not between this or that party but about whether one should, or should not, continue to play political games. On May 27th Harold Macmillan, a young conservative temporarily out of Parliament, had a letter printed in *The Times* in which he said:

> Faced with a startling and even spectacular calamity [the doubling of unemployment figures since Labour took office] Sir Oswald seems to have conceived a novel, and no doubt according to the accepted political standards of what are called 'responsible statesmen', incredibly naive idea. He drew up, and actually went so far as to present to his chief, a memorandum which suggested an attempt should be made to carry out at least some, if not all, of the pledges and promises by the exploitation of which the Socialist Party obtained power ...
>
> Is it to be the accepted rule in our politics that a political programme is to be discarded as soon as it has served its electoral purpose? Are we to accept the cynical view that a statesman is to be applauded in inverse ratio to the extent to which he carries out in office what he has promised in opposition? Must a programme always sink to the level of a fraud-ulent prospectus? Is a course of action, which in business affairs would end in the Old Bailey, in affairs of state to lead to Downing St and Westminster Abbey? ...
>
> I suspect that this is the real way that the game ought to be played. Only, if the rules are to be permanently enforced, perhaps a good many of us will feel it hardly worth while bothering to play at all. Sir Oswald Mosley thinks that the rules should be altered. I hope some of my friends will have the courage to support and applaud his protest.

The next day R. A. Butler, conservative MP in his first parliament, had (with three other signatories) a letter in *The Times* which said:

> We have read with interest and some surprise Mr Harold Macmillan's

letter published in your issue of today. When a player starts complaining that it is 'hardly worth while bothering to play' the game
at all, it is surely the player, and not the game, which is at fault. It
is usually advisable for the player to seek a new field for his recreation
and a pastime more suitable to his talents.

On 28th May Tom made his speech in Parliament to justify his resignation: this was his statement of belief that politics should be more than
a 'recreation' or a 'pastime'. He reiterated the points of the Mosley
Memorandum – an effective machinery of government had to be set
up to deal with the unemployment crisis; it was to the home market that
people had to turn for the solution to trading problems; after a short-
term programme of road building power had to be given to an
Executive Committee to control imports, prices, wages, and finance for
industry. He spoke without looking at his notes; there was a dazzling
display of figures; in a passionate peroration he begged that the country
should not be allowed to 'sink to the level of Spain' and exhorted
Parliament to give a lead. The message of the speech was epitomised in
a sentence half way through – 'the first duty of the government is, after
all, to govern'.

When Tom sat down he was cheered. It had been a magnificent
performance. The papers the next day were unanimous – 'A tremendous
personal triumph': 'one of the most notable parliamentary achievements
of modern times': 'the triumph of an artist who has made his genius
perfect by long hours of practice and devotion to his art'. But then, with
all these curtain-calls as it were – might it not be possible that after all
Tom had made a successful move in terms of the game?

He was taking his stand on being the 'honest man' of politics; in the
long run such an 'honest man' might have the best chance of winning
the highest honours. Tom of course felt this: other people after his
resignation began to feel it: Beatrice Webb wrote – 'Has MacDonald
found his superseder in Oswald Mosley? MacDonald owes his pre-
eminence largely to the fact that he is the only artist, the only aristocrat
by temperament and talent in a party of plebeians and plain men . . . But
Mosley has all this with the élan of youth, wealth and social position
added to them.' She added however in her usual warning style –
'Whether Mosley has Mac's toughness of texture – whether he will not
break down in health or in character – I have doubts.'

But one of the manoeuvres by which people who stick to the rules
of the game instinctively try to outwit those who do not, is by giving
them extravagant applause just when there is no particular danger to the

status quo: like this the rebels get carried away and overreach themselves. And would-be heroes anyway have primitive instincts ready to be tapped by applause. After his resignation speech Tom's mother had written to him:

> My darling Tom,
> So many judges and abler folk must have congratulated you on your masterly performance of last night my congratulations are almost absurd. But oh! my dear lad, I can never tell you what it meant to your old mother. I was so full of pride and joy in my man-child it almost choked me. It was wonderful. People of all shades and opinions were thrilled and staggered by 'the finest speech heard in the House for 20 years' ...

Tom had said 'The first duty of a government is to govern': but then, what was he doing resigning from government and putting on magnificent performances? Was he really now going to trust just his own rationality and rhetoric – and other people's rationality in being carried away by his rhetoric – in order to govern? Might this not be the mark of someone with such overweening confidence in himself that it would seem to have sprung from fantasies?

But if he was ever to have a chance of exercising practical power, Tom knew he had to form new loyalties. This was not going to be easy from the ranks of the Parliamentary Labour Party. Jennie Lee, a young Labour MP and one not unsympathetic to Tom at this time, wrote of her own reactions to her colleagues:

> What I was totally unprepared for was the behaviour of the solid rows of decent, well-intentioned unpretentious Labour back benchers. In the long run it was they who did the most deadly damage. Again and again an effort was made to rouse them from their inertia. On every occasion they reacted like a load of damp cement. They would see nothing, do nothing, hear nothing, that had not first been given the seal of MacDonald's approval.

When Tom resigned, the only back benchers who he was certain would be loyal to him were Cimmie and John Strachey. He soon got four other young labour MPs to commit themselves to some sort of an alliance – W. J. Brown, Oliver Baldwin, Robert Forgan and Aneurin Bevan. He also got young MPs from the other parties interested in talking about alliance – from the Conservatives Harold Macmillan, Bob Boothby,

Oliver Stanley, Walter Elliott, Henry Mond; from the Liberals Archibald Sinclair and Leslie Hore-Belisha. During the summer the unemployment figures rose to over two million: the battle more than ever seemed to Tom to be not between this party and that, but between anyone who seemed interested in getting something done and those who did not. Tom himself saw it in many respects still as a battle of the young against the old. In June he wrote an article in the *Sunday Express* in which he claimed that the young man of today was:

> a hard, realistic type, hammered into existence on the anvil of great ordeal: in mind and spirit he is much further away from the pre-war man than he is from an ancient Roman or from any other product of ages which were dynamic like his own. For this age is dynamic and the pre-war age was static. The men of the pre-war age are much 'nicer' people than we are, just as their age was much more pleasant than the present time. The practical question is whether their ideas for the solution of the problems of our age are better than the ideas of those whom that age has produced.

This was the language of some sort of heroism – of preparation for future battle; of appeal to the glories of the past. It was this that attracted would-be knights to Tom's banner. 'In those days Mosley's drawing room was an exciting place' Hugh Massingham, a journalist, wrote: 'the gay Bob Boothby flitted in and out: there was John Strachey who could be relied on to give the talk a Marxist twist: C. E. M. Joad, a philosopher of sorts, could be discovered cowering in a corner occasionally letting out a squeak of protest whenever the necessity of violence was mentioned which it usually was'. Harold Nicolson, himself a member of the group, wrote – 'They talk about the decay of democracy and of parliamentarianism. They discuss whether it would be well to have a fascist coup. They are most disrespectful of their various party leaders.'

Two politicians from the older generation were naturally attracted to such ebullience – Lloyd George and Winston Churchill. They occasionally joined in discussions. There were also the press lords Beaverbrook and Rothermere in the background; who by their vocation were interested in matters sensational or dynamic. Beaverbrook wrote to Tom, 'I am ready at any moment to make overtures in your direction in public if you wish me to do so'. Churchill made a speech at Oxford in which he echoed Tom's proposal that an Executive Committee should be set up 'free altogether from party exigencies and composed of persons possessing special qualifications in economic matters'. One reason why Churchill, Beaverbrook and Rothermere were interested in Tom was the fact that in his economic thinking he was coming to the conclusion that the closed economic area over which the government should have tight control should be expanded from the home market to include the Empire and Commonwealth. With all this talk and intrigue going on it could not have worried Tom much that the 'damp cement' of Labour was not following him. Beatrice Webb wrote 'He will be a great success at public meetings; but will he get round the Arthur Hendersons, the Herbert Morrisons, the Alexanders, the Citrines and the Bevins ... the natural leaders of the proletariat?' Tom and even Cimmie were even demonstrably not worrying: they went out a lot during that summer to parties: Tom seems to have felt liberated by the fact that he had staked everything like a gambler on forming his own group.

Bob Boothby wrote to him another of his long, marvellous letters setting out his opinions on gambling and the sort of odds a gambler has to face because there are rules even for adventurers.

My dear Tom,
If ever I signed on the dotted line I would play to the end – and beyond.

I think you know that.

But *in the meantime* I don't think the game is practical politics, and for the following reasons.

(1)   Our chaps won't play, and it's no use your deluding yourself that they will. You saw Oliver [Stanley]'s reactions last night.

Of the whole lot Walter and I would be most useful, because we have a territorial base and between us we could shake up Scotland. But Walter has spent the last twelve months consolidating his position in the Conservative party: he has won for himself a good deal of rank-and-file support: he won't give it up unless he's sure he's going to win. And he doesn't think this will win.

As for Oliver, his influence could, and almost certainly would, be countered by Edward Stanley. And so far as the Conservatives are concerned, Harold would be a definite liability. I know you think I'm prejudiced against him. I'm not. But even on the assumption he decided to play (a large one) how many votes can he sway.

Not one.

Who is left?

George Lloyd, generally regarded as the 'Super Diehard' and rightly or wrongly regarded in many quarters as a shit. And this brings me to the second point about our chaps, which is that they simply aren't good enough for the job (I include myself with becoming modesty).

(2)   Now what about your side? I agree you can sway more votes than any other contemporary politician.

But I don't believe, at present, that you can bring over any substantial section of organised Trades Unionism. And as for the Parliamentary Party, do you really think you can send Aneurin Bevan to the Admiralty to lay down more cruisers, and John Strachey to spank the blacks? I confess I doubt it. Who else is there? The mugwumps who comprise 95% of your party will be solidly arrayed against you. The intelligentsia of the Dalton–Baker school will be actively and venomously hostile.

(3)   We come now to the main source of strength – Beaverbrook, with the dubious support of Rothermere.

Beaverbrook's qualities are sufficiently obvious. I don't know him as well as you do. But I have long since come to the conclusion that he would be very nearly impossible to work with. And, as Oliver pointed out, he is in the impregnable position (which we are not and never can be) of being able to double cross and let down the side at a moment's notice without loss of power or even prestige.

If he were to do that we should be marooned, and ultimately sunk politically.

One other point.

What is going to be the reaction of the great British public to a Beaverbrook-Mosley-Rothermere-Lloyd-Macmillan-Stanley-Boothby combination?

I don't know. But they might conceivably say 'By God, now all the shits have climbed into the same basket, so we know where we are.' Would they be so far out? ...

(5)   Lastly, don't underestimate the power of the political machines. I believe that in the long run it far exceeds that of the press ...

On this assumption, the only game worth playing is to try and collar one or other of the machines, and not ruin yourself by beating against them with a tool which will almost certainly break in your hand.

To all this I make one qualification and one only.

If there is a really serious economic crisis this winter, there may be a widespread demand for a national government, new men, and new measures.

It must come from the country and be *interpreted* by the press. If it does come, then the situation will be fundamentally changed, and a game of a kind we cannot yet envisage may open out ...

Well my dear Tom, I've been very frank. I always will be with you, and I hope you don't mind. I happen to think you can do more for us than anyone else now alive – a view I've held, and from which I've never deviated, for six years.

Only for God's sake remember that this country is old, obsolete and tradition-ridden; and no one, not even you, can break all the rules at once. And do take care of the company you keep. Real shits are so apt to trip you up when you aren't looking. And flat-catchers who want to be hauled along are only an encumbrance.
No answer.

Yours ever
Bob

CHAPTER 16

Cimmie in Russia

At the beginning of 1930 Cimmie wrote in her usual style to Tom:

> Sweetie fellow, this is just a line to tell him on New Years' Day of
> all the wishes wished thoughts thought and resolutions resolved by
> her on New Year's Eve. Does hope 1930 will be a happy one for them
> both. Does hope he will go on loving her. *Sure* she will love him. Will
> try try to do everything she can to make it a success.
>> Success politically. Success fun and good times.
>> Success them 2 together ...

Cimmie was busy in local and national politics during 1930. She opened
nursery schools and art exhibitions in Stoke; spoke at a Labour Party
May Day rally at Alexandra Palace in North London; spoke in Parliament in favour of the Rural Amenities Bill which gave greater governmental powers to safeguard the environment, and in favour of the Bill
which ratified the provisions of the Court of International Justice at The
Hague. Her speaking voice, a reporter said, was 'like that of Cordelia
– soft, gentle and low: "an excellent thing in a woman".' She wrote an
article in the *Sunday Express* which considered whether or not rich
socialists should spend money on their children's education (her sister
Irene called this 'shattering bilge'): she gave an interview on the radio on
the subject of Social Conventions. In this she was eloquently in favour
of breaking conventions: 'I want to bring out the frightful danger latent
in *all* conventions, of their proving an obstacle to living thought and
self-expression, because that for me is the most precious thing in life –
lose that and you lose everything.' She got quite a few letters in response
to this broadcast – one from a 17-year-old girl who wanted to be a dirt-
track rider and asked Cimmie for the loan of £50 to set her up.

She backed Tom publicly in his struggles with J. H. Thomas: privately, in spite of her resolutions and perhaps because Tom was becoming increasingly under strain, their quarrels – and her own part in them – seemed to get worse. In April Irene was recording in her diary – 'That naughty Cim kept having awful gibes at Tom so unnecessarily as he was quite peaceful.' Then in July – 'Cim and Tom had a couple of sparring matches Tom as usual scoring in getting a raging rise out of Cim.' And later – after a dinner party in Irene's house with Cim and Tom and Sacheverell and Georgia Sitwell – Irene found 'Cim and Tom having a row about some stupid bill and he dashed off in the car in a rage and poor dazed Cim still could not see how it had all arisen'.

Two days before this myself, aged seven, had been taken to a nursing home for an operation for appendicitis. On the night of their row Cimmie stayed on in Irene's house and wrote to Tom:

> 3 Deanery St W.1.
>
> I don't know what you felt like when you got home but I know I have seldom felt worse, it is now 3 o'clock-ish and I am still sitting on my bed not having closed an eye – I cannot make out what it is all about, I am entirely bewildered, I just don't understand – why have you been so horrid to me, not only tonight but ever since I got up from chickenpox. As the sound of my voice and my presence (and you've seen so little of me) seems to drive you demented I resort to poor Irene's method of putting pen to paper ... You leave me *alone* in London for weekend to look after Nicky and go away with another woman for weekend. You never see Nicky from before his op Sat am till Mon evening ...

The woman whom Tom went away with might have been Georgia Sitwell, with whom Tom was carrying on about this time: there is a letter from her to Tom consisting of just one enormous O covering most of the page which seems to have been some symbol of sexuality. (It was Georgia Sitwell who said to Tom's second wife, Diana, later in life – 'Of course we all went to bed with him but afterwards we were rather ashamed'). One of the points of conflict now between Tom and Cimmie concerned a flat that Tom had got at 22 Ebury Street, about a mile from the family home in Smith Square. Ostensibly Tom had rented this flat in order that he should have peace to do his work as a government minister: but the flat consisted of one huge and very elegant room like a stageset for a bachelor's apartment; the bed was in an alcove at the back across which curtains could be drawn and (one of the occupants

remembers) at the press of a switch warm air be wafted in. Cimmie had
felt that the style of this was not aimed at entertaining Ramsay Mac-
Donald or J. H. Thomas.

Cimmie's letter to Tom, written from Irene's house, continued –

> I feel very lonely and unutterably depressed and so puzzled and tired
> it is difficult to think or even see much ... I know you'll make out
> it's all my fault ... I could not think why it went on and then you
> driving off after what you said. Why did you?

Tom was apparently clever at making out things were another person's
fault: also probably at using rows as a means of being able to get away
– and do what he wanted. And then, the next morning, he could think
about making things up again. He wrote to Cimmie:

> Darling Fellow,
> Terribly sorry if I upset you, but you did drive me almost demented
> – and he too was upset all right! It is that aggressive student talking
> about little things which (1) do not matter (2) could be settled in two
> minutes quiet talk – do be your own sweet self – a charming woman
> – and not a lawyer attacking a hostile witness. We are all rather on
> edge after a very tiring session and many worries – do try to make
> the little things of life easy and not more difficult. I do love you so
> and was so looking forward to seeing you again and longing to get
> off to the South of France with you away from all this turmoil – you
> can be the sweetest most feminine one in all the world, or you can
> be a real old nagging harridan which you were last night (but I do
> understand you too are on edge a little after Nick) ... I believe you
> are lunching out but we will dine together and I will ring you up at
> Nina's 7 pm if you are not in the H of C. So much love. Tom

It was true all this was happening at a time when Tom was increasingly
under strain in public life: he knew he might not be able to get back
into conventional party politics: he had chosen his role of gambler. He
probably felt it consistent that he should gamble on getting everything
that he wanted in private life too. He would have the power to ration-
alise to himself that it was not his fault if this sort of thing caused Cimmie
pain: he did his best to leave her free to do as she wanted. He would
probably not consciously have seen that one of the reasons why he had
strength as a gambler was because she, having suffered, was still there
for him to come back to.

People close to Cimmie and Tom were trying to 'get her to see she ought to stand up to him and give him a fright' (Irene): this presumably meant threaten to leave him. But Cimmie could not do this. It remained a mystery however about Tom and Cimmie why she as much as he insisted on their having 'fun' in places like Antibes and Venice – where one of the rules of the social game was simply that husbands should try to get off with other people's wives. But now at the end of the summer of 1930, they did plan, for a while, to go their separate ways. After the usual two or three weeks at Antibes (I myself, after my operation, had followed the main party with Nanny in a bath chair or being carried by porters) Cimmie went off on a trip to Turkey and Russia accompanied by her friend Zita James. Tom went with her as far as Venice, then returned to the South of France.

Cimmie's trip to Russia is of interest because it seems to have been her effort to gain some independence from Tom: for a time she seemed to be succeeding. Zita was one of two sisters (Zita and Theresa Jungman) who were in the social worlds of London and Venice and the South of France: she had recently married: she too was travelling apart from her husband. She kept a diary, which provides glimpses of Cimmie in her efforts to be herself apart from Tom. Cimmie and Zita met in Athens, where –

We went out to see the Acropolis at sunset. Of course it didn't come off again and Cimmie was bitterly mocking – I was rather annoying and kept giving details about blank bits of stone that I'd heard the guide saying days before. I felt rather like a governess but couldn't stop myself. I was annoyed that the sunset was so bad. In the meantime Cimmie had left a message for a Greek young man she knew about, and later as we were lying on our beds in the hotel shouting from one room to another a card came up to say he was waiting below so we hurried and Cimmie went on down. I found her drinking a cocktail with a very good looking Greek and a very American American called Francis Peabody Krane. After a good deal of gay talk and familiar badinage we finally decided to go in Peabody's car to a native restaurant on a hill far away.

They went on the American's yacht, they swam, they had picnics: 'after a huge meal Cimmie and Kartali (the Greek) went and lay down on the moonlit horizon and talked in whispers to each other while Peabody went miles to fetch me a cushion'. They went to see the church at

Daphne; they did not think much of the museum at Athens. They
travelled on by boat to Istanbul, where Cimmie wrote to Tom:

                    Hotel M. Tokatlian. Istanbul.   Sept 5th 1930
Darling Sweetie, you will never guess what I did yesterday. I think
something very exciting, but in order to get you all expectant I won't
tell you yet. We had hardly arrived before a very insignificant young
man called round from the Embassy to say Sir George Clerk [the
ambassador] was away in Ankara but he was to put a car at our
disposal so we arranged to have it for the next day ... We sight-saw,
but really there is nothing much: Mosques awfully ugly and Sophia
definitely disapointing. Afterwards heavenly time in lagoon and then
a row in caique up to Eyouli and a moonlight picnic in the
cemetery and coffee in the cafe where Pierre Loti used to sit. Yesterday morning more sightseeing; lunch at Embassy where we made a
great hit with Sir George who is taking us out all day on his yacht
today – and then we did the exciting thing. They all said at the
Embassy we would never pull it off.
    But we did!
    We went and saw Trotsky!!
    You know he lives on a small island called Prinkipo about hour
and $\frac{1}{2}$ away from here by boat. He is allowed nowhere else in the
world. So I thought – We'll go off to Prinkipo and try! Wrote a
lovely note and set off. Deposited outside iron gate at top of hill,
long straggling walk down between vegetables to a fountain small
pond court and square peeling white house. By this time a sec: had
popped out to ask us our business – he said it was *quite* impossible –
never done. I said well anyway could he not take my letter. No.
Well could he not read it himself – which he did. He then re-
considered and said he would go and see. In a few moments he was
back and said the great man would receive us. So up we went
through an absolutely bare hall absolutely bare staircase another
absolutely bare room except for thousands of newspapers knocked
on a door and there we were. Magnificent head, masses and swirls
of the most beautifully cared-for grey hair, the softest most soigné
rather sallow skin, *huge* eyes behind prince nez, large thick fleshy
mouth, moustache and imperial, immaculate snowy white suit and
beautiful hands – nails polished and shining. He was courteous and
charming and talked for about $\frac{1}{2}$ an hour, absolutely scathing about
English Labs. Very funny. And Clynes and Duchess of York got it
very hot.

Cimmie's description of her visit to Trotsky ends here abruptly. Her long letter then continues, for pages, to talk about her relationship with Tom. Other accounts of the visit to Trotsky are of interest however both on account of the incident itself (Trotsky had been outlawed from Russia the year before and had few contacts with the outside world) and because they confirm the impression that to Cimmie the visit was at least in part some dare-devil act which she could present as a trophy to Tom.

Zita had written in her diary about lunch at the Embassy the previous day:

> We could see the secretaries and wives sniggering as we told rather exaggerated stories of what up to now we had done, they thought us a little mad, so we piled it on and said the most startling things. Cimmie capped the lot by declaring that she was going that afternoon to see Trotsky. At this suggestion the whole table went off into a guffaw, several bets were placed against us achieving our object, and everyone winked slyly round the table and patronised our idiocy . . . We went back to the hotel where Cimmie composed a letter beginning 'Dear Comrade Trotsky' and ending 'Yours fraternally'. She took his book of memoirs under her arm and off we started for the ferry boat.

Trotsky recorded his own account of the visit in his published diary for 1935. He had made a reference to Tom as 'the aristocratic coxcomb who joined the Labour party as a short cut to a career'; and then reminisced:

> In September 1930 . . . Cynthia Mosley, the wife of the adventurer and daughter of the notorious Lord Curzon, visited me at Prinkipo. At that stage her husband was still attacking MacDonald 'from the left'. After some hesitation I agreed to a meeting which, however, proved banal in the extreme. The 'Lady' arrived with a female travelling companion, referred contemptuously to MacDonald, and spoke of her sympathies towards Soviet Russia. But the enclosed letter from her is an adequate specimen of her attitude at that time. About three years later the young woman suddenly died. I don't know if she lived long enough to cross over into the fascist camp.

But the letter which Cimmie wrote to Trotsky and which Trotsky printed in his diary showed something of her genuine enthusiasm and courage.

Dear Comrade Trotsky,

    I would like above all things to see you for a few moments. There is no good reason why you should see me as (1) I belong to the Labour Party in England who were so ridiculous and refused to allow you in but also I belong to the ILP and we did try our very best to make them change their minds; and (2) I am daughter of Lord Curzon who was Minister of Foreign Affairs in London when you were in Russia!

    On the other hand I am an ardent Socialist. I am a member of the House of Commons. I think less than nothing of the present government. I have just finished reading your life which inspired me as no other book has done for ages. I am a great admirer of yours. These days when great men seem so very few and far between it would be a great privilege to meet one of the enduring figures of our age and I do hope with all my heart you will grant me that privilege. I need hardly say I come as a private person, not a journalist nor *anything* but myself – I am on my way to Russia – I leave for Batoum – Tiflis – Rostov – Kharkov and Moscow by boat Monday. I have come to Principo this afternoon especially to try to see you, but if it were not convenient I could come out again any day till Monday. I do hope however you could allow me a few moments this afternoon.

Yours fraternally
Cynthia   Mosley

A few days after her exploit with Trotsky, Cimmie performed another feat which seemed aimed at demonstrating her energy and independence and reporting this to Tom. She swam across the straits of the Bosphorus from Asia to Europe – a distance of about a mile. Zita, who accompanied her by boat, reported – 'When she got about half way across it became more difficult as the current was so strong ... large steamers began to pass and their huge wash became very tiring. I kept screaming "Look out!" and Cimmie began to get a little cross. However after one or two desperate moments the heroic deed was accomplished.'

    Cimmie went back to her hotel to write immediately of this new deed to Tom. But there she found a telegram from him of which the words, it would seem, did not contain much beyond the usual reassuring and encouraging noises he used to make to her. But it made Cimmie write:

Sunday 7th   Hotel M. Tokatlian

Oh Billo, just to show you what an ass I am your wire has just come and I feel suicidal. Why. It came from Le Lavandou, what on earth are you doing there unless you have popped off with Paula? I have always longed to go to Le Lavandou, you never would – why now – only to hide. Darling darling you would have been better never to wire me or else to explain why you were there, it has just spoilt everything for me. Even when I am hundreds of miles away your shadow falls on me. How can I ever dare to have holidays away from you – and yet it may be nothing, you may be there with a large party. Then why not all sign the gram. No doubt you'll explain it away. But as the song says – 'How am I to know?' How fed up I am with love. I suppose I ought not to mind but I do so damnably I don't know what to do. Can hardly bear to face dinner and all the rest. Can't wire you as have no address.

Hell Hell Hell. If it's true, I think you and Paula unspeakable cads. If it's not true, then I do apologise, but wish you had not caused the unnecessary anguish – you might have said why you were there – I suppose you thought they wouldn't put where the tel: came from.

So you see all my talk about self sufficiency serenity peace etc – Balls Balls Balls
– goes in 1 second at the bare hint of an idea from you.
Ought (1) to trust you not to do such a thing, or –
         (2) not to mind if you did.
The first impossible, as I fear I have *never really* in my heart of hearts trusted you in that way. The second however much as I try I cannot help such a flame of misery jealousy resentment I can't cope.

Please forgive me if it is all nothing, perhaps I shouldn't even write and keep all my doubts to myself; but somehow I can't do that, it seems clearer to get it off my chest. And darling when I came in I was so gay and full of myself and elated and just sitting down to write you that I had just swum the Bosphorus from Asia to Europe against a strong current in 40 minutes – thought you'd be thrilled – I thought it so terribly in the Grand Style and Byronic and even rather Mosley – and now – those stupid names of tunes – they are so apposite –

> *What is* this thing called love
> How am I to know?

I don't, either.

I will wire an address from Batoum for you to write. Don't be angry if I am all wrong it's because I love you so awfully. Even if I am not wrong I suppose you'll pretend I am. What a farce it all is.

I wish you were here with me.

We are off to Russia tomorrow.
I'll try to forget about all this. Poor Tom
                              Poor Tim
My sweetie one.
                    Blessings.

                         Mum

Cimmie never spoke to Zita about any of this. The next day they got
on an Italian boat bound for Batum, in Russia, at the eastern end of the
Black Sea. They 'settled down into a sort of routine . . . we both adored
reading and hardly spoke to each other: we invented games and ate
rather a lot in view of the future' (Zita). They had a vague certainty that
in Russia 'we should be starved and imprisoned and probably shot and
at any rate never come out of the country the same as we went into it.
The Captain was horrified at the idea of our going to Russia and said
we ought to be at home with our husbands.'
    While she was on the boat Cimmie probably dwelt on the things
that seemed never to be far from her mind about Tom. The letter she
had written to him directly after her visit to Trotsky had continued, after
she had told him the news of her exploit:

> About our life. I will try, but also remember I *do* try all the time, it's
> when I am so tired of trying I get so difficult. I never seem to be able
> to let up trying. As to not having complexes about you oh how
> difficult – only because I care for you so much – that is what makes
> it difficult; and all the side of me you hate, the hard defiant knock-
> me-down, curiously enough is created by you – an attempt by me
> to clap on some pieces of armour – a sort of sanctuary inside where
> I was inviolate and you could not get at me – I might behave
> outwardly more sensibly but up to now I have not been able to
> preserve one solitary atom or portion of me that you could not get
> at and hurt almost beyond endurance . . .
>   I fear so awfully all my efforts to adjust myself to you so as not
> to be hurt result in the very symptoms that make you hurt me more
> – If I appear to 'don't care' by being 'don't care', you just get fiercer
> and fiercer and destroy me more and more: and to just submit to
> being hurt without putting up some show seems to me almost
> unendurable. So far I have only achieved not being hurt by you (and
> rarely enough at that) by thinking you a cad and a swine – by
> despising your methods – oh dear how difficult it all is! – as quite
> beyond question you matter more to me than anything in the world.

With the children when you are sweet to me I could die of joy. But as you say: in term-time you have to work so very hard – with other people: in hols you play hard – with other people. Where does Mum come in?

It's all very well to talk of the great life we could build up together but we never are together – and don't go off and say we are more together than any other married couple as that is bosh – in the sense I mean *together* we are very little. This may seem an ungenerous answer to you but these letters are no good unless they face facts – after all we have written them before, and the real life we can have – and I agree with you we can have it – must and can only come if we really take trouble about it. You must take some trouble about me. You will say I must about you – my answer is I never seem to cease bothering about you, tho' you may find that hard to believe ...

Always remember I adore YOU – tho' loathing the thing that masquerades as you every so often and is cruel and unkind and often despicable ... It's the same about me, the real ME is a dear, but the horrid student creature that I become is awful – but I only become it to fight the masquerading you. Let's both be YOU and ME. I swear I'll try.

But you MUST. I can't do it alone.

There is no way of knowing the words by which Tom 'destroyed' Cimmie more and more, since this was always done face to face with his cutting tongue and not by letter. In later life, when Tom wanted to be rude to people he was just rude; with his chin up, barking at people to 'get out', or stabbing at them with his heavy, relentless sarcasm. But Cimmie in her letter did seem able for the first time to stand back and see that a proper way of describing what was happening to her and Tom might be that there was in each of them something that took them over and made them helpless in their efforts to deal with themselves or each other by will. There was something in Tom that needed to protect himself by having her enslaved: there was something in her that, in pain, still could not escape from enslavement. Tom could not stand back from himself enough to talk to Cimmie in these terms; he was too successful with his manipulations.

Cimmie and Zita landed at Batum; they travelled by train and bus into the Caucasus; they got a boat from Batum to Yalta and from there went by train to Kharkov and Kiev. Their impressions of Russia were much the same as impressions of tourists have been for fifty years: they noted the delays, the inefficiency, the subjects that could not be talked about; at the same time there was 'that queer intangible new spirit, everyone equal, no classes' (Cimmie in a letter to Tom). Also – 'all the nonsense talked about only wearing old clothes so as not to be conspicuous, typhoid, the frightful food shortages, no soap – bunk from beginning to end'. From the Caucasus, Zita had written of 'The Children of the Night – the children who, directly after the revolution, without parents or guardians, infested the whole of Russia especially the south: they were the essence of vice, disease, crime and terror: there are supposed to be few left now, but this little band had the most terrifying faces I have ever imagined'. Cimmie on the coast of the Black Sea had admired the 'thrilling modern white blocks of sanatoria'. They both were rather impressed by the public nude bathing of both sexes. And they wondered why Stalin had thought it profitable to get rid of so many intellectuals.

In Kharkov they discovered from the Intourist office that Cimmie's sister Irene, in the company of John Strachey, had passed through the day before on their way down from Moscow. This rather dampened their feeling of being pioneers. They went on to Moscow where they found in a 'spotlessly clean hotel which 'looked almost normal' other Labour MPs, including G. R. Strauss and Jennie Lee. Cimmie found also a letter from Tom, in answer to the one she had posted in Istanbul.

Darling Baby Mutton,   22 b Ebury Street. S.W.1.
    What a mutt she is! What a let to write him – What an upset to give herself – and him because he felt she was upset! Toured the coast from Cannes to Toulon – *alone or with parties* – got Daisy's speedboat Fish (without owner included let me hasten to add) (and further only 300 francs a day) and had glorious time – shot to and fro just the king of every beach [drawing of pig or sheep] – met many people knew at various spots but much Byronic solitude (which is growing on him a lot in her absence – great feature!) St Maxim's and more especially St Tropez proved enormous fun on revisits. Marvellous man with concertina and all Cannes dancing in Marie Antoinette humours at your little restaurant. Found ever so many small cheap but charming places with lovely sand beaches for the children (needless to say the real object of his pilgrimage!) Thinks he hears a porker sizzling.
    Silly fellow, if he had been on such an expedition would he have telegraphed you from the rendez-vous? He may be wicked but he is not such a mutt as that. That place was lovely but I think better still Cavalaire which is nearer to St Tropez and has the same sand beach. Of course would never do it before, as had never had his fill of rest,

immobility and fun – a few days after return to Cannes however had more than enough – very hectic and most of nice people went – further in-solitude-Byron feature plus a speedboat.

What a clever mutt to swim the Hellespont – big and proud Byron mutton! [drawing of sheep swimming]. Sorry, good resolution, never make jokes. Kiss nose. Or pat bottom [drawing of a bottom with a caption 'verboten']. And he is lapsing already (but he loves her so much). Thought her letter did not go very far to meet his sweet and sympathetic gestures. So glad however she is having a lovely time and do hope it will last to the end.

Just been alone to see a flying film *The Dawn Patrol* – best yet – overdrawn in personal things but wonderful flying pictures – very reminiscent – moved and depressed. Seen only serious people in London and been mostly alone – rang up no one of friends – but expect have little tiny bit of various fun in Paris – where he wishes his Mutt was because he misses and loves her so. Resolved to be the perfect husband. She is not to be such a Porker and roarer because she can be sweetest one in world whom he loves. [Drawing of rather wild-looking sheep or pig with the caption 'The Corsair between Cannes and Toulon!!!!']

In Moscow Cimmie and Zita were taken to some show-piece prison in the company of other political tourists. Zita reported – 'The Head of the Reformatory was more than charming and seemed to be an angel of goodness with an immense paternal love and kindness for all his prisoners ... he explained Russia's theories about prison and punishment. He said that their idea was that crime was due almost entirely to environment, and that therefore all they needed was to remove the criminal and place him in another position.' However she did add 'Really I suppose they were completely under control.'

Cimmie, worrying about Tom, must have wondered, having received his letter, about the ways in which politicians use words with little regard for truth. But then, with politicians, what does one do for truth? There was no way of Cimmie knowing with whom, if anyone, Tom had been in the South of France: he had almost certainly been with someone. But then, there were his usual protestations of love. Cimmie seemed to be stuck – as perhaps some Russians might have been feeling stuck – with this endless, vaguely persuasive, duplicity of words. Cimmie had written to Tom from Kharkov – 'Oh I wonder when I will become any better about you: you have me tied up in one of those knots well nigh impossible to undo.'

Back in London Tom was preparing for the Labour Party Conference; which was to be his last conventional platform of appeal to people to listen to the logic of his words.

CHAPTER 17

The Mosley Manifesto

In one of his letters of the summer Bob Boothby had set out what he believed to be the alternatives facing Tom – '(1) Staying where you are, consolidating and strengthening your hold on the Labour movement in the country and persuading the workers that they will not always be betrayed; or (2) making another speech or two along recent lines and crossing the floor in the autumn. You would be amazed at the welcome you would get.' He had added – 'The former is the long term policy and involves a further bleak period in the wilderness: (2) assures power at an early date, but power limited by the Tory machine, and the knowledge that you can't change again.'

Bob Boothby believed that the Labour government was coming to an end because of its failure to deal with unemployment; that the Tories would soon get in with a huge majority. Liberals would be of no account. 'Two machines, and two only, right and left, will wield political power in this country in the years that lie ahead.' He assured Tom that, if he stayed within the fold of either of the party machines, 'I have not the slightest doubt that you would win through in the end'.

Tom's chance to get a hold on the Labour Party machine occurred at the party conference at Llandudno in October 1930. During the summer his prestige amongst party workers does not seem to have weakened: his stand appearing as the 'honest man' was bearing fruit. He had had copies of his Memorandum printed and sent to local Labour parties with the request that they should consider it and give their opinions on it at the Party Conference: this of course did not make him popular with party leaders. Professional Labour politicians have the gang-solidarity of people accustomed to fight as underdogs; they are particularly susceptible to feelings of betrayal.

At the conference Ramsay MacDonald 'made a wonderful speech: he said nothing whatever, but he said it so eloquently that the delegates were deeply moved' (John Scanlon). Then Tom spoke: he could match MacDonald for eloquence: he also had a policy which delegates could think they might fight for – or die for. In his peroration Tom told those who might follow him – 'at best they would have their majority; at worst they would go down fighting for the things they believed in: they would not die like an old woman in bed: they would die like men on the field – a better fate and, in politics, one with a more certain hope of resurrection.'

A journalist in the *Sunday Graphic* wrote – 'There was stillness save for Mosley's voice gathering in power. Boldly, challengingly, he gave his own plan to restore stability . . . The throng was hypnotised by the man, by his audacity, as bang! bang! bang! he thundered directions. The thing that got hold of the conference was that here was a man with a straight-cut policy. It leapt at him.'

Fenner Brockway reported that Tom got 'the greatest ovation he had ever heard at a party conference'. Tom was compared by one commentator to Hitler; by another to Moses. There was a vote taken on a resolution that the Memorandum should be submitted again for consideration by the National Executive Committee. Tom's supporters lost the vote by the narrow margin of 1,046,000 to 1,251,000 – the miners having at the last minute transferred their block vote away from Tom against the advice of their leader A. J. Cook. (There was a story that Cook himself had got held up in a taxi or he might have swayed the vote: there seems no hard evidence for this). But it did not seem to people in the hall that the vote much mattered anyway. The vote had been to do with a technical matter of loyalties: in emotion, party workers were overwhelmingly behind Tom. He was elected to the National Executive of the party: J. H. Thomas lost his seat on it. John Scanlon wrote:

In the Press and the Labour Movement itself the discussion now centred round the question of how long it would be before Sir Oswald became the party leader. Even without a crash in the Party's fortunes it was easy to see that changes must come soon. The controllers of the Labour Party, mostly old men, could not stay the inexorable march of time any more than ordinary mortals. No other leader was in sight. Mr Wheatley was gone. Mr Maxton had none of the pushful qualities which carry a man to leadership in Labour politics, and nobody in the trade unions showed the slightest sign of being able to take charge. Therefore every prophet fixed on Sir

Oswald as the next party leader. Even Socialists, who had no particular love for Sir Oswald, were saying nothing could stop it. All
the prophets, however, had overlooked the one man who could stop
it – Sir Oswald himself.

Tom himself used to say he might soon have become *de facto* party
leader under the nominal leadership of Arthur Henderson. But in order
to do this he would have had to work in with the party machine; to
humour it, tinker with it, play the political game. His refusal to do this
was made partly on an intellectual assessment – he believed that it was
the mechanisms of bureaucratic party politics that prevented anything
decisive being done – but it was also an emotional decision: he had no
natural taste, nor aptitude, for the painstaking and boring manoeuvrings of committees. What he liked, and was good at, was the manipulation of crowds by his oratory and of individuals by his reasoning and
charm. After the Llandudno conference it was these talents that he
wanted to exercise: he probably had little clear idea, at first, of where
the results might lead.

He was perfecting his style as a mob orator – that strange music by
which crowds are swayed like snakes. He would declaim – 'We are a
party with our eyes on the stars, but let us also remember that our feet
are planted firmly in the earth, on muddy soil, where men are suffering
and looking at us with eyes of questioning and anguish saying "Lift us
up from the mud! give us practical remedies here and now!"' For
practical remedies he was returning with renewed vigour to the matter
of trying to form political alliances in London. In his thinking he was
putting more and more emphasis on a policy of protecting and controlling trade with empire countries: this was indeed ensuring the interest
of the Tories: Stanley Baldwin remarked that Tom was 'now producing
ideas which I remember giving voice to in 1903'. But Tom's feelings
did not change that if ever he was to do anything decisive in politics he
would have to lead an alliance of his own. And in fact there seemed to
be more potential rebels in the Labour than in the Conservative Party.

In December 1930 a short four-page *Manifesto* appeared entitled *A
National Policy for National Emergency*. It was signed by seventeen Labour
MP's: amongst them Aneurin Bevan, John Strachey, W. J. Brown, and
the two Mosleys – and A. J. Cook, the miners' leader. It became known
as *The Mosley Manifesto* (as distinct from the Mosley Memorandum of
earlier in the year): it was obviously dedicated to Tom's ideas, though
it was written mainly by Strachey and Brown and Bevan. It's main
recommendation was that 'an Emergency Cabinet of not more than five

ministers without portfolios' should be set up and 'invested with power
to carry through the emergency policy'. The emergency was that the
unemployed had now increased to two and a half million: the policy
was that 'we should aim at building within the Commonwealth a
civilisation high enough to absorb the production of modern machinery
which for the purpose must be insulated from wrecking forces in the
rest of the world'. This policy was necessary, it was claimed, because
there was no other way that either conservatism or socialism would not
be at the mercy of the whims of what Tom later called 'international
finance'. Nearly all the signatories were young labour MP's in their first
Parliament: they had not had time to feel themselves dependent on
Parliamentary institutions. It was difficult for older MPs to be sympathetic towards the Manifesto because it was contemptuous of existing
institutions. Also for orthodox conservatives it was too socialistic and
for orthodox socialists too imperialistic. The manifesto got much
publicity: but discussion was apt to descend to the level of jokes about
who would be the five 'dictators'. All this confirmed Tom in his belief
that if anything was to be done he would have to lead some new political
alignment.

All this was according to reason: there remained the practical politics.
Tom saw that if he was to make anything of his 'New Labour Group'
(as those who agreed with the Manifesto had come to be called) then
he would have to equip it with a specific organisation and with funds:
this would require publicity: at the same time too much publicity might
alarm people, before the funds and embryonic organisation were there.
Tom was on a political tight-rope. Allan Young, Tom's political secretary, wrote to Cimmie – 'I am more content now to accept Tom's
leadership than ever before. He is made for the job that has to be done
... He has displayed all the qualities of intellectual courage and ability,
combined with the caution great actions demand.'

Tom had for some time been making soundings about whether it
might be possible to gain backing for his proposals from industrialists
or from financiers in the City – and for any organisation committed to
putting the proposals into effect. He had had one or two meetings with
William Morris, later Lord Nuffield, who had become interested in the
Mosley Manifesto. In January 1931 Morris sent for Tom and handed him
a cheque for £50,000 with the remark 'Don't think, my boy, that
money like this grows on gooseberry bushes.' This was a fateful moment
for Tom. He thought that other money would follow. He felt that it not
only made possible, but was a portent for now putting into effect, his
plans for starting his own movement.

Bob Boothby uttered his last precise cry of warning and lament.

Jan 30th 1931   Carlton Club
Pall Mall SW1

Dear Tom,

... Since you wrote and told me that you proposed to play your hand in your own way I never sought to enquire what you were doing. But I imagined you were devoting yourself to the task of building up and consolidating your position in the Labour movement.

If it be true that you are trying to raise money in the City then I feel I must say once more – and for the last time – that I believe this to be madness from your own point of view; and leave it at that.

I became uneasy from the first moment the word 'cash' was mentioned, because I never thought it could be raised except under more or less false pretences: and I don't believe that money, even in large quantities, can ever start a new political movement in this country (witness the fate of L.G., the Empire Crusade, and your own effort years ago with Cowdray).

You will remember that I left the dinner party given by Col. Portal at the Garrick Club because I so heartily disapproved of it.

You are, of course, right to pursue the course you think best.

But I too am entitled to my opinions which in this case are very decided.

Last night I turned up some notes that I made of the letters which I wrote to you during the course of last year.

I find that you have persistently disregarded every single piece of advice or suggestion that I have ever ventured to offer.

And so, my dear Tom, I cannot feel that you will greatly miss the benefit of a judgement which you obviously do not value highly. What I most sincerely hope is that neither you nor Cimmie will allow our political differences to interfere with a friendship which I think we all do value a good deal and which has survived sterner tests than this.

Yours ever
Bob

Events now happened fast. 1931 was the year which Arnold Toynbee called 'annus terribilis' in which 'men and women all over the world were seriously contemplating and seriously discussing the possibility that the Western system of society might break down and cease to work'. In January there were five million unemployed in Germany, between six and seven million in the USA, and two and a half million in Great Britain. Old political alignments were in any event cracking up. It so happened that the height of Tom's reputation and belief in himself as an almost magically potent political figure coincided exactly with the moment of twentieth-century history at which it was felt that in the face of almost certain chaos new and indeed almost magical leadership was called for. For once, Tom's natural impatience seemed undeniably suited to events. On February 4th Cimmie told Harold Nicolson that 'Tom is about to form a New Party'. On 20th February six members of the 'New Labour Group' who had signed the *Mosley Manifesto* decided to resign from the labour Party: these were Tom and Cimmie, John Strachey, W. J. Brown, Oliver Baldwin and Robert Forgan. This was the decisive moment in Tom's political life. All his political manoeuvrings up till now had been, however arrogantly or recklessly, still within the terms of some recognised political game: even his resignation from the government, his narrow defeat at the Party Conference, had in fact seemed to enhance his prestige. But if he resigned from the Labour Party itself (he had already resigned from the Conservatives) and formed his own party, he would be putting himself outside any known game.

It was agreed that the six MPs who were to resign should do so on different days to ensure the maximum publicity. Strachey and Baldwin resigned; and then Cimmie, on March 3rd. Ramsay MacDonald replied to her letter:

5th March 1931 10 Downing Street.
Whitehall.

My dear Lady Cynthia,

 I have to acknowledge the receipt of your letter of the 3rd instant, resigning your membership of the Labour Party. Had it not been announced days ago in the newspapers, I should have been surprised, but I am interested to be put in possession of your considered reasons for the step which you have taken. Needless to say I am very sorry.

 When you came in a year or two ago we gave you a very hearty welcome and assumed that you knew what was the policy of the predominant Socialist Party in this country, and that, with that knowledge, you asked us to accept you as a candidate and to go to your constituency and assist you in your fight. You are disappointed with us; you have been mistaken in your choice of political companions, and you are re-selecting them so as to surround yourself with a sturdier, more courageous and more intelligent Socialism for your encouragement and strength. You remain true, while all the rest of us are false. Whoever examines manifestos and schemes and rejects them, partly because they are not the sort of Socialism that any Socialist has ever devised, or because they amount to nothing but words, is regarded by you as inept or incompetent. We must just tolerate your censure and even contempt; and, in the spare moments we have, cast occasional glances at you pursuing your heroic role with exemplary rectitude and stiff straightness to a disastrous futility and an empty sound. We have experienced so much of this in the building up of the Party that we must not become too cynical when the experience is repeated in the new phase of its existence. Perhaps before the end, roads may cross again and we shall wonder why we ever diverged.

Yours very sincerely,

J. Ramsay MacDonald

P.S. This is not an official reply, as I am waiting for all the resignations to be in before I decide whether to publish anything, so I mark it as a purely personal communication which is not to be published.

Cimmie also received a letter from the chairman of her constituency committee, who told her – 'Whilst I have always felt you were sincere in your desire to improve the lot of the people, I think your secession from the Labour Party is a bad let-down for all those who worked so wholeheartedly for you in your contest.'

Tom, in the middle of all this, suddenly became ill: he retired to bed in his flat in Ebury Street with pleurisy and double pneumonia. W. J. Brown was also stricken: just before it was his turn to resign, the trades-union that employed him, the Civil Service Clerical Association, threatened to sack him; he got cold feet. Tom got himself driven to Brown's house in an ambulance and was carried in on a stretcher. There, Tom wrote later of Brown – 'his face seemed to be pulled down on one side like a man suffering a stroke and he burst into tears ... The very few men in whom previously I had observed this phenomenon had likewise usually rather emphasised their determination and courage before they found themselves averse to getting out of a trench when the time came.' Tom had himself carried back to his ambulance. He himself never resigned from the Labour Party: on March 10th when the news of the New Party had become official, he was expelled for 'gross disloyalty'.

Tom's illness lasted four weeks. He lay in bed in his flat in Ebury Street – where the warm air at the press of a switch might waft over him – and he ruminated, presumably, on what he had done. He had in his mind accused W. J. Brown of cowardice: he himself had seemed brave to a point of recklessness. But still, it was now Cimmie and John Strachey who were left to launch the New Party in the planned programme of speeches round the country. Tom had had faith in his rôle as hero: but there was evidence, as there had been before, that accidents happen to heroes at decisive moments of their histories; that it is more than will-power that decides who, and in what in what way, in fact gets out of a trench when the time comes.

CHAPTER 18

The Riddle of the Sphinx

The word 'hero' may seem ambiguous in relation to Tom. In common use it refers to someone of slightly superhuman qualities: it also has the suggestion of tragedy or death, or of someone who never quite grows up.

Tom had probably not set out to put himself beyond the rules of the political game, but there seems to have been something in him that would inevitably have done this. Heroes are fought or followed because of an air of inevitability about them: they achieve what is set out for them not by will, but by becoming legendary.

The next two years were the central ones in Tom's life and the last in Cimmie's. Tom did almost seem to be (as other 'heroes' have said of themselves) sleepwalking. He is remembered at this time as someone whom people 'fawned on': he continued to be attacked with violence: he also was increasingly ignored. People did not seem quite to know what attitude to take to him. It was as if a guerrilla fighter had appeared on a football field.

At the end of his life Tom was like Oedipus at Colonus – 'beyond the pale' in the sense of his seeming to have broken some fundamental rule which had rendered him taboo. The taboo was not on account of his having made a mistake or chosen evil: it was the penalty for some falseness attendant on possible success. Oedipus, in the myth, becomes an outcast not just because he has murdered his father and married his mother: he has assumed a false mantle of omnipotence, having solved the riddle of the Sphinx.

In the legend, after having unknowingly killed his father on the road to Thebes, Oedipus is challenged by the mythical monster the Sphinx. The Sphinx is part woman and part lion and part bird: she is that which devours people who travel hopefully: she is laying siege to the city of

Thebes, whose citizens are starving. The Sphinx will not let anyone pass unless they answer a riddle. The riddle is childish: it seems that anyone might answer it, but they do not.

The riddle is – What has four legs in the morning, two in the afternoon, and three in the evening. Oedipus answers the riddle – a man. Whereupon the Sphinx, instead of devouring him, throws herself over a cliff. Oedipus goes on his way and becomes the saviour of the city of Thebes.

What Oedipus saw in the solving of the riddle was that the Sphinx was playing a game with words: in two instances the word 'legs' is a metaphor; in one it is not: the words referring to time are all metaphors. The riddle was a riddle because in it metaphors and direct reference are mixed. To solve it, someone had to have the power to discriminate between the two.

The people who had not been able to solve the riddle had not been accustomed to see what is a metaphor and what is not: they used words in such a way that they did not question how they used them. So they were trapped by words: they could not break out. And Thebes was starving.

Oedipus had the power of discrimination: he could stand back from words: he could see some words are metaphors and others are not. He lifted the curse from the city of Thebes. But he was left with a false impression of omnipotence.

In the myth, he was crowned King of Thebes: he married Queen Jocasta. But then another curse came down – perhaps even worse than the first. There was a plague attendant on the city being ruled by someone who seemed to have magical powers; who had also, although unwittingly, and although people did not see this at the time, murdered his father and married his mother. Oedipus had solved the riddle of the Sphinx: what he had not solved – in fact what he had landed himself with – was the problem of someone who, when he has power over words, thinks he has power over himself and over reality.

Oedipus learned that he had overreached himself: he had solved a riddle about what were and were not games: he had thought that thus he could control reality. But in fact he had become trapped unconsciously at a deeper level: people cannot get away, ultimately, from the power of the rules of games. He had murdered his father and married his mother: this was a curse within himself; he might have had the wit to see it, if he had not been so carried away by his feelings of omnipotence.

A power to see what is games-playing and what is not is only a first step in coming to terms with reality. There is the further step, perhaps made possible by the first, which is to do not with the illusion that one is above the rules of games but with seeing the new patterns and even rules that are opened up by the fact that one can see patterns.

There are superficial parallels between the stories of Oedipus and of Tom: these are not the most interesting. Tom was the son of a bullying father whom he hardly saw and by whom he was rejected and of an adored and adoring mother who called him her 'man-child'. All this indeed when he was a child might have given him feelings of omni-potence: he could play upon his mother who seemed to be his world; there was no father to instil in him knowledge of limits imposed by morals and tradition. With such a background, a child might well have contempt for the rules of games.

What is of deeper interest is the way in which Tom seems to have come mythically towards his city of Thebes in which people were starving. In England, the plague was unemployment: there was some riddle that could not be solved not because a solution was too difficult, but because it was outside the usual terms of people's minds. Of course unemployment could be solved: a leader could say – You will be employed in this way or that or you will be shot. Most people did not think of this solution because it did not seem relevant: it might work, but they assumed it would be worse than the curse. But they could not quite say this, because it would seem they were not interested in solving unemployment – which they were. And so they said nothing. And they were devoured. And the city starved. The riddle was not solved not because it was too difficult, but because it was too undesirably easy. But what was also unpalatable was the fact that in that case perhaps the only solution was that there was no solution – one had to learn how to live with the curse.

Tom came along with his impressions of omnipotence and said – Of course you cannot solve the riddle if you stick to your customary attitudes of mind; but outside these, the solution is quite simple. The fact that you do not want to consider it means that not solving the riddle is in fact your game: you talk and do nothing about it. If you did, your game would be over: but this is your plague. If you want to cure unemployment then you have to pay the price: if you do not want to pay the price then you do not want to cure unemployment. This is a matter of logic: words refer to reality. If you really want to cure unemployment, then follow me. But you must step out of the rules of the game.

But then, Tom was trapped by the forces of a game on a deeper level, of which he was unconscious. He felt that he could order the world as he ordered words. But he could not step back from himself, as he had stepped back from words, and see what was the nature of human beings – in what ways they might need games-playing, even if there were ways they might not. He could not do this because he could not see what were needs, and helplessnesses, as opposed to powers, within himself.

Oedipus is forced to see that however clever he has been with his power and with his words, he has not been clever with himself – he has not been clever enough to see the riddles that he has been landed with by his own nature and his own history – not to solve them, because perhaps they are insoluble – but just to see them and learn to live with them. He has simply been clever enough, in fact, to think he can ignore all this; and so his power turns to ashes. At the illuminating crisis of his life he blinds himself; as if in some recognition of his failure to see. This does not mean that he is not a legendary hero. People are legends just because they can give light to others: they can still alter the way people think.

Tom, as he lay on his bed in Ebury Street plagued with fever, must have had some archetypal dreams and visions about all this. He had seen how much of what politicians said was rubbish: how everyone knew it was rubbish but carried on as if they did not know this: thus they suffered from plague. If you pointed this out to them their minds seemed to go blank: it was as if they were at home in the plague. Tom thought he could free them by discrimination, by reason; but then what was he freeing them into? On some level Tom must have known (or when people faced him with this did his mind go blank?) that you cannot have politics without paradoxes, riddles: there are always enigmas about authority and freedom: this is just what the business of power is like. It cannot be helped if it is like a plague from time to time: if you think you can do away with paradoxes, you bring down a worse curse. In the activities of power you are dealing with other people: if other people are to be respected then there have to be rules of games: if there are not, then other people are not respected. If you do want to respect people the highest emphasis cannot be on 'losing' or 'winning': losing is a lesser disaster than that of destroying the game. You only want to destroy the game if your feelings of omnipotence give you contempt for other people.

Tom claimed that he was involved in no game: that he could order reality. With this confidence he both did and did not deceive other people: he made them feel at moments it might be true. A more interesting question is, how much he deceived himself.

In his relationship with Cimmie he had always been ruthless with words: he used them without much relevance to what they might mean. He manipulated tenderness in order to keep her: he used rages in order to get away. But also, the tenderness and the rages happened naturally: his manipulations were efforts to make the best of what was there. All this involved some ability to stand back from the forces that were driving him: if he could use them, he was not quite at their mercy. What he lacked perhaps was an ability consciously to see himself doing this – and to see where his ability to manipulate might lead him. In fact, he was involved in some circle in that the more he succeeded the more he failed – his endearments placated Cimmie but made her not trust him: in the end he did not keep her and was desolate when he failed. He might have learned something of all this if he had not himself been so involved in the game of saying that in public life he was not games-playing.

Once or twice during the next two years Tom does seem to have thought about giving up politics – at least for a time. He said he wanted to relax; to think. If he had, what he might have learned was that the most successful way of dealing with riddles and paradoxes is perhaps to enjoy them; to savour them; not to dream that they are not there or can be eliminated. Then, perhaps, one can accept what is possible and what is not. Tom had an instinct about this in his private life: but people are victims of their talents – and circumstances. In public life he had enormous talent for histrionics; and this was a time when people were seizing on people like Tom and offering them power – or at least acclaim. It was in public life that he became a victim.

Cimmie was the one person who might have influenced him in all this – to learn something about himself. But Cimmie, in spite of glimpses every now and then of their both being taken over by forces stronger than themselves, herself was trapped by circumstances and her nature – not so much by the usual traps of class or money, as by the additional facets of her background which had made her believe that she was someone exceptional and thus too proud to believe for long in forces stronger than herself. Cimmie had realised she was apt to see Tom as a saint or a devil: a hero or a baby: that so long as she saw him thus he could make use of her: perhaps she wanted to be so used. But neither Tom nor Cimmie seemed to want to learn to treat the other as an ordinary human being. With Tom there was the baby-talk: with Cimmie the appreciation of this because thus she might feel he was her baby. If she challenged him he might become raging and dash off: but then in need, he might return to her. In a marriage a husband and wife either hold a mirror up to each other so that they can see themselves (this is rare) or each provide food for the other's fantasies. Tom perhaps felt safe through his power to hurt Cimmie: Cimmie in turn could say, almost cheerfully, 'I could die for you' or 'I could kill you'. She sometimes saw the irony of this and could say – 'What a farce!' But for all her life-giving qualities she had less and less enjoyment from the farce. She did not so often see things as she said she wanted to see them – as 'fun'.

Tom, with part of him, always did manage to see things as 'fun': he had an enormous zest for life; a talent for enjoyment. This is what made him personally, in spite of the distaste often engendered by his politics, so attractive to people – and a survivor. People loved to be with him: it was on this level that his life succeeded: he did become a happy old man; a legend. He could not of course easily accept this as his fate: part of his legend was, that politics were the whole of life to him. In some way it was probably his zest for life – even his sexual drives – that helped to render him politically ineffectual: politics are a boring game, requiring that other people should feel safe in one's presence. Tom, with the cutting-edge of his personality, seemed often to be almost knowingly self-destructive. But then – might he not in truth have wanted to become a legend – thus embracing the paradoxes he said he wanted to deny?

When Tom talked about wholeness or 'Ganzheit' this was for him not a matter of conscious integration but of balancing bits of his life at opposite ends of a pole as it were, while he stayed on a tightrope. Much of his contempt, his vituperation, was channelled into his politics: here he had no patience, no forbearance: he loved a fight. But then in private life there was room for open-mindedness, wit, laughing at himself, hilarity. People used to feel what marvellous company he was. He also, of course – again perhaps because of his sexual drives – hurt them.

One of his favourite quotations were the lines from Goethe's *Faust* where Faust makes his bargain with the devil – if the devil can show him a moment of such delight that he, Faust, will cry out for time to stop, then he, the devil, can claim Faust for his own. Tom would roll out this quotation at the dinner table like someone making a strike at skittles. He loved the sound of this; though he felt perhaps that he himself would be too hard-headed to utter Faust's cry: he might have hoped both to get the moment, and to trick the devil.

Cimmie did not want trickery: did not want balancing acts: she wanted wholeness in the sense of being all-of-a-piece and without guile. At least, she thought this was what she wanted. She made resolutions: she struggled: but then, when the resolutions failed, she did not learn:

when ideas and policies such as his were succeeding extravagantly in other parts of the world: these policies, and ideas, destroyed themselves at an enormous cost of human suffering. Tom never got off the ground as it were in the matter of causing much political human suffering: he had the private wit to see that his destructiveness remained largely symbolic.

Cimmie, like Tom, imagined she wanted outward life to be orderly: she did not have his sense of curiosity when it was not. She felt passionately: but she feared a lack within her: she blamed it on her relationship with Tom. She said that she could not change unless he changed: but it was not he who felt there had to be change to survive.

Neither Cimmie nor Tom had religion: Tom had faith in himself: Cimmie had faith in Tom. Then when she lost it, she seemed to have nothing. They both, in the way they saw things, thought that life should respond to their will: they both saw death as some sort of let-out. But Tom, knowing the complexities of things, was using a metaphor when he talked about 'going down fighting'. Cimmie did not see life as a metaphor: perhaps, if she could not find faith in herself, she felt death as a condition in which humans might at last be all all-of-a-piece.

she just made them, and the same mistakes, again. This wore away her faith in Tom: but why did she have this faith? From the first, she seems to have known what he was like. It was just his complexity, perhaps, that she had come to feel might contain her; that would give her simplicity something grand that she might attach herself to. She had written as a schoolgirl of her feeling of the necessity of a 'Big Solemn Comprehensive Idea'. And perhaps Tom had needed her simplicity to give him a thread through the maze of life. But then, he also now used her like some of his skittles to be knocked down. And then he could come for forgiveness and be comforted again. And she would feel reassured. This was their game. By staying in it, Cimmie in some sense colluded. But she got tired. Perhaps it is always a matter of luck how people do, or do not, get out.

In politics, Tom went on thinking that if you put a rational case to people you had done your job: they either followed or they did not. There was a real sense in which Tom was not interested in power – 'he was a complete professional in everything except the winning of power' (Robert Skidelsky). It was this that rendered him powerless, but also established the legend: in the circumstances this was actually a virtue. Beatrice Webb wrote of him 'He lacks genuine fanaticism: I doubt whether he has the tenacity of a Hitler'. At a slightly later date than the time to do with this book Tom wrote a letter to Lord Beaverbrook in which he himself said, in effect, that Britain was fortunate in having a fascist leader such as himself because another leader might have been more ruthlessly and successfully interested in power. Tom was capable of such irony: though not often, it is true, in politics. Trotsky, in his diary-entry about Cimmie, had called Tom a coxcomb; but there is something in Trotsky's history and character that is similar to Tom's: both men turned away, at crucial moments, from their chance to exercise power; they did this because they had some instinct about their ideals – or about their legends. Trotsky in his autobiography said the reason why he did not make a serious bid for power in Russia after Lenin's death was because he could not face the boring and squalid day-to-day procedures necessary for power: he too became ill (he got cold feet, literally, while duck shooting).

If Tom could not laugh at himself in public it was because he had put himself up on a stage and you cannot laugh at yourself on a stage or you destroy the illusion. Laughter is a sort of safety-valve which stops energy running away with itself: there is inevitably something self-destructive about people who cannot laugh. But legends are often to do with people who risk being self-destructive. Tom had a chance of power at a time

The family bathing at Savehay Farm

Cimmie's victory at Stoke, 1929

Ramsay MacDonald writing the Labour Party manifesto in the loggia at Savehay Farm, 1929

Tom fencing

Nicholas catching tiddlers

At Savehay Farm, 1930: Nicholas, Vivien, W.E.D. Allen and child, W.J. Brown, Countess Karoli, Aneurin Bevan; (right) Tom with Harold Macmillan

Venice, 1932: Cimmie, Tom Mitford, Doris Castlerosse, Diana Guinness, Tom

Rome, April 1933: Tom and (top right) Cimmie at the March Past

Last picture of Cimmie with her children; in the Rose Garden, May 1933

CHAPTER 19

The New Party

The New Party, which Tom started in March 1931, lasted for less than a year. It did not attract the number of people Tom had hoped for, and it failed dramatically and almost ridiculously: but the people most concerned did not seem to mind its failure, they appeared to see it as some sort of clearing-ground from which they could move on.

While Tom lay ill with pleurisy it was left to Cimmie and John Strachey and Oliver Baldwin (who in fact called himself an Independent) to launch the New Party: they undertook the speaking tour round the country which had been arranged for Tom. The *Manchester Guardian* commented 'Lady Cynthia contributes intensity, Mr Strachey states the case, and Mr Oliver Baldwin provides comic relief'. The 'case' was that set out in the *Mosley Manifesto* of a few months earlier: it was elaborated in yet another pamphlet under the signatures of Allan Young, John Strachey, W. J. Brown and Aneurin Bevan. The latter allowed his name to remain on the pamphlet although he had not resigned from the Labour Party. The pamphlet, entitled 'A National Policy', went into greater detail about the administrative machinery it advocated for putting its policy (or indeed any policy) into effect.

In general Parliament must be relieved of detail. Its essential function must be to place in power an Executive Government of the character to be decided upon by the nation at the last election; to maintain it in power until and unless it commits some action which in the opinion of Parliament is deserving of censure; in that event to turn it out by way of direct Vote of Censure and appeal to the Electorate . . .

It is essential that a small inner Cabinet Committee consisting of five or six men should be formed . . . This proposal has been described as an attempt to set up five Dictators. No accusation could be more

inept. There is nothing either more or less democratic about entrust-
ing the ultimate responsibility for the decision of the Government to
a Cabinet of five men who are free from all other work than entrust-
ing them as at present to a Cabinet of twenty men who are too busy
to give real consideration to their most vitally important decisions . . .

Broadly we say to the Electorate: Choose whatever Government
you like. But when you have chosen it, for heavens sake let it get on
with the job without being frustrated and baffled at every turn by
a legislative and administrative procedure designed for the express
purpose of preventing things being done . . .

Cimmie and John Strachey and Oliver Baldwin delivered this message
round the country: they attracted audiences of several thousands: but
they found that they were increasingly heckled, and that sometimes
their meetings were broken up by what appeared to be organised gangs
of Labour militants and Communists. The communist paper *The Daily
Worker* was in fact already referring to the New Party as 'fascist': the
militants were behaving with the special fury of people who feel they
have been betrayed by their old heroes. But the New Party, if it was
to get anywhere, depended on public meetings: it had little time to build
up an organisation that would be accepted to deal with the crisis.

Tom lay in bed with a temperature of a hundred and five. He wrote
to Harold Nicolson 'The illness has been a strange blow of fate – the
first serious collapse of my life, and what a moment!' At the end of
March he went with Cimmie to recuperate at Lord Beaverbrook's villa
in the South of France. Also with them was his sister-in-law Baba, who
herself had been seriously ill after the birth of twins and had been
recuperating with Tom and Cimmie at Savehay Farm.

Up till now Tom had had the naive and presumably Marxist idea that
an appeal to reason could always if necessary be made over the heads
of a stupid Cabinet, a cowardly Parliamentary Labour Party and even
a hysterical Party Conference, to an enlightened proletariat who in some
way would be a fair judge. Marxists had to think this because if they
did not – knowing as they did their non-proletarian colleagues – what
hope was there for reason? But now if this belief was to go or be
rendered ineffectual – if really it was members of the proletariat who
were shouting down or allowing to be shouted down the reasonable
exposition of New Party policy – what was there left?

Tom had, perhaps, been preparing for something like this. He had
for long been perfecting his techniques as a mob orator: he seems
consciously to have faced questions about the limitations of rationality

and the fact that the exercise of power is perhaps always to do with manipulations of emotion. Rationality puts a burden on people by asking them to think for themselves; it is apt to make them feel inadequate. The manipulation of emotion achieves some sort of power by making people feel that they belong.

It was remarked that Tom was different when he emerged from his sick bed: he was less patient; it was as if he had personally come to terms with having stepped outside the rules of games. The first big test of the New Party was to be at a by-election at Ashton-under-Lyne in Lancashire on April 30th 1930. Allan Young was standing as the New Party candidate. Tom had played no part in the run-up to the election: the brunt of the day-to-day electioneering had been borne by Cimmie. Jack Jones, a left-wing orator hired by the New Party at five pounds a week, wrote of Cimmie at the time:

> Cynthia Mosley was both able and willing. With me she must have addressed at least a score of very big outdoor crowds during the campaign, and also scores of 'in our street' talks to women. Whilst others in the first flight were looking important in the presence of reporters, or talking about the holding of the floating Liberal vote, the cornering of the Catholic vote, and preparing their speeches for the well-stewarded big meetings indoors each evening, Cynthia Mosley was out getting the few votes that were got.

Tom appeared on the scene six days before the election. His presence had an electrifying effect. He addressed an indoor meeting of six or seven thousand. Harold Nicolson reported:

> Tom then gets up to make his speech and profits enormously by a few interruptions from Labour supporters. He challenges Arthur Henderson to meet him tomorrow in open debate and this stirs the audience to enthusiasm and excitement. Having thus broken the ice, he launches on an emotional oration on the lines that England is not yet dead and that it is for the New Party to save her. He is certainly an impassioned revivalist speaker, striding up and down the rather frail platform with great panther steps and gesticulating with a pointing, and occasionally a stabbing, index; with the result that there was a real enthusiasm towards the end and one had the feeling that 90% of the audience were certainly convinced at the moment.

Harold Nicolson was a newcomer to politics. He had just resigned from the diplomatic service and was working as a journalist on the *Evening Standard*. He had been attracted to the New Party, he said, out of '(1) Personal affection and belief in Tom: (2) A conviction that a serious crisis was impending and that our economic and parliamentary system must be transformed if collapse were to be avoided.' He got carried along by the sense that Tom engendered of being in touch with great events; also by the sense of fun.

Another leading figure in the New Party was Peter Howard, captain of the England Rugby Football team. Harold Nicolson wrote to Cimmie 'Peter Howard I have a feeling is bowled over by your charms – but so are we all'. Peter Howard had organised a group of young men from Oxford to protect New Party meetings: these were referred to in the press as 'Mosley's Biff Boys' or 'strapping young men in plus fours'. The emphasis of the New Party was on youth: a journalist wrote of the party headquarters at Ashton-under-Lyne – 'Young men with fine foreheads and an expression of faith dash from room to room carrying proof-sheets and manifestos: I have seldom seen so many young people so excited and so pleased'.

When the election results were announced the Conservatives had got 12,420 votes, Labour 11,005, and Allan Young of the New Party 4,472 – just saving his deposit. This result was not discreditable to a party only two months old but it was not as good as Tom had hoped: he found, as he was so often to find later, that the enthusiasm he engendered as a one-man-band did not effectively last until his audience went to the poll. But it had lasted long enough, Labour supporters imagined, for the intervention of the New Party to have ensured that the Conservatives won what had previously been held to be a safe Labour seat. In fact, the New Party's intervention had probably somewhat lessened what was a general swing against Labour throughout the country. But political crowds want scapegoats, not analysis.

The crowd of Labour militants outside the Town Hall shouted for vengeance. Tom, standing on the steps, turned to John Strachey and said 'That is the crowd that has prevented anyone doing anything in England since the war'. John Strachey commented – 'At that moment British Fascism was born: at that moment of passion, and of some personal danger, Mosley found himself almost symbolically aligned against the workers.' Tom himself commented later that what he had meant was that 'dedicated agents and warriors of communism always play on the anarchy inherent on the Left of Labour to secure confusion, disillusion and ultimately the violence which is essential to their long term plan'.

In the Town Hall, Tom arranged for Cimmie to be smuggled out of a back door; then, in the face of the crowd which in Jack Jones's words 'had all the appearances of an American lynching crowd', Tom – 'white with rage, not fear' – led his small party through the mob 'howling at him and calling him names'. He 'smiled contemptuously' at them. Jack Jones added – 'An exciting experience it was.' Tom, to Jack Jones's apparent surprise, seemed 'almost cheerful'. ·

Through the summer discussions went on amongst the New Party leaders – there was an Executive Committee that met almost daily in offices in Great George Street – not so much about policy, as about what was to be done about the difficulty of getting the policy heard. Labour militants did not deny the attacks were organised: the hostility was not discouraged by Tom's old parliamentary colleagues: A. V. Alexander referred to the 'traitorous Mosley'; Emmanuel Shinwell to 'Brutus . . . responsible for "the stiletto in the back".' Young men who had come fresh into the New Party wanted to build up a Youth Movement into a force that would be trained to defend the speakers against physical attack: John Strachey and others continued to be alarmed at this. They agreed that it was right that meetings should be protected from organised disruption, but they feared that a group of young men trained in judo and boxing for this purpose would grow into a proto-fascist defence force. Also they seemed to feel that demonstrations by workers, however suspect, were in some way sacrosanct. But it was difficult to see how one could have the protection without the discipline. The activists seemed to have logic on their side: the intellectuals an instinct.

Everything depended of course on what sort of balance was struck between the two; or rather what sort of skill Tom had in appearing to control or to embrace the two. He announced that in the light of the violence directed against Cimmie during her speaking tour earlier in the year a body of young men would indeed be trained; but they would 'rely on the good old English fist.'

During summer there were weekends at which the intellectuals exercised their conundrums. In Hampstead, John Strachey, Harold Nicolson and Cyril Joad debated – What happens to the New Party, which is dedicated to dealing with a crisis, if the crisis does not come? Harold Nicolson suggested that the party should continue with a programme advocating 'Sacrifice, Discipline, Service, Courage and Energy of Thought'. Cyril Joad asked – 'But how can *we* put over such a programme?' At Savehay Farm there was a congress at which John Strachey delivered his 'good old Marxian speech' (Jack Jones); Tom spoke 'soulfully of the Corporate State of the future' and 'a young man called Winckworth called for a revival of the Attic Spirit' which would involve the New Party in attracting people with 'the heads of thinkers on the bodies of athletes'. Cyril Joad riposted 'Be careful you don't attract people with the heads of athletes on the bodies of thinkers'. Tom appreciated the wit: but he would have wished, as usual, to cut through the riddles. During the Congress at Savehay Farm, Harold Nicolson recorded – 'The Youth Movement swam'.

In a speech at the Cannon Street Hotel, in London, on June 30th 1931, Tom announced that his movement was trying to create 'a new political psychology, a conception of national renaissance, of new mankind and of vigour'. John Strachey and Allan Young were in the audience: they decided to make a positive show of their alarm. The next day Strachey addressed a meeting of the Youth Movement and spoke against the idea of any disciplined use of violence to counteract violence: a version of his statement appeared in the *Daily Herald*. At the next meeting of the New Party Executive Tom (according to Harold Nicolson) 'reprimands Strachey in terms which, if addressed to me, would have caused the most acute embarrassment'. But Harold Nicolson went on – 'I do not deny that I was impressed by the force of discipline in Tom's speech. It is quite evident that he will allow no independence to any member of the party and that he claims an almost autocratic position. I do not myself object to this, since if we are to be the thin end of the wedge we must have an extremely sharp point and no splinters. I wonder, however, how long other members of the Council will tolerate such domination.' And later – 'I think that Tom at the bottom of his heart really wants a fascist movement'.

One of the hopes that Tom was playing with at this time was that he, and some of his party, might be able to join Churchill and Lloyd George in making up a 'National Opposition' if, in the face of the continuing economic crisis, a National Government was formed by MacDonald and Baldwin. Tom drove to Archibald Sinclair's house to have talks with Lloyd George: on the way he told Harold Nicolson that he thought that Allan Young and John Strachey would be soon leaving the New Party: he said this with little regret. He called them the 'pathological element' – apparently because of their timidity in the face of violence. (Tom used to tease John Strachey by telling him he was 'governed by Marx from the waist up and Freud from the waist down.') Nothing much came of the talks with Lloyd George. Everyone on the fringes of power seemed to be trying to charm everyone else, and to be waiting to see what would happen. Perhaps no one, in the face of the frightening prospects of 1931, really wanted power.

John Strachey then produced a memorandum in which he advocated

making 'a progressive break with that group of powers of which France
and the USA are leaders' and entering into 'close economic relations
with the Russian government'. This was a direct challenge to Tom, to
test his left-wing or right-wing commitment. There was also a dispute
in the New Party Executive about unemployment benefit: it seemed to
John Strachey and Allan Young that Tom was not taking a strong
enough stand against proposed government cuts. Tom made con-
cessions here: but he rejected Strachey's pro-Russian proposals since
they 'contradicted directly the whole basis of the policy we have long
agreed together'. Then John Strachey and Allan Young resigned.

They prepared a joint letter to be made public: but each wrote
privately to Tom.

July 22nd 1931

7 North Street.
Westminster.

Dear Tom,

I think you will agree that the differences between us which have
become apparent during recent meetings are too serious to be left
where they are. In fact they are really so wide as to make argument
impossible. It is quite clear to me that your whole outlook is becoming more and more Conservative: already you regard any other
outlook as 'pathological'.

In these circumstances further collaboration between us would be
nothing but a handicap to both of us. So I send you my resignation
from the New Party and its Council.

I intend making this resignation public tomorrow unless you want
to talk about it first. If you do ring me up tomorrow morning at
North St (Vic 3681) But I don't see what purpose will be served by
such a talk – and frankly I dread it. One can't have worked as closely
with and for anyone as I have tried to work with and for you ever
since I came into politics, and not feel pretty smashed up by such a
separation.

We have obviously quite different conceptions of what the New
Party ought to be and of how it could succeed. Naturally it seems to
me that it is you who have changed. No doubt you feel that it is I who
have changed. What more is there to say? – except for me to thank
you very genuinely for all the kindness and I believe affection you
have shown me.

Yours
John

22nd July 1931   as from – 10 Brookland Rise
                                           N.W. 11

Dear Tom,

   ... Since your illness and the Ashton bye-election there has been a change in your whole attitude of mind which has disturbed me more than I can say. Your semi-public and private statements with regard to the Youth Movement, India, Unemployment Insurance, Russia, and the general function and purpose of the New Party has made me ashamed of my own association with it. Our difficulties in launching the party were due to the doubts and suspicions of our friends that you would succumb to the pressure and attraction of right-wing views. I contested this strongly at the time – placing reliance on your strength and judgement. Your attitude in the last two months seems to have proved me wrong and the critics right. From the beginning I have been aware of the dangers implicit in a movement such as ours. These dangers could only have been avoided by a leadership above suspicion as far as working-class interests were concerned. You have not given us that leadership but rather have provided grounds for the suspicion that the party would become Hitlerist, Fascist, and ultimately anti-working class. I cannot be associated with a party which is even open to that suspicion, and I now tender you my resignation.

   I will always remember with gratitude your kindness to me. But I must pursue the course which my conscience and intelligence dictates.

Yours,
Allan Young

Tom got in touch with Harold Nicolson who was working at the *Evening Standard* and asked him to go round to see John Strachey and Allan Young and to try to get them at least to postpone the public announcement of their resignation which was to be made at six o'clock that evening. Harold Nicolson did not manage to get in touch with them till 5.30 – they were apparently in hiding – then he found them in John Strachey's house, where:

Allan Young descends to the dining room looking pale and on the verge of a nervous breakdown. I say that Tom suggests that they should not openly resign at the moment but 'suspend' their resignation till 1st December by which date they will be able to see whether their suspicions of our fascism are in fact justified. Allan might have

accepted this, but at that moment John Strachey enters. Tremulous
and uncouth he sits down and I repeat my piece. He says that it would
be impossible for him to retain his name on a Party while taking no
part in that Party's affairs ... He then begins, quivering with emotion,
to indicate some of the directions in which Tom has of late abandoned
the sacred cause of the workers. He says that ever since his illness he
has been a different man. His faith has left him. He is acquiring a Tory
mind. It is a reversion to type. He considers socialism a 'pathological
condition'. John much dislikes being pathological. His great hirsute
hands twitch neurotically as he explained to us, with trembling voice,
how unpathological he really is.

Harold Nicolson failed to get them to withdraw or to postpone their
resignations. He commented – 'Undoubtedly the defection of John and
his statement that we were turning fascist will do enormous electoral
harm to the party. Politically however it will place Tom in a position
where with greater ease he can adhere to Lloyd George and Winston.'

Tom, however, was now only going through the motions of playing
at party politics; he was dreaming more and more of the time when he,
as an effective leader, might be in direct relationship to the masses which
he was sure was the only way of getting anything done. Harold
Nicolson recorded – 'Tom conceives of great mass meetings with loud
speakers – 50,000 people at a time'. For the organisation of them, the
Youth Movement would of course be vitally important. Tom drafted
a farewell note to Allan Young: 'I want just to tell you how sorry I am
our association has ended. It has meant more to me than most things
in my life. As we go on the sorrow of things deepens'.

Harold Nicolson told Cyril Joad that he was staying on in the New
Party because 'I felt it was the only party which gave to intelligence a
position above possessions or the thoughts of Karl Marx'. Cyril Joad said
he was leaving the party because it was about to 'subordinate intelligence
to muscular bands of young men'.

At the end of July the government received the report of a committee
it had set up to advise on the economic situation: the main recommendation was that unemployment benefit, already pitiful, should be
cut by twenty per cent. The New Party held a rally at Renishaw Park,
in Yorkshire, the home of the Sitwells, at which 40,000 people were
present. Tom declared 'We invite you to something new, something
dangerous'. Then politicians went on holiday.

Tom and Cimmie went, as usual, to the South of France. They left
Harold Nicolson virtually in charge of the office at home. He was

Rules of the Game

making preparations for the New Party weekly newspaper, *Action*, which was to be launched in the autumn and of which he was to be editor. The New Party had based its appeal on being the party that would be ready to deal with the crisis when it came: everyone agreed it was coming and it would be the worst economic crisis for a hundred years. Tom was all his life contemptuous of people who 'even for the few years at the height of their responsibilities cannot be serious'. But the trouble was that however accurate had been his forecast of the crisis, he had succeeded in putting himself in a position in which he had no responsibility for dealing with it. Harold Nicolson wrote to him:

> I recognise that people may say that at the gravest crisis in present political history you prefer to remain upon the Mediterranean. On the other hand, I do not see what you would do were you here at this moment; and I feel that it is more dignified to be absent and aloof than to be present and not consulted.

CHAPTER 20

Politics as Farce

The extraordinary position that Tom had got himself into – that of preparing for a crisis by finding himself able to do nothing about it when it came – was the result of two major assumptions: the first, that the old parties would disintegrate in the face of the crisis so that it would be better not to be tainted by their failures of responsibility; the second, that he himself would be in charge of a party so patently free of the farcical aspects of the old parties that people would soon turn to him and give him responsibility.

The nature of the crisis had seemed to him to be simple: if the welfare of every country in the world depended on its selling more than it bought on an open world market, then in fact only those countries would succeed which could sell the cheapest goods by paying the lowest wages. It was out of the question for British workers to accept ever lower wages: so there would be crisis. This might take the form of bankruptcy or even of war – by which other countries' economic competitiveness might be broken. But for this sort of crisis too the old parties were not equipped to deal: and in any case, any party led by Tom would be dedicated to preventing war.

The success of a party run by Tom in dealing with a crisis would hinge on a body of dedicated men who would run, without the supervision of Parliament, the 'closed' economic area of Great Britain-and-Empire by means of statutory powers to control wages and prices, industrial investment, a floating exchange rate and the bulk buying of raw materials. Everything would depend on the efficient, incorruptible nature of these 'new' men: without such characteristics they would just have more power to make more muddles and to act more deviously than the old. Tom for some time had recognised this: in his *Sunday Express* article of 1930 he had suggested that no political programme such as his could work without men of 'a hard, realistic type, hammered into existence on the anvil of great ordeal'. Now, a year later, the ordeal was here.

Half way through August an Austrian bank went bankrupt; foreign depositors called in their money from London; there was what is called 'a run on the pound'; gold reserves (Britain was still on the gold standard) were depleted; it was believed – this was contemporary economic dogma – that international 'confidence' could only be restored if there were cuts in public spending at home. This in effect meant the immediate implementation of the recommendations of the report which had advocated the cutting of unemployment benefit. A large proportion of the Labour Cabinet would not agree to this: they had however no practical alternative suggestions. Ramsay MacDonald suggested to the King that a National Government might be formed consisting of members of all parties: this would obviate everyone's tendency to wish to pass responsibility on to others. Also it might prevent Britain being forced off the gold standard; which eventuality would be, according to dogma again, a disaster. The King agreed. A general election could follow later.

The formation of a National Government under MacDonald cut from under the New Party much of the ground on which its appeal had been based – that of aiming to put in control of the country men who were above the customary game of party politics and in theory at least dedicated to the business of getting a job done. The only serious appeal that the New Party might now have against the National Government would be if it could be seen to be composed of the type of people more likely to do a job well.

Harold Nicolson had been to Manchester to interview prospective New Party candidates. He recorded in his diary:

> They vary from an old lunatic called Holden to a boy of 21 called Branstead who scarcely knows what the House of Commons is. Only one of the many we interview – a wild-eyed nymphomaniac called Miss —— is at all a possible candidate . . . The party has quite clearly not as yet attracted the better class of manual worker.

Slightly later Harold Nicolson reported to Tom in the South of France. His letter is dated August 13th – three days after Ramsay MacDonald had been recalled to London to face the 'run on the pound' and ten days before the public announcement of the formation of the National Government. Of the people mentioned in Harold Nicolson's letter

Sellick Davies was the New Party Treasurer, F. K. Box was the Chief Party Agent, and Dr Robert Forgan was, together with Tom and Cimmie and a recruit from the Conservatives W. E. D. Allen, one of the four remaining New Party MPs.

4 King's Bench Walk.

August 14th 1931   Temple W.C.2.

My dear Tom,

This is going to be a long letter and illegible in parts. It will also, at least at first, be a painful letter. The reason why it will be illegible is that I am using the typewriter of Mr Hamlyn, the Genera Manager of *Action*. To which I am not attuned. The reason why it will be painful is Sellick Davies. I begin with the bloody part. The rest will be cheery enough.

First the iniquities (so I am assured) of Sellick. Box rang me up today in a state of perturbation. Box was perturbed. It seems that he had received a request from Sellick who is now with the admirable Forgan at Berneval sur mer (that obscure Dieppoise resort where the unfortunate Mr Wilde retired after endurances of Reading Gaol). Sellick asked for £25 from the till. Box sent for the books. The books disclosed that Sellick had been withdrawing from from the said till sums which even to me appeared excessive. And for these sums he had provided vouchers which, although proof of his hospitable instincts, were by no means proof of his capacity as Treasurer. Box was shocked. So also, to a lesser degree, was I. I managed to convince Box that a chartered accountant such as Sellick was could scarcelz behave in such a manner unless there was some explanation. We must go careful like. Box was all for calling in other and less Welsh accountants at once. I urged him to consult you. And by this post you will receive a letter which will cause you much distress.

Anyhow we have refused to advance Sellick money for his amusements at the Dieppe Casino. And have done so in a manner which will cause him a certain uneasiness if guilty but no acute displeasure if innocent. The sums involved are not enormous. I think he has been a muddle head. But the fact remains that he is not competent to control our finances, and that som more chartered and less Welsh accountant will have to take his place.

This is unpleasant not only because we cannot face more resignations but also because Sellick has his points. Financial sensibility is obviously a rare quality and one possessed only by those who know nothing of finance...

So much for the bloody part. Now for other more cheering news. (1) The party. I find that the present crisis has enormously increased your prestige. People who treated us as a painful joke five weeks ago are now regarding us with a wild surmise. Men like Keynes are saying you were right all along. I find that 'West End Clubmen' (it is not for nothing that I spent eighteen months at the *Evening Standard*) have adopted quite a different angle towards your movement. People like Middleton Murray in this month's *Adelphi* speak openly in your favour. H. G. Wells today spoke with serious interest about the policy, and Leonard Woolf has written to me asking for full information and pamphlets. These may be straws – but they are straws in an important wind ... (4) *Action*: otherwise the paper which fills all mz thoughts and most of my time. I shall not bother you with details. It is going ahead like a speed-boat. I have engaged the staff and feel they are good. Mr Hamlyn the Manager is a Jew. Mr Joseph the assistant editor may also be a Jew but his point is that he will corrct my tendency to quote Aristotle. A clever young man ...

(the bore about this typewriter is that when I want to say 'Y' it sazs 'z'. The result is ungainly. 'Bz' is not a pretty rendering of the word 'by').

One more point. Would you wish to start off the paper with an article by yourself? 'HAVE I FIZZLED OUT?' seems the right note. It is not essential, but I think we should face that question and I think you can do it best. My God, Tom, if that paper is a dud then I am a dud. It WON'T BE A DUD ...

I think that for once events have moved to help you. Of course the Socialists have cornered Baldwin and are taking your programme leaf by leaf like an artichoke. But that merely increases your opportunity. I find that many people are saying that you will be tempted to join any coalition that is formed. I hope you will if you consider it right to do so and if you are assured of the necessary authority. People always accuse you of being out for yourself. I reply 'Yes, thank God¾ (it is very rude to write God¾ one ought to write God just like that) – I reply 'Yes, thank God, he is one of those people who feel a we should all feel – 'l'etat c'est moír' I mean 'moi'.

Tom – it is fun being with you since you understand where my nonsense begins and where my my sense begins.

But really everying is gling very well, and if we keep faith in ur own intelligence nothing can to wrong

Yours ever
Harold.

P.S. Did you get my memorandum on Foreign Policy? I sent it by registered post but have just discovered that I wrote Villa Uzes or rods to that effect beine memerised by the memory of little bo-peep alis Miss Gordon alias Duchesse D'Uzes. But I hope it turned up all right.

To this letter, surely unique in the annals of letters from editors to newspaper proprietors, Tom, from Antibes, replied – 'It is a joy to have you on the job: do not kill yourself'.

The centre of attraction at Antibes this year (apart from Tom and Cimmie themselves: it was true that they appeared ever more glamorous politicians the further they got from the drab corridors of power) was Michael Arlen, the author of *The Green Hat*, whom Tom, according to Irene, so inspired with New Party propaganda over dinner at Monte Carlo that he, Michael Arlen, considered becoming a party member. Life at Antibes went its usual way: Tom was pursuing someone called Lotsie: I, aged eight, was bitten on the head by a pet monkey: people 'massed again, booted and spurred, and in a relay of cars departed to the dirty pictures at Nice and on to Monte' (Irene).

The history of the New Party is crucial to an understanding of Tom: he stayed in the South of France because he had announced that party politics were absurd: he was acting logically according to his convictions. Even if he had had anything to do with the crisis he would have felt it better to wait, probably, until people turned to him; only then would he feel he had a mandate to put what was required into effect. And was it not the case, as people told him, that his legendary prestige was increasing so long as he remained aloof? But the question remained – what use, in the end, could he make of this prestige?

The affairs of the New Party went their own bizarre way. Dr Robert Forgan wrote from Berneval-sur-Mer:

Dear Tom,

Recent public events in England have more than justified the cry of 'crisis' that we raised so long before anyone else . . . unfortunately I have a crisis of my own. Ever since – imprudently or at least improvidently – I entered Parliament two years ago (and gave up moderately lucrative medical work) I have been in financial difficulties . . . I took to borrowing at ruinous rates of interest until now I find myself in such a mess that I must get the ground cleared somehow . . . Just at the moment the New Party can ill afford to lose another Member of Parliament . . .

There followed the request for a loan of £500. The letter ended somewhat disarmingly – 'Superintending the earth is, for me, far more interesting than keeping one's affairs in order!'

Tom arrived back from Antibes on 26 August, two days after the formation of the National Government. Harold Nicolson met him at Dover, and found him cheerful. Tom said that of course he would be pressing on with New Party plans: he hoped to get six members into the House of Commons so long as a general election did not come before February. But he recognized that it was possible the New Party might fail completely, in which case he would retire from public life for ten years. He explained – 'I have never led a civilised life at all since I entered politics as a boy. I can well afford to wait ten years, to study economics, and even then when I return I shall be no older than Bonar Law was when he first entered politics'.

In later life Tom used to say that he sometimes wished he had taken this advice to himself more literally: he knew that he was no longer interested in conventional manoeuvrings for power; he was interested in the presentation of the embodiment of an idea. For this, it was not clear how much there was urgency: what was important was the effort to formulate and give substance to the idea.

For the next four months the New Party end-game was played out to what must have been the bewilderment of a dwindling band of spectators. The first number of *Action*, edited by Harold Nicolson, came out on October 8th: it was a tabloid-sized paper of 32 pages and cost 2d. The tone was set by the first editorial: 'We have adopted certain watchwords – the first is truth: the second courage: the third intelligence: the fourth vigour.' Tom on the front page wrote 'We must create a movement which grips and transforms every phase and aspect of national life.' On the inside pages there was an article by Dr Forgan on old age ('The Commonest Disease in the Wide World') a science article by Gerald Heard ('From Faraday to Kapitza – Great Cambridge Dynamo') a gardening page by Vita Sackville West ('How To Plant And Design Beds') and book reviews of *The Waves* and *Sanctuary* by Harold Nicolson. The next few numbers contained 'Did the Werewolf Exist?' by Gerald Heard and 'Vagabond Camp – Tales of Great Journeys' by Eric Muspratt. Tom continued to emphasise the need to 'imbue the nation with a new idea and a new faith' and to insist that a 'virile group' should be returned to the House of Commons. The editor however announced as the general election approached – 'If, as is far more likely, the New Party has done extremely badly . . . the note will be one of quiet manliness; of resigned British pluck'.

Tom himself carried on powerfully as his one-man-band. On September 8th he made his last major speech in Parliament: he attacked Labour for having followed conservative policies of deflation: he advocated following Keynes's advice to borrow money to finance work for the unemployed: he perorated 'the way out is not the way of the monk but the way of the athlete . . . the simple question before the house . . . is whether Great Britain is to meet its crisis lying down or standing up.' On September 20th he was addressing a meeting of an estimated 20,000 people at Glasgow: he referred to the Labour Party as 'a Salvation Army that took to its heels on the day of Judgement': he was attacked by a communist group with razors. His bodyguard, including Peter Howard and the ex-welter-weight boxing champion Kid Lewis, fought off the attack, but a stone hit Tom on the head. (Tom used to tell the story how he had asked Kid Lewis why he had not punched more ruthlessly, and Kid Lewis had said he was afraid of killing someone). Tom's speech however had been heard through the use of loudspeakers: the meeting, Peter Howard reported, was 'really rather a success'. Afterwards Harold Nicolson noted – 'Tom says this forces us to be fascist and that we no longer need hesitate to create our trained and disciplined force. We discuss their uniforms: I suggest grey flannel trousers and shirts.' He also suggested the emblem of a marigold in the buttonhole.

Tom agreed with Harold Nicolson that it was important that the Youth Movement should not appear too military: on the other hand – 'the working class have practically no sense of being ridiculous in the way that we have, and their very drab lives gives them a thirst for colour and for drama'.

On the whole, however, I think that Peter Howard is just the man to hold the right balance. He must see that Mr Kid Lewis is invariably accompanied on his tours by Mr Sacheverell Sitwell – in a Siamese connection they might well form the symbol of our Youth Movement!

Through Harold Nicolson and *Action* Tom was in touch with the Sitwells, the Leonard Woolfs, with other writers and artists: he was also through the Youth Movement in touch with a growing band of toughs. But the true Siamese connection existed within himself. After a wildly enthusiastic and peaceful meeting at the Free Trade Hall the *Manchester Guardian* reported –

In his 35th year Oswald Mosley is already thickly encrusted with legend. His disposition and his face are those of a raider, a corsair ... We speak metaphorically; but who could doubt ... that here was one of those root-and-branch men who have been thrown up from time to time in the religious, political and business story of England.

Then after a meeting at the Rag Market at Birmingham, the *Birmingham Post* reported that it was the presence of the Youth Movement that 'immediately set up a militant feeling in the few who were out for trouble' with the result that there was such a fight that Tom and his bodyguard were afterwards charged with assault. They were acquitted: the magistrate agreeing with Tom's counsel's opinion about the un-likelihood of a speaker hiring a large hall for the purpose of beating up his own audience. Also prosecution witnesses were made to look ridiculous by saying that Tom's 'provocative attitude' was due to the 'smile on his face'. But the two sides of the legend were becoming established in people's minds – that of the hero and the thug.

The general election took place on October 27th. Six months ago the New Party had talked about putting up four hundred candidates: in the event it put up twenty four. All but two lost their deposits. Tom saved his, but came bottom of the poll with 10,834 votes at Cimmie's old constituency of Stoke. Harold Nicolson lost his deposit standing for the Combined Universities: Kid Lewis polled 154 votes at Whitechapel. Cimmie herself had not stood: she was said to be suffering from 'over-strain': she was also pregnant.

The New Party had been in a hopeless position in terms of practical politics at the election. It had campaigned on a programme of 'mobil-ising national forces to revive trade; linking up with the Dominions to help the export trade; scientific protection of the home market and a General Powers Bill to give the government powers of rapid action.' All these points with the exception of the last had been covered by the manifestos of the National Government; and there had been promises of decisive action of course too. The New Party could not even cam-paign as the party of opposition, because the Labour Party had broken away from Ramsay MacDonald and was itself in opposition to the MacDonald-Conservative-Liberal government. The New Party had nothing of substance to say to the electorate except that it had been the party which had foretold the crisis and that it was unlikely that the crisis would be solved by the people who had failed to prevent it.

Tom believed that the government of 'the old men who have laid waste the power and the glory of our land' would collapse within a short time and that then politicians would be faced by more strenuous problems than those of collecting votes. This conviction was not unreasonable. Shortly before, there had been the naval mutiny at Invergordon when sailors, faced with the proposal to cut their pay by ten per cent, had refused to turn out for duty. Already the Government had had to take Britain off the gold standard – which action it had ostensibly come into existence to prevent. People other than Tom felt that ordinary structures of society were cracking up; that battles for power would soon have to be won not at elections, but in the streets.

Against this background *Action* continued on its haphazard way. After the debacle of the election (there were no details printed in it of the election results) the editor wrote 'Are we downhearted? Yes we are!' and Gerald Heard's science article was on 'Will Eels Show Us Where Lost Continents Lay?' However in the next number there was a new feature by Peter Cheyney, the crime writer, whom Harold Nicolson had described in his diary as 'a Jew fascist – a most voluble, violent and unpleasant type'. This feature was entitled 'Cutting out the Bunk in Great Britain' and it referred to the 'Nupa Youth Movement' and the 'Nupa Shock Movement' – 'Nupa' being toughened-up jargon for 'New Party'. Peter Cheyney wrote:

In both these movements he [the young man of today] will learn realism as opposed to bunk, vibrant nationalism as opposed to sloppy internationalism, discipline as opposed to the post-war ideal of sloth, and a comradeship unknown to the Red 'comrades' of the sickly sickle . . . You will meet Nupa. It will find you in its own way. Its programme . . . aims at the establishment of a country-wide system of Nupa-Shock-Propaganda Controls by June 1933 and the completely organised Political-Shock-Youth Movement by June 1935.

Harold Nicolson's friends wrote amongst themselves in horror at this style (Raymond Mortimer to Edward Sackville West: 'When I walk in the streets and see posters – *Action* edited by Harold Nicolson – *The Prime Minister Needs Kicking* by Oswald Mosley – I desire to vomit'). But Raymond Mortimer himself still wrote an article for *Action* ('The Reasons Why I Prefer The Present'); and so did Osbert Sitwell, Peter Quennell, Christopher Isherwood, and Alan Pryce-Jones ('The World Is Neither Large Nor Remarkable'). The circulation had dropped from an initial 160,000 to 50,000 at the time of the election: by December it was under 20,000 and was losing £340 a week. There did not seem to be much point in its going on.

The last number appeared on December 31st. Harold Nicolson wrote – 'We recognise with cold calm that our failure is for the moment complete ... we were too highbrow for the general public and too popular for the highbrow ... The first number was a dud. We were thereafter not quick enough to reduce our printing order ... (People) accused the paper of lacking punch. Perhaps they were right. Yet it is difficult to punch fairly.'

Tom on the front page wrote:

We were never fools enough to delude ourselves into the belief that we could build a new political party of a normal character in normal conditions. We shall be a movement born of crisis and ordeal or we shall be nothing. If that crisis does not mature we shall be nothing, for the country for perfectly good reasons will not require us ... In that case we can all retire more happily to more congenial occupations, satisfied that at least we have done our best to meet a menace which might have overwhelmed this country but which fortunately did not mature.

However at the end – and printed in italics as if it were being pointed out to his readers that they were being involved in some sort of change of gear – Tom launched into one of his perorations. Under the headline 'We Are Pierced and Broken – We Advance', he wrote:

Better the great adventure, better the great attempt for England's sake, better defeat, disaster, better far the end of that trivial thing called a Political Career than stifling in a uniform of Blue and Gold, strutting and posturing on the stage of Little England, amid the scenery of decadence, until history, in turning over an heroic page of the human story, writes of us the contemptuous postscript: 'These were the men to whom was entrusted the Empire of Great Britain, and whose idleness, ignorance and cowardice left it a Spain.' We shall win; or at least we shall return upon our shields.

Tom's perorations were demonstrations of the style of his heart, of his dedication, in a more profound way perhaps than was his logic. The style was that of one who gets glory from battle: it had none of the vulgarity of Peter Cheyney's call for a Nupa Political-Shock-Youth-Movement; but the chords it touched were inevitably, if tragically, sometimes the same.

During the autumn in spite of (or because of) Tom's increasingly

apparent failure with the New Party there had been continuing moves
to try to get him back into the conventional political fold. For a time
the New Party MPs had sat on the Conservative benches. Then
Randolph Churchill had come to see Tom on a mission from his father
Winston to ask him whether he would still consider joining a band of
'Tory toughs' in opposition to the National Government. Tom had
asked Randolph why Winston wanted him: Randolph had replied
'Because without you he will not be able to get hold of the young men.'
(Harold Nicolson, who recorded this story, added 'Tom is very pleased
with that'). Tom also had had talks with Neville Chamberlain to see
whether the New Party could make some electoral deal with the
National Government. But it was still obvious that Tom wanted
seriously to be involved with none of these moves. Harold Nicolson
wrote 'He says that it would be impossible for him to enter the
"machine" of one of the older parties: that by so doing he would again
have to place himself in a strait waistcoat: that he has no desire for power
on those terms'. But by the end of the year the New Party had virtually
ceased to exist: the office in Great George Street was closed down. One
of the last manifestations of the party was, typically, the completion of
a propaganda film exhorting people to join it. In the film there were
shots of MPs asleep and then crowds rushing forwards shouting
'England wants Action!' The film was banned in cinemas on the grounds
that it might bring Parliament into disrepute.

With part of himself Tom might well have been happy, as he had said
he would be, to 'retire to more congenial occupations' while the crisis
did not come to a head in the way he had expected it to. He and Cimmie
were seen at a great many parties and night clubs that winter: he created
excitement and interest wherever he went. He had the style of the
temporarily defeated but still potentially justified hero. At the very end
of 1931, after cataloguing the disasters of the year and of his association
with Tom, Harold Nicolson could still write – 'yet in spite of all this,
what fun life is!'

Out of all Tom's political involvement for the past thirteen years
there remained only one practical manifestation – the embryonic
NUPA Youth Movement. This with its 'Rugger, Cricket, Boxing,
Fencing and Billiards' and 'Talks By Famous People Every Tuesday' at
122a King's Road, was the embodiment of that other part of Tom
which, whatever the circumstances, would always be concerned with
returning, or not, upon its shield.

CHAPTER 21

Steps to Fascism

Cimmie's practical involvement in politics virtually ceased after her efforts to launch the New Party during the spring and summer of 1931. After this she seems to have lost heart. She had written an article in the *Daily Sketch* in May – 'There is something in the very air of the House [of Commons], something indefinable, which daunts me. I think it is the thought that it does not really matter what you say, that it will have no effect on anyone at all, and that you might as well not say it.' In a letter to Tom she had written of 'the horrible dreary list of engagements and meetings at Stoke which seem 10 times worse as I am so absolutely wretched and miserable.' Almost her last public speech was at a Women's Peace Conference in June: she said 'There is only one way that people could stop war – by refusing to fight'. Harold Nicolson remarked 'Poor Cimmie cannot understand his [Tom's] repudiation of all the things he has taught her to say previously. She was not made for politics. She was made for society and the home.'

At the time of the split in the New Party John Strachey had written to Cimmie – 'To think of the inevitable separation from you is to me *by far* the worst part'. Some months later Allan Young wrote 'I want to meet you, and talk, and touch you, and feel everything is all right again'. She seemed to play a rather distant motherly role to people in the New Party. But in private life, too, there seemed to be something in her that was beginning to give up.

At Antibes in 1931 two days after Tom's return to England, Irene recorded – 'Cim drove herself home at 5.30 am and to my horror fell asleep at the wheel and hit the rocks on the hairpin bend mercifully not on the sea side'. In England, Harold Nicolson noted about Tom and Cimmie – 'They bicker as usual . . . she nags at him . . . but they are really fond of each other in spite of their infidelities'.

Cimmie wrote to Tom – 'I won't repeat any of the things I have said scores and scores of times – please remember them yourself – and I on my part will do everything I can try and think of your point of view . . . I am tired of talking. All I want is something doing, something happening.'

This was about Tom's private affairs. In public life, what Cimmie was at the moment objecting to was Tom's involvement with fascism. In December Lord Rothermere, owner of the *Daily Mail*, approached Tom and said that he was prepared to put the Harmsworth press at Tom's disposal if he, Tom, succeeded in organising a disciplined movement from the remnants of the New Party. Harold Nicolson recorded – 'Cimmie, who is profoundly working-class at heart, does not at all like this Harmsworth connection. Tom pretends he was only pulling her leg. Cimmie wants to put a notice in the *Times* to the effect that she disassociates herself from Tom's fascist tendencies. We pass it off as a joke.' Also – when Tom and Harold Nicolson were talking of the approaches made by Winston Churchill and Harold Nicolson had suggested that Tom was 'destined to lead the Tory Party' – Cimmie 'who is violently anti-Tory, screams loudly'.

Cimmie was by this time five months pregnant. She had not stood again for Stoke in the general election partly out of disenchantment with politics but mainly out of fear of another miscarriage. She was not well: she was having trouble with her kidneys. But she went out a lot with Tom to parties during that autumn. They were both now out of Parliament, and there was not much else for them to do. In this area, she could still try to keep up with Tom.

She talked to Harold Nicolson about Tom – 'about his incurable boyishness and *joie de vivre*. She welcomes his fencing as it serves as a safety valve for his physical energy. That in fact is what is wrong with Tom: his energy is more physical than mental.'

Cimmie also told Harold Nicolson that as a result of the Leiter Estate lawsuit which had gone against the Curzon and Suffolk branches of the family in America, and the huge expenses incurred by the New Party, she and Tom were now 'broke'. 'Tom has lost all his money and there are huge overdrafts': they had to live now 'at a rate of £1,000 a year.' During 1932 both Savehay Farm and the house at Smith Square were let; Cimmie and the children went to live in a mews flat behind Tom's flat at Ebury Street, which had previously been occupied by their chauffeur. Reports of their losses, however, were exaggerated.

Tom had taken up fencing again: this was indeed a means of exercising his exuberant energy. It was also probably an excuse, now the House of Commons was not available to him, to be away from home at all hours practising. At fencing he very quickly again became amazingly good. In 1932, at the age of thirty five, and with his injured leg, he was runner-up in the British épée championships. While in training for this he wrote to Cimmie:

> Tiger Boy! Clever lad!
> Army List team turned out with Epée won 2 matches drew one double hit. They asked fight foil after not having one in hand for six months. Among those he defeated 5pts to 2 Army champion and 4th in last world's championship.
> Won 2 matches with foil and lost one.
> Result 6 matches – won 4 lost 1 drew 1.
> Proud Porker. [drawing of a pig with its tail up]
> Hope after her meeting not [drawing of a downcast sheep].

Cimmie seemed to become more at ease with Tom as she advanced with her pregnancy. She had been told to rest, and she stayed at home, or sometimes went with Tom to parties. There was a fashionable craze that winter for watching all-in wrestling at the Gargoyle Club. She did not involve herself in Tom's preparations for fascism.

Harold Nicolson spelt out to Tom the dangers of fascism with a calm, warning voice like that of Bob Boothby the year before.

> I beg Tom not to get mixed up with the fascist crowd. I say that fascism is not suitable to England. In Italy there was a long history of secret societies. In Germany there was a long tradition of militarism. Neither had a sense of humour. In England anything on these lines is doomed to failure and ridicule.
>
> He answers that he will concentrate on clubs and cells within clubs; that a new movement cannot be made within the frame of a political party. I beg him to examine himself carefully and to make certain that his feelings are in no sense governed by anger, disappointment or a desire to get back on those who have let him down. I admit that disasters such as he has experienced in last year are sufficient to upset the strongest character, but I contend that the strength of his own character is to be tested by the patience and balance with which he takes the present eclipse. He says he feels no resentment: that he had expected that the effect of his defeat would be to throw him into a life of pleasure: on the contrary, he feels now bored with night clubs and more interested than ever in serious things. I say that he must now obtain a reputation for seriousness at any cost.

Before 1931 Tom does not seem to have thought much about fascism: he had been outspoken against Mussolini at the time of the invasion of Corfu: he had been in the neighbourhood of an English yacht in Venice which had been blown up by some 'festive young blackshirts'. But by 1932 Mussolini was emerging not only as someone who was giving the word 'fascism' a recognisable meaning, but as the leader of a nationalist revival about some aspects of which it was difficult for even the most sceptical politicians not to be admiring.

In the last number of *Action* it had been announced that Tom and other members of the New Party were going to visit Italy and Germany and 'probably at a later date Russia' to 'study the modern movement in all countries'. By modern movement was meant – 'new political forces born of crisis, conducted by youth and inspired by completely new ideas of economic and political organisation'. In January 1932 Tom set off for Rome: he left Cimmie behind staying with friends in the country and guarding her pregnancy. On his way he stopped off in Paris where he 'spent *reveillon* at the Fabre-Luces' and was 'kept up doing *jeux de société* till 8 am.' (Harold Nicolson). Concerning this, Tom wrote to Cimmie:

> Last night was just her party: wished she was trumpeting her instruction for the games and attendant swains . . . Much dancing in the dark: young Tommy coyly against the wall of course. Then a lovely romp at supper with little puff balls iced in champagne buckets and thrust down ladies' backs (in his mind's ear he could hear her bellows indignant if she had suffered!) Perhaps he better confess that he invented this game, which went with a real swing!

In Rome he was joined by Harold Nicolson and Christopher Hobhouse, a young recruit to the New Party. Tom and Cimmie continued to correspond while he was in Rome. In the background to their letters is the struggle between Tom's interest in fascism (what he called 'fascio') and Cimmie's continuing wariness about it (what he called 'fatio'). In the foreground is what Cimmie had called his increasing 'boyishness'.

January 6th 1932.

Darling Baby Squasher,
Completed 2 days in Rome and what days – yesterday dark and gloomy – today radiant sunshine – lay nudo in his room – flooding in – real sun bath – so wished she was here – nose squashed sideways – turtle on a rock – feel much better after sun.

Royally received and ushered into palatial apartments – thought at first was spontaneous tribute by regime to the British hopeful – learnt later that Quag [Quaglino] of London had written to Quag in Rome saying tiny T was a swell guy who always paid up – rather dashed.

In things that would interest you (roar!!) saw Jane [Princess Jane di San Faustino] last night – same as ever – same people – in same positions – backgammon substituted for bridge ... Jane addressed me as 'beautiful boy' which delighted me (a great Italian doctor next to me at lunch refused to believe I had been in the war and said I could not be more than 25) perfect country! Lunch tomorrow with Jane and a Hesse Prince who was there last night – said he was on Hitler's staff ...

Saw today the newly appointed secretary of the Party – they are arranging for us a resumé of the whole story and methods (trumpet crash!) Poor Tomby is so nervous – everywhere he goes hands go up; but as his tiny paw creeps upward in return he hears in his mind's ear [drawing of an ear] an indignant trumpet which pulls it down again – roar roar. I am seeing everyone and very interested – no panache or mum-indignant – but quiet interest. They all know about us. Except in Jane's drawing room, where I was asked if I was still Bolshevik!!

Thursday we go to the Pontine marshes to see the great reclamation scheme. When I asked why they did not publish their doings like the Russians they said 'We are more interested in achievement than in propaganda.' *One for squashland.* Another on the squasher – The Russians last year took 100 to 150,000 children to holiday camps – the Fascists 250,000. Roads rebuilt, land reclaimed, systems of child welfare and youth training – wa wa wa – (piling it on a bit, but a good show!!)

When Fatio and Fascio resume the stout debate he will be better armed. The most interesting thing is the new psychology – 'Opposition? we do not understand! we believe in "solidarita!"' Political career is then not only career in one's profession' etc. There are some trumpety reasons, but on the whole with stout prejudice she would yet be interested.

I am thinking of slipping up to Milan for fencing for a day or 2 and then back when Nach returns – unfortunately he goes tonight – I watched him training the Olympic foilists and sabreurs tonight – he is marvellous – I fight with them tomorrow – the épéeists are all at Milan. If I come back here to work with Nach I will go straight to Berlin on 21st via Munich (another little interruption trumpet

trumpet suspicious eye). We really learning a tremendous amount, and will be equipped more on return. [drawing of an outraged bird or turtle].

After Cimmie had got Tom's letter about the Fabre-Luces' party in Paris, she had written:

Darling old boy you are a scream —

I do wonder how Rome is going. Longing to hear that. Remember Fatio a bit, and not too Fascio. And do find out about 'the workers' and their conditions and what about wives and children.

Precious mutty you are the only one in the world for me. Bless you and bless you and love and love and love and happiness in abundance and fun and for old Mummy that soon too...

On 8th January Tom wrote from Rome:

Sweet Fatio [drawing of figure with arm raised in the fascist salute] Such a fascinating day. Started early to see great reclamation scheme in Pontine marshes where first time since days of Rome the Pontine waters rush to the sea (Hola Fatio!) escorted by Gelasio Gaetani younger brother of Sermoneta — qualified and worked in America as mining engineer — best type of aristo Fascist — great charmer — would undoubtedly be listed — accompanied by old McClure, G. Jebb, Murray of Embassy, Harold and Hobhouse — had lunch at one of Gaetani's houses — ruined town of Ninpha reclaimed after 5 centuries — 13th century castle of honey-coloured stone where a pope was crowned — complete ruined city of the middle ages — limpid stream with 9lb trout of type imported by Romans from Africa — lunch in castle — wonderful cakes and honey — saw reclamation scheme — fascinating country — buffaloes imported by Hannibal [drawing of a buffalo]: if they had been a little more bellowsome, would have made him quite homesick.

Gaetanis originally owned nearly all land from Rome to Naples and 200 castles — now going in with State in great consortium — the powers of the State are enormous — corporative system interferes immediately with inefficient ownership and management. Everywhere en route *Dopolavoro*, the state assisted club houses of the workers after work (come on fatio, just a sideline that).

Harold who was originally a little shaken by 'Solidarita' is visibly more and more impressed by constructive elements. Young Tom of course maintains a balanced view –

Hurried back just in time for an interview with Mussolini – who was charming and asked a lot of very good questions. He speaks English well. Tomorrow interview minister of Corporatives and later in day fence with crack Italians of Olympic sabre team. Yesterday fought one of the Olympic épéeists and was not at all overwhelmed. May go up to Milan for a day or two as the Olympic épée team train there.

Yesterday lunched with Jane and Prince Philip of Hesse (married Princess Matilda of Italy) was intelligent and is a great Hitler man ...

Rome very dead – backgammon and gambling – nothing else – we have no frivolity – work and read the whole time – all very interesting – WISHES HIS SQUASH WAS HERE – ... They all miss her and send love and happy sniffs XXXX.

Cimmie wrote from Sussex:

Darling Mutty boy,

You really are sweet the lovely letts you write me and I can promise you I simply adore them and look forward to them ever so. The first Rome one arrived this morning and cheered me up no end as I was feeling low-ish – very sick and faint – slightly coldy – and these cursed signs again ...

I had a long letter from Peter [Howard] from Birmingham and he said there was a good nucleus of keen serious young men to form a Youth Section ...

Do stay as long as you want my sweet, I am quite hap-chap and will have lots of people to see me in London and still one or 2 country visits I can arrange ...

Not on the warpath, loving him velly much, full of resolutions which she does hope will stand his return!! and weather 1932 triumph-antly ...

One of the joys of getting Tom's letters, Cimmie added, was that although he took immense pains to write clearly she had to 'read each page again and again before I get it all quite clear and even then there are some words I never get at all!' She did not think 'old Fascio' [Mussolini] sounded too bad: but she still worried about the 'WORKERS'. Tòm said – 'All the great men here look like undergraduates – they are so young and mostly listable'. 'Listable' meant they might go on Cimmie's 'list' of attractive men.

Christopher Hobhouse had come to Rome from Munich where he had talked with Nazis: this was a year before Hitler came to power. Hobhouse reported 'The Nazis think that we of the New Party have tried to do things too much on the grand: we should have begun in the alleys, not in Gordon Square.' Also – 'They think the fact that Tom is not a working class man will be a disadvantage to us.' Christopher Hobhouse said he saw the NUPA Youth Movement turning into something like the Nazi SS.

Argument went on in the Hotel Excelsior. Harold Nicolson insisted 'the party should be constitutional and Tom should enter Parliament'. He read fascist propaganda pamphlets: 'I agree that with this system you can attain a certain degree of energy and efficiency not reached in our own island. And yet, and yet...'

He and Tom went to dine in 'a lovely flat with a view one way to the Villa Medici and the other way all over Rome' Harold Nicolson wrote in his diary:

> Signora Sarfatti is there. She is the friend of Mussolini's whom we met at the Embassy yesterday. A blonde questing woman, the daughter of a Venetian Jew who married a Jew in Milan. It was there that she helped Mussolini on the *Popolo d'Italia* right back in 1914. She is at present his confidante and must be used by him to bring the gossip of Rome to the Villa Torlonia. She says Mussolini is the greatest worker ever known: he rides in the morning, then a little fencing, then work, and then after dinner he plays the violin to himself. Tom asks how much sleep he gets. She answers 'Always nine hours'. I can see Tom doing sums in his head and concluding that on such a time-table Musso cannot be hard-worked at all.

When Tom returned to England the New Party was formally disbanded and his association with Harold Nicolson came to an end. Harold Nicolson wrote 'He is prepared to run the risk of further failure, ridicule and assault, rather than to allow the active forces in this country to fall into other hands.' Also – 'If Tom would follow my example – retire into private life for a bit and then emerge fortified and purged – he will still be Prime Minister of England. But if he gets entangled with the boys' brigade he will be edged gradually into becoming a revolutionary, and into that waste land I cannot follow him.' Harold Nicolson, but not Tom, had been to Berlin after they had left Rome: he had recorded – 'Hitlerism, as a doctrine, is a doctrine of despair.'

This was the last time that Tom was talked about as a probable future Prime Minister. His 'last-chances' in conventional politics had been as numerous as the farewell performances of the most magnificent prima donna: but now this style of things was over. Tom knew he would have to start from the beginning again; building up from cells; parading in the streets. He wanted to do this because old forms of growth seemed degrading to him.

Mussolini sent him two messages from Italy: one was 'not to try the military stunt in England'; the other was to go ahead and call himself fascist. These injunctions seemed somewhat contradictory.

Fascism is a form of activity where what is usually contained in games becomes reality; where what is logic is forced into flesh; where rules are broken and are not replaced. It is a state of mind that does not see that words are different from things; that suggests that what in abstract argument might be desirable can be put into effect with people. Fascism denies that there is anything above decision and justification for decision that can judge their worth; it is a style by which activity seems to be a justification for itself. The drive is towards order: but in so far as there is glimpsed almost from the beginning the fact that orderliness may not be achieved, there are the safeguards of the rhetoric of returning upon one's shield. If the drive to orderliness is towards death, it is still the drive that matters.

There has for the most part evolved in human beings a feeling that however much words are used in justification for drives there is always something slightly different, and more important, at stake: this is a more subtle feeling than that of transcendence: it is a feeling of oneself being part of a whole; of the whole being something other than the sum of the parts of the whole; it is a feeling for the significance of something aesthetic. Fascism denies this sort of aestheticism; it feels no governing shape of the whole. Fascism is an immanence, a sorting out, a tidying-up; the elimination of some things for the ostensible sake of others. Of course, the whole structure may fall down. The point of aestheticism is that it tells what will not fall down: the shape of the whole is more important than the expansion of some of the parts. With fascism, the feeling of 'greatness' is an end in itself.

Tom knew that by embracing fascism he was making some move like a gambler staking all his fortune on one number at roulette: that whether he won or lost, he would never get back to the ordinary political game. The luck he required was that the sort of crisis he had envisaged would turn up: but in his acceptance of this he did not behave like a fascist, for he made few moves to try to bend the rules of the game. He took on all the trappings of fascism; he waited for the number, or the crisis, to turn up; but he did not, curiously, try to fix, as it were, the wheel. In this respect he was politically self-defeating; but he stayed alive.

The story of Tom's fascism is the story of another book. He was seen by orthodox fascists as a rather unsatisfactory fascist: it was to non-fascists that he sometimes seemed almost the most outlandish fascist of all. For how could someone get all dressed up for fascism and then not quite play the ruthless fascist game? Did not this put someone almost beyond belief?

Fascism is to do with ferment, with war, with the challenge of great events. But Tom was a fascist dedicated to stopping war. When he first became a fascist the established fascists called him a 'kosher fascist'. What was frightening about him was that he seemed to be playing some super-game with himself. He seemed to care not about becoming violent nor even ultimately victorious; but about seeing which way a legend might develop.

By the summer of 1932 few people in England were still thinking in terms of the immediate crack-up of the western world. The crisis had come and not of course gone, but was not so much talked about. Newspapers do not bother to report the end of a crisis. It suddenly is boring.

In Tom's private life too things suddenly seemed to be orderly. Cimmie had been ill, but was now ready to have her baby. On April 25th it was born by Caesarian operation – a boy, to be called Michael. Tom was being attentive to Cimmie: on the 11th May, their twelfth wedding anniversary, she wrote to him her most optimistic letter for some time.

> My darling darling – Have a happy time –
> I only want to send you a line at the end of *such* a happy anniversary to say how much I want the next year to be a happy one for us 2 as private people and a successful one for you publicly. How I long for it to be better than beastly 1931 and how much I want above all else for loveliness and understanding and sympathy to be with us and between us . . .

But some time earlier that spring, in his stalk like some knight-errant through the coverts of dinner parties and balls, Tom had come across, as if indeed she were a legendary maiden, a young married girl called

Diana Guinness. Their hostess had told them they would get on well
together: they did not in fact get on too well at first: (Diana was apt
to say at this time 'I'm just an old fashioned liberal'). But then, Diana
was a great prize – at the age of twenty-one she had already gained a
reputation for intelligence and beauty not only in the fashionable world
but in the literary and artistic worlds of London and Paris – and it would
not have seemed to Tom, since Diana appeared unique, that it mattered
very much if they did not get on well at first.

CHAPTER 22

The Greater Britain

People suggested in later life that Diana might have influenced Tom in his turning to fascism; but there is no evidence for this: Tom was virtually committed to fascism before he met Diana: Diana at twenty-one had not come across fascism and would have had little power to influence Tom if she had. What she did give him however was a chance to exercise his need and talent for risk and conquest: and so perhaps just by her arrival on the scene she created something of the atmosphere as it were of fascism.

Tom's pursuit of Diana was contemporaneous with his work on his book *The Greater Britain* which was to be his public statement about British fascism. The story of himself and Diana ran parallel to what he was trying to do in politics: he was trying to become responsibly committed both to Cimmie and to Diana: he was trying to start a fascist street-movement that would be respectable. It was not his ruthlessness or singlemindedness that made him at this time seem to be doing things that were taboo: it was the way in which he seemed to be both breaking the rules of games and at the same time trying to demonstrate he was keeping them. This seemed to involve a confusion of rules as it were on a higher level.

Diana was the third daughter of Lord and Lady Redesdale: she was a Mitford: the Mitfords were not then the legendary figures they have now become (1982). But Diana was in fact at twenty-one already something of a legend – with her beauty, her cleverness, her ability to seem both conventional and unconventional at the same time. When she was eighteen she had married Bryan Guinness, the eldest son of Walter Guinness, soon to become Lord Moyne. She had gone from her eccentric but somewhat restricted schoolroom straight into a world of freedom and riches: all this has become part of the Mitford legend chronicled by sister Nancy, her sister Jessica, by Diana herself. It was conventional of course in the world in which both she and Tom moved for married men to take out young married girls to lunch and even to dinner; it was conventional (though this was not spelt out) for them to have affairs. But the smooth running of all this – as in the world of conventional politics – depended on the participants observing rules – not even really questioning them. The rules of the social game were to do with there being no public scandal. There was little chance of scandal (newspapers kept to the rules in those days and people within the game did not talk) unless there was a question of divorce. This was the equivalent of, in politics, gangs taking to the streets.

At first in his pursuit of Diana Tom appeared to be doing no more than what he had been doing for years: he took her out; he talked; they went to his flat in Ebury Street. Then in June 1931 the Guinnesses gave a party in their house at 96 Cheyne Walk to celebrate Diana's twenty-second birthday. Diana recorded in her autobiography:

> A few things about this party dwell in my memory: myself managing to propel Augustus John, rather the worse for wear, out of the house and into a taxi: Winston Churchill inveighing against a large picture by Stanley Spencer of Cookham War Memorial which hung on the staircase and Eddie Marsh defending it against his onslaught. I wore a pale grey dress of chiffon and tulle and all the diamonds I could lay my hands on. We danced until day broke, a pink and orange sunrise which gilded the river.

What also happened at this party was that Tom made some formal proposal to Diana that their relationship should be of a more committed kind than could normally be covered by the terms of the game. He told her that he did not intend to leave Cimmie: but he was in love with her, Diana. Diana said she was in love too. She also said she wanted to be committed to him because he had convinced her about the importance of his ideas for altering the world. What would be the precise nature of the commitment could be worked out through the rest of the summer.

There is a home movie in existence of this time taken by Cimmie at the christening-party of Dick Wyndham's daughter Ingrid to whom Tom was godfather. There are the usual shots of people posturing, or performing, in front of a camera – Tom coming down a staircase and pausing with a hand on his heart; Dick Wyndham shaking a bottle of champagne so violently that it foams like a fire extinguisher. Then the camera moves to, and rests on, Diana: she is smiling and quite still; like some statue come across in a jungle.

There had always been something awkward, enthusiastic, schoolgirlish about Cimmie. She had grown rather fat and heavy: she seemed not to take much trouble now about her clothes or her appearance. People remember her at this time still with the exuberance that could light people up when she came into a room. But she was perhaps no longer elegant.

Diana wrote of this time that her life had seemed 'absolutely useless and empty' before she met Tom. Her great friends Lytton Strachey and Dora Carrington had just died. She had enjoyed her brief reign as one of the princesses of the smart social world: she had had two children, Jonathan and Desmond, within two years. But she wanted something more. When Tom came along he was not only 'handsome, generous, intelligent and full of a wondrous gaiety' but also 'completely sure of himself and his ideas: he knew what to do to solve the economic disaster we were living through'.

Tom and Diana made plans about what they should do in the summer holidays. Diana was going to motor down through France with friends; Tom and Cimmie were due to go this year to Venice. Cimmie was still not well enough to travel by car: it was agreed that Tom should drive, and Cimmie should follow by train with the children. Tom made a plan with Diana to run into her as if by chance at Arles or Avignon.

Cimmie does not seem to have realised yet that there was anything out of the ordinary about Diana. Tom had always gone after the socially most glamorous women: two years ago he had seriously upset her with Paula Casa Maury. But she had learned to believe he would always come back to her; probably to trust that what he said about the triviality of his affairs was true. Also now he was being particularly attentive to her. As late as August 3rd Cimmie was telling Irene that Tom 'had been exquisite to her since the baby and she had not been so happy for years'. But it is an ironic fact that when people are in love they are apt to make happy for a time the other people around them.

At Avignon Diana became ill suddenly with diphtheria and had to go to bed in a hotel. A doctor from the Institut Pasteur came and gave her 'enormous injections'. She was frightened lest a letter from Tom might arrive at the hotel desk and have to be opened. She got her friends Barbara Hutchinson and Victor Rothschild enrolled in the plot and a message was got through to Tom. New arrangements were made that they should all meet in Venice when Diana got well. Tom got Diana's message in Arles. He drove to Cannes, where he wrote to Cimmie:

His own darling soft-nosed wog-tail
... Rather slacked up last two days. From Lyons Thursday went to
Valence – tremendous lunch – bottle of beautiful Rosé – afterwards
began to write you very witty letter but remembering both you and
Lady D W [Lady de la Warre with whom Cimmie was staying in
England] were a little literal minded tore it up, in case produced as
evidence of insanity. Waddled on via Avignon to Arles – 'Tomby
you stand where Caesar stood: twenty centuries gaze down on you
and acclaim you'. [drawing of man doing fascist salute and saying
'wee wee'.] ... Got to Cannes 6 pm ... quickly landed by Lotsy and
a merry thing who pressed him to come to a grand gala at Monte
Carlo: he *refused* and had vegetable soup *alone* in *room*. Since striking
attitudes on moonlit balcony alternating between Missolonghi and St
Helena – very spacious apartment – asked very diffidently price –
they said loftily they would make him a special arrangement – must
be distinction of his appearance – always given much better rooms
when she isn't there (I feel my indignation rising within me, better
stop). THIS IS ALL A JOKE. Lots of love my sweet fellow misses
her so much. Love to all [drawing of four pigs of decreasing size].

From England Cimmie replied –

My sweet darling heart. Does wish you hadn't torn up that witty lett,
not *soooo* literal minded as all that, still absolutely loved the one she
did get. I am sitting in the sun and the gram is playing 'Goodnight
Sweetheart' which reminds me irresistibly of Lotsy and last year oh
dear oh dear I wonder if she's keeping you up all night, still really
I don't think I mind, as I do love you so and am pretty happy and
serene about you loving me at the moment, it makes me more happy
than anything in the world...

You know, given good weather England now is a knockout – the
lushness, the quiet, the colour... I'm not sure we shouldn't try a
summer or just a fortnight in Aug at Savehay once. There is something southern climates utterly lack; it's much softer and the birds
sing. I really don't envy the hurry and bustle of the Croisette one bit
and even the Excelsior seems garish and ugly when I think of it. I'd
like to have you and the children in a quiet place where it's green and
peaceful sometime...

Darling Darling Darling You are my heart's delight... I don't
know why I love you like I do, I don't know why but I do. I do I
do I do I do I do I do I do.

Love and kisses from the Porkers united and loving Wog Tail. I really am looking forward to Venice terribly. Let's have a beautiful time. 'I want to be featured by you' – words for new song by one of Tomki's girls!!

A week or two later, on the Lido at Venice, where Tom and Cimmie were staying, and the Guinnesses, and many of their mutual friends, for the first time what Tom and Diana felt about each other became apparent. They would go sightseeing in a group round the town; then they would disappear round corners, down alleyways, and would not be seen between lunch and dinner. Diana in her autobiography remembered this summer as one in which 'our countrymen were not on their best behaviour: at one party, a picnic on Torcello, there was a fight': at another Randolph Churchill called Brendan Bracken 'my brother' and there would have been another fight if Randolph Churchill had not 'snatched off' Brendan Bracken's spectacles and thrown them into the sea. Bob Boothby remembered a dinner party on the Lido at which all *dramatis personae* were present: Tom leaned across the table and said 'Bob, I shall need your room tonight before midnight and 4 am'. Bob Boothby, said 'But Tom, where shall I sleep?' Tom said 'On the beach'. Bob Boothby, recalling this story fifty years later, added with a great smile – 'And I did!'

Cimmie's children did not notice anything very unusual going on: were not grown-ups always jumping about and exclaiming and shouting? During this holiday Vivien and I were nominally under the care of Cimmie's lady's maid, Andrée: Nanny had stayed behind with Michael. An incident that stuck in our minds was when Randolph Churchill, on the beach, referred to us as 'the brats': nothing else seems to have pierced us so much during a fortnight in Venice.

During the summer, and concurrent with his pursuit of Diana, Tom had been engaged in writing *The Greater Britain* – a 40,000 word book in which he sorted out for himself, and presented to the public, his ideas about the nature of British fascism. In the second half of the book there were recommendations for Britain's economic recovery which were not different from those which he had put forward in his New Party and Labour days – the necessity for centrally controlled economic planning within a protected home-and-imperial market. But the important part of the book was its first forty pages, in which Tom outlined what he saw as the attitude and spirit of fascism.

The argument of *The Greater Britain* was that the crisis facing the world was of a more fundamental kind than that talked about in the terms of the current economic breakdown. The inventions of science and the products of modern technology had created a new type of world during the last hundred years: yet the political institutions to deal with it had scarcely changed at all. The machinery of life was once such that it could be handled by a leisurely system of balances: now complexities and pressures and the possibilities of destruction were so great, that mankind had to fashion stronger and tighter methods of control or else there would be catastrophe.

The problem was how to organise for this control while allowing for freedom: 'to harmonise individual initiative with the wider interest of the nation.' There was not much difficulty in doing this with words. The word 'fascist', Tom said, implied 'a high conception of citizenship': it 'recognises the necessity for the authoritative state' in which 'there is no room for interests which are not the State's interests'. But somehow at the same time 'wise laws' would allow human activity 'full play'. The desire of men 'to work for themselves' would be guided into 'channels which serve the nations ends'.

In practical terms – '*Government must have power to legislate by Order subject to the power of Parliament to dismiss it by vote of censure* (the italics are in the original). Fascism 'seeks to achieve its aim legally and constitutionally by methods of law and order, *but in objective it is revolutionary or it is nothing*'. So long as the power of an elected Parliament to dismiss a Government was retained, then 'the charge of Dictatorship has no reality'.

The naiveties of *The Greater Britain* were deliberate: the paradoxes concerning the use and abuse of power were commonplace: it was from their recognition that had grown the delicate system of democratic checks and balances. But it was specifically these that fascism was now claiming were dangerously out of date: fascism stated the paradoxes, and then ignored them. It said that there just *will* be freedom for individual energies within complete state control. It was using words in such a way that the things they referred to seemed equally malleable – and thus almost meaningless.

Fascism 'combines the dynamic urge to change and progress with the authority, the discipline and the order without which nothing great can be achieved'. The word which cuts through the paradoxes is 'greatness': it is in following this device held aloft like a sword that questions of individual freedom, of state authority fall away. 'Our hope is centred in vital and determined youth, dedicated to the resurrection of a nation's greatness and shrinking from no effort and from no sacrifice to secure that mighty end.' 'In every town and village, in every institution of daily life, the will of the organised and determined minority must be struggling for sustained effort.' Every now and then it is as if Tom remembered he must recognise he was dealing with paradoxes: 'Voluntary discipline is the essence of the Modern Movement': 'the beginning of liberty is the end of economic chaos': even – 'in a superficial paradox, it will be necessary for a modern movement which does not believe in Parliament as at present constituted to seek to capture Parliament'. But then the tone of voice goes back to that of the warrior who has broken through; who when he finds one side of a paradox being obstructive, throws it away.

Into the measured prose of *The Greater Britain* there comes from time to time – like fighting breaking out in the hall of a political meeting – the rhetoric of contempt. The favourite words of scorn are 'children' and 'old women'. Politicians of the old parties are 'like children in the dark ... [they] put their heads under the bedclothes rather than get up like men and grapple with the danger'. Orthodox economics are the remedy of the 'eternal old woman'. One of the most scathing words is 'Spain' – 'alive in a sense, but dead to all sense of greatness and to her mission in the world'. (This is odd in the light of the fact that it was Spain that was shortly to provide the one and only relatively successful fascist government.) Another contemptuous phrase for conventional politicians was 'united muttons' – odd, again, in the light of the fact that 'mutton' was one of his favourite words for Cimmie.

As well as the words there were the promises of activities to do with contempt. 'So soon as anybody, whether an individual or an organised interest, steps outside those limits [of the national interest] so that his activity becomes sectional and anti-social, the mechanism of the Corporate system descends upon him ... The State has no room for the drone and the decadent, who use their leisure to destroy their capacity for public usefulness. In our morality it is necessary to "live like athletes".'

In the last pages of the book, which return to the themes of the beginning in the style of one of Tom's perorations, his struggle to try to appear once more reasonably to embrace paradoxes results in his language becoming almost openly without content: 'We appeal to our countrymen to take action while there is still time and to carry the changes which are necessary by the legal and constitutional methods which are available. If on the other hand every appeal to reason is futile in the future, as it has been in the immediate past, and the Empire is allowed to drift until collapse and anarchy supervene, we shall not shrink from that final conclusion, and will organise to stand between the State and ruin ... In no case shall we resort to violence against the forces of the crown but only against the forces of anarchy if and when the machinery of state has been allowed to drift into powerlessness.'

What would have given such a statement meaning was, of course, a consideration of who was to be the arbiter of when such a moment of decision had come, and what would be the extent of the moves to deal with the crisis. It was Tom's total ignoring of such questions (or the assumption that of course the arbiter of everything would be himself) that rendered the reasonableness of much of his argument irrelevant.

In the eyes of most people in 1932 the worst of the economic crisis had already gone; it was only Tom, and his incipient band of dedicated followers, who were insisting that it was still coming. But whoever might, or might not, be proved right by history, to ignore questions about how the crisis would be judged was not just to trivialise the discussion but to make the whole form of it suspect. Tom made no secret of the fact that his whole movement was a preparation for (and in fact depended on) crisis: 'in a crisis the British are at their best: when the necessity for action is not clear they are at their worst ... a complete breakdown would be a stronger incentive to action than the movement, however cumbrous, of a crippled machine.' After breakdown it might be true that 'in the highly technical struggle for the modern state in crisis only the technical organisations of Fascism or Communism have ever prevailed, or, in the nature of things, can prevail'. But then, people might reasonably ask – might not Tom, with his 'organised and determined minority', if the crisis he insisted he foresaw did not in a time that suited him materialise, be tempted reasonably (since it would come anyway) to spur on the crisis himself? The irony of Tom's political career was that he deliberately put himself into a position in which reasonable men could hardly fail to ask such a question and be alarmed at the lack of a coherent answer: while Tom himself, without giving the question any publicity or apparently even much thought, probably gave to himself an answer that reasonable men might not have had all that much cause to fear.

What Tom did publicly go on stressing was 'the ferocity of struggle and danger' and the fact that the inevitable catastrophe would only be able to be dealt with by 'new men who come from nowhere'. It was only after these ferocious men had sorted out the crisis that once more (this was one of the paradoxes Tom most naively cut through and just left) 'rational discussion of the world's economic problems would supervene'.

Throughout *The Greater Britain* there is not one reference to Jews. In

Hitler's *Mein Kampf*, written ten years previously, it is explicit that Jews
are the enemy. In *The Greater Britain* the enemy is decadence. This
decadence is in society; in oneself.

There is a curious impression as one reads *The Greater Britain* that the
problems it presents are philosophical and psychological and have not
much to do with practical politics. In politics anyone can have high-
sounding ideals: anyone can slice with words through paradoxes about
authority and freedom. Practicalities depend on responses to events:
upon the style in which is discovered what is not possible and is practised
what is. The appeal of fascism was to a 'greatness' that would march
through human affairs like a column of ants: but this has not much to
do with what human beings are actually like; it is to do with a longing
of the psyche. Once the idea of 'greatness' is projected outside as a way
of cutting through paradoxes then there is in fact no control of them
but rather a helplessness – a runaway situation towards death. There is
no 'greater' challenge that a man can pit himself against than one with
the likelihood of death: this is a way in which life can in fact be cut
through.

A way in which it might conceivably have struck Tom and those
closest to him that what was being talked were paradoxes concerning
themselves was Tom's curious insistence on the need to eschew and even
destroy everything 'decadent' and to 'live like athletes'. For years Tom
and Cimmie had enjoyed during their leisure moments the company of
people who in any normal understanding of words 'use their leisure
moments to destroy their capacity for public usefulness'. Tom had
perhaps reasonably justified himself in this – on the grounds that it was
necessary for personal equilibrium that portentous human attitudes
should be balanced by some such relaxations at the other end of the scale.
But then why did not he, or those closest to him, see that such balances
or at least tolerances might be necessary for the equilibrium of society
– and that there was a likelihood of disaster if they were treated with
contempt? Diana might have seen this: before she had met Tom she had
been involved in some of the more bizarre incidents of the 'decadent'
age: she and her brother had put on an exhibition of paintings by Brian
Howard said to be by a German artist called 'Bruno Hat' and critics had
enjoyed the joke: Evelyn Waugh's *Vile Bodies* was dedicated to Bryan
and Diana Guinness. Throughout her life Diana has always seemed
personally to embody a balance between the passionately serious and
an enjoyment of the absurd. But she, at the time, seemed to insist on
some simple commitment: it seemed not to be fashionable anywhere
to think about balances in politics.

The result of this sort of failure – to see that all life depends on balances; that a definition of life is in fact that which has feed-back and response; that the simplicity, the drive to the doing away of balances, results in a runaway situation towards death – the result of this sort of failure is that it can affect the mind and heart as well as the outside world. Cimmie was the person who now suffered; who perhaps wanted at last to get out of the whole arena; who had her dreams of being with Tom and the children 'in a quiet place where it's green and peaceful sometime'. She was not getting well after the birth of her baby Michael; she was still suffering from her kidney disease and she had pains in her back. Then there had been the holiday in Venice when she had discovered the seriousness of the threat of Diana and had cried much of the time. In September she went to a spa called Contrexeville in eastern France. She was trying to get her health back. She took with her her two older children.

CHAPTER 23

The British Union of Fascists

Contrexeville is a place I remember quite well, perhaps because it was one of the few times Vivien and I were on our own with our mother – in the sense of there being no other grown-ups around by whom her attention would inevitably be taken away. In practical matters (we were aged eleven and nine) we were still 'looked after' by our mother's lady's maid Andrée. We were in a big hotel called Hotel des Etablissements, which was next door to a building called the Pump Room, where people drank water out of little metal mugs. After doing this they would walk about, or sit down, until it was time to go back to the hotel or to have another drink of water. There was a park where children went round and round on paths between flowerbeds on bicycles. Our mother would sit in a wicker chair with a writing pad on her knee and write to Tom, who was in London.

My dear darling,

I wonder what your plans are. I am afraid this place would bore you unbelievably, it is just BOREDOM personified – bourgeouis dreary self-satisfied – mediocre hotel, fairly good cooking, hideous revolting people, nothing to do. I drink a glass of water from 8 am every 25 mins for 2 hours, then am massaged for an hour, then go across the way and have Diatherm treatment then ionisation – then am finished except for more and more water and a diet.

In the pm we go out in the car – lovely country road. Today went to Domremy where Joan of Arc was born. I have no breakfast, no tea, lunch at 12.15, dinner 7.30. It is now 9, and after this letter I shall go to bed. There is a Casino but I have not been in, and a Cinny. I hope it really will do me good, and I will come home well and hearty . . .

Cimmie in these letters makes few references to her children. She makes
no direct reference to what Tom might be doing in London. It was as
if she were going more and more into her private world in which
nothing much mattered except the dream in which she and Tom would
somehow, some day, be all right together. It was this that signified to
her the recovery from her illness.

> I really feel we will have a good winter – you building up your
> organisation, coping with the sales of your book, having a happy time
> *with* your family – and some stolen moments with lovely sillies but
> not *too* many – mum seeing to household, coping with children,
> getting together nice intelligent Circle, arranging *fun* – does it seem
> a nice proposition. I hope so.

Children find it difficult to be aware of their parents' sicknesses: parents
are like the natural course of events: what happens when a course of
events gets out of joint? I remember getting on badly with my sister at
this time: we had ferocious fights: after one which went up and down
the corridors of the huge hotel like one of our father's street-fights my
mother came out of her room and admonished both of us equally. I was
outraged at this: I thought I was in the right: but anyway, where was
justice in a world that did not even enquire into rights? I rushed into
our bedroom and locked myself in the lavatory. I thought I would stay
there until I died; then the grown-ups would be sorry. My mother and
sister did come to the door from time to time and ask me to come out:
they even pushed food under the door for me: I pushed this back. It
seemed that I was in there for a vast stretch of time: I suppose in fact
it was no more than most of a day. I became aware after a time that
although I seemed to be winning there was in fact no such thing as
winning: I would lose face if I came out but if I stayed in I would die:
this might be some sort of victory, but I would not be there to see it.
This perhaps is a common romantic predicament. Eventually I emerged
tentatively at night and my mother appeared at the bedroom door and
held out her arms to me and I ran into them and cried. I remember this
well: it is almost the only time I remember my mother holding me.
  Tom wrote to Cimmie from London:

> His own darling soft-nosed wog-tail
> Glad to hear that Flexyville is not so bad – working very hard –
> organising sale of book and many statements on current politics etc.

Fencing every night and morning at RAC – seeing no one – practically! Might turn up at Flexyville at any time but do not wait as in a great turmoil. Rather enjoying it all. Directly I am satisfied organisation can run without me will go off on another trip. Forgot to tell you – an idea that B. Bracken (listen CM) and I should meet Winston and Lindemann on Como. Lots of love and happy squashes. [drawing of a gondola; then of a pig with its nose against a wheel]. Back at the grindstone – far, far away from Venice *pleasure* and *temptations*.

One of the expeditions that Cimmie took the children on was to the trenches and dug-outs of the first world war which had been preserved near Verdun. We were taken round the sand-bagged passages like sewers and the holes in the ground like those of rats: these were the memorials of man's urges to get rid of himself. We were aware that our father had been somewhere near here some sixteen years ago: that he cared passionately that there should be no more war. He was in London, we understood, doing something about an organisation which would prevent war; which would appeal to reason over the heads of mad politicians.

At times Cimmie seemed to be dealing with her own predicaments quite well. She wrote:

Bless you my darling right deep down I *have* confidence, my most secret soul knows we are all right, I love you and you love me till Death do us part; but various surface selves need encouraging now and then, need a little bolstering up, want a little public demonstration, want to show off a bit, and it is that part that gets hurt and upset. All the sweetness in the world isn't quite the same as a demonstration of affection and choice in public and my bowels yearn for the latter as well as appreciating the former.

Shan't expect you here more than 1 or at most 2 nights, would *love* that, but *at pinch* would understand none at all. Remember always how I love you.

But then again – as if she were indeed under some attack in war, or plagued by the illness she had come to Contrexeville to cure – the other part of her would come out on top.

My heart is not yet quite right about you, it hurts when I think of you, it misses you dreadfully, and is as jealous as hell. All the time I try to reason with it, with my head. Theories could hardly be improved on: practice not so good I fear. Still, Tom, doing some thinking and philosophising – how much it will stand any strain of events remains to be seen ... I hug you. I love you. What am I? I forget. Is it your soft-nosed squash-tail?

There are medical reports on what was wrong with Cimmie at the time it was decided she should go to Contrexeville: they were written in July 1932, just before the summer holiday in Venice.

Very briefly the history is that she had spinal curvature from childhood and in recent years this has been getting worse. Has had six attacks of lumbago in her life. For the past two years she has been stiff in the back.

In September last she fell out of a wagon loft and soon after had acute pyelitis with high temperature etc. The exact date of onset of the increase in the back is indefinite, but the pain definitely became worse at her last pregnancy, so that she even had to have morphia to relieve it. She was in bed three months in all. She was better after the child was born but the pain increased again as soon as she got up and she is now unable to take any form of active exercise ... Sneezing is agony. For history of kidney infection see (enclosed) note.

Lady Cynthia Mosley has a bacillus coli infection of her urinary tract which appears to date from Sept 1931 ... On several occasions the question of terminating the pregnancy arose. Since the Caesarian section the kidney has settled down; the urine still contains colon bacilli ...

It was to get rid of these, ostensibly, that she had come to Contrexeville. After a fortnight a report read 'Colon bacilli nearly disappeared'.

Tom announced his intention of coming out. 'Here is the plan of squash world – say if it is not porker – he will cross Saturday 10th, stay night in Paris, and come on to Flexyville next day. Porkers united!' There is a photograph of Tom at Contrexeville standing by his Bentley, and looking rather sad.

In London, he had been seeing to the publication of *The Greater Britain* which was to be put out by his own publishing company and was to coincide with the launching of the British Union of Fascists in October. Representatives were sent out all over the country with the book: this was to provide information for the cells of the 'organised and determined minority'.

The story of the British Union of Fascists will be told in another book: but the beginnings of it belong here, because they overlap with the story of Cimmie's life and death. Harold Nicolson had recorded in April that Tom did not want 'to allow the active forces of this country to fall into other hands': it was because of this he was prepared to 'run the risk of further failure, ridicule and assault'. By 'active forces' was meant, presumably, the fascist-type bodies already in existence.

The two main home-grown fascist groups were – The British Fascists, founded by Miss Lintorn-Orman who (it was often explained) was the grand-daughter of a Field Marshal, and to whom in 1923 the idea of saving the country from communism had come while she was weeding her kitchen garden: and the Imperial Fascist League, founded by Arnold Leese, who had been a vet specialising in the diseases of camels and whose anti-semitism had arisen (so the story went) from his objection to kosher methods of slaughtering animals. Throughout the nineteen-twenties there had been numerous schisms and splinter-groups from these bodies: for a time Brigadier Blakeney, previously an administrator of the Egyptian State Railways, took over the British Fascists; then he joined Arnold Leese, and both of them disassociated themselves from Italian fascism on the grounds that it was too favourable to Jews. There were splinter-groups called The British Empire Fascists, The Fascist League, The Fascist Movement, The National Fascisti, and the British National Fascists: it seemed that the number of bodies was limited only by the availability of names. None of the groups had much of a policy: they felt they existed to protect old fashioned virtues to do with patriotism and law and order against the world-wide conspiracies of people like Communists and Jews. They marched to and fro, and cared about uniforms and flags and badges.

When Tom came along and proposed a merger of all these groups into the British Union of Fascists he was objected to violently by Arnold Leese on the grounds that he was being manipulated by Jews – to divert attention from Leese's true anti-semitism. And in fact in March 1933 the *Jewish Chronicle* declared – 'The Mosley Fascists themselves are our best supporters in the fight against The Imperial Fascists League.' It was the latter who called the British Union Kosher Fascists; and claimed that Cimmie was Jewish. In a fight between Mosley fascists and Leese's Imperial Fascist Guard in 1933 Leese was beaten up and General Blakeney got a black eye: this was the only fight, Tom said later, in which his stewards got out of control. At the time he was soon claiming that the only fascists left outside his organisation were 'three old ladies and a couple of office boys'. But then – what kind of people were the fascists within his organisation?

It is easy to write slightly mockingly about early fascists: such an attitude is in reaction to Tom's own idealistic claim that he was discovering a 'new' type of man. They were mostly sincere idealists. The British Union of Fascists officially came into existence on October 1st 1932 when there was a flag-unfurling ceremony in the old New Party offices in Great George Street. Tom said 'We ask those who join us ... to be prepared to sacrifice all, but to do so for no small and unworthy ends. We ask them to dedicate their lives to building in the country a movement of the modern age ... In return we can only offer them the deep belief that they are fighting that a great land may live.' But the question of interest, as usual, was how successful Tom would be in putting his fine sentiments into effect.

The first public meeting of the BUF was on October 15th in Trafalgar Square. There was not much of a crowd. Photographs show Tom making his speech on the plinth at the bottom of the column: he is wearing a dark suit and tie and a white shirt: eight men with black shirts and grey flannel trousers are around him. Newspapers reported that Cimmic and her two older children were there. I have no memory of this.

A week or so later there was an indoor meeting in the Memorial Hall at Farringdon Street in the City. Here Tom, answering rather obstreperous questions from a group in the gallery, referred to 'three warriors of class war all from Jerusalem'. Fighting broke out: two of the questioners were ejected. Afterwards Tom was reported by *The Times* as saying 'Fascist hostility to Jews was directed against those who financed communists or who were pursuing an anti-British policy.' This was the first public reference by Tom as a fascist to Jews.

After the meeting there were further scuffles in the street. The scene was the prototype of what was to become an archetypal pattern of fascist and anti-fascist behaviour. *The Times* reported:

Sir Oswald marched in the midst of about 60 or 70 of his supporters along Fleet Street, the Strand, and Whitehall, to the headquarters of the British Union of Fascists at 1, Great George St, S.W. Of this party, all young men, many wore either grey or black shirts, without jackets, and nearly all were hatless. They roared patriotic songs and the rallying cries of their organisation in turn, and behind them walked a smaller party of men and women roaring revolutionary songs and slogans.

The sort of slogans that the fascists and anti-fascists used to sling to and
fro at each other like tennis-balls were:

> Two, four, six, eight,
> Whom do we appreciate?
> M.O.S.L.E.Y. – Mosley!

and:

> Hitler and Mosley, what are they for?
> Thuggery, buggery, hunger and war!

As a result of Tom's reference to Jerusalem in his Farringdon Street
speech (Irene recorded in her diary) Israel Sieff, a prominent Jewish
businessman, withdrew a tentative offer of support for Tom.

The British Union of Fascists was not in its origins a working class
movement; it was composed mainly of lower-middle-class men who
resented the inequalities and lack of opportunities under capitalism; they
also feared the prospect of repression of individualism under socialism.
They were mostly young: those who were not, looked back to a spirit
of youthfulness such as they had found in the war. They joined the
movement not so much because they cared about any policy but because
they wanted order; and they felt the disorderly paradoxes of life might
be solved if they handed responsibilities to a leader whose words seemed
to cut through difficulties like a knife.

In the first edition of *The Greater Britain* (5,000 copies had sold out
quickly) Tom had written 'Leadership may be individual or, preferably
in the case of the British character, a team'. In the second edition the
sentences were added 'But undoutedly single leadership in practice
proves the more efficient instrument. The Leader must be prepared to
shoulder absolute responsibility.' This was undoubtedly what he found
his followers wanted. A black shirt uniform for the BUF was designed
which was copied from Tom's fencing jacket: Tom was reported as
saying that the shirt was 'the outward and visible sign of an inward and
spiritual grace'. A uniform was useful for control if there was to be
fighting at meetings: also it did seem to be some sacrament (did Tom
realise the significance of his words?) by which his followers might feel
they were absolved from responsibility themselves.

Tom's activities in the streets brought forth comments from friends
and associates in his other world. Harold Nicolson wrote that he was
saddened by the thought of 'young Bermondsey boys with *gummiknüppel*

(rubber truncheons). Irene complained – 'I wish everyone would not come in and say Tom was a musical comedy fool with his blackshirt group'. Both Irene and Baba had been at the Farringdon Street meeting: afterwards they discussed it with 'rather broken hearts'.

> Baba said his speech had been so fine, why descend to the Jerusalem inanity, and really the little man in the balcony was quite inoffensive. She waited for Tom for hours at Smith Square and finally he swaggered in like a silly schoolboy only proud of some silly scuffles and rows whilst marching home and glorying over his menials throwing two lads down the stairs at Farringdon Street and possibly injuring them and all this swagger and vanity to Mrs Bryan Guinness and Doris Castelrosse – muck muck muck. When he is such a magnificent orator, and if he had vision, he could have carried the entire hall with him without descending to these blackshirt rows he seems to revel in, and none of his friends will tell him what a ludicrous figure he makes of himself.

But on the path that Tom had chosen for himself it was not ludicrous that he should chuck hecklers out of his meetings, nor that he should not be too concerned if there were scrimmages on his marches. He had a policy that he wanted to be heard: it was a fact that in his pre-fascist days people had defeated him by ignoring him. He believed that his economic policies might save the country: if he was to make himself heard, not only had he to ensure that he was not shouted down but he needed publicity. The sort of public image he wanted to project was that of someone who would guard law and order in the face of those who were out to cause disruption. Logically, all this made sense. And in Italy, fascists had in fact got power by presenting a tough, theatrical image. There was still the question of tactics – if all this in political terms was not to be turned against him.

Cimmie, now back in Smith Square, made designs for a fascist flag; she discussed with Tom the prospect of turning Sousa's 'Stars and Stripes' into a fascist anthem with words by Osbert Sitwell. (William Walton was later asked if he would write music). Cimmie went to Tom's meetings, but she did not appear on platforms nor take part in the marches. It was as if she still could not quite make up her mind about what was happening.

Diana, for all her seriousness and sophistication, might have found it easier to accept in the BUF what Irene called 'the musical comedy element': there was something in all Mitfords, as was later said about

Diana's sister Nancy, that saw the world as something of a 'tease', and that they might tease.

In his private life Tom seems to have been managing his juggling act quite well; he was keeping all his plates, or whatever, fairly harmoniously up in the air at the same time. On October 8th, a week before the BUF's inaugural meeting in Trafalgar Square, Cimmie, in a plane between Paris and London, wrote to Tom, who was staying (according to the address on the envelope) with the Guinnesses at their home at Biddesden, in Hampshire.

> Just want to send him love. Don't know yet of course whether she is to go on [this refers probably to the Trafalgar Square meeting] but if so will do best gladly and proudly for him: if not will come home determined to really try and both be happy and help meet to him. Bless your heart, if I do try and see your point of view, please be sweetie and see my p. of v. Be kind. Moo moo.

But Tom, involved in his public life with 'the ferocity of struggle and of danger', would not have had time for much kindness. The style of the task he had set himself was that you had to fight to stay alive: you attracted people to you by your ability to show off ruthlessly and win. A month after the Farringdon Street meeting newspapers reported one at St Pancras where 'some of the fascists had the shirts torn from their backs and received razor slashes': the battle with left-wing militants was once more under way. Each side said that they were fighting for what they believed in: but what they believed in was the struggle against the other: this was the nature of their power, and the chance of their extending it. Fascists and communists needed one another as enemies: if each did not have the other, then indeed they were ludicrous because they were punching at empty air. No one was talking much about Tom's economic proposals now: but then, not many people had wanted to talk about them before.

At the time of the launching of the New Party a year and a half ago it had been Tom who had become ill: he had perhaps glimpsed the nature of the path from which he would not be able to turn back. He was now on that path: he had gambled on gaining political power on his own terms, or nothing. In private life he was gambling too against almost impossible odds – for the perfect arrangement by which he could have Cimmie as wife and Diana as mistress and everyone be happy as he himself strode in and out of protecting rings of fire.

CHAPTER 24

Diana Guinness

In the autumn of 1932, when I was nine, I was sent to boarding school. My mother had taken trouble to find a suitable school: the one chosen was Abinger Hill, near Dorking in Surrey. It was known as being 'progressive': the sort of school rich socialists or ex-socialists might send their children to. What was progressive about it was that boys were allowed to do a lot of their work in their own time and in their own way, and a good deal of freedom was allowed to them in the surrounding countryside.

My father used to say he was haunted up to the end of his life by memories of how he had hated boarding schools; he was bitter against his mother for sending him away.

I look back on Abinger Hill with some gratitude. There were the usual squalors and miseries, but it gave a child a chance to learn, and to make, what adjustments were possible; and thus it did what all schools should do, which is to teach a child what are the terms of the grown-up world by which later he might feel free. What I remember about my first year at Abinger Hill was the way in which life on the mundane level seemed to be dominated by schoolboy gangs: the masters floated almost in another dimension like gods. It was comparatively easy to learn to come to terms with the gods: apart from a few compulsory lessons the work that boys did could be arranged by the boys themselves: when they had done a piece of work they were supposed to present it to a master who would judge it and then according to its quantity and quality would mark up a line on a graph in this or that coloured pencil. Each boy carried his graph around with him as the frontispiece of a loose-leaf notebook. It struck me almost at once that the most sensible way of dealing with this situation would be to lay in a store of pencils oneself — particularly those of the colours denoting 'good' or even 'excellent' – and to mark up, from time to time, one's own graph; thus doing away with the need for a lot of boring work and leaving time free for reading interesting things like *The Modern Boy* and *The Wizard* in the lavatory. (How much of childhood seems to have been spent locked for safety in lavatories!) When the time came for end-of-term examinations one could always mug up quickly all the work one was supposed to have done, and this was the only way work could be made interesting anyway; because it would be for a purpose and in response to a challenge.

The problem of the older-boy gangs of bullies was much more difficult. When I arrived at the school there was a ritual known (I have changed the name) as 'Brown's Daily Blub'. Brown was I suppose a rather unprepossessing boy, and each day after breakfast a column would form and would follow Brown through the passages and round the changing rooms chanting, as if it were one of the political slogans used at my father's marches, 'Brown's Daily Blub!': until, in the course of time, it became a self-validating statement in that Brown did, in fact, blub; after which the column would disperse. I remember being amazed at this: at first because I could not see the point of it; then because I could not understand the odd pleasures of joining in.

Even more alarming rituals were apt to take place in the woods on Sunday afternoons. One Sunday shortly after I had arrived the new boys were rounded up by the senior boys and were marched off into the woods and there we were split into two groups and one group was ordered to dig the graves of the other group and to bury them up to their necks. If anyone in the digging group demurred, it was explained, he would be put into the other group – or worse. This was indeed a sort of predicament about to become common in the grown-up world. I was, by luck, in the digging group. We dug rather shallow graves. Then one or two of the other group were told to lie in the graves and we were told to pee on them. I remember there was a bit of a remonstrance about this: I don't remember, perhaps mercifully, exactly the outcome. What I do remember is that some days later the whole school was assembled and the headmaster announced that it had come to his notice via a letter written by one of the new boys to his mother that certain of the new boys had been out in the woods burying others up to their necks and then – but the sequel was not mentionable. And so – for this, certain new boys were going to be beaten if not expelled. Nothing was said about any older boys. What I remember about all this was a feeling of the inexorability of it: there was nothing one could do: this was what life was like. Older boys took you into the woods and told you to do these things: of course it was against the rules to tell about the older boys: even the boy who had written to his mother had not told about them. He had broken a rule by writing to his mother; but then, at least he had been buried up to his neck. And so myself, and other boys, were beaten. One had to learn about the ways people behaved.

Boarding school was a place in which one learned that the world away from home was cold and damp and smelt of ink and herrings; in which one had to be cunning in order to survive; one of the ways of being cunning was to accept somewhat arbitrary injustices but if one did this there were magical moments of laughter at the awful ways of bullies and of gods. I do not know what the masters made of all this: perhaps, like wise gods, they thought it best to pretend not to know what was really going on and to let their children learn in their own ways. But at boarding school one learned one could not fight the system; the danger of this was, one might believe it of later life.

One of the agonising matters for boarding-school children is the appearance or almost existence of their parents: parents are required to be conventionally prosperous yet completely unremarkable. My first term at Abinger Hill coincided with my father's launching of The British Union of Fascists: this was such a profound embarrassment that it placed me as it were beyond usual categories of alarm. I was nick-named by a friendly master 'Baby Blackshirt': I had to make some virtue of this, or die. This was not impossible. I had loyalty and admiration towards my father: were not he and my mother outstanding after all: how lucky to be the son of someone so unique as a rich titled ex-socialist fascist! And how boring to be a child of unremarkable, conventionally prosperous parents! Somewhere floating around in the background, I suppose, was the gratefully accepted respectability conferred by the memory of grandfather Curzon. I built up a good deal of armour about all this: but was still vulnerable as it were to torpedoes below the consciousness line. My stammer, not bad when talking to friends, in any sort of school activity got worse.

A week or so after the incident of gravedigging in the woods I wrote home – 'Darling Mummy and Daddy, I am very happy here. Thank you very much for all your letters. I am not at all homesick. Yesterday 7 of us went blackberrying but we did not get much. We have very nice meals. Love from Nick.

Neither Tom nor Cimmie had much talent for noticing what life in fact was like around them: their talent was for ideas, for resolutions, for insisting that life should be what it ought to be; for making passionate gestures when it was not. Tom's very determination that a new type of society had to be built by a new type of man prevented him from looking and seeing what men actually were: Cimmie's faith that in the end she and Tom would be all right stopped her perhaps observing cunningly how to make them so. She endured: she complained. Tom was cunning: but there was danger of catastrophe in his use of cunning for his own ends.

After the somewhat public imbroglio about his private life at Venice Tom seems to have managed in his usual way to placate Cimmie while he continued with his amazing juggling act. But sometimes things went wrong; manipulations flew out of control.

Darling Tom, As I don't want to spare any time we may have together by nags and reproaches I write to explain about Sunday. If only you would be frank with me, that is what I beg. If when you refused Mereworth you had said it was because you thought you would like to take Diana out for the day Sunday I would have known where I was. I started by thinking it odd but as you said nothing about another plan I began to think it must be that you wanted to stay at home and just be with us and I was so pleased. Then you tell me about Sunday as if it was vague and only planned last night – and then I realise the whole thing was arranged before and you had been putting off telling me and letting me go on thinking we were going to have a lovely Sunday together and then jump it on me after the party last night. Even then you first say 'Go a drive for an hour or two' and I get adjusted to that; then this morning it's lunch and I rearrange my point of view but you say anyway back for evening; then you ring up and say whole bally day and night – well it's pure funking, why not tell me days ago, why not be truthful and honest. That is honestly and truly what I want – beloved Tom do believe that – but the feeling that you are not telling me, that you do things behind my back, that you are only sweet to me when you want to get away with something, gives me such a feeling of insecurity and anxiety and worry I am more nervy and upset than I ought or need to be.

The book I am reading says this: 'If John were extra sweet to you then he had something to hide' – very Tomki.

Oh darling darling don't let it be like that, I will truly understand if you give me a chance, but I am so kept in the dark. That bloody damnable cursed Ebury – how often does she come there? Do you think that I just forget all about her between the Fortnum and Mason party and last night? I schooled myself the whole week never to even mention her in case I should nag or say something I should regret.

And then I have the horrid feeling this morning you've let me down
– don't do that my angel please, I'm complicated because I feel
insecure and afraid. Don't be secretive and hidey – I love you so much
I'd cope if you were open with me.   Mutton

But human beings do not on the whole succeed in coping openly with
this sort of situation: openness succeeds with simplicity: when complexity is at stake what is demanded is self-sufficiency, or some style.
Cimmie wrote to a woman friend (Mary Pearson) to ask for advice. She
got the reply:

> It is natural and essential to mind unfaithfulness. It should always be
> done a la Victorian without the knowledge of the other party. We
> place an intolerable and mad psychological strain on ourselves with
> all this so-called frankness. If Tom wishes to have affairs he is welcome
> – but you shouldn't know ... It's 'contrary to nature' as the old
> women used to say ...

This was the old aristocratic attitude. But it was just this that Cimmie
had spent her life trying to break away from. And she did not seem to
have the resources, now, to re-build a life on her own.

During the autumn Tom went again to Rome for a fascist anniversary: he wanted to keep the visit secret. From Rome he wrote the last
letters that are in existence from him to Cimmie: after this, when he was
not with her, he seemed to think it better to keep quiet.

> His own darling fellow
> What a roarer – no harm in a few pictures!
> Rome very interesting. Celebration and illuminations – the reception
> of M tremendous – a great tribute to the system – very interesting
> accounts of the 10 years work in the papers which I will bring home.
> Have not seen any friends yet but have heard from some of them.
>   [series of squiggles as if ending the letter]
> Was rather cross, but opened this again to say he loves her very much
> – not to be a goat because he adores her and she is his own sweet one
> he loves. Darling fellow, they could have such a lovely life together
> if his little frolicsome ways did not upset her. She does mean so much
> to him and he does so appreciate her. She is such a great fellow. He
> loves her so.   [drawing of a piglet]   X

Enclosed in this letter were two advertisements cut out of newspapers.

The first was headlined *The Wolsey People Have Got At Poor Matilda* and went on 'No self-respecting sheep is safe. Let it once be observed that her fleece is really first rate, and away it may go at any moment to the Wolsey mills ...' Above this Tom had drawn two illustrations – one of a sheep with its wool on beside which he had written 'But he prefers –': and the other of a shorn sheep beside which Tom had written 'Sad effects of getting in a stew about nothing.'

The other advertisement was of a charging rhinoceros with the headline *Nature In The Raw Is Seldom Mild*: and beside which Tom had written 'Fatty finding out after a few peeps.' (It is not known what were the 'pictures' referred to at the beginning of the letter).

Tom's second letter to Cimmie from Rome was:

His own darling fellow [drawing of piglet]
Has a really great regret did not bring her with him. Suppose could not have foreseen. But does really regret it awfully. Might have had a *lovely honey squash.* Seeing some of friends tomorrow – may have to wait longer for others – everyone so terribly busy over anniversary ...

One great regret I did not bring her – how one wastes life and yet so difficult to foresee – should really have settled definitely stay a week – always see you amid such turmoil of work or if a holiday of other things. Would have liked this to be a sweetly sweetly lovely time – misses her so much wiffling and sniffing about! Really loves her very much indeed, sure she is the one for him, glad she still loves him, sorry he is such a Porker. Feeling very calm and rested now, my life is so strenuous and hectic, I must recapture a little calm. Very ill and wretched on arrival – caught chill on boat – but all gone now. First lovely sunshine. I hope anyhow return before end of week but will wire you. Would be ever so happy if she were here. As it is rather sad and down. But hopes see her soon. Loves my darling fellow. Think sweetly of him who loves her!
[huge drawing of a piglet]

Tom meant this when he wrote it: no one who knew him ever denied that he meant it when he said he loved Cimmie: what people questioned was how he could both mean this and behave as he did. This was the peculiarity about Tom – how he did not seem restricted by other people's inability to hold opposites at the same time; and he did not feel guilt. It is probable that he had stopped feeling sexually attracted to Cimmie: she had often been ill in the last two years and had grown heavy. But even if he had continued to be sexually attracted to her he had shown often enough he could be involved in this way with more than one person at once. What was happening now was that he loved two people at once.

That Tom felt little guilt can be seen by the calmness with which he justified himself all round: to Cimmie he referred to Diana as part of his 'little frolicsome ways': he would not have told Diana of the re-assuring things he said to Cimmie. This was, in the circumstances, reasonable. But Diana would not have known how Cimmie suffered. What other people could not forgive Tom for was his lack of guilt.

Cimmie was helpless because she was lulled by his sweet reasonable-ness, by what seemed his simplicity, by his baby-drawings hung out like bait on the end of a line. Then when she found he also loved someone else the bottom fell out of her life. She did not have the capacity – as many people do not have – to accept the terrible complexities of love; that in such areas things can both be and not be at the same time.

What was destructive about Tom was that in spite of his manifest complexities he still, in the matter of words, insisted on doing his simple baby-talk with Cimmie: he hardly ever helped her to attain her own complexities of mind. He had probably learned that this was the best way of preventing her protesting too strongly about his 'frolicsome ways': but in so doing he was allowing some outrage to fester inside her.

Cimmie kept on trying to make her calm, serious decisions about learning to accept Diana as she had accepted other women in Tom's life. She kept on being defeated because the extent seemed never ending of what she had to accept.

At the end of 1932 Tom and Cimmie rented a house at Yarlington, in Somerset – Savehay Farm was still let. There we had a family Christmas with Cimmie's sister Irene and her sister Baba with her three children: for some reason Uncle Fruity Metcalfe was Father Christmas this year and the children at last all guessed who he was because of his unmistakable Irish brogue. Tom and Cimmie planned a New Year's fancy-dress party with many of their old friends. Irene reported 'a lot of talk about how to conceal it from those foul gossip writers who had already written it up and asked to come down and photograph the guests'. Friends who lived in the neighbourhood such as Cecil Beaton were to bring their house parties. The last time that Tom had been pursued by newspapers had been after the razor attack on him at St Pancras. It was odd that he should have wanted to give such a party now – when he was in the business of building up the image of the hard, 'new' man. But then – might not in fact a 'new' man be someone who took pride in being all things to all people? Among Tom and Cimmie's own house party guests was Diana Guinness.

The party was rather wild – Tom got over-excited and threw an éclair which hit Syrie Maugham on the head. She had hysterics: the newspapers duly reported the scene. The *Daily Worker* commented – 'The above picture of fascists at play should remove once and for all any lingering doubt as to the superman nature of Mosleyini self-cast for the role of the future dictator of Britain.' This was a subtle conclusion to be drawn from the evidence of a thrown éclair: it does not always suit Marxists to link fascism to images of effeteness. But it was probably true that Tom was at the height of his superhuman feelings just then – thinking he might get away with everything.

Some time before the new year it had been agreed between Tom and Diana that she would leave her home and set up house on her own so that she and Tom could see each other more easily. People's jealousies were making it difficult to abide by any rules of the game. And in fact Diana anyway wanted to 'nail her colours to the mast'; to 'throw in her lot' with Tom (the phrases are hers): it was one of her characteristics, as it was one of Tom's, that when emotions and beliefs became serious she would want to throw over the boards of games. Tom himself probably wanted publicly to be seen to carry off some great prize: this would be a compensation for other disappointments. But above all, Tom and Diana were involved in a grand passion: they thought they were made for each other, and continued to think this for fifty years.

Diana's sister Nancy Mitford wrote to her in November – 'You know, I feel convinced that you won't be able to take this step ... everybody that you know will band together and somehow stop you ... I believe you have a much worse time in store than you imagine.' However – 'Whatever happens *I* shall always be on your side.'

In January Diana moved with her two small children and a nanny into 2 Eaton Square – a house made available to her rent free by the Grosvenor Estate on condition that she repaired it and redecorated it – she was even given a grant for this purpose. This does not seem to have been done as a special favour to Diana: with economic conditions such as they were in January 1933 (the unemployed had reached nearly three million) it was just that it was difficult to find suitable tenants for empty houses in Eaton Square.

Diana's friends continued to predict nothing but disaster for her in her relationship with Tom. Her three younger sisters were forbidden to visit her house. The taboo that she had broken was to have set herself up openly as Tom's mistress: Tom had broken the taboo of accepting this while remaining openly married to Cimmie. Tom seemed to be claiming simply that he had the right to have two wives – a state of affairs traditionally indeed held to be taboo. Moreover one of the wives had been for years a favourite of society because of her enthusiasm and charm, and the other was the currently most sought-after young beauty of the tribe. Tom could not have been surprised that there were strong feelings against them.

Irene recorded in her diary:

My heart was in my boots over the hell incarnate beloved Cim is going through over Diana Guinness bitching her life wanting to bolt with Tom and marry him and the whole of London getting at me and Baba with the story he had gone with her and needless to say every Redesdale up in arms and Walter Guinness only wanting to 'crash' him and this blithering cow-faced fool insanely ditheringly recklessly trying to ruin Cim's life for her 19-year-old crush on that vain insensate ass Tom.

In fact Lord Redesdale and Walter Guinness (Diana's father-in-law) did try to scare Tom off: they went in a deputation together to his flat in Ebury Street. Tom was with Randolph Churchill before they arrived; he said 'Those two old men are coming to see me': Randolph Churchill said 'What are you going to do?' Tom said 'I suppose wear a balls' protector'.

It was not true that Diana expected to marry Tom: he had made it clear that he would not break his marriage to Cimmie: he had made this clear to Cimmie herself. It was just that 'the whole of London' (Irene's phrase) could not believe that Diana would have left her husband on those terms. But this was, of course, one of the great attractions of Diana: that she would stake her life, as Tom was doing, on something she believed in but which was unlikely to go all her own way. In fact she expected to see Tom only 'when he could spare time from his all all-absorbing political work and the family to which he was devoted' (this was Diana's description in her autobiography). And Tom's engagement diary for 1933 does bear out that this is roughly what happened: he would see Diana for lunch or dinner two or three times a week; he would also enter his dates for lunch or dinner with Cimmie. He also entered the dates he had with Cimmie's sister Baba. Sometimes he would see all three on the same day – 'January 6th: Lunch Cim; Baba 4.15; Dine D.'

Cimmie, in her few remaining letters, seems to have alternated between faith that in the end Tom would be left more hers than anyone else's as had happened before – 'My darling one, my own sweet love, just a line to say I am happy and all is well and I am looking forward to all being back at Smith Square': and the old schoolgirlish rage which, God knows, Tom could hardly now think he could placate with baby-talk. 'What an idiot you are, really, Tom, going through the fencing prints to stick up in Ebury this p.m. ....' (this is the only letter from Cimmie that seems to have been censored: the page is torn off below this point.) But then Cimmie would be making her resolutions and requests again (Tom in letters was now silent); and in one case Cimmie wrote as if she were forming an inscription on a tombstone:

I herby make a
Solemn Vow &
Covenant
not to again what you call nag
I will really
TRY & TRY & TRY
& can only ask in return a certain measure
of kindness and decency as to *Provocation*
Herby sealed and signed the 26th March
by
Cynthia Mosley
Do let's start off by having a lovely happy day
today so sunny and birds twittering. Help me
my darling.

CHAPTER 25

The Death of Cimmie

It became fashionable in later life for people to say that my father was responsible for my mother's death. I remember the scene when this was first suggested to me: I was in the nightnursery at Savehay Farm: I was twelve or thirteen: I had been trying to get Nanny to explain why she would never speak to my father's friend Mrs Guinness who was staying in the house. Nanny said — Well, if it had not been for — whatever it was — she did not think my mother would have died. Nanny had her back to me by the washbasin: there were blue and white striped curtains in front of a cupboard. I remember thinking even then — But you can't say something like that is a *cause* of why people die: I mean, there is that sort of thing, isn't there, and people don't die? I suppose I was quite a clever little boy. I had also, for years, thought that much of the grown-up world was mad: that they liked not liking one another. It seemed to me the most striking thing about this bit of news was that it showed how people must hate my father: I was glad that he seemed so impervious to this. And anyway — if people thought that my mother had died because of whatever my father was up to with Mrs Guinness, what about her children, did people think she had cared more about that sort of thing than about them?

Tom was a fool, I suppose, to imagine he could go on juggling with people as if they had no hearts to fall and break: he could not have foreseen such a bitter nemesis. Many people get into the same sort of situation as Tom and Cimmie and Diana: not many, in fact, die. Cimmie became ill; she had an operation: there could be conjectures about what weaknesses were in her to make her not equipped to get well. But weaknesses are not a cause of death. If Cimmie had not died, Diana did not believe that Tom would ever have left her. In time she, Diana, might have got tired and left. Or Cimmie and she might eventually have made friends.

The reason why people felt so bitter about Tom was not rational but symbolic: if Tom had put himself outside the rules of the social game it was inevitable that he should be blamed for any nemesis. He himself was always curiously unaware of such bitterness: for the most part he thought life so wonderful himself, that he could not believe others might need bitterness.

It was suggested also that Cimmie had been losing heart because of Tom's fascism: but here again there is little evidence. She liked Mussolini: she called him 'that big booming man': she would have been content, probably, to wait and see what would happen to Tom's politics. It is true that she seemed to have become increasingly distrustful of Tom's power with words – his belief that he could manipulate people, and the world, just by his skill with words – but she might have learned to live with her distrust. There was however some joint inability with her and Tom to face the reality of the forces of darkness or helplessness within themselves; and thus in the other, and in the outside world. Cimmie perhaps began to lose heart because she could not get away from her innocence: if she began to, she did not know where she was: 'What am I? I forget: am I your squash-nosed wog tail?'

Tom wanted to alter the world; it is such wilful dreamers who do sometimes alter the world: but the whole perilous edifice of fascism was some demonstration of how things are not, rather than how they are. Before the demonstration people did not know this: they believed that human society and even human nature could be altered by reason and will: that if it could not, than at least people might die splendidly in the attempt. One demonstration of fascism was of the style in which people do in fact die in this attempt. Tom was an odd exponent of fascism because in spite of his talk about returning on his shield he did not in fact do so: there was always a part of him that was not taken in by his own romantic rhetoric. This did not prevent his being taken, by others, symbolically to be responsible for deaths.

In January 1933 Hitler came to power in Germany. There was an immediate outcrop of public brutality in which people who it was thought would not fit into the regime were sorted out as if they were dirt. Other people might have learned from this, then, if they had wanted to. Once the power of the party in Germany had been thus established public violence for a time calmed down. Perhaps it had been too sudden, and too arbitrary, for people to have been able to take in what it meant.

Harold Nicolson in his diary never suggests anything except that Cimmie was opposed to fascism (he wrote to her jokingly about his godson Michael 'Does Mikki have a swastika on his crib? that would be the worst crib of all'). But Tom maintained she had come round to the idea before she died: she was certainly accepted as Tom's wife as part of the early fascist scene. There is a letter to her of January 1933 from the Battersea Branch of the BUF beginning 'Hail! Lady Cynthia' and asking for the loan of furniture and crockery to help set up the Area Office. But then at the same time came a letter from Russia from one of her friends of two years ago – 'Have you studied Marx yet? You would find it a tremendous help in clearing up doubts which continue to arise.'

In February there was a debate at the Friend's House in Euston Road in which Tom and James Maxton of the Independent Labour Party argued against each other with Lloyd George as chairman. There was a large audience containing many of Tom's and Cimmie's social friends. Fascism was still on the edge of being respectable. It was thought that Tom won the argument; but then, when people went away, there was still the question of what the winning of an argument meant.

In the middle of April Cimmie at last went to Rome with Tom, to take part in the celebrations around an International Fascist Exhibition. Starace, the Secretary of the Italian Fascist Party, presented a banner to the British Union of Fascists delegation: the banner was black with a Union Jack in the top corner and in the centre the fasces symbol (a bundle of bound sticks and an axe) around which were the words – *The British Union of Fascists For King-Empire and International Justice*. It was intended that the British delegation should be given the honour of sharing with Mussolini the saluting platform at a march past of contingents from all over Italy; but at the last moment it rained, and Mussolini retired to a covered balcony some distance away. Tom and his seven men stood to attention in front of the platform holding their banner while behind them in a stand – there are photographs of this – Cimmie looked down on them as if from a great height, rather bewildered and amused. She wore a raincoat and a sort of schoolmistress's brown felt hat. The other occasion during this trip to Rome of which a photograph has survived was of an official visit to the Roman Royal Academy. Tom and Cimmie are surrounded by frock-coated dignitaries and they both look absurdly young. Tom was thirty six. Cimmie was thirty four.

While she was in Rome Cimmie received a letter from a young admirer she had met at the Embassy:

... Unemployment being the big problem and the British Fascist's opportunity, surely the job is to strike the English imagination. What about voluntary labour battalions? I don't know anything about the finance and organisation side, but it seems to me that if the fascists were to form battalions of unemployed (all classes) headed by determined young men who would march on the places where a job needs doing – building sports' grounds, clearing slums – and work scientifically and like hell, they'd capture the imagination of the public by a manifestation of ENERGY ...

I'm not going to chop words – the English are afraid Mosley is out for himself: they don't see that belief in oneself and belief in oneself as an instrument are different things. When they see a man who has actually got hold so to speak of a spade and is digging away with his pals it'll change the attitude a lot ... Mosley probably talks excellent sense on unemployment, but so many people are talking: let him form these labour battalions and choose definite and if possible spectacular jobs which can be done in record time ... It's the man who *does* something that is going to capture the imagination ...

No *physical* offensive. Defensive and if necessary *passive* in suffering. An example of *doing* in the physical sense and enduring in the spiritual.

This was the sort of good advice that Tom took at no time in his life: to him politics were a matter of oration, of argument: the matter of doing, though he talked about it so much, seldom seemed to get past the stage of making sure that his words could be heard. He was from now on never in a position of power from which he could put his words into direct effect: he did not see the strength of an action as a symbol. He never recognised for instance the harm that the activities, however logically justifiable, of the stewards at his meetings were doing him: he would not have seen the good that the rather absurd but symbolic use of voluntary labour battalions might do him. It would certainly have been some sort of anathema to him to have had to consider the idea of victory through suffering.

When Tom and Cimmie got home from Rome at the end of April Tom continued to visit Diana at 2 Eaton Square: Cimmie continued to fail to keep for long her 'solemn vow and covenant' not to show how much she suffered. She was encouraged by friends to have an affair of her own: she said she did not want to. Tom himself (so he told the story) encouraged her to have an affair: the lover he suggested for her was Dick Wyndham.

There is a story of this time that once when Tom was talking to Diana she asked him why Cimmie was so upset about her, Diana, when he had been involved with so many other women; Tom replied that Cimmie had probably not known about most of the other women. Then the thought struck him (after all, rationally) – might it not help Cimmie to know about the other women because then it would help to take her mind off Diana? So he went home and told Cimmie a list of his women: and Cimmie said 'But they are all my best friends!'

The follow-up to this story was told by Bob Boothby. He and Tom were both at the same dinner party that night and Tom asked him, as one of Cimmie's greatest friends, if he would go to Smith Square after dinner and comfort her, because she was upset. Bob Boothby said 'What have you done to her now, Tom?' and Tom said 'I've told her all the women I've been to bed with since we've been married.' Bob Boothby said 'All, Tom?' and Tom said 'Well, all except her stepmother and her sister.'

In the spring holidays my sister and I were home from school and we were back again at Savehay Farm. My mother, for something to do, began to clear a two-acre wood at the end of the garden on the banks of the river. I helped her with this work: we dragged brushwood and fallen logs, and made bonfires. We did not often talk. Perhaps this was my mother's attempt to be 'doing in the physical sense and enduring in the spiritual'. I liked the work: it seemed more sensible than most things I had been part of in the grown-up world.

In early May there was school again and my mother drove me there in my father's dashing Bentley. After she had said goodbye and was going back past the rhododendrons she turned to wave – in her brown felt hat like the cup of an acorn – that figure which I suppose meant much of the world to me. I went off into the world of changing-rooms where boys were lethargically bashing one another up. Cimmie went to spend the weekend with Tom at Savehay Farm. At least, they had intended to spend the weekend together; but they had a terrible row on Sunday night – so Nanny later told Irene – and Tom walked out. Nanny heard Cimmie crying during the night.

On the morning of Monday 8th Cimmie wrote her last letter to Tom.

Darling heart, I want to apologise for last night but I was feeling already pretty rotten and that made me I suppose silly. Anyhow I had a star bad night of feeling wretched and this morning was all in with sickness and crashing back and tummy ache I can't think what it is. The Dr says my 'wee' shows slight recrudescence of coli bacilli but he thinks it must be a chill. No temp, so it's nothing to worry about, but it's just as painful and ill-making a feeling as if I were 106. Enough of myself.

My darling precious if you can remember that it's a sort of crazed for-the-moment-off-her-balance and all-her-good-resolutions-gone Cim who 'nags' and just be kind to it – not fight back – I always regret so bitterly after, I could kill myself. I wouldn't have married anyone else for the world, I am ever so proud of being your wife, I do love and adore you so – that's the trouble – as much as 13 years ago and in a way more frightenedly as then I had confidence and was happy and now I cannot figure anything quite out any more. But I love you, love you, love you, want to look after you, help *you*, be with you: be a joy and assistance – an 'ever present help in trouble' instead of which half the time I am the exact opposite. I am feeling too done in to cope more now. Don't, I beg of you, say unkind things to me, and however much I drive you to it don't compare me unfavourably with the other one. You have no idea how desperately I mind and I am trying and fighting every min: of the day. I never have a 'let-off' to speak of.

My beloved darling darling Tom I love you so wholly as a wife and a mum, but also I want you as a lover and sweet companion and want to be 'gay bird' with you as well as 'stress and strain of public life'. I want the sun and the stars and the moon and they are all called Tomki. I still thought I had them right up to last Xmas in spite of everything. Perhaps I still have, who knows.
I wonder how the ancients acquired wisdom.
How tired you'll be with this my mutti-one.
Lotsie is coming for this weekend and I am getting ahead with the party.
Let's have a radiant day Thurs: without one cloud.
X O X O X O X O X O

that is a hug and these are loving thoughts
///////////////////////

Thursday May 11th was the thirteenth anniversary of Tom's and Cimmie's wedding. On the evening of May 8th, the day on which she had written the above letter, Cimmie was rushed to a nursing home in London with acute appendicitis; the appendix had perforated; she was operated on that night. There was a danger of peritonitis. (This was before the days of penicillin). For a few days the danger did not seem too great. Then it did.

The story of Cimmie's death is taken from Irene's diary. Irene was not an impartial witness; she wrote in her usual emotional, anarchic

250 of the Game

style. But this was the sort of style that must have surrounded Cimmie from childhood; that she had hoped to get away from in marrying Tom. It is perhaps not inappropriate that Cimmie's death should be recorded in a manner in which it might seem that childhood was reclaiming her.

Irene was abroad in Switzerland when Cimmie became ill: she had just become engaged to be married at the age of thirty seven. She wrote a letter to Cimmie telling her of her engagement; and saying that she longed for her, Cimmie, to come to the wedding which was to be quietly in Switzerland but she did not want her other sister Baba to come; so could Cimmie please not tell Baba.

Irene learned of Cimmie's illness when she read about it in the *Continental Daily Mail* of May 11th. She sent a telegram to Tom, who replied that there was no need for her to come home as all was well. Then three days latter – 'A wire from Tom bombshelled me with utter horror: it said that Cim very seriously ill ... peritonitis has set in.' Irene and her fiancé, Miles Graham, caught an aeroplane from Zurich and arrived in London on May 15th. They were met at the airport by Baba, but were too late to see Cimmie that day. The next day Cimmie was worse – she was having saline injections because she was too weak for blood transfusions. Irene went to the nursing home but she still did not get into Cimmie's room: 'Baba held the fort and sat outside Cim's door'. Then – 'Tom came in and said I must decide whether or not to see my Cim: it might kill her, and whilst there was life there was hope: and was it not better to remember her always as lovely, not now, ill and drawn.' And so – 'I refrained from going into that tragic bedroom.' Irene waited outside with Tom's mother, 'Ma'. She spoke to the doctors about Cimmie.

> Oh that afternoon of horror! Dr Kirkwood then divulged – she had never fought from the start, and her gaiety on the second day was a bad sign: both mentally and physically she had never lifted a finger to live. Ma, Andrée and I crouched outside that door whilst my angel breathed out her last few hours. Poor Tom came out once or twice and said he could get nothing through to her: if only the doctor had warned him she was going he has so much to tell her, and now he was trying to get through to her how magnificent her life had been in its splendour and fulfillment. She had said to him that morning 'I am going, goodbye, my Buffy' – what she always said when he walked away through the garden at Denham. Baba sat in broken solitude in the bathroom and try as I would to hold on to her hand she turned away from every advance. Ma told me alas! alas! Cim had

got her to read my last letter to her and so of course she read – 'I only want you not Baba at my wedding'!!

My precious got weaker and weaker and oh! her stertorous breathing in the last $\frac{1}{2}$ hour was torture to hear through the crack in the door where I could just see the mirror: Tom murmuring to her his last words of love. I shall *never never* forget the pure ruthlessness of the pretty young nurse attendant on her all day: she stood outside that door going in and out and never even shed a tear though another little nurse by me was weeping sadly. I knew my love's spirit had fled by the sudden quiet and I saw Tom laying her beloved hands out. Baba went in and I ran to tell the men to get on to poor Nanny. I made plans for her to tell Viv and go at once and fetch Nick and I would be at Denham by the time they got back from Abinger. Tom came out after a bit, he hugged Baba pathetically, and thanked her for being there, and if I had not kissed him on the stairs he would have passed me by. But I saw so clearly Baba had been in the picture, I came in late, I could only stand and wait till needed. I went round to Dr Kirkwood's and waited there whilst he went to get luggage for Denham. Dr Kirkie said he had purposely written up all the slush of Tom's love at Cim's bedside because of so much Guinness scandal talk going about. I then sobbed and sobbed on the floor till Miles came back for me. I would not be able to get into my house because I had lent it to Elsie Fenwick for a debutante cocktail party party for Una!! Miles took me in his car to Denham. Oh! how the beauty of the place hurt me . . . Her bedroom I went to pray in to help her children for always. But oh! she was everywhere – everywhere – and yet gone: the place was crying out for her. I met the children about 8.30 and took them up to their suppers. Nanny had told them and they had cried all the way back. I chattered over their ovaltines and God sustained me not to break down; and Micky Mouse awake in his bed got over sweet Nick getting into his. I then knelt by sweet Viv and explained to her Mummy was tired and would have been an invalid and God had given her perfect rest by taking her away but she was always so near us and around us. I then lay on the bed and the housemaid sustained me with sal volatile. Tom then appeared alone to walk hopelessly in the garden. Miles did such a good thing, he got the revolver out of Tom's room as I told him I felt Tom might do something dreadful. Ma then phoned would Tom go back as Cim was looking so lovely.

At Abinger Hill, in my dormitory, I remember the headmaster coming in and saying Nanny was downstairs and would I go to her; and I was so pleased, so pleased; I had been back at school for about a week; I had been told my mother was ill, but children do not quite believe their parents' illnesses. (I had written to her two days before. 'How are you feeling? And is your tummy still aching?') I ran down to the head-master's drawing-room and there was Nanny on the sofa and she told me my mother was dead and there was the feeling of the bottom falling out of the world, space and time going, and a terrible fear that this might not be bearable. I cried. Perhaps it is true that I remember so little about my mother because of what was not bearable.

I do not remember my Aunt Irene at Denham when we got back: my Aunt Irene was very good to us, but I suppose children have an instinct about what is required when things are falling. Nanny and my sister Vivien and I sat in a little heap by the nursery fire. Then our father came in and held out his arms to us. I don't think he could have done better.

Nanny told Irene about the last weekend at Savehay Farm before Cimmie went to the nursing home: it was presumed that Tom had gone to Diana when he had walked out on Saturday night. Irene wrote – 'Oh God what a terrible doom for Tom! and to think that Cim is gone and that Guinness is free and alive and oh! where is any balance or justice!'

Diana remembered the day when Cimmie died as being one of the worst of her life: many of her friends realised this, and wrote to her, and sent her flowers. Tom came round to see her briefly that night: he said that they would not be able to see each other for some time. She wondered if she would ever see him again. But he told her – It will be all right.

The 'slush' that Dr Kirkwood said he had 'written up' about Tom because of the 'Guinness scandal' came out in the papers the next day. The *Daily Telegraph* reported the doctor saying about Tom:

> Through the days and nights he never left her. He kept a ceaseless vigil by her side, and his devotion to his dying wife was the one bright spot in a losing fight. There was something perfect and beautiful about it ... how Sir Oswald stood the anxious strain I do not know ... Before Lady Cynthia lost consciousness it was wonderful to see them whisper encouragement to each other. She must have meant far more to her husband than the world knows. It may seem a rather strange thing to say, but they had a very beautiful time together during their last few days.

This was not the feeling amongst those who had once been Cimmie's and Tom's friends. Irene recorded that Nancy Astor was 'defiant and adamant in her opinion of Tom ... all this theatrical grief would pass like a mirage ... it was unbelievable the hatred against him and Cim's death in the House of Commons.' Irene herself 'tried to see it was best she had gone to suffer no more at Tom's hands'. Baba however explained (in Irene's words) 'Cim would rather have lived for her children and all the hell he put her through for one of the short elysian heights he and she definitely attained now and again.'

It was planned that Tom would build a tomb in a memorial garden for Cimmie in the wood by the river at Savehay Farm which she and her children had been clearing during the easter holidays. Until this was ready the coffin would lie in the chapel of the Astors' house at Cliveden a few miles away. There was a funeral service around the coffin at Smith Square for just Tom and his mother and Irene and Baba: at the same time there was a memorial service at St Margaret's Westminster for her friends. These had been told that Cimmie had wished that no one should wear mourning; so almost the only people who turned up in black were members of the BUF in their new shirts. Tom had asked that the organist should play the *Liebestod* from *Tristan and Isolde*, which had been played at their wedding thirteen years ago. The children were not taken to either of these ceremonies: it was thought that 'the sight of the coffin might shock them and mummy locked inside it'. Irene recorded that we were kept at Savehay Farm doing basket-work with her secretary: but I remember going out with my fishing net to the river and wondering about the damned grown-up world that did not teach you to know when your mother was dying and made it so difficult to say good-bye when she was dead.

After the service in Smith Square, in a room full of flowers, Tom sat for hours 'gazing and gazing at her coffin'. No one close to Tom at this time thought his grief was not genuine. Baba was called round to Ebury Street by a mutual friend that night because he was 'frightened for Tom'.

Tom made up bunches of flowers, and photographs, and messages, to lie on Cimmie's coffin while it remained at Cliveden. The messages were written on tiny bits of paper like confetti. After Tom's death I found them in an envelope with Tom's writing on it – *Not to be touched*. On these scraps that are like petals fallen from trees there is written – My love's last present to me on the anniversary of our wedding last Thursday May 11th – Tiny Pres for my darling love I love you so always and for ever – Happy kippers my own darling one with love for ever misses her so – Come over Denham my darling where you are with me always and I love you for ever. And at the bottom of each note there is one of the tiny drawings in Tom's wild, child-like hand that were the talismans of his and Cimmie's life together – the sheep, the turtle, the piglet.

CHAPTER 26

Beyond the Game

Whatever was destructive about Tom's and Cimmie's life together was the result of their trying for too much, not a failure to do enough. Tom had the crazy belief that he could get away with almost anything – adoring wife, passionate mistress, goodness knows what else – keep everyone happy when he wanted them to be happy and avoid them when he wanted to get away. He wanted to create and run a revolutionary political movement that when he chose might seem conventional: that would both break and not break the rules. He evolved some sort of philosophy about all this – in later life he tried to write it – it sprang from a genuine conviction that old forms of life, social and personal, were dying, and that some new type of society and of human being had to emerge if there was to be hope for humanity. He took his pessimism about the old world from Spengler and his optimism about what might be new from Nietzsche: but he thought he could 'go beyond' Spengler and he misread Nietzsche (or did not read him enough): he imagined that Nietzsche was talking about politics when he was talking about states of mind. Nietzsche had found that to talk about a new type of man required a new style of language: this language was often ironic: it half mocked the so desperately serious things it was trying to say. Nietzsche thought that some such style was necessary if one was to face truth about human affairs and not get carried away or overwhelmed by the vision. This style, possibly might be the mark of a new type of man. But there would still be rules, on a higher level, of a new type of game.

Tom with part of himself picked up this style: he was unusually witty: he was sometimes humorous about himself. But then some sort of curtain would go up and he became like a ham actor on a stage; he became roaring, runaway, all-of-a-piece, savage; he was like a bus with no brakes going down a hill. It was always a bit of a mystery why he let himself go like this. Rudeness was perhaps some sort of relief when the pain of looking at the truth of things became too much.

The image that Tom built up for himself was that of Faust: of someone always striving, always searching, because that was what a human being was for. This was his justification for his arrogance and his energy: it was not just for himself, but was part of a training by which 'great' things could be achieved. But the only justification for this justification is that he should have been ready to face, to examine, everything: he should not have picked what results of his experiments he should pay attention to and what he would not. When he went roaring off on his hobby horses it was as if he were turning his back on pursuers. Protection is an activity natural to politicians: it has nothing to do with Faust.

Cimmie could not free herself from Tom whatever he did or did not do to her: this had given him security to go roaring off. The more he went his own way the more Cimmie heroically put up with it: by increasing his confidence, she increased her pain. This circle went on running away with itself until, suddenly, there was a death. It is difficult to see, perhaps, another outcome. Cimmie does not seem to have been able seriously to consider the possibility of her leaving him: until she could do this Tom would always have been able to hurt her. And so she would nag at him, and so he would have an excuse to get away from her: and so it would go on; but it was to herself the nagging caused too much pain.

After Cimmie's death Tom's great grief was genuine; but he used his grief, as he had once used her love of him, to spur himself on. Tragedy was not something that might make him change his ways. He built his memorial to her in the garden at Savehay Farm: he told Harold Nicolson that he 'now regards his [fascist] movement as a memorial to Cimmie and is prepared willingly to die for it'. There was nothing in fascism that could not assimilate images of death.

Another memorial was planned for Cimmie: there was to be a children's Day Nursery in south London named after her, and subscribed to by her friends. This was organised by Irene and Baba. An appeal went out over the signatures of Ramsay MacDonald, Stanley Baldwin, George Lansbury and Lloyd George.

Tom became involved in attempts to 'get through' to Cimmie by spiritualist mediums: these were organised by one of his mother's sisters. There was one quite striking result when a medium came up with the word engraved on the inside of Cimmie's wedding ring which was thought to be known only by Cimmie and Tom. Most of the messages that came through however were, as usual, strangely impersonal; though they did often have a peculiarly political content – 'Tom pursues a good course by going to Manchester: he should try to fight Salford and a better spirit will prevail'. One such message, passed on in a letter from his aunt to Tom, had even a weirdly prophetic ring: 'I feel he will never be able now to manage to move near another new policy while he gives stiffs all the more important posts'. The medium was asked twice if 'stiffs' was the right word: the reply each time was 'Yes'.

Tom took up again the reins of his fascist movement: his mother 'Ma' emerged from the shadows and became leader of the woman's section of the British Union of Fascists. She announced 'When my son married Lady Cynthia, she took her place by his side. Now she is dead there must be someone to help him in his work and I am going to do my best to fill the gap.' In July Tom and his mother led a big fascist march round London which began, whether by chance or design, close to Diana's house in Eaton Square. Irene reported:

> Saw Tom amassing his fascists in Eaton Square and Ma the women: then from Colin Davidson's window in Grosvenor Place we watched the March Past along with Zita, Beatrice Guinness, Patrick Hepburn, and Hitler's jester lover 'bugger' Hanfstaengl – a magnificent type of man who plays the piano beautifully, is anxious and oily and utterly evasive on any real question. At first with Colin and Zita and then alone I followed on foot, car and taxi Tom's march all round London to see no harm came to him: it was a splendid show and no trouble and I greeted him when he came back to H.Q. and he made a short speech from the top of a car.

Tom's ex-sisters-in-law were being very solicitous about him at this time: they stopped talking about his 'musical comedy' blackshirts. With Cimmie dead, they were trying to comfort him: they saw that he was doing his best to be a good father to his children. 'Nanny said Tom was very sad yesterday and his sweetness with the children hour after hour Sunday was wonderful.' But above all what Baba and Irene and 'Ma' seemed to be getting together about was a determination to try to prevent him seeing Diana.

> Baba and I were scared stiff when we learned Tom had gone up for dinner Sunday night and was back by 1 a.m. and was doing the same tonight. Who could it be but Diana Guinness. Baba and I, I know, were both sick with terror.

The reason ostensibly given for this attitude was that any further association between Tom and Diana would in some way be hurtful to Cimmie: Baba 'could not make him see the cruelty of it to Cim first and foremost'. But even Irene, with her haphazardness of mind and style, must have found it difficult to continue to convince herself that hers and Baba's feelings were as grandiose as this. A plan was made that later on in the summer, while Irene took the older children on a holiday, Baba should go on a motoring trip in France with Tom to give him further comfort – having 'asked for a fortnight's leave' from her husband Fruity. Irene consulted Tom about this: 'I definitely sensed he wanted Baba alone or no one, and I saw his point about this'. Fruity, however, seems to have seen a less blinkered point: to Irene he 'muttered about all this Tom hysteria and Baba's sacrifice to him watching and guarding him – he saw it as all bunk and false' – here Fruity even got out a bit of resentful rage '– when Tom had killed sweet Cim in cruelty and mental torture'. People were becoming involved in the sort of manipulations, conscious or unconscious, that they blamed Tom so bitterly for.

In early May Diana had asked for a divorce: this had been agreed: moreover it had been arranged that her husband would, according to the gentlemanly conventions of the time, appear to be the guilty party so that Diana need not be accused.

Tom went to see Diana again in June: Eaton Square was only three minutes walk from Ebury Street. He came after dark. He said – referring to her proceedings for divorce – 'Have you jumped your little hurdle yet?' Diana replied 'It's my whole life!' They had a terrible row; and Tom went away.

Irene and Baba and Ma were all on the telephone about this.

When Baba rang him up he had gone to London – there could only be one – and we were scared stiff. I had a talk with Ma over the phone and she told me she was worried – that the horror had sent for Tom after her divorce coming up ... It puts Baba in a fearful fix about motoring in France with Tom as if he is seeing Diana none of us could have the heart to deal with him: the idea is utterly unthinkable. Zita could give us no gossip on her; she had seen her at 2 dinners doing the grim-wan-dead-white-face line ...

But Tom, as was his way, seems to have used the row with Diana to give his ex-sister-in-law and his mother the assurances they required:

He had asked Ma to tell Baba and me he never contemplated meeting Diana after his trip with Baba. Ma had told him what gossip she had heard about the girl saying she was going to get him now and that those who knew her said she was the most determined minx and that she talked to everyone. Tom refused to believe the tales and said she was dignified and sweet and would never gabble. Ma cried and said Tom was so marvellous to his children and that perhaps Cim had died to save his soul: I wondered!

Tom's assurance to Diana – they soon made up their quarrel – was that it would be useful to themselves if it became known that he was seeing a lot of Baba: during the long period before Diana's divorce became final he and Diana had to be careful about their being seen together and so a 'cover' would be useful: these were the days when any hint of adultery on the part of the petitioner or so-called 'not-guilty' party could, if it was brought to the attention of an official called the King's Proctor, render a divorce invalid.

Tom told Baba (Irene reported) that he had to see Diana occasionally because he could not 'shirk his obligations'. All this intrigue was representative of something which had presumably always been going on but which Cimmie by her good nature had rendered almost innocent. This was now the conscious style of life around Tom: the permutations of passion and deception and self-deception seemed endless:

When I saw Baba later although she could not tell me details as she has been sworn to secrecy by Tom I knew he had killed something in her after all these months of devotion and sacrifice to him as she could not reconcile and told him so this frenzied love for Cim trying now to get mediums and the horror of seeing Diana on and off – dining with her as he says platonically – and she still could not make him see the cruelty of it to Cim ... I knew she felt she could hardly start on the motor trip now if at all ...

Baba had had lunch with Tom and had fairly let fly about Diana whom she loathes and she tried to make Tom see that if he went on like this he would be utterly killed and his future smashed as people would not stand for it but he seemed more smashed over having hurt Baba and was asking her to tell him what to do – anything to restore that confidence ...

I cannot get over Tom's consideration towards Babs ... I pray this obsession with her will utterly oust Diana Guinness ...

What was happening, of course, was that Tom was once more managing to do his juggling act of keeping people and passions in the air at the same time. There was even a curious incursion from his private world into his public world, which people apart from Tom seemed to view with the deepest suspicion:

> Ma was harrassed by Unity Mitford now joining the Fascist cause, and she was sure she was doing it to spy on Tom in the office as she had asked such curious questions of Lady Makgill ... This wretch is wanting to sell blackshirts and walk in parades and attend all meetings – for what reason?

Tom and Baba went off on their motoring trip through France: Irene and Vivien and Nicholas and Andrée, Cimmie's ex-lady's-maid, set out on a cruise to the Canary Isles: Nanny and Michael went to the Isle of Wight. Diana and her sister Unity went on a journey to Germany which, Diana said later, changed Unity's life. In Munich they met Putzi Hanfstaengl – he whom Irene had just previously described (in words not literally but perhaps metaphorically apt) as 'Hitler's jester lover bugger'. Putzi Hanfstaengl – 'a huge man with an exaggerated manner' (Diana's description) – took them to the Nuremberg Parteitag, the first huge Nazi rally after Hitler had come to power. Diana wrote – 'A feeling of excited triumph was in the air, and when Hitler appeared an almost electric shock passed through the multitude.'

This is the moment to end this book; with the characters abroad and getting ready for their new parts and re-alignments. The story of the next thirteen years is the story of Tom's fascism; of his attempt to prevent war; of his new and extraordinary private juggling acts; of the passions and duplicities surrounding these but also of the bright, violent feeling that followed my father wherever he went; as he made stands about crucial events; as he occasionally dallied on the Mediterranean; as he marched his blackshirt army against the blank wall of war. His children had to learn to come to terms with all this: not only with a world in which their mother had died and people suggested their father had killed her (and their father told them how wonderful his marriage had been) but with a world in which now their father was apt to march down Oxford Street at the head of people who if you looked at them in one way were magnificent and if you looked at them in another were like soldiers from Selfridge's toy shop. Also – why was the world going towards war? And why were people so angry at my father for trying to stop this? As an adolescent, one built up one's own defence works;

came up against one's own brick walls. There were not so many refuges now in the hidey-holes of childhood. Some sort of acceptance, or technique, had to be worked out in the mind.

Tom's energy seemed to carry him over difficulties like someone on a flying carpet. He went on perfecting his marvellous powers with words: he lifted people off their chairs with them. Part of his appeal as a fascist was that he seemed to be a single, lonely figure taking on all the challenges of the world. But then, he was too powerful for people to think they might really help him. He did perform some service by getting what he had called the extremist forces of the country in his hands: violence in England, unlike that on the continent, was for the most part symbolic.

His children learned something from Tom about how to trust themselves: but how might they explain this? Part of what they learned was that the power of words was both wonderful and terrible.

There is a photograph of myself and my sister Vivien and my Aunty Irene at this time: we are on our cruise ship between the Canary Isles and Southampton: we are at one of those fancy dress balls so beloved by people with nothing to do. Aunty is dressed in what she referred to in her diary as her 'white lace veil as a mantilla'. Vivien is in 'her mummy's turkish harem dress'. Nicky is just 'in his burnous'. We do seem to be involved in some journey through purgatory: I at least am dressed for the part. When we got back from our cruise we went to join Nanny and Micky in the Isle of Wight: then Daddy and Aunty Baba came down and told us of their wonderful motoring trip through France: and everything was much as before, except that 'Tom was getting up and handing the vegetables round' and it was now Tom and Viv who 'went bang bang at each other with the coltish smacking and chaffing which I hate' (Irene). But what about Uncle Fruity? This however was the sort of question one did not ask grown-ups: they were apt to shoot at each other hurt glances, like that time for instance when I had told Nanny an amusing limerick I had picked up at school. It was better, I had learned, if one wanted to find out about life, to wait to talk with people of one's own age; who seemed to have the gift to laugh and be serious and be curious without deluding themselves or dying because they were hurt.

Notes on sources and acknowledgements

Material for this book was for the most part provided by my father's papers which, after his death, were put at my disposal without reserve by my stepmother Diana Mosley; to her I have the greatest gratitude.

Secondly my thanks are to Robert Skidelsky, whose biography of my father (*Oswald Mosley*: Macmillan, 1975) deals with his politics with the most admirable judgement and comprehensiveness.

I am grateful to Lord Boothby for permission to quote at length from the three letters he wrote to my father in the early thirties: also the letter he wrote to my mother in 1925.

I am grateful to Zita James for permission to quote from her unpublished diary of 1930.

The diaries of my aunt Irene Ravensdale, from which I quote, are in my possession.

Of published works, apart from Robert Skidelsky's biography, I owe most to my father's autobiography (*My Life*: Nelson 1968) and to Harold Nicolson's *Diaries and Letters 1930-39* (Collins, 1966). I was also helped by being allowed to read Harold Nicolson's unpublished diaries in Balliol College Library.

I owe much to *The Fascists in Britain* by Colin Cross (Barrie and Rockliff, 1961); *John Strachey* by Hugh Thomas (Methuen, 1973) and *A Life of Contrasts* by Diana Mosley (Hamish Hamilton, 1977).

I have quoted from the following books: *Portrait of the Labour Party* by Egon Wertheimer (Putnam, 1936); *Decline and Fall of the Labour Party* by John Scanlon (Peter Davis, 1932); Volumes I and II of the *Diaries of Beatrice Webb* (1952 and 1956); *I Fight to Live* by Robert Boothby (Gollancz, 1947); *Tomorrow is a New Day* by Jennie Lee (Penguin, 1947); *Unfinished Journey* by Jack Jones (Hamish Hamilton, 1938); *J. H. Thomas: a Life For Unity* by Gregory Blaxland (Muller, 1964): *Diary in Exile, 1935* by Leon Trotsky (Harvard University Press, 1976); *Diaries and Letters: 1930-39* by Harold Nicolson (Collins, 1966); *A Life of Contrasts* by Diana Mosley (Hamish Hamilton, 1977); *In Many Rythms* by Baroness Ravensdale (Weidenfeld & Nicolson, 1953).

For my chapter on *The Riddle of the Sphinx* I am indebted to Charles Hampden-Turner's admirable *Maps of the Mind* (Mitchell Beazeley, 1981).

Last, but not least, I am grateful to my sister Vivien (who has allowed me to use some of her photographs) and to my brother Michael, both of whom have generously assisted with what is to them the unearthing of old stories.

N.M.

Index

Sir Oswald and Lady Cynthia Mosley are referred to here as Tom and Cimmie. (For these nicknames, see pp. 3, 10.)